Pennsylvania

*Four Complete Novels from
the Heart of Colonial America*

Kay Cornelius

BARBOUR BOOKS
An Imprint of Barbour Publishing, Inc.

Love's Gentle Journey © 1985 by The Zondervan Corporation.
Sign of the Bow © 1994 by Kay Cornelius.
Sign of the Eagle © 1994 by Kay Cornelius.
Sign of the Dove © 1994 by Kay Cornelius.

ISBN 1-58660-503-8

Cover photo: © PhotoDisc, Inc.

This Barbour edition is published by special arrangement with Kay Cornelius.

All Scripture quotations, unless otherwise noted, are taken from the King James Version of the Bible.

Published by Barbour Books, an imprint of Barbour Publishing, Inc., P.O. Box 719, Uhrichsville, Ohio 44683, www.barbourbooks.com

Member of the
Evangelical Christian
Publishers Association

Printed in the United States of America.
5 4 3 2 1

KAY CORNELIUS

Kay Cornelius grew up in Winchester, Tennessee. As a high school senior, she won a four-year college scholarship in a national civic organization's essay contest. She used the award at George Peabody College for Teachers in Nashville, Tennessee, where she graduated with a B.A. in English and a "Mrs.," having met her husband, Don, there. They lived in France while he was in the army, then moved to Huntsville, Alabama, where Don worked for the Army, NASA, and Lockheed-Martin. Feeling called to teach, Kay spent twenty-five years in secondary classrooms in Tennessee and Alabama. During that time, she earned a master's degree in secondary English education from A & M University in Huntsville and taught many in-service and other workshops on creative and technical writing on the local, regional, and national level.

While her years in the classroom were rewarding, Kay felt that God wanted her to do something with her own writing. The result was her first inspirational romance, *Love's Gentle Journey*. The idea came from a relative of her husband's, who mentioned that their common ancestor had left Europe with his wife and three young children, only to have his wife fall ill and die during the long sea voyage. His ancestor (and several of Kay's as well, although she didn't know it at the time) landed in Philadelphia and made his way to Lancaster. After **Heartsong Presents** published Kay's *More Than Conquerors* and asked for more from her, she returned to the McKay-Craighead family and followed members of the next generation through the French and Indian War in *Sign of the Bow*, and the Revolution in *Sign of the Eagle*. By the time she wrote *Sign of the Dove*, Kay's research into her own family history had revealed a great-great-great-great-grandfather who migrated from Pennsylvania into Kentucky, where he fought against the British, and then into North Carolina. One of his Yadkin Valley neighbors there was Daniel Boone, whom he followed into Kentucky. While the fictional characters in the Pennsylvania books are not based on her relatives as such, she used family letters and other sources to recreate their times. In those days, pioneers worked hard, but they always relied on God to guide and help them through the perils they often had to face.

Kay and Don have two grown children and four grandchildren. She leads the senior ladies' adult Bible study class in her church and enjoys learning, traveling, and volunteer teaching. Her most recent writing has been five nonfiction books for children and young adults. She continues to enjoy research and reading, with special interest in Native American history.

Love's Gentle Journey

To God be the glory

Chapter 1

Ann stood on the deck of the *Derry Crown* and looked about her, overwhelmed by the mixture of sights, sounds, and smells aboard the square-rigged sailing vessel and compelled to let its many new sensations wash over her without making any attempt to sort them all out. In the month since her father's decision to leave Ireland, she had often wondered what this day would be like. Now it was here and nothing was as she had imagined.

"Come, Lass, help yer mother below," said William McKay as he set down the last bundle of their small store of worldly goods.

Ann helped her mother rise from the trunk where she had been sitting. The winter of 1739–1740, just past, had been harsh, and she was alarmed that her mother's cough still lingered.

Despite the older woman's pallor and the dark shadows under her eyes, the resemblance between them was striking. Both women were blessed with gentle features and great dark eyes; though, at seventeen, Ann's figure was still girlish and only hinted of the beauty she would become. Sarah McKay, just over twice her daughter's age, moved slowly as if trying to conserve her meager energy.

Suddenly she stopped and looked anxiously about the deck. "Where is Jonathan?"

"O'er there," her husband replied, nodding toward the aft rigging where the seven year old's curly head was bent in earnest conversation with one of the sailors. "There's much for th' lad t' see."

"Look to him, William. I believe I'll rest a wee bit before we sail."

Leaning heavily on Ann's arm, Sarah moved toward the narrow passageway leading to the cramped quarters that would be their home for the next two months. The McKays had been given a set of double bunks near the foot of the stairs, though the close confinement did not even allow one to sit on the lower bunks. Indeed, only curtains of some coarse fabric separated them from the next family's allotted space.

Ann eased her mother onto the bottom bunk and spread her shawl over her. "I'll go help Father with our things if there's naught else I can do for ye now," she said.

"No, don't go just yet, Daughter. I would have a word wi' ye. Pull up that stool yonder an' sit down."

Ann did as her mother asked, taking the frail hand the woman extended to her. "I can see that ye are grieving o'er this journey," Sarah began, and although Ann shook her head in denial, her eyes filled with tears.

"Our life at Coleraine was all I ever knew. I just feel. . ." She paused, not knowing how to describe her turmoil since her father's decision to emigrate to the American plantation country.

Like most of their neighbors, the McKays were Scots, and although the family had lived in Ireland for three generations, they clung to their Scottish ways. From the porridge they ate in the morning to the Border ballads they sang each evening, the Scots, who had been brought from their lowland homes to curb the papist influence of the native Irish, had retained their own ways. Living in a land where the dispossessed Irish despised them and their absentee English landlords exacted a heavy toll for the right to use their land had not been easy, but they had always made the best of their situation.

Therefore, it was a surprise to learn that William McKay was ready to cast his lot, and that of his family, with the others leaving the green-gold hills of Ulster for the colonies in the new world. A surprise—and a bitter disappointment.

"Take heart, Daughter," Sarah encouraged softly, squeezing Ann's hand. " 'Twas hard for me to leave Scotland when I wed your father. 'Twas hard t' leave our wee ones who sleep in th' kirk yard. But we are together in this. Yer father had na choice, for a man has t' make a living for his family. It is best for us t' accept what must be."

Accept it she must, but she would miss the bonny cow she milked twice a day, the soft, fluffy fleeces of the spring lambs, and the downy yellow chicks she raised and sold at the market. Ann had tried to imagine what America was like, but she could not, any more than she was able to picture the Scots town where her mother had been born and to which she had always longed to return. Ann had been to Coleraine, and the village of Downready, and last year she had bought some bright hair ribbons at the Cleary Fair, but she had never been to Londonderry, or ridden in a carriage, or sat in a boat. And of all these unfamiliar things Ann was afraid. She listened as her father led their family prayer time by thanking God for the way they had been shown and asking Him to grant them a safe passage, and she was not comforted.

"I dinna mean to complain," Ann said, her eyes downcast.

"Ye must have faith, Ann, an' trust that God is workin' in all o' it."

Ann was silent, feeling the hot tears squeeze through her closed lids. To her, the God of the church had always seemed a remote, silent Judge. The small kirk where Reverend Duffie preached the Calvinist creed had never comforted her. She could not follow the long sermons, and the backless benches that served as pews grew harder and harder. Out-of-doors, where the storm clouds moved with awful majesty and the covenant of the rainbow arched over the Ulster hills, Ann could feel a peace in the wonder of God's creation. But He had never seemed a guiding Presence in her life as He obviously was in her mother's. Even William, though he attended Sabbath services and dutifully led their daily prayers, was not as devout as his wife.

"I would like to believe that God is guiding us," she said in a weak voice.

Sarah sighed. "Ye will need more than your own strength t' help Jonathan an' your father when I am gone."

"Hush, Mother!" cried Ann in alarm.

"Listen to me now, Child. I want ye to have my Bible. Keep it wi' your things."

"But—"

"Read it, Child, and keep its words in your heart. 'Lean not unto thine own understanding,' the Scriptures tell us. Will ye promise t' do that?"

"Aye," Ann said faintly.

"Now ye should go back to your father, Dear. This time together has done me good. And, Ann," Sarah added, touching her daughter's face tenderly, "ye are not t' worry him. Do ye understand that?"

Ann nodded, too near tears to speak. *Father must know,* she thought, and even Jonathan could see that their mother had not recovered her health—indeed was growing weaker by the day. Ann could only do as she was instructed. . .and hope.

The brightness of the morning sun, in sharp contrast to the dimness below, caused Ann to blink as she climbed to the upper deck. *If anything, the confusion here has increased,* she thought. The docks teemed with sailors, passengers, agents, and hawkers, all moving amidst general noise and confusion. Swarthy sailors came and went, hauling aboard great casks and wooden crates. Occasionally, some of them would glance her way, exchange a comment in some unknown tongue, then laugh uproariously. Ann felt uncomfortable and ducked into a more secluded passageway where she could view the happenings unseen.

She tried not to stare at the women who thronged around the sailors, hanging onto their arms and even touching their laces. Their bodices were cut astonishingly low, and their lips and cheeks were unnaturally red. Ann had heard rouged women spoken of in whispers, but she had never before actually seen any. She glanced at Jonathan, but he was absorbed in watching a sailor with a beautifully colored yellow-and-blue bird perched on his shoulder.

Here came other seamen and passengers up the gangplank, carrying sacks of provisions and barrels of grog and water. A few live animals were being prodded aboard, bawling and mooing their protest. Ann felt a momentary stab of sympathy. The poor things understood even less than she their sudden change of circumstance. Looking about for a glimpse of her father, she spied the bright red head of Isabel Prentiss.

"Hello, Ann!" the girl called, waving her hand. "I was wonderin' if ye had come aboard yet."

The Prentiss family had arrived in Londonderry about the same time as the McKays and with the same intentions. Although Isabel was just past sixteen, she already had the full figure of a woman. Today, dressed in a frock of vivid blue, she looked even older than her years, and Ann felt dowdy by comparison in her own drab homespun. Despite the differences in age and appearance, however, they had become friends, and Ann felt her heart lift a bit at the greeting.

"Oh, Isabel! Aye, we've been here for several hours now. My mother needed time to settle in afore the crowds gathered."

"Have ye ever seen the likes of so many men!" Isabel cried, her eyes bright. "Why, there are more fine-lookin' young chaps in one place than ever set foot in Coleraine. . .or Londonderry, either, I'd vow. Mayhap this voyage won't be so bad, after all. A girl ought to be able to find a husband wi'out half tryin'!"

"Most of the men I have seen are sailors an' look to be a rough lot," Ann observed.

"Aye, but there are lots o' single men here, on their way t' America, maybe even some rich ones wantin' to invest in the colonies."

Ann glanced at Isabel, wondering if she had intended to make a joke, but the girl seemed quite serious. "Ye want a rich husband, then?"

"Why not? I'd like to have nice things an' not be scolded if I spent a ha'penny now and again. How about ye, Ann? What sort of husband do ye seek?"

"I have na given it much thought," Ann said, half-truthfully.

"Well, ye ought to think about it," Isabel said firmly, with a characteristic toss of her red head. "If ye don't mind, ye'll likely wind up wedded wi' a poor crofter and never have two coins ta rub together. Look what's comin' now!" cried Isabel, nodding toward the gangplank. Ann turned to see a party of men being escorted aboard ship. "Do ye suppose those are the prisoners bein' transported?"

It had been rumored that a number of convicts would be sailing with them, some of whom had asked to be sent to the colonies instead of remaining in Irish prisons. Others had been given no choice in the matter. There were at least a dozen of them, carefully guarded by red-coated soldiers carrying muskets.

"They aren't in chains," observed Ann, "but it appears that those soldiers are making certain they are safely aboard."

"They don't look like such a bad lot, do they?" Isabel mused, taking a closer look.

Most of the men were young and poorly garbed, but not any more so than most of the passengers.

" 'Tis a shame. My father says many men who are transported come from debtors' prison. . .that their only crime is poverty." Ann shuddered, wondering if her father might have shared their fate.

The soldiers, having turned over their charges to a burly seaman with a look of authority, disembarked and stood on the dock at attention, evidently awaiting the launching of the ship.

When Ann looked back to the deck, a man was speaking to her brother, Jonathan. Plainly but neatly dressed, he was smiling at something Jonathan was saying.

"Should your brother be talkin' to a convict?" asked Isabel.

"Mother would be much displeased, I'm sure," Ann agreed. "But here comes my father. He'll attend t' it."

As William started toward them, the man tousled Jonathan's hair and moved on toward the passageway leading to the deck where the sailors and single men were quartered. Unlike the others who carried cloth or canvas duffel bags, he was holding a large wooden box. Ann wondered what it might contain.

"Oh, let's listen t' the captain, Ann. He's about ta speak." Isabel interrupted Ann's thoughts and moved nearer the upper deck, where the captain had taken a position near the wheel and was calling the noisy crowd to attention.

"Hear ye! Hear ye! I wish to see the head of every household, the eldest males traveling with families, and all other single men here on the wheel deck. We sail with the tide to Cork. There we'll pick up two other vessels to form a convoy. Then we're bound for the port of Philadelphia. May the good Lord grant His mercy on our voyage."

A few scattered "amens" were heard as the men pressed toward the designated meeting place. Jonathan and Sarah, who had left her bunk, were standing by Ann. She tried to count the men as they passed by, but soon gave up. Of the women and children who were left on the lower deck, there seemed to be around thirty, more than she had expected could be comfortably accommodated on a vessel as small as the *Derry Crown*.

"I wonder what the captain is sayin'," said Isabel.

"He might be tellin' them about *pirates*," Jonathan suggested, so solemnly that the girls laughed.

"Ye an' your pirates!" Ann exclaimed fondly. "Such notions ye have! And I suppose ye'll be disappointed if we don't see any the whole voyage, won't ye?"

"Ye jest, Mistress Ann, but I heard the sailors talkin' of it," young Samuel Prentiss put in. "They said pirates like the English ships best but will take a merchant ship like ours if it suits their fancy."

Mistress Prentiss joined them in time to hear her son's statement and nodded. " 'Tis true, what the lad says. I heard the captain say we are meetin' the other ships at Cork because there's some safety in numbers."

"I know what a pirate ship looks like," Jonathan volunteered. "She flies the Jolly Roger flag, wi' a cannon on every deck."

"Aye, and we have a cannon, too. Did ye notice?" asked Mistress Prentiss.

"It looks like a toy," shrugged Isabel. "I doubt it has ever been fired."

"And let us all pray that it need never be," Sarah said quietly.

"The captain must be through instructin' the men, for here comes Father now." Ann was glad for the diversion. The conversation seemed to be taking a morbid turn, and her mother needed no further worries.

"Well, at last we are ta get underway," he said with a cheerful air. "With fair winds and God's grace, we should make Philadelphia in eight or nine weeks."

Noting how pale and drawn Sarah looked, Ann felt that nine weeks would be quite a long time, but she kept silent, fearing to make bad matters worse. Isabel, on the other hand, was not so cautious.

"Well, I, for one, don't know how we shall endure it. But I suppose the sooner we begin, the sooner we arrive."

They watched as the ropes securing the vessel to the dock were released. The anchor was raised, and the rigging came alive with clambering sailors, maneuvering the sails to catch the freshening wind. A few people on the dock waved and shouted farewells to relatives aboard ship.

Keenly aware that she might never again see her native country, Ann watched the green hills slip from sight. Her vision blurred, but she was determined not to cry.

"Look, Jonathan, the seagulls are followin' us," she called to her brother.

Wild and free, they soared above the billowing sails. She watched them, wondering what it must be like to live untethered to the earth. Then the gulls, too, returned to shore, and Ann resigned herself to the brave ship that plowed on, through the trackless ocean that stretched forever ahead.

Chapter 2

L ife at sea, at first novel and exciting, quickly settled into a routine. As planned, the *Derry Crown* met two other ships, the *Star* and *Regent*, at Cork, and the sight of their white sails moving along on either side was vastly reassuring.

The passengers soon found that the agent had exaggerated their vessel's virtues and neglected to mention its faults. The food rations, while adequate for sustenance, often left them unsatisfied. The passengers soon learned that it was best not to expend energy unnecessarily.

After a poor start of sleepless nights, the McKays finally adjusted themselves to the unaccustomed motion of the ship and to their cramped quarters. William often slept upon deck, and Sarah was allowed the most convenient bunk, the middle one, to herself. When William slept below, Ann and Jonathan shared the bottom bunk.

The boy seemed to enjoy everything about the voyage. Despite his father's warnings to be careful, Jonathan wandered freely about the ship, talking to everyone who would listen and asking endless questions.

The single men, including the group being transported, were quartered with the sailors, one level below the family deck. They generally used the port side of the upper deck, although no restrictions had been placed on any of the passengers.

Ann and Isabel found a sheltered spot on the starboard side of the deck, where they sometimes watched the single men as they took the air. Although Isabel had dismissed them as unlikely marriage prospects, some of the men were young and attractive.

A few days into the voyage, the man who had spoken to Jonathan the day they boarded nodded to them. Much younger than Ann's father, he appeared to be perhaps a dozen years her senior. With his expressive gray eyes and broad brow, he was what many would call handsome, yet his air seemed unusually grave. The man was holding a book, and, as they watched, he leaned against a bulwark and began to read.

"I wonder what he did t' be transported," Isabel said. "He looks like a real gentleman, compared ta the others."

"Oh, he isna one o' them," Jonathan volunteered. "I think he's a schoolmaster, because he asked me if I thought Father might allow him to give us lessons."

"A schoolmaster!" Isabel exclaimed. "Perhaps he'll take th' boys in hand, then!"

"Aye, the children on board need somethin' to fill their time and keep them frae mischief," agreed Ann.

"I'll go ask him about it," said Jonathan, and was gone before Ann could open her mouth in protest.

When Jonathan returned, he was wriggling with excitement. "I am to tell Father that Mr. Craighead is willin' to teach any who wish it," he said importantly.

At his son's urging, William conferred with the schoolmaster that morning.

"He seems ta be a good sort," William told Sarah later as the family gathered for prayer. Subject to the captain's approval, Caleb Craighead would commence teaching the very next day. "Mayhap Jonathan will learn some of his letters by th' time we reach Philadelphia."

"I know some o' them already," Jonathan boasted, "and I know lots o' numbers and things."

"Ye still have much to learn." Sarah smiled fondly. "Aye, William, it is good for th' children to be occupied in a useful manner. Surely the captain can have na objections."

Captain Murdock readily agreed to the proposal, provided Mr. Craighead would keep the younger children out of the sailors' way. The next day six boys and four girls, ranging in age from seven to fourteen, assembled on the aft deck for their first session.

Ann and Isabel stationed themselves nearby, pretending to be fully absorbed with their knitting, but sharply aware of all that was going on around them. Mr. Craighead's black box, which had caught Ann's attention as he came on board, yielded a variety of interesting materials. In addition to textbooks of the kind used in the school Reverend Duffie kept in Coleraine, he had a Bible, a Psalter, and the Westminster Catechism, which most of the older children had already learned to recite from memory.

Mr. Craighead also had a shallow sandbox, in which the young ones practiced shaping their letters, using their forefingers. The sand could be smoothed again with a shake of the box, and even the older children, using feathered quills, used it to practice their handwriting. Sometimes Mr. Craighead set sums for his students, making the numbers in the sand and letting them take turns ciphering out the answers.

The only reader was the Bible, and often Mr. Craighead read it to them himself, in a firm, resonant voice that, with its Scots burr, was quite pleasant to hear. Ann and Isabel, though several years older than the pupils, listened along with them, glad for the diversion.

The school had been underway for some two weeks when the fair weather finally broke, and squalls of wind-driven rain kept the passengers below. Mr. Craighead tried holding lessons in the cramped family dining area, but the light was poor, and as the storm grew more intense, the motion of the ship made reading impossible.

"I had thought a spring passage would be calmer than fall or winter," William commented on the second day of their confinement.

For the first time, the movement of the ship made Ann feel ill, and she stayed in her bunk, grasping its sides as the vessel tossed and pitched. How long could the groaning timbers of the ship stand such buffeting without splitting asunder?

Twice daily a sailor came down to the family deck, carrying a bucket of water and another filled with the thin gruel the captain had ordered as their storm fare, but few of the passengers even attempted to partake of it. The sailor Jonathan called Ian brought them some hardtack on the third day of the storm, and at his urging they each broke off a piece and chewed it gingerly. "We should be out o' this blow by dawn," he assured them. "The wind has shifted direction, and the clouds are breakin' up."

❧

Just before sunrise the next morning, Ann, feeling weak and light-headed from the combined effects of the lack of food and the rankness of their quarters, stumbled up the stairs to the deck and leaned weakly against the rail, breathing in the fresh air. Some half-dozen others had come up onto deck by the time the sun appeared, and Ann saw that the schoolmaster was among them.

"Good mornin', Mistress McKay," he greeted, walking over to stand beside her. "How has your family withstood the storm?"

Ann looked up at Caleb Craighead, suddenly overcome with shyness. In all her years, Ann had never held a conversation with a man alone. His gray eyes were quietly reassuring, and Ann yearned again for an appearance that matched her years and for the facility to converse with him as easily as he was speaking to her. It seemed a very long time before she managed to say anything.

"We have all survived, thank ye," she finally said. "But for a time I feared I wouldna." Then, afraid her remark had been too personal, she blushed.

Apparently, Mr. Craighead did not notice her discomfort, for he continued. "The captain says we must expect at least one more spell of bad weather before we make port."

"Can th' ship withstand another storm?" Ann asked, alarmed at the thought of repeating their recent experience.

"It has done so many times before," he assured her. "Tell your brother and my other pupils that lessons will resume today for all who are able to come."

"Jonathan was th' least affected of us all," Ann said. "He will be happy to be occupied again."

"And I shall be glad as well. I am unaccustomed to idleness." Mr. Craighead touched a hand to his forehead in a gesture of farewell, wished Ann a good day, and walked away.

As Ann watched him go, her head was still light, but a strange warmth filled her heart. *He thinks of me as a child,* she mused, knowing full well that Isabel would have known just what to say—and how. As she went below, Ann found herself hoping that he would seek her out again.

Jonathan was taking breakfast when Ann returned to their quarters, and William was attempting to persuade Sarah to eat a bowl of gruel.

"I canna swallow a drop," she protested, but at her husband's encouragement she managed a few spoonfuls.

"The sun is out, an' it promises ta be a beautiful day," Ann told her mother. "Let us help ye up on deck. Ye'll feel better for havin' some fresh air."

"But she must na be chilled," William warned. "Wait until th' sun is higher and th' air warms."

By then, the deck was crowded with all the passengers who were able to walk. Most of Caleb Craighead's pupils were back, and he entertained them with stories of various biblical storms, while Sarah and Ann sat nearby, listening along with the children.

When he finished and had set the children to various tasks, Sarah spoke to him. "Mr. Craighead, the way ye tell those stories puts me in mind o' a pastor I knew in Scotland in the old days. Have ye e'er felt a call to the ministry, by any chance?"

Ann had never known a minister who looked—or sounded—like Mr. Craighead, and she was surprised when he nodded.

"I have, Ma'am. In fact, after serving as a schoolmaster for some years, I have only recently been ordained to the ministry. It is my intention to preach in America, as God leads me."

"Ah," said Sarah. "Then perhaps ye can lead us in worship of a Sabbath on this ship?"

"If Captain Murdock has no objections and will tell us when the Lord's Day is." He smiled. "I fear that I may have lost a day during th' storm."

"Please ask him," Sarah urged. "We all need t' hear the Word proclaimed, na matter where we may be."

❧

"I do hope Mr. Craighead willna be long-winded," Isabel said as she and Ann waited for him to begin the first service two days later. "Our pastor always spoke at least two hours and never said anythin' I could remember two minutes later."

"Mayhap his preaching will be as interestin' as his teaching," Ann replied.

"Well, in any case, we canna leave if we don't like it. 'Twould be a long swim back ta Ireland," Isabel proclaimed, tossing her head and smiling. Then she took a quick look about to see if any of the men were noticing.

Caleb Craighead, minister, looked no different to Ann from Caleb Craighead, schoolmaster, except for the white linen shirt replacing his usual brown one. Either he lacked a black ecclesiastical suit or had chosen not to wear it.

Standing on the captain's deck, Caleb looked out over his makeshift congregation. Nearly all of the passengers had gathered for the service, including most of the men who were being transported, and even a few of the sailors. His voice was firm and clear as he led in a long prayer and then asked one of the men to line out a hymn from the Psalter. Another read from the Scriptures, then Caleb Craighead began his sermon. All listened with attention as he began to talk in quiet, almost conversational tones of God's grace and mercy, of His ability to protect them if they trusted Him utterly.

Reverend Duffie had never preached with such force or quiet conviction, and as Ann listened, she thought about what this unlikely young minister was saying. *Does God really care about us?* she wondered. *Does He know, right now, this instant, that this band of people are here, on this tiny ship in the midst of a vast ocean?* There could be no doubt that Caleb earnestly believed that God was with them, but it was almost too much for Ann to accept.

"Well, that dinna take too long," Isabel said after the benediction. "Do ye think Captain Murdock'd lend us his spyglass? I want to see if the other ships are still wi' us."

"I am sure they are," Ann said, turning away. She did not want Isabel to see her face; she was not even sure what was written there herself, but whatever it was, she meant to keep it private. "I must see to Mother's bedding before she comes below," she added, and hastened away before Isabel could reply.

❦

The next week continued mostly calm and fair, but there was often a chill in the air, and Sarah had begun to cough again, so she rarely ventured on deck. Ann spent much time with her mother, reading aloud Psalms and Scripture passages that Sarah knew from memory. Each day when his lessons were finished, Caleb Craighead came to sit at Sarah's bedside, and Ann looked forward to his visits, although he rarely spoke directly to her. Caleb spoke of his childhood in Scotland, not far from where Sarah had been born, and of going up to the university at Edinburgh. Often a fit of coughing would seize Sarah, and although she turned her head away from them, Ann could see the crimson stains in the cloth her mother held to her lips, and her heart ached. It was apparent that Sarah was worsening daily.

"Father, is there naught we can do?" Ann asked one evening after Sarah had suffered a particularly violent spell of coughing. "I feel so helpless."

"Aye, Lass," William agreed sadly. "There's na surgeon onboard, and such physic as the captain has canna heal but only ease pain."

"She says she feels na pain, but her eyes tell a different tale. Perhaps ye could ask Captain Murdock for some laudanum."

William nodded and went in search of the captain, but when he returned with it, Sarah would not take the draught.

"Fetch Mr. Craighead," she asked. "I have need o' his prayers tonight."

When Caleb Craighead arrived, prayer book in hand, Sarah motioned to her family. "Leave us alone now."

Ann bent down and kissed her mother's wasted cheek, her throat tight with the burden of unshed tears. Then she and William went up on deck, where Jonathan sat with the Prentisses.

"I saw Mr. Craighead go below," Jonathan said. "Is Mother worse, then?"

William did not reply but patted his son's thin shoulder.

"I think we should offer prayer now, also," Mr. Prentiss suggested, and as they bowed their heads, he hesitantly began to recite the Lord's Prayer.

" 'Thy will be done,' " Ann repeated with them, but she did not understand what that really meant. How could she pray to a God whose will could take her mother from a family that needed her sorely, when she had ever been His servant? Yet she could not help murmuring over and over, as if the mere repetition could help, "She must live; she canna die; she canna. . ."

Ann did not know how much time passed. The Prentisses drifted away at dusk, and it was fully dark when she heard the minister's steps on the deck. He came to them, saying nothing, and embraced William. He picked Jonathan up and held the boy, murmuring to him, then turned to Ann, still holding her brother. She could not see Caleb's face, but the cheek he touched to hers was damp—from his tears or the others', she could not tell.

"It is over," he said softly, and Ann felt the deck slipping away under her feet—and a long fall into darkness.

Chapter 3

When Ann regained her senses, she was lying in Isabel's bunk, and Mary Prentiss was bending over her, pouring something down her throat. She began to choke and gasp.

"There, Lass, 'twill do ye good. Swallow it down, now. That's a good girl."

"Where is Jonathan? And Father?" Ann asked, trying to rise. "I should be wi' them."

"Just lie still and rest. Everything has been seen to, and th' others are asleep. Your father thought it best that ye bide wi' us for the night."

Ann looked at the drawn curtains around her family's bunks and saw that everyone else below seemed to be sleeping. "All right," she agreed. She wanted to ask what they had done with her mother's body, but she could not bring herself to speak of it.

Mrs. Prentiss patted Ann's hand and rose. "I'll just douse this candle, then," she said, "and crawl into the bunk above ye. Try to rest, and call me if ye have need of aught."

Ann murmured her thanks, but she did not think she would sleep. The ship creaked and groaned as it usually did, the noise always more ominous during the long hours of the night. One of the babies fretted and was hushed. Mr. Simmons was snoring again, and Ann recalled with a pang how she and her mother, both awakened by the noise the first night out, had stifled their laughter. Now Sarah would never hear anything, nor ever laugh again. Tears formed in Ann's eyes and rolled unchecked down her cheeks. Her mother was dead. She would never feel her tender touch, never again hear her soft voice. Ann had asked God to spare her, but her plea had not been heard.

Why? she asked, forming the word silently in the darkness. No answer came, and eventually Ann fell into an exhausted slumber.

❧

It was not yet quite dawn when Ann was brought up to the deck for her mother's funeral. Some of the women had laid Sarah out in her good black wool dress, and she looked as if sleeping on the deck of a ship at dawn were the most natural thing in the world. A small number of their company gathered around the trestle of boards in the center of the deck as the captain conducted the ceremony. He seemed to be accustomed to the role, seldom referring to the book

19

he held. Ann barely heard Mr. Craighead's brief eulogy, though she caught his reference to Sarah as a woman whose children "rose up and called her blessed," a woman who loved and feared the Lord and walked ever in His ways.

Ann stood between her father and Jonathan, who stared straight ahead, his face expressionless. Her brother was strangely quiet, and for his sake, she held his hand tightly and willed herself not to cry. William had aged ten years in the uncertain morning light, and he kept rubbing his eyes with the back of his hand, as if dust had blown into them.

The captain's voice droned on: "Let not your heart be troubled: ye believe in God, believe also in me. In my Father's house are many mansions: if it were not so, I would have told you. I go to prepare a place for you. . . . I am the resurrection and the life: he that believeth in me, though he were dead, yet shall he live: And whosoever liveth and believeth in me shall never die. . ."

Ann heard the words, comfortless. A cool breeze sprang up and she shivered. As the last prayer was said, the captain signaled two sailors, who covered Sarah's body and moved the catafalque to the rail.

"Unto Thy depths do we commit the body of Thy servant, Sarah McKay," the captain pronounced, and the boards were tilted, sending their burden into the sea. There was a faint splash, then silence. The sailors and the captain began going about their business, and the passengers who had ventured up on deck for the service began to scatter, most pausing briefly to express their sympathy.

"We thank ye," William said to Caleb Craighead when he joined them, "for your kind words."

"She was a fine woman," Caleb said, "and there can be na doubt that she is wi' the angels this morning."

"Can Mother see us, then?" asked Jonathan, gazing up at the brightening sky as if he half-expected to see her smiling down at him.

"Perhaps," the minister replied.

"But we shan't ever see her again?"

"Nay, Lad, not on this earth. But come, ye are learning the catechism, and it tells us that the souls of believers are at their death made perfect in holiness, and do immediately pass into glory; and their bodies, bein' still united to Christ, do rest in their graves 'til the Resurrection. Do ye not recall those words?"

"Oh, I know all o' that," Jonathan replied, then paused. "I just don't understand it yet."

"Aye, Son," William said, half-smiling at the remark, "and neither does any man. But come along now. We must go below."

With a nod in Caleb's direction, William steered Jonathan toward the stairs, but Ann made no move to follow them.

Caleb moved quietly to her side.

"I was thinkin' that if there had been a surgeon on this vessel, my mother might still be alive. She should not have been taken," she said, her voice faltering.

"Someday, perhaps all ships will be required to carry surgeons," Caleb replied. "But until then, we must do the best we can. I have some stores that will be useful if a general fever breaks out—wormwood and rue to cleanse. As closely as we are confined, one fever can become an epidemic."

"Mother was ill before we left home, but we thought she was getting better. She did nothin' t' deserve her punishment," Ann said bitterly.

"Ah, Lass, dinna be angry. Ye have sustained a great loss, but ye must be strong for your family."

"But ye knew my mother. How could it be God's will ta take her, kind and loving as she was?"

"I have not the answer to that. Ye know the catechism as well as I. If we knew the intent of God, He wouldna be better than ourselves. Better to ask Him for strength than to question what canna be changed."

Tears came to Ann's eyes and she could not speak. Caleb was looking at her with such pity and concern that she felt ashamed.

"God will help ye, though I canna," he said, taking her hand in his.

"There's no help for it," she said in a choked voice. " 'Tis hard."

"I know, Lass. Now go to your family, as your mother would want ye t' do. Ye need one another now."

For several days, Ann lay belowdeck on the bunk that had been her mother's deathbed and grieved, sometimes with tears, but often without. Fitfully she tried to pray, but her heart was not in the effort; God seemed too far away and remote for any words of hers to have any effect. *Maybe one day I can accept what has happened, but not now, not yet*, she thought. She continued to keep to herself until one afternoon when Jonathan was at his lessons and the others were taking the air on deck.

Ann forced herself to open the leather trunk that held her mother's things to sort the contents, knowing she must decide what to do with each item.

She could certainly use the winter cloak, the sturdy boots, and the petticoats. Sarah's dresses, like most of the family's clothing, were made of material she had spun herself: the linen, from flax they had grown; the wool, from sheep they had raised and shorn. The dresses were a bit long for Ann, but they would do: She would keep them all. The cloth from one could be recut for Jonathan, who would need warm clothing for the winter.

Ann set aside the garments and looked at the rest of her mother's small store of earthly goods. Ann had helped her pack these things—was it only a few short weeks past? Now, in this place, each was a sad reminder of the past. Her mother's only jewelry was a golden locket that had belonged to Ann's grandmother. It enclosed a ringlet of hair, and as Ann touched it, she realized that as a girl, Sarah's hair must have been very near the shade of Ann's own, a rich chestnut brown with shades of auburn.

Next, Ann found the blue cashmere shawl that William had given Sarah as a wedding gift, and which she had worn only on special occasions. A small parcel held some baby clothes, yellowed from age, that Ann had not known her mother had packed—hers, perhaps, or maybe even Sarah's, made with dainty stitches long ago.

Underneath it all, carefully wrapped in linen, lay the parts of Sarah's spinning wheel, along with her distaff and the carding combs. Their loom, too large and bulky to fit in their allotted luggage, had been sold, but Ann was glad they had brought the wheel. She had no idea if the packet of flax seeds William had brought would grow in their new home—wherever that might be—but if they could keep a few sheep, Ann knew she would be able to use the spinning wheel to help keep them warmly clothed.

"Oh, Ann, Mother was wondering if ye wanted us to do that," Isabel said, and Ann looked up to see her friend standing beside her, looking concerned.

"There's really naught t' be done," Ann replied. "We sold most of what we had afore we left home, includin' the coverlets and linens. Mother had na much that was her own."

"I know she set a great store by that Book," Isabel said, nodding toward the Bible on the table.

"Aye, an' she told me when we were still in port that I was ta have it. She knew then that she'd na survive this voyage."

Isabel was silent for a moment, then remembered her errand. "Ann, I've been sent to bring ye up to th' deck."

Ann pushed the trunk back under the lower bunk and stood. "Why? Is there trouble?"

Isabel lowered her voice, glancing back at a curtained area midway in the family passenger section. "The Fletcher boy is taken wi' a fever, and his baby sister is verra ill wi' the same sickness. The captain told Father he doubted it was serious, but he said not to stay too close to them, all th' same. I came to fetch ye to join the rest o' us."

Ann followed Isabel up the stairs. On deck, she could not help glancing at the spot where Sarah's body had been let down into the sea. *Where is it now?* she wondered. Had it sunk to the bottom, or was it perhaps floating on top of the waves, like the drowned man Ann had once seen in Bailley Creek? She walked over to the rail and looked down at the foamy green water.

"Mistress McKay! Mistress Prentiss! Would ye come over here, please?"

It was Caleb Craighead calling to them from the midst of a circle of children.

"What is it?" Isabel asked as the girls reached him.

"Would ye help wi' the lessons whilst I hear Mavis's catechism?"

Isabel looked uncomfortable. "I canna read to them," she said.

"That is fine—just trace letters for the little ones and watch to see if they can do them after ye. Here; shake the sand smooth first. Mistress Ann, would ye read to the older ones?"

"I can try," she said. He handed her a well-thumbed copy of *The Pilgrim's Progress,* which she had heard him reading to the children earlier.

"Begin here," he directed, and moved to one side with Mavis McCarty.

Ann began to read the story of Christian, who trespassed on the grounds of Doubting Castle, where Giant Despair imprisoned Christian and his friend, Hopeful. At last, after being beaten, tormented, and threatened with death, Christian remembered a key called Promise in his bosom. Using the key, he and his friend managed to escape, whereupon Christian and Hopeful offered prayer for their deliverance. The children were intrigued with the adventure and begged for more when she ended the chapter. But Caleb was back now, and when she tried to return the book, he insisted she take it.

"Keep it for a time," he said. "Perhaps ye will be kind enough to read again to the children. Ye should read it yourself, if ye have never done so."

"I have na read it, and I thank ye."

"And thank ye both for th' help. It was a pleasant change for the children."

"I can teach letters," Isabel said as they walked away, "but I could ne'er read aloud as ye were doing. All those big words!"

"Mother made me read to her as soon as I half-learned how," Ann said. "Her eyes were weak, and she had trouble making out the words. We had na books, though, just Mother's Bible."

"The same wi' us," Isabel said. "Father says that's the only book fit to be read, anyway," she added.

"I think I'd like to read more of this book now, if ye don't mind," Ann said.

"Och, no, I don't mind. I'll just see what I can find in th' spyglass."

But when Isabel had left, Ann sat with the book closed and watched Caleb Craighead. And more than once, she caught him returning her glances.

❧

In the next few days, everyone seemed intent on keeping Ann and her family occupied. William joined in the men's endless talk about America to pass otherwise idle hours. Ian, one of the crew members, gave Jonathan a bit of wood

23

and was teaching him to carve it into a ship. At his mother's urging, Samuel Prentiss began to spend more time with Jonathan after their lessons, and Ann was glad to see him enjoying the companionship of the older boy. Such activities filled his hours and reduced the pain of his mother's death. Ann, too, was glad for the time she spent helping Caleb Craighead with his school.

The Fletcher children were not much improved, however; and Caleb, who had gone below to see them, privately advised the parents quartered nearby to continue to keep their children as far away from the Fletchers as possible. Still, the fair weather was holding, and the mood of the passengers was optimistic.

"Ian said we could use his spyglass," Samuel told the girls one afternoon, "ta see if we can find th' other ships." Since the storm, the sails of the *Star* and *Regent* had been sighted infrequently, although the captain assured them that both ships had weathered it well and were reasonably close.

"Be careful," Ann called with a mother's concern as the boys began climbing the rigging of the mizzenmast.

"Och, look at them!" Isabel exclaimed as they watched their brothers scampering up the rope ladder like monkeys.

"Jonathan's not used to heights," Ann said anxiously. "I hope Ian is watching out for them."

"They're not likely to fall." Isabel shrugged. "But he could catch them if they did."

Samuel, looking through the spyglass aft of the ship, exclaimed that he could see a sail.

"The *Regent* be there," Ian said, pointing to the far horizon, "and summat t' port, the *Star*."

"No," Samuel said, lowering the glass. "I can make out th' lines well enough to see it's neither."

"Sail ahoy!" the lookout shouted from the crow's nest.

"What could that mean? He hasna ever done that before," Isabel said, alarmed.

Immediately, Ian ordered the boys to come down, took the spyglass from Samuel, and climbed up some ten feet, hanging onto the ropes with a practiced hand while he peered in the direction the lookout was pointing. By the time he returned to the deck, Captain Murdock had appeared; and he, too, surveyed the horizon.

"What do ye think it is?" Ann asked, but Samuel shook his head.

"I dunno. She's not flyin' any flag that I could see."

"Maybe it's a pirate ship!" Jonathan exclaimed.

"I most certainly hope not," Isabel said firmly.

"Go back to the main deck now, mates," Ian told them. "We'll soon know what the vessel be."

Hearing the commotion, some of the passengers stood about, shading their eyes and peering out to sea but seeing nothing.

"Father, Samuel saw a ship!" Jonathan cried, running to William.

"So I heard. There be many ships in the Atlantic trade. 'Tis not unlikely that we'd chance to meet one from time t' time."

" 'Tis a good place for pirates to be, as well," Tom Prentiss murmured.

"Mid-ocean?"

"Why not?"

"But we are travelin' wi' other ships," William pointed out, "and like us, they are armed."

"I can fight pirates," Jonathan said, earnest enough to bring a laugh from the men.

"Ah, Lad, and I am sure ye could," William said fondly. "But that ship, if there is really one out there, is probably another merchantman, just as curious about us as we are about her."

A stir of activity on the wheel deck signaled that all was not well, and it was not long before the passengers realized their course had been altered. Still, nothing was visible on the horizon when the captain called for an assembly of the men on deck.

"We must assume the vessel is unfriendly since we are not close enough to make out her colors. At present, however, we're in no danger. She seems to be making for the *Regent*."

"Is that why we changed direction?" Ann asked.

"No, Daughter. We are making for the *Regent* as well, and the *Star* is na doubt right behind us."

"The younger men are seein' to the magazine, just in case," Mr. Prentiss murmured under his breath to William.

But Jonathan overheard the exchange and jumped up and down in excitement. "The magazine! Will they fire th' cannon, then?"

"That will be done by the sailors if need be, Son," William replied.

"What about us?" Isabel asked. "What are we t' do?"

"Don't worry, Lass," her father said. "There be weapons for the men to use, and the women and children will be safely belowdecks in case o' trouble."

"But we aren't expectin' any," William said quickly, seeing the alarm in Ann's eyes.

"All we can do now is wait," Tom Prentiss said, "and pray that the ship is friendly."

It was dusk before the familiar rigging of the *Regent*, which had veered in their direction, hove into view. Beyond it, some thought they could see the stark profile of a third vessel.

"Is that the *Star* followin' there?" William wondered.

Caleb, who had emerged from his meeting with the captain some time ago, shook his head.

"We were sailin' in the middle of the three, so the *Star* is still to our starboard, unless she saw our maneuver and changed her own course."

Across the deck, the first mate was scanning the seas with a spyglass but could see nothing in the gathering gloom.

"By now someone should have made out that ship," Mary Prentiss said uneasily. "We ought to be told what is happenin'."

"The captain will tell us in his own good time," her husband replied. "We must be patient and not think th' worst."

"Come on, ye pirates! I'll gi' ye a fair fight!" Jonathan exclaimed, waving an imaginary broadsword.

"I think 'tis time the lad went below," William told Ann, and when she moved toward him, she saw that his eyes seemed unnaturally bright.

"Let me stay up here," he pleaded. "I want ta see th' pirates."

"Jonathan, your face is verra warm," Ann said, putting her hand to his cheek. "Do ye feel ill?"

"He got dizzy on th' riggin'," Samuel volunteered, but Jonathan insisted that nothing was amiss.

"I want ta sleep on deck again," he said. "I don't like it below. It's hot, an' there are strange shadows down there." The last few mild nights the children had been allowed to bring their pallets to the deck, a novelty they welcomed.

"Not tonight, Jonathan," William said firmly. "Go below and eat your supper. We'll have prayers presently, then ye must be abed."

Chapter 4

I think Jonathan may be feverish," Ann told Isabel when she returned to the deck.

"Maybe 'tis nothing," Isabel replied. "He was so excited today. But if that is a pirate ship out there. . ."

She broke off, and thoughts of pirates—looting, killing, marauding, kidnapping—troubled their minds.

"We are a poor lot," Ann said. "The Spanish ships would be better game."

"But the pirates have no way of knowin' that," Isabel said. "Besides, poor as we are ourselves, the ship may carry a rich cargo, for all we know."

As the men dispersed from the captain's deck, Ann and Isabel stood waiting for their fathers to join them, eager to hear the latest speculation.

"Ye shouldna be above deck," William cautioned. "Cap'n Murdock advises all women and children to stay below until further notice."

"Is it a pirate ship, then?"

"He fears so, since the vessel flies na flag. But he has hope that our presence will prevent its attack on th' *Regent*."

"In any case," Tom Prentiss added, "it is unlikely that anythin' will happen before dawn, an' we are prepared."

"Will ye be armed?" Mary Prentiss asked fearfully, and her husband nodded and touched her arm in a comforting gesture.

"Where is Mr. Craighead?" Ann asked, suddenly realizing he was not among the men. Lately she had found herself noting his whereabouts, as if his presence were somehow reassuring.

"He stayed to meet further wi' the captain," William replied. "But come now; 'tis pitch-dark, and ye need to get some rest. I'll see ye below."

When they reached their quarters, Jonathan was already asleep, but his face was flushed, and he was breathing harshly through his open mouth.

"I don't like the way he looks," Ann said, but William did not seem to share her concern.

"Likely it's just the excitement, and th' boy will be fine tomorrow. I'll take a pallet up on deck and bed there tonight. Try na t' worry," he added, but his own face was drawn; and Ann knew that he, too, was missing Sarah, who would have known just what to do for the boy.

27

"Do ye think he has the fever like the Fletchers' bairns?" she asked Mrs. Prentiss when she dropped in to check on Jonathan.

"Might be," Mary Prentiss replied, laying a practiced hand on his brow. "Wet a cloth, wring it out, and put it to his forehead to bring the fever 'round. Keep his lips dressed wi' lard—the sailors can give you some—and see that he has as much of water and gruel as ye can get down his gullet."

"How are th' Fletchers?" Ann asked.

Mrs. Prentiss paused and shook her head. " 'Tis hard ta say. The little one is taken bad, I fear. Jonathan may have the same fever, or he may not. In any case, most fevers will take care o' themselves in a few days time," she added, seeing that Ann was close to tears.

"Thank ye for the help," Ann said. "I'll see to gettin' the water now."

The sailor Ian immediately brought a basin of water and a lump of fat the size of a guinea egg, promising to see that she would have gruel for Jonathan whenever it was needed. Having done all she could for the moment, Ann lay on her bunk, sleeplessly awaiting the uncertain day ahead and wishing with all her heart for her mother's calm and peaceful spirit.

❧

At dawn, those who had been able to sleep awoke to the sound of distant cannon fire. In the darkness of night, the *Regent* had become separated from the *Derry Crown* and was now apparently under attack by the unidentified ship.

Above them, Ann could hear the barking of orders and the shuffling of feet on the planking—then the thunder of their own cannon. Though the attacking ship was too far away for their fire to be effective, William had explained that the captain wanted to assure the *Regent* that help was forthcoming.

Jonathan awoke briefly and drank some water, but his fever remained high, and despite the noise and confusion, he seemed frighteningly unaware. Mrs. Prentiss stopped by to see how Jonathan was faring and confirmed the rumor that the Fletchers' infant daughter had died during the night.

"But the Fletcher boy's fever has broken, an' he spoke this morning," she added brightly.

Ann nodded, taking small comfort in Mary Prentiss's words. She had watched her mother sicken and die, and now her brother was thrashing in delirium, his face red and his breathing labored. He turned his head when she tried to put wet cloths on his face, and he would not swallow the gruel she offered. As the morning wore on, the quarters below deck became stifling, and one of the women opened the hatch above the stairway, heightening the sounds of the battle and confusion above.

"Ye look almost as flushed as Jonathan," Isabel told Ann when she brought her some bread and cheese at noon.

"It's the heat," Ann said, brushing damp tendrils of hair from her face with the back of her hand. "I'll be fine."

"Ye ought to walk about some, anyway. I'll sit wi' Jonathan for a time."

"Unfortunately, there isna anyplace to go, but I will stand up and stretch a bit. What do ye suppose is happenin' out there?"

"From what I hear, I judge we are movin' around the *Regent* now so we can have a clear shot at the pirate ship."

"Then we might draw fire as well."

"I suppose so. I don't think the pirates have boarded the *Regent,* although I heard someone say they were rigging a battering ram."

Ann shuddered. "And how are the others—the women an' children? Seems I can hear nothing but the cannonade in the distance."

"Oh, you won't hear a thing out of anyone down here, I'll vow. We're all too frightened to do anythin' more than pray and wait!"

"I wish we could go on deck." Ann sighed. "Even a breath of air would help."

"Go to th' top of the stairs, at least," Isabel urged. "Ye look fair done in."

As she stood, Ann managed a faint smile. "Maybe we can take turns breathin'. There's hardly any air left."

As Ann reached the top of the stairs, there was the familiar sight of sailors heaving on the rigging. Nothing seemed amiss, until she caught the glint of metal from the long knives stuck through their belts. Just then Mr. Craighead came into view. He, too, was armed with a brace of pistols. Ann was taxed to imagine his using a weapon, but at that moment the schoolmaster looked grimly determined enough to do so, at that.

"Mr. Craighead," Ann called softly, not wanting to give away her presence in a forbidden area. "Can ye stop for a moment?"

"Mistress Ann, don't ye know ye're in danger here?" But the tender expression on his face belied the stern tone of his voice. "And how are ye farin' below? I know 'tis warm and likely to be warmer yet ere this day is ended."

" 'Tis hot and close there, true enough, but we can stand it for a time. Did ye know that Jonathan is ill?"

"Your father said he might be. What ails him?"

"I think he must have caught the fever. The Fletcher bairn died in th' night."

Caleb shook his head sadly. "I dinna know—I should be down there wi' them, but just now every man may be needed, and I must not leave."

"Can ye tell me what is happenin'?"

Caleb repeated the story Isabel had told Ann, adding that shortly they would be in firing range of the pirate ship. "If ye hear anyone order the hatches shut, be certain to pull the bolt from the inside," he warned, "and stay away from the stairway. When ye hear our cannon firin', go to your bunks and stay there. I'll come down as soon as I can. Will ye be all right?"

Ann wanted to say some brave words, but all she could manage was a nod, and with a touch of his hand to hers, Caleb walked away.

"You there! Away from the hatch!" the first mate called, seeing her at last.

"Things may soon be gettin' noisier, when our cannon is fired," she told Isabel when she returned to their quarters.

"Noise is fine," Isabel said, tossing her head, "as long as I know who is makin' it."

An earsplitting exchange of cannon fire, punctuated by much shouting and firing of smaller arms, convinced them that the pirates must be waging a full-scale attack. During a lull in the fighting, one of the women—Ann could not tell just who—began reciting the Twenty-third Psalm, and one by one, others joined in. Suddenly Ann recalled Caleb's warning about the hatch. She was halfway up the stairs to bolt the door when it opened, and Caleb himself bounded down the stairs toward her.

"Everythin' is fine," he assured them. "We have fired on the pirates and they are in retreat. The captain says ye are all to have an airin' now, but ye must be ready to return below at a moment's notice."

The women and children needed no urging, but Ann hung back, eager for a word with Caleb.

"I must speak t' the Fletchers," Caleb told Ann, "then I'll come back an' see Jonathan."

She waited, hearing the murmur of his voice and the soft sobbing of the bereaved mother. Evidently, Caleb had persuaded her to leave her sultry quarters, for she went out past Ann and up the stairs, and Caleb came to stand by Jonathan's bunk.

"He has been like this since last night," Ann said.

Caleb put his hand on the boy's forehead, then on his chest, and shook his head. "Aye, he looks just as Danny Fletcher did at first, but Danny's much better now, and soon Jonathan will be, too."

"I have been puttin' wet cloths on his head, but the water is all gone. Can ye ask someone to bring more?"

"I'll see to it myself. But try to rest, Lass. Ye look done in yourself."

"If anythin' happens to Jonathan. . .after. . ." She could not finish, nor did she try to stop the tears.

"I am goin' to ask God to spare Jonathan and to comfort and strengthen ye," Caleb said. "Will ye pray wi' me?"

Ann nodded, unable to speak for her tears, and knelt by the bunk. Caleb began to pray. He asked for healing for Jonathan, safety for all of them during the remainder of their journey, and peace for Ann. "Amen," he finished, and rose to his feet. "I'll bring the water and sit wi' the boy so ye can go on deck awhile. I'll return soon."

Ann dried her tears, strangely moved by Caleb's prayer. His strength had flowed through her, lifting and warming her. Strangest of all, the peace he had prayed for seemed to be settling upon her. Then another part of Ann's consciousness acknowledged the man who had done the praying. No one in all her life had ever affected her so.

When Caleb returned with the water and took her place by Jonathan's side, Ann joined the other passengers crowding the rail. From the distance of several hundred yards that separated them from the *Regent*, Ann could see the smoke of several fires burning on the vessel's deck. Most of the ship's sails were down, whether from having burned or by plan, she could not tell. Beyond the *Regent*, she could barely make out another set of sails, but the pirate ship was now too far away for its guns to be any threat.

"How is Jonathan?" William asked anxiously, seeing Ann.

"About the same. Mr Craighead is wi' him now. Do ye think the pirates will return?"

"I doubt it, but we'll stay close by the *Regent* in case they do."

"It must have been fair sportin' to see!" said Isabel, her vivid blue eyes sparkling.

"They are well-fitted to do battle," William replied, "but had we not been able to join her so soon, the *Regent* would be in the pirates' hands, wi'out a doubt."

Noting an edge of excitement in her father's voice, Ann realized that he had enjoyed the encounter with pirates. What was it about danger that men found so attractive?

"Ye all look so dangerous, with those knives and big pistols," Isabel said. "Were the transported men given arms, as well?"

"Aye, they were," Isabel's father answered. "There would be na reason to refuse them the right t' defend themselves. Most of the men are being transported from debtor's prisons and were never ordinary criminals, anyway."

"And they'll be free in America, when we get there," William added.

"Well, not exactly," Tom Prentiss corrected. "They'll serve five years' indenture before they're on their own. But 'twould be against their own best interests to cause any trouble aboard ship."

"Mr. Craighead has done a good work wi' those men," William remarked. "He has them sayin' their prayers every night, I hear."

"He has been kind to *everyone*," Ann said, "and we mustn't take advantage o' him. Father, I should go back to Jonathan now and let Mr. Craighead rest."

William glanced at the sky, which was rapidly darkening from the east. "We may all be joinin' ye soon. Looks as if our fair spell of weather may be comin' to an end."

Thunder rumbled across the sky as if to confirm William's prediction.

"Thank God that's not cannon fire," Tom Prentiss said fervently.

" 'Twill help put out the fires if it rains," Ann heard someone say as she went back to the stairway.

When she reached Jonathan's bunk, Ann saw that Caleb had fallen asleep, his head resting against the bulwark. With eyes closed and face unguarded in sleep, the somewhat stern lines around his mouth were barely noticeable, and he looked younger—vulnerable now, and very human. For a long moment, she studied those faint lines as if some vital secret might reveal itself there. For the first time it occurred to Ann that no one gave comfort to this man who gave so much to others. *Surely he must need encouragement sometimes,* she thought. Or was his faith and trust in God so complete that it filled his whole life, with no need for anything or anyone else?

" 'Could ye not watch with me one hour?' " he quoted ruefully, opening his eyes and smiling at her in chagrin at being observed.

"Ye need to rest, too," she said, flustered. "Ye ought to go and get some food now."

"I will," he said, rising to his feet. "Send for me, though, if Jonathan seems worse or if ye need aught."

"We owe ye a great debt already—more than can ever be repaid."

"Nay," he protested. " 'Tis the other way 'round." Caleb put a hand to Ann's cheek for a moment and then, almost before she had time to realize he had touched her, he was gone.

Outside, the thunder crashed, and the ship began to roll as the wind freshened and the billowing waves rose. The storm broke, sending the women and children streaming back into the family quarters, but Ann scarcely noticed.

Isabel found her standing by Jonathan's bunk, her hand pressed to her face, eyes staring into the distance.

"There'll be a rough night ahead," Isabel said. "Ye'd best get ready to hang on."

"Aye," Ann replied. "I will." She climbed into her bunk and watched the shadows deepen into darkness. This night, too, would pass. And tomorrow—tomorrow she would see Caleb again.

Chapter 5

The *Derry Crown* pitched and tossed for two days, and once again Ann felt the wretchedness of seasickness. To her surprise, however, she began to recover even before the storm's fury was spent. William could take no food, but he stayed nearby, seeing to it that she and Jonathan had whatever was needed. Kegs had been placed on the deck to catch rainwater, and William, with Ian's help, brought down enough to their quarters to last for several days.

"The water that was put on at Londonderry is na longer fit to drink, but this is fresh," William said as he handed Ann a cup. "I'll lift the boy up, and ye try to make him swallow a draught."

Despite the motion of the ship and Jonathan's restless thrashing, Ann was able to get a bit of the water down his throat. She took some comfort in the knowledge that Jonathan was at least no worse, a fact that Caleb Craighead confirmed on his visits. Because so many were now ill, he never stayed very long, but he stopped by several times a day, a calm and reassuring presence in the midst of the turmoil.

On the third morning, when the storm seemed to be waning, Ann awoke with the feeling that it would be a critical day for Jonathan's illness.

"How is he this mornin'?" asked Mary Prentiss, herself wobbly from seasickness, when she saw that Ann had opened the curtains around their bunks.

Ann laid her hand on Jonathan's cheek. His hair was matted and his eyes darkly circled, but his color was better. "He seems less feverish," she said cautiously.

Mrs. Prentiss nodded. " 'Twas about this time that Danny Fletcher came to himself. Jonathan will surely do th' same."

Ann said nothing. Neither of the women would utter the thought that was in both their minds—that during this same crisis period, the Fletchers' baby girl had died. Ann remembered, too, so vaguely that she was not certain whether she had dreamed it, her mother's sitting at the bedside of two dead infants, clasping her Bible in her lap and never shedding a tear. In the hope of a measure of comfort, Ann took Sarah's Bible from the table and held it. Instead of consolation, however, it was a grim reminder of her mother's absence. Sarah would have known what to do. If she had not died, Jonathan might never have become ill at all. *I should have died*, Ann thought, *I should be ill now, instead of Jonathan*. So deeply was she absorbed in her dark thoughts that at first Ann did not realize Caleb was standing beside her.

"Are ye all right?" he asked.

Startled, she turned to face him. "Oh! I dinna ken ye were there! I was woolgatherin', I guess. . . . Jonathan looks some better this mornin', don't ye think?"

William, who had gone for more water, returned with it and watched as Caleb touched the boy's forehead gently. "I dinna know what we'd do if we lost him, Mr. Craighead," William said thickly.

It was the first time Ann had heard William admit the possibility that Jonathan might not recover. *If Mr. Craighead says we must accept God's will, I'll scream!* she thought.

"Let's pray together," he suggested and knelt with them around Jonathan's bunk. As Caleb asked God to heal Jonathan and strengthen them all, Ann took her brother's hand, which now seemed but little warmer than her own. Had she imagined it, or had Jonathan's hand moved in hers? She opened her eyes as the prayer ended to find Jonathan, clear-eyed, regarding them with curiosity.

"What's the matter?" he asked, seeing that they were on their knees, and then, remembering, he sat up so suddenly that he almost struck his head on the bunk above. "Th' pirates! Are they still out there? Can I go see them?"

Ann sank back on her heels, tears of joy stinging her eyes.

William and Caleb both laughed, relieved, but Caleb answered the boy kindly. "Nay, Jonathan, I think the pirates have left us for better game. How do ye feel?"

Jonathan lay back, his forehead suddenly damp with perspiration. "Tired," he said. "I would like some water, please."

Caleb touched Jonathan's forehead again and nodded. "God be praised; the boy's fever has broken."

"Don't take too much o' this," William warned as Jonathan eagerly seized the cup of water he had poured. "Ye have not had much food or drink these several days, and too much now willna stay down."

"Several days?" Jonathan echoed, looking puzzled.

"Aye, Son, ye had a long sleep, but wi' a bit of rest, ye'll soon be good as new."

"I had some strange dreams," Jonathan said, his face clouded. "I was wi' Mother up on Maunder Hill just as the sun was goin' down. But then she went away, and everythin' got dark, and I was afraid. I called and called, but she didna come back."

" 'Tis all right," Ann said, hugging Jonathan to her. " 'Twas just a bad dream. Rest and I'll see what I can find for ye to eat."

"Thank ye for lookin' in on us," William said as Caleb got up to leave. "The Lord most surely heard your prayers today."

"No more than yours. Or. . . ," Caleb said, looking at Ann, "yours. I must go now and tell the captain the good news. He has been much concerned about the boy."

As Ann fed Jonathan some broth, her relief at his recovery was almost eclipsed by the pain that his mention of Sarah brought her. She would be here now, smiling at her son, if God had heard Ann's prayer.

"Ann?"

"Aye, Jonathan. What is it?"

"When I thought ever'body had left me in the dark, I was scared. I ken Mother won't be back, since she's in heaven, but I don't want ye to go, too."

"Hush, now," Ann soothed. "Those were just feverish dreams ye had. Ye were never alone, not for a moment, an' I promise that I'll never leave ye."

Jonathan nodded, stretched, and yawned. "All right," he said drowsily, "but next time, wake me up. I wanted t' see the pirates."

When Ann was satisfied that Jonathan was sleeping peacefully, William sitting alongside, she ventured on deck for the first time in several days. The sky was clearing, with no sign of another sail anywhere on the horizon. A brisk wind was moving the *Derry Crown* along at a good pace.

" 'Tis good to be out again, isn't it?" Isabel greeted her. "Mr. Craighead told us that Jonathan was mendin'—we are all greatly relieved."

"As are we," Ann replied, "and I'm glad to see that the ship is underway again."

"We were blown off course in the storm, accordin' to Ian, and no one has seen the other ships since."

"Includin' the pirates?"

"Yes, thank heaven. We lost a day's sailing maneuverin' around the *Regent,* but wi' fair weather and a holdin' wind, we should make port in another ten days or so."

"This is our seventh week out, isn't it?" asked Ann, amazed she had not completely lost her sense of calendar time. "Father wasna expectin' that we would make port on the announced day, but I for one will be verra glad to set my feet on dry land again."

"We may not be able to walk by then." Isabel smiled. "After the pitchin' of this deck, people may think we are tipsy." Then her expression grew serious, and Isabel squeezed Ann's hand. "I wish we could stay together when we reach America."

"So do I," Ann replied, "but our destination is uncertain."

"I have heard that the colonies are huge past all imaginin', wi' more than enough room for everybody in Ireland and Scotland as well, but Father will go where a merchant is needed."

"And we'll be goin' wherever the land is available. We have th' name of a wool merchant in Philadelphia, a man from our county, who can give Father advice."

"I doubt we'll stay in Philadelphia," Isabel said, "since it is a large city and already full of merchants. But I do hope we settle where people are nigh."

"So do I," Ann agreed, but in reality she had not given much thought to what would happen when they reached their destination.

Suddenly, she realized that she was not looking forward to the end of the voyage. As tiring as the journey had been, as tragic the circumstances, there was at least a predictable pattern to their lives. In addition, the little community of passengers, with Caleb Craighead as their unofficial leader, had forged friendships, strengthened by the bond of shared hardships.

Resuming the threads of family life without her mother would be an overwhelming task. Ann knew that with the void left by Sarah's passing would come the burdens of everyday life. Would she be equal to the task? Physically, Ann knew her strength excelled her mother's, but Sarah had always relied on inner resources that gave her abilities beyond that dictated by her poor health. Ann hesitated to admit her fears, particularly to Isabel, who had obviously never concerned herself about spiritual matters. And certainly Caleb Craighead's faith seemed unshakable.

Caleb resumed the children's lessons, once again enlisting the aid of Ann and Isabel, but she never saw him apart from the others. And so the days quickly passed, and Ann kept her thoughts to herself.

☙

The weather held, the wind continued fair, and one morning Ann awoke to the sound of seagulls come out to greet the ship, wheeling and calling above the sails. Everyone crowded to the rail, eagerly searching the horizon for their first glimpse of land, but it was not until that afternoon that the first faint smudge appeared on the western horizon.

"Is that Philadelphia?" asked Jonathan, who had been allowed to spend several hours each day on deck. He was still weak from the illness, but his curiosity was undiminished.

"Nay, Lad," said Ian, overhearing Jonathan's question. "That land ye see is far to the north of where we're bound. Ye'll see that we'll turn more southerly now and lay for Delaware Bay."

"When will we get there, then?" asked William.

" 'Tis two days to the bay, then we wait for the health inspector to row out to the boat and clear us to land. After that, we come in wi' the wind and the tide."

"Will we see Indians in Philadelphia?" Jonathan asked.

"Ye're not likely to see any savages in the city," Ian replied, "but once in the country, ye'll see a few."

"We've heard that the Indians in Pennsylvania are a peaceful lot," William said. "I hope 'tis true."

"The Penns are always treatyin' wi' the Indians," Ian said. "Bein' Quakers, fightin' is agin their religion, so mayhap they've worked a bit harder for peace than some of the other colonies. For my part, I don't rightly hanker t' live amongst 'em, though."

Overhearing the conversation, Caleb Craighead joined them. "I know the Penns, as proprietors of the colony, have always respected freedom of religious choice, as well," he said. "William Penn was a Quaker, aye, but he never set out to make it the religion everyone else had to follow."

"And where will ye be goin' when we land, Mr. Craighead?" asked William. "I don't believe we've heard ye say."

"I am not sure," the minister replied. "Since I am a redemptioner, I must raise my fare within three days of landing or be indentured."

"Indentured! I should think the church would have paid your way, and gladly, with so many of us comin' o'er these days."

"I didna ask it," he replied. "I can always earn my keep as a teacher, if it comes to that."

"But for a minister not to follow his callin'—"

"I have reason to believe that certain ministers in Philadelphia will help me," Caleb interrupted. "In any case, I am already a servant of the Lord and in His hands."

"What would your term of indenture be if ye canna raise your fare?"

"It depends on what the captain asks. For the men bein' transported, it is five years. In my case, I think he could get my fare for a three-year term."

"Three years!" exclaimed William, expressing aloud the alarm that Ann felt on hearing Caleb's words. " 'Tis a long time not ta be your own man."

" 'Ye are not your own. . .ye are bought with a price,' " Caleb quoted from Scripture. "The Lord will provide," he added, and looked at Ann with an expression she could not fathom. "Utter trust comes only from utter dependence."

"A hard lesson," William murmured, shaking his head. "Jonathan looks tired, Daughter. You had best take him below now. He ought not look peaked when th' inspector sees him."

Ann did as she was told, picking up the light burden and starting for the stairs.

"I wish Mr. Craighead was coming wi' us," said Jonathan, to whom the talk of indenture meant nothing. "I feel lots safer when he is nearby."

"Aye," Ann agreed, thinking how well Jonathan had put it.

The man seemed to impart a quiet strength to all whom he touched. Certainly, of all the passengers aboard the *Derry Crown*, Caleb Craighead was the one man she would never forget.

Chapter 6

There were cheers from the weary passengers of the *Derry Crown* when ocean-bound colonial fishing vessels and merchant ships passed by, some so close that the features of those on board could be clearly seen. Then the *Regent* sailed by, bound for Charleston Harbor, and, in a few hours, the *Star*. As the ship neared the coast, they could make out houses and trees and could see spirals of smoke rising from cooking fires.

Two days later the *Derry Crown* lay at anchor just inside Delaware Bay, tantalizingly close to the city that was its destination. Those who ventured on deck with the first light of dawn were rewarded by the sight of the sun gleaming on distant, red-brick buildings and shimmering on newly leafed trees. As the city awoke, the ship's spyglass revealed a panorama of horses and wagons, herds of cattle being driven from the city to graze on common ground, dockworkers, sailors, merchants.

Now that their journey was over, Ann felt as though she could not endure another delay to feel dry land beneath her feet. Still, the ship could approach no nearer until the inspector gave his approval. Impatient, the passengers had packed up their belongings and they now stood, like so many refugees, at the rail.

As the hours passed and the inspector did not appear, Captain Murdock announced that a hearty meal would be served in the evening, as there were still ample rations.

"I certainly hope to be on shore before then," said Mary Prentiss. Like the others, she had packed her family's belongings and stood on the deck by the luggage, watching for the inspector's arrival.

"The captain seems easy enough about it," William remarked. "Ye would think he'd want to be about his business, as well."

"Ah, but the more that know the *Derry Crown* is landin', the better the crowd for the auction, when the unconsigned goods and the convicts are offered," Tom told them, passing along what he had heard Ian say. "Likely the notice will be posted today that we are in port."

"Then we'll not leave the ship today?" Mary Prentiss asked, disappointed.

"We could, if the inspector comes in time and approves it."

I wonder how they feel? mused Ann, looking at Caleb who was conversing with some of the men facing auction. "Do they know they are about to lose their freedom?" she asked aloud.

"Those men were prisoners," William reminded her, "and, besides, indenture isna permanent. With a fair master, they'll be taken care of for their terms, and then have a fresh start."

"Still, it sounds like an uncertain business," Ann replied.

"Look!" called Jonathan, who had stationed himself at the rail with Ian's spyglass. "A boat is rowin' this way."

"Here, let me look," said William, taking the glass.

A man, bewigged and looking quite official, was being conveyed by rowboat. Presently the portly gentleman, in flowered waistcoat and dark knee breeches, clambered up the rope ladder that had been lowered for him. After disappearing into the captain's cabin, the inspector emerged some moments later waving a sheaf of papers and began a perusal of the sailors who had been mustered for his inspection.

"And are these all of your passengers? Are there any below?" he asked, glancing at the family groups gathered on the deck. Captain Murdock glanced inquiringly at Caleb, who nodded his head in confirmation.

"My passengers are all here, Dr. Elliott," the captain said. "Of course, you may check the quarters if you like."

Ann tensed, not knowing what to expect. There were few physicians in their part of Ireland, and to her memory, no one in her family had ever been attended by one. Even though the sun had put some color back into Jonathan's cheeks and he was no longer running a fever, he did not look entirely well, and she feared the inspector's diagnosis.

She caught her breath when he paused before Jonathan.

"You, Lad! Are you ill?"

"No, Sir," said Jonathan faintly.

"Put out your tongue," the inspector directed. He tilted the boy's head, pulled up his eyelids, then put an ear to his chest before he was satisfied. "Captain Murdock, you must carry more victuals in your hold," he said, moving on to the next group. "I have seen scarecrows with more meat on their bones."

"He dinna ask about the fever," William whispered. "Now if he sees nothing amiss wi' Danny Fletcher, we should all pass."

Older and stronger than Jonathan, and with the advantage of several more days of recuperation, Danny looked as well as the rest of the children. Everyone had lost weight and had come to think of their gaunt frames as normal. Only now, as the doctor scrutinized them, did Ann notice anew the prominence of hipbones and the hollowness of cheeks among the passengers.

In ten minutes more the surgeon general, having taken a quick look below the decks for form's sake, placed his seal on the passenger manifest and with a final wave for the captain, returned to his boat.

"When can we land?" The single question sprang from several throats.

"First tide tomorrow," Captain Murdock called to them, "if we've a bit of wind to help us. Mr. Craighead, whilst we are all assembled, I think it would be fittin' if ye would offer our thanks for a safe passage."

Even those who had not attended the Sabbath services fell to their knees as Caleb raised his arms and closed his eyes. The atmosphere was heavy with emotion as the passengers, soon to be parted, were united once more—in relief that the long voyage was over and in uncertainty of the future.

As Caleb called on God to continue to lead them on their separate paths, Ann wondered what the next days would bring for him. If he felt apprehensive about his own future, he gave no hint in his voice, which was firm and positive.

The prayer ended, and the passengers dispersed to prepare for their final night on board ship. Ann, remembering that she still had Mr. Craighead's copy of *The Pilgrim's Progress*, went below for it and returned to find him packing his books.

"I almost forgot to return this," Ann said, holding the book out to him.

"Did ye have an opportunity to finish it?" he asked, making no move to take it from her outstretched hand.

"I have na read it all," she confessed.

"Then keep it, and share it wi' others as ye go," he said.

"Oh, I couldna do that!" Ann protested, aware of the book's value. In Ireland, such a book would cost a working man half a month's wages.

"Sit down," Caleb invited, closing the lid of the box to make a seat. "Do ye know how this book came to be written?"

"I think Reverend Duffie told us it was written from a prison."

Caleb nodded. "Aye, John Bunyan spent twelve years in prison because he refused to stop preaching. Christian's search for the Celestial City represents our journey of life, wi' the temptations and problems everyone must face."

"From what I have read, it is a sad story," Ann said. "Everyone tries to stop Christian, or hurt him, and there are so few who are willin' to help."

"Ah, yes, but did ye note the ending?"

When Ann shook her head, Caleb took the book from her, and quickly turning the pages, he began to read aloud:

> *"Now I saw in my dream, that these two men went in at the gate;*
> *and lo as they entered, they were transfigured; and they had raiment on*

that shone like gold. . . . Then I heard in my dream, that all the bells in the City rang again for joy; and that it was said unto them, 'Enter ye into the joy of your Lord'. . . . Now, just as the gates were opened to let in the men, I looked in after them; and behold, the City shone like the sun; the streets also were paved with gold; and in them walked many men, with crowns on their heads, palms in their hands, and golden harps to sing praises withal. . . .'

Caleb closed the book. "The heavenly city is the end of Christian's journey. Just as we have reached the end of our voyage, having been beset by various woes, so one day when we reach the end of this life's journey will we go to claim God's promises. That is the message of this book." He held it out to her once more. "Please take it."

"I canna accept it."

"Accept its message, then."

Ann dropped her eyes and felt the blood rushing to her face. While she was still attempting to frame a reply, Caleb spoke.

"Your mother knew that her family would grieve for her, and she asked me to give all of ye what comfort I could. Your father has great resilience, and Jonathan, though a child, has fared well, wi' your help. But I have sensed that ye—"

Ann spoke quickly. "Ye have been a great help to us all," she answered him, meeting his level gaze with difficulty. She could not let him know how spiritually empty she was and risk his scorn, or worse, his pity.

"Not as much as I should have been," he said, "especially not for ye. I was hoping—"

"We are all most grateful to ye," she interrupted. "Please dinna concern yourself about us. Whatever happens, we'll manage."

Caleb looked as if he would say more, but Ann turned and left him standing there, holding the book and gazing after her with an expression that would have surprised her had she looked back.

❦

There was little time for prolonged farewells the next day when the *Derry Crown* eased up to one of the new wooden docks that had just been built for the burgeoning Atlantic–West Indies trade. Except for Caleb and the men who were being transported, all of the passengers and their belongings were off the ship before nine o'clock.

The McKays and Prentisses shared the expense of a freight wagon to carry their luggage to the city. Ann, Isabel, and Samuel walked along beside it, while Jonathan was allowed to ride on the seat with the teamster.

"The grass here is not as green as in Ireland," Isabel noted as they passed a meadow where cows were grazing. A boy little older than Jonathan, attending the cattle with the aid of a long stick, waved to them, and Jonathan waved back.

"The soil does not seem t' be so rocky, either," Ann observed. "Father always said that stones were Ireland's best crop."

"And the land is flat, as far as it can be seen."

After passing a scattering of partially constructed buildings along Dock Street, the driver turned the wagon onto the widest street they had yet seen, with wooden market stalls and stores selling every kind of item imaginable. Although the roadway was unpaved and the sandy soil was already dusting the hems of their dresses, broad flagstones stood before each house, and most had hitching posts set in them.

"Philadelphia certainly doesna look much like Londonderry," Isabel said, comparing it to the only other city either of the girls had seen.

"The houses are finer than I expected," Ann said. Although there were some buildings constructed of stone and a few of wood, the majority seemed to be of brick made from red clay, a material seldom seen in their part of Ireland.

"Cap'n Murdock said we could lodge here cheaply and in comfort," Tom Prentiss said presently, ordering the drayman to stop before a two-story house, identified by a brightly colored signboard as the Swallow Inn. The owners were a Quaker couple who dressed plainly and whose speech was liberally sprinkled with "thees" and "thous," a novelty that greatly interested Jonathan.

After they had unloaded their luggage, William asked the way to the wool merchant Josiah Pendleton's shop, and finding that it was but a short distance, decided to visit him at once.

"Ye'd best put Jonathan abed," he told Ann. "I'll see what the merchant advises."

Although he protested that he was not tired, Jonathan fell asleep almost instantly. Ann left the door open to their room and went across the hall to see Isabel.

"Let's go to the auction this afternoon," suggested Isabel. Tom Prentiss was readily persuaded to accompany them while his wife stayed at the inn in case Jonathan should awaken.

A fair-sized crowd had already gathered when they reached the designated site, and Ann saw Captain Murdock's agent conversing with the men who would apparently conduct the sale. The cargo was put up first and quickly sold. Then the agent appeared, accompanied by the men from the ship.

"Oh, look, there is Mr. Craighead as well!" exclaimed Isabel, craning her neck for a better view.

"I thought he had three days to raise his fare," Ann said. "Surely the agent is not goin' to bring him to the block today."

"The sale has begun," Mr. Prentiss said, shushing the girls. They listened attentively as the agent read a claim that the first man was healthy and strong and had formerly worked in the stonecutting trade.

"Four pounds!" called a man with powdered hair and wearing a rust-colored velvet suit.

"Six pounds!" cried a gentleman with a wooden walking stick and elegant silver-buckled shoes.

When no further bids were made, the auctioneer brought down his gavel. "Done!" he shouted.

The sale continued, until at last the agent pointed to Caleb Craighead.

"This man is a redemptioner," he said, "but he's a schoolmaster with a university education. Should any of ye want to pay his fare today, see me after the sale. If he's not redeemed, he'll be offered here day after next."

Even here, surrounded by strangers and in trying circumstances, Caleb had lost none of his quiet assurance. Ann longed to go to him and speak some words of encouragement, but her action was unneeded. She watched as he bid farewell to the men whose fate he might well share, then made his way to where they stood.

"How awful—bein' inspected like a cargo of fish!" Isabel declared.

Caleb smiled at her indignation. "The agent was only doin' his job," he told her. "It happens that schoolmasters with any sort of university education are in short supply in the colony, and he thinks I would fetch a good price."

"I don't see how ye can look so unconcerned, Mr. Craighead," Tom Prentiss said. "I'd think ye'd be on your knees askin' for deliverance."

"The Lord is acquainted with my situation," he replied quietly.

"Well, I still think 'tis a disgrace!" said Isabel, tossing her hair.

"Can you dine with us this evenin'? We are all stayin' at the Swallow Inn, just up a few blocks on Market Street," Mr. Prentiss invited.

"If I am back in time, I should verra much like to join ye," he said. "I have been given leave to seek out some of my fellow ministers, and am to go to a place called Neshaminy. I have no notion how far it is, nor how long 'twill take to get there."

"May your errand be successful." Ann spoke for the first time. "If we were rich folk, we would pay your fare ourselves."

"There was some talk of it on the ship, but Mr. Craighead wouldna hear to it," Tom Prentiss said. "I still say if we'd all ha' given a bit, it could ha' been done."

"And I appreciated th' offer greatly," Caleb replied, openly touched by Tom's sincerity. "Now if ye'll all excuse me, I must be about findin' my way to Neshaminy."

"Poor Mr. Craighead," said Isabel as they walked back to the inn. "What do ye suppose will happen if he canna raise his fare?"

"I don't ken," Ann replied, wondering what would happen if he did.

❧

William returned from Josiah Pendleton's shop just before the supper hour. As they ate, he told the others what he had learned.

"There's land to be had, all right, but not in these parts. Mr Pendleton suggested we head south and west—o'er the mountains."

"And is the land really free, as the agent claimed?" asked Tom Prentiss.

"Officially, land fetches sixteen pounds an acre in the Pennsylvania colony, with a quitrent o' a ha'penny an acre."

"That much!" exclaimed Ann, thinking of the slender sum that must support them in this new land.

"Aye," William explained, "but the quitrent is seldom collected on small acreage. It seems that the proprietors are so anxious to have land cleared and settled that they look the other way when squatters move in on an unoccupied grant."

"And how will ye reach these lands?" Tom inquired.

"Mr. Pendleton said I should buy oxen and a cart here, since I'd have need of a team to clear the land when we arrive, and they're not to be found in the West. Then we travel ta Lancaster."

"How far is that, Father?" asked Ann, wishing their journey would soon end.

"Several days hence," he replied. "First thing tomorrow I must see the merchants who can supply our needs. Mr. Pendleton was kind enough to give me directions and the names of men in Lancaster who can help us further."

Ann knew her mother would have felt Josiah Pendleton's assistance was a sign that Providence was looking after them, and no doubt Caleb Craighead would agree. *If only I, too, could believe it,* she thought, *I might find peace.*

❧

Caleb Craighead did not come to the Swallow Inn that Tuesday evening, and by Wednesday afternoon Ann had resigned herself to the probability that she would not see him again. The thought brought both relief and disappointment. On the one hand, she was afraid he would embarrass her by continually questioning her spiritual state; but at the same time, she longed to see him again. Something—she was not sure what—lay between them, unfinished.

Late Wednesday afternoon, when Jonathan was taking a nap and William and the Prentisses were gone to the market, the indentured maid-of-all-work at the Swallow Inn knocked on Ann's door and announced there was a caller to see her.

It must be Caleb, Ann thought at once, feeling her pulse leap. Glancing at her reflection in the pier glass, she patted the bit of ribbon she had used to hold her hair back and wondered if Mr. Craighead would find her appearance changed. She was wearing a dress of her mother's that had recently been altered to fit her and thought perhaps it made her look older. Walking down the stairs, she slowed her pace and tried to adopt a composure that would befit a more mature image.

Her efforts at entering the room gracefully were for naught, however, for Caleb stood with his back to the stairs. Hands behind him, he was looking out the window at the busy street and turned only when he heard her footsteps on the plank floor. When he saw her, he regarded her with some surprise in his clear gray eyes, and Ann's heart was wrenched at the signs of dust on his clothing and the lines of fatigue around his mouth.

"Everyone else has gone to the market except Jonathan, and he is asleep," she said quickly, already uncomfortable under his steady gaze.

"I am sorry to miss seein' them, but ye can tell them my news."

"We have all been hopin' that ye would raise the fare," she said, and he nodded.

"That I have—with the help of Reverend William Tennant and some of his friends. He asked me to stay and teach in his college, but when he realized I felt a different call, he wanted to help."

"Where will ye go then?"

"Where God has need of me," he answered simply. "Reverend Tennant mentioned that more and more settlers are venturing west, most of them with none to minister to them, so that direction would seem to be the most likely."

"I am glad ye will not be indentured," Ann said. "We shouldna have wanted to see ye sold."

"Nor I!" he agreed. Caleb smiled, the quick upward lift of his mouth that only momentarily changed his usually sober expression, and Ann returned his smile, unable to think of anything to say to him. It was then that he reached into his cloak and brought out a small parcel, which he handed her.

"I want ye to take this," he said. "And make no argument," he added, seeing that she seemed ready to protest. "There is probably much that I ought to say to ye about God's dealings, but ye have heard it all before. The mind is often aware of a matter before the heart is ready to act upon it. My prayer for ye is that soon ye will find God's peace, as your mother did."

Ann remained silent, holding the package he had given her and making no effort to return it. She had dreaded the time when Caleb would reopen this subject, dreaded even more the moment he would leave. And still she could not speak.

"Your mother loved ye very much," he went on. "And just before she died, she asked me to look after ye. Although I am not in a position to do that now, I do not want to lose contact with your family. Do ye know where ye will settle?"

"No, only that we will go west. The wool merchant, Josiah Pendleton, told us to go to Lancaster and inquire there. We are to leave in the mornin'. Mr. Pendleton does business wi' many of our countrymen, and we are to tell him when we find a settlin' place."

"I will be in touch with him, then." Caleb reached out and took Ann's hand. "I have th' conviction that we will meet again."

"Perhaps we will," Ann replied, making an effort to return his steady gaze. Still holding her hand, Caleb pulled her to him, pressing his lips to her forehead.

"Good-bye, Child. God be wi' ye," he murmured, and was gone before she could speak. For a moment Ann considered calling after him, her arms longing to return his brief embrace. But he had called her "child," and Ann felt that she would be foolish, indeed, to believe that a mature man like Caleb Craighead could think of her otherwise.

Ann unwrapped the package he had given her and found Caleb's copy of *The Pilgrim's Progress*. Opening the book, she saw that to his name and the words *Edinburgh, 1730,* had been added a fresh inscription: "For Ann McKay, whose pilgrimage is just beginning."

Ann closed the book and hugged it to her, happy to have something of Caleb's. *It will be a talisman for me in the days ahead,* she thought. And one day, perhaps it would bring him back to her.

❦

When the others found that they had missed seeing Mr. Craighead, they were disappointed, but all were happy to hear that he would not have to be indentured. Although Ann did not tell anyone about Caleb's gift, Isabel apparently sensed that something had happened between them and tried to find out what Ann was feeling.

"If Mr. Craighead already had a church, do ye think he would ask ye to marry him?" asked Isabel.

"Certainly not!" Ann replied, wondering where Isabel had gotten that notion. "For one thing, he thinks of me as a child; and in any case, wi' Father and Jonathan to look after, I've no time to be concerned with marryin' anyone."

"You will, though. Over here, women are in short supply, and any girl can just about have her pick."

"Who told ye that?" Ann asked, eager to steer the conversation into a neutral topic.

"Sally, the servant girl here at the inn. Of course, she still has time left on her indenture and canna marry until her term is up, but she says she's already had several offers."

Ann thought of the servant girl's pockmarked face and plain features and wondered if Sally had spoken truthfully. "Well, in that case," Ann said, "ye should have a husband and a houseful of bairns by the next time we meet."

"If only we could travel together!" Isabel said, growing serious. Tom Prentiss had decided to go down the Delaware River in search of a likely placc to sct up in trade, and, like William McKay, he did not yet know where he would settle.

"Father has his heart set on farmin' his own land, and when he makes up his mind to a thing, there's na way to turn him frae it. It's unlikely that we would be in th' same area."

"I know. But I'll miss having a friend like ye to talk to."

"And we'll miss ye all as well," Ann replied, aware that she and Jonathan would both feel the loss of Mary Prentiss, who had become a second mother to them and whose advice and aid would be sorely missed.

There were tears in Mary Prentiss's eyes that night as the families said their farewells. "Ye're a brave lass, and ye'll do fine on your own, I've na doubt," she told Ann. "Remember that your father may have to have your needs brought to his mind from time t' time, not being used to managing wi'out Sarah. Ye know that Jonathan is not well," she added, lowering her voice so that he would not hear her, "and when the hot weather fever comes, he'll bear close watchin'."

"I'll do my best," Ann replied. She had been surprised at the resilience of her brother's spirits, which had remained high despite the loss of his mother and the weakening effects of his illness, but she knew that he, too, would miss Mrs. Prentiss. And from all accounts, their land journey to Lancaster, a distance of some seventy miles, would be almost as arduous as the sea voyage had been, though not as lengthy.

"We'll not see ye in the mornin'," Tom Prentiss said at the door of the McKays' room as he paused to shake William's hand. "But Godspeed to ye all, and may we someday meet again."

"Amen," murmured William, and turned aside, unable to say more.

❧❧

The wagon William had purchased to carry their goods to Lancaster was little more than a two-wheeled oxcart, and by the time their possessions were placed on it, there was barely enough room left for Jonathan. A bit of space remained at the rear of the cart where Ann could ride if she became too weary of walking, but she could tell even before she tried it that it would not be comfortable.

Jonathan was still half asleep when William brought him down at dawn, and he hardly seemed aware of what was happening when he was placed in the cart. The early morning air was chill, and Ann wrapped a shawl about her head and shoulders as they walked through the waking city. William had been told to make his way to the western edge of Philadelphia to find the road to Lancaster, and with the rising sun behind them, they began the journey that would take them several days.

As they picked their way around the stumps and ruts of the Minqua Indian Path, they decided the Prentisses had been wise to travel by water. Walking along, each lost in thought, Ann wondered what was troubling her father. Never a jovial man, he had become moody and withdrawn since their arrival in Philadelphia.

"Father?"

"What is it?"

"How long do ye think it will take before we find our land?"

He was silent for a moment, then he shook his head. "The Lord only knows," he replied. "All we can do now is get to Lancaster. Then we must proceed from there on faith."

It was what Sarah might have said—but somehow William's voice did not ring with the same assurance.

Chapter 7

Rain began falling early in the morning of their second day on the road, and while the heavy canvas that William had bought in Philadelphia protected most of their belongings and kept Jonathan reasonably dry, the resulting quagmire slowed their progress considerably. Even her mother's boots and cloak couldn't keep the damp from crawling into Ann's very bones; and as the shower settled into a steady downpour and the air grew cooler, she wondered how long she could continue to walk. The sandy clay soil sucked at her feet, making every step an effort. Ahead of her, William walked by the oxen, the steam rising from their straining backs. From time to time he glanced in her direction, as if to assure himself that she was still there.

The land through which they had been passing had been settled for some time now. Already visible in the fields were greening shoots of buckwheat and other grains, and occasionally Ann glimpsed a few houses and handsome stone barns. But gradually they had left the more populated countryside and were approaching an isolated section of road beside dense woods. For miles they met no other travelers, nor saw any sign of settlement.

William had been assured that there were no unfriendly Indians in those parts, but he kept an uneasy lookout nonetheless. The knowledge that William had bought a rifle in Philadelphia brought Ann little comfort. It lay wrapped in a protective cover in front of the cart. Before he could reach it, fill it with powder, and work the flint to fire a charge, she realized, even a lone Indian would have time to overpower him. Two or more would surely be able to kill them all. Ann shivered, as much in fear as from the cold. The *Derry Crown* passengers had made it abundantly clear—Indians could not be trusted, treaty or no treaty.

" 'Tis a lone stretch," William said at length, when it seemed that they would never see open land again.

"Do ye suppose there might be an inn along the way? We canna spend the night in the wet like this."

"If we dinna come to an inn soon, perhaps we can shelter in a barn like those we passed earlier. Are ye able to go on for now?" William asked, peering anxiously at Ann.

She nodded her head, sending a freshet of rain cascading from the hood of her cloak. "I can stand the weather, but I dinna like the looks of this road. Suppose we met a highwayman?"

"Where is th' highwayman?" Jonathan, presumed to be asleep, raised his head from the canvas and looked around expectantly.

"I was just makin' light," Ann said hastily. "There's na one else about, nor likely to be in this weather. Now put your head back under that canvas, before ye get a proper soaking."

"I'm hungry," he complained. "When are we goin' to eat?"

"When we get t' a dry place. Here, chew on this," William said, tearing off a sinewy piece of beef jerky for the boy. He offered some to Ann, but she declined, having discovered the day before that it yielded very low returns for the time and energy spent on chewing it. Still, if it was all they could get, she would eventually have to eat it.

Perhaps another mile farther, while negotiating a tight turn in the trail, they found themselves face-to-face with two young Indian braves, in long-sleeved shirts and leggings of deerskin, their heads bared to the weather. One carried a bundle of pelts, wrapped in a single deerskin and tied with a deerskin thong. Over one shoulder the other was holding a deerskin bag, which Ann guessed to contain provisions.

William, warily eyeing the knives in their belts, made no move toward his weapon, but urged the oxen on. Ann prayed that the wheels of the cart would not choose that moment to mire down. But in making the turn in the trail, the oxen pulled too far to the side, and one of the wheels stopped, its forward progress arrested by a large stump. The snorting team halted, and Ann knew that it would take many minutes of tedious maneuvering to free the wheel. Such a thing was bad enough when the road was dry. Here, in the rain and mud and with the Indians looking on impassively, the vulnerability of the little wagon train was frightening.

"Get behind th' cart and push," William directed. Ann, making a deliberate effort not to look at the intruders, did as she was told; but this time the ground was too muddy to afford traction, and she could exert no force. "Try again," William urged, prodding the oxen. From the corner of her eye, Ann saw one of the Indians drop his bundle and take the knife from his belt, speaking something in a strange tongue to his companion.

"Look out, Father!" she cried, and Jonathan's head came up again, his eyes widening in surprise as he saw the Indians.

Still, William made no move toward his weapon.

The Indian turned and left the trail to enter the woods behind him, returning a short time later with several boughs cut from a long-leafed pine tree. As Ann backed away, he laid the branches under the cart wheel, and both he and his companion pushed, one on either side of the cart. The wheel hesitated momentarily before rolling over the boughs to a spot on the other side of the stump.

"We thank ye," William said to the man with the knife, speaking loudly as if that might help to make himself understood.

"You have trade?" the Indian with the pouch asked, pointing to the cart.

"I don't understand," William replied, shaking his head and speaking slowly.

"You trader?" the Indian asked.

"No, not a trader. I am a farmer."

At this both men laughed. "Squaw work," one of them said. "Better trade. Cloth, salt."

"We have some salt," Jonathan said, suddenly finding his tongue and the courage to use it.

"Hush!" Ann whispered, still unsure of what these savages might do with them. She hated to think what might happen if they lifted the canvas and found William's rifle.

"Ah," said the Indian with the pelts. "You trade—salt, fine beaver?"

"No," William said. "We have only a little salt, and we will be needin' it ourselves."

The Indians conferred in their strange language, unlike any Ann had heard on the docks of Londonderry or Philadelphia, and apparently reached a decision. "No salt, no beaver," the one with the knife said, and Ann noted with relief that he had replaced the weapon in his belt.

"No trade," the other one said, and although he did not smile, neither Indian looked particularly menacing.

William called to the oxen, used his stick on their backs, and the cart lumbered on. Ann walked alongside, trying to make Jonathan stay under the canvas, but he sat rigidly upright, staring back at the Indians until they had disappeared around a bend in the trail.

"Our first Indians!" he exclaimed, having looked in vain for some in Philadelphia. "I wasna a bit afraid of them, either."

"Put your head down; and should we see any others, do not speak t' them," Ann instructed. She tried to sound severe, but the relief in her voice was obvious.

"Mind your sister," William said sternly.

"They seemed friendly enough," Jonathan said, scooting back under the canvas. "I wish I had a shirt like that, an' leggings, too."

"Perhaps ye will one of these days," Ann replied.

William cast a speculative glance about, and Ann knew that he, too, half-expected to see the Indians following them. Thinking of their knives, Ann hoped that they were not being stalked. She had heard tales of how skillfully an Indian could lift a man's scalp and the man live long enough to know the full horror of his death.

In the rain and the mud of that isolated trail, Ann suddenly felt very far from home, and very, very much alone.

Much to Jonathan's dismay and Ann's infinite relief, they saw no more Indians and few other travelers. At night, they were able to shelter in stone barns near the trail, where sweet hay made a welcome bed. Its fragrance reminded Ann of their barn at home and she wept, remembering. Once a German farmer gave them food, and even though his words were strange, his message of hospitality was clear. *So,* Ann thought as they plodded along for what seemed to be forever, *there are good people in this land—people who help each other.*

Near Lancaster a trader with full beard and hair braided Indian-fashion caught up with them. The man, who said his name was Paul Yancey, was leading two packhorses laden with goods he hoped to trade with Indians in return for pelts. He glanced at Jonathan, but his gaze lingering on Ann brought a blush to her cheeks.

"Where are ye bound wi' your goods?" William asked the trader.

"On to the southwest, to the banks of the Susquehanna River."

"And do ye find tradin' a better life than farmin'?"

"I'm no farmer, man," the trader said with a coarse laugh. "I learned that when I was indentured to a planter in Virginny. Soon as my time was out, I bought a few trinkets and set out a-sellin', which I been at ever since."

"Then ye must know the land hereabouts well. Is it all as fertile as this?"

The man nodded. "All the land that was easy to get to is taken up. To keep on goin' west, though, you have to cross mountains, and that's hard goin' for a team. It's bad enough for a man on foot with packhorses, like myself."

"But is there a road to follow?"

"Indian trails, maybe this wide," the trader said, gesturing with his hands. "There's no place you might ever want to go to that don't have an Indian trail leadin' to it."

"We're from Ulster, and I was told there was land beyond Lancaster a man could settle on wi'out a grant."

"Donegalians, eh? I'm swanned if the Irish and the Dutch have any left to home at all, so many are comin' to Pennsylvania. Yes, the land beyond the ridges can be had, if ye're not afeared o' Indians and hard work."

William described their encounter with the Indians. "They wanted salt, but they didna try to take it frae us. Are the Indians really trustworthy?"

Mr. Yancey scratched at his stubby beard reflectively. "I didn't meet up with that pair, but as to whether Indians is friendly or not, I'd have to say yes and no, both. The ones around here have pretty much been forced out, what with the treaties takin' land they been usin' and all, an' most of 'em have gone on west. Some o' the ones there don't hold to no man's treaty, and ever' now and again, they go a-rampagin' against any whites they can find. They don't bother me none, though," he added, " 'cause I got things they want."

"We were warned that 'tis best not to trust any savage," William said.

"Mebbe," Yancey agreed, "but I wouldn't turn my back on lots of white men I know, neither. There's some rough ones around; I can tell you that."

He left them near Lancaster, casting a final look at Ann. Ann's discomfort in no way resembled the feelings she had experienced when Caleb looked at her. Still, she wondered what this man would have said or done had not her father been with her.

Lancaster was larger than Ann had expected, and they had no problem finding an inn. After the German proprietor had seen to the animals and taken Ann and Jonathan to a room, Ann used the waning light to read from the book Caleb had given her. Her understanding was still lacking, but the knowledge that Caleb had often held this book, in hand and in heart, gave a small measure of comfort to the yawning uncertainty of the future. As she had so often in the past, Ann thought of Caleb, trying to imagine where he was and what he was doing. Above all, she wondered if she would, indeed, ever see him again.

Chapter 8

During the three days they stayed at the inn, William talked with several men about his best course of action. His uncertainty increased with the information he gleaned. Striking out with a young girl and a frail boy, with no clear notion of where he was going or what he would do when he got there, suddenly seemed foolish.

Jonathan continued to look pale and hollow-eyed, and at night he often coughed. Although it was not mentioned, the sound of his coughing brought the chill suspicion that the boy might carry the sickness that had taken his mother.

Finally, after a second visit with James Andrews, a prosperous merchant who, while not an Ulsterman, was acquainted with Josiah Pendleton, William returned to the inn and announced that he had made his decision.

"James Andrews is a fine man, an' he has made an offer that will be of great assistance to us."

"And what is that?" Ann knew from the way that William was pacing about the room that he was uncomfortable.

"Mr. Andrews's wife, Martha, is not well. He believes that ye might be a suitable companion for her. If so, he is willin' to take ye and Jonathan inta their home until such time as our plans are set."

"Ye would leave us here and go on alone?" In all her idle speculation about the future, that possibility had never once occurred to Ann.

"It would only be for a short while, Lass. Under the circumstances," and he paused, eyeing Jonathan playing quietly on the lawn, "I think it would be best for all o' us."

"What is Mrs. Andrews like?" she asked resignedly.

"I have not met her myself, but I am sure she is a fine lady and would be good to the both o' ye. We are t' call there directly, so ready yourself up and come along."

❧

The Andrews house, like most of the dwellings in Lancaster, was of a single story, but the eight windows on the front of the house and the imported fanlight over the front door attested to the prosperity of its inhabitants.

Mr. Andrews answered the door himself and greeted them cordially. Ann immediately liked the man. His direct look and hearty manner were qualities

Ann had always thought bespoke honesty.

When he conducted them into the sitting room, she found cheerful whitewashed walls and rich furnishings, including several pieces of upholstered furniture. Mrs. Andrews was sitting in a wing chair by the fireplace, a quilt covering her legs. In contrast to her husband's ruddy complexion, Mrs. Andrews was somewhat sallow, with dull, listless eyes. Her mouth, turned down at the corners, gave her the appearance of one who has just bitten into sour fruit, and she did not smile as she was introduced to the McKays.

"You, Boy," she said, pointing a plump finger at Jonathan, "are you noisy?"

Perhaps because of her pronounced English accent, or perhaps because he did not understand her meaning, Jonathan did not immediately reply, and this seemed to irritate her. "I asked you a question, Boy. Are you noisy?"

"Noisy?" Jonathan repeated, still unsure of what he should say.

"I cannot tolerate noise," she warned. "Most young boys are entirely too loud."

"Jonathan is a quiet lad," William said, putting a hand on the boy's shoulder. "He took a fever on the passage over and has not quite recovered his strength, but he will make ye no trouble, I can promise that."

Mrs. Andrews looked at Ann dubiously. "And you, Mistress, are you strong enough to help me get about? I cannot walk without aid."

"I believe so," Ann replied, although she was far from certain. Mrs. Andrews was taller than Sarah, and more than a little on the plump side. Still, feeling that it was important to make a good impression for William's sake, she added, "I am stronger than I look."

"My daughter Elizabeth is about your size," she said, her eyes measuring Ann. "Since she married and went to live in England, I have been quite alone. My husband tells me that you can read and write. Is that so?"

Ann nodded. "Aye, Ma'am, I can do both."

"And needlework?"

"I can spin and card, both flax and wool, and work a loom. I knit, but I've done no fancy work."

Mrs. Andrews sighed. "Well, I suppose if you can mend and fit material, that will be sufficient."

"Well, Martha, what about it?" asked her husband. "Will the girl do?"

"She looks frail to me," Mrs. Andrews said, as if Ann were not present, "but she does seem willing enough."

"Fine," said James Andrews. "Come along with me," he said to Ann and Jonathan, "and I'll show you around."

They followed him down a hall to a bedroom wing on the right, and he opened the door to a room at the rear of the house. "This was Elizabeth's room."

Jonathan, who had been cautioned before they left the inn not to speak unless he was directly addressed, appeared to be keeping quiet only with extreme difficulty. When he looked inside the small but sunny room, he could contain himself no longer. "Look, a real bed!" he cried when he saw the sturdy four-poster, strung with stout hemp, covered by a rolled-up feather mattress.

"There's a trundle underneath," Mr. Andrews said, pulling a small bed out onto the wide-planked flooring. The room had a few pegs on the walls for hanging clothes, a table with a candlestand next to the bed, and a chest bearing a basin and pitcher, over which was hung the rarest of luxuries in the colony, a real glass mirror.

"It's a verra nice room," Ann said, trying not to stare at her reflection.

"The room across the hall belongs to our son, John," Mr. Andrews said, waving toward the closed door. "He is reading law in Philadelphia, so we seldom see him these days. Since the children left, and with having the fever of a summer, Martha hasn't been at all well." Looking at Ann, he added, "She needs the company of someone who can take her out of herself and cheer her up. Do you think you will be adequate to the task, Mistress McKay?"

"I will do my best," Ann replied, rather doubting that her best would be good enough to please Mrs. Andrews, but he nodded, seemingly satisfied.

"Come and see the rest of the house, then," he invited, and pointed toward the summer kitchen, detached from the main house for use in hot weather. "Here is the regular kitchen," he said, leading them through a dining room with real chairs—not just backless plank benches—into a small, hot room where a huge brick fireplace almost filled the rear wall. A stout woman acknowledged their presence with a curt nod and continued to stir something simmering over the fire. The aroma of spices hung in the air, and Ann realized that she was hungry.

"This is Agnes, who does our cooking and cleaning," Mr. Andrews said. The woman's face was red, whether naturally or from the heat Ann could not tell, and her puckered mouth testified that she had lost most of her teeth. Her manner belied the somewhat fierce appearance she presented and, from the compassionate look she gave Jonathan, Ann knew he would have a friend in the kitchen.

As they returned to the sitting room, James Andrews asked William if he was satisfied with the arrangement, and he in turn looked at Ann. "How about it, Daughter? Will ye bide wi' the Andrews for a time?"

"If I am acceptable to them."

"Then it is settled," Mr. Andrews said. "Martha, Mistress McKay has consented to stay with us." When his wife made no reply, James turned to William and shook his head. "I think it best that you bring their things over right away. This young man looks as if he could use a nap in his new bed, eh?"

Jonathan, realizing that William would not be staying there with them, burst into tears. Ann laid a comforting hand on his shoulder and led him from the room, hoping she might forget her own sorrow in trying to still his. Yet, when William brought their belongings from the inn and was ready to move on, it was Jonathan who solemnly shook his father's hand, and Ann who clung to him, sobbing, until William gently pushed her away.

"Dinna take on so, Lass," he said. "I'll be back for ye both as soon as I can. 'Tis but for a little while that we'll be apart."

Ashamed, Ann dried her eyes and managed a weak smile, but as they stood in the doorway of the Andrews house and watched William walk away, Ann feared that it might be a very long time before they saw him again—if, indeed, they ever did.

❧

Dealing with Mrs. Andrews was not as difficult as Ann had feared it would be, although it could hardly be called pleasant. She was expected to be at the woman's beck and call from breakfast until suppertime, except for a period in the afternoon when Mrs. Andrews rested. During those hours, when the house had to be absolutely quiet, Ann often took Jonathan outside as the weather permitted and gradually extended their walks until they knew every street in Lancaster. After the evening meal, James Andrews usually sat with his wife, unless he had brought home guests, other merchants and artisans of Lancaster, or an occasional visitor from Philadelphia or London.

At such times, Ann and Jonathan stayed in their room, and Ann finally finished reading *The Pilgrim's Progress*. She kept the book on her bedside table, along with Sarah's Bible. After a few weeks, feeling that Jonathan needed something to occupy his mind, she began to use the Bible to teach him to read, as she herself had been taught. But her efforts only called Caleb to mind and made her long to hear one of his comforting sermons.

She had learned of a church in Lancaster, with a native-born pastor, but Sundays proved to be the same as any other day to the Andrews, who, according to Agnes, were nominal members of the Anglican Church. Mr. Andrews often used the Sabbath for mysterious errands of his own, leaving Ann to perform her usual duties. Asking permission to attend church services seemed futile.

Ann and Jonathan tried to settle into the life of the Andrews household unobtrusively, but its ways were foreign to them, from the food they ate to the beds on which they slept. Jonathan sometimes had nightmares in which he cried out for his mother, and Ann would lift him from the trundle bed and hold him until he fell asleep again.

Certainly Ann could not complain about their living conditions, by far the most luxurious she had ever experienced. The fare was hearty and rich, and, under Agnes's watchful eye, Jonathan gradually lost his gaunt look. Ann could only hope that it was a good sign, for he still coughed when he played too hard. But, having a neighboring boy to pass the time with, Jonathan was content enough.

Ann, too, had put on weight, so much that the dress she had worn on the ship no longer fit at all, and she cut it apart to make an outfit for Jonathan. The change did not escape Martha Andrews's attention, and one Saturday she had Agnes find a box of clothing left behind by Elizabeth.

"I notice that you seem to be outgrowing your clothes," she said. "These dresses should fit you."

"Will your daughter not someday want these things?" Ann asked, overwhelmed at the thought of having so many dresses at one time.

"Not these. Now that Elizabeth is living in England, she can have the best and the newest fashions. These would not be good enough for her, even if she should ever come back here, which is highly unlikely."

Ann put on a dress of the softest homespun wool, dyed with the precious indigo that was now being grown in the South Carolina colony, and stood before the mirror. From the tiny mother-of-pearl buttons on the fitted bodice to the deep flounce at the hem, the dress had an elegance that Ann had never seen nor thought to have for her own. Regarding her reflection critically, Ann realized that just in the short time they had been with the Andrews, her girlish angular thinness had been replaced by a woman's softly rounded contours, accentuated now by the fit of the new dress.

"You look different," Jonathan said, coming in from outdoors.

"Well, I am." Ann smiled, turning to show off the dress. "I have three new dresses, just like a fine lady. What shall we do this afternoon?"

"David has some new kittens," he said. "I thought maybe we could go o'er and play with them."

"I don't believe I care to do that, but ye may go. Just be careful not ta track mud when ye come in. The ground's still soft frae last night's rain, and we mustna make extra work for Agnes."

After Jonathan left, Ann walked down the hall to Martha Andrews's room and knocked softly.

"Come in," she called, and Ann entered the dim room. The shutters were always tightly closed, even on the warmest of days.

"I thought I might take a walk this afternoon. Is there aught ye need before I leave?"

Mrs. Andrews sighed. "Well, if you are going to be about, find Mr. Andrews and tell him I am nearly out of my elixir. He can bring it home when he comes this evening."

"Aye, Ma'am." Ann reached over to plump Mrs. Andrews's pillows and check to make sure she had fresh water.

"I see that you are wearing one of Elizabeth's dresses," Mrs. Andrews said. "It seems to fit you well enough."

"Aye, thank ye. Even Jonathan took notice of it."

Mrs. Andrews frowned and shifted her ample weight, rising on one elbow with some difficulty. "And he will not be the only male who does, I am certain. A woman walking alone on the streets may be misunderstood. Do not tarry on your errand, and speak to no one."

"Nay, Ma'am, I won't," Ann promised, but she was not sure she understood what Mrs. Andrews was trying to say. *She called me a woman,* Ann thought as she left the house, and the mirror had told her she had a woman's form. But inside, Ann still felt like a somewhat frightened little girl and wondered when she might begin to feel that she had really grown up.

Ann found James Andrews at his place of business, and he stopped talking to his clerk to come around to the front of the office and greet her.

"It is well that Martha remembered the elixir today," James said when she had explained her errand. "Tomorrow I must go to Philadelphia, and it will be at least a week before I can conclude my business and return. Do you think that you and Agnes can care for Mrs. Andrews while I am away?"

"I am sure of it," Ann replied. "Tell me, will ye see Josiah Pendleton in Philadelphia, by any chance?"

"No doubt I will, as I have some business to transact with him."

"Then would ye please tell him that Jonathan an' I are here in Lancaster at your home? He said we should let him know where we were, in case someone inquired."

"Certainly," he agreed, "although I wish I could also tell him where your father is. I take it that there has been no news today?"

"Nothing. It has only been a month, though," she added, "and he warned me that we must not grow impatient, as he expected it could take him some time to locate suitable land."

"Of course. I am sure he is fine. Now, if you'll excuse me, I'll see to the elixir."

Ann walked back to the house, unmindful of her surroundings. Usually she took pleasure in listening to the polyglot population of Lancaster in conversation on street corners and around the marketplace, but today her mind was occupied with the possibility that, through Josiah Pendleton, Caleb Craighead might find out where she was and seek her out. It was a frail hope, but all she had; and feeling that she was still very much a stranger in a strange land, Ann clung to it.

Chapter 9

When James Andrews returned from Philadelphia, he brought welcome news.

"I saw John, and he is planning to pay us a visit within the week. It seems that Mr. Otis is going to New York to look at some property, and he gave John leave to come to Lancaster while he's gone."

"How did he seem?" Mrs. Andrews asked, with unaccustomed enthusiasm.

"He is well but up to his eyebrows in debt," Mr. Andrews replied cheerfully. "I gave him a bit of cash, but I venture to say it'll soon be gone."

"He should not be in Philadelphia," Mrs. Andrews said. Her tone and the expression on her husband's face told Ann this was an old controversy. "I don't know why he couldn't have stayed here, since he wouldn't go to England and read at the Inns of the Temple."

"Now, Martha, you know there's hardly a lawyer fit to practice in this town, much less to teach anyone else the profession. When John finishes his studies, he may decide to come back here to practice, but in the meantime, you should be grateful that we see him from time to time. Had he gone to England, we would not have had that privilege."

"He could come home more often." Martha pouted, but her petulance faded as she directed the household in a frenzy of cooking, cleaning, and polishing in honor of the impending visit.

"Ye'd think the governor himself was comin'," Ann said to Agnes as she helped her put fresh linens on John's bed.

"Ah, that you would," Agnes agreed, "but he's always been fussed over. A little prince couldn't a' had more than that lad. He's a charmer, he is."

"Have you been with the Andrews long?" Ann asked.

Agnes shook out a sheet and turned her head to one side, counting silently. "Well, lessee, I come here to work when the Andrews arrived, fresh off the boat from England. Must be nigh unto nine years now. Yes, Master John was eleven then, and Miss Elizabeth was going on ten."

"What is John like?" Ann asked, but Agnes only shrugged.

"Like no one else you'll ever meet. You'll see."

Still, Ann was unprepared for the laughing young man who flung himself into the house the next day and picked his mother up and whirled her around.

Then he kissed Agnes, all before he had so much as set down his riding crop.

"And who is this?" he asked, turning from Agnes to see Jonathan regarding him with awe.

Ann had time to note the crisp blond hair, pulled back but unpowdered, and the well-tailored riding clothes. His smile, so unmistakably his father's, brightened what could, in repose, otherwise be a sullen expression.

"You remember my telling you about the McKays?" James said. "This is Master Jonathan, and this is your mother's companion, Mistress Ann."

John turned to see Ann standing behind him, and she wondered if he recognized his sister's dress. Smiling broadly, John bowed from the waist and, taking her hand, kissed it. *"Enchanté,"* he murmured, and turned to his mother. "That is how one greets a lady in London, is it not, Mother? You always wanted me to acquire proper English manners."

"Your manners are far from English, whatever else they are," Martha said with some asperity. "A gentleman would leave his dusty cloak with the groom and clean his boots before he entered a house of quality."

John bowed. "Ah, I see you still know how to put me in my place," he said. "Excuse me, please, and I shall see to my horse. Young man—Jonathan, is it? Ah, yes, well, Jonathan, would you care to assist me?"

Enthralled, Jonathan followed him outside, and Ann helped Agnes take water to John's room. *How strange,* she thought, *that the son is so unlike his parents in temperament.* Even though John physically resembled his father, there was an air of recklessness about him that she could not imagine in James Andrews. And the way he had looked at her—it was not exactly the way the trader they had met on their way to Lancaster had looked at her, but it disturbed her nonetheless. Anyway, she told herself, John Andrews would soon be gone, and in the meanwhile, she resolved to stay out of his way.

❧

Planning to avoid John Andrews proved to be easier said than done. One never knew when he would stay at home, talking to Martha, teasing Agnes, holding a skein for Ann, or showing Jonathan how to make a whistle from a blade of grass. He would leave at odd hours, sometimes just before meals, and some nights he would come in long after everyone else was in bed.

Four days after John's return, when the others were out and Martha was taking her afternoon nap, he surprised Ann at her loom in the summer kitchen wing. Quite certain that John knew she was alone, Ann tried to keep her eyes and her attention on her work.

"What are you making?" he asked, taking a seat opposite her.

"Linen towels for th' household," she said, holding up the part she had finished for his inspection.

"Very pretty," he said, not looking at the work but at Ann. "What good luck that fate put you on the Andrews doorstep. I can tell a great difference in my mother since my last visit."

Ann never knew how to respond to the infrequent compliments she received, so she said nothing. It didn't matter if John Andrews thought his mother's servant dull, she decided.

"Your mother's death must have been very difficult," he ventured.

She nodded. "Aye, it was."

"I'm sorry about your loss but pleased with our gain. You and Jonathan have certainly brightened this house."

A cautious glance at John's face was rewarded by a broad smile. In spite of herself, Ann found that she, too, was smiling.

"That's more like it," he said, taking one of her hands. "You are quite lovely when you smile. You must smile more often—there, you've stopped. Come now; this won't do. Let's see that smile again."

In spite of her confusion, her lips turned up once more. This time they were immediately covered by his, in a brief and gentle kiss. "A smile is much better than a grim mouth, don't you agree?" he said, dropping her hand and standing. "I promised Father I would look in on him this afternoon. I'll see you at supper tonight."

Ann sat immobile for some moments after he had left, reflecting on what had passed between them. The kiss had been brief, but it was her first, and the fact that she had enjoyed the touch of his lips on hers disturbed her. How could she face John again? She had made no protest, and Sarah's vague instructions concerning matters of romance had implied that a girl must not encourage a man's improper behavior. Was she guilty of such encouragement?

She almost decided to stay in her room during the evening meal, but she finally put on the buff linen dress that was her favorite and helped Martha Andrews into her chair. John and his father arrived in time for John to seat his mother at the table with a great deal of fuss.

During dinner, he regaled his mother with so many amusing stories about Philadelphia that Mrs. Andrews neglected her food. At the meal's end, John and his father excused themselves to go to the Blue Boar Tavern, so Ann was not put in the awkward position of having to talk with him directly.

The next morning, at breakfast, John announced his impending departure for Philadelphia.

"You must stay at least one more day," Martha insisted. "We've hardly seen you the past few days; you've gadded about so much."

"Ah, Mother! Well, for you, maybe just one more day. What shall we do with it?"

"What do you usually do with your time and your money?" Martha asked, making a great effort to look cross. "You waste it and then wonder where it went, expecting to be given more."

"You are a wonderful philosopher," John said, kissing his mother's cheek. "Mr. Franklin ought to copy your adages for his almanack. I am quite willing to let you have the entire morning if I can have the afternoon."

"To do what?" Martha asked, smiling in spite of herself.

"I'd like to try my hand at fishing down by the Conestoga, and I'd like to take Jonathan and Mistress McKay along. Have you ever put a line into the water, Jonathan?"

The boy shook his head, his eyes bright with excitement. "I would like to try it, though."

"And, Father, how about you? Can you leave the gods of commerce long enough to practice the ancient angling arts with us?"

James smiled but declined the invitation. "You know I have a shipment to get out today," he said. "A lawyer may be able to take a holiday whenever the fancy strikes him, but I must make a living. Go along, though, and enjoy yourselves. The river is lovely this time of year."

"Then it's settled," John declared. "Agnes, come out here."

"Yes, Master John?" She appeared from the kitchen, wiping her hands on her apron.

"Be ready to fry fish tonight, Woman. With three sturdy anglers here, we should bring home an ample supply."

Agnes sniffed. "That's as may be," she said, "but there'll be stew on the hob, nevertheless."

John returned his full attention to his mother. "Now, let me help you up, and we'll adjourn to the sitting room."

❧

Ann stayed with Jonathan all morning so that mother and son could visit in private. Occasionally, the sound of his laughter reached them through their closed door.

She was looking forward to their fishing expedition—though she had had no say in the matter—as a pleasant break from their normal routine and a treat for Jonathan. But also, she had to admit that she simply enjoyed being around John. His good humor and light manner lifted her spirits. On the other hand, she was not certain what he really thought of her, and she did not want to appear to be forward. She had chosen to wear one of her mother's dresses, not wanting to risk soiling any of her new things or appearing to dress up for him. But at the last moment before emerging from her room, she tied her hair back with her brightest ribbon.

"You say you have never fished before in your entire life?" John asked Jonathan as the three of them walked to the river at a leisurely pace.

"I went to the mill creek wi' Father once or twice, but I were too small to do aught but bait the hooks."

"And what about you, Mistress Ann? Are you as talented at fishing as you are at the loom?"

"Father never took me wi' him."

"Then I must teach you all there is to know," John said, and his look warned her that he might not only be talking about fishing. She tried to dismiss the faint prickling of apprehension associated with the memory of his lips touching hers and resolved to focus her thoughts on the bright and pleasant day.

Reaching a shady and secluded spot that John pronounced acceptable, they set down their creels and poles. Ann and Jonathan watched as John opened a packet of oiled paper and extracted some fat worms. "Let's see if the fish will find them as attractive as we do," John said, noting Ann's expression of repugnance. A farmer's daughter, she was no stranger to worms, but seeing them in a field that had been newly turned to the plow was quite different from picking them up and impaling their wriggling bodies on hooks.

"Here, Jonathan," John said, handing him a pole. "Sit down and let your line float in along the water. If you feel a tug on the pole, that means you have hooked a fish."

"What do I do then?" he asked, concentrating on holding onto the pole with both hands.

"Just pull it in gently—don't jerk it, or the fish will get away from you."

John repeated the hooking process for Ann and motioned for her to take the pole. "Here, put your line out, not too close to Jonathan's." One of John's arms went around her waist, the other on her hand, helping her guide the pole into the water. He stood close to her a moment longer than necessary, then moved away to prepare his own line.

"Nothing is happenin'," Jonathan complained after only a few moments had passed.

"Shhh," whispered John. "You must be quiet, or all the fish will know that we are here. Be patient. One will find that juicy worm, then you'll have a nice fish to show Agnes."

After a few more minutes passed, Ann looked dubiously at John. "Are ye sure there really are fish here?" she whispered.

"Trust me," he whispered in return. "In any case, it's a lovely day, and you're out of that stuffy house."

So he knows how it is, she thought. *He knows how difficult his mother can be, and he's doing this for me and Jonathan.* Ann felt a rush of gratitude at his kindness and smiled at him.

Just then Jonathan yelled, "A fish!" John quickly handed his pole to Ann and went to help the boy with his catch.

"It's awfully small," Jonathan said when the fish was out of the water and lay flopping, gills heaving, on the grassy bank.

"Shall we throw him back in and wait for his big brother?" John asked.

"Oh, aye, let's do," said Ann, disturbed by the fish's imminent death.

John looked at Jonathan for instructions about the catch, and at the boy's shrug, he smiled and threw the fish back into the water.

"You are much too tenderhearted, Mistress Ann," John chided when they had all resumed their fishing.

Ann withheld her protests as other catches were made, and eventually they had caught five fair-sized trout. When their bait was exhausted, John and Ann put their poles down and sat side by side with their backs to a large willow that overhung the riverbank and almost hid them from view. Jonathan had fallen asleep with the pole still clutched in his hand, and as far as they could see, no one else was in sight. Except for the quiet murmur of the river and the occasional call of a bird, all was quiet.

"I am not looking forward to returning to Philadelphia tomorrow," John said at length. He pulled down one of the willow branches and began absently stripping its leaves.

"Your parents will miss ye," Ann said. "Ye are the most important thing in your mother's life, ye know."

John made a gesture of dismissal with his hands. "More's the pity," he said. "She ought to live in Philadelphia, at least, or preferably, back in England. But Father thinks he can make his fortune here and then move back there. I hope he doesn't take too long to do it to help Mother."

"Why did your father come to the colonies?"

"My grandfather gave my Uncle Martin, the eldest son, all the land he had. He gave Uncle Paul, the second son, a ship, and he's in the Indies trade. He gave Father, the third son, enough money to start his business here, but Mother has never become acclimated."

"She is heavy," Ann ventured, choosing her words with care, "and that makes it hard for her to move about, but apart from that—"

"You've not yet seen her with the fever," John interrupted. "When it comes back upon her, it takes two strong men to tie her down on the bed—otherwise, she would shake so hard she might fall out onto the floor and injure herself. The fever seems to be associated with swampland, and once you have it, it doesn't let go. She'll need your help when the next spell hits her."

"When will that be?"

"Usually in the heat of the summer. Maybe in two or three weeks, maybe a month. When it comes, I hope you'll be strong enough to handle her."

"So do I," Ann said, her light mood shattered by his words. Mr. Andrews references to his wife's fever had been rather vague, giving no hint of its seriousness.

"Here, here," John said, taking one of Ann's hands and using his other hand to lift her chin. "That smile has disappeared again. We can't have that happen."

"I am concerned about your mother," she said, but she attempted a weak smile.

"That's much better," he murmured, and drew her face to his. This time his kiss was not brief. And when he put both his arms around her waist and held her closely, she encircled his neck with her arms and held them there until he released her.

"Ah, Ann," he said softly. "How sweet you are."

Suddenly embarrassed at her actions, Ann rose quickly to her feet, brushing at her skirt to hide her confusion. "Jonathan should not be lyin' in the damp grass," she said. "We must go home now."

"In a moment," John said, standing and reaching for her again. This time he held her tightly without making any attempt to kiss her. "Will you be here when I come back?"

"I don't know," Ann replied, resisting the urge to add that she hoped she would be.

"Be here for me," he whispered urgently and released her. He turned to pick up their gear and retrieve the fish they had caught. Ann gently awoke Jonathan. She and John said little on the way back to the house, and they were never alone again the rest of the evening.

The next morning, Ann awoke to hear muffled farewells and the sound of John's horse as he rode away.

"I hope John will come back soon," Jonathan said. "He said next time we could take a ride on one of Mr. Andrews's rafts."

"That would be nice," Ann said absently, remembering John's smile and the mingled pleasure and shame she felt as she thought of the touch of his lips. She knew that, somehow, she would never be the same again.

Chapter 10

I ndians. . .Tolliver Station. . .killed three people. . ."

On her way to the market with Agnes, Ann stopped at the fringe of a knot of people gathered around a bearded man in deerskins. She had caught only a few words.

The growing crowd kept questioning him, but the trader threw up his hands and motioned toward the Blue Boar Tavern, where he had apparently been headed when the crowd stopped him. "Got to wet my whistle," he called out. "I've tol' yer all I know, anyhow."

The trader went inside, with some of the men following, but most remained where they were, talking among themselves about the news he had brought. Agnes saw a woman she knew and asked her what had happened.

"Injun trouble," the woman replied and spat disdainfully. "Some hot-blood Irish out to Tolliver Station killed a brave and his squaw, for no good reason but the sport, it seems. Next day some Injuns came in and burned three cabins down the creek and took some scalps."

"Who were they?" Ann asked.

"He didn't say, but I sure wouldn't want to be nowhere near that place, no siree."

"Where is Tolliver Station?" Ann asked Agnes.

"Somewhere west o' here, on t' other side of the mountains. Don't worry none about Injuns, though," she added. "Here in town, yer safe as a baby in a cradle."

"It's not myself I'm worried about," Ann replied, looking toward the tavern. "I think I recognized the man who was talkin'," Ann said. "We met him on the trail. He might know if Father was involved. I've got to ask him."

"Yer can't go into the tavern, Missy!" Agnes exclaimed.

"Then I'll just stand here and wait until he comes out."

"That might take all day," said Agnes. "And yer can't stand about here alone."

"Then go inside wi' me, Agnes."

"Mrs. Andrews would have my hide if she knew of it."

"Well, we won't tell her," Ann declared, starting for the door. "I must find out if he has seen Father."

The Blue Boar Tavern featured a high bar and plank tables and benches in a large front room, with small private dining areas in the rear, where the gentlemen of the city could do their drinking and gaming in relative privacy. The trader stood at the bar, holding a pewter tankard. Along with every other man in the place, he looked up with interest as Ann and Agnes entered.

"Well, well, here are some mighty thirsty females, for sure," someone yelled, and there was a great deal of shuffling and laughter.

While Agnes sent glaring darts in several directions, Ann ignored everything else and walked straight to the trader. "Mr. Yancey? I believe ye may remember seein' my father with my brother and me on the road inta town some few weeks back."

The trader looked at Ann appreciatively, his eyes moving up and down in a lingering glance that brought the blood to her face. "Sure, Missy. I don't forget no faces. It 'pears like you've put on a mite o' flesh since then, eh?"

"I heard what ye said about Indian trouble at Tolliver Station. I was wonderin' if ye might happen to have seen my father again or heard aught about him."

"Yer pa ain't here in Lancaster?"

"She is under the protection of James Andrews," Agnes put in quickly, seeing the man's lecherous leer.

"And yer father?"

"He left about six weeks ago to look for a place to live. He has not contacted us since. I hoped ye might remember seein' him along the way somewhere."

"No, but when I go back, I might ask around, as a favor to a purty gal."

The man was insufferable, but Ann tried to ignore his attitude. If he had any information about her father, or could procure any, he must be tolerated.

"The people the Indians killed—do ye know their names?"

"Perkins, I think it was, Irish folks like you, red-haired. Man and wife and one other, grown boy or man who happened by there; no one knew for sure."

"Thank ye," Ann said, aware that Agnes was plucking at her sleeve, impatient to be gone.

"Anytime, Missy," he said. "Tell y' what; I'll look ye up next trip, and mebbe you and me can have a little fun, eh?"

"That's an evil man, Miss Ann," Agnes said darkly, as they made their way outside. "If ever he shows his face around the house, he'll be sent packin' in a hurry."

"I don't like him, either, but he may be able to find out where Father is. I am beginnin' to be worried that something terrible has happened, or he would at least have sent a message to us."

"Ah, that's easier said than done," Agnes told her. "There's no regular post through Lancaster, and with fever season upon us, folks don't travel more'n they have to. You'll hear in good time."

"I hope ye're right," Ann said. John had told her that his mother's fever attacks were severe, but until now, it had not occurred to her that she or Jonathan might also become ill.

❧

As June wore on, the weather grew warmer than even the hottest days in Ireland. Ann watched Jonathan anxiously for any sign of sickness. Mrs. Andrews showed no signs of fever, but as the heat increased, her bulk and relative immobility caused her great discomfort. She became more irritable than usual, finding fault with everything and everyone that chanced her way.

So at first when she asked Ann for her shawl, in spite of the heat, Ann was convinced she was only demanding more attention. Nevertheless, at the woman's insistence, she rose to retrieve the shawl, and when she returned she found Mrs. Andrews in the throes of a hard chill—the signal that the dreaded fever had once again recurred. A surgeon was hastily summoned, and as Ann watched his leeches gorging themselves on Martha Andrews's blood, she was thankful there had been no surgeon aboard the *Derry Crown* to give Jonathan the standard fever treatment.

She, Agnes, and Mr. Andrews worked to secure the delirious woman's arms to prevent her from injuring herself, and Ann began caring for her day and night.

At length, the violent stage of the illness spent itself, and Martha Andrews was pronounced out of immediate danger. Mr. Andrews took over the close watch on his wife and urged Ann to get some needed rest.

Walking to her room, Ann put a hand to the small of her back and stretched, trying to ease the pain of muscles kept too long in one position. She opened the door carefully, not wanting to disturb Jonathan's rest, and stood by his bed for a moment, suddenly overwhelmed by her love for him.

Ann slipped out of her dress and decided to lie down in her petticoat and take a short nap. The heavy feather bed had nearly smothered her when the warmer weather came, and Agnes had replaced it with one filled with cornhusks. It made a cooler bed, but a noisy one, and as Ann cautiously eased down onto it, the crackling of the husks woke Jonathan.

"I wondered where ye were," he said, stretching and sitting up. "I dreamed that Father came back, and he had Mother wi' him, and we were all goin' somewhere wonderful in a big coach with four white horses. Then I woke up, and it was dark, and ye weren't here."

"I was wi' Mrs. Andrews all night, but she is better. Ye must be quiet now, and perhaps ye can go back to sleep."

70

"Agnes said I should not make any noise and that I must say a prayer for Mrs. Andrews's soul. I tried to be quiet, but I didn't ken how to pray for anybody's soul. I was afraid I might make her die."

He looked so woebegone that Ann gathered him into her arms and hugged him. "Ye have been a very good boy to be quiet and stay out of the way. But it would not have been your fault if Mrs. Andrews was worse. Such things are not in our control."

"I prayed for Mother, as hard as I could, and she just kept gettin' sicker."

"It wasna your fault," Ann said. "Didna Mr. Craighead talk to ye about it?" Jonathan nodded. "I liked Mr. Craighead. I wish he would come t' see us."

"Perhaps he will," she said quietly. "Now let's lie very still and rest, shall we?"

Ann laid Jonathan back in his trundle bed and lay down again. When she closed her eyes, she saw Caleb as he had stood before her in the inn. "I have the conviction we will meet again," he had said. Drowsily she thought that Josiah Pendleton could have told him where she was, if he had wanted to know. All she could do now was wait. . .for her father, for Caleb Craighead, for John Andrews. . . .

❧

"The post rider brought this today from Philadelphia," James Andrews said to Ann, handing her a letter. "I knew you would want to have it right away, so I brought it over. Is Martha resting?"

"Aye. She has had a rather difficult day," Ann replied as she took a slender folded paper from his hand. She had never before received a letter of her very own, and in her haste to break the seal and open it, she tore a corner of the page. The writing was clear and neat, instantly recognizable as Caleb Craighead's hand. Five days had passed from the date he had written at the top of the page. She read:

> *Dear Mistress McKay:*
>
> *I have this day called upon Mr. Josiah Pendleton, who has given me the intelligence that you are residing in Lancaster. He thought that perhaps by now your father would have found his land and made arrangements for you and Jonathan to join him. In any case, it is my hope that Mr. Andrews, in whose care I send this, will know where you have gone, and can direct me to you.*
>
> *The Lord has greatly blessed my efforts in Philadelphia, and I shall have much to tell you when I reach Lancaster the latter part of the month.*
>
> *In the meanwhile, it is my prayer that you and Jonathan are well and happy in God's care.*

"I hope that your news is pleasant," James Andrews said when he saw that she had finished reading the letter. He had politely withdrawn with his copy of the newspaper, but as she tucked the letter into her apron pocket, he put aside the *Pennsylvania Gazette* and looked at her.

"Aye, thank ye. It is from the Reverend Caleb Craighead, who befriended us on the voyage over. He will be comin' to Lancaster soon, he says. He kept a school on the ship—Jonathan will be glad to see him again."

"And, I wager, so will you," he said, noting her pleased expression. "You say that he is a schoolmaster? We could use him in Lancaster, then. My children had a tutor, but most of the young ones are growing up almost totally illiterate—a great shame. Tell me, does he plan to settle here?"

"It is my understandin' that he intends to go on to the new settlements where there are few ministers as of yet."

"Well, there's no money in that," Mr. Andrews declared. "But I do business with several men who trade six days and preach on the seventh and manage both quite well."

"I doubt that Mr. Craighead would make a merchant," Ann said, smiling faintly at the thought.

"Still, he should know about the possibility," Mr. Andrews said. "He would be serving people two ways, and a man could do worse."

"Thank ye for bringin' the letter. If ye will excuse me, I must find Jonathan and share this news. He could use some cheering."

❧

Over the next few days, Ann read and reread Caleb's letter until she knew it by heart. She was almost afraid to meet him again. She knew that her physical appearance had changed in their months apart, in a way that any man was likely to admire. But her spiritual state, which had concerned him so much, was virtually unchanged.

With Mr. Andrews's permission, she had recently started going to hear the Reverend Mr. Alexander preach on the Sabbath. American-born and poorly educated, he knew neither Hebrew nor Greek, and his sermons tended to be dull and repetitious. Yet she saw to it that Jonathan was enrolled in the catechism class, and each day she spent a portion of their prayer time in quizzing him on it. The catechism reminded her anew of the beliefs their mother had held so dearly, and which she could understand on an intellectual level.

But there was a measure of belief that she had not achieved, a plane of her existence that was not satisfied. Most of the time she was able to put it from her mind, but she felt sure that once he looked into her eyes in that penetrating way he had, Caleb was bound to know that she still lacked her mother's faith.

That evening, after Jonathan had said his prayer and was asleep, Ann took her mother's Bible from the table, and by the dim light of the single candle, turned to the Gospel of Matthew and began reading.

❧

Never had time passed more slowly. The heat had been aggravated by drought, and everything baked in the relentless sun. Agnes kept the kitchen garden alive with the aid of gallons of well water, drawn and applied with a gourd dipper early each morning. No one could work out-of-doors by suppertime, for the mosquitoes that had hatched earlier in the wet season made a vicious, biting attack on any foolish enough to venture outside. Ann had grown to dread their singing around her ears in the night, a sure sign that she and Jonathan would awaken the next morning to new itching welts. The goose grease that Agnes gave them to use as an ointment was messy and rank, but Ann used it and insisted that Jonathan do so, too.

"No one told us how hot it gets in America," Ann said to Agnes one morning as she was helping her weed the garden. "Or about these pests," she added, slapping at a persistent sweat bee.

"That's so," Agnes agreed, "but still I'd not trade places and be back in the hovel I come from, and that's a fact."

"I shouldn't complain, either," Ann admitted. "I know there was na future for us in Ireland, nor likely there would ever be. But I do miss th' old ways and the old places, and I miss havin' the family together most of all."

"What you need is a husband," Agnes said with her grimace that passed for a smile. "Yer must be close to eighteen already, or I miss a good guess."

"I'll be eighteen in September," Ann said.

"Ann! Agnes! Where is everyone?" Mrs. Andrews called from the house, and Ann rose hastily, wiping her hands on the light shift she wore for outdoor work.

"Comin', Mrs. Andrews," she called back. "She'll be wantin' her breakfast now, Agnes. Ye had best stop that and have it ready directly."

Agnes straightened up with difficulty and groaned, holding her back. "I'm too old to be doin' a man's work," she muttered. "Mr. Andrews ought to buy indenture papers on a man-o'-all-work t' help us out."

"Perhaps he will if ye keep remindin' him of it," Ann suggested.

"Have you been outside again without your bonnet?" Mrs. Andrews asked by way of greeting.

"Aye, but the sun was barely up when we started workin', and I had no need of it. Then we were so busy with our weedin' that it slipped my mind."

"Humph!" Martha Andrews exclaimed. "Seems to me you find it convenient to let it slip your mind entirely too much. A young lady must not allow her skin to become discolored, and yours is dangerously close to that condition already."

"Aye, Ma'am," Ann said meekly, having learned long ago that diplomatic agreement was the wisest way to handle Mrs. Andrews's notions.

While Martha rested that afternoon, Ann filled a basin with cool well water and sponged her own perspiring body, exchanging the shapeless shift for the lightest of Elizabeth's castoffs, a fine lawn dress in soft rose. In deference to the heat, she piled her hair atop her head, holding it with three tortoiseshell combs that Elizabeth had left behind. A few damp tendrils of hair curled around her face, softening it. Looking at her reflection, Ann found herself wanting Caleb to see her as she was now—no longer a skinny young girl, but a maturing woman. She smiled at her reflection, but the result seemed stilted and artificial. Her natural expression was good enough, she decided. If John found it too serious for his liking, she doubted that Caleb would.

Chapter 11

I t's Mr. Craighead!" Jonathan cried in the late afternoon of the following day. "He's here!"

Martha Andrews covered her ears and glared at Jonathan. "For heaven's sakes, Boy, do calm yourself!" she admonished.

"Aye, Jonathan, slow down," Ann said, so occupied with soothing him that Caleb was well into the room before she saw him. Her first impression was that she had forgotten what a striking figure he made, then she realized that she was seeing him in clerical dress for the first time. His black coat and square white linen stock were quite befitting the quiet dignity with which he greeted Mrs. Andrews.

"I do apologize for this intrusion, Madam," he said, giving her his full attention and bowing formally. "It was certainly not my intention to disturb your household."

Somewhat mollified by his tone, Martha Andrews held out her hand. "You must be the minister Mistress McKay has been telling us about. She mentioned that the boy was looking forward to seeing you again."

"And I was hoping to see him as well," Caleb replied, laying a hand gently on Jonathan's head.

"Have you come from Philadelphia today?" Mrs. Andrews asked.

"No, I stopped yesterday at Donegal, where I delivered some messages to a minister there. Today I came into Lancaster and left my belongings with the Reverend Alexander, where I shall bide tonight."

"I do hope you are free to take the evening meal with us," Mrs. Andrews said.

"It is kind of ye to invite me," Caleb said. "I'll accept the hospitality wi' thanks."

"Very well. Ann, if you will assist me, I will speak to Agnes."

"Aye, Ma'am," Ann said, and with some assistance from Caleb, conducted Mrs. Andrews to the kitchen, grateful that she was giving them some time alone.

As Ann returned to the sitting room, Caleb was still standing, listening as Jonathan told a rather embellished version of their meeting with the Indians on the Lancaster trail. Caleb looked at Ann with a slightly amused expression, but she could see no hint that he had noticed any difference in her.

"Please sit down," she invited, and Caleb took the large chair with carved arms, deeply upholstered in maroon velvet, usually occupied by Mr. Andrews. Jonathan sat on the floor at his feet, and Ann took her usual seat, a comfortable Windsor chair, the only one in the room completely without upholstery.

"From what Jonathan has been tellin' me, ye have had several adventures since last we met," Caleb said.

"Most of them were in the gettin' here. Except for the few weeks when Mrs. Andrews was ill wi' the shakin' fever, our lives here have been quite calm."

"And your father? What have ye heard from him?"

Ann shook her head, her expression sober. "Nothing. About a month ago I asked a trader we met to see what he could find out, but he has not contacted me, either."

"David Zimmer says the Injuns prob'ly have him, is why we've not heard," Jonathan said earnestly.

"Your friend has a good imagination," Ann replied. "I am quite sure there is a good reason for his silence that has nothing to do wi' Indians."

"No doubt ye are right," Caleb murmured, and quickly changed the subject. "I am glad to see ye both lookin' as if ye have fully recovered from the rigors of our voyage."

"Aye, we have an abundance of good food to eat here, and so far we have both escaped the summer fevers."

"Reverend Alexander tells me that the Andrews household is among the finest in Lancaster, but I have observed that even the most ordinary households in the colony set a good table. It is truly a blessed land, and everyone I have met has been most gracious."

"I wish ye'd stay here," Jonathan said. "I like ye lots better than Reverend Alexander."

"Jonathan!" Ann exclaimed.

Caleb smiled slightly, but his tone was firm when he spoke to Jonathan. "Reverend Alexander is a fine man, and he takes his duties quite seriously. He told me that ye attended preachin' services and his catechism class, and I am glad to hear it. Remember that we do not attend a service to honor the minister, but the God whom he serves."

"Aye, Sir," Jonathan murmured, somewhat chastened. "But I'll always like ye best."

"Your letter mentioned that ye had much to tell us," Ann prompted. "Does that mean ye have raised the funds ye need?"

"Well, as I mentioned, people have been most generous. I stayed with Rev.

Isaac Drumlie, a man I knew at Edinburgh, and through his introductions I was able to visit many churches in the Philadelphia area. The people, not being forced to pay a tithe to any religion, are more generous to the causes of the church than any I have ever known. From the collections that were taken on my behalf, I have been able to buy both a packhorse and a riding horse, with enough funds to sustain me until I am settled."

"And have ye determined where that will be?"

"Not exactly, but I have na doubt that God is leadin' me to a place of service in the western lands. By all accounts, there are hundreds of our people who have taken up grants in those areas and have no one to minister to them. When I come to such a group, there will I bide."

"Perhaps as ye travel ye can inquire about Father," Ann said hopefully.

"I shall do that," he promised. "And when I do see William, I know he will be relieved to hear how well ye both are."

Just then, Agnes called Jonathan to run an errand for her, and as soon as she and Caleb were alone, Ann felt her old shyness and discomfort returning. She could think of nothing to say. After a moment, he broke the silence.

" 'Tis true that Jonathan looks like a different lad," he began. "But I must also add that I perceive that ye, too, have experienced a change, Mistress Ann. Ye canna have had a light burden here, wi' William away and in a strange new land, yet I sense that ye are far calmer and at ease wi' yourself than before. Ye wear that new responsibility well."

As she listened to him speak, Ann felt ashamed that she had thought Caleb would remark on her physical appearance. He still spoke to her as a minister to one of his flock, not as a man to a woman.

"I have tried to be brave, for Jonathan's sake, but there have been many times when I fear that he will become ill again, or that somethin' has happened to Father and we will see him no more. Lately I have tried to read the Bible and have had prayer with Jonathan each night. For a long time, I couldna bring myself to read the passages that Mother loved so much. I am tryin' to get over that."

"Ye must continue to study the Word and t' seek to do God's will. Your mother set a most excellent example for ye, and now ye must do the same for Jonathan."

"I know," Ann replied, unable to bring herself to promise more.

"While we have this time alone, there is another matter that I wish to discuss," Caleb began but was interrupted by the arrival of James Andrews. Ann had scarcely completed making the introductions when Agnes announced that the evening meal was served and they adjourned to the dining room.

Agnes had already placed the food on the table, not the elaborate fare that might be prepared for the special guests that Mr. Andrews entertained for business reasons, but what would have been considered a feast in Ireland. In addition to thin slices of pink ham, there were side dishes of new potatoes in cream, tender garden peas, fragrant cheese, and a tray of pickles and relishes. This was served with crisp corn cakes and buttermilk, cool from the cellar. A sponge cake waited on the serving board for dessert.

"I can certainly see why the McKays look so well," Caleb commented after being asked to return thanks for the meal. "A nobleman could not provide a better board."

Martha Andrews warmed to Caleb's compliments and soon began to regale him with questions about Philadelphia.

"Our son, John, is reading law with Mr. Otis on Fourth Street," she said. "Perhaps you might have noted their establishment?"

"Is it in the vicinity of Arch Street? The Reverend Drumlie showed me a magnificent public hall that Mr. Franklin and some of his friends—Mr. Otis among them, I believe—are building at Fourth and Arch Streets so that preachers of any religious persuasion will be able to address the people of Philadelphia. I thought it quite a remarkable achievement."

"No doubt it is," Mrs. Andrews replied, "but I fear that such an invitation may well be abused. When there are too many who claim to be preachers, the people tend to confusion. It seems to me that there is more harmony in a place with one established church and one belief, to which all men subscribe."

"There are many such towns within the colonies, but I am told that almost any religious persuasion can be found in the city of Philadelphia, and that all are equally tolerated."

"That is why many people came to the Pennsylvania colony in the first place, Martha," Mr. Andrews said, aware that Caleb Craighead did not need a lecture on the merits of a state church. "Lancaster has many faiths, too, Mr. Craighead. I should think that a man of your education would prefer to stay in Philadelphia, or even settle here, rather than to rush off to the wilderness."

"I was not city-born, and I would miss the freedom of being close to the out-of-doors. I suppose that is one reason that America appealed to me."

"You would be welcome enough in this town as a schoolmaster," Mr. Andrews said. "But if you are determined to go on to the western lands, might you consider becoming a trader, at least until you have a church organized? I employ several men who have done that, and with great success."

"I believe that the Lord will provide," Caleb replied, "and so far, He has not called me to be a merchant. If He does, I am certainly willin' to try it."

"Do you really believe that God calls people to their professions, Reverend Craighead?" Martha Andrews asked, her tone dubious.

"I believe that there is a plan for every life, Mrs. Andrews. The happiest people are those who, whatever their occupations or stations in life, have yielded themselves to His will and operate within it."

"And what of those who are not of the flock?" Mr. Andrews asked. "Can they never be happy?"

"They may appear to be, and may even believe that they are happy, but in fact they are the most miserable of all men, for they have no hope of possessing eternal life."

"Reverend Craighead was invited to dine with us, not to dispute theology," Mrs. Andrews said, stirring uncomfortably.

"Sometimes I think talk of religion or politics ought to be universally banned around the dining table," said Mr. Andrews with a smile. "Will you have a slice of this excellent sponge cake, Reverend?"

"Thank ye," said Caleb, "but I fear I have already had more than I should. The meal was most enjoyable, and I appreciate your hospitality."

"I must bid you a good evening," Martha Andrews said, "and ask Mistress McKay to assist me to my room. But please stay on as long as you wish, and come again whenever you are in Lancaster."

"I must return to the Reverend Alexander's before dark," Caleb replied, "but first I should like to spend some time with Jonathan."

"Certainly," agreed James Andrews. "You and the boy may have full use of the sitting room."

"I feel unwell," Martha Andrews complained after Ann had helped her into bed. "See if you can find some fresh mint leaves for my indigestion."

Obediently Ann went outside, where already the lengthening shadows foretold that the day was almost done, and picked several sprigs of mint from the garden, washing them in water she drew from the well. The rest of the bucket she brought into Mrs. Andrews's bedroom and used to fill her bedside pitcher. "Is there anythin' else I can do for ye?" Ann asked, hoping that there would not be.

"I suppose not." Mrs. Andrews sighed. "And in any case, I can see that you long to be sitting with your minister. He's a handsome man, I grant you that; although he could use a more pleasant manner. You ought to persuade him to stay here and keep a school instead of traipsing off into the wilderness."

❧

"Jonathan tells me that he is quite a fisherman," Caleb said, rising as Ann entered the sitting room.

"He has gone once, when John Andrews was here, but the size of his catch seems to increase wi' the passage o' time."

"It was kind of him to give ye both an outin'," Caleb said, rather formally.

"Next time John comes, he is goin' to take us for a raft ride on the river," Jonathan confided.

"That could be dangerous if ye don't swim," Caleb replied. "I hope young Mr. Andrews will exercise caution." Glancing at Ann, he added, "He seems to be a bit reckless."

Before Ann could respond, Caleb added, "Reverend Alexander will be anxious if I stay longer."

"Will ye come again tomorrow?" Jonathan asked.

"No, Lad. I'll be on my way in the mornin'."

"Should ye come across Father—" Ann began, but seeing that she was close to tears, Caleb interrupted.

"I'll make inquiries as I go," he assured her. "In any case, I have not forgotten my promise to your mother, and until ye are all settled, I'll keep in touch."

"Was there somethin' else ye had to tell us?" Ann forced herself to ask, seeing that Caleb was determined to leave. He looked at her with an expression she could not quite identify—sorrow, or disappointment, perhaps—and shook his head.

"No, not now. Perhaps the next time we meet, when we are all more certain of our course." He put his hand to hers for a brief moment, murmured, "God bless ye both," and left the house. Jonathan walked with him to the street, and Ann watched numbly as Caleb lifted the boy in his arms and kissed his forehead, then strode away without a backward glance.

"Why are ye cryin'?" asked Jonathan when he returned.

"Because. . . ," Ann said, and stopped, not fully able to understand what had happened, but aware that something had gone terribly wrong.

"Are ye sad that Mr. Craighead is leaving?"

"Aye, I am. I had expected that he would stay in Lancaster for a few days."

"I wish he would, too. We talked some about it."

Ann wiped her eyes and looked at Jonathan, a suspicion slowly dawning. "Just what did ye and Mr. Craighead discuss whilst I was gone?"

"First we talked about the catechism, and he said I was doin' well on the memorizin' but didna know some of it perfectly yet. He asked me how I liked Lancaster, and I told him about my friends, and about John."

"What did ye say about John Andrews? I know ye told him about the fishin' trip, but what else did ye say?"

"That we liked him, and that I hoped he would come back soon."

"Is that all?"

Jonathan looked uncomfortable and did not speak for a moment.

"Jonathan, what else did ye tell him?"

"Just that he kissed ye some," he admitted.

"Oh, Jonathan!" Ann exclaimed, in anger and frustration. It was apparent that her brother had only pretended to be asleep the day they went to the river. But to tell Caleb. . .no wonder he had seemed so distant.

"Are ye angry wi' me?" he asked, seeing her distress.

"Ye shouldna have said that, Jonathan. Ye know that Master John is full of high spirits and likes to tease. He kissed me because it was a fine day and we were all verra happy. It was wrong for ye to pretend that ye were asleep, too."

Jonathan's eyes brimmed with tears. "I'm sorry," he said contritely. "I was just playin' a game. I didna mean to hurt ye."

"I know ye didna," Ann said, her anger replaced by humiliation. "But I am afraid that Mr. Craighead must have a very poor impression of me now."

"I don't see why," Jonathan said. "What does that have t' do wi' his bein' our friend?"

"He is still our friend, but ye must learn to hold your tongue in the future." She sighed and added, "What's done is done, and there is no need ta worry about it. Now wash your face and get ready for bed, and let's say no more about what happened tonight."

Had Jonathan's thoughtless words spoiled any chance for something more than friendship between her and Caleb? What would he have said to her had Jonathan remained quiet? Ann lay awake far into the night, pondering the questions along with the bitter realization that Caleb was more important to her than she had realized. More important than he would possibly ever believe.

Chapter 12

Ann awoke after a fitful sleep to find that the sky was just lightening toward dawn. She lay still for a few moments. *I just can't let him leave with the wrong notion,* Ann told herself. Once resolved, she hastily drew on her clothes, and holding her slippers in one hand, tiptoed out of the house, taking care to avoid the floorboards that always squeaked underfoot. She was not sure what she would say to Caleb, but she did not want their relationship to depend solely on a promise he had made to her dying mother.

Cutting through the dew-drenched lawn to the rear alleyway, Ann hurriedly covered the distance to the church, meeting no one along the way. The Reverend Alexander's home was a log house beside the church, and even with several additions and glazed windows, it was a far more humble dwelling than most of the houses in Lancaster.

The sun was breaking through a ragged fringe of orange-tinted clouds as Ann went to the rear of the house, where a rough shed sheltered the livestock. The grass showed signs of having been walked upon recently, and fresh hoof marks led to the street. There was no sign of Caleb or his packhorse anywhere.

Ann leaned wearily against the side of the shed. She was too late. Caleb had gone, and she had missed the opportunity to speak to him once more.

"Who goes there?" a voice called, and Ann looked up to see Mrs. Alexander standing at the rear door of the house.

"It's Ann McKay," she called back. "Has Mr. Craighead gone?"

"My, yes, with the first light," she replied. "But come inside and have a bit of breakfast with us." Mrs. Alexander held the door open for her. The minister's wife was wearing a severely cut gray dress, the only color Ann had ever seen her wear. The Alexanders, both in their early forties, Ann judged, had three lively children who were apparently still sleeping.

"I canna stay to eat, but I'm obliged to ye for the invitation. I had hoped for a word wi' Mr. Craighead before he left."

"I believe you met one another on the voyage over from Ireland, did you not, Miss McKay?" the Reverend Alexander asked. In his plain morning clothes, and without his clerical collar, he could have passed for an ordinary laborer.

"Aye, and his presence meant a great deal to all of us on the vessel. He intends to look out for my father as he goes west."

Reverend Alexander poured his tea into a saucer and blew on it, taking a swallow before speaking again. "Are you sure you'll not join us?" he asked. "Our fare is plain, but there is quite enough."

Ann looked at the coarse bread he was crumbling into curdled milk. "No, thank ye. I should go now. I'm sorry to disturb ye so early in the mornin'."

"Nonsense," Jane Alexander said. Both she and her husband were natives of the colony, and they spoke in a somewhat flat, nasal tone that Ann sometimes had trouble understanding. "I'm just sorry you missed your minister."

"So am I," Ann replied. "Do ye have any idea how far he'll have to travel to find a congregation?"

The reverend looked amused. "He'll not find a *congregation* waiting for him anywhere, far or near," he told her. "Those who go west are settling on four-hundred-acre grants or double grants if they buy their land. Some parts are thickly settled, but many are not. People have taken up land all the way from the Delaware to the Susquehanna and in every direction in between, mostly following the Indian trails and the creeks. He could stop almost anywhere and find people who needed him."

"Do ye suppose Mr. Craighead will be lettin' ye know when he finds his stopping place?" Ann asked.

"He may," the reverend said, looking keenly at Ann, "but I've no doubt that he will be in touch with you, in any case."

Mrs. Alexander smiled and looked knowingly at Ann. "Mr. Craighead asked us to keep an eye out for you and your brother in his absence."

"When did he say that?"

"This morning, just as he left," Mrs. Alexander replied. "He seems to be a true man of God, filled with the Spirit and anointed to preach the gospel, but when it comes down to it, he can't do his best alone. He needs a helpmeet."

"That is quite true," Reverend Alexander said, nodding in agreement. "A minister needs a good wife by his side. Our doctrine teaches that celibacy is dishonoring to women and dangerous to men. Mr. Craighead is aware of that obligation; we discussed it with him yesterday."

Ann felt her face grow warm. Mrs. Alexander gave her a knowing smile. "Don't you be concerned about Mr. Craighead," she said, following Ann to the door. "If the Lord is in it, he'll be back."

If only I could have seen him, Ann thought as she walked back to the Andrews's house. The uncertainties of her life were becoming increasingly difficult to her. Mrs. Alexander had meant to be comforting when she said Ann would see Caleb again if the Lord were in it, but there was no solace there for her. "I am na good enough to be his wife," she said aloud, and the admission brought tears to her eyes. "What a mess I have made of things!"

❧❦

Three days later, while Ann was carding flax and Agnes had taken Jonathan with her to the market, a dirty-faced boy, little older than her brother, came to the kitchen door and asked to see Mistress McKay.

"What is it that ye want?" Ann asked, thinking that the boy could use a hot meal and a good scrubbing.

"Are ye Mistress McKay?" he asked, peering in for a closer look.

"Aye."

"I have a message for ye," he said, "in private."

"Come inside," Ann invited. "Would ye like somethin' to eat?"

"No'm," the boy mumbled. "I'm not to come inside, but t' tell yet t' come wi' me now, if ye want word o' yer father."

"Who sent ye?" Ann asked, feeling a surge of hope.

"I ain't allowed ter say," the boy replied. "Yer t' come wi' me now," he added, as she hesitated.

"I must let Mrs. Andrews know I am leavin'," she said. "At least tell me where we are goin'."

The boy shook his head. "Yer t' come wi' me now, and none's ter know," he repeated stubbornly.

"All right," she agreed, looking out to see if there was any sign of Agnes and Jonathan, but the alleyway they usually took to the market was empty. "Wait and I'll get my bonnet."

Martha Andrews was taking her afternoon rest, and Ann decided not to risk disturbing her and hoped she would not be needed before her return. Taking her bonnet from its peg, Ann walked out into the heat of the summer afternoon.

"What is your name, Boy?" Ann asked as they walked down the alley, away from town.

"Tad," he replied, volunteering no other information. He led Ann toward the river where John Andrews had taken them fishing. As they passed the last house, Ann became increasingly uneasy.

"How much farther are we goin'?"

"Just down t' the ferry," Tad said, pointing. "See it?"

Up ahead on a wide expanse of the river, a flat barge, poled by a large black man, was slowly drifting toward the opposite side. A crude shed, built of rough-barked logs, stood on the near bank of the Conestoga, and the boy indicated that she should enter it. No one else was in sight, and the boy turned back toward town, his mission apparently concluded. For a moment Ann considered running after him, but having come this far, and wanting news of her father, curiosity overcame her fear, and she walked to the cabin.

"Come in, Missy," a male voice called as she reached the door, and she recognized it as belonging to the trader Yancey. He sat sprawled on a puncheon bench inside the cabin, bottle in hand, dressed in a soiled white linen shirt, open nearly to the waist, and ragged breeches.

"Why didna ye come to the house?" Ann asked, standing just outside and casting an anxious eye toward the raftsman, who had just reached the opposite bank. She wondered if a scream would carry across the river, and feared it might not.

"Ah, Missy, surely ye can see that I ain't dressed for town," he said, chuckling. "Besides, we can visit here a whole lot better, and nobody'll know our business."

"If ye have some news of my father, I would verra much like it," Ann said nervously, and again he laughed.

"I'll just bet ye would," he said, "but first, come on in out o' that hot sun."

As she gingerly entered the cabin, he stood and held out the bottle to her. "This is prime rum—have some."

"No, thank ye," Ann replied, wishing that Yancey were sober. "Now, what do ye know about my father?"

"Well, Missy," he began, "I had ter go out of my usual way on my last trip; had some trouble with my lead horse. A blacksmith told me there was a passel o' Irish around Shawnee Creek that was down with the fever, so many that some were lyin' unburied. Some of the Shawnee Kishacoquillas come through that way and found 'em."

"What does that have to do wi' my father? Do ye know that he was one o' the sick?"

"The smith didn't know no names," he said, and took another swallow from the bottle before continuing. "But I saw a cart that looked like the one yer pa had when he come here to Lancaster. When I asked the man where he got it, he said he bought it off an Injun. I figure it was likely stole from yer pa."

Ann felt stunned, and she wondered if she dared believe his words. "There must be many oxcarts like ours," she said slowly. "By itself, that doesna mean anythin'."

"Have yer heard from your pa, then?" he asked, moving closer. Ann backed away and did not answer.

"I thought not," he said, draining the bottle and wiping his mouth with the back of his hand.

"How can I find out for sure?" she asked.

"Likely ye could find somebody around Shawnee Creek that's seen the cart, and probably yer pa, too."

"Where is this place?"

"That's hard ter say. If yer take the Conewago Creek trail ter Tolliver Station and then turn south and follow Shawnee Creek fer a day, yer'll come to the blacksmith. He can tell yer from there."

"How long ago were ye there?"

The trader seemed to be having trouble reckoning the time, finally holding up five fingers. "This many days," he said. "If all goes accordin' to plan, I'll rest up awhile and restock and head out again. Thought yer might like to go with me, Missy."

Ann was silent, wanting to turn and run from the disgusting man. But if he could help her find her father, she did not want to antagonize him.

"I must think about it," she said.

"Ye can't let old man Andrews know," he warned. "He'd tie yer up afore he'd let yer go with me, and that's a fact."

"He promised my father that he would look after us," Ann said, aware that the trader's words were likely true.

Yancey laughed. "That's a joke. There ne'er was a bigger crook in the colony than James Andrews. Respectable as the Sabbath, he is, and crafty as a serpent."

She ignored his assessment. "If my brother and I went with ye—"

"Not the boy," he interrupted. "He stays here, or you don't go, neither."

She paused. "If I decided to go with ye, then there must be certain conditions on your part, as well."

"Of course," he said. "Yer'll find that Paul Yancey is a man o' his word, even if I ain't a fancy gentleman. Tell you what, Missy. You think over what I said, and let me know in a day or so. 'Twould be out o' me way to go back to Shawnee Creek, but I feel a bit sorry fer ye, and I'd see that you got there safe. Word'll get ter me at the Red Lion, just outside town. I won't be here long, though—don't miss yer chance."

In another moment Ann was safely out of the cabin, and she hurried back to the Andrews' house, her mind in a turmoil.

When Ann arrived, her duties kept her occupied until Agnes had the evening meal prepared. Ann had resolved to tell James Andrews about her encounter with Yancey, seeing no alternative, but he did not appear for supper, nor had he come home by the time she got Jonathan ready for bed.

"Ye can read tonight," Ann said, handing him their mother's Bible. She had opened it to Psalm 61, which had been one of her mother's favorites, and Jonathan remembered it, as well.

" 'Hear my cry, O God; attend unto my prayer. From the end of the earth will I cry unto thee, when my heart is over. . .' " He stopped, and Ann supplied the rest of the word. " '. . .whelmed.' " He continued. " 'Lead me to the rock that is higher than I. For thou hast been a shelter for me, and a strong tower from the enemy.' " He stopped reading and looked at Ann. "Ann, do ye really think we'll ever see Father again?"

"O' course we will," she assured him, although far from certain of it herself.

"Mr. Craighead said we should ask God to help us," he said. "But I wish there was somethin' else we could do to find out where he is."

"So do I," Ann replied, "and maybe soon there will be. In the meantime, we must try to be brave, as Father would want us to be."

"I'm glad ye are here," Jonathan murmured when Ann kissed him good night after they had prayed together for their father.

🙦

Sometime in the night Ann awoke, aware of the distant rumble of thunder and oppressive heat in the room. She got up, the cornhusk mattress rattling beneath her, and crept to the window for air. So low at first that she thought she had imagined it, she heard a voice calling her name. Thunder muttered again, and sheet lightning briefly illuminated the landscape. She saw no one outside her window but quickly lifted her robe from its hook and left the room. She wound her way quietly to the kitchen door and looked out, straining to see into the darkness. Ann had just decided it was her imagination when a form slipped from the shadows, and with a swift motion grabbed her, covered her mouth, and half-led, half-dragged her out of the house toward a seldom-used shed across from the rear yard.

She wriggled desperately trying to see her captor's face, until he spoke. And then there was no longer any doubt who he was.

Chapter 13

I hope I haven't hurt you," John Andrews said, taking his hand from her mouth, "but I feared you might wake the household."

"What on earth are ye doin' here in Lancaster in the middle of the night?" she asked as they entered the shed. Lightning flashed again, and thunder roared on its heels as the storm approached.

"I had a bit of trouble over a debt and had to leave Philadelphia," he said.

"And ye are ashamed to face your father?"

"There is more to it than that," he said, and in the flash of a brilliant streak of lightning, Ann could see the drawn, defeated look on his face. In a flat tone, he continued his story. "There's no need to go into the details, but what it amounts to is that a certain gentleman wanted me to pay a debt I owed him. When I could not get the money immediately, he placed me in the position of having to defend my honor against him. It did not go well."

"Ye mean ye fought a duel?" Ann asked, astounded. In Ireland, the men of the McKays' acquaintance used their fists to settle their arguments, leaving duelling pistols or swords to the landed gentry. "Isna that against the law?"

"Yes, and so is thievery," John said. "But goods are stolen and duels are fought, all the same." He sank to the dirt floor of the shed and rested his head against a pile of lumber. As the first raindrops peppered down, rattling the tin roof, he put his head on his drawn-up knees and made a sound very much like a sob.

"Ye say the duel did not go well—what do ye mean? Are ye hurt?"

His reply was lost in the drumming of the rain, and Ann moved closer and knelt beside him. "I couldna hear ye. Are ye hurt?"

"Not as much as my opponent," he said bitterly. "I am told he may be mortally wounded."

Shocked, Ann drew a deep breath. It was difficult to believe that John Andrews, so lighthearted and pleasure-loving, could actually have caused someone's death. "But ye—are ye in pain?" she asked, and he nodded assent.

"We used his weapons, since I had none—a brace of matched derringers. We must have fired at the same instant, because I heard only the report of my own pistol. I felt a stinging in my left side, but I still stood. He lay on the ground and didn't move. My seconds dragged me away to an inn, and when I saw the blood on my shirt, I realized that his charge must have grazed my side."

"Then how were ye able to ride all this way?" Ann asked, recalling the hardships of the journey from Philadelphia. "Ye must be half-dead."

"One of my seconds is a surgeon's apprentice, and he bound the wound well enough so I didn't lose much blood. But then my opponent's man said he thought the other was dying. Under that condition, I had no choice but to leave."

"What will ye do now?" Ann asked. "Your father is certain to find out."

"True, but I prefer to keep it hidden as long as I can. My father can be a very hard man when he chooses, and I have no desire to put my mother in the position of harboring a fugitive."

"Surely no one will come all the way from Philadelphia after ye, will they?"

"That is not the way things are done in the colony. There will be a public announcement posted in town and run in the *Gazette* to the effect that one John Andrews is afoul of the law, and that any citizen who apprehends him can be assured of a reward. Once that comes out, I will be in great danger, because there are those who make a handsome living from chasing runaway slaves and indentured servants—and criminals. I had to ride hard to put distance between me and the newspaper."

"Ye still have not said what ye aim to do."

"I will," he promised. "But first do you think you could find some food? I've not eaten all day."

"Of course!" she said, turning for the door. "I should have realized your need."

In the kitchen, Ann found bread and a pastry, filled with apples and spices in the German way, and added cheese and mutton and buttermilk from the cooling slab in the cellar. The rain had subsided to a soft drizzle as she returned to the shed, her arms so full that she had to walk slowly.

John sat where she had left him, so still that at first she feared that he had fainted. "Here," she said, spreading an apron to serve as a tablecloth. "I was afraid to draw water, the well-chain rattles so; but I found a half-crock of buttermilk."

When he had eaten most of the food, she spoke again. "Now, tell me what ye plan to do."

"There isn't much I can do, except push on to the new lands until this business is forgotten."

"When do ye think ye can go back?"

"Not for months, maybe even years. In the meantime, I'll be fairly safe on the frontier."

"But how will ye live?" Reading law was a poor preparation for breaking land, she knew.

"I can't tell Father what happened, and I can't ask him for help; but I know where he keeps the stores he sells to traders, and I know how to get to them."

His words called to mind another trader. "Do ye know a man named Paul Yancey?"

"A rough fellow, fond of rum, as I recall. Why do you ask?"

Ann told John of her encounter with the man. "I was goin' to ask your father to help me trace the truth of his story, but he was not at supper."

"Do you know if he came home at all tonight?" John asked.

"No, I don't. Your mother retired to her room directly after supper, and Jonathan and I were in ours before full dark. He was not home by then. Is it important?" she asked, sensing his anxiety.

"It could be," he replied and hesitated. "Ann, I will tell you something about my father, but it must be held in the strictest confidence. You must promise that you will never mention it to anyone else."

"Ye should not be telling me anythin' like that," Ann said uneasily.

"Ordinarily I wouldn't, but you should know that my father is not exactly what he seems to be." He paused, and for a moment the only sound in the shed was the rain dripping from the roof. "I found out by accident several years ago that Father is engaged in illegal trade with the French. I understand how it began, and I have reason to believe that he would like to end it now, but he has been threatened with financial ruin if he does not continue to do as they wish. Yancey is one of the go-betweens in the trade, and there is no love lost between them."

Ann remembered Yancey's words—"James Andrews is crooked as a serpent"—words she had discounted as the rantings of a drunken man. Although she knew that Mr. Andrews hoped to accumulate as much wealth as he could, she had never seen him behave in an unseemly way, and she told John so.

"Do ye think Yancey means to do your father harm?" she added.

"Not as long as Father is useful to him. But Yancey has no loyalty to anyone, and if he thought there was a profit in it, he would sell his very soul."

"I don't fully trust Yancey myself," Ann said. "But he has information about where my father might be, and at this point I am almost ready to believe him."

"I think you should avoid the man," John said bluntly. "It is my guess that he and Father are moving stores tonight in secret. They smuggle cargo by water every few months."

"How will ye get your stores, then, if your father is at the warehouse tonight?"

"I'll have to wait until he has finished, that's all. Now, let's consider what you should do."

"What I should do?" Ann echoed, surprised. "I should think that ye'd be too concerned with your own problems t' bother yourself wi' mine."

"Maybe we can help each other," John said. "You want to find your father, and with the word soon out that there is a price on my head, I need to go to the frontier. The authorities will be looking out for a man alone, not for a couple. With some work on changing our appearances, I think we could escape notice. Suppose you received a letter from your father, telling you to join him," he said slowly, "and saying that Jonathan should stay here, because of his health."

"But Father would never ask me t' travel alone," Ann protested, "and I wouldna leave Jonathan here by himself, anyway."

"If he went with us, there would be greater danger of detection," John pointed out. "He could easily give us away by saying the wrong thing."

How well she knew her brother's tendency to speak when he should be silent. "I couldna just go off supposedly on my own, anyway," Ann said aloud. "Your father would never permit it."

"I'll grant you that," John agreed. "There must be some way that we can invent an escort for you."

"We could invent any number of things, but I have no way t' travel anywhere at the moment."

"Do you ride?" he asked.

"When I was a child I would sometimes sneak into the lord's pasture and ride bareback, but I've ne'er sat a saddle. Anyway, where would I get a mount? I have very little money."

John sighed. "It's very late, and I'm almost past thinking. I'll sleep here in the shed tonight, and stay behind this lumber during the day. As soon as you can get away tomorrow, bring me some food. By then I should have worked out a plan for us."

"Will ye be all right? Shouldna your wound be attended?"

"It doesn't hurt so much, now that I'm off that jolting excuse of a horse—and in any case, I can't afford to let anyone know I am in town."

"What did ye do with the horse?" Ann asked.

"I left him at the Watters stable, with no one the wiser. I can get him back, and a mount for you as well, if need be."

"Are ye sure ye won't come inside?" Ann asked. "It seems to me that your parents would want to help ye."

"They must not know about this," John said emphatically. "Can I count on you to keep my secret, sweet Ann?"

It was the first time that night that he had said anything personal to her, and for a moment he almost sounded like the John Andrews she had known before. But then his voice grew more serious. "My life is in your hands." He sounded so desperate that she felt she had no choice.

"I will not tell your parents," she promised, "and I'll bring food to ye tomorrow when I can."

Back in her room, Ann lay still a long time, pondering her and John's predicaments. A fragment of Scripture came into her mind, and she repeated it several times: "In all thy ways acknowledge Him, and He shall direct thy paths." She desperately needed direction, but as light returned to her room, Ann was no nearer to knowing what she should do than she had been before.

❧❧

Called away on a business matter. . .that was Mrs. Andrews's explanation for her husband's absence from the breakfast table the next morning.

"And what ails you this morning?" Mrs. Andrews asked, when Ann made little response to her declarations. "Are you coming down with something? I'll not have you get sick on me! Agnes can prepare a posset—"

"No," Ann interrupted, attempting a smile. "I'm quite well, thank ye. It's just that the storm kept me awake, and I'm a bit tired."

"Well, I still say you look unwell," Mrs. Andrews declared, returning her attention to her food. "And I think you should stay in the house today and not go gadding about in the heat as you seem to have formed the unwise habit of doing."

When Ann went to the kitchen to fetch Mrs. Andrews a second cup of tea, Agnes commented on the missing food. "I put it away myself, from supper."

"I'm afraid I ate it," Ann said, her eyes downcast.

"Yer needed a bit o' flesh on yer bones when yer come here, I'll grant," Agnes said earnestly. "But overdo it, and yer'll have trouble catching a man."

"I'll remember your advice," Ann said, smiling. Despite her rough ways and appearance, Agnes was good-hearted, and Ann knew that she would do her best to care for Jonathan if Ann were not there to look after him. But she still could not accept the idea of leaving him with the Andrewses while she went to look for their father.

The morning hours seemed to crawl by. At both breakfast and dinner she had managed to sneak some bread and cheese into her pocket, and Ann hoped that it would suffice if Agnes did not leave the kitchen and give her a chance to raid for more.

Finally Mrs. Andrews was settled for her afternoon rest, and Jonathan was off to play with his friend, leaving Ann with her first free time of the day. "I'm goin' to take a walk," she told Agnes, tying on her bonnet. "I won't be gone long."

Agnes looked up from the potatoes she was peeling and grunted. " 'Tis a strange time o' day to be goin' out," she said. "Mind you watch where you walk."

"I will," Ann promised. "It's much cooler today, and I just want to get out o' the house for awhile."

"Go, then," Agnes said, resuming her work.

When Ann entered the shed, John Andrews put out both his hands and took hers in greeting. In the light of day, dark shadows under his eyes and the stubble of beard covering his face changed him from the carefree young man he had been only a short time before. When he dropped her hands, Ann brought the food from her pocket. "This is all I could get today. Agnes missed what I took last night, and I had to tell her that I ate it myself."

John unwrapped the cheese. "Thank you. I didn't intend trouble for you," he said, taking a bite before continuing. "I have formulated a plan for us. It may take a few days to work it all out, but we can make a start laying the groundwork right away. You need to receive a letter from your father saying that he is near Harris's ferry and that he wants you and your brother to join him there. At the same time, my father must receive a letter asking him to finance your trip, to be repaid on whatever terms he chooses. He will ask Father to find a trustworthy escort for you both, say a family traveling in that direction. I'll stay around here in the woods by the river until I know what arrangements have been made, then I'll ride out west alone. Somewhere along the way, I'll meet you and say that I have been sent to take you to your father, and we'll leave the west trail and go on to Shawnee Creek together. How does that sound?"

"It might work," Ann admitted, trying to follow his reasoning, "but I wouldna feel right, askin' Mr. Andrews to pay our way."

"Don't worry about that—you work very hard around here, just for your board. You've earned more than enough to finance your trip."

"But what if Jonathan recognizes ye when ye join us?"

"I will try to disguise my appearance, but Jonathan is old enough to obey you if you tell him he must not appear to recognize me. He might enjoy the game, if it's put to him that way."

"And the letters from Father—how will ye manage that?"

"I think you should write them. I will get the necessary materials tonight and leave them in the shed. Then I will come back tomorrow night to pick up the letters."

"How will ye get them to me and your father?"

"That can be arranged—the ferryman on the Conestoga can find someone to deliver them for a few coppers, with no questions asked."

"So we could be ready to leave in a few days," Ann said, calculating the time involved.

"I should think so. Families pass through Lancaster on their way to the West every day. It shouldn't take Father long to find one that you can travel with."

"But suppose your father doesn't agree that we should go? Suppose he says he can't find us an escort?"

"I know that he will not welcome the news that you are leaving, but you came with the understanding that it was a temporary arrangement, and whatever else my father may be, he has always been a man of his word in a business arrangement."

"What else should the letter say?" Ann asked. She did not like deception and felt herself stalling. "Won't everyone wonder why Father waited so long to write?"

"Not if he had just found his land when he came down with the fever and has just now recovered. You'll know how to word it. Come to the shed tonight as soon as everyone else is asleep."

It all seemed to be happening too quickly. There were too many unanswered questions, and Ann felt an uneasy fearfulness growing in her. She spoke once more. "Makin' all of these arrangements," Ann began haltingly—"well, I know ye'd be better off just goin' alone. Perhaps that's what ye'd best do."

"Do you want to find out what has happened to your father?" he asked.

"Of course. But what will we do if we can't find him? Or if we find that he is. . ." She stopped, unable to voice the possibility that had more and more haunted her in the past few weeks.

John put his hands on her shoulders and looked into her eyes. "In any case, you and Jonathan will at least have me," he assured her. "I will see to it that you are taken care of, and that's a vow."

"I don't want ye to feel obligated to us."

John spoke in a low voice. "I need your help, Ann. Can I count on you?"

She nodded. "I'll come for the paper tonight."

Chapter 14

James Andrews appeared at the supper table, looking tired, but quite solicitous of Martha. Ann found it hard to believe that he had been regularly breaking the law for years. She had never known her father to do less than the law required, and although William McKay had never been able to lavish his family with the comforts that James Andrews provided, his integrity was his treasure. She knew that John did not hold his father in such high regard, and she felt genuinely sad that he could not.

James Andrews retired early that evening, and Ann sat up with Mrs. Andrews for some time. Finally everyone was in bed, and even though it was well before midnight, Ann decided to visit the shed and see if John had already left the writing materials for her.

He was there, waiting, when she stepped inside. He had brought several sheets of heavy paper, a quill, and a small container of India ink. "You'll have to seal the letters with candle wax. Leave them here, under this board, tomorrow night," he directed. "Then, leave a note for me here as soon as Father has received the letters and made some plans."

"Be careful," Ann cautioned.

"And you, too."

❧

Ann had no scrap paper on which to practice the wording of the letters, so she thought them through before she dared commit them to paper. Afraid to work by day, she waited until Jonathan was sleeping soundly before she dipped the quill into the ink and began to write by candlelight. She held the quill at an awkward angle and formed the letters more vertically than in her usual writing, trying to imitate William's hand. She purposely crossed out a few words, and misspelled a few others in both letters, and when she had finished, she reread them and was satisfied. It was not a perfect forgery by any means, but close enough, she hoped, for James Andrews to accept without question.

She blew out the candle and slipped out of the room, making her way quietly to the shed. After placing the letters under the board, Ann looked out the door in all directions to be sure she had not been observed. In the light of the waxing moon, she could detect nothing. As soon as she was back in the house, she waited by a window, watching, and saw a shadow detach itself from the wall of a neighboring house. A lone figure entered the shed, emerged a moment later, and was soon swallowed up in the night shadows.

Ann sighed and got ready for bed. For better or worse, John's plan had been set into motion. She thought of praying, but she wasn't at all sure God approved of such a plan. She felt quite sure Caleb would not. In the end, all she could do was wait and wonder where their actions would lead them.

❧

The next day dawned heavy with clouds, and a steady rain more typical of early spring than summer fell all morning. As Ann and Jonathan were eating their noonday dinner with Martha Andrews, a light rap sounded on the front door, and presently Agnes came into the dining room and handed Ann a folded paper. It was so creased and soiled that at first she did not recognize it as her work.

"Is it from Father?" Jonathan asked eagerly, leaving his place at the table to stand beside her. "What does he say?"

"Aye, it is from Father," she said, her heart pounding. How could she manage such a pretense! She continued after staring at the paper for a moment. "He says he has had the fever but has recovered, and he wants us to join him."

"Where is he?" Mrs. Andrews asked.

"I don't know," Ann answered, grateful for that bit of honesty. "He says we are to come to Harris's ferry."

"Merciful heavens!" Mrs. Andrews exclaimed. "That's many days' journey from Lancaster. How does he expect a lone girl and a little boy to make a trip like that? The man must still be feverish even to think of such a thing."

"He says that he is also writin' to Mr. Andrews, and that perhaps he can arrange a way for us to go there."

"Well, it doesn't sound sensible to me," Mrs. Andrews responded. "And, anyway, what am I going to do when you leave me? I'm afraid I have become quite dependent on you, Mistress McKay."

Jonathan began dancing around the table, emitting war whoops, until Ann had to excuse herself and take him from the room. She welcomed the opportunity to leave Mrs. Andrews. John's plan seemed to be working so far. They should soon be on their way.

The other letter that Ann had written was delivered to Mr. Andrews while he was taking his noonday meal in the company of Karl Watters, owner of the livery stable.

As James told Ann that evening, Karl's brother and his wife were planning to go to Harris's ferry quite soon, having decided to set up a gristmill in the vicinity. She and Jonathan would be able to travel with a respectable family. "Of course, they're only a few years away from the Palatine, and their English is still rather poor. That might cause you some problems."

"I could speak for them when English was needed," Ann said.

"And I know some German," Jonathan added. He had been playing with several German children and had learned quite a few words, as Agnes discovered one day when he brought home some German phrases she recognized as most unsuitable.

"Karl Watters seems to think that you could go with his brother practically free—for a keg of flour, some salt, and a bit of other provision. Do you want me to arrange it?"

"Oh, aye!" Ann exclaimed.

"We really don't want you to leave us," James Andrews said, putting a hand on the boy's shoulder. "Your presence has been a great help to Mrs. Andrews, and she will miss you sorely."

"And I will miss her, too, and your lovely home. But we long to see our father, and we are all he has now."

"I understand," James said. "And tell your father that I am happy to do this for him in lieu of wages you might have been paid for your work."

"That is kind of ye, and I thank ye for him," Ann said.

❧

"Shouldna we say a prayer of thanksgiving, like Mr. Craighead did on the ship?" Jonathan asked at bedtime.

"Aye, we should," Ann murmured. How long ago it seemed since they had all bowed together in sight of their new land, grateful they had been delivered from the hazards of the voyage! But tonight, though Ann was grateful they would soon be on their way, she felt equally apprehensive about their next journey, and what they would find at the end of it.

Chapter 15

James Andrews was as good as his word, and he came home at noon the next day to tell Ann that the Watterses had agreed to take her and Jonathan to Harris's ferry.

"A carpenter is making a frame to carry the millstone, and it should be ready tomorrow. Karl said they plan to leave Lancaster early the next morning."

"This is entirely too sudden for my liking," Martha Andrews complained. "Whatever am I going to do without Ann?"

"I have given the matter some thought, and I believe that I can find a suitable replacement for Mistress McKay, and some help for Agnes, as well. It will necessitate a trip to Philadelphia, but if I leave tomorrow morning, I can be back in a few days with a pair of servants," James Andrews said. "How would that suit you?"

"I'm not sure," Mrs. Andrews replied. "I'll not have any with rough manners or who cannot speak decent English."

"I will look for a suitable couple who will consent to indenture," he assured her.

Ann realized he was bound to find out about his son's disgrace when he reached Philadelphia and tried to visit him. So far, no copy of the *Pennsylvania Gazette* had arrived in Lancaster. Erratic in its delivery, it usually could be counted on three days after its Philadelphia publication. Surely the next issue would carry notice of John's duel.

Ann felt compassion for father and son, though she did not condone the act of dueling nor understand how John had come by the debts that had led to it.

That afternoon Ann wrote a brief note to John, giving the date of their departure, and adding "Leave *now*." She put the unsigned note under the board in the shed.

Afraid that Jonathan's high spirits were disturbing Mrs. Andrews's rest, Ann decided that they should get out of the house for awhile.

"We should let the Alexanders know we are leavin' and that ye'll not be in the catechism class tomorrow," she told him, suggesting they pay a visit.

❧

While Jonathan played with the youngest Alexander child, Jane Alexander invited Ann to take tea with her.

"I know you will be happy to join your father," she said when Ann told her their plans. "But you must know that we will be sorry to see you leave our congregation."

"Thank ye. Everyone here has been kind to us, and I am certain we shall always remember Lancaster fondly."

"Well, you must come back for a visit one of these days. Tell me, does Reverend Craighead know about your latest plan?"

"No, he doesna." Ann realized that the Alexanders could tell him her true destination. "If ye do hear from him, tell him he can inquire for us at a place called Shawnee Creek, just south of Tolliver Station. I am not exactly sure where Father is now, but I'll leave word there in case anyone should inquire."

"Tolliver Station," Jane Alexander repeated, and looked disturbed. "Seems that I heard of some trouble there recently."

"There was news about settlers killin' some Indians and then bein' killed in revenge."

"Oh, yes, I remember now. Terrible business, that was. But out there in the new lands, you never know what any man will do, red, black, or white. It's all the same. The unredeemed human heart is utterly depraved and capable of any crime." Mrs. Alexander spoke with the calm assurance of one who had long since made peace with God.

Ann envied the woman's complete composure. "Mrs. Alexander, did ye ever have any doubts—about God or His care for ye?"

"Doubts?" she echoed. "The catechism tells us that both mind and nature reveal God's existence. His Word and Spirit work to convict man of his sin and reveal the salvation of Christ. But you've been nurtured in the faith from childhood, Mistress McKay, and you must already know those things. Reverend Craighead told us that your mother was one of the strongest Christians he has ever known."

"But I am not as strong as she was," Ann confessed, "and sometimes my faith is verra weak."

"We are also taught that if we pray for more faith, it will be given to us. That is the only way any of us can be strong—in the strength of the Lord."

"Ye remind me of my mother," Ann said. "She always said that I must be strong, too, but I have ever felt weak and powerless, instead."

"I shall pray for you," Mrs. Alexander said sincerely. "But I can tell you this much—you will never be able to draw on God's strength until you have put your trust in His Son, Jesus. If you have not done that already, I pray that you will not delay further."

"I have always attended church," Ann said, "and I understand the doctrine of salvation. I just have never been certain that I have experienced it."

"The Bible teaches us that those who come to Him He 'will in no wise cast out.' But you must take the first step, in faith, of your own free will. When you have completely yielded your life to Christ, without any doubts or reservations whatsoever, you'll know His peace. You'll feel it *here*," she said, touching her heart.

"Ye have given me much to think on," Ann said, rising to leave. "And I thank ye for your words and your prayers, as well. My brother and I will have need of them before our journey is ended."

"You're most welcome," Mrs. Alexander replied, taking one of Ann's hands in both of hers and kissing her lightly on the cheek. "I think you are closer to God than you realize. He has a plan for you if you will but seek His will."

"I will write you and Reverend Alexander when I reach my father."

"Please do, and may God protect you all."

Ann's physical journey might end soon, if she found her father. *Could it be,* she wondered, *that like Christian, my spiritual journey is nearing its end, as well? Or did one ever reach the end of that pilgrimage in this life?* In the midst of questions, one thing was certain: Jane Alexander's words would stay in her mind.

❧

Ann spent her last day in Lancaster with Martha Andrews, finishing some sewing for her and listening to her complaints about the couple James Andrews proposed to bring home from Philadelphia. James had left early that morning, after calling Ann aside and pressing some coins into her hand.

"These are gold pieces, to be used in case of emergency," he said. "Hide them on your person and let no one know you have them. Sometimes thieves stop travelers in the forest, where they can take what is easy to get and disappear into the trees. With the millstone, your party will move slowly, and you must stay alert. Don't let Jonathan out of your sight."

"Thank ye, and I'll remember your advice. But I canna take the money. Ye've been more than generous already."

"It's no more than you deserve, and I insist that you take it," he said firmly and turned away.

So Ann had made a pouch for the coins and tied it to the top of her petticoat. By evening everything had been done that could be to prepare for their journey, and in a few hours they would be on their way.

It was still light and Ann had just listened to Jonathan's prayers when she heard loud voices, one of them Agnes, apparently from the kitchen. Then they faded, and when Ann walked out into the rear garden, she saw Agnes coming back toward the house—and the trader Yancey retreating down the alleyway.

"That man Yancey," Agnes sputtered, her face more than usually red. "A lower dog ne'er walked."

"What did he want?"

"Well, first he asked to see Mr. Andrews, an' when I tol' him he wasn't home, he said he'd see *yer* instead. The very idea! Yer can b'lieve that I sent him off, and that in a hurry."

"Did he say what his business was?" Ann asked uneasily.

"He said he had news about Master John, then he said to tell yer he was leavin' soon as he talked to Mr. Andrews, as if yer'd care a pin what the likes o' him did."

"How strange," Ann said. "What do ye suppose he meant about John?"

"Prob'ly just an excuse to get in the door," Agnes said. "Well, the master'll be in Philadelphia soon enough and can get the straight of it from John himself. Likely he's run up more debts for his father to pay."

"I suppose that it takes a great deal of money to live in a city like Philadelphia," Ann offered.

"Humph!" Agnes grunted. "That it may do, but Master John has his own reasons for needin' money."

"What do ye mean?" Ann asked.

"I mean that he has the gentleman's fondness for gamin' without much talent for winnin'."

"John gambles? Is that why he is in debt?"

Agnes laughed. "Mercy me, yes, he gambles regular, he does. One o' these days he'll get it out of his system, mayhap; but in the meantime, he's cost his father a pretty penny."

"I am sorry to hear it," Ann said, disturbed. It had never occurred to her that John's debts were related to gambling—the greatest of all vices, according to William McKay.

"Well, yer have enough to think on, what wi' yer trip and seein' yer pa again. As I tol' yer before, Master John is a charmer. He'll come out on his feet, just like a cat dropped out of a tree."

As soon as she could, Ann crept back out to the shed and lifted the board where she had hidden her note. It was gone, and so, she presumed, was John.

Later, sleep proved elusive. Ann's mind kept turning over Agnes's words and those of Jane Alexander. Since their journey was founded on deception, she felt it would almost be blasphemous to ask God to bless it. When at last she slept, her dreams were of Caleb. Although she could see him clearly, she could not speak to him and tell him where she was.

Chapter 16

Agnes, up before her accustomed hour, had prepared a lavish farewell breakfast of fried ham, eggs, thin buckwheat cakes cooked on an iron griddle, and a quantity of honey.

"Heaven knows when yer'll see another decent meal," Agnes said when Ann protested at the amount of food they were served. "Yer may as well eat hearty one more time."

"We'll miss your cookin'," Ann said. "I really think it saved Jonathan's life."

Agnes looked fondly at the boy and sighed. "Well, he does look better'n what he did when yer come here. And maybe travelin' with the Germans, yer'll be well-fed. They do like their victuals."

"Food is the least of my concerns now," Ann confided after her brother left the table. "Last night Jonathan put Indians and pirates in his prayers, askin' to be protected from both. There could be some renegade Indians about, and Mr. Andrews said somethin' about watchin' out for thieves. I just hope that Mr. Watters will be able to defend us if need be."

"If he's aught like his brother Karl, he will be," Agnes assured her. "They're strong men and brave as they come. Now let me help yer get yer belongings outside afore yer come for."

Ann took a breakfast tray in to Mrs. Andrews. "I thought ye might like to bide in bed awhile longer this morning," she said, setting the tray on a bedside table.

Mrs. Andrews's expression was unusually dour. "Ah, Mistress Ann, it is a sad day for this household. Even now, I wish you would change your mind about rushing off into the wilderness and stay here with us."

"I must go to my father," Ann said. "Soon Mr. Andrews will be bringin' ye a new companion and some help for Agnes, as well. That is somethin' ye can look forward to. And just think how peaceful it will be around the house without Jonathan's noise."

"It will be more lonely than peaceful," she declared sadly. "With my children so far away, this has been a desolate house. For at least a little while, you and Jonathan brought some life into it. I do not begrudge your father the right to have you back, but I wish it did not have to be this soon. And, should anything go amiss with him, I hope you will remember that you will always have a home with us."

It was possibly Martha Andrews's longest and kindest speech ever, and knowing that the woman would soon hear the bad news about John, Ann felt a rush of pity for her. Bending over, she kissed her cheek. "Thank ye for takin' us in when we needed a home," she said. "Jonathan and I may never see ye again, but we'll never forget ye for that."

Agnes summoned her, and Ann went outside to find the livery man standing in front of the house, holding the reins of a laden packhorse.

"Mornin', Mistress," he said in thickly accented English. "Mine brother is vaiting for you and der boy."

With a final embrace for Agnes, Ann and Jonathan followed Karl Watters to the edge of Lancaster, where his brother awaited them.

Klaus Watters was about thirty, a huge man, standing over six feet tall and well-muscled, obviously a valuable ally in a fight. His wife, Maria, made up in girth what she lacked in height. She wore her glossy black hair in braids close to her head, and her deep-set eyes were dark and alert. Her plump, rosy cheeks and generous mouth, which turned up at the corners, gave her a look of perpetual amusement. Both husband and wife greeted Ann and Jonathan warmly as Karl introduced them.

"Now ve start," Klaus said, heaving Ann's trunk effortlessly onto the cart containing the Watters' household goods. A yoke of oxen pulled the cart, a larger and heavier version of the one that had brought the McKays to Lancaster.

Another yoke of oxen was attached to a triangular wooden frame that held the millstone that would assure the Watters' livelihood at the end of their journey. This contraption was not fitted with wheels, but was designed so that only one small point of the triangular frame touched the ground. Ann had never seen anything like it, but as they got underway, she saw that it moved the heavy stone quite efficiently. In addition to the packhorse Karl Watters had brought to the Andrews' house, two other packhorses made up the procession, and one riding horse was tied to the back of the cart.

"Der boy can sit der horse if he vants," Karl Watters told her as he bade them farewell. "It is a gift to him from James Andrews."

"Oh! Please thank him for us." Ann was surprised at the gift, but she accepted it, thinking they might need a horse when John joined them.

The sun was well up and at their backs, promising a hot and dry day, when the little caravan finally got underway. Klaus led the team that pulled the millstone. Ann and Jonathan walked along beside Maria, who directed the team pulling the cart by voice commands and a hand on the yoke when necessary.

The terrain was, at first, identical to that which they had encountered as they came to Lancaster from Philadelphia. On the road ahead of them, cultivated land alternated with patches of dark woods; the trees on either side of the trail formed an overhead canopy that provided a welcome relief from the heat of the sun.

At their first rest stop, with several hours' travel behind them, Klaus Watters unfolded a crude parchment map of the area, marked with streams and names in a few places. At the far left-hand margin, designated with an X, was Harris's ferry. Other drawings indicated the location of springs and likely camping places. Although she tried to make out all of the names, Ann did not see either Tolliver Station or Shawnee Creek, but she did note the location of Conewago Creek, the stream that the trader Yancey had mentioned. It appeared about halfway between Harris's ferry and Lancaster. She wondered how many days away it was.

By late afternoon of the first day's journey, the land began to change, from flat to gently rolling to steep, winding upward seemingly forever. Twilight deepened into night, and when Ann had despaired of ever reaching the summit, they rounded one last turn in the trail and came upon open ground. Ashes of old campfires, evidence that others had used this place before them, dotted the broad meadow.

In the light of the campfire, with Maria moving about preparing their evening meal, Jonathan crept close to his sister and put his head in her lap. He was tired, as was she, but he was still excited about their trip. "Do ye think that Father camped here, too?" he asked.

" 'Tis likely. How do ye feel?"

"Weary of walkin'," he admitted, "and I'd like to ride tomorrow, if ye'll let me."

"Sittin' in a saddle may not be as comfortable as ye think, but ye can try," Ann said. When John came for them, she would have to ride, too, and she would like to practice a bit first. As they settled down to sleep that night, she wondered where John was, and if he, too, had camped in this meadow.

❦

Ann found the Watterses surprisingly easy to understand. Like most of the German settlers in those parts, they spoke only German at home, in their churches, and with their fellow countrymen, but they had learned enough English to get by in most ordinary situations. Klaus's wife, who seemed naturally reticent, wept as she haltingly told Ann of their voyage from Rotterdam, through the North Sea and then across the Atlantic, on which two of their children had died. Since coming to Lancaster, another child had been taken by the fever, and their last son had drowned early that summer in the millpond.

"So ve go away from der place where is trouble," Maria explained.

Ann told Maria of losing her mother on the voyage over, and a special bond of understanding was forged between them.

That bond was strengthened by prayers and Bible reading. The Watterses' massive Bible, printed in heavy Gothic lettering, fascinated Jonathan; their prayers, spoken in German, touched Ann. She did not understand their guttural tongue, but their invocation, their God, their faith was universal. Prayers and praise really did rise to heaven from every tongue. In that wild land, still largely untouched by the hand of man, Ann felt the assurance of God's presence.

On the third day of the journey, their slow but steady progress was halted by a downpour that forced them to seek shelter under the cart. Ann watched as Klaus traced their route on the map, pointing out a small square that appeared to be near their present location. "Ve stop by here next," he told them. "Is trading post. Ve sleep dere."

"In a real bed?" Jonathan asked. The novelty of sleeping out-of-doors had worn off, and the monotony of the journey was dampening his spirits.

"Vell, in a house vit a roof and walls," Klaus replied, hiding a smile.

"How far are we from here?" Ann asked, pointing to a wavy line labeled "Conewago Cr."

"Mabby vun day. Vy do you ask?"

"My father knows someone who lives near there." She knew she should begin to prepare the way for John's appearance.

"Mabby ve see him, den," Klaus said, folding the map and replacing it inside his shirt.

With some hours of daylight still remaining after the rain ceased, they were able to reach the trading post.

Sturdily built of notched logs, and far smaller than a regular inn, the dwelling provided shelter from the elements for several travelers. The wiry owner proudly told them his name was Walters and that his was the first permanent dwelling to be built west of Lancaster.

Ann asked him if he had seen William McKay.

"Well, now, people stop here almost every day," he told her. "Some days I've had as many as four families sleeping in the cabin and more camped out in the shed. I seldom recall a name."

"What about a minister, a man about thirty, ridin' alone with one packhorse? He could have passed this way within the past ten days."

"There's been no one claiming to be a minister, though several would fit that description, otherwise. Last night, it was a young man with a yellow beard, who took supper with us like he hadn't et in a month, then rode off like a spook was after him when one of John Penn's men rode in from

Philadelphia on a survey run. Most would have stayed to hear the latest news of the city, but not that one!"

Seeing that the Watterses and Jonathan were occupied with livestock, she took the opportunity to inquire about Tolliver Station.

"It's not on the western trail," he said. "About three hours due west of here, you'll come to a branch. If you bear north and to the west, you'll be going toward Harris's ferry. Go south along Conewago Creek, and you'll come to Tolliver Station directly. There was some trouble there lately. Some fool hot-headed Irish broke a treaty that was scarce a year old, and now nobody is sure what the Shawnee will do."

Ann wanted to ask him more questions, but he was needed outside and left her to think on his words. Ann was almost certain that the man who had fled from the post the night before was John. He had probably been watching them from the woods for several days, and when he learned of the Philadelphia surveyor's arrival, feared he would be recognized from the latest fugitive notices. He must be somewhere ahead of them, waiting.

When Walters came back into the cabin, Ann asked if he had any newspapers, and after some rummaging, he produced the tattered remains of a *Pennsylvania Gazette*.

"What happens in the city doesn't mean much out here," he said, and Ann took comfort in his indifference.

❦

Klaus Watters was already outside, hitching the oxen to the cart when Ann awoke at sunrise, and after a breakfast of cornmeal mush, they got under way.

The trail was overgrown and travel was slow. They climbed or descended one small ridge after another until late afternoon. When they finally reached a valley clearing, Ann thought she could make out a fork in the trail ahead, just before it disappeared into the beginnings of yet another pine-covered ridge. Threading through the valley was a flow of ankle-deep water. The sides of the creek bed were steep and rocky. Klaus halted the oxen and took out his map.

"Conewago Creek," he said, showing Ann the mark.

"Ve must cross now," Klaus added, scanning the sky. Rolling thunder and rising wind threatened a storm, and Ann realized, as the first few sprinkles fell around her, that a heavy rainfall could fill the stream, making the crossing with the huge mill wheel almost impossible.

Klaus would lead the packhorses across first, followed by Ann leading the riding horse, with Jonathan astride. Then Klaus would return to bring the cart and the millstone across with his wife's help. It was a plan they had utilized in fording several small streams the day before, and it had worked perfectly each time.

However, by the time they reached the creek and were positioned for the crossing, heavy rain was falling, and even as Ann took her first step down the side of the creek bank, the stream was already beginning to rise. "Hang on," she called to Jonathan, her words snatched away in the din of the thunder and the roar of the rain.

Ahead, she could barely see the packhorses as they picked their way through a curtain of rain. So much lightning flashed around them that it was difficult to distinguish any separate strokes. The horse Ann was guiding laid back his ears and tossed his head nervously, but Ann pulled on the lead, and then the bridle itself, forcing the animal on. An eternity later Klaus held out his hand to help Ann climb up the slippery bank on the other side. He lifted Jonathan from the horse's back.

"Keep down!" he yelled as lightning struck a pine tree a hundred yards away, flaring briefly like a fiery torch until the rain quenched it. Ann sank to her knees, sheltering Jonathan as well as she could while holding onto the horse's reins.

Klaus quickly waded back to the opposite shore, through water that had risen almost to his knees. Ann strained forward, trying to see through the driving rain.

Surely he won't try to cross in this downpour! From bank to bank, the distance was perhaps fifty feet, but with the stream filling rapidly from runoff coming down the ridges, it had become a swift-flowing torrent.

As Ann watched, the oxen moved forward, prodded by Klaus into the turbulent waters. The cart lurched sideways as it caught the current, and Ann held her breath as Klaus struggled forward. She was certain with his every step that all would be swept away, yet with his sheer size and strength—and the dogged determination to keep going—Klaus was inching his way toward them.

A shout sounded above the wind, and Ann saw a horseman hesitate only a moment before urging his mount forward into the water. It struggled for a foothold, then spurred on by his rider, the animal reached midstream. The rider steadied the cart that the current was threatening to wrench away and helped bring it safely to the edge of the bank. That reached, he dismounted and waded into the water to help Klaus push the cart onto the land.

The rescuer was completely enveloped in a dark cloak, with a broad-brimmed hat obscuring his features. But as he bent over the rear of the cart, Ann glimpsed a yellow beard. *John Andrews!*

"My vife is on the other side," Klaus shouted as the cart came to a stop.

"I'll ride over for her," the man offered, and was gone before Klaus could say more. Once on the other side, he lifted Maria up behind him. As he urged his horse back into the water, Maria's long skirts billowed out, becoming thoroughly soaked. In a few moments she stood huddled by Klaus, shaken but safe.

"I never saw vater rise so fast," Klaus declared, "or rain stop so suddenly." Droplets of water falling freely from leaves of the surrounding trees were the only evidence of the downpour.

"Vat about our stone?" Maria asked anxiously.

"Ve get it later," Klaus said. "Praise God ye have not all drowned. You come at a needful time," he added, addressing the horseman.

"I'm glad I could be of help. I am looking for Mistress Ann McKay and her brother. Might they be with your party?"

Chapter 17

A nd whom might you be?" Klaus asked.

John had managed to disguise his voice in such a way that, with his hat pulled down over his face and cloak turned up, his own mother could not have recognized him.

"A friend of William McKay's, sent to fetch his son and daughter to him. My name is Jeffrey Lewis."

Klaus looked at John, puzzled. "Mr. James Andrews asked us to take them to Harris's ferry," he said.

"And that is where Mr. McKay was at one time," John replied easily. "He has now removed to land south of Tolliver Station and has asked me to take his children there."

"I don't know," Klaus said doubtfully. "I vas told they went to der ferry with us."

John reached inside his cloak, brought out a scrap of paper, and handed it to Klaus. "This is a note from Mr. McKay. He heard from a trader that Mr. Andrews had engaged a German miller to bring the children to him, and he thought to make it easier on them to come directly, rather than to go out of their way, since he is no longer at the ferry."

Klaus scowled at the words on the paper, and Ann guessed that he could not make them out. "Vell, I don't know," he said again, scratching his chin thoughtfully. He handed the note to Ann, and she looked at it carefully.

"This man is my father's friend," Ann said. "This note says that he has changed his plans, and we are to go wi' Mr. Lewis."

"I don't understand vy Mr. McKay did not come himself, den," Klaus said.

"He has had a fever," Ann put in quickly. "That is why he dinna come for us before. He probably thought he shouldn't travel any more than necessary for fear of a relapse."

"Yes, that's right," John agreed. "He wanted to come himself, but I persuaded him to let me come in his place."

"If that is vat you must do, then I think that ve should all go," Klaus said.

"Oh, no!" John exclaimed, then added quickly, "The trail to the Station is steep, and with your heavy load, it would be far too difficult. Mr. McKay will appreciate your concern, but I will see to it that they reach him safely, and

109

you can be on your way with an easy mind."

"Vell, first I must have my stone," Klaus said, looking back across the creek where the oxen waited patiently. "Soon comes dark, and ve must bring it over while ve can still see."

"I think it is safe to bring it across," John said. "The current is not so strong now."

"Ve get it, den," Klaus said, and the men waded into the creek.

Jonathan remained quiet for a moment after they left, then looked steadily at Ann. "Why is John Andrews callin' himself something else? And did he really come from Father?"

Ann glanced at Maria, but she was busy untying the cover on the cart and apparently had not heard him. "There are reasons, but I canna tell ye all about it now. Just trust me when I say that John is goin' to make every effort to get us to Father as soon as he can. In the meantime, we must pretend that we do not know who he really is until we are away from the Watterses. It will be like a game. Can ye do that for me?"

The urgency in her voice must have communicated to him, for he nodded and said nothing as Klaus and John returned with the millstone.

"Ve must have a fire and dry out, *ja?*" Klaus said, seeing that Jonathan was beginning to shake with cold.

"I'll gather some wood," Ann volunteered. As she walked away, she heard John tell Klaus they would camp there that evening, and start for Tolliver Station at dawn.

"We should be there by suppertime tomorrow," he was saying in his strange new voice.

❧

Sometime in the night, while everyone else slept, Ann crept away from the campfire and walked into the forest. Her doubts about the plan had melded into a leaden feeling of sinfulness inside her. She could no longer bear the weight of it. She remembered the words of her minister's wife, that it was never too late to pray, to ask Jesus for help. So now, even though she was coming to Him out of desperation, unsure of her future, and her bridges burned behind her, she had to believe that He would not reject her. She had tried making it on her own and was weary with the effort. It was time she let Him guide her life.

Kneeling in the damp pine straw, she acknowledged that she had done wrong, and she asked for forgiveness. For the first time, she committed her entire being to Christ, and almost immediately she felt a strange warmth in the chill, wet forest.

Direct me, O Lord, she prayed. *Show me what I must do.*

❧

Sodden blankets and the fog that wrapped around them like damp cotton caused the entire party to awaken the next morning stiff and miserable.

Jonathan was listless and ate little of the hot mush Maria prepared for them. Ann prayed that she had not been the cause of bringing illness to her brother.

"We have enjoyed travelin' with ye both," Ann said sincerely, after Klaus secured their luggage onto the packhorse.

"You must come to see us at der ferry," Maria said. "Maybe your father will have grain to grind, *ja?*"

"I hope so," Ann replied, embracing Maria. In their short time together, she had become quite fond of this calm, good-natured woman.

"Are you sure this is vot you should do?" Klaus asked in a low voice as he lifted Jonathan onto the saddle.

"Yes, it will be all right," Ann said, trying to reassure him.

"Dot man—there is something I don't like."

"I feel we are under God's care," Ann said with new conviction. "He will work things out for us." With a final wave to the Watterses, Ann and Jonathan walked with John toward the fork in the trail that would take them to Tolliver Station.

The fog persisted well up into the morning, muffling all sounds and lending an eerie stillness to the landscape. Ann looked up toward the treetops, obscured by the mist. *That's the way I've been living,* she thought, *with the truth hidden away in the mist of doubt I created for myself.* But even though the fog was all around her, she felt a new clearness of vision that not even the chill dampness could diminish.

They journeyed for some time in silence, and it was John who finally spoke. "I wasn't sure that man was going to let you come with me."

"Klaus Watters is a good man," Ann replied. "He only wanted to protect us from harm and do what he saw as his duty. I am sorry that I lied to him."

Lowering his voice, John moved closer. "You should watch what you say," he warned. "Jonathan can hear you."

Ann looked at Jonathan, whose eyes were regarding her steadily. He looked frightened, and Ann patted his leg and smiled reassuringly before she returned her attention to John.

"He knows who you are. He recognized you immediately, as I feared he would. I have promised to explain the situation to him later, and I will. But for my part, I regret that I ever agreed to your plan, and the sooner the truth comes out, the better 'twill be."

"I told you in Lancaster that I wanted to help you," John said, dropping his new accent. "If your father can be found, I'll leave you and Jonathan with him and you'll never be bothered with me again, if that is what you want."

"And if he isna there?"

"Then we will find him, or find out what happened to him, one way or the other. I promised that I would take care of you, and I will."

"I think it best that we just get on to Tolliver Station and say no more for the present."

"If that is what you want," John replied stiffly. "But I don't see why you are so angry now."

"I am more angry with myself than with ye," Ann said, her tone softening. "I will try to explain it to ye when I have sorted it out a little better for myself."

And so they walked on, following the creek along a trail over several ridges. The trader Yancey had told Ann that some settlers had been killed near Tolliver Station, and then that many had died from the fever on Shawnee Creek, a day's journey past the Station. He had not told her how isolated the area was or how devoid of any evidence of human life it seemed to be.

By the time they stopped at midday, the fog had finally dissipated; the remnants were a mere wispy wreath about the tops of the tallest trees along the ridge. The Watterses had given them more than ample provisions for several meals, but since they had no cooking utensils, they ate some cheese and picked blackberries from the prickly bushes that grew in abundance along the trail. When they were underway again and had descended the next ridge, they found themselves in another narrow valley, a spidery crisscrossing of paths giving first evidence that others had traveled there before them.

"The trader said the stream led south to Tolliver Station," Ann said as John seemed to be considering which of the paths they should follow.

As they continued by the stream, the path widened somewhat, but there was no sign of life anywhere along it. Finally, when Ann had almost given up thinking they would find it, they came to a cleared area where three cabins stood close together. There could be no doubt that they had finally reached Tolliver Station.

A yellow dog sleeping in the sun roused at their approach. His frantic barking summoned a man in a fringed buckskin shirt from the rear of the central cabin. Even though his grizzled hair and beard gave him a rather fierce expression and his voice sounded harsh and rusty, as if he lacked many opportunities to use it, his welcome was warm.

"Is your name Tolliver?" John asked.

"This place is known as Tolliver Station, but the Tollivers moved on south some time back. My name's Lemuel Smith."

John again introduced himself as Jeffrey Lewis and explained that they were looking for William McKay.

"Do ye know aught of him?" Ann asked.

"Maybe, though not by name. A few weeks back, a lone man was found on the Shawnee Creek trail, sick with the fever. The Stones took him in, but what's happened to him since, I ain't heard."

"How far is that from here? Could we get there today?"

Smith scanned the sky, mentally measuring the angle of the sun's rays, and shook his head. "It's doubtful, since you don't know the lay of the land. You'd best bide here tonight and start out fresh in the morning. I'll be right glad o' the company," he added, seeing that Ann looked disappointed.

"The boy is tired," John said, "and we could all use a good rest. I think we should stay here."

"I suppose ye are right," Ann said reluctantly, torn between her impatience to continue their quest and concern for her brother's welfare.

"You'll feel better after a good feed," Mr. Smith declared, and when Ann shared their stores with him, he put their food with some game he had just brought in and produced a pungent stew.

"Are there many settlers in the valley?" Ann asked. "It seemed so deserted along the trail from Conewago Creek."

"There's more people in this valley than you'd think, and more coming in all the time. They don't all walk in, though. Lots come up the Susquehanna. Some are goin' south, too, down into the Virginny lands, particularly the Irish. I've been here nigh on to three years, and I've seen more folks in the last two months than all the rest of the time put together. Why, there's so many families coming into the valley now, a blacksmith's set up at Shawnee Creek, and we even have a preacher once a month."

"A preacher?" Ann repeated, her heart leaping at the words. "Do ye happen to recall his name?"

Mr. Smith frowned and scratched his head. "A tall fellow, rides a blaze horse. I b'lieve his name is Grayson, but I ain't for sure on it. He'll be around again in a week or so."

So it wasn't Caleb. Ann chided herself for daring to hope.

"You folks must be dead tired. Mistress, there's a lean-to in the back with room for you and the boy to spread your blankets."

"I'll take him in there," John said, scooping the sleeping boy up in his arms and laying him on the blanket Mr. Smith put down.

Bone-weary herself, Ann knew she had to talk to John before she slept, and they walked outside into a brilliantly clear night in which the heavens seemed crowded with stars. Somewhere an owl called, and a dog barked in the distance. Ann sat on an upended tub beside the cabin, with John on the ground by her side.

"You have been behaving oddly these past two days," he said. "I thought you agreed that what we are doing was the only way that you could find out about your father, but now you act as if it were something you want no part in. What has happened?"

Ann took a deep breath and began speaking, earnestly hoping he would understand how she felt. "I always knew in my heart that what we are doin' was wrong, but I suppose I was so concerned about Father that I ignored the warnin' signals. But I've had a chance to do a lot of thinkin' since I left Lancaster, and last night I realized that a right thing canna be accomplished in a wrong way. I canna be proud of my part in the deception, and as soon as I can, I intend to ask your parents' pardon."

"Pardon for what?" John exclaimed. "You did nothing to harm them!"

"I did much to harm them," Ann said. "I knew about your troubles, and I remained silent, thus wrongin' both ye and them. Ye should have shared your problems with them from the first, and I should have seen to it that ye did. Then when Agnes told me that ye were often in debt because of gamblin', I realized that ye had deceived me, too, in a way and that gave me somethin' else to consider."

"You must hate me," John said sadly.

"Nay, I don't hate ye," Ann assured him. " 'Tis not my place to judge any man or what is in any man's heart. I know your family isn't churchgoin', but perhaps ye know that Jesus said, 'Judge not, that ye be not judged.' Last night I asked Him for forgiveness for all the wrong that I've done and put my life in His hands. I feel absolutely certain that I have been redeemed."

Ann stopped for a moment, wondering how she could possibly relay to John the peace that had enveloped her the instant that she yielded her will to Christ. In the back of her mind, she knew Caleb would understand.

"My mother once told me that she was prayin' that I would find God's peace and claim His promises for myself. I didna understand what she meant for a long time, but last night I was able to do it; and even if I don't find Father, I have na doubt that God will care for me. I just wish that ye could have the same assurance for yourself."

John sighed wearily. "Ah, Ann, how easy you make it all sound! Tell me, will your newly found conscience permit you to continue to travel with a sinner like me?"

"I am afraid ye don't understand a word I've said if ye think that."

"Well, don't worry. I promise I'll not burden you much longer," he said, standing. As they went back into the cabin, Ann's heart ached to see the pain and hurt in his face. As she spread her blanket beside Jonathan, she said a prayer—an action that now seemed natural—for John to find the peace she had found and for her to accept whatever result the search for her father would bring.

The next morning they were on the trail an hour after sunrise. Mr. Smith directed them to follow the creek until they came to a path that led up a rolling hill and into a hardwood thicket. On the other side was a clearing, he said, where they could inquire about the man who had been found on the trail nearby. "Watch for three notches in the trees just before you reach the path," he added. "Those cuts show where the Stones' land begins. Turn west, and you'll be on Stone land all the way to their clearing."

John and Ann did not talk as they made their way, and Jonathan, apparently sensing the importance of this final part of their journey, was silent as well. By midmorning they entered a large cleared area. Two cabins stood there, one completed and the other being worked on by a half-dozen men.

A chorus of barking dogs greeted them as they rode into the open, and the men stopped their work to stare at them. Ann slid down from her horse and reached for Jonathan as John swung him down to her. A woman came to the doorway of the completed cabin, shading her eyes against the sun's glare. One of the young men put down a large log he was fitting into one of the walls and came over to them. When John explained their errand, the man turned and, as if in answer to Ann's desperate prayer, pointed toward the woman in the cabin door.

"You need to talk to my mother, Hannah Stone," he said, indicating a sturdy woman of middle years with even, regular features and sun-browned skin. When Ann introduced herself and explained their mission, she smiled down at Jonathan.

"So this is the boy," she said. "Your father sets a great store by you, Lad."

"Ye know him then!" Ann exclaimed. "Is he here?"

Mrs. Stone took Ann's hand in hers. "Yes, I know him, although it was just a few days ago that he was able to tell me his name. My son found him on the trail, half-dead from the fever, and brought him here for me to nurse. I never thought he'd live through the day. Two babes and a husband I've seen taken by the fever, and I've had it myself, but I've never seen anyone so sick for so long who lived through it."

"Is he all right now?"

"He's alive, and that's remarkable in itself. My son had to tie him down; he was so wild at first. He'd talk about you and his boy and someone called Sarah. Then he was unconscious for weeks. It was just three days ago that he came to himself and told us his name."

"Can we see him now?" Ann asked.

"He's mighty weak yet," Mrs. Stone warned. "I think it best that you let me talk to him first. The shock of seeing you so suddenlike might do some damage."

"Of course," Ann said and looked down at Jonathan. "Did ye hear that? Father's here, and soon we shall see him."

Jonathan began to cry, and tears filled Ann's eyes as well as they clung together, John standing silently beside them. Spontaneously, Ann voiced her joy: "Thank Ye, Lord, for leadin' us safely here."

❧

William, wearing a coarse but clean homespun shirt, lay on a built-in bunk along the side of the cabin wall. His features had been sharpened by the weight he had lost, and his eyes seemed sunken and lusterless. It had been some weeks since he had shaved, and the beard was strange and unfamiliar. Yet he was William McKay; there could be no doubt of that, and the way his eyes lighted when he saw his children showed that he recognized them as well.

"How came ye to find me in this place, where I hardly know where I am myself?" he asked when he could speak again.

" 'Tis a long story," Ann began, wiping her eyes, but Jonathan interrupted her.

"We asked God to bring us to ye, and He did."

"We had some human help, too," Ann said, smiling, and called John to come inside. "Ye must meet my father."

John took William's thin hand gently. "My name is John Andrews, James Andrews's son."

"What happened to Jeffrey Lewis?" Ann asked, lowering her voice.

"He doesna exist anymore," John whispered back.

"I lost all our things, Lass," William said sadly. "Everythin' was gone when they found me, cart, oxen, all."

"It doesna matter. We have found ye, and that is the important thing."

After some minutes, Mrs. Stone decided that her patient had need of a rest and suggested that they leave him for a time.

"We should see to the horses," Ann told her father, "but I'll be back to sit with ye in a bit."

"Isn't it strange how this has worked out?" she said a few minutes later, helping John unload her packhorse. "It's almost as if Father really did write that letter to me."

"I'm glad that you have found him," John said sincerely. "Now that you have, I'll be riding on. Jack Stone told me I could make it to Shawnee Creek tonight. From there I can raft to the Susquehanna."

"And where will that take ye?" she asked quietly.

"To Philadelphia. I hardly slept at all last night, thinking about what you said. I know you're right and that I can't keep running away from what I did."

"Oh, I am so glad!" Impulsively, Ann threw her arms around John's neck and kissed his cheek.

"I may hang, you know," he said. "Is that why you are so pleased that I am going back?" But his tone was light, and he once again sounded almost like the John Andrews she had first known.

"Of course not," she replied. "But if ye turn yourself in and plead for mercy, I verra much doubt that ye'll hang."

"So do I, now that I have had time to consider the matter. Mr. Otis has his faults, but he's an excellent lawyer and a fair man; and if he won't defend me himself, he can find someone who will."

"I am sure your parents will stand by ye, as well," Ann said. "Ye just never gave them the opportunity."

The amused look faded from John's face. "That remains to be seen," he said. "And that will be the hardest thing of all to face."

"How did ye ever get started in on gamblin'?" Ann asked, feeling that his gambling debts were the cause of his present trouble.

"Oh, it was exciting at first, and it passed the time. I was lucky enough to keep winning for months, so I went for higher stakes, and then I began to lose. I borrowed money, thinking to make it all up, but I just got deeper into debt instead. I never intended to harm anyone by it, and I'll never gamble again, believe me."

"Good," Ann said and smiled.

"Are you still sorry that you came with me?" he asked.

"I am not sorry to find my father, of course, and I thank ye for your part in it. But I believe if I had told your father what Yancey told me, he would have found someone to bring me here, and the result would have been the same. I meant what I said earlier—I handled the whole thing badly."

"I would like to think that perhaps you have some small regard for me," John said, regarding her steadily. "Could you love me just a little bit, sweet Ann?"

Ann was able to return his gaze. "I know now that I love someone else. I may never see him again, but he will always be in my heart."

John dropped his eyes. "I wish, with all my heart, that things could be different between us."

"And I wish ye happiness, John," she said gently.

Chapter 18

Her first days at Stones' clearing were strangely bittersweet for Ann. Along with her newfound peace of mind and great joy in being with her father again was a nagging concern about their future.

Both Hannah and Jack Stone assured Ann that she and Jonathan were welcome to stay as long as they liked, but she felt that they were disrupting the Stone household. Mrs. Stone and her son had given up their bunks to sleep on the floor of the new cabin. Hannah Stone would not hear of changing the arrangement, however, nor would she take the money that Ann offered to help with living expenses.

Hannah shook her head emphatically. "We've had a good year, and we have no need of cash money for the present. Seeing your father well and strong is all the payment we need or want."

"At least let me help ye with the household work, then," Ann said, believing it must have been more difficult for the widow than she was letting on. "I recently nursed a woman with the fever, and I know ye've not had an easy time of it with Father."

"Well, I am a bit behind on some of the outside chores," she admitted. "If you want to do a bit of spinning as you sit with your father, I've some things that need seeing to elsewhere."

Ann readily agreed, and as she busied herself about the cabin, she was pleased to note that her father seemed to be gaining strength each day. Less than a week after their arrival at Stones' clearing, William stood and took a shaky step, and they wept together with joy. Encouraged, Ann asked him if he had given any thought to what they would do when he had regained his health.

"I have thought of little else," he said cautiously, "from the time I first felt the fever comin' upon me. I thought I was goin' to die there on the trail with none around me, and I prayed that God would look after my children. I dinna expect that He would spare me, too, and when I woke up in this place and realized that He had given me back my life, I figured it must have been for some reason. The Stones are good people, and they've a large grant that needs much work. Since his father died, Jack has had more to do than he can handle alone, and he has asked me to stay on and help him."

William paused, glancing away for a moment, and then looked back into

Ann's eyes. "Would ye think ill of me if I took Hannah Stone to wife?" he asked.

The idea that her father might marry again had never occurred to Ann. When, in her surprise, she did not immediately reply, William continued to speak. "I know ye're thinking about your mother, and the day never passes that I don't miss her, too. No woman could ever take Sarah's place. I believe Hannah understands that, being a widow herself, but we've each a need the other can fill. I should be able to help with the harvest this year, and it won't be long until Jonathan can do a full share, as well. In all, I can only think that Providence brought us to this place."

Ann left the spinning wheel to kiss her father's cheek. "I have lately felt the same," she said. "And Hannah Stone is a fine woman. I wish ye much joy together. And I think it is time that I told ye how we happened to come here."

Ann sketched the series of events that had led to her and Jonathan's departure from Lancaster. "At the time, I believed that circumstances justified what John and I did, but soon I began to have doubts. And when I met John at Conewago Creek and heard myself lyin' to Klaus Watters, I knew I had done a great injustice to everyone involved. That night I asked God to forgive me, and I feel that He has. I kept thinkin' of Mother, and how she always told us to have faith in God's will. I had never been able to do that, because I had not given Him my life. Now I have, and I know somethin' of what she must have felt."

" 'In all thy ways acknowledge Him, and He shall direct thy paths,' " William quoted from the Bible. "My illness has made me realize how much I need to rely on Him, too. We mustna dwell on the wrong that might have been done but look forward to walkin' in the light from now on."

"I know," said Ann, "but it grieves me that I might have hurt the Andrews. I'd like them to know how I feel."

"Then write to them, and let Jack take the letters when he goes to Shawnee Creek," William suggested.

"I'll do that," Ann said, and the thought occurred to her that she should also write to the Alexanders. She wanted Jane Alexander to know that her words had borne fruit, and it could do no harm for them to know where she was, just in case Caleb might someday return to Lancaster and inquire about her.

Later that day, Ann stopped on her way to the spring for water to talk to Jack, who was smoothing logs with a broadaxe. She asked when he was planning to go to Shawnee Creek again.

"As soon as I finish building Mother's bunk—probably tomorrow. Why do you ask?"

"I want to send some letters to Lancaster, and Father suggested that ye could take them to Shawnee Creek and find someone there to send them on."

"I'll do better than that—I'll give them to a merchant on the Susquehanna, and they'll be on their way much sooner."

"Oh, I'd not want ye to go out of your way on my account," Ann protested. "That's another half-day's journey from Shawnee Creek, isn't it?"

Jack Stone nodded, then smiled. "It is, but I was intending to go there anyway to see someone."

"Father told me that ye have a sweetheart," Ann said. "Is that where she lives?"

"Yes. She's a merchant's daughter, newly come to the river, and I've not had much time for proper courting. But now that the new cabin's up, I plan to ask for her hand."

"And do ye think she will consent?"

"If I didn't, I wouldn't be making the trip," he said. "She's a bit of a wild thing, being Irish and red-haired to boot, but I think we'll get on."

"What is her name?" Ann asked, amused at his confidence.

"Isabel Prentiss," he said and was about to add more when Ann's delighted exclamation stopped him.

"Jack, how wonderful! Our families crossed together from Londonderry."

"So you know her then!"

"Isabel's the only really close friend I have ever had," Ann said. "How I would like to see her again!"

"Then ride along with me," Jack invited. "Maybe you would be willing to put in a kind word for my cause."

She smiled. "I'll see what Father thinks about it."

William, too, was amazed to hear of the Prentisses, and he agreed that Ann should accompany Jack on his visit. When Jonathan heard of it, he wanted to go, too.

"I want to see Samuel," he wailed. "There isn't anyone around here for me to play wi'."

"Hush that, now," William said sternly. "Wi' Jack away, Mrs. Stone will have all the work on her shoulders, since I'm not able to do much yet. I was hopin' ye could help us out, but I see ye're still too much of a bairn to do a man's work."

Jonathan stayed his tears. "I'm no baby! I'm big enough to see to anythin' that needs doin'."

Ann was suddenly sobered by the realization that her brother would have to do a man's work at an early age here, just as he would have if they had stayed in Ireland. But here, at least, he could work toward being independent, and when the time came, he could leave the Stones' grant and claim land of his own. It was one of their father's dreams for him, and Ann could see that it would come to pass.

The Stones were not much for letter-writing, Hannah said, but after some searching, she found paper that Ann could use. Ann thought a long while before she penned a letter to the Andrews expressing her appreciation for their help and asking their forgiveness for any pain she had caused. She added that she had not used the gold coins, and she intended to return them to James Andrews as soon as she found a safe means of doing so.

To the Alexanders she described her newly found spiritual peace, without going into the details of what had precipitated it, and thanked Jane Alexander for her valuable counsel. She concluded both letters with detailed directions for reaching Stones' clearing and added that it seemed likely that they would stay there permanently.

Ann added a prayer of her own to William's that night, that in the days ahead, God's will would be done in all their lives.

The next morning Jack and Ann departed for Shawnee Creek, where he stopped at the blacksmith's to leave a tool that needed repair. As she watched Jack conversing with the man, Ann realized that it had been the blacksmith's comment to the trader Yancey that had begun the chain of events that culminated in her finding her father. She did not mention the incident to the blacksmith, however, and she told Jack only part of the story as they rode on toward the river.

"The man that brought you to the clearing—might you be writing to him, by any chance?"

"John Andrews? No, but one of the letters is to his parents. All of us owe them a great debt. We'd never have found Father wi'out the Andrews' help."

"Are you going to marry John Andrews?" Jack asked.

"No," Ann replied.

"That will be good news for the other bachelors around here," Jack said with a smile. "There are plenty of men who'd like to wed if they could find a girl. That's one reason I want to get things settled with Isabel, before someone else comes along and takes her away from me."

Ann recalled that Isabel had wanted to marry a rich man, but she knew that her friend would be happy with Jack, and she was glad for them both.

"What is the Prentisses' store like?" asked Ann as they drew nearer.

"It's not just a store," Jack explained. "It's part inn, part tavern, part freight depot, and the church where the minister holds services when he makes his rounds. There's a dock behind it, where barges and fishing boats and canoes tie up, and a shed on one side where the cattle and horses are kept. There must be eight or ten cabins in the village already, and more being built. Pretty soon it'll be a regular town."

"How often does the minister come? Mr. Smith said a Reverend Grayson would be in Tolliver Station in a week or so."

"We don't usually know, but he always stays around for a week or so; when the word gets out, couples come in to be married, and sometimes he even has a funeral service for all who have died since his last trip. I figure he ought to be back at least once more before winter comes."

It was almost full dark when Jack and Ann rode up to the store, and candles had already been lit inside. As they entered, Ann was reminded of the Blue Boar in Lancaster. Only this place had shelves filled with all manner of goods, running the length of one wall, and plank tables and benches were set in front of a large hearth.

No fire burned in the large fireplace this evening, however, and Ann could see that food was being prepared in a room at the rear. Although both mother and daughter were enveloped in aprons and crowned with white mobcaps covering their hair, Ann immediately recognized Mrs. Prentiss, and then Isabel. When she saw Ann, Isabel screeched and almost dropped the platter of fried fish she was carrying.

"Look what I brought you," Jack said to Isabel.

"I can't believe it!" Isabel cried, as the girls fell into each other's arms. Hearing the commotion, Mary Prentiss, and then Samuel, crowded around Ann, all talking at once.

"How well ye look!" Mrs. Prentiss exclaimed.

"How is the rest of the family?" Tom Prentiss asked. "Are they with ye?"

"And how came ye to know Jack Stone?" Isabel demanded.

"She'll gladly tell you all, but first might we have a bite of supper?" Jack put in, with a broad smile at Isabel. "It's been a good day's ride we've had, and not even a woman can talk on forever without some nourishment."

"Well, food we have," Mary Prentiss said. "And better than the fare on the *Derry Crown;* I can assure ye. Sit down, Lass, and eat. Then we want to hear it all."

Ann's condensed version of what had befallen them since their parting with the Prentisses concluded with the news that she expected her father and Hannah Stone to marry.

"It's God's own miracle," Mary declared, her eyes moist. "I canna tell ye how often we've thought o' ye and the others we traveled with, and wondered how all were farin'."

"We often thought of ye, as well. How did ye come to be in this place yourselves?" Ann asked. "The last we knew, ye were to go down the Delaware."

"Aye, we did that," Tom Prentiss said. "All the way to the Chesapeake Bay. Then we heard about this post on the Susquehanna that could be bought cheap. It's not much now," he added, looking around as if comparing it to his shop in Ireland, "but it's all ours, free and clear, and with the peltry trade this winter, we should do well."

They sat around the table and talked until the candles began to sputter and go out, and Tom Prentiss declared that they must call it a day. Jack went off to share Samuel's bed, and Isabel and Ann climbed a ladder into an attic, where Isabel slept on a straw mattress.

"It gets stuffy up here when the day's been hot," she said. "But at least we have some privacy. Now tell me about Caleb Craighead."

"I told ye he came to see us in Lancaster," Ann replied. "I don't know where he is now, or whether I'll ever see him again. When ye marry Jack and come to live at Stones' clearin', we'll have more time to talk together."

"What makes ye think that I'm goin' to marry Jack Stone?" Isabel asked with a twinkle in her eye. "Have ye forgot that I want a rich husband?"

"No, but I think it's unlikely ye'll find one of those around here, and in the short time I've known the Stones, I have been impressed by them both. Jack and his mother saved my father's life, and I'm sure he'd make a fine husband."

"Don't ye dare tell him I said so," Isabel said in a whisper, "but I was afraid he wouldna ask me—we've not had much chance to get to know one another."

"Well, rest assured; he will ask ye," Ann said, hugging Isabel. "And I couldna be happier for the both of ye."

❦

Ann and Jack set out for Stones' clearing after two days at the Prentisses' post. In that time, Jack had asked for and won Isabel's hand in marriage, and Ann's letters had been put into the hands of a bargeman who promised to see that they would reach Lancaster.

"I will let ye know as soon as the minister arrives," Tom Prentiss assured Jack, and Ann promised to return for the wedding.

"There is much to be done before my cabin is fit to receive Isabel," Jack said. "I want her to find everything she needs when she comes into our home." Once again Ann realized that Isabel was fortunate to be marrying such a considerate man.

"Could we make it a double ceremony, then?" William asked when Jack shared the news of his and Isabel's upcoming wedding. "I'd be honored if Hannah'd be my wife."

"Well, Mr. McKay," Hannah replied, obviously pleased, "it's a dangerous business to say such a thing before witnesses. You'll have no way to back out of it."

"I'll not take it back, but first ye must say that ye will agree to it."

"And that I can gladly do."

"It looks as if we'll have to get the neighbors back over here and build on to this cabin," Jack declared, surveying it with his eyes. "How about three more rooms—one for Ann, one for Jonathan, and one just for cooking? That ought to take care of everyone."

Yes, Ann thought as she listened, *everyone was taken care of—almost.* Her prayers were for the patience to await God's good time in revealing His purpose for her life.

As the extra rooms were being added to Hannah Stone's cabin, Ann made bedding for the new bunks, stitching homespun linen together and stuffing it with cornhusks and straw, then making pillows with feathers Hannah had saved. When finally they were finished late one morning, Ann tied on her bonnet and walked up the ridge west of the cabin, her copy of *The Pilgrim's Progress* in hand. She had discovered that from the top she could see the surrounding countryside rather well. The Stones' cabins were the only dwellings in sight, and only a small portion of the trail was visible as it crossed an open area to the south. The land was wild and demanding of those who sought to tame it, but Ann already felt deeply attached to it. How far they had come and how many things had happened in the past few months!

Settled in her favorite spot, she opened the book once more and began reading, thoughts of her own spiritual journey suddenly seen in a new light. When Christian fell into the Slough of Despond, he was rescued by Help, who told him that every virtuous man sometimes falls into the mire of doubt. Later, when he had been captured by the giant, Despair, and taken to Doubting Castle, Christian was freed by using the key of Promise, and fled with Hopeful as his companion. Eventually, Christian reached Mount Zion to be greeted by angels.

Like Christian, Ann had set out on a journey full of hazards, and like Christian's, many of her worst fears had never materialized. It was true that she had lost her mother, and nearly her father, but both she and Jonathan were safe; they had not succumbed to fever or been attacked by Indians, after all. She had much to be thankful for, not the least of which was her experience of salvation.

So lost was she in thought that the sun passed its zenith unnoticed and made its way into the west to cast her shadow in front of her. As she looked up from the pages of her book, she realized suddenly that she had missed the noon meal, and her continued absence might cause her father alarm.

As Ann stood, she saw that a horseman wearing a black hat and cloak was approaching rapidly from the south, raising dusty plumes as the horse's hoofs churned the dry trail. Just before he was lost from view in a grove of trees, Ann caught sight of a glimmer of white at the man's throat. A white shirt, perhaps, or—her breath caught sharply—a clerical collar. She ran down the hill, heedless of the brambles that caught at her skirt and clawed her ankles. She arrived at the clearing breathless, her bonnet askew, her skirt covered with sticktights and briar snags. Still she ran, down the path into the thicket leading to the trail. *The rider must have reached the blaze marks on the trees,* Ann thought. In a moment, if he kept on the trail, he would soon be out of sight, and she might never know who it was. Or he might turn west and come up the path to Stones' clearing. The clatter of hoofs grew louder, and Ann stopped, her heart hammering, as the horse and rider came into view on the path. Her head swam and she was nearly faint as she looked up at the rider. At first his head was down, but when he raised it, she saw that it was Caleb Craighead.

In an instant he reined in his horse, dismounted, and came toward her, and then his strong arms encircled her. She began to cry, and he cradled her gently, rocking her tenderly in his arms as if he were soothing a child.

"I feared I would never see ye again," Ann said when she could speak.

"I told ye once that I felt convicted that we would meet again," Caleb said, looking intently into her eyes. "Did ye not believe me?"

"All I could do was hope," Ann said. "How did ye know where to find me? Or did ye happen here by accident?"

"It was no accident," he assured her. "When I left Lancaster, I thought ye loved another man and would be happy with him, and that it was best that I let ye be. But I couldna forget ye. Two weeks ago I was on my way to preach at Drumore when I met John Andrews, and he told me everything that happened." He pulled Ann to him again and held her tightly. "He said ye had found God's peace, and that ye wanted that for him as well. We prayed together, and John asked Christ to rule his life."

"I am so glad," Ann murmured. "I have prayed that he would. Oh, Caleb, I was so ashamed of what I did—" she began, but he would not let her continue.

"Hush," he said gently. "Whatever you did, God has forgiven, and ye have never wronged me in any way. The important thing now is that we do God's will."

"Aye," Ann whispered and felt fresh tears of joy as she cradled her head on his shoulder.

Tenderly, Caleb lifted her chin and looked into her eyes. "Will ye marry me and share my work, Ann?"

"Aye, Caleb," she said, smiling. At last, she knew the direction her life would take. She was about to start a new journey, one ordained by God and one that she prayed He would lead every step of the way.

Sign of the Bow

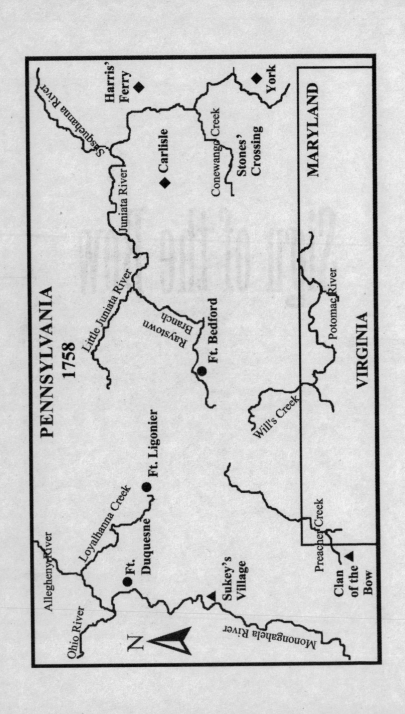

PENNSYLVANIA
1758

Susquehanna River

Harris' Ferry

York

Carlisle

Conewango Creek

Stones' Crossing

MARYLAND

Juniata River

Little Juniata River

Raystown Branch

Ft. Bedford

Potomac River

Allegheny River

Loyalhanna Creek

Ft. Ligonier

Ft. Duquesne

Will's Creek

VIRGINIA

Sukey's Village

Preacher Creek

Clan of the Bow

Monongahela River

Ohio River

N

Chapter 1

Pennsylvania, 1758

S arah McKay Craighead knelt beneath a huge oak, gathering bits of what the settlers called squawroot. Her fine brown hair fell into her face, and impatiently she brushed it away, leaving streaks of black earth on her forehead and cheeks.

When she judged that she had collected enough, Sarah laid the squawroot in a moss-lined willow basket, then stood and stretched. It was a fine June morning, and she was in no hurry to get back to the cabin on Preacher Creek where her family had lived for several years.

Sarah walked slowly, enjoying the peace of the woods, but with a watchful eye for forest creatures. Panthers hadn't been seen in their part of Pennsylvania lately, but dangerous bears and wild pigs still inhabited the wilderness in large numbers.

She moved through the dappled sun and shade with the easy grace of young womanhood. The moccasins Tel-a-ka had made her were silent against the forest floor as she walked, and the hem of her homespun shift whispered against her calves.

Only that week, her mother had declared that Sarah must have a new dress. "I maun get ye some cloth when Jonathan comes by again," she had said.

At the time, Sarah had been more pleased at the prospect of seeing her uncle again than in having a new dress. Her homespun shifts—linen for summer and wool for winter—were comfortable, and in the wilderness surrounding them, there were few settlers to see what she wore. The only whites who sought out the Craigheads' small cabin were fellow settlers who wanted her mother's healing skill or her father's prayers. Occasionally, a couple came to be married, but as a rule, unexpected visitors usually meant trouble.

For that reason, Sarah felt a prickle of apprehension when she came into the clearing and saw a pair of horses tethered to the lean-to by their cabin.

It's too early for Miz Warfield to be brought abed, she thought. She had gathered the squawroot for her mother to take to the Warfields' cabin, several hours' ride away, but Teresa Warfield's baby wasn't due to come until the full moon now riding the night sky had waned by a quarter.

Sarah stopped at the open cabin door and looked inside, curious to see who had come to call. Two men stood with their backs to the door, each cradling a rifle in his right arm. Before them, Sarah's mother sat on a low stool by the fireplace, holding Sarah's two-year-old brother, Adam, on her lap. Her father sat at the table, the Bible he had been reading still open before him.

Sarah stepped onto the doorstone, and immediately the taller visitor spun around and aimed his rifle squarely at her.

" 'Tis only our Sarah," her father said quickly. The man lowered his gun, his bearded face split by a sudden grin.

"Aye, and a comely lass she is, too, Reverend Craighead. I wonder that she's still to home wi' ye."

Sarah's cheeks burned, although the man's bantering tone made it clear that he wasn't serious.

Her mother smiled faintly. "We're in no hurry for our firstborn t' leave us," she said.

As her mother spoke, the other visitor turned toward Sarah. "Mayhap Mistress Craighead aims on weddin' one of your Indian neighbors. Looks like she's already wearin' war paint."

Sarah brought a hand to her dirt-daubed cheek, then dropped it as the speaker removed his hat, revealing flaming red hair that she recognized instantly.

"Joshua Stone!" Sarah took a half step toward him, then stopped. "Are ye here because something is amiss at the Crossing?"

"Nay, Daughter. They bring news closer to home," her father said, his even features more than usually sober.

Sarah put down her basket and walked over to stand by her mother, making an effort not to stare at Joshua. His eyes were as blue and his hair even redder than she remembered; but now he was more than a head taller than she, and his skinny boy's frame had filled out to a man's. Her first impulse had been to tell him that he'd turned out some better than she would have expected, but they weren't children anymore—by her calculation he was nearly twenty to her sixteen years—and Sarah sensed that this was not the time for jesting.

Joshua nodded toward his dark-haired companion. "This is Nate McIntyre. We came across Jonathan McKay a few days ago while we were scouting for Colonel Burd. He told us you had settled in these parts."

" 'Tis a strange place ye choose to live, hard by a Delaware village," Nate said. "More and more of the savages are sidin' wi' the French, raidin' bold as ye please where white men have lived in peace these many years."

"The Lenni-Lenape are our friends," Sarah's mother said. "They would never harm us."

"So the others thought, afore they parted wi' their scalps," Nate said darkly.

"As I was sayin' to Reverend Craighead, ye'd best go on and fort up whilst ye have the chance."

"And do ye agree, Joshua?" Sarah's father asked.

Joshua shrugged. "You may trust your neighbors, but there's plenty of other Indians out there ready to fight. The French give them rum and it ruins them."

"Where are the people hereabouts forting up?" Sarah asked Joshua, but again her father answered first.

"From what these fellows tell us, nowhere yet. But we'll find a likely place, should it be needful."

"It will be, Reverend," Nate said emphatically. "Mark ye my words; too many Indians have forgot they ever spoke words of peace in Philadelphia."

"Joshua, where was my brother when ye saw him?" Sarah's mother asked, apparently eager to change the subject.

"Hard by the Monongahela, several days northwest. He said he means to look in on you when he comes east with his next load of pelts."

"I thought he would be wearied wi' the wilderness by now. 'Tis time the lad found himself a wife and settled down."

Sarah caught the sudden look that passed between their visitors and wondered if her mother had also noticed it.

"Now ain't that jest like a woman, wantin' to marry off every free man in the whole world!" Nate exclaimed, grinning.

Sarah's mother wrinkled her brow. "Nay, Mr. McIntyre—other men don't concern me, but my brother ought to have a good woman lookin' after him. He was never strong as a lad."

Joshua smiled. "I don't think you need to worry about that, Ma'am. Jonathan McKay is as hearty a man as I've ever seen."

"Aye? That's good news, then. But tell us, Josh, how fare your folks? I've missed your mother every day since we left Stones' Crossing."

Joshua nodded. "I'm sure she feels the same. The last I heard, all was well there. But I've not been home since—" He paused and frowned as if trying to remember.

"We've been scoutin' together for nigh onto a year," Nate put in, and Joshua nodded.

"Yes, it must be that long since I saw them. Little Jack and Billy were almost big enough to be a big help to Pa, and Belle had just started to take a few steps."

"Aye, I'd love to see them all again," Sarah's mother said wistfully.

"Then you ought to go to Stones' Crossing for a time," Joshua said. "At least it's fairly safe around the Susquehanna now."

Ann Craighead stood and handed Adam over to Sarah. "That's enough such talk," she said. "I know the Lord watches over us, and I'm quite willin' to leave Him in charge whilst I prepare us some food."

"We'd be much obliged to break bread wi' ye before we leave," Nate said quickly. "But we canna tarry."

"Surely ye can stay and visit awhile!" Sarah's mother exclaimed. "We seldom have visitors here, much less see an old friend."

"No, Ma'am," Joshua said, and Sarah thought he looked genuinely sorry. "We have important information for Colonel Burd—but we'd be much obliged for a hot meal before we go."

"If that's the case, sit ye down and rest now," Sarah's father invited.

Nate McIntyre leaned his rifle by the door, then settled down on the split log bench and began to talk with Sarah's father. Joshua came over to where Sarah stood.

"I wish ye could stay longer," she told him.

Joshua's blue eyes regarded her steadily. "So do I. I'd like to hear all about what you've been doing since you left the crossin'."

Sarah shrugged. "Nothing but traveling, mostly, for the first few years. Father never stayed long in any one place in those days. Just before Adam was born, we heard that the people who built this cabin had moved on. We've lived here ever since."

Joshua's glance took in the sparsely furnished room, then nodded toward the overhead sleeping loft.

"Your sister Annie and your brother William—where are they?"

Sarah lowered her head. "I thought ye knew—they sickened and died not long before Adam was born. Did Jonathan not tell you?"

Joshua shook his head. "We hadn't much time to talk, meeting on the trail and both needing to press on. I'm sorry—but your little brother seems fit enough."

As if to prove it, Adam leaned forward and grabbed a fistful of Joshua's abundant red hair. He pulled it hard and laughed in glee as Joshua hastily drew back.

"Ouch! That hurt!" Joshua exclaimed, and Sarah smiled at his offended surprise.

"My brother's a lively one, all right," Sarah said. "Tel-a-ka says he will make a mighty warrior."

"Tel-a-ka?" Joshua repeated. "From the village yonder?" He pointed toward Preacher Creek and Sarah nodded.

"Yes. The Indians there call themselves the People of the Bow. They have been very kind to us. Tel-a-ka is the chief's son, and his grandmother saved Mother's life when Adam was born. They've taught us much about finding herbs and making possets."

"Maybe so, but be careful around all Indians, Sarah—I've seen what they've done to other settlers."

"You don't know these people as we do," Sarah said, and the set of Joshua's mouth told her that he disapproved of her defense of the Indians.

"Here, Lass, fetch some trenchers for our guests," Sarah's mother interrupted, ending their private conversation.

All too soon, Sarah stood with her parents on the doorstone, watching Joshua and Nate mount up and start to ride away. They stopped at the edge of the clearing to wave farewell, and Joshua shouted a final warning. "Watch the woods!"

"I wonder if they are right when they say that trouble is coming," Sarah's mother said. Her husband put a comforting arm around her shoulders.

"Don't ye worry yet, Wife. 'Tis na wisdom to borrow trouble."

Sarah's mother almost smiled. "Och, Reverend Craighead—'tis true that we've enough troubles of our own—we dinna need to borrow more! But come now, Sarah. 'Tis time to brew up the squawroot."

Sarah brought her gathering basket to the fireplace, where her mother's herb pot simmered. "You're making this infusion a long time ahead," Sarah commented as she handed the squawroot to her mother, who carefully folded it into the water along with some dried herbs.

" 'Tis better to be prepared than sorry—more than one babe has come into the world ahead of time with the full moon, and in any case, the hidey-hole is cool enough to keep the draught for some time."

"It certainly isn't cool in here," Sarah said a few minutes later, when she had twice strained the last of the squawroot infusion and poured it into a wide-mouthed crock.

"Then take this on to the hidey-hole—that should cool ye off."

The hidey-hole had been little more than a shallow ditch when they had moved into the cabin, but her father had dug it deeper, creating a cool haven where food, roots, and herbs could be safely stored. With the leather door latch pulled to the inside, it also made a good place of refuge.

After placing the crock on the ledge, Sarah sank down on the cool earth, drew her knees up under her chin, and thought about Joshua Stone. His words of warning hadn't disturbed her nearly so much as seeing him again had. She recalled many happy days at Stones' Crossing when her family had lived with Sarah's grandfather, William McKay, and his second wife, Hannah Stone. Hannah's son, Jack, had married Isabel Prentiss, Sarah's mother's best friend, at the same ceremony that had united Sarah's parents, and they had all lived side by side at the crossing. Not only had Sarah Craighead always known Joshua Stone—she'd been a fair-sized girl before she'd realized that they weren't blood kin.

"For which I thank heaven!" Joshua had declared then, making fun of the younger Sarah. Soon afterward, they'd gone their separate ways, Joshua to school in Lancaster, and Sarah into the wilderness. Joshua was now a man grown, while she—

Sarah sighed and smoothed her shift, already patched in several worn places. *I hope Uncle Jonathan comes by soon*, she thought. She'd like to have a dress made out of real bolt cloth, especially if they forted up. There was no telling who would show up at a forting-up—it was like a combined revival meeting and play-party, and since no Indians had ever actually attacked during any forting-up Sarah had known, she had always enjoyed the experience. And if by chance Joshua should happen by again, she'd like to look nice.

The hidey-hole door opened, startling Sarah.

"What were ye studying on so seriously, Daughter?" her mother asked.

"Nothing—I was just thinking about Joshua and his friend," Sarah said.

Her mother sat down by Sarah. "I'm not surprised. Joshua Stone cuts a fine figure, but mind that he's still young—and ye are younger."

Sarah felt a blush come to her cheeks and averted her eyes. "Age has naught to do with it. I pray that Joshua and Mr. McIntyre will journey safe."

Her mother sounded amused. "I'm sure ye do, at that. I've a feeling we've not seen the last of that pair."

I hope you're right, Sarah thought but said nothing.

Their companionable silence was broken as a commotion erupted somewhere in the forest.

"What on earth is makin' that racket?" Sarah's mother asked, sounding more annoyed than fearful.

"Ann! Sarah! Where are ye?" Sarah's father yelled from the cabin, his words punctuated by Adam's frightened howls.

"We're comin' from the hidey-hole now," Sarah's mother called back.

As they climbed out, Sarah heard the urgent tattoo of a horse's hoofs, then saw a lone figure burst from the forest and ride into the clearing.

Her first impression was that the man was far too tall and lank to be Joshua, so it must be his companion.

Something must have happened to Joshua, she thought.

Sarah's heart lurched, and she held her breath as the man reached them and swung off his horse.

Chapter 2

Teresa's took real bad, Miz Craighead," the man said by way of greeting. At his words, Sarah felt a surge of relief. It wasn't Nate McIntyre, after all.

"Is your wife alone, Mr. Warfield?" Sarah's mother asked, and he nodded.

Jake Warfield's buckskin shirt was sweated through and covered with a fine film of dust. His eyes were red-rimmed and his mouth set in a grim line as he spoke.

"Yes, Ma'am, she is. I hated t' leave her, but she begged me t' fetch ye quick as ever I could. She don't look good, Miz Craighead."

Sarah's mother laid a comforting hand on his arm. "She'll be fine. The first babe is always the hardest, especially if it comes a wee bit early. Daughter, see that Mr. Warfield gets food and water whilst I pour up the squawroot and ready my other things."

"Did ye note any Indians as ye rode along?" Sarah's father asked as they entered the cabin.

"Nay, Reverend, just two riders a bit up the trail who said they'd come from here. There may have been some Indians a-watchin', though—I heered some mighty strange birdcalls."

Sarah gave their visitor a gourd dipper of water, but he refused the offer of a trencher of squirrel stew.

"I've no stomach for food today, and that's a fact," he said.

Sarah's mother finished her preparations and tucked her bundled midwife's stores under one arm. "Ye'd best take along some jerky, anyway, Mr. Warfield. I'm ready to leave now."

Sarah's father, who had been sitting at the table holding Adam, now stood and handed him to Sarah. "I'll go wi' ye this time," he told her mother.

She cast a worried look at her children and shook her head. "We canna leave Sarah and Adam here alone. This matter may take some time."

Her husband nodded. "I agree. I'll stop by the village and ask Old Woman to watch out for them."

"Are ye certain—" she began, but stopped, silenced by the set of her husband's jaw.

Sarah's father turned to her. "Now mind ye stay close, Sarah. Should ye note aught strange, make straight for the hidey-hole and take in the latch."

Sarah nodded. "I will. Don't worry, Mother. We'll be all right," she added.

It took only moments for the horse to be brought from the lean-to and saddled. Sarah's father helped her mother onto the animal's broad back; then with a final wave, he mounted and they rode away with Jake Warfield.

It was a scene that had often been repeated in the months they'd lived on Preacher Creek, as her mother or father went off on their separate missions. But something about this time seemed different, and Sarah turned back to the cabin with a sense of foreboding. Missing his mother, Adam began to wail, and Sarah held him close and rocked him in her arms until he forgot his loss.

She had scarcely settled her brother at his play when a shadow fell across the floor, and Sarah looked up to see Bel-a-ka at the open door. Her twin brother usually accompanied her, but this time the Indian girl was alone. As always, she refused to enter the cabin. Sarah stood on the threshold as they exchanged formal greetings.

"Ili kheleleche," Bel-a-ka said.

"Ili kheleleche," Sarah responded.

From the time Sarah had first seen the slender, copper-skinned girl in fringed deerskin, she had admired her. Slightly older than Sarah, Bel-a-ka had already taken her place in the women's lodge as the ranking princess of the Clan of the Bow. Bel-a-ka sometimes treated Sarah as vastly inferior, but she had also shown Sarah where the best medicinal herbs could be found. The twins had taught Sarah much, including a smattering of their Delaware tongue, and in return, they had added to the English they had picked up from traders. Since Sarah rarely saw whites her own age, the Indian twins had become her best—and only—friends. They called her "Sa-la" and visited her almost daily.

"You are alone," Bel-a-ka said.

"Yes."

"Did you find the squawroot?"

Sarah nodded. "It was where you said. Mother is taking it to Miz Warfield."

"If she live to use it," Tel-a-ka said as he joined them. When Sarah had first come to Preacher Creek, she and the twins had been almost the same size, but in the past year Tel-a-ka had grown almost a head taller. Soon, Bel-a-ka said, her brother would enter the medicine lodge for the ritual that would make him *netopalis,* a warrior. After that, Sarah knew that she and Bel-a-ka would rarely see him.

Sarah turned to Tel-a-ka. "Why do you say that? What do you know of such things?"

Tel-a-ka's dark eyes regarded her steadily. He stood with his arms crossed, cupping his elbows in his hands. His chest was bare, save for a breastplate made from the bones of many small animals, arranged in a diagonal pattern that only the son of a chief could wear. "Old Woman knows there is trouble. She has said it."

"I have heard that some Delaware are raiding," Sarah said.

Tel-a-ka shrugged. "The People of the Bow do not raid," he said. "I do not know about others."

"Some of the Lenni-Lenape favor the French," Sarah went on, unwilling to let any opportunity pass to gain information. "Such a thing makes much trouble."

Tel-a-ka scowled. "What does a *Yengwes* know of war? Have our people not lived in peace these years? I will hear no more of it."

It was the first time Tel-a-ka had ever called Sarah "English," and his angry tone surprised her.

Bel-a-ka frowned at her brother, then turned to Sarah. "Enough of this talk. Come and watch the contest with the bow now."

"Adam and I ought to stay here," Sarah said, glancing back at the cabin as if some visible orders had been left there for her.

"No. *Allogagan Nehellatank* told Old Woman to send for you."

The Indians' name for her father, translated as "servant of the Lord," had at first seemed almost sacrilegious to Sarah, but now she accepted it as a token of respect. Among the People of the Bow, Sarah's mother was known as "the God Woman," and Sarah and Adam as "the God Children."

"And so ye are," Caleb had said when Sarah told him of it. "We're all God's children, even the savages who call me by a name they ken not."

"I wish they could know our God," Sarah had said then.

"So do I, Lass, but for now I maun be content to let those called to the savages preach to them. I've enough to do to help our own through this world."

"I think they'll understand one day," Sarah had said, but as the twins either changed the subject or remained silent when she tried to speak of her faith, she sometimes wondered when that day would arrive.

Bel-a-ka held out her hand to Sarah. "Come—let us go now."

Sarah picked up Adam, and with one last look around the cabin, she closed the door behind her. "I have not seen the contest with a bow. What is it like?"

As they walked toward the shallows of Preacher Creek, where they could cross the stream on boulders placed there long ago, Bel-a-ka explained it, then added, "It is the last for Tel-a-ka. *Netopalis* do not play games."

"Then you must win," Sarah said, but Tel-a-ka merely glanced at her and said nothing.

"We watch from here," Bel-a-ka said a moment later. She stopped at the edge of a meadow that was already knee-high in early summer hay, while Tel-a-ka went on to the village.

Though she had never seen the contest of the bow, Sarah understood it immediately. A half-dozen boys, a few about Tel-a-ka's size and one or two a little smaller, stood in a cleared area behind the village and took turns shooting their arrows at a large, deerhide-covered target. The entire village had turned out to watch as practice ended and competition began in earnest.

"What do they say?" Sarah asked, unable to understand the speech each boy made before taking his stance and starting mark.

Bel-a-ka smiled. "They talk how great they are."

"The time for that is after they win," Sarah said.

Silence fell as the first contestant flexed his bow. "Watch!" Bel-a-ka whispered.

The boy stood absolutely still for a moment, then with a blood-curdling yell, he pulled on the bowstring and sent an arrow flying.

"Ahh," the watchers breathed in unison as the arrow hissed through the air, only to fall just short of the target.

Immediately jeers arose, and Sarah guessed that missing the target was a great shame. The boy postured and turned to face the crowd, yelling words that made Bel-a-ka smile.

"He says he saves his best arrow for the last. Three times they shoot. Only the best counts."

Sarah watched as the other contestants took their turns, with Tel-a-ka the last. Of the six, only two had hit the target solidly the first time, Tel-a-ka and a boy whose chest was covered with an unusual red breastplate that matched his headband.

"An-we-ga did well," Bel-a-ka remarked after he struck the target's center.

"He is not from your village," Sarah said, knowing she hadn't seen him before.

"No. But he will take a wife from our Clan of the Bow."

You, perhaps? Sarah wondered, noting how intently Bel-a-ka watched his every move.

In the second round, once more only An-we-ga and Tel-a-ka's arrows found the center of the target, with An-we-ga's closer to the mark. As the final round began, Sarah realized that Tel-a-ka might lose to this challenger from another village, a defeat that would mean a great disgrace for a chief's son.

"Why do your people seem to want An-we-ga to win?" Sarah asked when he was loudly cheered as he postured before his final try.

"It is just good sport. Watch, now!"

Bel-a-ka leaned forward, her eyes shining, as An-we-ga turned to face them and held out his bow as if inviting Bel-a-ka to cross the meadow and take it. Everyone grew quiet until Bel-a-ka raised her right hand high and nodded, bringing cheers from most of the onlookers.

Slowly An-we-ga placed an arrow in his bow, then pulled it back until the sinews on his forearms trembled from the effort. He released it with a loud cry, and it sliced through the air and dug itself shaft-deep into the heart of the target.

Tel-a-ka was the center of attention as he walked to the target, pulled out An-we-ga's arrow, and broke it across his thigh. Then he motioned for the target to be moved farther back.

The villagers gasped, then were quiet as Tel-a-ka went back to the starting place and turned toward Bel-a-ka and Sarah, lifting his bow toward them. Sarah expected for Bel-a-ka to signal him to begin, but she remained motionless.

"You," Bel-a-ka said, touching Sarah's forearm. "Do what I did."

Somewhat embarrassed that all watched her, Sarah raised her arm high. Everyone cheered except An-we-ga, who stood to one side, his arms folded across his chest, his expression grim.

Sarah wondered briefly what would happen if Tel-a-ka lost. She had seen village games in which losers ran a gauntlet of women and girls who whipped them with willow switches while the rest of the men and boys looked on and jeered. Sarah couldn't imagine proud Tel-a-ka undergoing such indignity, and she watched intently as he fitted his final arrow to his bowstring.

All eyes were upon Tel-a-ka, every breath held as he pulled back on the bow. There was a universal groan when, at the last moment, he turned aside without releasing it.

"Something is wrong," Bel-a-ka murmured, looking past the contestants. Almost immediately, the air filled with a confusion of shouts and screams.

"Seneca!" Bel-a-ka exclaimed as several dozen painted warriors burst from the forest into the village and quickly surrounded both contestants and onlookers.

From their vantage point across the meadow, Bel-a-ka pulled Sarah and Adam down into the tall grass and motioned for them to stay there.

"What is happening?" Sarah whispered after the screams and shouts died down and Bel-a-ka had raised her head for a cautious look around.

"My father and their chief will smoke the pipe now. The Seneca must not see you."

"Why not?" Sarah asked.

Bel-a-ka spoke matter-of-factly. "The French give much wampum for white scalps."

Sarah swallowed hard and tried to form a coherent prayer for their safety. "When the Seneca go into your father's lodge, I'll take Adam to our hidey-hole," she said aloud.

"No!" Bel-a-ka's voice was sharp. "Stay here. I must go now. I tell you when to go."

Adam began to whimper when Bel-a-ka left, but Sarah finally managed to soothe him. The late afternoon sun glared down, but by shading Adam with her body, Sarah managed to lull him to sleep.

Still Bel-a-ka did not return. When Adam awoke, cross and crying from hunger, Sarah knelt in the grass and peered across the meadow. She watched the village people gather around the chief Seneca warrior, who spoke in a loud voice. Too far away to hear his words even if she could have understood them, Sarah could tell that they weren't peaceful. He held a feathered war stick in his right hand, and each time he shook it, his warriors shouted. Soon even some of the Delaware shouted with them, so contagious was the enthusiasm generated by the Seneca speaker.

Then Tel-a-ka's father came to the center and began to talk, making many gestures with his own war stick. The villagers were silent at first, then they began to shout at the Seneca, who moved menacingly toward them. Sarah watched helplessly as a pitched battle erupted, scattering the women and children. In the confusion, Bel-a-ka made her way back to Sarah and took her hand.

"Hurry! You must go."

"What is happening?" Sarah asked.

"The Seneca want our warriors to raid with them."

"And what says your father?"

"He will not go with them. There will be trouble. Go to the squawroot tree and wait there."

Before Sarah could say anything more to Bel-a-ka, the girl had started back to Old Woman's lodge, nimbly dodging several fighting groups.

Holding Adam tightly, Sarah breathed a silent prayer as she began to run. Bent low, she splashed through Preacher Creek, then passed the cabin and fled into the cover of the forest.

Adam wailed in protest as underbrush scratched his arms and legs, but Sarah didn't stop until she had reached the huge oak tree under which the squawroot grew.

"Hung'y, Sa-wa!" Adam cried, and after she had caught her breath, Sarah carried him to a nearby tangle of honeysuckle vines, where the nectar from the blooms would temporarily satisfy him.

As the afternoon shadows lengthened into twilight, Sarah still waited—

for what, she didn't know. Night fell, and Adam whined and fretted for a time, then snuggled close to Sarah and fell asleep. Through the trees, the sky glowed red with reflected flames. No campfire could be that large, that bright.

They must be burning our cabin, Sarah thought numbly, but without tears.

Then, as the glow continued to light the sky, Sarah realized it was far too large to be caused from the Craigheads' cabin alone.

The Delaware village is burning, too, she realized.

Apparently, the entire village was being punished for their chief's refusal to raid with the Seneca. Sarah wondered what had happened to Bel-a-ka and Tel-a-ka, to their father the chief, and Old Woman. Then she thought of her own parents, and sudden tears stung her eyes. Suppose they returned to find their cabin burned and their children gone? She had to go back and watch for them.

Burdened with the weight of her sleeping brother, Sarah slowly retraced her steps through the forest until she reached the edge of the clearing. Dry-eyed, she saw the pile of ashes where her home had stood. On the other side of the creek, the thatched lodges of the Delaware still smoldered. Sarah closed her eyes and bowed her head in prayer. "Protect us all, Lord," she whispered.

When Sarah opened her eyes, the light of the full moon revealed that the clearing had filled with many armed warriors, who quickly surrounded her. One wrenched Adam from her grasp as another put his hand over her mouth, pressing down brutally. The men spoke in low tones in a guttural language Sarah did not understand, and her blood ran cold as she realized that she and her brother had fallen into the hands of the fierce Seneca.

Trying to fight back, Sarah forced open her mouth and sank her teeth into her captor's thumb. There was a loud exclamation, then Sarah felt a blow to her temple and heard the sound of her own voice crying out. The clearing spun around her, and she felt herself falling as the shadows began to fade to blackness.

Chapter 3

I *will not faint,* Sarah vowed. Struggling to stay on her feet and fighting a rising tide of panic, she tried to take deep, calming breaths as her arms were twisted behind her and tightly bound.

Adam was nowhere in sight; the Seneca who had taken him had apparently departed with most of the others, leaving only four of their number behind.

"What have you done with my brother?" she asked the nearest Seneca.

"Hile!" he warned, grabbing Sarah's arm and pushing her roughly into the dark forest.

The small party moved silently through the gloom, the Indians with assurance and Sarah haltingly. A warrior walked before her and another behind her, with one on either side forming a guard, marching her through the night to some unknown destination.

Sarah assessed her situation and her chances of getting out of it alive. Although she feared what might await her at the hands of the Seneca, Sarah knew she had no present hope of escaping her captors. Even if she could manage to get away from them, she'd be alone in the wilderness and, with her hands tied behind her, helpless as well.

Unable to use her arms to balance herself, Sarah stumbled so often that the Indians finally slowed their pace. Then an owl called in the darkness, and Sarah shivered in apprehension. Perhaps other Seneca were signaling to her captors. Or perhaps warriors from Tel-a-ka's village had followed them. If so, there would surely be a fight.

Sarah began to whisper the Shepherd's Psalm, but instead of comforting her, it only reminded her of the many times she'd heard her father line it out, and tears came to her eyes. Would she ever see her parents or her brother again?

If only I had stayed by the squawroot tree, Adam would still be all right, she told herself. *This is all my fault.*

Only when someone touched Sarah's shoulder did she realize that the others had stopped. Wearily she knelt to the ground, the Seneca making a silent circle around her. Apparently, they had also heard the owl's call and had stopped to listen for it again. Since none of the Seneca had responded to the call, Sarah thought perhaps it had come from the Lenni-Lenape. She held her breath, listening with them.

The cry came again, even closer, followed at once by the flapping of wings as a quite real owl swooped overhead. The Seneca murmured quietly among themselves, then moved on.

They are in enemy territory now, she realized. The Seneca probably wouldn't rest until they reached their own camp, wherever it might be. They walked on and on into the night, until Sarah's legs trembled with fatigue and she felt she couldn't take another step. Finally they stopped, and almost as soon as she was allowed to sit down, Sarah slept.

When she awoke, dawn had broken, and only one Seneca remained to guard her. Underneath his war paint, Sarah saw that the man's face was deeply scarred from smallpox, making him appear even more sinister.

"Auween kachev?"

In the Delaware tongue, Sarah asked the Seneca who he was. Her uncle Jonathan had once said that most of the Woodland Indians understood Delaware, no matter what their own native language. However, the Seneca merely pulled Sarah to her feet and gestured that she was to continue to walk.

Now that it was light, Sarah looked in vain for any familiar landmark. Her family always used well-worn Indian trails whenever they went anywhere and avoided the deep woods, which to Sarah all looked the same. Eventually the trees began to thin out, and as they climbed a high ridge, Sarah realized that they were leaving the forest.

Her captor walked faster, pulling Sarah after him through a wild blackberry bramble. He wore rawhide leggings, but her bare legs, already scratched the night before, were soon a mass of bloody cuts. She knew from experience that the pesky chigoes that lived in the brambles and high grass would add to her misery. With her hands tied behind her back, she couldn't even scratch their bites.

But at least I still have my scalp. She tried to take comfort in the thought that, had the Seneca intended to kill her, they would surely already have done so.

Beyond the blackberry bramble lay a stretch of forest from which many trees and nearly all of the underbrush had been removed. A crude camp, their apparent destination, occupied the center of the cleared area. They entered it, and several curious Seneca warriors crowded Sarah. She looked at their faces, wondering which of them had burned her cabin, and praying that whoever had taken Adam had brought him safely to that place. The warriors stood aside only when an ancient, toothless woman came slowly forward to greet Sarah's captor.

"Alle, Niskitani," she said, and he nodded.

"Alle-shema, Nad-ta-ka."

The man pointed to Sarah, then to the old woman, gesturing for Sarah to go with her. As Nad-ta-ka approached her, the mingled scents of bear grease, wintergreen, and the pipsissewa shrub assailed Sarah's nostrils, proof that the old woman was using several common rheumatism remedies.

Hoping that Nad-ta-ka's infirmities might allow her to escape, and eager to be away from the warriors, Sarah readily followed. Some of the Seneca reached out to touch her, and the tone of their remarks caused Sarah to blush angrily, even though she didn't understand their words.

"*Hile!*" Niskitani shouted, and the men turned and slunk away, so much like cowardly dogs that Sarah had to stifle the impulse to smile. Her light mood was short-lived, however, as Nad-ta-ka pushed Sarah into a dark, cramped, makeshift, pole lean-to.

"Is there a child in the camp? A little boy?" Sarah asked, hoping that the old woman might understand English.

"*Nime!*" Nad-ta-ka hissed.

Sarah flinched when the old woman pulled a knife from the tie around her waist and came toward her, then felt relief when the old woman used it to cut the bonds that had chafed and all but cut off the flow of blood to Sarah's hands.

"Thank you," Sarah said aloud.

Nad-ta-ka frowned and held her hand to her lips in the universal sign for silence, then slowly lowered herself to sit opposite Sarah.

Pain throbbed in her wrists, but Sarah uttered a silent prayer for herself and her family. Almost immediately she felt her heart lift. Even though the Seneca held her body captive, her spirit and soul they could never harm.

Nad-ta-ka might be old, but Sarah soon discovered that her guardian was sharp enough to anticipate any move toward escape that Sarah might think of making. Nad-ta-ka put her to work almost immediately, hauling water and carrying wood. Then she set Sarah at the task she disliked the most, chewing deerhide until it was soft and supple.

It's no wonder the Indian women lose all their teeth, Sarah thought when she realized that every scrap of deerhide the Seneca used to make their clothing had first been prepared by being chewed. When Nad-ta-ka had first showed Sarah what she must do, Sarah had gagged and refused, but after understanding that she would get no food unless she did as she was told, Sarah had reluctantly complied. She remembered seeing the Lenni-Lenape women chewing rawhide strips and thinking that they must enjoy it, as Bel-a-ka and Tel-a-ka liked to chew the tops of the cup plant. Now she knew better.

However, Sarah had to admit that the method worked well. She looked down at the surprisingly comfortable deerskin shift that had replaced her badly torn homespun dress. With her hair in a single braid down her back and too-large Seneca moccasins on her feet, Sarah knew she must be a strange sight. On the rare occasions when she was allowed to leave the twig-and-pole lean-to, the Seneca pointed at her and laughed if Niskitani wasn't around. Sarah was always closely guarded, and with each new day of captivity, she wondered more and more why they kept her there and what they had done with her brother.

By Sarah's reckoning, she had been in the camp for seven days when, going to the creek for water, she noticed that the camp seemed strangely empty. There had never been more than several dozen warriors there, plus a few old women who prepared their meals, but on this day, no one was in sight.

The Seneca must be raiding again, she thought. Other captives might be brought back to the camp—or worse, perhaps they'd return to display scalps they had taken.

"Where is everyone?" Sarah asked Nad-ta-ka, her gesture taking in the silence of the camp.

"French fort," Nad-ta-ka said.

Surprised that the woman had both understood and spoken English, Sarah stopped short in the path, sending Nad-ta-ka stumbling against her. "The French fort?"

The old woman half-closed her eyes. "Not *Yengwes*. Niskitani go to French."

"Why?" Sarah asked.

Nad-ta-ka's hands moved rapidly, imitating the motion of a tomahawk being thrown, then circled Sarah's head in a gesture that she understood all too well. "War," she said simply. "Much wampum."

So the Seneca were helping the French make war against the English, just as Joshua said. "What about me? I am *Yengwes*."

Nad-ta-ka's mouth creased in a wrinkled grin as she pointed to Sarah. "*Yengwes* squaw to Niskitani."

"No!" Sarah exclaimed.

Nad-ta-ka frowned and with surprising strength pushed Sarah down the path toward the stream, muttering rapid Seneca.

I must get away before they return, Sarah thought as she knelt to dip the water. The creek was fairly shallow; she could probably wade in it quite a distance and not be easily tracked. Nad-ta-ka would be unable to come after her, but from the corner of her eye Sarah saw that the pair of warriors left to guard her still watched her every move. Escape would be difficult, but she had to try it, and soon. She had no intention of becoming Niskitani's squaw.

Late that afternoon, Sarah noticed that the deep quiet and the warmth of the day had combined to lull Nad-ta-ka to sleep. The old woman's head rested on her shrunken chest, and she didn't stir as Sarah crept to the lean-to's entrance and peered out.

One of the guards stood a few yards away with his back to her. Not seeing the other one, Sarah had decided to make her move when a strange birdcall from the forest behind them broke the silence, and the guard turned toward the sound. Sarah stepped aside as the other guard appeared, but neither glanced her way as they readied their weapons and moved away, out of her sight.

Sarah took a deep breath, then bent low and ran around the side of the lean-to. From there she scanned the camp but saw nothing. Again the bird called, followed by a rustling in the underbrush to her right.

Had they heard it? Sarah stayed still for a moment, then when the call wasn't repeated, she began to walk backward with only an occasional glance behind her until she reached the cover of the forest. Then, thinking only of putting distance between herself and the Seneca camp, Sarah turned and ran as fast as she could. From the sun signs, she knew the Seneca had traveled north-northwest to reach the camp, so the way back home must lie south, away from the French forts to the north and west.

Home! Sarah thought, and her heart sank. She had no home now. The cabin on Preacher Creek was in ashes, as was the Lenni-Lenape village beyond. But there were a dozen families in the area who would take her in, could she but find them.

When she was too winded to continue running, Sarah rested under a huge oak tree. Was she still going the right way? She looked up at the sky, all but obscured by overhanging tree limbs, and tried to fix her direction from the position of the sun. Although it lay too low on the horizon to be seen, the sun was setting to her right, casting long shadows that pointed east. If she walked at right angles to those shadows, Sarah reasoned, she'd be heading south.

I can't spend the night in the woods alone, without even a fire to keep the wild creatures away, she thought. But what other choice did she have?

Unbidden, a fragment of Scripture came to Sarah's mind: *In all thy ways acknowledge Him, and He shall direct thy paths.*

Although her condition hadn't changed, Sarah felt encouraged. God hadn't been left behind at Preacher Creek—He was still with her. She would keep going as long as she could see, then she would find a sturdy tree and climb into it. Not even a panther could get to her if she went high enough.

"I'll be all right," she said aloud, more bravely than she felt.

But Sarah knew she had no time to waste. She walked rapidly into the lengthening shadows until a sound ahead sent her seeking the protection of a bramble bush.

She expected to see a squirrel or some other creature of the woods, but the form that emerged from the southeastern shadows was no wild animal. As it grew closer and took human shape, Sarah gasped in surprise. The man's face was painted vermilion and yellow and he wore his hair in a warrior's top-knot, but Sarah recognized him at once and ran from her hiding place.

"Tel-a-ka!" she exclaimed.

"*Sehe!*" Tel-a-ka warned. He put the hand that held a tomahawk to his lips and gestured with the rifle in his other hand for her to join him.

Sarah followed Tel-a-ka into the forest without question. Where he had come from and how he had managed to find her were questions that could be answered when they were well away from the Seneca. In the meantime, Sarah was content to walk behind him as the twilight deepened and the woods grew ever darker.

Tel-a-ka walked rapidly, turning his head constantly to survey the terrain, which had become increasingly steep. Then he stopped suddenly.

"Go there," he whispered, pointing in the direction of a rock outcropping.

"Why?" Sarah whispered back.

"*Sehe!*" he warned again. "Go!"

Quickly Sarah made for the rocks. Crouching behind them, she peered into the gloom and attempted to see what had alerted Tel-a-ka. Some animal, perhaps, although it was still too early for the night creatures and too late for those that hunted by day. But then several human shapes emerged from the west, and Sarah's heart sank.

Four Seneca warriors, led by Niskitani. No doubt they had somehow tracked her and had come to return her to captivity, not reckoning she'd have an escort.

Look out, Tel-a-ka! Sarah cried silently.

Almost as if he had heard her, Tel-a-ka stepped behind a bramble bush, but a split second too late.

Half-paralyzed with fear, Sarah watched in helpless horror as the Seneca warriors headed straight for Tel-a-ka.

Chapter 4

With a blood-curdling cry, the Seneca raised their tomahawks high. *Surely Tel-a-ka will be scalped*, Sarah thought numbly, dreading what was about to happen, yet unable to look away.

"God, help him," she whispered at the same moment that a young deer ran out from the underbrush directly in front of the bramble bush. The startled Seneca stopped where they were, and Tel-a-ka seized the opportunity to dart from his hiding place and run to Sarah.

Wordlessly he took her hand and pulled her after him, with the shouting, angry Seneca following only a few steps behind. Although the way grew ever steeper and her lungs burned, Sarah dared not slow down. She took in great gulps of air as they gained the crest of the ridge and started down on the other side. Then she had to struggle to keep her feet as she half-slid, half-stumbled down the hill, still in Tel-a-ka's iron grip. About midway down the slope, he pointed to an outcropping rock ledge and motioned her toward it.

In near-total darkness, Sarah found a shallow cave underneath the rock's overhanging ledge and huddled in its protection. She'd thought Tel-a-ka was following her, but he had disappeared, swallowed up by the night shadows.

He should have stayed here, Sarah thought uneasily. Taking on four armed Seneca in darkness would be folly even for a skilled warrior, much more so for a novice like Tel-a-ka.

What is happening to him? Sarah couldn't hear or see anything to give her a clue. What the Lenni-Lenape called the Honeybee Moon waned almost by half. By its light she saw a lone figure reel and stagger drunkenly past, only a few yards from her hiding place.

Something Joshua had said came to Sarah's mind: *The French give the Indians rum and it ruins them.* Niskitani and his companions had been to the French fort—perhaps they had drunk enough spirits there to cloud their judgment. In that case, Tel-a-ka might have been able to defeat them, after all.

Sarah waited until she was certain the man had gone before she crept cautiously from the cave and stretched her cramped muscles. Hearing a faint sound borne on the night wind, she stood still and listened. A moment later it came again, clearer and more urgent.

"Sa-la!"

Welcome relief washed over Sarah. *Tel-a-ka is alive, after all,* she thought. *Thank God for that, at least.*

"Where are you?" she whispered back, but there was no answer. A gust of wind rattled the leaves of a nearby sassafras tree, then all was silent.

Cautiously Sarah made her way in the direction of Tel-a-ka's call, struggling to keep her footing in the dark.

Help me find him, dear God, she prayed, and a few moments later the tip of her moccasin encountered something soft and yielding. Gingerly she reached down until her hand touched deerskin—and something else. Something warm and wet and sticky.

Sarah snatched her hand away, frightened and repulsed by the blood that covered it.

Steady, she told herself. This was no time to behave like a foolish child. She was the daughter of a healer, and she knew what must be done.

Sarah took a deep breath and knelt beside the still figure. When her fingers found Tel-a-ka's wrist and felt a thready pulse, she breathed a prayer of thanks that he still lived. However, she knew from the force of the warm tide still flowing from his upper arm that he had lost a great deal of blood. Quickly Sarah unwrapped the rawhide around one of his leggings and tied it tightly above his wound. The other rawhide thong she placed loosely around the wound in a crude bandage, and soon the steady flow of blood stopped. Sarah put her hand on his face, which felt cold and clammy, and she guessed that underneath its layer of war paint, Tel-a-ka's skin was as pale as her own. For the present, Tel-a-ka must be kept warm. She had seen her mother wrap blankets around blood-loss victims, even in the hottest weather, until their skin had lost its pasty whiteness and regained natural color. Sarah wished that Tel-a-ka had carried a blanket, as many warriors did.

Having done all she knew to do for him, Sarah lay down close beside Tel-a-ka, hoping that the warmth of her body might help to ease the shock of his wound. She did not feel particularly afraid at that moment. If the Seneca came back or if some night creatures prowled around them, Sarah wasn't entirely defenseless. She had Tel-a-ka's knife and rifle, and if she had to, she could use them.

More important, though, was Sarah's belief that, somehow, in His own way, God would take care of them. For the present, that was comfort enough.

Sarah stayed awake a long while, straining to see the slightest movement that might be revealed in the dim moonlight, but eventually fatigue overcame her, and she slept deeply. The daylight that awoke her also served to confirm that Tel-a-ka was, indeed, very badly wounded.

The scratches on his face suggested hand-to-hand combat, and a jagged shoulder cut had shattered part of his new warrior's breastplate. But Tel-a-ka's worst wound, the one that had bled so freely the night before, was in his upper left arm. A bit of red still seeped from the rawhide covering it, and Sarah knew that the wound ought to be cleansed and packed with honey, then properly bandaged with linen. But knowing what should be done and having the materials to do it were two different things.

Gently Sarah touched Tel-a-ka's face and was gratified that it seemed warmer. Yet he didn't respond to her touch, and Sarah knew that the longer he remained unconscious, the less likely was his full recovery.

Sarah closed her eyes for a moment, praying for wisdom to do the right thing, and opened them to such a strange sight that she had to blink and rub her eyes to make sure she wasn't dreaming.

A woman dressed much like Sarah, her legs wrapped in rawhide, walked out of the west, directly toward them. She carried a pack and held a long walking stick in one hand. Her hair, a dark black that seemed almost blue in the sunlight, was parted in the middle and pulled back in twin braids that reached almost to her waist. A young woman, Sarah judged, older than she but still beautiful in the way that frontier women, white or Indian, so often were before hard work aged and wore them down.

Who is this Indian woman who walks the forest alone?

As if she had read Sarah's thoughts, the woman stopped and looked all around, listening intently. Sarah held her breath, aware that she could probably hear even that slight sound. But when she resumed walking and came closer, Sarah sighed in relief.

She isn't Seneca, Sarah realized when she saw that the woman wore wampum like Bel-a-ka's. Then Sarah made out something else—a crudely carved cedar wood cross hung from a strip of rawhide around her neck. Was the cross hers, or had it been some unfortunate settler's?

The woman stopped, and Sarah knew she had seen them.

"*Auween kachev?*" Sarah asked without moving.

She wasn't prepared for the woman's laugh, a musical sound deep in her throat. "*Auween kachev,* yourself, *Yengwes!* Who is the *netopalis?*"

Sarah stood and wondered at this English-and-Delaware-speaking Indian woman who had seemingly appeared from nowhere. "My name is Sarah, and this is Tel-a-ka, a Lenni-Lenape. Will you help us?"

The woman nodded. "That is why I come," she said simply. "My people call me Sukeu-quawon." She knelt and put her ear on Tel-a-ka's chest. He moaned but did not open his eyes. "He has lost much blood."

"I stopped it as best I could," Sarah said.

Sukeu-quawon ran her fingers over Sarah's makeshift rawhide bandage.

"You did well, but this place not safe. The Seneca have many war parties in these parts."

"Tel-a-ka is too weak to travel," Sarah said, then felt a moment's uneasiness when Sukeu-quawon withdrew a knife from the belt around her waist. "What are you going to do?" she asked.

"You see. Stay here," the woman ordered, then disappeared into the forest.

Sarah settled back and wondered what their rescuer could do for Tel-a-ka. At length she heard a rustling in the underbrush, then Sukeu-quawon emerged, pulling three slender saplings behind her. Looped around her neck like some primeval necklace was a garland of stout vines, cut from the trees on which they climbed.

"Is that for a shelter?" Sarah asked, thinking that Sukeu-quawon intended to hide Tel-a-ka and return for him later.

"No. Help me take off the leaves."

Deftly Sukeu-quawon took the stripped saplings and notched the smallest so it could be lashed to the others with the vines. When the frame had been made, she took a blanket from her pack and tied it to the corners. Satisfied that the crude litter was secure, she placed it on the ground next to Tel-a-ka and motioned for Sarah to help her position him upon it.

"He's heavy," Sarah said as she lifted his feet.

"He will grow leaner on the long hunts. He is new *netopalis*."

"How do you know that?" Sarah asked.

Sukeu-quawon pointed to the double bow carved on Tel-a-ka's chest so recently that it hadn't yet healed, and which Sarah had failed to notice.

"That is the sign of the Clan of the Bow—and the cut is still fresh."

"The Seneca burned his village seven or eight days ago. Tel-a-ka must have found another medicine lodge after that."

Sukeu-quawon nodded. "I heard there was much trouble. But now we must go from this place."

After Sukeu-quawon had tied Tel-a-ka to the litter with rawhide thongs from her leggings, she took a frame pole in either hand and began to walk forward, dragging Tel-a-ka behind her. Although his body was jostled, his eyes remained shut.

"Can I help you carry him?" Sarah asked, but Sukeu-quawon shook her head.

"Walk behind and watch. Tell me when his eyes open."

Sarah obeyed, marveling at the woman's strength as she maneuvered the litter to avoid the worst of the rocks and tree roots. *Whoever this Sukeu-quawon is, she seems to know what she's doing*, Sarah thought, and although she was tired and hungry, she thanked God for this woman's help.

Soon the sun became obscured by clouds, and a cool breeze bent the tree-tops. Sarah thought they were still walking south, although the sun offered no friendly guidance. She wondered where they were going and hoped they would soon get there.

Sarah was quite tired when Sukeu-quawon finally stopped by a small stream and took a deerhide pouch from her pack. Opening it, she gave Sarah several slivers of venison jerky and a handful of parched corn. With that and the clear stream water to slake her thirst, Sarah felt revived.

"Where are you taking us?" she asked, but her companion merely laid a cautioning finger to her lips.

"Soon you see," she said.

As the day wore on, Tel-a-ka began to drift in and out of consciousness. When Sukeu-quawon stopped again in the late afternoon, he opened his eyes and asked her in Delaware who she was and where she had come from.

"Ta-koom?"

"Sehe!" she cautioned.

When he persisted, Sukeu-quawon repeated her name but said nothing more. Tel-a-ka gestured that he wanted to get out of the litter, and although Sukeu-quawon frowned, she untied the thongs that bound him.

At Tel-a-ka's first attempt to stand, he swayed so that Sarah feared he would faint. Sukeu-quawon used her knife to cut the vines that had bound the litter, then handed Tel-a-ka the shortest of the litter poles to use as a walking stick. She rolled up the blanket and returned it to her pack, then scattered the rest of Tel-a-ka's temporary litter into the underbrush.

"We go on now—we there soon."

They walked at a much slower pace for another few minutes, then emerged from the forest to a wide meadow east of the largest stream Sarah had seen in years. In the distance was an Indian village that reminded Sarah of Tel-a-ka's. She glanced at him and wondered what he was thinking. But no matter what he felt, it would not be the Indian way for Tel-a-ka to show it.

"Monongahela?" Tel-a-ka asked, pointing toward the water, and Sukeu-quawon nodded.

She turned and motioned for Sarah to walk between them as they covered the last few hundred yards to the camp.

Sukeu-quawon spoke in rapid Delaware to Tel-a-ka, and Sarah caught the word *meteu*. She guessed that Tel-a-ka would be dispatched to the village medicine man, who might or might not be of much help. In Tel-a-ka's own village, Old Woman was a much better healer than the *meteu*, who was long on ceremony but short on actual benefit.

Tel-a-ka's scornful tone made it clear that he didn't consider his injuries to be serious, but Sarah knew that only by sheer dint of will was he still on his feet. Although he had lost a great deal of blood and hadn't eaten in many hours, Tel-a-ka managed to walk into the village with his head held high, as a warrior should.

"*Ili kheleche, muchomes,*" he said to the village elder who came out to meet him.

"*Ili kheleche, lenni quis,*" the man responded.

Sukeu-quawon waited until the elder had finished greeting Tel-a-ka before she turned to Sarah. In Delaware she told the elder that Sarah was no *tschepsit,* or stranger. Asked if she spoke Delaware, Sarah understood the question but replied in English.

"I know only a little Delaware, *muchomes.*"

"Where is Pimoca?" Sukeu-quawon asked, and the old man gestured toward the largest lodge in the village, then to Tel-a-ka.

Sukeu-quawon took Sarah by the arm and led her away from the men. "We go to my lodge now," she said, more as an order than an invitation.

"What about Tel-a-ka?" Sarah asked. "His wounds—"

"In time. First he shares the peace pipe. The chief must know where he comes from and why he is here."

A few children followed them until Sukeu-quawon chased them away. "They think you give them something," she said. "To them, all *Yengwes* carry gifts and things for trade."

As they walked through the village center and past racks of drying deer-hide and jerky strips, the odors of food cooking on a dozen fires reminded Sarah that she was hungry.

Ye probably don't want to know what the savages eat, her mother had once said, but the twins often shared their food with Sarah. They seemed to thrive on it, and never once had it harmed Sarah.

"Here," Sukeu-quawon said when they reached a solitary lodge on the far side of the village. Sarah stooped to enter a lodge that was similar to Old Woman's, but smaller. The floor was covered with soft bearskin rugs, and all around were piles of deerskin and an abundance of hunting and trapping equipment such as Sarah had never before seen.

"Sit," Sukeu-quawon said. She went outside and returned in a moment, bearing wooden trenchers heaped with aromatic fish and some sort of corn pudding. "Eat," she directed.

Automatically, Sarah bowed her head and repeated the prayer that her father always said before meals. She looked up to see Sukeu-quawon regarding her with mild curiosity.

"I do not know those words," Sukeu-quawon said.

Sarah leaned forward and touched the woman's cross. "Do you follow Christ?" she asked.

The woman closed her hand around the crude twig cross and nodded. "I do not have the Word, because there is no man of God here, but I believe it."

"The Word?" Sarah repeated, then realized Sukeu-quawon must be referring to the Scriptures. "I'm afraid I don't have the Word anymore, either. The Seneca burned our cabin and everything that was in it."

Sukeu-quawon laid a comforting hand on Sarah's forearm, a gesture of genuine sympathy that moved Sarah to tears. "Yes. But God will care for you," she said.

"He already has, letting you find us. But if there is no minister here, how do you come to know about God?" Sarah asked.

Sukeu-quawon sat back on her heels and smiled. "My man teach me."

Sarah's gesture took in the hunting equipment around the lodge. "He must be a mighty hunter," she said.

Sukeu-quawon nodded. "Yes. And wise, as well. He come back soon, I think. Eat now. We talk later."

For the first time in many days, Sarah felt a ray of hope. Sukeu-quawon's man must be a Christian, and perhaps he would be willing to help her. When Tel-a-ka was strong enough, they would go back to look for Adam and her parents.

What they might find, Sarah preferred not to dwell upon. For now, it was enough to know that she would at least be able to look for them.

Chapter 5

Sarah's optimism served her well for two days, but by the third day, with Tel-a-ka nowhere in sight and Sukeu-quawon away on mysterious errands much of the time, she began to grow impatient.

"I have not seen Tel-a-ka since we got here. Do you know that he is all right?" Sarah asked Sukeu-quawon at midday.

"Yes. He is at steam house to cleanse himself."

"When will he be back?" Sarah asked.

Sukeu-quawon smiled faintly. "You *Yengwes* ask much questions."

"I know little," Sarah said. *Never fear to ask a question, Lass—'tis the way for ye to learn,* her father had often told her. "I don't even know where we are now. Does your village have a name?"

"*Alleghi sipu achgook.* Do you know the words?"

"River something—but what is *achgook?*"

Sukeu-quawon made a spiral motion with her hand, imitating the movement of a snake. "Ser-pent," she said, separating the syllables so much that at first Sarah didn't understand what she meant. "Like the story in the Word," she added.

"Oh, the serpent—the tempter of Eve. How did you hear that story?"

Sukeu-quawon's lips lifted at the corners in the way she had of almost smiling. "My man knows many stories. Is Tel-a-ka your man?"

Her question caught Sarah off guard, and misreading her expression, Sukeu-quawon again seemed amused.

"No," Sarah said. "I have no man."

"You need *netopalis* to look after you," Sukeu-quawon said.

"I can look after myself, but I do need someone to help me find my brother. We were taken together, but he was not in the Seneca camp with me."

"Seneca have many villages. Some stay at French fort."

"Then Adam could be anywhere," Sarah said.

"A-dam?"

"Yes—my brother's name is Adam, like Adam in the Word. You must have heard that story, too," Sarah said.

Sukeu-quawon was about to reply when the sound of Tel-a-ka's voice stopped her.

"Sa-la!"

Sarah scrambled to her feet and went to the door of the lodge just as Tel-a-ka reached it. His breastplate and clothing had been mended, he had renewed his war paint, and although he held his wounded arm somewhat stiffly, he looked remarkably well.

"*Ili kheleche*. I am glad to see you," Sarah said formally. Tel-a-ka inclined his head and spoke rapid Delaware to Sukeu-quawon, who glanced at Sarah with her now-familiar almost-smile.

"I go," she said, leaving them alone.

Tel-a-ka's gesture took in Sarah's Indian garb. "You Delaware now."

"No. I will always be *Yengwes*. I want to go back to Preacher Creek. I must find Adam and look for my parents."

Tel-a-ka folded his arms across his chest and slowly shook his head.

"Adam not there. *Allogagan Nehellatank* not there. You stay here—I look."

"Do you know what happened to them?" Sarah asked. Something in Tel-a-ka's manner suggested that he might know more than he was willing to tell her, and Sarah fought against the fear that made a knot in the pit of her stomach.

"Seneca take you; go this way. Seneca take Adam; go that way. I take Bel-a-ka and Old Woman to village of An-we-ga. I track Seneca to camp and find you. Now I must help my people."

"If you know where they took Adam, tell me—I must get him back!"

"Boy is *nimat* to Seneca—not hurt."

"Brother?" Sarah said, translating the Delaware word. "No, Adam is *my* brother. He cannot be brother to Seneca."

Tel-a-ka's sober expression never wavered. "I have said it—you can do nothing."

His air of finality chilled Sarah. "I can do nothing alone; that is true. But if you will go with me—"

Tel-a-ka unfolded his arms and made the cutoff sign with his right hand. "No! Sa-la stay here."

"When will you come back?" Sarah asked, but as he had so often done, Tel-a-ka chose not to answer her question. Without another word, he turned and left the lodge.

Sarah hurried outside and watched Tel-a-ka walk away. He spoke briefly to Sukeu-quawon as he passed her, then stopped to accept his rifle and powder horn, offered with much ceremony by the village chief. Then, without a backward glance, Tel-a-ka was gone.

"What can I do now?" Sarah said aloud, more to herself than to Sukeu-quawon. The last link to her previous life had just walked out, and she had no idea what course of action she should pursue.

In all thy ways acknowledge Him, and He shall direct thy paths, Sarah reminded herself.

She did believe it—but how and when would that direction come?

❧

"You are sad," Sukeu-quawon said to Sarah a few days later. She had been helping Sarah mend her moccasins, much the worse for her recent forest treks.

"I will be sad until I find my family," Sarah said. "Tel-a-ka should have let me go with him."

Sukeu-quawon shook her head. "No, Sa-la. He must help his family and build new village for his people."

"Surely there must be someone here in this village who could go with me," Sarah said. "Even you—"

Sukeu-quawon made the cutoff sign. "No." Then seeing Sarah's stricken look, she softened her words. "My man come soon. He will know what to do."

Maybe he will, at that, Sarah thought. Several times, Sukeu-quawon had mentioned that her man had told her about God, so Sarah presumed he must be one of the Delaware that had been converted by the very few missionaries to the Indians. However, as far as Sarah could tell, Sukeu-quawon seemed to be the only one in her Serpent Clan village who professed Christ. They had prayed together, and Sarah had taught Sukeu-quawon a grace to say before their meals. However, Sarah wasn't sure that the Indian woman really understood everything that she told her.

"Where is your man?" Sarah asked.

"East," Sukeu-quawon replied. "He comes when the Moon of Milk Corn is new."

❧

But the Honeybee Moon had waned and the Milk Corn Moon was already well past the crescent, and still there had been no sign of Sukeu-quawon's man. If she felt worried about him, she didn't show it, going about her work calmly and quietly. Then one afternoon when all the village dogs began to bark at once, Sukeu-quawon rose from her corn-grinding and went to the door of the lodge, the corners of her mouth lifted in a welcoming smile.

"My man," she told Sarah.

"I will leave you alone," Sarah said, and made as if to go. But before she could reach the lodge doorway, it suddenly filled with a man dressed in the manner of a trapper. On his head was a cap made from the skin of a small animal—a raccoon, Sarah guessed. He wore a long buckskin tunic, richly fringed, and lighter-colored buckskin trousers topped by boots.

But it was the man's face that struck Sarah. The skin that wasn't covered by his curly brown hair and beard was tanned, but obviously as white as her own. His hazel eyes widened in astonishment as they met hers. Then he spoke, removing any doubt about his identity.

"Is it really ye, Sarah?"

He took a step toward her, and Sarah ran to him and threw her arms around his neck. "Oh, Uncle Jonathan! Surely God brought you to this place!"

"More like that He brought ye, Lass," he replied.

Sukeu-quawon had stood aside when he entered, but now she came over to where Sarah wept quietly in her uncle's loose embrace. Placing a hand on each of their shoulders, she spoke softly.

"Welcome home, Husband."

Sarah pulled away and wiped at her eyes with the back of her hand.

Husband? Then she recalled the look that had passed between Nate McIntyre and Joshua Stone when her mother had spoken of her brother's need to marry, and she knew it must be so. Sukeu-quawon's man was her uncle Jonathan, and he was the reason she was a Christian.

Jonathan embraced Sukeu-quawon and whispered something to her, then he released her and turned to Sarah.

"I see ye have already met my Sukey," he said.

"Sukey?" Sarah repeated, and Jonathan smiled and brushed Sukeu-quawon's hair with his hand. "Sukeu-quawon means 'black hair' in Delaware, and while 'tis a lovely name, I think Sukey suits her better."

"Whatever her name, she saved my life, and for that I am truly grateful," Sarah said.

Jonathan looked puzzled. "Saved your life? What do ye mean? Where are my sister and Caleb—and Adam?"

"I don't know," Sarah said, once more almost overwhelmed with the leaden weight of sorrow. "There was a Seneca raid—"

"Aye, I heard of it, but I had no idea—did the Seneca take the others?" he asked anxiously.

"No, just Adam, as far as I know. Mother and Father were away at the time, and the Seneca burned our cabin. I heard that Adam is probably in a Seneca village."

"That raid was about a month ago—how did ye get here, then?"

Sarah nodded. "When the Seneca left to go to the French, I ran away. Then Tel-a-ka—a friend from the Clan of the Bow—came looking for me and was hurt fighting some of the Seneca. Sukeu—your wife—found us in the forest and brought us here."

"Ye were in the forest alone, Sukey?" Jonathan asked, disapproval in his tone.

Her mouth lifted in a small smile and she put a hand on her husband's arm. "Nay, Jonnie. God was with me," she said.

"We'll speak more of this," Jonathan said. "As for now—"

Jonathan stopped speaking as someone else entered the lodge—a man almost as tall, but considerably younger, a man whose bright red hair gave him away instantly.

"Jonathan, where do you want me to put—" he began, then seeing Sarah, he stopped abruptly.

"Joshua!" Sarah exclaimed, while he seemed past speech.

"This is Joshua Stone, Sukey," Jonathan said. "He was a neighbor at Stones' Crossing."

"Glad to know you," Joshua said, looking at Sarah over Sukey's head.

"You are welcome here," Sukey said.

Joshua turned toward Sarah and slowly shook his head. "When I saw you last, I accused you of havin' a bit of war paint on your face, but now it seems you've taken on the whole garb," he said.

Sarah's face reddened. "It is the best I can do the way things are," she said.

"What has happened?" he asked, his tone more serious; and briefly Sarah repeated her story.

"Well, I tried to warn you," Joshua said.

"The raid happened the same day you were by—we wouldn't have had time to reach a fortified house, anyway," Sarah said, somewhat nettled by Joshua's attitude.

"That's neither here nor there," Jonathan put in. "We must plan how we can find Ann and Caleb—and get little Adam back."

"When can we leave?" Sarah asked.

Jonathan looked at Sarah as if she had taken leave of her senses. "We, Lass? Surely ye don't think that I'd take ye into that sort of danger!"

"Why not? It's my family, and I can take care of myself," she said.

Joshua's face darkened. "In the face of a raiding party? I think not," he said.

"You must think I'm still a child," Sarah said, an edge of anger in her voice. "Believe me, Joshua, I can load and fire a rifle as well as a man, and Tel-a-ka even taught me to throw a tomahawk."

"Really? And how many scalps have you seen lifted?"

"That's enough!" Jonathan exclaimed, making the cutoff sign. "The both of ye are too old for such childish temper."

"It's not a matter of temper," Sarah started to say, but Jonathan held up a warning hand.

"Hist, Girl! 'Tis na safe for ye to go, and there's no more that needs to be said. In the place of my sister and your father, I maun do for ye as I ken best.

'Tis dangerous here—ye will go back to Stones' crossing."

"I am not a child, Uncle," Sarah said with all the dignity she could muster. "I don't want to go to the crossing. I can stay here with Sukey."

"No," said Jonathan flatly. "I will look for your family whilst Joshua takes ye back to the Crossing."

"What?" Joshua turned to Jonathan, consternation plainly written on his face. "I was glad enough to help you bring the trade goods back, but I ought to get back to my duty."

"Ye heard me, Joshua. The good colonel can spare ye for another week or two, I'm sure. When ye've seen Sarah safely there, I'll rest much easier myself."

"Why can't I stay here?" Sarah persisted.

Her uncle sighed and took both of Sarah's hands in his. "The Lenni-Lenape have been good to us. I canna place them in the position of keeping a Seneca captive. They don't lightly lose prisoners, and should they come lookin' for ye—"

Sukey interrupted Jonathan and spoke so softly that only he could hear her. When she had finished, he nodded and looked back to Sarah.

"My wife agrees with me. She says she can help you look like a trapper's squaw so if the Seneca should happen by on the trail they'll pay ye no heed."

"When must I leave?" Sarah asked, already dreading the long trip east.

"As soon as we can find ye a horse and gear. Ah, don't look so sad, Lass. As Caleb would na doubt say, ye should put the matter into God's hands."

"Don't worry, Sarah. I promise to get you there safely," Joshua said. His words were small comfort, but knowing the effort that it must have cost for him to say it, Sarah tried to smile.

"I take promises seriously, Joshua."

He looked levelly at her, not returning her smile. "So do I."

"Then the matter is settled," Jonathan said with the air of a man who has just solved a knotty problem. "Now bring us some food, Sukey. 'Tis been a hard trip, and I'm nigh unto starvin'."

Chapter 6

Sarah and Sukey stood together the next morning in the pale light of dawn and watched as Jonathan and Joshua prepared to ride out again.

" 'Twas a short visit, but I'll make it up to ye later," Jonathan promised his wife.

Not wanting to intrude on their farewells, Sarah and Joshua stood a few paces away. When her uncle embraced Sukey, Sarah looked away from them and spoke to Joshua.

"Where will you go to get my horse?"

"Up north a ways. Last week Nate and I saw an Indian with a string of horses he probably stole from the French—most of them had military saddles. I'm sure he'll be willin' to make a trade for one of them."

Sarah sighed. "If you can't get one of those horses, just about anything with four legs will do. I can even ride bareback if I have to."

Joshua frowned, and Sarah had the distinct impression that he wished he didn't have to worry about her at all. However, his words somewhat belied his sour expression.

"Yes, I recall how you used to sneak out to the glen and ride your grandfather's horse. It would serve you right if I took you at your word. You'd look strange enough tryin' to ride some of the four-legged critters around here—"

"Never mind that," Sarah interrupted. "Just get me something to ride and come back soon. Uncle Jonathan ought to be looking for my folks right now, instead of riding off with you again."

As if he had heard her, Jonathan released Sukey and called to Joshua. "Come along now, Lad. 'Tis high time we got started."

"God go with you both," Sukey said. Jonathan kissed his wife one last time before swinging into his saddle.

"Be careful," Sarah said, knowing even as she spoke how useless her words were against the weapons of marauding Indians.

"Don't worry about us—we can take care of ourselves," Joshua replied unsmilingly.

"How long do you think they'll be gone?" Sarah asked after the men rode out of sight.

Sukey shrugged. "Two, maybe three days. They go north and west, where the French make danger."

Sarah was silent, thinking of the stories she had heard about the way the French had used the promise of guns and firewater to incite some Indians to fight even their own people. She knew Joshua and her uncle would be in dangerous territory.

Sukey touched Sarah's arm. "Come, let us eat. Jonnie always says that a wee bit of food makes things seem better."

Sarah glanced at Sukey, whose composed features betrayed no sign of anxiety or sorrow. Was it the Indian way again, or did Sukey really have such inner peace?

"I'm not hungry," Sarah said.

Sukey nodded. "I know, but you eat. Our men will come back."

They entered the lodge, where Sukey divided the rest of the breakfast she had prepared for Joshua and her husband. She handed Sarah a trencher of cornmeal mush and sat down opposite her.

"Now Sa-la say the prayer for food," Sukey said.

Sarah bowed her head and recited the grace she had taught Sukey, then added a brief petition that God would keep her uncle and Joshua safe.

She opened her eyes to find Sukey looking at her with a strange half-smile. "I think Jonnie's friend is good man for you," Sukey said.

Sarah felt her cheeks grow warm. "Joshua is not my man," she said. "I have always known him—he is my friend."

Sukey nodded. "Jonnie is my friend, too. Should be friend before husband."

"Tell me how you happened to meet my uncle," Sarah said, seizing the opportunity to change the subject. "The way some whites have treated your people, 'tis a wonder that you'd have aught to do with any of us," Sarah said.

Sukey put down her trencher. For a long moment she gazed into the fire as if remembering things too precious for mere words.

"In the old days, my people live in the east, by the big river. They hunt in the fall and winter. They plant in different place every spring. No white men and no guns and no firewater."

"That would have been long before your time," Sarah said. "Whites came many years before you were born."

Sukey nodded. "Yes. But the Old Ones know how it was. They tell the Young Ones so we will not forget."

"Did they tell you that the whites were evil?" Sarah asked.

Sukey looked at Sarah and shook her head. "They had no need to do that," she said. "We all knew."

"Yet everyone in your village has been friendly to me. What made them change their minds?"

The half-smile returned to Sukey's face. "Jonnie," she said simply. "Several winters ago, the snow came early and very deep. Our people had no meat. Many warriors had the white man's sickness and could not hunt."

"The white man's sickness?" Sarah repeated.

Sukey tapped her fingers against her cheeks. "The red spots killed many children and old people and even some warriors. My rabbit snares gave us some meat, but it was never enough."

"You hunted rabbits?"

Sukey smiled at Sarah's incredulous tone. "Aye, and deer, too. That is how I met Jonnie."

"You had a rifle?"

"No. Our people had old muskets but no powder or lead. My brother die; I take his bow into the forest. I follow fresh deer track for half a day. Then more snow come, cover the tracks. I start to go and see something move. My hands stiff from cold, but I shoot arrow true enough."

"You killed a deer?" Sarah asked.

Sukey smiled. "No. I hit something brown, but not deer. It was Jonnie."

"I take it that he wasn't badly hurt," Sarah said.

"No. My arrow hit this way," she said, demonstrating that the angle of entry had merely dealt his side a glancing blow.

"What did he do then?"

"I thought he would kill me. I began the Death Song. Then he laughed."

"Laughed? I'm not sure I could have laughed in his place," Sarah said, trying to imagine the scene.

Sukey nodded. "He told me a squaw should not try to hunt. He said I should be at home by the fire."

"He spoke to you in Delaware?"

"Aye. Jonnie know much Delaware. He trap with Lenni-Lenape in the forbidden lands."

"The land west of the mountains where the English aren't supposed to settle?"

"Aye. That same day he come to my village and every day for the next month he hunt food for us. He take pelts to trade and bring powder and lead and other stores. He live in chief's lodge as blood brother to my people. He tell me about his God. He go away in spring."

"When did you marry?"

"After the next harvest. He take me down the river for white man to marry us."

"My uncle always talked about wanting to settle on land of his own. Do you know of this?"

Sukey made an impatient gesture and spoke with more emotion than she usually showed. "My people do not understand these things. Who owns the land? The white people move into places where we hunt and fish. Our chief says we can go beyond western mountain and white man will not follow. I know this is not so—the white man always go where he wants."

"What about Uncle Jonathan? Does he want to move over the mountains?" Sarah asked.

"No. He speaks of land to the south. There people of all our tribes hunt for many years. He says we go there one day."

"How about you, Sukey? Will you leave your people?"

"Jonnie is my people now. All my family die before Jonnie come. Now I go where he wants."

"The rest of your people don't seem to be Christians," Sarah said, broaching a possibly delicate subject. "Have you talked to them about it?"

"Aye. Some Young Ones are already believers, but for the Old Ones it is hard. My people have many names for the *michabou*. To them, Jesus is just one more. They see no reason to change what has always been."

"But you did, and so can they," Sarah said.

Sukey shrugged. "I have told you of my people—what about yours?"

"What do you mean?" Sarah asked.

"Jonnie said they came from the land beyond the morning sun in the same big canoe. Were you with them then?"

Sarah shook her head, trying not to smile at Sukey's word choice. *She speaks better English than I do Delaware*, she reminded herself.

"No," she said aloud. "That was before my parents married. My grandmother took sick and died on the way here. My mother and brother and my grandfather were apart for a long time. She and Uncle Jonathan lived with a family in Lancaster. Then he and my mother found Grandfather McKay, and they all lived together at Stones' Crossing."

"Now Joshua take you there. Jonnie says we go someday, too."

Sarah sighed. "I want to see Grandfather again, but I would rather look for my family."

"But you will do as Jonnie says," Sukey said.

Of course I will, Sarah thought. She had no other choice.

❧

The fair weather broke the next day, and after several hours of lowering clouds, the first early summer thundershower descended upon the village late in the afternoon.

"Come; we gather greens now—they will be fresh after this rain," Sukey said as soon as the thunder and lightning had moved on across the river.

The young women made their way into the meadow on the other side of the village just as the sun came out from behind a bank of clouds and pierced the mist that still shrouded the distant eastern hills.

"Oh, look!" Sarah exclaimed. A shimmering rainbow began to take shape and arched all the way across the sky directly before them.

"A good sign," Sukey said.

"Did Uncle Jonathan tell you about the rainbow?"

"Aye. Our people have a story about how a great turtle saved many people on his back during the great flood. He said the Word has a story about a flood and a rainbow."

"Yes. God became so angry with people doing wrong that He sent a flood to destroy them. But He saved a good man, Noah, and his family. Then God promised that He would never destroy the earth by a flood again. He sent the rainbow as a sign of that covenant."

"What is cove-nant?" Sukey asked.

"It's a promise God makes to His people, or that His people make to each other. When Uncle Jonathan took you to wife, that was a covenant."

Sukey was silent for a moment. "I not understand all the words of the man of God, but I feel them here," she said, touching her breast.

Tears came to Sarah's eyes—tears for the beauty of the rainbow, for the obvious tender love that her uncle had found in his wife, for herself and the challenges that lay before her.

"Tel-a-ka's people took the Sign of the Bow for their clan," Sarah said aloud. "Maybe one day they will understand what the covenant really means."

"You can tell them," Sukey said. "That *netopalis* likes you."

"Maybe I can, one day," Sarah said.

As Sarah and Sukey watched, the bright colors of the rainbow gradually faded to pale pastel, then disappeared altogether. A cool wind sprang up, and in silence they returned to their gathering.

Chapter 7

"We have much to do before you go," Sukey told Sarah the next morning.

"Like what?"

Sukey put her own bronzed arm beside Sarah's, paling Sarah's deep tan into sallow, obviously white skin. "See? Dress not cover this."

"Maybe I should wear a blanket," Sarah said.

"In summer? No. I fix. Come."

Sukey picked up the largest basket in the lodge and motioned for Sarah to follow her. At the edge of the village, she paused at a pit heaped high with a mound of green-jacketed walnuts and began to dig through the pile with a stick. "Find split ones," she instructed.

Sarah didn't have to ask what the walnuts were for. Before she had put a half-dozen into Sukey's split-oak basket, her fingers already bore dark stains. Recalling the times her family had gathered walnuts together brought a lump to Sarah's throat. Now she was preparing herself for a trip that would take her even farther away from them.

"Suppose it rains?" Sarah asked, forcing herself not to dwell on her ever-present heartache.

"Take with you. But this strong, and we put on much times."

"What about my hair?" Sarah asked, touching the single long braid she had been wearing since the Seneca first seized her. The sun had put golden streaks into its honey-brown hue, making it appear even lighter than usual.

"I know special bark, make black dye. You do like me," Sukey said, indicating that Sarah needed two braids.

"My eyes—" Sarah began, aware that she'd never seen any Indian with hazel eyes.

Sukey tilted her head and put a hand out to Sarah's cheek. "Pretty, like Jonnie," she murmured. "You look this way; no one sees."

Sukey demonstrated, then flashed a quick smile. Sarah practiced a demure downward glance, bringing a nod of approval from Sukey. Sarah had noticed that Indian women seldom looked directly at people they didn't know; Sukey's boldness the first time they met had been a notable exception.

"I teach you other things," Sukey said.

All that day and the next, between repeated walnut rubbings that stung Sarah's skin, Sukey showed Sarah how a trapper's squaw made a fire and cooked simple meals on the trail.

"Do you travel with Uncle Jonathan?" Sarah asked.

Sukey looked down, busying herself with tying a bundle of jerky and parched corn she was preparing for Sarah to take with her. "Not now. Since the last trouble, I stay here. Once we go to O-hio, beyond the western mountains." Sukey paused and sighed. "Next time, we not come back here."

Sensing the sadness Sukey would surely feel when she left the only home she had ever known, Sarah put a comforting hand on her arm.

"That might be a long time yet," she said.

Sukey shook her head. "No. Not long," she said.

Not long enough, you mean, Sarah thought.

Uncle Jonathan had vowed to find her family. When that was done, he and Sukey would probably head south. With sadness Sarah realized that once they left, she might never see her uncle or Sukey again.

But by then I'll have the rest of my family back, she told herself and added a prayer that it would be so.

For two days Sukey labored on Sarah's transformation, until at last Sarah's skin was as dark as repeated applications of walnut stain could make it, and her hair, washed several times in a brew of black bark and crushed berries, was many shades deeper, though not nearly so shiny as Sukey's.

"I hardly know myself," Sarah said when she bent to see her reflection in the village water trough.

Sukey nodded. "Good. Now come to the lodge."

There she handed Sarah a long doeskin skirt, split down the middle, and a pair of sturdy leggings, laced with rawhide. "You ride in this," she said. "With blanket roll, you make Delaware squaw."

The material felt smooth and soft against Sarah's hand, and she knew Sukey was giving her the best she had. "It's lovely," Sarah said, touched at her generosity. "I'll see that Joshua brings it back to you."

"You keep," she insisted. "Always remember Sukey that way."

Impulsively Sarah hugged her uncle's wife. "I will never forget you, no matter what. After all, you saved my life."

Now outfitted for travel, Sarah waited impatiently for the men to return. The two days that Sukey had predicted their trip would take grew into three, then four, and still they did not return.

"I'll be white again if they don't come soon," Sarah complained on the morning of the fourth day.

"It is long way to the north and west," Sukey said in her usual calm manner. "They come soon. You see."

Around midmorning, all the village dogs began to bark to signal the men's arrival. Sarah and Sukey stood outside their lodge and watched them ride in. Each led a saddled horse, one gray and one a dark chestnut.

"Where's Sarah?" Jonathan teased after he had dismounted and kissed Sukey.

"I think she might be under all of that—that _stuff_," Joshua said, shaking his head at the results of Sukey's artistry.

"But will I pass as an Indian?" Sarah asked.

"In the dark, perhaps," Joshua said.

Her uncle turned a searching look on Sarah. "Ye look close enough now, but what happens when it rains? Ye canna stay away from storms this time of year."

"Sa-la knows what to do," Sukey said to Jonathan. Her expression grew more serious as she turned to address Joshua. "Sa-la Delaware now. Do not talk to her where others hear."

"And mind ye don't ride side by side," Jonathan put in.

"I have seen Sukey ride that way with you," Joshua said.

"Not on dangerous trails. Trust what Sukey says—she knows about these things."

The gray mare Joshua had led into the village snorted and tossed her head as if to remind them of her presence, and Sarah smiled at the animal's sudden show of spirit.

"Did you have trouble getting the horses?" Sukey asked her husband.

"No, but Black Bear had traveled quite a ways since last we met. We had to go far into Shawnee country to find him. Tell me, Sarah, which one do ye fancy?"

"The gray reminds me of the horse I learned to ride on," Sarah said.

"Then she is yours," her uncle said. "The other is for Sukey, when we go south."

"Now that we all have horses, why can't we just ride back to Preacher Creek together?" Sarah asked.

The look on her uncle's face confirmed his disapproval even before he could voice it. "Nay, Lass, ye know I won't hear of that. Tomorrow ye start back to Stones' Crossing, and I'll go on my way to Preacher Creek alone. 'Tis the only safe thing to do."

"I will pray for you, then," Sarah said. She had expected his reaction, but she had to keep trying as long as there was any hope that her uncle might change his mind.

"You had best pray for our journey, as well," Joshua said quietly. "Even traveling east is dangerous enough these days."

Sarah lay awake a long time that night, thinking about what might lie ahead. Apart from the journey itself, there was the fact that she and Joshua would be together almost constantly. She knew he didn't want to take her, and she half-dreaded, half-anticipated the time they would spend on the way to Stones' Crossing. It was the journey of a week in normal times, Uncle Jonathan said. A lot could happen in a week, both good and bad.

Which will it be? Sarah wondered.

❧

By dawn the next morning, Sarah and Joshua already had their saddlebags packed, ready to leave the shelter of Sukey's village. Despite her determination to be as stoic as the Delaware, Sarah's eyes filled with tears as she tried to thank Sukey for all she had done to help her.

"God go with you," Sukey said. Although her expression was somber, she remained dry-eyed as her husband embraced Sarah.

"When you find my parents and Adam, will you bring them to Stones' Crossing? You and Sukey could head south from there," Sarah said with a great deal more assurance than she felt.

Jonathan shrugged his shoulders. "Ye are assumin' a great deal, Lass. It may be that they'll have no wish to leave. The last I spoke with your father, he repeated that he was certain God meant for him to preach in the wilderness. I doubt losin' his cabin has changed his mind about that."

"Maybe not, but remind Father that he and Mother haven't seen Grandfather McKay in several years. Besides, if the wilderness isn't safe, they mustn't stay on there."

"I agree, but ye must be patient. Findin' them might take awhile."

"Send word to me any way you can in the meantime," Sarah urged. "I won't rest easy until all the Craigheads are gathered safe under the same roof again."

"I have some trapper friends who travel east right regular—they'll see that ye get my news." Jonathan turned to Joshua and clasped his hand. "Remember the things I told ye, Lad. Ye are to get Sarah to the Crossin' as soon as ye can, then send word here that ye have done so."

"Yes, Sir. I'll surely find someone coming this way when I get back to Colonel Burd."

Jonathan nodded. "Enough talk—ye'd best be on your way. Godspeed to ye both."

Silently Joshua and Sarah mounted their horses. Despite the early hour, many villagers came out of their lodges to see them off. At the chief's lodge they stopped, and in her best Delaware, Sarah thanked him for his help. In return, he handed her an amulet, which Sarah accepted with the appropriate gestures of appreciation.

At the edge of the village, Sarah turned to look back, but Jonathan and Sukey had already returned to their lodge. Soon, Sarah knew, her uncle would leave on his own journey.

Help him, Lord, Sarah prayed. *And us, too,* she added. She had no doubt that she and Joshua might need all the help they could get before they saw the familiar cabins of Stones' Crossing again.

They rode side by side in silence across the dew-splashed meadow that Sarah had last crossed with Tel-a-ka and Sukey. The waters of the Monongahela gleamed in the morning sun. They waved at several village children who stood on the bank, casting nets for their families' breakfast. The scene was so peaceful that once more Sarah felt a pang of regret that she could not stay there longer. As if he understood her mood and wanted to distract her, Joshua spoke.

"What did the chief give you?"

Sarah took the amulet from her saddlebag and handed it to him. "Some kind of good-luck charm, I think. It looks like the one that Tel-a-ka's grandmother insisted on putting around Mother's neck before Adam was born."

Joshua looked closely at the beaded deerskin pouch and nodded. "That's what it is, all right. Wear it around your neck—it might help."

"Surely you don't believe in good-luck charms!" Sarah exclaimed.

Joshua shook his head impatiently. "No, but Indians seeing it might recognize that you have the protection of a chief."

"How do you know that?" Sarah asked.

"It's a soldier's business to know these things," Joshua said, his tone so self-assured that Sarah laughed.

"If you're a soldier, why don't you wear a fancy scarlet coat and white trousers? And where is your sword?"

Joshua did not return her smile. "You know good and well that Nate McIntyre and I are scouts, not regulars. Anyhow, Colonel Burd's Pennsylvania Volunteers don't turn themselves out like English soldiers. We know better than to make ourselves a target in the forest—and a sword is the last thing we need."

"I thought you had finished with scouting when you came home with Uncle Jonathan."

"No, I haven't. That river may look peaceful enough now, but a ways up north on it the French are building up Fort Duquesne."

"Is that where you'll go?" Sarah asked. Joshua hadn't told her anything about the duties he was so eager to return to fulfill, but she knew that the British had tried unsuccessfully to take Fort Duquesne several years ago, when it was an even smaller outpost.

"Perhaps. The French must be stopped before they can turn any more Indians against us, and that seems as likely as any a place to start."

From what she had heard her father and uncle say, Sarah was well aware that Colonel Burd's volunteers would have a hard and dangerous time against the highly trained French soldiers, and Sarah feared for Joshua's safety.

"You're a volunteer—you don't really have to go back to Colonel Burd."

They reached the edge of the forest, where Joshua halted his horse and glanced at Sarah. "You don't know me very well if you think I would turn my back on a fight," he said quietly.

Sarah felt her face grow warm. "It's not that—I just thought perhaps you might be willing to take me to the crossing by way of Preacher Creek, if you had time."

Joshua looked annoyed. "You know it's not a matter of time—I promised your uncle to see you safely to the crossing, and I intend to do that. It'd be wrong for me to go against his wishes."

"He didn't say *how* we were to get to the crossing, though," Sarah persisted, clinging to her lost cause as long as she could. "It couldn't be much out of your way."

Joshua leaned over and took Sarah's arm, startling her. "Look here, Sarah, I've tried to be patient with you, but if I hear one more word about going to Preacher Creek, I'll pull you off that horse and give you the spanking you deserve. Even if I thought it'd do you any good to go there—and I don't—I wouldn't disobey your uncle."

Sarah's cheeks flamed, more in resentment of being talked to as if she were a child than in Joshua's argument. Even worse, she knew he was right.

"You just try to lay a hand on me and see what happens," she said, her eyes challenging his.

Joshua glared at her for a moment, then threw his head back and laughed unexpectedly. "Ah, Sarah! I recall how well you fight, but I believe I'd rather save my strength for now. Are we still friends?"

It was what they had said when they'd fought as children. Sarah's grandfather had taught them to shake hands afterwards and to say that they were friends. Although it had been many years since she had done so, Sarah extended her hand to Joshua.

"Friends," she repeated. "But I wish you'd quit treating me as you did when we were children and you were older and stronger."

Joshua grinned. "Oh, I'll always be older and stronger. I think that's what makes you so angry," he said easily. "But come now; we won't get to the Crossin' or anywhere else at this rate."

Sarah rode in silence for a few moments. "I suppose I should thank you for taking me," she said, "but I wonder why you were with Uncle Jonathan if you're so eager to be with the army."

"Watch that fallen limb," Joshua said, carefully guiding his horse around it. "Not that it's any of your business, but when your uncle and I met again at Gist's Station, he asked me to help him carry some of his supplies so he wouldn't have to make another trip. He knew I intended to rejoin Colonel Burd, as Nate McIntyre went on to do."

Sarah was silent for a moment. "I hope you don't blame me for keeping you from doing that. You should know I'd rather go with Uncle Jonathan or stay with Sukey and let you be on your way."

"I do know," he said, sounding almost sympathetic. "But Jonathan is right—he can find your folks a lot quicker by himself, and the wilderness isn't safe just now."

Almost as if to prove Joshua's words, the stillness of the forest morning was broken by the sound of nearby hoofbeats.

"What should we do?" Sarah asked.

"Nothing. Ride behind me and keep looking down. It's probably just some village braves on their way home."

But if it isn't, we ought to try to hide, Sarah thought. However, she had no time to voice the idea as several riders broke through the intervening trees and spotted them.

Sarah looked up quickly, then down again. What had been revealed in her brief glance made her heart hammer so hard that the chief's amulet fairly danced upon her chest. The riders were Indians, all right, but they weren't from Sukey's village.

And from the way they were garbed, Sarah knew they weren't Delaware, either.

Chapter 8

Sarah's quick glance had revealed five or six Indians, decked out in war paint and carrying rifles. She had to use all her willpower not to watch as Joshua rode toward them. After a moment, Sarah dared to raise her head slightly to see what was happening. Whoever the Indians were, they seemed to be peaceful enough for the moment. They met too far away for her to make out what they were saying, but the man who seemed to be their leader wasn't shaking his war stick, and none of the Indians' rifles were pointed at Joshua.

After what seemed a very long time, the group broke up and Joshua rode back to her. The war party—if that was what it was—continued on toward Sukey's village.

"What was that all about?" Sarah asked.

"I'm not sure," Joshua said. "They claim to be Seneca who want to fight the French because they broke some promises to them. I tried to tell them if they rode east they could join Colonel Burd, but as you can see, they're still heading north."

Sarah felt uneasy. "I hope Uncle Jonathan and Sukey won't be in danger," she said.

Joshua laughed without humor. "From a half-dozen renegades? I think not."

"Why do you say they are renegades?" Sarah asked.

"For one thing, there are too few of them for a full-fledged war party. For another, they all look very young. I doubt if any have ever been in a real fight yet."

"I wish I could have talked to them," Sarah said. "They might know something about what happened to Adam."

Again Joshua's expression and tone grew serious. "You must never speak to any of the Indians we meet, Sarah, no matter how friendly they may seem. Anyway, I don't think they would have understood either of us enough to ask about Adam. They were talking mostly in French, a tongue I dislike."

"Maybe not—but perhaps Uncle Jonathan will ask them. He knows many languages."

"So he does. I just hope that the Seneca he asks about Adam will give him the chance to talk."

Sarah was quiet for a moment. "You don't think he's going to be able to find my brother, do you?"

Joshua looked at Sarah with something akin to compassion. "As your father, the good reverend, might say, miracles do happen. I think it far likelier that he'll find your parents, however," he added when he saw her stricken look.

"I pray that Uncle Jonathan will find them both," she said.

"You'd better pray that I can keep you alive long enough to see them all again," Joshua said. "You did well this time—just remember to keep quiet and let me talk. If we should happen to be attacked, you must get away and keep riding east. Follow creeks wherever you can—they'll eventually bring you to a settlement."

"Or to an Indian village," Sarah said, voicing what she knew to be true.

"I see that you still like to look on the bright side," Joshua said, teasing her again.

"Somebody needs to," she replied tartly.

"Things will begin to look bright to me when you're safely delivered to Stones' Crossing," he said. "In the meantime, we've got a lot of ground to cover."

Twice more that day they heard riders in the forest but did not actually encounter them. Late in the afternoon, Joshua and Sarah stopped at the top of a hill and saw that, below them, a large group of Indians had apparently stopped to make camp.

"They're not Delaware," Sarah noted.

"Shawnee, maybe," Joshua said. "This isn't their usual hunting ground, but judging from their war paint, I don't think they've come to hunt."

"What's that on those poles?" Sarah asked, leaning forward in her saddle in an attempt to see better.

"Let's get out of here," Joshua said abruptly.

They turned and rode on, but not before the realization of what she had seen hit Sarah with an almost physical impact.

Scalps. The poles held the bloody souvenirs of some tragic hunt. Sarah's stomach lurched and a wave of nausea swept over her.

Ahead, Joshua turned back to look at her. "Are you all right?" he asked.

Mutely Sarah nodded. She knew there was no time for anything else.

"Good girl," he said. "I'm going to ride as fast as I dare—we should cover as much ground as we can before we have to stop for the night."

Sarah followed in silence, trying not to think about what she had seen, trying not to think about the twilight that deepened around them. She had never really liked sleeping on the trail. In the days when her family had traveled almost constantly, there had been some comfort in the blazing campfire that her father always built, even in the hottest summer weather. It was to keep panthers and other night creatures away, he had told her. But long after her father had heard her prayers and she had settled down in her blankets to sleep, Sarah had often stayed awake, fearing that some evil awaited in the wilderness. If she closed her eyes, it would seek her out and carry her away.

"We can't risk a fire," Joshua said when, at length, he had found a relatively safe place to make camp.

"We don't need it for cooking," Sarah said. "Sukey packed enough food for several days."

Sarah slid down from her horse and removed one of the saddlebags. Spreading her blanket on the soft forest floor, she arranged their evening meal on it while Joshua tended the horses.

He sat down opposite her and nodded his approval.

"Will you say grace?" Sarah prompted when it seemed obvious that Joshua had no intention of doing so.

He bowed his head and repeated the words Sarah had taught Sukey, then added a few of his own. "Lead us safely on our way and be with Jonathan on his journey, too. Amen."

"Thank you," Sarah said.

Joshua half-smiled. "No one will ever mistake me for a reverend, but I still know how to ask for help when I need it."

Cold springwater from their water bags accompanied the food Sukey had provided, and as they ate in silence, Sarah felt enveloped by a great peace.

But soon afterward, when the darkness was almost total and she lay down to sleep, Sarah was again reminded that danger still surrounded them.

"Here," Joshua said, handing her a knife. "This is yours. Keep it handy, day and night."

Sarah looked at the knife, a twin to Sukey's, and swallowed hard. "Do you really think I could use this?" she asked.

"I don't know and I don't want to find out. Try to sleep now—we have a long journey ahead."

The next day was very much like the first, except that the skies clouded along about noon and eventually produced a steady, chilling drizzle that caused Sarah to huddle under the protection of her blanket. In a few more hours they left the forest and rode along a trail that Joshua told her had been made many years before.

"See the signs on those rocks?" he asked.

Peering through the mist, Sarah made out a crude symbol that had been carved into the stone itself. "What does it mean?" she asked.

"I have no idea, but it was supposedly made by Woodlands warriors on their way to fight Catawbas and Cherokees."

"I've never heard of those tribes," Sarah said. "Where do they live?"

"A long way to the south. The Cherokee don't usually come this far north, although they did make an alliance with the British in Philadelphia a few years ago."

"Why were the Indians fighting?"

"I think it had something to do with their hunting territory. To the south and west the land is said to be much richer than this. No Indians live there."

"Why not, if it is such good land?"

"Many tribes—Seneca, Shawnee, Delaware, Cherokee, among others—hunt over it but don't live there. That was agreed a long time ago, maybe after some of the tribes fought over it."

"If the land is that good and there are no Indians, why don't whites go there?" Sarah asked, thinking it sounded like the kind of land that her uncle might like.

"For one thing, they'd be squatters. There are no land grants for that territory now. Indians don't live there, but they still hunt the area in large numbers. Also, it's still pretty much unexplored."

"But it probably won't stay that way for long," Sarah said, knowing that the same thing had once been said about the land through which they now rode.

Joshua nodded. "True enough. In fact, some time back I met one of Colonel Washington's wagoners, a young fellow named Boone. All he could talk about was the huntin' in the Kain-tuck, as some of the Indians call it. I think he means to live there one day."

"What about you, Joshua? Surely you don't intend to scout for the Pennsylvania Volunteers the rest of your life. Will you claim land then?"

Joshua looked away and said nothing for a moment. "To tell the truth, I've not really given much thought to what I'll do when we get the French out of the way. But when the time comes, I'll know."

" 'What will be, will be,' " Sarah said, quoting one of her father's favorite Presbyterian creeds.

"What will be is what we make it be," he corrected. "And right now, we must leave this trail."

"Why?" Sarah asked, following Joshua into the rougher underbrush to their right.

"The ground is soft from today's rains, and I see many tracks that were likely made today. Since we don't know if the riders of those horses are friendly, the best thing is to stay out of their way."

"But what makes you think they are anywhere near here now?" she asked, reluctantly following him where the underbrush would mean much slower going.

"They may not be, but others are," Joshua said. "I can hear them, and if you'd be quiet long enough, so could you."

Sarah intended to say that she had only been talking because he was, but before she could open her mouth, she also heard the muted beat of approaching horses.

Joshua didn't have to tell her to stop where she was and say nothing. Sarah sat motionless as he dismounted and walked through the underbrush. He crouched down and looked toward the trail they had just left. She heard, but could not see, the riders pass, riding fast; and her blood chilled as she realized that, over the horses' hoofbeats, she could make out distinct war whoops. The last time Sarah had heard that sound, the Seneca had captured her.

A moment later Joshua returned to her side. "I know about a fortified house not too far from here," he said. "Maybe we'll have time to get there before a war party finds us."

"What kind of Indians were they?" Sarah asked.

"I don't know for sure. But they had at least two or three prisoners who seemed to be white."

"And scalps?" she forced herself to ask, already knowing from his expression that he had probably seen those, as well.

"Perhaps. They passed in a hurry and I just caught a glimpse of them. We'll have to risk the trail again for speed's sake, but if you see me leave it, follow immediately and don't say a word."

They resumed riding, with Sarah following a few feet behind Joshua. Eventually the skies cleared, and as Sarah stowed her blanket, she noticed that the rain hadn't seemed to lighten her walnut-stained skin.

Thanks to Sukey, she thought, and wished she could see her again. Even though Sarah had known Sukey for a short time, there was a bond of belief between them that could never be broken. It was comforting to know that, wherever Sarah might be, Sukey prayed for her.

After an hour of steady riding, Joshua pointed toward a nearby stream, and they stopped in a thicket by its banks.

"We'll rest here and water the horses," he said.

"Are we nearly there?"

"We're closer than we have been. We'll have to skirt the trading post that's down this path about two miles, then we'll turn east again. We should get there before dark."

"Why don't you want to go to the trading post?" Sarah asked, thinking that someone there might have some news of her parents.

Joshua leaned close and looked at Sarah's skin. "You're still dark enough, but we can't risk havin' the wrong people see you up close. Even if there aren't any Indians hangin' around, the old man runnin' it would know right away that you were white, and I'd just as soon not have to explain anything."

Sarah sighed. "This is more complicated than I thought it would be," she said.

Joshua nodded. "Things usually are. But we're doin' all right so far."

In a few minutes they resumed traveling, riding in silence, parallel to the main path. Sarah was grateful for the thick leggings that protected her legs from being scratched by the underbrush, but she was far from comfortable. Joshua had added padding to her French saddle, making it somewhat more bearable. Still, by the end of her second day of unaccustomed riding, Sarah was sore and bone-weary. The thought of resting under a real roof again grew more appealing with each passing hour.

"I hope we're almost there," she said when Joshua stopped and looked about as if seeking his bearings. The sun had set, and its dying rays cast long, fantastic shadows across their way. Even with the lengthened June day, night would soon overtake them.

"Do you smell that?" he asked, turning slightly to the east.

Sarah hadn't, but when she lifted her head and took a deep breath, she was immediately aware of an acrid, unmistakable odor. "Something must be burning."

"So I would say."

Joshua resumed riding, and almost immediately they saw the smoke, a spiral column rising above the trees, perhaps a half-mile ahead.

"Is it the fortified house?" Sarah asked, voicing the fear that she'd felt when she first smelled smoke.

"I don't know. When we get to the top of this rise, I might be able to tell."

But the hill was not very high, and a line of trees between their vantage point and the source of the smoke blocked the view. Joshua maneuvered his horse to a sturdy oak tree, then motioned for Sarah to dismount and join him.

"Hold my horse's head and try to keep him still," he directed.

"What are you going to do?" Sarah asked.

"Get a better look."

Carefully Joshua put first one foot, then the other, on his saddle, and stood slowly. Sensing that something unusual was happening, the horse shifted slightly, and Sarah tightened her grip on the bridle. Standing upright on the saddle, Joshua was able to grasp a limb and pull himself up into the tree, where he climbed to a dizzying height before he stopped and peered out through its foliage into the dwindling daylight.

"What do you see?" Sarah called up to him, but Joshua remained silent until he had reached the lowest limb.

"Move my horse away now," he said, then dropped easily to the ground.

"Well?" Sarah prompted.

"I see that you don't have any more patience now than you did at the crossin'," he said.

Sarah sighed in exasperation, but she felt relieved. Surely Joshua wouldn't be teasing her if the fortified house lay in ruins. "And you aren't any nicer, either," she said. "Tell me what you saw."

Joshua rubbed his chafed hands together and shook his head. "I'm not sure. The smoke is from some kind of structure, all right, but it's not in the right place to be from the fortified house I have in mind. Something else must have been built there since Nate and I last passed by."

"But if Indians burned that—" Sarah began.

"No sense in borrowin' trouble," Joshua interrupted. "We'll be there soon enough if we don't stand here and talk until night takes us over."

"Then let's be on our way," Sarah said.

Less than a half hour later, they saw the comforting bulk of the fortified house topping the next hill, and Sarah breathed a prayer of thanks that it still stood intact.

"It's bigger than most of the fortified houses I've seen," Sarah said as they rode toward it side by side.

"It's different from most in these parts, too. It's not just one house but several cabins enclosed by a barricade, more like a small fort."

The land around the fortified house had been clean-cut, so that anyone who approached it could be clearly seen from a distance. As they rode closer, Sarah could make out several armed men at the corners of the high fence surrounding a two-story house. To her consternation, the men pointed their rifles at them when they were still several hundred yards away.

"Surely they're not going to shoot us!" Sarah exclaimed in disbelief.

"Of course they're not," Joshua said, but she noticed that he didn't sound very convinced. He removed his hat and began to wave it, his red hair shining like a beacon in the deep twilight.

"Hallo!" he cried, his voice echoing hollowly from the hill behind them. "I'm Joshua Stone, Colonel Burd's Pennsylvania Volunteers."

The men stayed where they were, their rifles still trained on Sarah and Joshua. Another armed man stepped from the massive main gates, which had been made from whole tree trunks sharpened to a point on the top.

"Stop where you are!" the man ordered, and Joshua and Sarah instantly obeyed.

"We are travelin' east and seek shelter," Joshua called back. "Do we have permission to enter?"

Another figure appeared at the gate, and there was a brief consultation before the first man turned back toward them.

"The man Stone can come in," he called back. "The squaw is not welcome."

"Sukey would be pleased at how well her disguise worked," Sarah said, with an ironic smile at the unintentional humor in her rejection.

Joshua cast an impatient glance at her. "It's nothing to smile about," he said. "Stay here—I'll go talk to them."

All the while that Joshua rode toward the gate, Sarah was uneasily aware that she was still in the sights of the riflemen atop the barricade.

What do they think I could do to them, even if I really was an Indian? she wondered, irritated that the settlers wouldn't accept her even though one of their own vouched for her.

Joshua stood at the gate a long time, and as each minute passed, Sarah guessed that the parley wasn't going well. Finally, he turned back to face her, but instead of giving the expected signal to come ahead, Joshua rode back to her.

"What now?" she asked when he was close enough to hear her.

"It seems that they don't believe that you are white and they don't want to let you in to prove you are."

"That's ridiculous!" Sarah exclaimed.

"They have good reason to mistrust Indian women," Joshua began, but Sarah didn't wait for him to finish his sentence.

In the knowledge that at least three rifles were still trained on her, Sarah took a deep breath and dug her heels into the gray mare's side. Joshua could stay outside all night if he wanted to, but she intended to get inside the fortified house.

With the shouts of Joshua and the riflemen ringing in her ears, Sarah lowered her head and rode toward the gates as fast as she could.

Chapter 9

Halt or I'll fire!" someone cried. Sarah reined in her horse, then realized that the words were meant for Joshua, who had apparently started after her. She rode on toward the gate again but got only a few yards before one of the men at the gate ran out and grabbed her horse's bridle.

"Get down!" he ordered, and Sarah obeyed. He grabbed her arm and waved his rifle menacingly. "Walk nice and slow to the gate—and no Indian tricks."

"I'm not an Indian," Sarah said, but he paid no heed.

Hearing the racket, several other armed men came outside the gates and moved quickly to surround Sarah as she reached them. One stepped forward and plucked the knife Joshua had given her from her belt.

"Nice Injun knife," he said, his dark eyes glaring at her.

"I'm not an Indian," Sarah repeated.

"Sure she ain't," one of the other men said, and they all laughed.

"Looks mighty much like the squaw that set up that ambush against us over at the Samuels'," a short, portly man said.

"And I'll wager that man with her's a Frenchy, too," someone else said.

As Sarah turned around to see what had happened to Joshua, the man standing nearest her struck her on the cheek. Sarah put her hand to her face, feeling shock, then anger.

"Joshua Stone is no Frenchman, and if you'd just really look at me, you'd see I'm as white as any of you."

"Ease off, Jenkins," one of the other men said to the man who had hit her and who now held her arm in his iron grip. He took a step toward Sarah and stopped. "Her eyes don't look Injun," he said as if she weren't even there, "but I never saw skin that color on any white woman."

"Or Indian, fer that matter," the man called Jenkins said. He let go of Sarah's arm and tugged at the top at her shift, revealing white skin below her collarbone.

"Do ye see that, boys?" another of the men cried, reaching out to touch her throat.

Sarah jerked away as if she'd been burned. Taking a deep breath, she tried

181

to speak calmly. "My name is Sarah Craighead. Some of you may know my uncle, Jonathan McKay. Seneca burned our cabin and took my little brother away. I don't know where my parents are. Joshua Stone is taking me back east to Stones' Crossing. He and my uncle thought I'd be safer from the Indians if I appeared to be one of them."

"She tell da truth," one of the men who hadn't spoken previously said, stepping forward for a closer look at Sarah.

"Don't I know you?" she asked, aware that something about the way the man spoke seemed familiar.

"*Ja,*" he said. "You vonce stay many days at der Stegmans'."

"I had a fever and you took us in," Sarah said, recalling those hard first days in the wilderness. "I was just a child then."

"And she's still acting like one," Joshua said.

"I am not!" Sarah turned to glare at Joshua, who did not look at her.

"Sorry, Mr. Stone," the man who seemed to be the leader said as he extended his right hand to Joshua. "I'm Fischer Brown. We're all still pretty spooked by some of the tricks the Indians have pulled lately. It wouldn't be the first time they used a squaw to get into a fortified house—and what the heathen did then ain't fit to tell."

"I can imagine," Joshua said. "We must have seen five or six war parties since we left the Monongahela."

Fischer Brown nodded. "We want to hear about it, but we'd best get back inside."

The gates opened to admit the party. Their horses were taken away to be cared for, and Joshua and Sarah were led to the two-story cabin, the largest in the enclosure.

Sarah stopped in the doorway and gazed at the roomful of people, mostly women and children. A child laughed, and Sarah's heart stopped as a little boy toddled across the floor, chased by a slightly older girl.

Adam! she thought, but the hope was short-lived as the child turned his head toward her, and she saw that his dark brown eyes and straight nose were a far cry from her fair brother's features. He was the first white child she had seen in many weeks, and the sight wrenched her heart.

"Folks, these here are Joshua Stone, one of Colonel Burd's boys, and Mistress Sarah Craighead. They're headin' back east," Fischer Brown said.

Sarah's first thought as she looked around the cabin was that it had been a long time since she'd seen several dozen white people in the same place at the same time. Her second thought was that she had never been stared at so thoroughly, not even by the Seneca.

A stout, pink-cheeked woman stepped forward and spoke directly to

Sarah. "I'm Catherine Brown, and this is our place. Most of these other folks live around here—you can sort them all out later. Right now, the both of you look like you could use a hot meal."

"Yes, thank you, Ma'am. That would be nice," Sarah said.

A tall, spare woman gasped and covered her mouth with her hand. "I never saw an Indian that could speak English like that," she said.

Catherine Brown turned to the speaker and shook her head. "For heaven's sakes, Tillie, didn't you hear a word my man said? This girl is no more Indian than you are, despite the garb she's a-wearin'."

"Mebbe not," the woman muttered, "but I can't forget that it was a squaw like that who killed my boys. 'Tis a strange way to be traipsin' about the wilderness with things like they are."

"Well, it sounds like a good idea to me," one of the younger women said, flashing a timid smile at Sarah. "I'd like to know how you got your skin so dark."

"Time enough for that later," Catherine Brown interrupted, then turned to Sarah and Joshua, who still stood just inside the doorway. "Come on in. Sit yourselves down at that yonder trestle table and take a trencher of stew. If I do say so myself, today's mess turned out right good."

The others parted and allowed Joshua and Sarah to walk to a long table that had been set up before a large fireplace. Seeing the stew pot on the hearth and the familiar fieldstone chimney, Sarah felt an almost physical longing to be back with her parents in the cabin where they had lived in peace for so many months.

"It's nice to see a fire in a chimney again," Sarah remarked to Joshua.

He scowled. "You're lucky you lived long enough to see it."

Joshua looked so much like a pouting child that Sarah had to stifle a smile. "I don't know what you have to be so mad about," she said. "If I hadn't let them see I was white, we'd still be on the outside."

"There were safer ways to do it," he began, then stopped talking when Catherine Brown set a steaming trencher before him.

"Here's a scrap of pan bread to sop with," she said, drawing a coarse, crumbling loaf from the ample pocket of her apron. Then she turned and gestured to a towheaded boy who had been silently staring at Sarah. "Silas, go fetch the folks some water."

"I'm not sure I'm that thirsty," Sarah remarked when the boy returned bearing a wooden bucket almost as big as he was.

"I ought to pour it on you," Joshua muttered.

"Pour it on your own head," Sarah returned tartly. "Maybe it'd clear your thinking and make you sensible again."

"Sensible!" he exclaimed. "You're a great one to talk of being *sensible,* taking off like you did in the face of at least three flintlock muskets. You must know that a single musket can fire up to thirty shots and hit a target a long way off—and at close range, they're deadly."

"But they didn't fire. We're here and we're safe. I see no reason to talk about it anymore."

"I do," Joshua began, leaning closer to Sarah. Then one of the older women came up to Sarah and put a hand on her shoulder, and he drew back.

"So it is you, after all," the woman said softly. "It seems chust a day or two before that you come to our cabin, on fire vit fever."

Sarah rose from the bench and embraced Rosa Stegman. "It has been many years, though, Frau Stegman. And since then, many things have happened."

The woman nodded. "I vant to hear all about it, but sit you down und you und your young man, you finish the eating. Then ve talk."

"And so will we," Joshua said darkly when Rosa Stegman left them.

"I can wait," Sarah said, knowing her indifference to his anger only fueled it more, yet refusing to defer to him when she knew she was right.

Although no one else interrupted their meal, the moment that Sarah and Joshua finished eating, they were led into the center of a circle of settlers and invited to tell what they had seen on the trail since they left the Monongahela. The adults in the fortified house sat on the floor or on benches around the log walls. The children had been dispatched to the second floor, where from time to time their play became so noisy that the women had to call to them to be quiet. But when Joshua started telling what he had seen of the frontier, even the children stopped to listen.

"And so here we are," he concluded. "Now it's your turn," he said, looking at Fischer Brown. "What happened to bring you folks here?"

"Several things, none of them good. When the Stegmans got burned out after living on Indian Creek without any trouble for years, some of their neighbors decided to make for the nearest fortified house. They'd no more than gotten there than this squaw come by, sayin' her man was a trapper in trouble down the way. When some o' the men went out to help him, she come in and burned the place down."

"Are you sure about that?" Joshua asked.

Many heads nodded in assent. "No doubt she done it," Fischer Brown said. "Furthermore, some Shawnee was waitin' in ambush for the men that went out to help that trapper. The ones that got out alive rounded up their families, pretty well scattered when the house started burnin', and all made a beeline for here. That was nigh unto three weeks ago, and no one's tried to go back to their homes yet."

"What happened to the squaw?" Sarah asked.

Catherine Brown made a sound of disdain. "Nobody knows, but I'll guarantee she'd better never show her face around here again."

"That's not all," one of the men who had held a gun on Sarah said to Joshua. "You been gone awhile from the army, I reckon, or you'd a'heared about what happened at Duquesne."

"The last time I talked to Colonel Burd, he said the British officer in charge was planning to send a reconnaissance force to Fort Duquesne to measure the French strength."

"Aye, and the British tried to do that, but they lost a lot of men before they even got anywhere near to the fort. There's too many Indians spyin' for the French for anything the British do to go unnoticed."

Joshua looked worried. "I had no idea things were so bad," he said. "I knew there was unrest, of course—"

"Unrest!" Fischer Brown laughed shortly. "From Will's Creek west, there's not a settler that can lay his head down to rest of a night without wondering if he'll wake up with his scalp still on it the next day. Your Colonel Burd's men ought to be out here helpin' us right now—where are they?"

"I don't know," Joshua admitted. "The Pennsylvania Volunteers are a small group. Mostly we scout for the British Regulars who don't know the country at all."

"Protectin' settlers is more important," one of the other women said, speaking for the first time. "I wish you'd tell that to your colonel."

"That's so," another woman agreed, and soon the whole room was abuzz with a dozen different simultaneous conversations.

"I should have stayed with Colonel Burd," Joshua said, as much to himself as to Sarah. "It sounds like he needs all the scouts he can get."

"You couldn't have stopped the British soldiers from being turned back," Sarah said.

"Maybe not. But I'd certainly know better than to lead them into an ambush, which is what I imagine must have happened. The British have no experience with wilderness terrain. They make mistakes."

"Quiet!" Fischer Brown called, and abruptly the noisy groups of conversants broke apart. "Arguin' about what should've been done don't do us a bit o' good out here—and there's not a man among you that didn't know when you come this way that it'd be some dangerous. For now, it looks like we're goin' to be here awhile longer, and we'll need to talk about goin' out for supplies. Joshua Stone, you meet with us men in the next cabin whilst the womenfolk get the little ones down for the night."

Without another word to Sarah, Joshua followed Fischer Brown and the other men. She turned back from watching him leave and almost collided with a middle-aged woman.

"I'm Agnes Barber," she said. "Did I hear that your name was Craighead?"

"Yes, I'm Sarah Craighead. My father, Caleb, is a minister. Do you know him?"

The woman turned her soft, dark eyes away from Sarah as if she couldn't bear to look at her. "Not exactly. But just afore we left our cabin the first time, a man and woman stopped by and asked if we'd seen their children. They was lookin' for a grown girl with light brown hair and a towheaded boy just walkin' good. I'm almost sure they said their name was Craighead."

"It must have been my parents!" Sarah exclaimed. "How long ago was that?"

Agnes Barber shook her head and turned her sad eyes back to Sarah's. "Three, four weeks past—they said their cabin had been burned and they didn't know where their children were. After they rode on, my Sam said he thought the Indians had probably killed their children."

"Which way were they riding?" Sarah asked.

Mrs. Barber frowned as if trying to recall. "Northwest, I s'pose. The woman kept sayin' she knew her babies was alive, and the man said it was all in the Lord's hands. He preached for us afore they left."

"That sounds just like them both," Sarah said. Her initial elation that her parents hadn't been taken in the raid that had destroyed their cabin faded as Sarah realized that they might have been ambushed later.

Tears came into Agnes Barber's eyes. "It was the last time my Sam ever got to hear a prayer. The next day we went on to the fortified house and it wasn't hardly two days later before that squaw tricked the men into goin' outside—"

She stopped, too overcome to continue speaking, and Sarah put a comforting arm around the woman's shoulders.

"I am so sorry," she murmured. "Thank you for telling me about my parents."

Agnes nodded. "I must go now and see to my babies—please excuse me."

"How many children do you have?" Sarah asked.

"Three—girls six and five, and a boy that's just turned three. Your mother cried when she saw him."

"I think I saw him earlier tonight—he's a bonnie lad, and about the size of my brother," Sarah said. "Your children must be a great comfort to you."

"A comfort and a burden, too, poor fatherless mites that they are. But I pray that your parents will find you and your brother soon."

"Thank you," Sarah replied.

The woman walked away, her frail shoulders stooped as if the burden she carried was far too great, and Sarah felt great compassion for her. *No wonder the settlers were hesitant to let me in,* she thought. *That squaw, whoever she was, certainly caused a great deal of grief.*

"Sarah? Sarah Craighead?"

Sarah turned as a woman who had just entered the cabin spoke to her, but this time both the voice and the face were familiar. Abby was the sturdy wife of Ian McKnight, who had often sheltered the Craigheads before they'd settled on Preacher Creek. Her plain, round face beamed as she opened her arms and pressed Sarah to her ample bosom.

"Is it really you?" Sarah asked, returning Abby's hug.

"Aye, it is, and a sight for sore eyes ye are, too, Lass. Although I must confess that in that get-up, ye don't look much like the Sarah Craighead I always knew."

Sarah glanced down at her doeskin dress, so jarringly out of place amidst the long linsey-woolsey and ginghams of the women. "I was to have a new dress, and I'd planned to wear it to my next forting-up," Sarah said ruefully. "Now I'm dressed like the enemy you're all running away from."

"Aye, but it's kept ye safe so far," Abby said. "If only Ann Craighead could see ye, she'd not care what ye wore!"

"I'd like to see her, too," Sarah said. "Agnes Barber said my parents had come by their cabin after the troubles began, so I know they were all right then, at least."

Abby McKnight patted Sarah's arm. "And last week, as well," she said.

"Last week! You saw my parents last week? Where?" In her excitement, Sarah reached out and clutched Abby's arm.

"On the trail. We were heading east, and they were going west. We tried to persuade them to come along with us until things were a bit quieter, but they were determined to go on until they found you and Adam."

"Do they know how to get to this place?" Sarah asked.

Abby nodded. "Aye, and they did promise to come here if they saw that it was too dangerous to continue."

Thinking of the possible white captives Joshua had seen as they'd traveled that same trail only a short time ago, Sarah shivered. "They should have already been here by now, then," she said. "It can't get much worse out there than it already is."

"Och, Lass, but they are all right; I know it. Dinna the reverend always say that he'd let the Lord do his worryin' for him? Ye should do the same."

Sarah smiled faintly. "Aye, but now I think there's more than enough worry for all of us to have a wee bit."

"Well, here come the men back—and I'm sure they have a thing or two to say about what must be done."

Abby left to go to her husband's side, and Sarah waited impatiently for

Joshua. When at last he appeared, she went to him and motioned him outside.

"What happened?" he asked. "Did you just get a bag of gold?"

"Gold would be of less use to me than the news I've just heard," she said.

"And what news was that?"

"What I heard means that I must stay here," she said.

"I didn't plan to leave in the middle of the night," Joshua replied, obviously unmoved by Sarah's excitement.

"But now I don't want to leave at all," she said impatiently.

"I didn't think this place was all that impressive," Joshua said.

"Just listen to me," Sarah said impatiently. "Mother and Father have been seen twice by people staying here, the last time just a week ago."

"I suppose that is good news," Joshua said cautiously.

"Well, of course it is! But even better, there's a good chance they'll come back here soon."

Sarah couldn't see Joshua's face in the darkness, but she guessed that it wore the familiar look of exasperation she had been seeing since they were children. "Then perhaps you'll see them before we go on," he said.

"But don't you see? I can't leave now!" Sarah cried. "I'll stay here with the McKnights until my parents come back, and you'll be free to go on to Colonel Burd."

Joshua spread his hands on top of Sarah's shoulders and gripped them hard, as if he would much rather shake the nonsense out of her. He spoke deliberately, an edge of anger in his voice. "You can't stay on here and hope that your parents might happen by. They've probably already found another fortified house by now, but even if they did come here, the Browns will tell them where you went. I promised Jonathan to take you to the Crossin' and I intend to do it, whether you like it or not."

"But—" Sarah began.

"Hush!" he said sharply. "I'll get back to Colonel Burd soon enough, never fear. In the meantime, I expect you to behave yourself and do what I say. Is that clear?"

Sarah was glad that the darkness hid the tears that stung her eyes. Mostly they were for her parents and her brother's safety, but not entirely. Some were tears of anger and frustration for herself, that Joshua treated her as a wayward, backward child he reluctantly had to save from herself.

"Perfectly clear," she said stiffly.

His hands still rested on her shoulders, and deliberately Sarah wriggled free from his grasp and started back inside.

You may not get your way yet, Joshua Stone, she silently predicted. Sarah knew they'd have to stay at the fortified house at least for the next few days. She hoped that her parents would come there before they had to move on. But even if they didn't, Sarah knew that, despite his promise to her uncle, Joshua wanted nothing more than to be rid of her and go back to the Pennsylvania Volunteers.

Sarah sighed. She had only a few days to persuade him to do what she wanted—and to make him believe that doing so had been his own idea. It wouldn't be easy, but as she went back into the cabin where the women slept, Sarah was determined to try.

Chapter 10

At first the sound was so faint that Sarah wasn't sure she heard anything at all. She opened her eyes to find that some of the other women sleeping on the floor of the main cabin must have heard it, too, for some were already sitting up. They rubbed their eyes and whispered fearfully to one another.

"What's happening?" Sarah asked Agnes Barber, who had just come back inside. From the thin beam of silver that entered the cabin when the door opened to admit her, Sarah could tell that the moon still rode high in the sky; dawn was yet a long way off.

"The men are looking to their weapons," she whispered back. "We must bring the children downstairs now."

As quietly as they could, the women sorted out their children from the tangle of sleeping bodies in the second-story loft. Sarah went up to help fold the bedding and peered through one of the openings into the silent night, not expecting to be able to see anything. Yet on the brow of the same hill where she and Joshua had stood only hours ago, Sarah could make out what seemed to be many figures, moving quietly and deliberately toward them. They came on foot, not by horseback. Still, it would only be a matter of minutes before the intruders reached the Browns' fortified house.

Sarah wondered what would happen then, but she didn't dare answer her own question.

With a minimum of quiet conversation, the men climbed the second-story ladder and thrust their rifles through the slits in the walls that served as windows when the house was at peace. Sarah went back down to the first floor.

Suddenly wanting Joshua's reassuring presence, Sarah was on her way to look for him when he came into the cabin, carrying his rifle.

"I saw something on the hill yonder, heading this way," Sarah told him.

"I know. We're going to try to hold them off, but if they break through the barricade, it'll be every man for himself. We have to be ready to get away immediately. Can you saddle the horses and bring them to the back gate?"

Sarah nodded. "I think so, but I didn't know there was any other way out."

"I hope whoever's out there doesn't know it, either," Joshua said. "It's just a small gate the Browns use to let livestock pass through. It backs up to a hill with deep woods on all sides. The plan is for everyone to scatter into the forest in case we can't hold them off. If you see even one Indian come over this wall, you must ride out into the woods and hide."

"But how will we find each other?" Sarah called after Joshua, who had already started to go back outside.

Joshua stopped and turned to face her. "Do you recall the way your grandfather used to call for us when we'd gone too far from the crossin'?"

"He made a sound like a mourning dove," Sarah said. How long ago that whole life now seemed!

"That will be my signal, then. Promise you'll leave the second that things get out of hand here."

"Yes," Sarah managed to whisper.

"Mind what I told you, Sarah—your life may depend on it."

After Joshua hastened away, Sarah gathered her blanket roll and saddlebags, her sole earthly possessions. Looking around the confused scene inside the cabin, Sarah saw mothers settling their children by the interior walls, where they'd be safer from stray bullets and arrows. Sarah felt a pang that there was nothing she and Joshua could do to help them.

"Lord, care for us all," she murmured, realizing as she did so that it had been too long since she had really taken the time to pray. *I'll do better when we are out of this danger,* Sarah promised.

She slipped away without speaking to anyone, aware there was no time for farewells. Outside, the scene was hectic and confused. Men carrying rifles and powder went back and forth between the cabins and the barricade walls in eerie quietness. Sarah guessed that they hoped to surprise and repel the invading Indians before they got anywhere near the walls, but she also knew they hadn't much time to do so.

Sarah made her way around the men and hurried to the livestock area. She found their horses easily enough amid the oxen, milch cows, and squealing pigs, but it took her several precious minutes to locate the tack. Once she had found it, Sarah had the difficult task of lifting the heavy saddles and putting them on the backs of the restless horses in almost complete darkness. Finally she got Joshua's horse saddled, but before she could finish her own, the strange stillness was broken. The sound of war whoops and the sharp report of muskets firing into the night told Sarah that she was running out of time.

With trembling fingers, Sarah cinched her saddle girth and threw her blanket over it. Just as she led both horses around the side of the cabin, the first Indians appeared atop the barricade wall. Although they were picked off immediately, others soon took their places, and with alarm Sarah realized that there was no way the handful of settlers could hold out against such an overwhelming force. And, as she reached the rear gate, she also knew that it was just a matter of time until it, too, would be discovered by the marauders.

Where is Joshua? Sarah removed the rawhide loop holding the rear gate shut and hesitated, looking back in the vain hope that he would suddenly appear. Instead, the mingled screams and war whoops which now seemed to be coming from the cabin told her she had no more time to wait. Acting on a sudden impulse, Sarah stripped Joshua's saddlebags from his horse and added them to hers, then looped Joshua's horse's reins around one of the barricade poles. Mounting her own horse and praying that Joshua would soon join her, Sarah rode out alone into the night.

Although she couldn't see the invaders well enough to tell their tribe, their war cries echoing in her ears painfully reminded Sarah of the day the Seneca had burned her home and Tel-a-ka's village. She wondered what had happened to Tel-a-ka and Bel-a-ka, the best friends she'd known in the peaceful time on Preacher Creek. Did Tel-a-ka still raid against the French and the Seneca? Perhaps even now he and Bel-a-ka's new husband were seeking those who had led the raid on the village of the Clan of the Bow.

And what of her uncle and Sukey? From what she had seen so far on their trip east, Sarah feared that no part of the frontier was safe. Surely they must be in danger, as well—and she didn't want to think about what could have happened to her parents. As for Adam, Sarah had to believe that Tel-a-ka was right—that he was being treated well by his Seneca captors.

Sarah rode as far into the forest as she dared before she dismounted and walked into the protection of a sheltering grove of trees. She had come too far to hear any sounds from the fortified house, but she was still close enough to see flames flaring up.

They're burning the Browns' house, she realized numbly. In horror, Sarah watched the sky redden and prayed that the others had somehow managed to get away as she had.

The flames burned brightly for awhile, then gradually subsided. Pushed toward her by a light wind, the acrid odor of smoke filled Sarah's lungs and made her eyes water, until finally she turned away in anguish. She stood perfectly still, straining to hear the call of a mourning dove, but it did not come. And, she realized, it might never come.

Sarah imagined Joshua standing at his place on the barricade, firing away at the Indians, refusing to leave until it was too late, and her heart ached.

If something should happen to me, you must ride east, Joshua had told Sarah after their first encounter with a band of Indians.

She would do it if she had to, but for the time being, it was too soon for Sarah to admit that something had happened to Joshua. She tied her horse to a nearby sapling, then spread her blanket on the ground. She lay very still and stared, dry-eyed, into the star-spattered sky. With her eyes thus on the heavens, Sarah prayed for God to show her the right direction.

❧

"Sarah? Are you all right? Wake up!"

From what seemed to be a long way off, Sarah heard her name being called. Reluctantly she opened her eyes to find Joshua bending over her, his red hair a bright splotch of color against the gray of the early morning fog.

"I thought you were—" Sarah began, but she couldn't bring herself to say the words. She rose to a half-kneeling position and barely resisted the urge to throw her arms around Joshua. He had his faults—a great many of them, as a matter of fact—but Sarah certainly hadn't wanted to go on without him.

As if he feared that she might be about to embarrass him, Joshua stood and took a step away from her. For the first time, Sarah noticed the dark stains on his buckskin jacket and several cuts and bruises on his face and hands.

"What happened back there?" she asked.

Joshua turned his hat in his hands and sighed. "I think you know—you must have seen the fire from here."

Sarah thought of the women and children she'd left behind, and her throat constricted. "Did anyone else escape?"

To her relief, Joshua nodded. "Yes. Brown had dug a pretty big cellar under the main cabin. Most of the women and children got to it before the Indians broke through."

"And the men?"

Joshua's forehead creased, and he shook his head. "I don't know how many casualties there were. I helped Fischer Brown bury four or five men. Others were hurt, but we killed more of them than they did us."

"What tribe were they?"

Joshua shrugged. "I don't know—they could have been Delaware or Shawnee or Seneca, maybe Iroquois. But from the way they burned the place without botherin' to take anything first, I'm thinkin' it was a revenge raid."

"Revenge? For what?"

"Who knows? Whites sometimes kill Indians without much reason, especially in times like this when everyone's on edge. Get up—we need to move on."

Sarah stood and looked around, puzzled. "I left your horse at the rear gate like you told me to. Didn't you find it?"

He shook his head. "No—it was gone by the time I got there. Someone else no doubt made good use of it."

"You don't seem to be very worried," Sarah said, puzzled that Joshua would take the loss of his horse so lightly, considering the distance they still had to cover.

"There's no sense in cryin' over spilled milk, as my mother used to say. Besides, I've still got my scalp and, thanks to you, my saddlebags."

"You saw them, then," Sarah said. She wondered how long Joshua had been there before he'd awakened her. The thought that he had watched her sleeping was vaguely disturbing.

"Yes, and I also saw that we don't have much of Sukey's food left for the hike ahead of us."

"Hike?" Sarah repeated, as if she had never before heard the word. "We're going to *walk* to Stones' Crossing?"

Joshua seemed amused at her consternation. "Yes and no. Yes, we are going to walk—at least most of the time, although if you behave yourself, I'll let you ride some of the time. But we aren't going on to Stones' Crossing just now."

"Then where *are* we going?" Sarah felt suddenly light-headed, as if trying to keep up with what Joshua Stone might do next had begun to addle her senses.

"Here, let me have that," Joshua said. He took the blanket from Sarah and folded it neatly before placing it across the gray mare's back. "With things like they are, it's not safe to travel at all. We're going to a real fort, not just a fortified house."

"I didn't know there was a fort in these parts," Sarah said.

"There isn't. Fort Bedford isn't exactly in these parts, but it's the closest. I figure it might take us two days to get there, providin' the weather holds and the Indians leave us alone."

"Then what will happen?" Sarah asked.

Joshua shrugged. "We'll see when we get there, which we never will if we keep standin' around here. Let's go."

They walked into the morning sun until they came to a small creek, where Joshua stopped and told Sarah to mount the horse.

"It'll keep your feet dry," he said in response to her questioning look.

For some time he led the gray mare through the shallow, rocky stream, and Sarah guessed he wanted to be sure they couldn't be tracked.

"Do you think the Indians who raided the fortified house are still in the neighborhood?" she asked.

Joshua did not turn back to look at her. "They may be. I hope you've still got your knife."

Sarah touched her waist, where the knife rested securely in her belt. Her fingertips brushed the cool metal and sent a shiver through her body. "Yes, it's right here. I'd rather not use it, though," she added.

"If you can just manage to keep quiet and do what I say, you shouldn't have to."

"*Yes, Father,*" Sarah wanted to say, but she managed to hold her tongue.

If Joshua insisted on playing the adult and casting her in the role of a child, she'd let him, no matter how it rankled. But she didn't intend to put up with his arrogance and condescension a moment longer than was absolutely necessary. Once they were out of danger, Sarah intended to put Joshua Stone in his place. The mere anticipation of it gave her something to look forward to as they traveled on.

Joshua kept his rifle at the ready and often reconnoitered ahead, making Sarah wait while he climbed to the top of a hill and surveyed the countryside before moving on. Only once did they encounter any Indians, and they proved to be friendly. The Shawnee warriors used Delaware and a strange version of English to tell Joshua that they were on their way west to Fort Ligonier, where they wanted to fight the French. The men looked at Sarah with ill-concealed curiosity, but she stood quietly apart from the parley and didn't look at them, and they went on without questioning whether she was truly Indian.

The weather was not quite as peaceful, however. After fair weather on the first day, in the afternoon of the second day the heavens opened, and a crashing thunderstorm sent Joshua and Sarah huddling against the protection of a rock outcropping as lightning flashed throughout the forest around them.

As a child, Sarah had never been afraid of storms, primarily because her father had explained to her that they were God's way of showing a tiny part of His majesty. "The God of glory thundereth. . .He maketh lightnings for the rain; He bringeth the wind out of his treasuries," her father had read from the Psalms.

"That was close!" Joshua exclaimed as the boom of thunder merged with a blinding explosion of light less than a hundred yards away.

Sarah felt the hair on her arms and head prickle. She drew her blanket closer around her shoulders and shivered.

"Do you smell something strange?" she asked.

Joshua lifted his head and sniffed the air. "That's the scent of lightnin', all right. Sometimes you smell it first and then hear it strike. 'Tis better to smell it after the stroke—that way, you know you're still alive."

Sensing that Joshua thought she was afraid, Sarah forced herself to smile. "God is putting on quite a show. I suppose He intends to remind us of His power."

"I was convinced of that a long time ago," Joshua declared. "He can let up anytime now."

Although Joshua had spoken lightly, Sarah felt that he was sincere. She was so totally convinced that no one could survive in the wilderness without God's help that it was always a shock when she encountered the occasional doubter.

" 'The fool hath said in his heart, There is no God,' " she said, her words almost lost in the roar of the storm.

"What?" Joshua asked, leaning closer.

"Nothing," Sarah replied.

Suddenly Joshua threw his head back and began to laugh.

"What is it? Have you taken leave of your senses?" she asked in the annoyed way of one who fails to see any humor in a situation.

Still convulsed by laughter, Joshua pointed in the direction of her chest. "Your hair—" he began but was laughing too hard to finish.

Sarah looked down at the dark streaks that now ran down from her braids and dripped into her lap. The hand that she touched to the top of her head came away covered with blue-tinted droplets.

"Sukey didn't tell me her dye would wash off," she said, setting Joshua off into another gale of laughter.

"There's nothing funny about it," Sarah said crossly.

"You should see yourself," he said when he could speak again. "If this rain keeps up much longer, every bit of Indian about you will be completely washed away."

Sarah rubbed at her forearm and saw the skin whiten underneath her fingers. It was quite unlikely that anyone would mistake her for an Indian now, she realized.

"You won't laugh so hard when the next Indians we meet see that I'm white," she said tartly. "I hope you'll have time to explain it to them before they take my scalp."

Joshua's laughing spell subsided to an occasional chuckle, then stopped. Gently he touched the top of Sarah's head.

"I'm sorry," he said, not sounding at all contrite. "But I've seen drowned kittens that looked better. At least their fur didn't change color."

"You're an awful person, Joshua Stone!" Sarah exclaimed. "You may take pleasure in drowning little kittens for sport, but I'll not be made fun of. Is that clear?"

Seeing the sparks that flew from Sarah's eyes, Joshua's expression sobered.

"I never said I drowned kittens. And I didn't mean to make fun of you. Friends?"

Sarah looked at Joshua through the curtain of rain between them and sighed. Reluctantly she extended her hand.

"Friends," she repeated. "But I warn you—"

"The storm's passed on," Joshua interrupted. He reached for her other hand and pulled her close to him, and suddenly she realized that he wasn't talking about the weather at all.

"I don't want to fight with you," Sarah said in a low voice.

"Then don't," Joshua said, his voice sounding strange.

An odd sensation washed over Sarah. She felt a fleeting dizziness as she looked into Joshua's unsmiling face. He moved closer, and she drew back.

Immediately Joshua dropped her hands and stood. "It's not much farther to the fort now—we should be there by dark. You can ride the rest of the way if you like."

Sarah pulled her blanket around her shoulders and shook her head. "No, thank you. I can walk."

"Suit yourself," Joshua replied, matching her tone.

Not wanting Joshua to see her staring at him, Sarah looked to the heavens. The western sky was rapidly clearing, but on this day no bow would form in the sky.

I really would like to have a sign, Sarah thought and wondered what Joshua would say if she told him so.

However, his expression seemed to indicate that he didn't want to talk, so in damp and bedraggled silence, they went on to Fort Bedford.

Chapter 11

Although Sarah had never seen an actual fort, she had some notion of how Fort Bedford would look. It would have a palisade and towers, perhaps a moat and a drawbridge, and from its topmost point, the red, white, and blue flag that marked His Majesty's outpost would proudly fly. With those images in her mind, Sarah was disappointed when they reached the edge of a clearing and sighted Fort Bedford. In reality, it proved to be an irregularly shaped wooden structure that didn't look much larger than the Browns' fortified house.

"Is that all there is to it?" she asked Joshua.

"Fort Bedford isn't the largest outpost on the frontier," Joshua admitted, "but it's well-run, and we'll certainly be safer there."

"How long will we have to stay?" Sarah asked, already dreading the prospect of more delay and close confinement.

"That depends on what I find out from Captain Hawkins. But it won't be as bad as you think," he added, correctly reading her expression. "Mrs. Hawkins is here with her husband, and she should be some company for you."

"If they let me in, that is," Sarah said ruefully. Although she hadn't been able to see herself, she knew her face and hair were streaked where the hard rain had worn away some of Sukey's coloring.

"Stay here," Joshua said when he judged they were just out of the range of any possible rifle fire. "I'll walk in and report to the duty guard. Watch the main gate. When I wave, you can ride in."

"I suppose they'd open fire if they saw me first," Sarah said.

"I hope not, but that story about the squaw that caused so many to be ambushed will be all over the frontier by now, and there's no need to take any chances. Just don't come any closer until I say so, all right?"

"Of course I won't. Last time was—different."

Joshua gave her his now-familiar look of exasperation. "Every day is different out here, Sarah. Since we never know what to expect, we have to be prepared for anything. Remember that."

"I don't need any more lectures," Sarah said stiffly. "Hurry up and get us inside that fort."

Joshua's grin irritated her even further. "Patience, my dear Miss Sarah!

All things in due time."

If I had anything to throw at him I would, Sarah thought as he walked away. Why did Joshua keep on treating her as if she didn't have good sense, when she had shown him time and time again that she could handle herself in a crisis?

As clearly as if her mother had spoken the words beside her, Sarah remembered her saying that men sometimes got strange notions and there was nothing a woman could do but to go along with them. Of course, Sarah's father had disputed the claim.

" 'Tis the woman who shilly-shallies and always changes her mind, Lass," he'd said.

"And the man who's too hardheaded to do so, even when he knows he's in the wrong!" her mother had replied, setting off a brief debate which Sarah had watched in amusement. Her parents had had disagreements, but they always settled them without rancor. Sarah knew that her parents cared enough for each other not to fight over who would have the last word.

Sarah sighed and shook herself as if trying to dismiss her parents' image. She found herself thinking of them often, thoughts that always made her feel the sadness of her loss.

When she looked back at the gate again, Sarah saw that Joshua stood before it, signaling to her. Quickly Sarah mounted and rode to join him.

"Things have changed a bit since I was here last," he told Sarah as she dismounted. "But Captain Hawkins is still in charge. We must report to him now."

Sarah and Joshua followed a guard through a narrow passageway and into a large courtyard thronged with uniformed British soldiers, a few Indians, a number of men dressed like Joshua, and several women and children.

"There are more civilians here than usual," Joshua remarked to the guard.

"Aye, that there are," the ruddy-faced man said, the burr in his voice betraying his Highland origins. He turned aside down another passageway and stopped to rap lightly at a door about halfway down the corridor. "Joshua Stone and a lady to see ye, Sir," he called out.

"Bid them to enter, Corporal," an obviously cultivated British voice called back, and Joshua and Sarah stepped inside the command room.

A tall, strongly built man in his early thirties sat at a plain table, where he had evidently been writing with his quill pen. When he rose and came forward to meet them, his blue eyes widened in astonishment, and he seemed to be having some trouble controlling the smile that twitched at the corners of his mouth.

"It is good to see you again, Sir," Joshua said, making a half-bow in his direction. "By your leave, may I present Miss Sarah Craighead? Sarah, this is the fort commandant, Lieutenant Walter Hawkins."

The officer bowed and murmured something that could have been an expression of pleasure, but he was trying so hard not to laugh that most of what he said was swallowed up in the effort.

"I know my appearance must be quite peculiar, Sir," Sarah said. "Go ahead and laugh if you like. I won't take offense."

Captain Hawkins smiled. "On the contrary, Miss Craighead. I was just thinking how happy I am that it is only your clothing that is Indian. Perhaps you have heard about the unpleasantness such a woman recently caused?"

"Yes, Sir, we both know the story," Joshua said for her. "She's dressed like this because her uncle, Jonathan McKay—I believe you know him—thought she'd be safer on her way back east. We didn't know how rough things had come to be when we left the Monongahela."

Captain Hawkins nodded. "I always enjoy the hunter McKay's visits, but it has been some months since I last saw him. But as for Mistress Craighead's being safer in Indian dress, I must say I have my doubts."

"I had nothing else to wear, anyway," Sarah said. "Some Seneca burned our cabin and took me captive with only the clothes on my back. The Delaware woman who is my uncle's wife gave me some of her clothes and tried to make me look like an Indian."

"It worked well enough until we were caught in a heavy rainstorm this afternoon," Joshua said.

"Perhaps so, but there is no reason for you to continue it here," Captain Hawkins said, never taking his eyes from Sarah. "You look to be about my wife's size—you should be able to outfit yourself with her things quite well."

"Oh, no, Sir, I couldn't presume to do that," Sarah protested. "She might object."

The corners of the captain's mouth tightened, but otherwise he showed no emotion. "My wife died some three months ago. Actually, I should like to dispose of her effects. They are an unwelcome reminder that presently do no one any good."

"I didn't know, Sir—please accept our condolences," Joshua said, breaking an awkward silence.

"Yes, well, I'm afraid Betty was never suited for garrison life. I had already made plans to send her back to Philadelphia when she took ill." He paused for a moment, then squared his shoulders and turned to Sarah. "Mr. Stone and I must confer. While we do so, outfit yourself from my wife's trunk. It would please her to know that someone enjoyed her things."

"That is very kind of you, Sir—" Sarah began, but Captain Hawkins's gesture of impatience silenced her. Opening his office door, he summoned the corporal who had led them there.

"Show this young lady to my quarters and see that she has what she requires," Captain Hawkins said. "Miss Craighead, I trust that you and Mr. Stone will dine with me this evening."

Sarah nodded and murmured her thanks before following the Scot down yet another passageway to another, much smaller room.

The fort commandant certainly doesn't live in luxury here, was Sarah's first thought. Her second was that the room was totally lacking any evidence that a woman had lived there.

"Will ye be wantin' some washin' water?" the corporal asked, and Sarah nodded.

"Please, and some soap, too."

"Yes, Ma'am. I'll see what I can find."

While she waited for him to return, Sarah looked around the captain's room. There was but one window, a rough opening covered over with heavy oiled paper that admitted a little light but no air. A square wooden trunk that she presumed had been his wife's stood under the window. Sarah went to the trunk and lifted its lid.

Immediately, a familiar fragrance filled the air, and she leaned over to savor it. Lavender—her mother had grown it at Stones' Crossing but never had cuttings to start at Preacher Creek. Feeling like an intruder, Sarah moved the sachet bundle aside and reached into the trunk. The topmost garment was a plain day gown, made of some kind of patterned cloth that Sarah had rarely seen. *Calico,* she thought. It had a set-in waist, rather than falling straight from the shoulders. She'd never worn a dress with a fitted waist, and she wondered what it would look like on her.

A knock sounded at the door, and almost guiltily Sarah lowered the trunk lid and opened the door.

"Here's water—and a bit o' soft soap. Ye'll find bath linens in the press yonder. Is there aught else ye need?"

"No, and much thanks."

The corporal poured some of the water into a bowl on the bedside table and put an egg-sized lump of soap beside it. "I'll be back to fetch ye to supper at retreat."

Sarah went back to the trunk and found a shift and petticoat. Quickly she removed her doeskin dress, which had stiffened as it dried, and vigorously scrubbed her forearm. After she'd rinsed it and wiped it dry, Sarah saw that most of the walnut stain was gone, leaving her skin glowing pinkly. She finished bathing and donned the unfamiliar undergarments, wishing that she had enough water to wash her hair.

At least I can undo the braids, she thought, and hastened to do so, separating the heavy strands as well as she could with her fingers. Then Sarah remembered having seen a silver-backed hairbrush in the trunk and rummaged around for it. She felt a moment of uneasiness when she noticed several light strands of its former owner's hair. But her hair needed care, and this brush was available. Not to use it would be foolish. As she worked the snarls from her hair, Sarah recalled Captain Hawkins's words.

It would please her to know that someone enjoyed her things. From the contents of the trunk, Betty Hawkins must have loved bright colors, and from the quality and number of the dresses she had owned, she must have been well-off, too.

The trunk held five dresses, so many that Sarah found it hard to decide which to wear that evening. The first one she'd seen was far more serviceable, but Sarah chose a slightly more elaborate gown of soft yellow linen, trimmed with a wide white collar. She slipped it over her head, relishing the unaccustomed softness of the material against her body. Although Sarah laced the bodice loosely, the dress revealed soft curves she had scarcely been aware were there. She wished for a looking glass, then chided herself for her vanity. Looking down, Sarah chuckled when she saw that the skirt fell several inches short of the floor, revealing her bare feet in all their glory. Vain or not, she'd wear the dainty kid slippers she'd seen in the trunk. They weren't practical, but they suited the dress far better than either moccasins or bare feet would.

As Sarah closed the lid of the trunk, she heard some sort of commotion outside. She thought that Fort Bedford had come under Indian attack and realized that she was poorly dressed for a fight.

Immediately, someone rapped at the door, and as he called to her, Sarah recognized the corporal's voice.

"Are ye ready to take supper now, Ma'am?"

"Yes," Sarah called back. "Come in."

The corporal opened the door, then stopped when he saw Sarah. His ruddy face paled. "Oh, my," he said, barely audibly.

"What is it?" Sarah asked, then as he continued to stare at her, she realized that seeing her in Mrs. Hawkins's clothing must have upset him.

"I'm sorry, Ma'am," the corporal said, recovering his composure. "Ye look so different—like it wasn't ye, but her ghost."

"The only ghost I believe in is the Holy Ghost," Sarah said quickly. "I hope my appearance won't upset Captain Hawkins—if I really look that much like her, perhaps I shouldn't wear his wife's dress at all."

"No, Ma'am," the corporal reassured her. "Ye don't favor her at all, really. Miz Hawkins was fairer and some shorter; and anyhow, I'm ordered to take ye to the lieutenant straightway. There's no time for ye to change."

Sarah sighed. "I hope you're right."

Once more she followed the corporal, this time to a room near the commander's office. It was furnished with two plank tables and benches, a few chairs, and a sideboard bearing a joint of meat and several other platters of food.

"Ah, there you are, Miss Craighead," Captain Hawkins said as Sarah entered. "Pray enter and be seated. Mr. Stone will join us presently."

Sarah watched the captain closely but saw no sign that her clothing upset him. He looked at her with more interest than concern, and if he thought she looked like his dead wife, it didn't seem to bother her.

"Thank you, Sir," Sarah said as he offered her a chair at the end of the table.

"I see that I was right—you are a bit taller, but Betty's dress fits you well."

"She had many beautiful things," Sarah said.

The captain nodded. "Yes, I fear that was her weakness. I do hope you will take whatever you want with you, Miss Craighead."

"Your offer is most kind," Sarah said, trying to match the commander's easy elegance and feeling she only sounded stilted. "However, we have only one horse. We can't carry anything we don't absolutely need."

"Yes, I know. However, I have promised to provide Mr. Stone with a horse in return for a favor."

"Oh? And what is that?"

"My line of communication with Colonel Burd has been disturbed lately. Having been his scout, Mr. Stone knows how to find him. He has agreed to take vital intelligence to his outpost."

Sarah felt a twinge of alarm. "How long will Joshua be gone?"

"Ask him yourself—here he is," the captain said.

"Ask me what?" Joshua said.

Sarah half-turned. In a clean linen shirt, with his unruly red hair combed into place, Joshua Stone made a handsome and imposing appearance.

"Captain Hawkins says you're to take a message to Colonel Burd. I wondered how long you'd be away."

As Sarah spoke, Joshua's eyes widened and his jaw dropped in astonishment.

"Is that really you, Sarah?" he asked, his tone so incredulous that even Captain Hawkins smiled.

"Of course it is," she replied with some asperity. "Who else did you expect it to be?"

"With your hair down like that—and the dress—" Joshua stammered. "You certainly don't look like a squaw now."

Sarah touched her hair, which fell in waves halfway down her back. "I didn't have enough water to wash my hair—I imagine it must look very odd."

"Well, being two colors, it does look something like a skunk's," Joshua said, recovering from his initial shock.

Captain Hawkins raised an eyebrow and smiled at Sarah. "You may wash your hair whenever you like, Miss Craighead. Fort Bedford has an excellent water supply."

"Thank you, Sir." She turned back to Joshua, who still stood to her right. "I asked how long you'll be gone on your errand," she reminded him.

Joshua shrugged. "It's hard to say—a few days, at the most."

"Don't look so alarmed, Miss Craighead," Captain Hawkins said. "Mr. Stone knows what he's doing. He'll be back in time to take you wherever it is you want to go."

"Where my uncle wants me to go, you mean," Sarah corrected, looking at Joshua.

Puzzled by their conversation, Captain Hawkins shrugged. "At any rate, you were invited to dine with me tonight, and that we shall do. Be seated, Mr. Stone. The corporal will serve us."

Throughout the meal, as Joshua and Captain Hawkins discussed the perfidy of the French and the fate of mutual acquaintances, Joshua kept glancing at Sarah as if he'd never seen her before. Something in the way he looked at her brought color to Sarah's cheeks and made her feel awkward.

At length the meal concluded, and Captain Hawkins rose from the table.

"Please excuse me now, Miss Craighead. I would prefer to stay and enjoy the pleasure of your company, but I must prepare my dispatch to Colonel Burd, since Mr. Stone will be leaving at dawn. The corporal will show you where the women sleep. I must apologize that I have no better quarters to offer, but with the refugees that have poured in lately, the fort is a bit crowded."

"Not at all," Sarah returned. "You have been more than kind already."

"You don't need to call the corporal, Sir. I'll see Sarah to the women's quarters," Joshua said.

Captain Hawkins almost scowled. "See that you do just that, Mr. Stone. Good night, Miss Craighead."

Sarah's cheeks felt warm as Joshua took her hand and helped her from the table with an unaccustomed show of manners. In other times she would have commented on it, but tonight something about the strange way Joshua looked at her kept Sarah silent.

They walked down one dim corridor, then turned into another. Joshua stopped and pointed toward a door behind which a number of feminine voices seemed to be engaged in animated conversation. "The women stay in there," he said unnecessarily.

Sarah started toward the door, but Joshua's hand on her arm stopped her. "Wait," he said.

It was too dark for Sarah to see the expression in Joshua's eyes, but there was no mistaking the seriousness in his voice.

"What is it?"

"I'm sorry I have to leave you, Sarah."

Joshua took a half step toward her. Sarah's heart hammered against her yellow bodice, and she swallowed hard.

"I understand," she said faintly. "Be careful. If anything should happen to you—"

He moved still closer, and Sarah trembled as he put his hands on her upper arms.

"Don't worry. I'll be back in a few days."

Sarah nodded, dangerously near to tears. Tentatively, she put her hand to the side of his face.

"Promise?" she whispered.

Joshua drew Sarah into a gentle embrace. They stood, quiet and unmoving, with her head resting on his shoulder for a long moment. Aware of the slow, steady rhythm of Joshua's heartbeat, Sarah wondered if he could feel the rapid fluttering of hers.

Then Joshua moved away from her, just far enough for his lips to seek hers for a long, sweet kiss. Sarah's arms tightened around his neck, and she clung to him, accepting and then returning his kiss. Finally Joshua pulled away, leaving her dizzy and shaken.

"Promise," he said, and then he was gone.

Chapter 12

Promise? . . . Promise.

The words echoed and reechoed in Sarah's ears for hours after every other woman in Fort Bedford had found sleep.

Sarah touched her fingertips to her lips and shivered. Joshua had kissed her, and she had allowed him to. Not only that, she had kissed him back. And what was worse, she'd enjoyed every second of it. But—

Sarah sighed and turned over, trying not to think of the image of herself in Joshua's arms. She had to forget it, to pretend that it had never happened, as Joshua surely would.

What had made him kiss her? *Maybe it was the shock of seeing me in a real dress,* Sarah told herself. Maybe that was why Joshua had looked at her like that, why he had wanted to hold her in his arms. When he saw her in the cold light of day, wearing her Indian disguise and with her hair in braids again, everything would be as it was before between them. Surely that would be better—and safer—for both of them.

Never before had Sarah felt so happy and confused and sad, all at the same time.

Oh, Joshua, what has happened to us? she cried silently.

As if in rude reply, a rather large woman sleeping on the floor near Sarah began to snore, softly at first and then with increasing volume.

"Turn her over," someone mumbled sleepily. Stifling her sudden laughter, Sarah managed to do so, although with considerable difficulty.

Then she returned to her blanket and finally slept.

When Sarah awoke, most of the women were up and stirring about, and Joshua had been gone for some time.

It's just as well, she told herself. Now that it was morning, Sarah could almost believe that she'd merely dreamed that Joshua had kissed her. And even if he had, it may have meant nothing.

To occupy her time, Sarah helped nurse some of the sick and injured women and children and entertained the older children, who were growing increasingly restless in the confines of the fort. Later in the day, Captain Hawkins sought her out and urged her to take three of his wife's dresses, another pair of slippers, and her set of tortoiseshell hair combs.

"I want you to have them," he repeated at her protestations, and not knowing what else to do, Sarah had folded two of the dresses, including the yellow one, away in her saddlebags. She wore the morning gown, the plainest of the dresses, around the fort and washed her doeskin shift and worked it with her fingers until it was soft and supple. It would be more practical for travel, regardless of whether she adopted an Indian disguise again.

Sarah had been surprised to see so many Indians living in and around the fort, but Captain Hawkins explained that they were friendly to the British and therefore were tolerated. A few were Delaware, but Sarah's inquiries revealed that none came from the Clan of the Bow or the Clan of the Serpent.

Late that afternoon, as Sarah sat in the courtyard drying her hair in the sun, another party of Indians entered. She looked up to see one of them staring at her, and then realized that his face also seemed familiar.

"An-we-ga!" she exclaimed, rising to meet him. *"Ili kleheleche!"*

He frowned as if trying to place her.

"I am Sa-la, friend of Bel-a-ka and Tel-a-ka at Preacher Creek," Sarah said slowly. "Tel-a-ka helped take me from Seneca."

An-we-ga scowled. "Seneca! Seneca burn Bel-a-ka village, no good."

"Is Bel-a-ka all right?"

An-we-ga nodded. "Bel-a-ka now An-we-ga squaw," he said, pointing to his chest. "Bel-a-ka and Old Woman live with my people."

"Good. But what about Tel-a-ka? Is Tel-a-ka all right?"

"No see Tel-a-ka."

"He went from the Monongahela to help his People of the Bow," Sarah said.

An-we-ga shook his head. "No, Sa-la. Tel-a-ka not come back. Bel-a-ka sad, Old Woman sad."

Sarah frowned, disturbed by An-we-ga's report. If Tel-a-ka hadn't gotten back to the Clan of the Bow, then something must have happened to him. "I am happy that Bel-a-ka and Old Woman are well," she said. "Tel-a-ka says Seneca have Adam—my *nimat*. Do you know of this?"

An-we-ga repeated her gesture and shook his head. "*Matta*, Sa-la. We go fight Seneca now."

They were joined by Captain Hawkins, who had overheard at least part of their conversation and now asked An-we-ga why he had come there.

"We want powder, mighty chief of whites. We kill much French, much Seneca, take much scalp."

Captain Hawkins glanced at Sarah, then addressed An-we-ga.

"Yes, I am sure that you do. Come and let us discuss the matter."

"I don't think he understood you very well," Sarah said to the captain.

"We have an interpreter," he said, his tone making it clear that she must not interfere in his business. "I see that you found enough water to wash your hair," he added, lifting a damp strand. "Such a pretty shade of brown it is. What a pity to hide it under that dark stain."

Sarah's face reddened and she brushed her hair back with her hand.

"By your leave, Sir, I would like to use your interpreter to talk further with An-we-ga when you finish. He may know something concerning the whereabouts of my parents and brother."

Captain Hawkins nodded. "Very well, Miss Craighead. I'll send the corporal to fetch you directly."

As he and An-we-ga walked away, Sarah wished she hadn't had to ask Captain Hawkins for another favor. She feared that An-we-ga knew nothing about her parents, but she wanted to find out when he had last seen Tel-a-ka and if his people had known where he had gone when he'd rescued her from the Seneca. They deserved that much, at least.

Less than a half hour later, Sarah was brought to the fort's command room. There she found An-we-ga, Captain Hawkins, and the interpreter, a half-breed Delaware scout.

"What is it you wish to know of this man?" he asked, and for the next few minutes he patiently translated her questions and An-we-ga's answers.

When she had told An-we-ga how Tel-a-ka had come to her rescue and was certain she had learned all he had to tell, Sarah asked the scout to tell An-we-ga that she would be praying for them. Then she thanked him and Captain Hawkins and turned to go.

"Wait a moment, Miss Craighead," the captain said. "Corporal, you and the scout take this man to the magazine and see that he gets the standard issue of rifle and powder."

When they were alone, Captain Hawkins rose from his chair and stood beside Sarah, staring down at her with a strange expression.

"Miss Craighead, did I understand you to tell that savage that you were going to pray for him and his people?"

"Yes, Sir, I did. They were our neighbors on Preacher Creek, and his wife was my best friend."

Captain Hawkins shook his head. "Am I to presume that your father is some kind of Indian missionary, then?" he asked.

"No, Sir. The Clan of the Bow are as yet unconverted."

The captain crossed his arms over his chest and smiled faintly. "I wish you would not persist in calling me 'sir.' I still consider myself to be a fairly young man, although if I have to spend much more time in this forsaken place, I may begin to doubt it myself."

Sarah felt her face flush. "It is a mark of respect, Captain Hawkins. I meant no offense."

The captain leaned down and took Sarah's hand, which he pressed to his lips. Sarah had never in all her life had her hand kissed, and although she knew it was an acceptable custom in what her mother described as "society," it took all her willpower to keep from snatching her hand away from him.

"I am sure you didn't, Miss Craighead," he said, removing his lips from her hand but continuing to hold it. "And neither do I. But you have no idea how lonely I have been since my wife—" He broke off, and Sarah seized the opportunity to reclaim her hand.

"I must go now," she said, standing. "I do appreciate all that you have done for us, Sir, but—"

"Is it young Stone?" Captain Hawkins interrupted. "Oh, I noted the way he looks at you. But he's a mere boy with no future, Miss Craighead. On the other hand, I expect a colonelcy when this posting is over, maybe even duty back in England. I would enjoy showing you London—"

Sarah didn't wait to hear anymore. She turned and ran from the room and never stopped, even though he called after her, until she had reached the crowded, noisy haven of the women's sleeping room.

I'll stay here until Joshua comes back, she vowed. When the corporal sought her out later to tell her that the captain wished Sarah to dine with him, she told him she was unable to do so.

The corporal frowned. "Captain Hawkins won't like to hear it," he said.

"Perhaps, but that is what you must tell him."

After the corporal left, Sarah half-feared that the captain might come in person to ask her why she declined the pleasure of his company. To make herself less accessible, Sarah sought out Mary Trent, the large woman who snored and who, having lost her own children, had taken an interest in Sarah. The two prepared their evening meal in the courtyard. She'd stay with Mary until Joshua returned, Sarah decided, and try to avoid Captain Hawkins altogether.

Lord, bring Joshua safely back and send us on our way soon, Sarah prayed with special fervor that night. It couldn't happen too soon to suit her.

On her fourth day at Fort Bedford, Sarah awoke to a medley of sounds denoting a great deal of activity within the fort.

"What's happening?" she asked Mary Trent.

"The captain's taking a patrol out to chase some Injuns that fell upon a refugee train comin' from Fort Ligonier."

"Where's that?" Sarah asked, immediately fearing for Joshua's safety.

"Fort Ligonier's about a day and a half northwest o' here. It's some bigger than Bedford."

Sarah went to the door and watched the troop ride out together, led by a color guard bearing the guidon of the Royal Americans.

"I hope Captain Hawkins has left enough men here to defend us," Sarah said.

Mary Trent cast Sarah a sidewise glance. "In an attack, we all have to do our part. Can you fire a rifle?"

"Yes. I have an Indian knife, too."

Mary Trent threw her head back and laughed, her several double chins quivering. "I can jest see you a-scalpin' an Injun, Missy. Nay, you'd best trust a rifle, lest your knife be turned agin you an' you lose your own scalp."

"Do you really think we might be attacked?" Sarah asked anxiously.

Mary put a comforting hand on Sarah's shoulder. "No. Anyhow, your man will be back soon, and you'll be well out o' all this."

"I hope so," Sarah said, but she took little comfort in the woman's words. She didn't bother to correct Mary's impression that Joshua was her man, a notion everyone at the fort except Captain Hawkins seemed to share.

Joshua should have been back long before now, Sarah thought but did not say so aloud.

After supper, Sarah drew apart from the others and sought a quiet place. It was time, she realized, to do some serious praying.

That night as she tried to sleep, Sarah wondered what she would do if something happened to Joshua. If she'd had her way to begin with, Sarah wouldn't have been traveling with him in the first place; she would have gone back to Preacher Creek with her uncle. Perhaps by now he'd located her parents and maybe even gotten Adam back. But as it was, Sarah knew that if Joshua didn't return in a reasonable amount of time, she'd be forced to look for someone else going east. From what she'd seen on the way there, Sarah knew she couldn't travel alone. Mary Trent had mentioned that traders and scouts came by all the time—and the courier who'd brought the pouch from Philadelphia would probably go back there soon. Maybe he would let her ride with him.

In all thy ways acknowledge Him, and He shall direct thy paths, an inner voice reminded her. Sarah sighed and closed her eyes, quite willing for the moment to turn her problems over to a higher authority.

"Sarah! Where are you?"

The whispered words brought Sarah awake instantly.

"Over here," she called softly, her heart beating in anticipation. By now, Sarah knew Joshua's voice well enough to recognize it anywhere.

Mary Trent snorted as Joshua nearly tripped over her sleeping form in the near-total darkness.

"Hush up, there!" someone else called out sleepily. Sarah stood and groped toward the sound of Joshua's footsteps until their hands touched.

"You're back!" Sarah cried.

Joshua held her hands tightly. "I told you I always keep my promises," he said. "Let's get out of here."

Under the faint illumination of the stars, they made their way to a far corner of the courtyard beneath the fort's outer walls.

"I see that you've become a squaw again," Joshua said, pointing to Sarah's doeskin shift.

"Only at night."

They reached the wall and Joshua motioned for Sarah to sit down, then he joined her. "I couldn't wait to tell you the good news."

"Have you seen my parents?" Sarah asked.

"No, but I met a trapper who'd just come from the Fort Duquesne area. He saw a white boy about three years old with a group of Seneca camped across the river from the fort."

"Adam!" Sarah exclaimed, clasping her hands together in her excitement. "Is he all right?"

"Yes, as far as the trapper knows, he's fine. He thought the boy had probably been there for some time."

"I wish there was some way we could get that word to Uncle Jonathan," Sarah said.

Joshua shook his head. "That wouldn't help. The Seneca might kill Jonathan on sight—the man I talked to barely escaped with his scalp."

"Then how can we get him back?" Sarah's elation faded, leaving her more desolate than ever.

Joshua reached for Sarah's hand and squeezed it. "I've come up with a plan."

"What is it?"

"Colonel Burd has to take action against Fort Duquesne sooner or later. He's held back until he could build up his forces and get a supply line established from the east. But he can't wait forever. If I join his army—"

"You can't!" Sarah cried. "I won't let you leave me again!"

"Hear me out," Joshua said, a sharp note in his tone. "Fort Bedford's as safe as anyplace on the frontier right now. After we take Fort Duquesne, I'll find Adam and bring him back here, then we'll all go on to the crossing."

"If you're not scalped in the meantime," Sarah said tartly.

Joshua's look of exasperation returned. "Trust me—I don't intend to get scalped."

"All right, assuming you're right, how long would all this take?"

"I don't know," Joshua admitted. "Colonel Burd is awaitin' word from

Philadelphia that his supplies and reinforcements are on the way. After that, it shouldn't take very long at all."

"A courier from Philadelphia came a few days ago, but of course I have no idea of his business. Captain Hawkins wasn't here to receive him—he left the day after you did."

"Oh? For what reason?" Joshua asked.

"Something about a party of settlers that had been ambushed between here and Ligonier. I thought maybe you knew about it."

Joshua shook his head. "I went northwest—I had no reason to stop at Ligonier. In any case, Captain Hawkins will probably be back soon. Will you agree to stay here awhile longer?"

Sarah leaned back against the wall, her head reeling as she considered her answer. She wanted to get Adam back as soon as possible, of course; but that was the only part of Joshua's plan that appealed to her, and it was too vague and uncertain. In no way did she want to be left at Fort Bedford at the mercy of Captain Hawkins's protection.

Sarah leaned toward Joshua and spoke earnestly. "I'd rather go on to Stones' Crossing. You told Uncle Jonathan you'd take me there, and you're still bound by that promise. Then you can still join Colonel Burd and find Adam."

"I can't believe my ears," Joshua said, obviously surprised. "I thought you'd want me to go after Adam."

"I do! But not like this. How soon can we go on to the crossing?"

"That depends in part on when Captain Hawkins gets back. I can't leave until I give him Colonel Burd's messages."

Sarah stood and smoothed her shift. "Very well. I'm ready to go on anytime."

Joshua stood and looked intently at Sarah, searching her face in the dimness. "I don't understand what's happened to you," he began, but Sarah interrupted him.

"Nothing has happened," she said brusquely. "I'm glad you're back, and I'll be even happier to be on our way to the crossing again."

Joshua briefly brushed Sarah's cheek with the back of his hand. "You're definitely not the Sarah I started out with."

"You aren't the same Joshua, either."

They stood for a moment in silence, neither moving, the eyes of each questioning the other.

Finally Joshua spoke. "Friends?"

Sarah nodded, unsmiling. "Friends."

But as they walked in silence back inside the fort, Sarah's heart knew better.

Chapter 13

As Joshua had done the evening before, Captain Hawkins also returned to Fort Bedford in the middle of the night, but so quietly that Sarah didn't know that he was back until the next morning.

"I overheard one of the men sayin' they was ambushed and barely made it back wi' their scalps," Mary Trent told Sarah in a low voice as they worked together serving the children's breakfast.

"I suppose it's still dangerous out there," Sarah said.

Mary Trent laughed without humor. "I reckon you could say that, all right. Looks like you and your man may have to stay around here awhile longer."

"I certainly hope not," Sarah said.

Later that morning when she looked for Joshua, Sarah was told that he was conferring with Captain Hawkins. Sarah stationed herself where she could see the captain's door and waited impatiently until, almost an hour later, Joshua finally emerged. Behind him were Captain Hawkins and the Philadelphia courier. Not wanting the captain to see her, Sarah hastened to hide behind a pile of stores until the men were out of sight. It was another quarter hour before she saw Joshua again, and from the look on his face, Sarah knew that Captain Hawkins hadn't told him anything good.

"What's happening?" she asked.

"Several things," he replied. "Let's go where we can have some privacy," he added, noting the curious stares of the nearby women and children.

"In this fort? I don't think such a place exists," Sarah said.

"You just have to know where to look."

Joshua led Sarah to the area where the animals were quartered and pointed to a black horse with a white blaze. "Captain Hawkins said I could have the loan of that horse yonder," he said.

"Does that mean we'll be leaving?" Sarah asked.

"Almost. The courier will be ready to ride out at first light tomorrow. Because of the recent trouble and also to help bring back and protect the supplies, Captain Hawkins is sending a small patrol with him. He said I could travel with them."

"Then we can start back to the crossing tomorrow," Sarah said.

"Yes, but Captain Hawkins agrees that you'd be better off staying here until Colonel Burd has taken Fort Duquesne."

"I'm sure he did!" Sarah exclaimed, then bit her lip when she saw Joshua's expression.

"The captain seems to be quite taken with you," he said, his tone suggesting he found the idea astonishing. "He asked what my intentions were toward you."

"I don't believe it!" Sarah exclaimed. "What did you tell him?"

Joshua laughed. "What do you think I told him?"

Sarah looked at the ground and blushed. She wasn't really sure she wanted to hear what Joshua had told the captain. "To attend to his own business, I hope," she said.

"Not quite." Joshua's smile faded. "Actually, I think Captain Hawkins is concerned for your safety. His patrol came across what had been a party of sick and wounded people traveling under escort from Fort Ligonier. All thirty had been scalped."

Sarah shuddered. "Did the Seneca do it?" she asked.

Joshua shrugged. "Who knows? Captain Hawkins thinks it was the work of a scattered band of renegades, not a concentrated drive sponsored by the French. At any rate, there's still danger out there."

"But with a group of soldiers to escort us—" Sarah began.

"There were soldiers with those people, too," Joshua said. He took both of Sarah's hands in his and looked into her eyes. "Jonathan will understand if I don't take you to the crossin' right away. He wouldn't want me to put you in unnecessary danger."

Sarah squared her shoulders and looked back at him. "I'm not afraid. I want to go there now."

Joshua sighed. "I hope you're right. But if we get into any trouble—"

"You can say 'I told you so,'" Sarah said, trying to end their conversation on a light note and not quite succeeding.

"If I'm still around to talk afterwards, that is. All right, Sarah, ready yourself to ride out tomorrow. I hope you know what you're doing."

As she thought he might do, Captain Hawkins sought Sarah out later that day and chastised her for her decision.

"It is rash and foolhardy of you to leave the relative safety of Fort Bedford," the captain told her.

Sarah stood her ground and looked him in the eye. "Do you know for a fact that this fort won't be attacked and overrun, Sir?"

"Of course not, but—"

"And can you tell me when it *will* be safe to travel in these parts?"

Captain Hawkins folded his arms across his chest and shook his head. "Are you really so eager to get away from me, Miss Craighead? I had hoped to get to know you much better."

Sarah felt her cheeks warm and stifled the imprudent reply she wanted to make. "Sir, I do appreciate your hospitality and all that you have done for us. But it's quite possible that my parents have already made their way to Stones' Crossing, and since that is where my uncle plans to contact me also, I must go on."

Captain Hawkins sighed. "Why is it that you females are so stubborn? A man would at least listen to reason."

Sarah nodded. "Perhaps so, Sir, but after a man listens to reason, he usually does whatever he wants to, anyway. I don't see much difference."

Captain Hawkins laughed, and Sarah was relieved that this time when he kissed her hand in farewell, the gesture seemed more friendly than romantic.

"Come back to Fort Bedford anytime, Miss Craighead, and if there is ever anything I can do for you, just say the word. If it is in my power to do so, I'll grant it."

"Thank you, Sir. I'll keep it in mind."

But as Captain Hawkins walked away, Sarah hoped she'd never have to ask him for another favor, even if their paths did somehow cross again.

❧

As planned, Joshua, Sarah, and the patrol left the next morning just as the sun came up over the horizon, rimming the lacy clouds with gold. Sarah wore her Indian dress for comfort, but this time she saw no reason to try to darken her skin and hair. The night before, Mary Trent had braided Sarah's hair in a new way one of the German women had taught her, pulling the hair so tightly to her head that Sarah almost felt that she was being scalped.

While it was still dark, Sarah crept from the room before any of the other women awoke, not wanting to say good-bye to them. She had hoped that Captain Hawkins wouldn't rise early enough to see them off, but just as Sarah prepared to mount her horse, he suddenly stepped forward to help her.

"Have a safe journey, Miss Craighead," he said. "Remember what I told you." Then he turned to Joshua. "Take care of that horse, Mr. Stone. I shall expect you to bring it back here within the week."

"Yes, Sir. Thank you for your help." Joshua put his hand to his brow in the semblance of a salute. Pennsylvania Volunteer scouts might not have official rank as such, but regular army officers still expected them to be respectful, if not subservient.

"Mind you, look lively," Captain Hawkins said to the sergeant in charge of the patrol. "The Glades Road seems to be fairly safe for the present. But mind that you post advance and rear guards at all times."

"Yes, Sir, Captain." The sergeant saluted, then turned in his saddle and motioned for the gates to be opened. In silence the small party rode out, crossed the clearing, and headed east on the narrow road that had been cut several years earlier between the British outposts. Only the jingle of the horses' tack and the muffled stress of their hoofs broke the silence of the summer morning.

Sarah glanced at Joshua, riding beside her, and wondered what he was thinking. The easy intimacy of the earlier part of their journey wouldn't be possible now, surrounded as they were by Captain Hawkins's men. And as soon as he had seen her to the crossing, Joshua would return to help Colonel Burd, so they would not have much more time together. Sarah already knew that she would miss him, but if Joshua regarded the prospect of parting from her with the same regret, he certainly hadn't shown it.

They continued riding in silence for several hours, the soldiers speaking in hushed voices and only when necessary. Although they constantly scanned the road and its environs, there were no signs that Indians might be stalking their trail or lying in wait over the next hill.

Dear Lord, let it be like this all the way to the crossing, Sarah prayed, and for a long while it seemed that would be the case. The army patrol traveled faster than she and Joshua had by themselves, and although she felt quite tired by the time they finally stopped to rest, Sarah was gratified that they seemed to be covering so much ground.

Joshua sat down beside Sarah and spoke to her for the first time since they'd left Fort Bedford. "What was that with Captain Hawkins all about?"

Sarah looked at him inquiringly. "All what?"

Joshua's jaw tightened. "You don't need to act like you don't know what I'm talkin' about, Sarah. Just what is it that the captain wants you to remember?"

Why, Joshua sounds almost jealous! Sarah thought. She found the notion pleasing, but she'd never let him know it.

Sarah shrugged and feigned indifference. "Oh, when Captain Hawkins came to say good-bye last night he said something about letting him know if I ever needed any help—just polite talk, really."

Joshua didn't look convinced. "Maybe it's just as well that we're away from there," he said.

"Why do you say that?"

"I heard some things about his wife—I don't think he was very good to her."

"I don't know what business that is of *ours*," Sarah said, stressing the last word.

Joshua gave Sarah an inquiring look, then shook his head. "I think you know very good and well, Sarah Craighead. But be that as it may, it's likely the captain may take pains to see you again. If that happens, I hope you won't let him turn your head."

Sarah's pleasure that Joshua might be jealous of Captain Hawkins quickly faded, replaced by annoyance that he was once more treating her like a girl in need of the guidance of an older, wiser man. "You worry about your own head and let me worry about mine, Mr. Stone," Sarah declared. She stood and went back to stand by her horse, her heart beating rapidly.

I shouldn't let him bother me, she tried to tell herself. But Sarah hadn't forgotten that Joshua had once kissed her and that she had returned his kiss with pleasure. Had that meant nothing at all to him?

Sarah sighed. From the way Joshua had behaved lately, he must regret having kissed her. In any case, he certainly didn't seem eager to repeat it.

When they resumed their journey, Sarah was almost glad that Joshua volunteered to ride as advance guard. But when he came back a short time later with the news that he'd spotted a small war party riding north, she wanted him back by her side again.

"Did they see you?" the sergeant asked.

"Of course not," Joshua replied, somewhat indignant that the sergeant could think he'd be so careless.

"In that case, we'd best stop here. Stone, you and Corporal Johnson watch them and report back when they've cleared the area."

"How far east do we have to go to be safe from these Indians?" Sarah asked the sergeant after the scouts left.

"I reckon you don't meet many Injuns in the middle of the Atlantic Ocean."

"Then even Stones' Crossing might not be safe," Sarah said.

"I wouldn't say that, Ma'am," the sergeant said quickly, seeing that his words had disturbed Sarah. "We're almost out o' the country that's had the most trouble—by noon tomorrow we should be able to breathe some easier."

The war party Joshua had seen went on its way, apparently not knowing or not caring that British soldiers were in the vicinity, and once more the patrol rode on. After only one other brief stop, they made camp on high ground before full darkness. Sarah took comfort in the knowledge that at least two soldiers would take turns guarding them throughout the night. However, Joshua's behavior still puzzled her. He seemed to be preoccupied and barely spoke to anyone. After spreading his blanket near hers, Joshua volunteered to take the first guard shift when darkness fell, leaving Sarah no opportunity to talk to him.

Physically tired but not sleepy, Sarah lay down with her eyes open. Seeing Joshua silhouetted against the rising moon, she prayed for his safety when he went back into danger, and that he would be able to find and return Adam to her. It was a big request, but Sarah had no doubt that God would carry it out, if it were in His will. Once when she was a child, Sarah had questioned why all her prayers weren't granted, and her father had cautioned her that she must not presume on the plans of the Almighty.

"God is omnipotent, Sarah—that means He is all powerful—He can do anything He chooses. But He's also omniscient—He knows everything, including what the consequences would be if we got certain things we might want enough to pray for. Ye must trust that His plans for ye are the right ones and will be carried out at the right time."

I wonder if Joshua Stone might be in God's plan for me, Sarah thought drowsily, but she fell asleep before it could be framed into a prayer.

Sarah awoke refreshed the next morning. As they started east again, she felt more optimistic than she had in many days. Yet by midmorning, as the party traveled over rough terrain and through a forest that could have hidden a hundred painted warriors as easily as one, Sarah remembered the massacred patrols and found herself growing increasingly edgy.

Something is going to happen. A feeling of nameless dread, mixed with vague anticipation, sent shivers down Sarah's spine, and she surveyed the bordering woods with new apprehension.

Noticing Sarah's restiveness, Joshua dropped back to ride beside her. "What's the matter?"

"I'm not sure. I just have a strange feeling that I can't shake off."

"Perhaps the sergeant should post more advance guards," Joshua said.

Sarah half-smiled. "Do you mean to tell me that you think I might be right?" she asked.

"Well, it's a slender chance, I admit; but to tell the truth, I've felt a little spooked myself lately. Anyway, it can't hurt anything."

Joshua rode ahead to confer with the sergeant, leaving Sarah alone in the rear of the column. She had just spurred her horse in an effort to catch up with him when she heard horses' hoofs coming from behind them, apparently closing the distance between them at a rapid pace.

"Do you hear that?" she asked when she reached Joshua and the sergeant. The sergeant jerked his mount to a halt and swiveled in his saddle to look behind them. "Sounds like one or two horses in a big hurry."

"Time to scatter into the woods," Joshua said. "Those red jackets make mighty temptin' targets."

Using hand signals, the sergeant motioned for his men to spread out, and in seconds they had done so.

"I'll ride back and take a look," Joshua said. "Get behind the biggest tree you can find," he added to Sarah.

"Don't go, Joshua!" she called out, but her words were swallowed up in the staccato beat of his horse's hoofs.

A force that she did not understand made Sarah ride after him. She had just reached Joshua's side when the hoofbeats that had been approaching them reached a crescendo, and a lone Indian topped the hill just in front of them.

He and Joshua raised their weapons at the same time, but in the split second before either could fire, Sarah lunged desperately at Joshua and knocked his rifle sideways. It discharged into the forest, its report reverberating like a hundred council drums calling braves to war.

"Are you trying to kill us all?" Joshua shouted.

Sarah's horse reared, startled by Sarah's sudden movement and the loud noise that had accompanied it, and she had to dig her hands into its mane to keep from being thrown off.

"Don't shoot again," she gasped. "It's Tel-a-ka."

"Tel-a-ka?" he repeated, as if trying to recall the name. "I can't fire at him now, anyway—he's gone."

As soon as she had her mount under control, Sarah looked into the forest and saw that Joshua wasn't entirely correct. Tel-a-ka had hidden himself behind screening vines, but his warrior's topknot was clearly visible.

"It's all right," Sarah called out. "You can come out now."

At first she heard nothing, then Sarah felt a cold chill throughout her body as a faint, high-pitched voice, one she had longed to hear many times in the weeks since they had been apart, called her name.

"Sa-wa! Sa-wa!"

Dumbfounded, Joshua looked at Sarah. "Can that be your brother?" he asked.

Beyond speech, Sarah could only nod.

At that moment the patrol, having heard the report of Joshua's rifle, approached, brandishing their weapons.

"Look over yonder—it's an Injun!" a soldier shouted. At the same moment, Joshua turned sharply and maneuvered his horse, placing himself between the patrol and Tel-a-ka.

"Don't fire! He's friendly."

For a fraction of a second, time seemed to stop, suspending everyone in the positions they had last assumed. Sarah sat motionless, frozen with horror that Joshua's warning had come too late, and that both he and Tel-a-ka would be shot before the sergeant understood the situation.

Then the sergeant shattered the silence. "Hold your fire!"

With no more forethought than the impulse which had made her follow Joshua, Sarah immediately rode toward Tel-a-ka, dimly aware but not concerned that a number of things seemed to be happening around her.

For the moment, all Sarah could see or think about was reaching the child who still called out her name.

Chapter 14

B y the time Sarah reached Tel-a-ka, he had dismounted and stood waiting for her, ready to place Adam in her outstretched arms. As Sarah took her brother, Tel-a-ka stepped aside, reluctant to intrude upon their reunion.

"Oh, Adam, thank God you're all right!" she exclaimed, holding him away to look at him, then clasping him tightly to her. He was clad only in a breechcloth and some sort of deerhide vest. He was dirty, his skin was covered with scratches and insect bites, and he had lost weight. But considering all he had been through, Sarah thought he seemed to be in good physical condition.

However, as Adam wound his arms around her neck and clung to her with continued sobbing, Sarah knew that it might be a long while before the child could forget his harrowing experience. Her tears briefly mingled with Adam's, then Sarah realized that she hadn't yet spoken to Tel-a-ka. Wiping her eyes with the back of her hand, Sarah turned to him.

"*Ju kella!*" she exclaimed with gratitude. "Thank you for Adam's life. How did you do this thing?"

Tel-a-ka looked deeply into Sarah's eyes, and in his own Sarah read far more emotion than she had ever before seen there. "I do for Sa-la," he said simply.

By this time, Sarah became aware that she and Adam and Tel-a-ka formed the center of attention of the soldiers, who stared at them in silent amazement.

Sarah gently pried Adam's arms from around her neck and turned his dirty, tear-streaked face toward the men. "This is my brother, Adam, who was taken by the Seneca some weeks ago. And this is Tel-a-ka, a warrior of the Lenni-Lenape, who has brought him to me. Tel-a-ka is my friend," she added somewhat unnecessarily.

His eyes suspiciously bright, Joshua came up beside them and put out a hand to Tel-a-ka, who hesitated briefly, then took it. "I want to hear how you got him away from the Seneca," he said.

"That can wait," Sarah said. "Adam's been through a terrible ordeal. I want him to get to Stones' Crossing as soon as possible." She turned back to face Tel-a-ka. "You must come with us. There is much to say."

"Yes," the sergeant echoed, nodding at Tel-a-ka. "Come along. My outfit can always use a good Injun scout."

Tel-a-ka shook his head. "No. I must stay with my people. For now, I go with Ad-am."

Unwilling to part with her brother again so soon, Sarah insisted on having him ride with her. Equally unwilling to let his charge out of his sight, Tel-a-ka rode along at Sarah's right. Joshua rode on her left, and as they traveled east, Adam fell asleep and Tel-a-ka haltingly began to tell how he had managed to rescue Adam.

With a few interruptions from Sarah and Joshua to clarify some of the details, Tel-a-ka said he had gone to the medicine lodge in An-we-ga's village to purify himself on returning from the Monongahela. There, after the usual period of fasting, Tel-a-ka had seen Adam in a vision. A voice told him he must go after Adam alone, unarmed, and tell no one. It had taken him many days to find the right Seneca camp, and then several more before he was able to go in and take Adam.

"You just walked into the Seneca camp and they let you have him?" Joshua asked, incredulous.

Tel-a-ka shook his head. "I make like Seneca with firewater." He swayed in the saddle and assumed a drunken expression. "Seneca not know Tel-a-ka, not know Tel-a-ka *netopalis* of Lenni-Lenape. I give old squaw with Ad-am firewater and sleep-weed. She sleep, I take Ad-am."

"How did you know where to bring him?" Sarah asked.

"I go back to Monongahela," Tel-a-ka said. "Sukeu-quawon say you go east. She mark trail for me with stick."

"It's a miracle that we met like this," Joshua said.

"The whole thing is a miracle," Sarah said. "God's hand has been in it from start to finish."

"*Michabou* make big medicine," Tel-a-ka said, using one of the many names that the Delaware called their supreme being.

"That is what you call it, Tel-a-ka. When we get to Stones' Crossing, we will speak more of this."

"You'll be wasting your breath, you know," Joshua said, too low for Tel-a-ka to make out the words. "If your father couldn't convert Tel-a-ka's people, I don't see why you think you can."

"Father never tried, for one thing." Then Sarah turned to Tel-a-ka and asked if he knew anything about her parents.

"No, Sa-la. I not go Preacher Creek. I hear nothing. I not see Bel-a-ka for much weeks."

"I know something about her," Sarah said and recounted her meeting with An-we-ga at Fort Bedford.

"So An-we-ga fights the French, too," she concluded.

Tel-a-ka frowned. "An-we-ga should go back to village now and make meat for winter," he said. "Women alone, not good."

"He had only a few warriors with him. He said Bel-a-ka and Old Woman are all right."

"It is good," Tel-a-ka said, and they rode on in companionable silence.

As the day wore on, Sarah began to recognize a few familiar landmarks. They passed a cabin where her father had once preached, then came to a broad meadow which she also remembered.

"Why are we stopping now? We're almost there," Sarah said when the sergeant called out the order to make camp.

" 'Tis still a bit farther than you think," Joshua told her. "There's no way we can get there before dark, and 'tis never a good idea to ride into a settlement at night, particularly when everyone's expectin' trouble."

Sarah smiled. "I can picture Grandfather coming at us with that ancient musket of his—heaven knows what would happen if he ever had to fire it."

Joshua chuckled. "Yes, but by now Grandmother may have taken it away from him, as she always threatened to do."

Tel-a-ka had been listening to their conversation and turned to Sarah with a puzzled look. "Josh-u-a is *nimat?*" he asked, gesturing from her to Joshua.

"No, Joshua's not my brother," Sarah said, suppressing a smile. "His grandmother and my grandfather are married to each other now."

"What happen his grand-father? Your grand-mother?"

"They both died many moons ago," Sarah said.

"Ahh," Tel-a-ka said, apparently understanding.

"Let's stop here and I'll tie the horses to those trees yonder," Joshua suggested.

Sarah halted her horse and handed a still-drowsy Adam down to Tel-a-ka's waiting arms. Joshua led their horses away, leaving them alone.

"I'm afraid Adam won't sleep at all tonight," Sarah said as she spread her blanket on the ground.

"He sleep. He much tired," Tel-a-ka said knowingly.

"Let's get a look at you, little brother," Sarah said, motioning for Tel-a-ka to put Adam on the blanket. "You're dirty enough—the Seneca must not believe in washing."

"Tel-a-ka make Ad-am dirty. Make him look Indian."

In spite of his serious expression, Sarah laughed. "What about Adam's hair? It still looks pretty light to me."

"Rain wash mud off," Tel-a-ka said matter-of-factly. "He look Indian to get by Seneca."

"Oh, Tel-a-ka, I don't mean to make fun. You did well to bring him to me, and I thank you, truly, I do." Sarah scrambled to her feet and hugged him impulsively.

Tel-a-ka might not have understood every word that Sarah said, but when she put her arms around him, he seemed to be having a hard time maintaining his usual passive expression. Tel-a-ka gripped her upper arms, then backed away. "I go find water," he said and left.

"Indians can be a strange lot," Joshua said when he returned. "I've never known one to do so much for a white. That Tel-a-ka must be countin' on gettin' some kind of big reward."

"Tel-a-ka didn't do this for a reward—I told you that his people were our friends. He's always been fond of Adam, too."

"Maybe, but I don't think he did this for Adam," Joshua said.

"Anyway, I have my brother back, and that's all that matters."

Sarah knelt beside Adam and moved aside the deerskin vest that covered his chest.

"Hurt, Sa-wa!" Adam cried. At the same moment Sarah gasped, seeing the jagged wound across his chest.

"I'm sorry, Adam," she said, trying to steady her voice. "I see the hurt place. How did you get it?"

"Cut, Sa-wa—man hurt A-dam," he said, then began to cry again.

"How could they do such a thing to a child!" Sarah exclaimed angrily.

"They make Ad-am Seneca *nimat*," Tel-a-ka said, joining them. He knelt beside Sarah and offered her the water jug.

"Cutting is a strange way to make a brother," Sarah said.

"Tel-a-ka's right," Joshua said. "I've seen such marks on Indian captives before." He bent closer and traced the wavy outline with his fingers.

"Lightning," Tel-a-ka said, his finger tracing a jagged line in the air. "Sign of Seneca clan."

"The flesh is unhealthy and must be cleansed," Sarah said. "I can do nothing to help him until we get to the crossing. Why can't we press on there tonight? There's still quite a bit of daylight left."

Joshua laid his hand on the boy's brow and touched each of his cheeks in turn. "He may have a bit of a fever, but surely a few more hours will not make that much difference."

"He's definitely ill," Sarah said, pouring water into her hand and wiping Adam's face with it. The boy twisted and groaned under her touch. "That's why he's been so drowsy. We must go on to the crossing tonight." Sarah turned to Tel-a-ka. "Will you ride with me?" she asked.

"That would be foolish," Joshua said, also addressing Tel-a-ka. "We can leave at first light and be there soon. It's not safe to ride at night through strange country."

"It's not strange country to us," Sarah reminded Joshua. "The moon is almost full tonight, and as I recall, the way is fairly level until just before the crossing."

Joshua shook his head, the familiar look of half-exasperation on his face once more. "You do beat all I have ever seen, Sarah Craighead. First you don't want to go to the crossin', then you can't get there fast enough. Just what is it that you think you can do for Adam tonight that couldn't wait until tomorrow?"

Sarah pointed to the angry red skin around the cut and spoke softly so that Adam wouldn't hear her. "That's proud flesh, full of corruption. It needs to be opened and treated with healing herbs. The longer before it's opened, the more likely it is that the sickness will spread over his body. He could even die from it."

Tel-a-ka nodded. "Sa-la speaks true," he said. "This bad medicine."

Joshua nodded, his expression resigned. "All right; I'll tell the sergeant we're movin' on. But don't expect him to go with us."

"We don't need him and his soldiers, anyway," Sarah said confidently. "Fetch the horses so we can get started." Soon arrangements had been made.

"Let Tel-a-ka carry the boy," Joshua suggested when they were ready to mount and ride out, and reluctantly Sarah agreed.

"He sleeps," Tel-a-ka said, easing the child down onto the blanket in front of his saddle.

"That's a blessing," Sarah said. "Sleep is the best thing for him now."

"But not for us," Joshua said. "I'll lead the way, and I don't intend to stop until we get there—mind you don't nod off."

"I'll stay awake," said Sarah, who had never felt more alert.

It was barely dusk when they rode out of the meadow after exchanging farewells with Captain Hawkins's men, but full darkness soon overtook them. The road was reduced to a narrow silver ribbon often almost totally obscured in shadows. They dared not ride at full gallop but settled into a steady canter that would bring them to the crossing in a matter of two or three hours if all went well.

No one else seemed to be on the road, nor did Sarah ever sense that anything lurked in the woods, waiting to pounce on them. Their greatest danger came not from Indians or wild animals, but from the frantic barking of the dogs all settlers kept to warn when someone approached. They had to pass several settlers' cabins, and even though none of the occupants ever came out to fire at them, Sarah always breathed easier when the sound of the barking dogs faded into the distance.

Finally, they reached the last ridge before Stones' Crossing, where they slowed their horses to a walk up the steep hill, then kept them tightly reined as they made their way down the other side. Then the road flattened out, and in the distance, Sarah spotted the path that turned off to the south. Only a few hundred yards farther lay Stones' Crossing.

"We're almost there," Sarah said. She had felt tired about an hour ago, but at the comforting sight of the crossing's cabins, Sarah felt fresh and fully awake.

"And here come our greeters." Joshua swung down from his saddle and spoke to the barking dogs that rushed toward him, calling a few by their names. Apparently recognizing his scent, the dogs jumped and fawned on Joshua, totally ignoring the other riders.

As they approached the first cabin, all was dark. Then through the window, a light appeared and widened as the cabin's front door opened. A figure in a long, white nightshirt came to the doorstone and peered out into the darkness.

"Who goes there?"

Followed by the frolicking dogs, Joshua stepped into the dim light in front of the cabin. "It's Joshua, Grandfather McKay; and Sarah Craighead's with me. We've come home."

Chapter 15

The next hour passed in a confused jumble of greetings, exclamations, and tears as the inhabitants of Stones' Crossing, roused by the barking dogs, gathered in the McKay cabin.

"We don't have time now to explain everything that's happened," Sarah said. "Adam was captured by the Seneca, and Tel-a-ka got him back, but they cut him in some kind of ritual and his wound must be tended immediately."

Sarah's grandfather had pulled on a pair of trousers and sat before the hearth beside his wife, Hannah, who had draped a blanket over her long nightgown.

"Ye talk too fast, Lassie," Grandfather McKay complained. "I'll ne'er sort all this out if ye don't slow doon a wee bit."

Sarah held Adam on her lap, gently washing his face with the soap and linen provided by Joshua's grandmother. "The sorting out can wait, Grandfather. Aunt Isabel has gone to fetch some herbals. As soon as she comes back, Adam's wound must be opened."

Her grandfather frowned and passed a hand over his eyes as if to clear his vision. "Adam? Can that dirty child really be my Ann's son?"

"Yes, Grandfather. Look—where I've washed him, you can see how white his skin is. Adam's fair, like Mother."

The door opened and Isabel Stone, her red hair still as bright as her son's, entered the cabin, carrying a stone jug and a cloth-wrapped bundle.

"I brought a fresh infusion of plantain and some dead nettle," she said.

"Good," Sarah said. "Is there bandaging material handy?"

"Right here." Hannah McKay pointed out a basket of linen strips.

"All right. I'll need some cloth wrung out in hot water for cleaning the wound. Now, who has the sharpest knife?"

Jackie Stone, the older of Joshua's two brothers, stepped forward and held out a slender blade for Sarah's inspection "I honed this 'un on the wheel this mornin', Sarah."

"It'll do, but first it must be heated in the flame until it glows red. Can you do that without burning yourself?"

"Better let me do it," Joshua said. He took the knife from his brother's hand and thrust the blade into the hottest part of the fire.

"Are you gonna stick him with that knife?" Joshua's other brother, Billy, asked, his eyes huge with disbelief.

Belle, the youngest member of the Stone family, began to wail and ran to her mother.

"It won't hurt him," Sarah said reassuringly. "Just a prick of the point of the knife to let the bad things out. Otherwise, he could be very sick."

Joshua returned from the fire and stood next to Sarah. "I think you'd best lay the boy on the table to do this," he said.

"Yes, I mean to do that," Sarah said.

"I'll move him." Jack Stone picked up Adam, who whimpered and looked back at Sarah as if he feared she might abandon him.

"Do you really intend to do this yourself?" Joshua asked Sarah, doubt clear in his tone.

"It has to be done, and I know how," Sarah said. Adam's soft cries wrung her heart, but resolutely she took the knife from Joshua.

God, help me do this right, she prayed silently.

Jack Stone put Adam on the table, where he lay with his eyes half-closed, sobbing but apparently not fully aware of what was happening. "I hope you know what you're doin'," he said.

"Hush with that talk!" his wife returned sharply. "Better ask her how ye can help the child than to make her doubt her healin' skills now."

"I'm sorry, Sarah. I guess I don't like to see the lad hurtin', and me helpless to do anything about it."

"Seems to me like there's one thing we can all do. It's time we prayed about this," William McKay said.

Sarah nodded at her grandfather. "Of course. Will you lead us, Sir?"

All but Adam, who still whimpered softly, and Tel-a-ka, who watched the proceedings with interest, bowed their heads and closed their eyes as William McKay invoked the presence and blessings of the almighty God on this company in general and upon Sarah and Adam Craighead in particular. Compared to some of her grandfather's other prayers, it was mercifully short, and when it ended in a chorus of amens, Sarah felt a great sense of relief and strength flood through her body.

With a steady hand, Sarah took up the knife and approached Adam. "Hold him down," she said calmly.

Joshua and Jack Stone stepped forward to take Adam's arms, Isabel Stone and Tel-a-ka grasped his legs, and Hannah McKay stood by with the bandages.

"Hurry up," Joshua said as Adam struggled weakly in their grasp.

Sarah gently probed the wound to find the most swollen area, then sank the point of the knife into Adam's angry red flesh. Immediately, a foul-smelling mixture of pus and blood spurted forth.

Adam screamed and jumped when the knife first pricked him, but as Sarah gently sponged the corruption issuing from the wound, he gradually relaxed and there was no further need to hold him down.

"It's all right, Adam," Sarah said soothingly. "The bad stuff inside is all gone now. You'll sleep now, and tomorrow you'll feel much better."

"That certainly needed doing," Isabel Stone remarked as Sarah packed the wound with dead nettle and bandaged it.

"Yes. If we'd waited much longer, it might have been too late."

"Sa-la make strong medicine," Tel-a-ka said.

"So does Old Woman," Sarah said. "She would have done just the same if she had been here."

"What old woman?" Belle asked, removing her thumb from her mouth just long enough to speak.

"Tel-a-ka's grandmother," Sarah said. "She was our friend on Preacher Creek."

"Come now; we must get this wee laddie to bed now and let him rest," William McKay said. "Sarah, put a pallet down for the both of ye here by the fire, where ye can see to tend him in the night if need be."

"And Joshua, you come along with us now—and your friend can sleep in the haymow if he's a mind to," Jack Stone said, glancing at Tel-a-ka.

Tel-a-ka looked over at Sarah, who nodded. "That is a good place. Come here in the morning and take breakfast with us."

He nodded. "I see Ad-am then," Tel-a-ka said and followed the Stones out into the night.

"Well, well," Hannah McKay said. She rummaged around on a shelf over the bed and found a feather tick, which she put on the floor for Sarah. "This has been quite a night."

"For Adam and me, it's been quite a few weeks," Sarah said.

"We want to hear all about it, but don't you want to get out of that Indian garb now?"

Sarah looked down at her dress. "Uncle Jonathan's wife gave this to me. I hope you can meet Sukey soon—she is a wonderful person."

Grandfather McKay sighed heavily. "When Jonathan wrote that he'd taken an Indian to wife, it was hard to bear, I can tell ye. What ye say about her is welcome news."

"I owe her my life, and my uncle could never find a better wife anywhere. But you're right—I am tired."

"Here's a night shift. You can wash up in the lean-to, then off to bed you go," Hannah McKay said.

After a sketchy bath, Sarah put on Hannah McKay's gown and lay down beside Adam, immediately falling into a deep and dreamless sleep.

❦

Stones' Crossing looked about the same as always, Sarah decided when she ventured outside the next morning. Hannah McKay had helped her take down her braid and brush her hair, which now fell in waves down her back. The yellow dress was somewhat wrinkled from being rolled up in the saddlebag, but Sarah had put it on, anyway, bringing tears to her grandfather's eyes because, he said, she looked so much like her mother.

"I'll go draw some water," Sarah had said, knowing if she stayed any longer she, too, would weep.

Smoke rose from the fieldstone chimneys of two of the three cabins in the clearing; the third, in which Sarah and her parents had lived for a time, seemed to be unoccupied.

As Sarah reached the well, Joshua's mother emerged from their cabin and hurried toward her.

"How is Adam? As soon as I saw you I couldn't wait to find out."

"He seems to be much better," Sarah said. "He still feels too warm, but that awful look in his eyes is gone."

"Praise God for that! Joshua has told us some of what ye've been through the past weeks—I don't see how ye were able to do what ye did last night, as tired as ye must have been."

"Without God's help, I couldn't have," Sarah said.

Isabel Stone smiled and laid her hand on Sarah's cheek. "I'm so glad that God led Joshua to ye out there in the wilderness, and that ye're still friends, just as back here in the old days."

Friends. Sarah felt foolishly disappointed that Joshua had spoken of her only in terms of friendship.

"Things are far different now," Sarah said. Then, to change the subject, she pointed to the cabin where she had been born. "What are you doing with our old place? It looks deserted."

Isabel turned back to look at it. "Nobody lives there, although I'd be glad enough to have your folks come back to it. For now, Jack stores goods he buys at the river there. A few neighbors buy or trade for them."

"Maybe he could open a store," Sarah said. "It should do well, with all the settlers coming into these parts."

Isabel tossed her head in the characteristic way that Sarah remembered from her childhood. "No, thank ye! Ye may recall that my parents had a trading post on the river—and I couldna wait to get away from it. I'd a-wed the first man who came along and asked me—luckily, it was Jack Stone."

"Yes, Mother told me the story," Sarah said, then stopped, overcome by the realization that her parents might never again return to the crossing.

Isabel reached out to Sarah and hugged her to her ample bosom. "Ah, don't ye worry, Lass—I know your mother. Ann McKay won't give up. Likely we'll hear from them soon." Then she stepped back and smoothed her apron. "I must get back and see to our breakfast. 'Tis awhile since I had my first-born's feet under my table."

"Did Joshua say how long he'll be here?"

His mother shook her head. "Not long enough. Jack and I both told him he ought to give up this chasin' around with the army."

"Maybe he will someday," Sarah said, but as Isabel Stone walked away, Sarah was almost certain that Joshua didn't intend to live at Stones' Crossing again, even after he left the army.

"Sa-la."

Sarah turned to see Tel-a-ka walking toward her. *"Ili kheleche,"* she said in greeting.

"Ili kheleche. You not Indian now," he said. Tel-a-ka had never seen her wearing anything as splendid as this yellow dress, and he stared at her in surprise.

"I still wear moccasins," Sarah said, putting a foot out to prove it.

"How is Ad-am?" he asked.

"Awake and hungry. Come and take breakfast with us."

Tel-a-ka took the bucket Sarah had just filled and followed her to the cabin. Inside, Hannah McKay held Adam on her lap, spooning thick oat porridge into his mouth.

Recalling that Hannah McKay had force-fed her the same way when she was his age, Sarah made a face. "Adam must be feeling better to eat oat porridge so readily."

Adam looked up at her and smiled. "Sa-wa—Tel-ka," he added, holding out both arms to them.

Tel-a-ka spoke in Delaware to Adam, and he replied in the same tongue.

"He glad to see Tel-a-ka," he translated.

"I suppose Adam's learned some Seneca words, too; more's the pity," Sarah said.

"Sit and eat, the both of you," Hannah McKay invited, as if having an Indian at her breakfast table was an everyday occurrence.

Sarah bowed her head and said grace, then accepted a trencher heaped with bread and savory meat. "Wheaten bread!" she exclaimed. "This is the best I've tasted since Mother's yeast starter went bad a few months back."

"Mr. McKay took the news that Ann and Caleb are missing mighty hard,"

Hannah said. "He's taking his feelings out on the woodpile."

"I know, but I still have faith that my parents are safe. They may have gone to a fortified house when they saw that the cabin had been burned. By now, Uncle Jonathan has found them and they know that I'm all right."

"I told your grandfather we'd probably hear something soon, but he's determined to ask Joshua to look for them instead of going with the army."

"I'm sure he'd like to, but Joshua promised Colonel Burd he'd rejoin him as soon as he can. Some sort of big action is planned against the French, and he wants to help."

Hannah shook her head. "I'll never understand why men seem to be so fond of fighting. But at least you and Adam are safe, and for that I do thank God."

Tel-a-ka remained silent throughout most of the meal, exchanging a few words in Delaware with Adam and then translating them for Hannah McKay. As soon as he had eaten, he stood and half-bowed to Hannah McKay.

"Tel-a-ka go now," he said. He touched his breast. "*Wdee* thank Grandmother."

"He says he thanks you from his heart," Sarah said.

"Tell him he doesn't have to go yet," Hannah McKay said, touched by the gesture. "He must be tired—he should rest awhile longer."

"He understands you well enough," Sarah said, glancing at Tel-a-ka for confirmation.

He nodded. "*Lenape m'hackney*," he said. "Tel-a-ka belong with Clan of the Bow."

"He says he is an Indian. Tel-a-ka is a chief of his people now, and he has been away from them a long time. I'm not surprised that he won't stay."

"Tel-a-ka go now," he repeated. He started out of the cabin, and Sarah followed him.

"Wait," she called.

He walked steadily on toward the stable, stopping only when he had reached it. Without looking at her, he reached for his saddle. "Tel-a-ka go," he said once more.

"Please let me thank you, at least," Sarah said. "I know you don't understand everything I say, but look at me, Tel-a-ka."

She touched her right hand to her heart, then gestured toward him as she had seen Sukey do.

His eyes met hers and he stood impassively for a moment, his arms crossed over his chest in the posture that was so familiar to her. Then Tel-a-ka dropped his arms and closed his eyes. He murmured something she could not understand, then spoke her name.

"Sa-la," he said quietly. "You make strong medicine. You save Tel-a-ka from soldiers. How you do this things?"

231

"I have told you about our *michabou*. I prayed to God that Adam would be all right. He sent you the vision when you fasted. You have many names for Him, but there is only one true God."

Tel-a-ka stared at her. "Why you not say this to me before?"

"I tried to, many times, but you and Bel-a-ka never wanted to hear it."

"I hear now," he said.

Sarah took a deep breath and prayed for the right words. "Many of your stories are really about the same God. You just call Him by a different name. The Lord God Jehovah made the earth and all that is in it. He made man and woman and gave them rules to live by. Once people became very bad, and God sent a flood. Only a few good people were saved, and God said He would never send another flood that would destroy the earth. The sign of His promise is the rainbow—the same as your clan sign."

Tel-a-ka touched the bow on his chest and looked back to Sarah. "My people should hear these stories."

"They will, I promise—my father will see to it."

"If he live," Tel-a-ka said.

"I believe that he is alive," Sarah said. "But even so, my father's spirit will always live. God takes all Christians to heaven when they die."

Tel-a-ka shook his head. "This is hard," he said. "I not know."

Tears of frustration came to Sarah's eyes, and she stepped forward and touched Tel-a-ka's forearm, wishing she had a better way to explain her beliefs to him. "It is a hard thing to know God. So God sent His Son, Jesus, to live on earth as a man. His words tell us that God wants us to love and care for each other."

Tel-a-ka turned away briefly and busied himself with his saddle. "Tel-a-ka love Sa-la," he said, almost too low for her to hear.

Sarah swallowed hard. *Is it possible that Tel-a-ka means that?* Then he turned back and looked into Sarah's eyes, and she knew that he did.

"I love Tel-a-ka in the Lord, too," Sarah said, aware that he did not yet know what that meant.

Tel-a-ka took a step toward Sarah and put his arms around her. She felt his breastplate pressing against her as he held her close for a moment. Then he stepped back and dropped his arms.

"Tel-a-ka chief now, take squaw from Lenni-Lenape. Josh-ua and Sa-la have many sons."

Sarah's tears ran down her cheeks and splashed on her white collar. There was so much she wanted to say to Tel-a-ka, and yet no words were adequate to express her gratitude and love—not the kind of love that led to marriage, but that between tender friends.

"Oh, Tel-a-ka—" she began, but his face impassive once more, Tel-a-ka made the cutoff sign.

"Tel-a-ka go now. I look for *Allogagan Nehellatank*."

Sarah nodded. "I know you have to go. And when you find my father, say you want to know about God. He can tell you much better."

"Sa-la tell much," Tel-a-ka said. "Watch Ad-am."

"I will."

Sarah followed Tel-a-ka to the edge of the clearing, where he turned back to wave at her before he rode away.

Sarah's heart felt heavy as she walked back to the cabin.

Tel-a-ka might be out of her life, but she knew she would never forget him. And someday, God willing, they would meet again.

Chapter 16

When Sarah came back into the cabin, Adam sat on the floor, listlessly playing with some wood scraps Grandfather McKay had smoothed into blocks. Sarah touched her hand to his face and found that it was warm with fever.

"Does the rainbow weed still grow in the glen, Grandmother?" Sarah asked.

"I suppose so, Child—I've not been able to climb the hill to get there since the misery got into my legs these months past."

"Adam's wound needs an infusion of rainbow weed."

"Take my gathering basket and go before the sun gets higher. I'll ready the water."

The glen had always been Sarah's favorite retreat and the place where she and Joshua had once played. Sarah glanced toward the Stone cabin as she passed it, wishing she could see Joshua, yet dreading having to tell him good-bye.

Sarah climbed the hill south of the clearing and descended to the glen's cool and shady haven. She walked along the stream, looking out for the plant that took its name from the many shades, from rose to purple, that graced its spiked blossoms. Its green leaves would make an infusion to help heal Adam's wound. Sarah found one plant and stripped its leaves, then moved on. Intent on her search, she didn't notice the figure sitting on the creek bank until she almost fell over his feet.

Sarah looked up in surprise. "Joshua!"

He seemed equally startled. "I see you still have that yellow dress, although this is a strange place to be wearin' it. What brings you to the glen so early?"

"I'm gathering rainbow weed for Adam."

"What will it do for him?" he asked, peering into the basket.

"When put into boiling water, rainbow weed leaves make a potion to keep wounds clean and help them heal," she explained, adding, "I didn't expect to see you here, either."

Joshua tossed a twig into the stream and watched until it disappeared. "I had to get away. I'm not used to bein' around so many people, all talkin' or wantin' me to talk."

"I know," Sarah said.

"Sit down," Joshua invited, patting the mossy ground beside him.

Sarah obeyed, but rather than look at him, she concentrated on picking leaves from a nearby rainbow weed plant. "When will you leave the crossing?" she asked.

"Soon. I see that your Indian has already left. I thought he might ride back west with us."

"Tel-a-ka said he had to get back to his people. Then he'll look for Mother and Father."

"So will I, first chance I get."

"I'm not sure Tel-a-ka thinks they are still alive," Sarah said.

"Tel-a-ka!" Joshua exclaimed, and once more he looked at her with exasperation. "You think entirely too much of what he says."

Sarah's eyes challenged him. "You forget that he saved my life and probably Adam's, too. I owe him a great deal."

"True. And he won't ever let you forget it, either."

"Tel-a-ka's not like that—he's never asked anything in return for his friendship."

"Friendship?" Joshua repeated, his expression dark. "Is that what it is, Sarah? Or is it something more?"

"I don't know what you're talking about," Sarah said, not entirely truthfully.

"I'm talkin' about following the example of your uncle and marryin' an Indian. Don't tell me that the thought never crossed your mind."

Sarah rose to her feet and glared down at Joshua. "What right do you have to say such a thing to me! Who I marry certainly isn't any of *your* business."

She turned and began to walk away, her heart hammering in mingled indignation and anguish.

That was not what I meant to say, she thought, wishing that she could call back her words.

"Wait, Sarah!" Joshua caught up with her and put a detaining hand on her arm. "I'm sorry—but I saw the way Tel-a-ka looked at you. I feared that you might return his feelings."

Sarah turned to face Joshua. Her chest felt tight, as if the breath were slowly being squeezed from her. "What is it to you if I do?"

Joshua's face reddened. "Oh, Sarah, you know how I feel about you—" he began, then stopped as if the words were too hard to say.

"No, I don't." The bands around Sarah's chest eased as Joshua stared down at her, his eyes searching hers.

His sigh was almost a groan. "You do beat all, Sarah Craighead! After all we've been through together, you must know—!"

Again he stopped without finishing the thought.

"What must I know, Joshua?" Sarah asked, her voice soft.

He took a step forward and put his hands on her upper arms as if he intended to shake her. Surprised, Sarah dropped the gathering basket and swayed, off-balance.

"That I love you, of course! Don't try to pretend you didn't know it," he said almost angrily.

"I wasn't sure."

"Do you know now?"

Sarah read the answer in his eyes. "Oh, Joshua—"

They moved toward each other at the same instant, coming together in an embrace of such force that Sarah's head reeled. Her arms tightened around his neck for a long moment, then he bent to kiss her forehead, her cheeks, the tip of her nose, and, finally, her mouth.

"I love you," he said hoarsely.

"I love you, too," she confessed, but his lips closed over hers in a long, sweet kiss almost before she could finish saying the words.

"How can I let you leave now?" she asked when he finally pulled away.

"I have to go, but it won't be for long. Then we'll always be together."

Her eyes bright with tears, Sarah tried to smile. "Promise?"

Joshua swept her into his arms again, then lifted Sarah's hand to his lips and kissed it. "Promise," he said.

They walked back up the hill, hand in hand, until they neared the top. There they stopped to kiss again.

"When will I see you again?" Sarah asked.

"Soon. I'll gather everyone together and tell them."

"Tell them what, Joshua?" Sarah prompted, and his face reddened.

"Why, that we're gettin' married, I guess. We are, aren't we?"

"I haven't heard you ask me to be your wife," Sarah said demurely.

A brief look of exasperation crossed Joshua's face, then he took her right hand in his and knelt on one knee, looking up at her almost grimly.

"Sarah McKay Craighead, will you do me the honor of bein' my wife?"

"I will, and gladly. But stand up—you should bow your knee only to the Lord."

Joshua took her into his arms again and groaned softly. "Oh, Sarah! I do thank God for bringing us back together."

With a final kiss, they reluctantly parted. By the time she reached the cabin, Sarah's initial elation began to ebb away, replaced by the dread knowledge that soon Joshua would leave her.

It was just past noon when the families met together at the McKay cabin to tell Joshua good-bye.

"I wish ye'd change your mind, Son," Isabel Stone said, well knowing

236

that her words would fall on deaf ears.

"I can't, Mother, you know that. Most of the trouble that's happened this summer has been caused by the French, and if we don't stop them now, the death and destruction will only get worse. I can't turn my head and pretend it isn't happenin'—I'd take no pleasure in livin' the life of a coward."

Joshua looked at Sarah as he finished speaking, and she had to glance away. She realized that his words had been said for her as much as to his mother, and she knew he was right.

"I understand," Jack Stone said, coming forward to clasp his son's shoulder. "I pray you'll succeed."

"What are your plans after this battle, or whatever it is?" his mother asked, struggling not to cry.

"Right now, there's only one thing I know for sure." Joshua turned to Sarah and held out his hand to her. Her face warmed as she walked over to stand beside him and take his hand. "I intend to take Sarah to wife."

There was a split second of silence, then everyone in the cabin talked at once. From the loud "Hurrah!" from Joshua's brother Billy to Hannah Stone's soft "Praise the Lord!" approval was unanimous. Their families crowded around, offering congratulations, until Adam, forgotten in the confusion, began to wail.

"I'm afraid he's getting spoiled," Sarah said, leaving Joshua's side to pick up her brother.

"Take good care of him, Sarah. I hope to bring his parents back with me soon."

"It's time to pray for Joshua," William McKay said, rising to his feet.

When he concluded his lengthy petition, everyone followed Joshua outside for a final farewell.

"Come back soon," Sarah said after Joshua had spoken with each of the others in turn.

"I will."

"Promise?" she asked, attempting to smile through the tears that threatened her resolve not to give in to them.

"Promise," he said.

"Ain't you goin' to kiss her good-bye?" Billy Stone asked.

Surrounded by their families' laughter, Sarah and Joshua exchanged a brief kiss.

"I'll do better next time," he whispered.

"You'd better!" Sarah replied.

With that, Joshua swung into the saddle and rode out of the clearing. He left Stone's Crossing, taking Sarah's heart with him.

But he had promised to come back, and for the present, his promise would have to be enough.

In the days that followed Joshua's departure, Sarah settled into a routine that kept her occupied. Yet the work never made her forget Joshua or her parents, and she prayed daily for their safety.

ॐ

August was already well advanced when Jack and Isabel Stone took Sarah with them to the trading post that had once been owned by Isabel's parents.

"I don't know when I've seen so many travelers," Jack Stone remarked as they made their way homeward late that afternoon. There had been no rain for a week, and the dust churned up by passing horses hung in the air and soon coated their clothing.

Some of the travelers were soldiers marching to the west, but most were families on their way back east after being burned out by Indians.

"We was lucky to git away with the hair on our heads," one of the men said.

"Where did you come from?" Jack Stone asked.

"Up around the Loyalhannon," he replied. "Ain't none of that country safe these days."

"I think that's the area where Joshua said Colonel Burd was camped," Sarah said when the family had gone on its way.

Isabel took her hand and squeezed it. "He's all right," she said, trying to make her conviction match her hope. "God is with him."

When the Conestoga wagon finally turned into Stones' Crossing, Billy and Jackie ran out to meet them, both shouting at the top of their voices.

"What is the matter with you two?" Jack Stone braked the wagon to a stop in front of the McKay cabin, to which the boys pointed as they shouted.

With both talking at once, Sarah could make out only a few words.

"Indian!" one of the boys said.

"In there!" the other cried.

Jack reached for his rifle at the same moment that the McKay cabin door opened. Hannah McKay emerged, followed by a shadowy figure.

"See the Indian? I tole you an Indian was here!" Billy exclaimed.

For a moment Sarah felt her heart stop. Her first thought, that hostile Indians had somehow overwhelmed the Crossing, quickly gave way to another.

Tel-a-ka must have come back.

Chapter 17

Sarah held her breath as a buckskin-clad figure stepped from the shadows into the twilight. It came closer, and Sarah saw long black braids and a fringed doeskin shift. With a cry of joy, she climbed down from the wagon.

"Sukey!" she exclaimed, embracing her uncle's wife.

"Is good to see you, Sa-la," Sukey said when Sarah released her.

Sarah looked past Sukey with expectation. "Where is Uncle Jonathan?"

Slowly Sukey shook her head. "He not come," she said.

"Is he all right?" Sarah asked.

"Oh, yes."

Sukey turned away to look back into the cabin, from which two figures emerged and hastened toward them.

"Sarah!" her parents exclaimed in unison as they enveloped her in their joint embrace. Overcome by emotion, Sarah was incapable of speech.

"It's all right, Daughter," Caleb murmured as she sobbed against his chest. "We're back together now."

"Thank God," Sarah said when she regained her voice.

"We do, indeed," her mother replied.

"Come, let's go inside—there is much to talk about," Jack Stone said.

Everyone gathered around, and in a voice that quivered with emotion, Ann Craighead told how she and Caleb had said good-bye to Sarah and Adam and gone to the Warfields' cabin, where they had stayed two days. "Her poor wee babe was stillborn, but we stayed to be sure Miz Warfield was all right before we left."

Ann paused a moment to wipe her eyes, and Caleb continued the story. "When we got back the next afternoon and found the cabin burned and Sarah and Adam gone, it was the darkest hour of our lives."

Sarah touched her father's hand. "What did you do then?"

"When we couldn't find any trace of ye or the Clan of the Bow, we went around to several fortified houses, but no one knew anything. After barely escapin' a raidin' party, we made it to the fortified house at Will's Creek. That's where Jonathan found us. He told us that Sarah was safe and on her way back here, and that Adam had been taken by the Seneca."

"When did you know Adam was all right?" asked Hannah McKay.

"Only last week. Tel-a-ka found out where we were from Jonathan and came to tell us that Adam was safe at the Crossing. He said Jonathan wanted us to wait there for him," Caleb said.

"We expected Jonathan to come back east with us, but he sent Sukey instead," Sarah's mother added.

Sarah turned to Sukey. "Where is Uncle Jonathan? Why didn't he come with you?"

"He go fight the French," she said. "Say he come back after."

"I hope he and Joshua are together," Sarah said.

"Your grandfather tells me that ye and Joshua plan to marry," Sarah's mother said, her tone making it a question.

"Yes." Sarah glanced at her father. "Joshua wasn't able to ask you for my hand in the old-fashioned way, but I hope you'll give us your blessing."

Caleb's brow creased and he shook his head. "It all seems too sudden. Ye've not seen Joshua for years, and now to be marryin' him—or to be marryin' anyone—it's a bit hard to take in, with all else that's happened."

Sarah took her father's hand and looked at him fondly. "Joshua and I have been through a great deal together. We know our minds."

"Ye have to admit she looks grown-up enough to wed," her mother said, smiling faintly. "Where did ye get such a fine dress, Sarah?"

"While we were at Fort Bedford, Captain Hawkins gave me some of his late wife's clothes." Sarah turned to Sukey. "However, my favorite dress is the one Sukey gave me when I started back here with Joshua. Wait until you see it!"

"Does anyone care to eat, or do you intend to fill your mouths with words instead?" Hannah McKay asked.

"I could stand to take nourishment," Caleb admitted. " 'Tis awhile since we last had a hot meal."

For awhile, at least, the pace of conversation slowed but never entirely stopped. Hannah McKay maneuvered around the unaccustomed number of people, too many to feed at a single sitting. Sarah and Isabel helped with the preparations, but Ann had other orders.

"Sit you down there and keep Adam out of my way," Hannah McKay told her.

"He wants me to hold him all the time," Ann Craighead commented, but it was far from a complaint.

"Adam certainly is happy to see you," Sarah said.

"Not half as happy as I am," she declared. "All the way here, I prayed that he hadna forgotten us."

"Sukey did a fine job in leading us here," Caleb said. "I dinna know what we'd have done without ye, Lass."

Embarrassed, Sukey bowed her head.

"We all owe Sukey a debt of gratitude," Sarah said.

"Marryin' her was the best thing my son ever did," said William McKay, who had listened in silence all evening. "I admit I wasn't sure about ye when I first heard it," he said to Sukey. "Indians once robbed me and left me for dead. If it hadn't been for Hannah here," he went on, gesturing toward his wife, "I'd a-died right there on the trail. But she took me in and nursed me back to health."

"So of course he had to marry me," Hannah said with a smile. "What he's trying to say is that lately he's changed his mind about Indians."

"Nay, I just changed my heart. There's no doubt that God's Word tells us to be brothers and sisters in the Lord."

Sukey put her hand on her heart and then motioned toward her father-in-law. "I thank you for your welcome to me. I try to make good daughter."

"You already have," William McKay assured her. "Now if I just had Jonathan and Joshua safely back, I'd be content."

"Wouldn't we all!" Hannah exclaimed.

They continued to talk far into the night, until finally William McKay ordered everyone to bed. Even then, there was drowsy conversation until, too overcome with fatigue to say another word, all slept.

After spending one night in the McKay cabin, the Craigheads moved back into their old cabin. Jack Stone put his extra stores inside the stable, and he and William planed logs and made beds for them all. With Sukey sleeping in the McKays' loft, everyone had enough room.

The warmth of her family's reunion continued to fill Sarah with joy, but it was tempered by the absence of Jonathan and Joshua.

"Surely Colonel Burd has moved on Fort Duquesne by now," Sarah said one day after her parents had been back at the Crossing for several weeks.

"News is usually slow to come east," her mother reminded her. "Perhaps ye ought to pray for patience."

"I'd prefer to pray for action," Sarah replied.

"Isabel said that Jack went to the river today—he may bring us word."

Jack Stone's news wasn't encouraging, however. A large British reconnaissance on Fort Duquesne had been turned back on September 15, but there had been no battle. Sarah turned away, despondent.

"Come with me," Sukey invited, holding her hand out to Sarah. "We talk."

Silently, they climbed the hill to a spot where Sarah often went to watch the road. The late September sun was still warm, but Sarah shivered in the chill breeze.

"What is it?" she asked when they had settled themselves on a sun-warmed boulder.

Sukey flattened her hands against her stomach, and for the first time Sarah noticed the slight thickening there. "Baby come in spring," Sukey said.

Sarah hugged her. "That's wonderful! Does Uncle Jonathan know?"

Sukey shook her head. "No. How your family feel?"

"It will please them," Sarah assured her.

Sukey gazed into the distance as if seeking something there. "I not know what Jonnie think."

"He'll be happy—I'm sure of it."

"I pray much that it is so."

"Don't worry, Sukey—we'll take good care of you."

That's another reason the men should come back to us soon, Sarah thought as she and Sukey came back down the hill.

❧

As September gave way to October, the glory of autumn surrounded the Crossing but failed to lift Sarah's spirits. Jack Stone heard that an October 12 attack by the French on Fort Ligonier had failed, but there had been no further news from the West.

In the meantime, their lives were busy. After Sarah told her father about her encounter with Tel-a-ka, he asked Sukey to teach him the Delaware language.

"It's clear that the Lord bids me to take the Word to Tel-a-ka's people—He's even provided a way for me to learn how," he said. Caleb and Sukey began the slow process of translating some of the Bible into Delaware, while Sarah copied their work onto stiff paper that Jack Stone went all the way to Lancaster to buy. Always they prayed for the safe return of Jonathan and Joshua.

Yet the news about Fort Duquesne that Jack Stone brought to them on a frosty day in late November was almost too good to be believed.

"It seems that most of the Indians helpin' the French deserted them when the trade goods they were promised didn't arrive. The French just up and left Fort Duquesne without a fight—and the British marched in and occupied it on the twenty-fifth."

"That was four days ago—the men may be on their way home even now!" Hannah McKay said.

Standing side by side, Sukey and Sarah grasped each other's hands.

"Let us pray that it is so," Sukey said in a low voice. For the first time, Sarah saw tears in Sukey's eyes.

The weather warmed the next day, bringing rain, and Sarah stayed inside, spinning linsey-woolsey. Late that afternoon, over the persistent murmur of falling rain, she heard the dogs begin to bark. Sarah threw a shawl over her head and ran outside in time to see two men dismount in front of her grandfather's cabin.

"Joshua!" Sarah called. He ran to her, picked her up, and twirled her around three times before setting her back down.

"Oh, Sarah! I never want to let you out of my sight again!" With a shudder, he drew her to him.

"Looky there! Joshua's kissing Cousin Sarah!" exclaimed Billy Stone, but they scarcely heard.

"I told you I'd do better when I came back," Joshua said when he let her go.

Sarah smiled. "I like kept promises."

"And I like to keep them for you," he said, bending to kiss her again.

A few feet away, Sukey and Jonathan stood together in a similar embrace, until Sukey suddenly drew back and pointed toward the eastern sky.

"Look!"

A small part of the setting sun had emerged from the surrounding clouds, and as its beams filtered through the misting rain, a shimmering rainbow formed over Stones' Crossing.

"I never saw a rainbow in December," Jonathan said.

They watched in awe as its colors dimmed, then disappeared.

"It faded so quickly," Sarah murmured.

"The bow is sign of God's promise," Sukey said.

"So it is," Jonathan replied.

Joshua took Sarah's hands in both of his and kissed her gently on the forehead. "God's greatest sign isn't the rainbow, though," he said.

"Oh? What is it, then?" Sarah asked.

"Love. It's the greatest sign of all."

Sarah stood drenched to the skin in the cold rain but warmed by the love she and Joshua shared, a love that would forever be their own covenant sign of the bow.

Sign of the Eagle

McKays of Pennsylvania

William McKay (1700-1770) **m.** Sarah Macpherson (1704-1740)

- Ann (1723-) **m.** Caleb Craighead (1712-)
  - Sarah (1742-) **m.** Joshua Stone (1738-)
  - Adam (1756-)
- Jonathan (1729-) **m.** Sukeu-quawon (1740-1768)
  - David (1759-)
  - Susannah (1761-)
  - Matthew (1763-)
  - Mark (1765-)
  - Luke (1766-)
  - John (1768-)

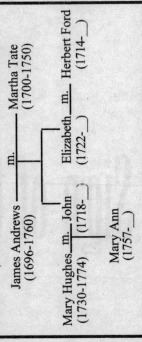

Andrews of Lancaster & Philadelphia

James Andrews (1696-1760) **m.** Martha Tate (1700-1750)

- John (1718-) **m.** Mary Hughes (1730-1774)
  - Mary Ann (1757-)
- Elizabeth (1722-) **m.** Herbert Ford (1714-)

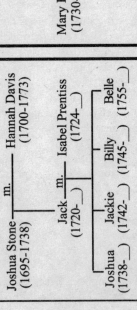

Stones of Stones' Crossing

Joshua Stone (1695-1738) **m.** Hannah Davis (1700-1773)

- Jack (1720-) **m.** Isabel Prentiss (1724-)
  - Joshua (1738-)
  - Jackie (1742-)
  - Billy (1745-)
  - Belle (1755-)

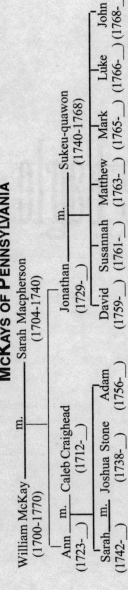

Chapter 1

Even the youths shall faint and be weary, and the young men shall utterly fall:
but they that wait upon the Lord shall renew their strength;
they shall mount up with wings as eagles; they shall run, and not be weary;
and they shall walk, and not faint.
ISAIAH 40:30–31

A spectacular golden sunrise promised a fair April day as Mary Andrews alighted from her cabriolet and surveyed the crowded Philadelphia docks. Mary always enjoyed coming to the harbor, where the ever-changing sights and sounds told of a wider world, but on this day she had a special reason to be there. Her friend Hetty Hawkins was returning from six months in London.

Mary breathed deeply of the warming, salt-tanged air. *Hetty has a lovely day to come home,* she thought. The early months of 1775 had brought various troubles to her family and to the Pennsylvania Colony, but on this sunny April day it was easy to believe that nothing would ever again go wrong.

"Mistress, are y' sure this is the right place?"

Polly Smith, the Andrews' young bond servant, stood beside Mary Andrews. Gnomelike in her black dress, she peered nearsightedly at the scattered ships which rode at anchor in the Philadelphia harbor.

Mary shaded her brown eyes with her gloved hand and squinted into the early morning sun. "Yes, I'm positive. The paper said the *Sea Pearl* would discharge its passengers and cargo this morning."

" 'With a stock of fine lace from Belgium and many willin' hands,' " quoted Polly. Because of Mary's tutelage, the young servant was able to read anything she came across, and she welcomed any opportunity to display her new skill.

"Yes, and the Hawkins family, unless something happened in London to prevent their sailing. Oh, I do wish I'd thought to bring Papa's spyglass."

"Mayhap we can get closer, Miss Merry," Polly said, calling her mistress by her childhood nickname.

"Or climb higher." Mary pointed to a nearby stack of wooden crates awaiting loading. "Those should make a fair vantage point."

"Miss Merry! Watch out—if y' should take a fall from there—"

Polly's alarmed voice called after Mary, but her warning went unheeded as Mary found a small box and used it to step up onto a sturdy carton. From her impromptu platform, Mary had a wide view of the harbor.

"This is wonderful!" Mary exclaimed. "I can make out four sailing vessels in the harbor, and two of them are discharging passengers. Come and see," she added, holding out a hand to Polly.

"No thank ye, Mistress—yer makin' enough of a spectacle fer the both o' us."

Mary looked away from the harbor in time to see several people in the crowd point to her and laugh.

"Momma! Look at that funny girl! Why is she up there?" a child called out.

Mary's cheeks reddened, and reluctantly she stepped down from her vantage point.

"I tole you, Miss Merry," Polly said, wagging her head.

"The child called me a *girl*," Mary complained.

Polly's glance took in Mary's aproned morning dress, whose hem stopped a few inches short of her ankles. "Well, y' act like one, climbin' up on them boxes. I tole y' that skirt was gettin' too short, but as usual y' paid me no heed."

Mary tugged at her skirt as if that would make it longer. "It was fine last time I wore it. Surely I should have stopped growing by now."

"Y' and Miss Hetty was allus of a size—I wonder me if she's growed, too, these six months."

"I'm sure she will be some changed," Mary said. In the weeks since she'd known when Hetty was returning, she had wondered if they would still be best friends. "Come on, let's get closer," Mary added. She and Polly pressed through the crowd toward the double gangplank which all debarking passengers would have to use.

"Mornin', ladies," a man in somewhat tattered knee breeches said, doffing his three-cornered hat and moving as if to block their way. "If ye're lookin' for a good man, I'm at yer service."

Mary opened her mouth to deliver an appropriately scathing reply, but Polly pushed her past the man, whose laughter followed them.

"What a rude lot o' men is about these days! Y' can't trust none o' them!"

Mary chose not to answer Polly, whose words reminded her of things that her mother had often said. Mary's mother had died suddenly eight months earlier, and the loss had left a hollow place in Mary's heart that still ached whenever she thought of her.

"You mustn't go to England, Mary—I can't lose you, too," John Andrews had told his daughter when Mrs. Hawkins had proposed that Mary should travel with them and visit her father's sister, who had lived in

London for many years.

"You won't ever lose me, Papa," Mary had reassured him. She hadn't really felt up to going with Hetty herself, but someday Mary hoped her father would take her to England.

"Here they come!" someone in the crowd cried, and Mary and Polly stopped to watch several dozen passengers step from a small launch and make their way onto the dock.

"There's Miz Hawkins—an' Miss Hetty, too!" Polly cried a moment later when a group of red-coated soldiers parted, revealing an attractive woman and a blond young lady flanking a splendidly uniformed British officer. As soon as she spotted Mary, Hetty Hawkins left her parents and ran to her, kissing the air beside Mary's cheek in a ritual of greeting.

"How good of you to meet us, Merry!" Hetty exclaimed. "How are you?"

"Quite well, thank you." Mary held Hetty at arm's length and admired her fine dress and satin-lined traveling cloak. "Did you come back with a whole new wardrobe?"

Hetty nodded. "Some of my old things were unfashionable anyhow and getting too short—so when Father obtained his generalship, Mother celebrated by calling in Queen Charlotte's own dressmaker. She barely finished this before we sailed."

Agatha Hawkins joined the girls and linked her arm in her daughter's. "Hello, Mary. You're out terribly early, aren't you? Have you kept well? And why is your father not with you?"

It was a habit of Hetty's mother to ask several questions at once, so that Mary never knew quite how to answer. "I'm fine, Mrs. Hawkins. Papa's away attending to some business."

General Hawkins joined them and half-bowed to Mary. "I must say this is quite an unexpected honor."

"Hetty wrote that you'd booked passage on the *Sea Pearl,* and when I saw it would dock today, I was determined to welcome her home," explained Mary to her friend's father. His manner always made Mary feel that he subtly mocked her. She never felt truly comfortable in his presence.

"Surely you aren't on foot?" The general's tone registered his disapproval.

"No, Sir—there's Thomas with the carriage now. By your leave, we can take Hetty home."

"Oh, please, Father!" Hetty plucked at her father's sleeve and smiled engagingly.

"Very well, then—but mind that you go straight to the house. The servants should be expecting us."

The general helped the girls into the Andrews' cabriolet for the brief ride to Hetty's house. The servants had evidently been watching for the return of their employer, for all four had come outside before Hetty could alight from the carriage.

Hetty turned to Nancy, the housemaid. "Have our trunks arrived?"

"Yes, Miss Hetty. The drayman brought them late last night. I put the gowns in your clothespress."

Hetty slipped her arm in Mary's and smiled. "Come up and see my new dresses. Brew us a pot of tea, Nancy—and in honor of the occasion, you and Polly may take a cup, too."

"Real *tea?*" Mary questioned. Like most Philadelphians, she and her father had not drunk English tea for many months.

"Father had some shipped home while we were in England," Hetty said.

Mary followed Hetty to her room at the top of the stairs, the largest, airiest bedroom in the house. Hetty opened her clothespress, revealing a rainbow of fabric. She removed a dark blue taffeta dress draped with side panels of velvet and stood before a pier mirror, holding it to her.

"This is my favorite, I think," she said. "Do you like it?"

The dress accented Hetty's blond hair and china blue eyes. Her heart-shaped face and small, even features reminded Mary of porcelain dolls she'd seen in shop windows, dolls too dear for even a prosperous merchant like her own father to buy. However, there was nothing doll-like about Hetty otherwise. She and Mary were still of a size, both slender, both half a head too tall to be considered petite.

"It's lovely!" Mary exclaimed. She stood beside Hetty and gazed at their contrasting reflections in the mirror. Mary's dark hair, brown eyes, and olive complexion had been inherited from her mother, but her rounded chin, wide-set eyes, and generous mouth were her father's. Hetty, on the other hand, had her father's blond coloring and her mother's delicate features.

Hetty waved at the drifts of satin, lace, velvet, and taffeta still in the clothespress. "Look at these—have you ever seen anything so *delicious* in all your life?"

Overwhelmed, Mary sank down on the bed and watched Hetty exhibit one gown after another, each more elaborate than the last. "They're all lovely, but where will you go in them?"

Hetty held a pale pink satin gown with lace inserts in the bodice to her waist and twirled around. "There will be dozens of dinners and dances in Philadelphia this season—and now that Papa is a general, we're certain to be invited to many of them."

"You'd better be! Where else would you need such elegant gowns?"

Hetty put aside the dress she held and came to sit beside Mary, her expression suddenly serious. "In London, perhaps. If Papa could get into a regiment there, we'd not stay in the colonies."

"But isn't it a great honor for a colonial to be made a general?" Mary said, repeating what she had heard others say.

"Oh, yes—and you can be sure that many regular British officers are furious that he made the rank before they did. But Papa says his reputation will be assured when he leads the Crown's forces against its enemies. Then he can have his choice of posts."

"You sound different—you weren't talking that way when you left Philadelphia," Mary said, steering the conversation away from a subject not to her liking.

"I hope not! London society looks down on colonials who speak with a provincial accent. Mother engaged a tutor to help me master the King's English."

"But now you'll sound strange to Philadelphians," Mary pointed out. "With so much anti-English feeling about these days—"

"Pshaw!" Hetty said in disgust. "What do I care what rude colonials think? I am His Majesty King George the Third's loyal subject, and I'd much prefer to be taken for English-born than an ignorant provincial."

Mary threw up her hands and slid off the bed long enough to curtsy. "Yes, Your Highness! Your gowns are exquisite, and I'm sure you'll look wonderful in them."

Hetty nodded as if in agreement. "Thank you. But now it's your turn. What has happened since your last letter? Surely you must have a suitor or two by now."

Mary shook her head. "No. A few seemed interested, but Papa chased them all away."

Hetty laughed. "Really? Did he go after them with his blunderbuss?"

"Almost. You know how fathers can be—they think no one is good enough," Mary said, unwilling to disclose the real reason for her father's animosity to several who had sought to court her. "What about you? I thought you might have snagged a duke or earl by now."

Hetty smiled, briefly showing the dimple in her left cheek. "I did meet some titled gentlemen in London, but they were all so *boring*. Actually, to London ladies, there's nothing more interesting than a native-born colonial wearing buckskins."

"London society must be very strange if it admires backwoodsmen but objects to their speech," Mary said. "I can't say that I've given frontiersmen any thought," she added, truthfully enough.

"Well, do so—we must find out what the fuss is all about," Hetty said cheerfully. "Now, do start at the beginning—you must tell me absolutely everything that's happened in Philadelphia since October."

Chapter 2

Spring had come early to the Pennsylvania forest. Dark evergreens framed a palette of pastel blooms and golden leaves. Underfoot, the soft forest floor was brightened by maypops and trillium.

Adam Craighead scarcely noticed the beauty of his surroundings, however. To cover the last few miles to Stones' Crossing, he had left the heavily traveled main road. He rode at a steady pace, but without urgency, his thoughts his only companion. He'd already come a long way from the settlement on the Monongahela where he'd lived most of his life. Adam lifted his head and sniffed the air. The fresh scent of the spring woods now carried with it an acrid pungency that could mean only one thing—a nearby fireplace; campfire smoke wouldn't be so concentrated. The crossing couldn't be much farther.

Before him a twig snapped, then another. Adam reined his sturdy chestnut horse to a halt, his hand ready on his rifle. "Who goes there?" he called out.

"A friend," a voice answered, and a moment later another rider emerged from the forest and stopped a few yards away.

Facing one another, the two made an interesting contrast. Both wore long hunting shirts and buckskin trousers and were armed with long-barreled rifles and Indian knives. Adam sat tall in the saddle, rangy and square-jawed, with long blond hair and hazel eyes. The newcomer was younger, half a head shorter and more stocky, with Indian-straight, long black hair and dark eyes. A smile lifted the corners of his generous mouth, and Adam recognized him.

"*Ili kleheleche, woapalanne-tit,*" the newcomer said in Delaware.

"David McKay!" Adam exclaimed. He rode close enough to grasp his hand. "So you got to the Crossing first, eh? I'm not 'Little Eagle' anymore, even among the Lenni-Lenape."

"Then I'll call you Adam. I'll be glad for your company when I trade our load o' pelts. I'm glad we can make th' trip together."

"I'm surprised to see you here, though. How'd you know I'd come by the woods?" Adam asked.

David shrugged. "I had a hunch you might—and anyhow, I thought I might find somethin' to bring home for th' Stones."

"Are they all right?"

David turned his horse back toward the direction from which he had

252

come. "Come and see for yourself—they've been lookin' for you to get here for two days now."

"It's a long way from here to the Monongahela," Adam said.

David nodded. "I remember. How are Aunt Ann and Uncle Caleb?"

"Tolerably well. Father took a bad cough in the winter and still has it, but he won't give up his preaching and catechism classes. Mother can't do a thing against it. How about your folks? They still in Carolina?"

"Yep. Pa and I went trappin' together this past winter—we had a good year. Susannah and the Gospels still live with Aunt Sarah and Uncle Joshua."

Adam smiled faintly at David's mention of Matthew, Mark, Luke, and John, collectively known as the Gospels. David's younger brothers and sister had joined their aunt and uncle's family soon after their mother's death several years before. "Susannah's near to marrying age—seems like she could keep house by herself."

David nodded. "She could, but the Gospels like it at the Stones', and Aunt Sarah'd miss them something fierce if they left, too."

"Too?"

"I'm thinkin' of leavin' home for good," David said.

"So am I," Adam said.

David glanced at his cousin. "Why?"

Adam shrugged. "It's time. There's no future for me at Craigheads' Station."

Karendouah's face swam before him, and with clarity Adam remembered how she'd tenderly placed the bracelet she'd woven on his wrist, then wept and told him she would marry the son of An-we-ga and Bel-a-ka. Even now, six months later, his heart felt heavy with the memory.

"What're you goin' to do now?" David asked.

"I might ask you the same thing."

"I asked first."

"I haven't decided. Mother thinks I might find work in Philadelphia. Father would like for me to take up the ministry, like him."

"The ministry!" David's sidewise glance and his tone showed his amusement. "You don't look like a preacher to me."

"Or to me, either. Now, what about you? What are your plans?"

"I'll sell th' pelts and take trade goods back to Pa, then I don't know. A lot of our neighbors talk about goin' to the Kaintuck. I might take a look-see myself."

"Kentucky? I hear it's quite a good hunting ground, but I don't know about trying to live there."

"Huntin' like you never saw in your life—buffalo so thick you can't count 'em, and all sorts of game at the salt licks. Land so rich, crops all but grow by themselves, they say. A man could get fair rich in a hurry, and that's a fact."

Adam shook his head. "Hunting and growing food to live on is one thing—doing it year in, year out for a living—I don't think I want to do that."

"What do you want, then?"

David spoke seriously, but Adam smiled. "To get to the crossing first and sit down to a hot meal."

"I reckon I can get there pretty quick," David replied, grinning and spurring his horse.

"Not any quicker than me, Davy." Adam urged his horse forward, catching up with David as they broke from the forest and raced toward Stones' Crossing.

❧

John Andrews came home just in time to take supper with Mary. The spring twilight had all but faded, and as he greeted her, Mary thought her father looked exhausted.

"Tell me, Mistress Mary Ann, what has passed while I was away?"

"You hardly ever call me 'Mary Ann' anymore," Mary said. "What made you do so tonight?"

Her father shrugged. "I didn't even realize I had until you pointed it out. I suppose certain recent events must have reminded me of the days when I knew the Ann who was your namesake."

"Was? Is she dead, then?" Mary knew she had been named for a friend of the family, someone she'd never met and whose last name she'd never heard.

Her father shrugged. "I don't know. I haven't seen her in years. But back to my question—something tells me you've been up to no good."

Mary matched her father's mock seriousness. "As usual, you're absolutely right. Hetty and her family have returned from England—Thomas took Polly and me to the docks to meet them this morning."

"In the cabriolet?"

"No, Papa, it was such a lovely morning we decided to walk," Mary said, her smile betraying her effort to sound serious.

John Andrews did not return her smile. "You may use the carriage, as long as Thomas and Polly are with you. But I'll not have you going about alone."

Mary's smile faded. "That is not my custom," she said, only slightly stretching the truth. Mary usually went alone to Hetty's, the distance being short, and occasionally to the market.

"I should hope not! So, tell me—how did the Hawkins family fare in London?"

"Very well, I should say. Colonel Hawkins is now a general, and to celebrate he had the queen's dressmaker make Hetty a completely new wardrobe."

"I'm sure that pleased Hetty and her mother," her father said with some asperity.

Mary looked down at her plate and said nothing. She knew her father disliked Hetty's parents, from whom he kept a polite distance.

"Do you envy Hetty?" he asked after a moment.

Mary frowned as she considered his question. "I don't think so. Hetty's changed—but in a way that I can't say I envy."

Mr. Andrews smiled ironically. "Life in London would be enough to change anyone, I suspect. I'm sure I'd hardly recognize my own sister these days."

"Do you suppose Aunt Elizabeth will ever come back from England?" Mary asked. "I should so like to meet her."

"I doubt it. Her husband has such a high post that, from what she writes, the whole British economy would collapse if Herbert Ford ever left the country."

Mary smiled. "Then perhaps we should urge them to pay us a visit—I'm sure your business would be much improved if that should happen."

Rather than laughing with her, as her father usually did when Mary made light of a subject, he frowned. "You must never say such a thing, even in jest," he warned.

"Such a thing as what?" Mary asked, bewildered at her father's reaction.

"As saying aught against the Crown. We may have our private opinions— we certainly cannot help that—but treason against the Crown is a crime, and its punishment isn't light."

"Are things really that bad, then?"

Her father set his mouth in a grim line. "These are hard times, and the British seem bent on making them worse. Not always knowing who is friend and who is foe, 'tis best to keep your own counsel."

"I understand," Mary murmured, although she wasn't entirely certain that she did.

"Good. I'm afraid I must absent myself again for a few days." Mary's father rose and came around to help her from the table.

"Not already! You just got here!" she cried. "And what about your promise that we'd go to the Lancaster house?"

"I'm sorry, Mary, but I didn't conclude all my business—I must go out of town again for a short while. But I promise to take you to Lancaster as soon as I can arrange it."

"Will you sign a contract to that effect?"

He gazed down at his daughter. "Who could resist such a sweet request, so sweetly made? Lancaster it will be."

"Or what? What penalty will you pay if you forfeit?"

Her father opened his palms in a gesture of resignation. "Perhaps you'd like a new gown or two?"

"Miss Elliott is already making me some, remember? I know a better one—my own riding horse."

He shook his head and bent to kiss Mary's forehead. "I'll be back in a few days and we'll go to Lancaster. There'll be no forfeit."

Her father had resisted letting her have her own horse for far too long—whether they went to Lancaster when he returned or not, Mary definitely intended to pursue the subject.

"We'll see about that," Mary said.

Chapter 3

Adam Craighead and David McKay rode from Lancaster toward Philadelphia, making their way past slow-moving Conestoga wagons and groups traveling on foot. Ever since leaving Stones' Crossing two days earlier, they had encountered more traffic than either of them had ever seen at one time.

"For awhile there I was a-feared that Uncle Jack was comin' with us, no matter what," David said as they passed an older couple who somewhat resembled the Stones.

Adam smiled. "Aye, and if Aunt Isabel hadn't told him he couldn't leave her alone to tend the store with all the spring travelers about, he'd be riding alongside us this very minute."

"Uncle Jack thinks that this war business will get worse," David said. "Do you agree?"

Adam scanned the skies with a practiced eye. "I know nothing about that, but I'd say we might run into some rain before we make Philadelphia."

David shook his head. "The wind's not come fresh from the west yet—there'll be no rain tonight."

Adam laughed at the seriousness with which his cousin made the pronouncement. Despite his engaging smile, David was a rather grave young man, little given to making jokes. "Have you been reading Mr. Franklin's almanack, perchance? I hear it gives the weather for a whole year ahead."

"I've heard tell of it, but I've never seen a copy. What I know about weather I learnt mostly from Ma. She could read signs in the clouds as well as Pa, sometimes even better."

Mention of Sukey, as David's Indian mother was generally known, made Adam feel sad. He hadn't known her as well as he did his uncle Jonathan, who always stayed with them for at least a few days during the hunting and trapping season, but he'd enjoyed her rare visits. When she died soon after the birth of their sixth child, his uncle had taken it very hard. "Losing your mother must have been terrible," Adam said after a moment.

David compressed his mouth to a thin line but said nothing. *He is Indian enough to keep his feelings to himself,* Adam thought and was sorry he'd said anything. "Do you know where to take your pelts?" he added after awhile.

David nodded. " 'Tis the same place Pa's done business with for years. I went with him once when I was nine or ten years old—I can find it easy enough."

"If not, we can ask my mother's friend—that is, if I can locate him."

"You said she writ you a letter of introduction—what does that mean?"

"Wrote me," Adam said, unconsciously correcting his cousin's error. "Mother knows a businessman in Philadelphia who might be willing to take me on as his apprentice—or send me to someone else who would."

"Seems to me that twenty is a mighty old age to be 'prenticed," David said.

Adam nodded. "Aye, but a man can't live without some kind of trade."

"You say you have another letter?"

"Oh, the other's to Father's friend in Neshaminy, where there's a school of sorts for ministers. He and his friends raised the money for Father's passage so he didn't have to be indentured."

"I'd not want to be bound out for any four or five years," David said, shaking his head at the prospect.

"Neither would I," Adam agreed. "If that's all Mr. Andrews has to offer, I'll not stay long in the city."

Adam and David reached Philadelphia late in the afternoon. The sun lay low behind them and cast fantastic shadows before them. As soon as their horses' hoofs hit the unfamiliar cobbled pavement, the animals nickered uneasily and shied.

"We ought to lead them until they get used to these stones," Adam said, and he dismounted.

At the same moment, muted sounds of some sort of disturbance grew ever closer, and by the time David had swung down from his saddle, they were all but overrun by a seething mass of fighting men. Between blows, the men shouted oaths and imprecations at one another, and Adam caught the words "Traitor!" and "Tory!"

"What's happening?" David cried.

"They seem to be having a quarrel—and since it's none of ours, grab your horse's bridle and let's get out of here!" Adam shouted over the din.

But escaping from the mob—for that was what the several dozen fighting men had become—wasn't easy. It was only when Adam's horse shied and kicked its rear legs that a hole opened for them to pass through, and even then Adam's only cloth shirt was all but torn off.

"What do y' think that was about?" David asked when they were a safe distance away.

"I suspect British Loyalists and Patriots were having it out," Adam said. "Uncle Jack warned there was much bad blood between them here."

"I thought Philadelphia calls itself the City of Brotherly Love," David said, shaking his head. "Some love its citizens show, bashin' each other about."

"Well, we've no help for it. Whatever they do is of no matter to us. We'd best try to find the Andrews' house before dark overtakes us."

They pressed on, and after getting directions at an inn where they also had a hasty supper, Adam and David soon stood before the Andrews' town house. The three-story brick structure was flanked by others identical to it but made unique by its bright green shutters. Suddenly apprehensive of what might lie behind the solid oak door, Adam hesitated for a moment before letting the heavy door knocker fall. When there was no immediate response, he repeated the action.

"Maybe no one's to home," David said, just as the door swung open and a servant girl dressed in black, accented by a white apron and a mobcap, stared at them as if they were some sort of very unpleasant vermin.

"Is Mr. Andrews in?" Adam asked.

The girl scowled and backed away, evidently ready to shut the door in their faces. "We don't 'low no walkabouts here. Go away!" she cried in a shrill voice.

Her action galvanized Adam, who grabbed the door and kept it open. "Wait, please, Miss—we're not beggars. I have a letter of introduction for Mr. Andrews. Is he here?"

"No, he ain't, and neither will the likes o' you be in two shakes, or I'll—"

"What is it, Polly?"

Adam heard another voice, this one much softer, then he saw the loveliest face he had ever encountered. Adam opened his mouth and tried to speak, feeling like the crow in the fable that thought it could sing but could only croak.

"They say they want to see Mr. Andrews," Polly said, her tone disdainful.

The vision stepped onto the threshold and stood in the doorway looking down at them, framed as perfectly as a portrait. "I am Mary Andrews. What is your business with my father?"

"I have a letter of introduction to him, Ma'am," Adam replied, never taking his eyes from her face.

"I hope it wasn't in your shirt," she said, and Adam's face reddened as he realized how disreputable he must look. It was no wonder that the servant hadn't wanted to admit them.

"No, Ma'am. It's yonder in my saddlebag," he said, nodding back toward his horse, which he'd tethered to a hitching post beside the doorway.

"Then fetch it and come inside," she said. "Polly, get these gentlemen some refreshment. If I'm not mistaken, they've traveled a long way today."

"What makes you say that?" Adam asked, following her into a dim hallway.

"Philadelphia's paved streets don't make the kind of dust that's on your clothes. Come in here," she added, leading them to a small drawing room off the main entrance.

Another smaller room that seemed to be an office of some kind was to the left of the door. From the front hall, stairs led to the other two stories. Narrow though it might be, the Andrews' house was still the grandest that Adam and David had ever seen. Adam tried not to gape at the upholstered furniture, the leather fire screen, and the lace window curtains, but he couldn't resist surveying the room. When he glanced back to Mary, she was staring at him.

"What happened? Have you two been a-brawling?" she asked.

"Not us. Some people were fighting around us and we had a hard time getting away," Adam said, meeting Mary's direct glance.

Mary stepped closer to Adam. "Is that a wound that needs to be treated?"

Adam looked down at his chest as if he had never seen it before and tried to pull the ripped fabric to cover the jagged, red mark. "No. It's just an old scar."

"What caused it?"

Adam wasn't accustomed to having a woman ask about his scar, and his face betrayed his uneasiness. He cleared his throat before answering. "The Seneca took me when I was about two. This is their mark."

Mary put out her hand as if to touch Adam's scar, then drew back, apparently thinking better of it. "You were raised by the heathen?" she asked, having heard many such tales over the years. *That would account for his buckskins and wild hair and that odd leather bracelet on his right wrist,* she thought.

"No, Ma'am. I didn't stay long with the Seneca. And the Indians I grew up with aren't savages. My father saw to that—he's a missionary among the Delaware. My name is Adam Craighead."

Mary looked from Adam to David. "And him? Is he one of your Indian friends, then?"

"I'm David McKay, and Adam is my cousin," he said quickly.

"Oh," Mary said, as if surprised that David had understood her question, much less answered it in English.

"There's refreshment in the kitchen. If you'd like to clean up, I'll show you to the pump," Polly said, directly addressing Adam and David.

"Thank you, Ma'am," Adam replied in the same tone he'd used with Mary.

Mary sank down in her father's favorite chair and stared after them. They were frontiersmen, no doubt about it, perhaps the very kind that Hetty said caused a stir in London. She'd seen many frontiersmen on the streets of Philadelphia, wild, bearded fellows clad in fringed buckskin, carrying rifles taller than some of them. She'd always stayed as far away from them as she could. None had looked like this pair, however. The shorter, dark one was at least half-Indian, she was certain. But the tall, golden one—he must be just the sort of frontiersman that Hetty wanted to meet.

What should I do with them? Mary wondered. If Adam Craighead had a letter of introduction to her father, he should be treated as a guest, no matter how odd his appearance. John Andrews would want that. However, inviting complete strangers, and male ones at that, to use the guest bedchamber was out of the question. On the other hand, the carriage house was comfortable enough—they could stay there.

Satisfied with that decision, Mary called Polly and bade her to make the arrangements.

The Andrews' carriage house, located across a narrow alley from the red brick house, was a two-story frame building. The horses and carriages were kept on the ground level, while upstairs there were a jumbled storage room and an unoccupied room where, Polly said, the coachman used to stay.

"What happened to him?" Adam asked.

"His time was up, so he left," Polly answered. Then seeing that Adam hadn't understood, she went on. "He was bound, like me. One o' these days, I'll be leavin', too."

"This is a nice room," Adam said, noting it actually had a window with glass in it.

Polly grunted. "Humph! Had y' to stay here in the cold o' the winter or heat o' the summer, y'd not think so. Y' can sleep on those quilts yonder. Mice got into the feather tick an' Miss Merry made me throw it out."

"It will do nicely. And thank your mistress for putting us up."

"Humph," Polly said again, obviously not wanting these strange-looking young men to lodge under any part of the Andrews' roof. "If y' plan t' sit up past dark, there's some candle ends in the tack room. But y' must use your own flint to light 'em."

Adam nodded. "We'll not be sitting up tonight—we've had a long journey."

Polly turned to go, then stopped at the head of the steps. "Y' can come to the kitchen for breakfast if y' like, but wait 'til the sun's up good," she added grudgingly.

"Aye, that we will," David said. He smiled at her, throwing the girl into complete confusion, and she turned and fled down the steps.

❧❧

"Did you get them settled?" Mary asked later when Polly came into her room to brush her hair.

"They're in Tad's old room, sleepin' on the quilts y' told me they could have. I only hope we don't wake in the mornin' an' find our scalps missin'."

Mary laughed. Taking off her cap, she ran her hands through her thick brown hair. "I daresay even a tomahawk would have a hard time cutting through this mane," she said lightly.

"All the same, those two bear watchin'," Polly said.

"That they do," Mary agreed, but the reasons she was thinking of to watch Adam and David were hardly the same as Polly's. "Please try to be quiet while you brush my hair. I don't want to hear your chatter tonight."

Polly compressed her lips. In the two years she'd been trying to anticipate and fill her mistress's every whim, Polly had learned two things: Mary Andrews was as hardheaded as they come, but she could also be strangely softhearted. *A bad combination,* Polly thought as she moved the brush through Mary's heavy hair. Someday it was bound to get them all in trouble.

❧

Despite his fatigue, Adam stayed awake a long time. He and David talked for awhile in the darkness, but eventually David fell asleep in the middle of a sentence, leaving Adam wide awake. He rose from his quilt pallet and walked to the window. Through its streaked pane he could make out the dark bulk of the Andrews' house. Either Mary had retired for the evening herself or, more likely, her room was on the front of the house, overlooking the street. The kitchen was on a lower level in the rear, an arrangement Adam had heard about but had never seen. In fact, he realized, there were many things about city life that he hadn't suspected. Sighing, he returned to his pallet.

Could I live here all the time? Adam asked himself. It would take some getting used to, no doubt about it. Then he thought of Mary Andrews and her dark hair and searching eyes. She was the first woman he'd noticed since his painful parting with Karendouah, and she was definitely a part of the city in which she lived. *Philadelphia can't be all bad if it raises the likes of her,* Adam told himself as he drifted off to sleep.

Chapter 4

Have our guests broken their fast yet?" Mary asked the next morning when Polly brought her usual hot scones, jelly, and "tea," made from herbs found at the market.

"Yes, Ma'am. The one wi' the torn shirt asked the loan of needle and thread so's he could mend it."

Annoyed, Mary put down her scone. "Oh, I knew there was something else I should have done last night—Papa has some old shirts that he can have. I'll look into it straightaway."

"There ain't no rush," Polly said. "He's got on one of them long buckskin shirts this mornin'. Claims it's more comfortable than the linen, if you can feature that."

"Papa gave me some buckskin boots once," Mary said. "I recall they were very soft and warm."

"But not a'tall fit for a lady," Polly said, with the air of a final authority on fashion matters. "What will y' be wearin' today?" she added, moving to the wall where Mary's dresses hung on pegs.

"The brown, I think."

Polly cast Mary a quizzical glance. "Your silk dress? Will y' be goin' callin' today, then?"

"No, but Hetty said she and her mother will make calls today. I should receive them properly."

Polly said nothing, but the shake of her head clearly expressed her opinion.

As usual, Mary ignored her somewhat sour servant. It was true that the Hawkins might come to call. It was also true that Mary would see the two frontiersmen. In either case, looking nice wouldn't hurt anything.

❧

"I sure would like t' get rid o' these pelts today," David said later that morning. The bundles had been brought inside as a precaution against theft, and their distinctive odor filled the room.

Adam looked up from the linen shirt he was struggling to mend. "Maybe we will, but I still want to see Mr. Andrews first. From what his daughter said, he should be back soon."

"I hope so," David said. "I've groomed the horses half to death an' beat a

263

peck o' dust out of my buckskins. I can't think of another thing to do."

"You might stitch on this for awhile," Adam said, holding his torn shirt up to the light. Although he had been working on it for some time, he still had a long way to go. And what he'd already done was puckered and imperfect, reminding Adam of the scar on his chest. *In men and shirts alike,* he thought, *once an injury is sustained, some mark of it always seems to remain.*

"No thanks. I'd ruin it fer sure."

"Someone's coming," Adam said, hearing footsteps on the coach house stairs.

As Polly entered the room, David stood and bowed low. "Good mornin', Miss Polly," he said pleasantly, bringing a blushing scowl to the servant's face.

"Mistress Andrews will see you at your pleasure," she said, addressing Adam.

"Myself alone?" he questioned.

"The both o' you, I suppose. But hurry on now—Miss Mary's expectin' quality company in a little while."

"We'll be there right away," Adam said.

"Quality company?" David questioned when Polly had left. "What does *that* mean?"

Adam laughed and rose, laying the shirt aside. "It means that Miss Polly doesn't think much of us."

"What about her mistress?"

Adam shrugged. "She let us stay here last night—she must see some good in us."

"Still, we ought to plan to move on. I don't want to be beholden to anyone, much less a female."

"You're right. But for now, Cousin, we mustn't keep the lady waiting."

When Adam and David appeared in the drawing room doorway, Mary stood and handed Adam a cloth-wrapped bundle. "I should have given you these last night," she said, her soft brown eyes meeting his. "They are my father's—I hope you can wear them."

Adam opened the bundle and took out a shirt. Holding it up, he saw that it was made of fine lawn, but also that it was far shorter than the shirt he'd been mending.

"I appear to be some taller than your father, who might not want you to give away his shirts in any case," Adam said. He handed the bundle back to Mary, who gestured for Polly to take it. Mary's face reddened, and Adam hoped his refusal hadn't angered her.

"Yes, I suppose you are some taller," she said.

"When can we see your father?" Adam asked.

"I'm not sure," Mary said. "He—"

Mary broke off speaking as the door knocker sounded.

"David and I will leave now," Adam said as Polly swept past them to answer the door, casting a meaningful glance in their direction. "We have some other calls to make, then we'll stop by later. Perhaps Mr. Andrews will be back by then."

"Don't go!" Mary said. She could hear Hetty's voice, and Mary knew her friend would never forgive her if she didn't let her meet these genuine frontiersmen.

Adam had turned to leave but stopped at her words. "We can't impose—" he began, but then Hetty and her father were in the hall, and it was too late for him and David to leave gracefully.

"General Hawkins, what a surprise!" Mary said in a bright tone of voice far different from what she had used with Adam and David. "Hetty, Dear, how did you manage to get your father to come with you to call?"

"The same way she gets me to do anything," General Hawkins said. "Those blue eyes of hers can be very persuasive."

"Oh, Papa!" Hetty said. Then she turned and saw Adam and David, and her mouth fell open in surprise. She looked back to Mary and waited to be introduced.

"General Hawkins, Hetty—may I present Adam Craighead and David—"

"McKay," David supplied, and again Mary was embarrassed that she hadn't recalled his name.

Adam noted that the general's eyes were as blue as his daughter's, and that he was tall and well-built, resplendent in his new, bright red uniform, trimmed with gold braid. There was an awkward moment before General Hawkins extended his hand, first to Adam, and then to David.

"Craighead and McKay, eh?" he said. "From around the Monongahela, perhaps?"

"I am, Sir," Adam replied. "David lives in North Carolina."

"Won't you sit down?" Mary invited, gesturing toward the drawing room.

Everyone followed Mary into the drawing room, where David and Adam sat together on a sofa. The general sat opposite them, while Hetty and Mary seated themselves in wing chairs flanking the sofa.

General Hawkins leaned forward and looked closely at Adam and David. "I believe I might know your father," he said to David. "Did he ever hunt around Fort Bedford?"

"Yes, Sir—all through that area. He's a hunter to this day."

"And you, young man—from your garb, I presume you hunt, as well?"

"Not for a living," Adam said.

"Perhaps you'd both be interested in signing on with the British Army, then." General Hawkins looked directly at David. "Am I right in assuming you have Indian blood?"

"My mother was from the Delaware," David said.

The general looked pleased. "I thought so! I had charge of Fort Bedford in '58. Later I recruited and trained native troops to defend against the French. Splendid fighters they were. I should like to do the same thing again. Someone like you, intimately bound by blood to the Indians' language and customs, would be invaluable to the Crown."

"I'm not a soldier, Sir," David McKay said levelly. "I've no interest in makin' war."

"It's not a matter of interest but of patriotism," General Hawkins said. "We're all subjects of His Majesty the King. The colonies are merely branches of Britain, which has spent a great deal of money and effort on providing them with its protection."

"Oh, Papa, please don't start a tiresome lecture!" Hetty exclaimed.

"A lecture? Nonsense! I am merely making a legitimate offer of employment to some fellows who look as though they could use it."

"Thank you, Sir, but we don't need your help," Adam said, trying hard to be polite for Mary's sake. He had no experience with Philadelphia drawing rooms, but he knew that a man shouldn't insult another when both are guests of a lady. Not even the worst of the "savages" he had been raised among would be so crude.

"Mr. Craighead has a letter of introduction for my father," Mary said quickly.

General Hawkins looked back to Adam and frowned as if trying to remember something. "Craighead—seems I've heard the name before."

"My father is a missionary among the Delaware," Adam offered. "Perhaps you've heard of his work."

"No, it wasn't that—" General Hawkins furrowed his brow, then shook his head. "I'll not rest until I can recall the connection, but for now, it eludes me."

"I have an older sister named Sarah. She once stayed at Fort Bedford during the trouble with the French. Perhaps you met her then," Adam said.

General Hawkins's face cleared and he nodded. "Of course! Sarah Craighead—came to Bedford dressed like an Indian—a pretty young woman. As I recall, she was on her way to some crossing or station. Where is she now?"

"In North Carolina with her husband, Joshua Stone. He was with her at the fort, I believe."

"Yes, I recall such a man, although I had forgot the name. Well, young men, I repeat my offer. You must know that I am in a position to secure you both good postings with His Majesty's troops."

No one said anything for a moment, then David spoke. "Much obliged, Sir, but as a matter of fact, I've not decided whose side I'd be on if it came to a fight. I'd best stay away from anyone's army for now."

"And you, Mr. Craighead? Are your sentiments the same?"

Adam matched the general's direct gaze. "They are."

"Then there is nothing more to say." General Hawkins's voice was distinctly cool.

Recognizing they were being summarily dismissed, Adam and David stood and bowed to the ladies before taking their leave.

Mary followed them into the hall and laid a restraining hand on Adam's sleeve, her voice urgent. "Don't leave yet—my father would be very upset to find that I had let you get away."

"Thank you, Ma'am, but we're not fish to be reeled in. I think it best for us to move on," Adam said.

"At least stay here another night," Mary begged. "One more night—then if Papa still hasn't come home, you may go."

"What about it, David?" Adam asked. He turned to his cousin, who shrugged.

"I reckon we can stay—as long as I don't have to see *him* again," David said, nodding in the direction of General Hawkins.

Mary looked pleased. "Polly will call you to supper. Good-bye for now."

As Mary returned to her guests, Adam and David went back to the carriage house.

"I wouldn't work for that man for a pile of gold," David said.

"Neither would I," Adam agreed. "I hope we don't run into him again."

David glanced knowingly at Adam. "One member of that family'd like to see y' again, though."

"I don't know what you're talking about."

"That Miss Hetty's got the bluest eyes I ever saw—and she never took 'em off you, even for a second."

Adam shook his head. "I think you're daft," he said flatly.

But on one thing he had to agree with David. Hetty Hawkins did, indeed, have exceedingly blue eyes.

Chapter 5

"Y ou mustn't let that pair get away, Mary."

General Hawkins had gone on to make some calls of his own, leaving his daughter with Mary, and Hetty wasted no time in broaching the subject of the men she'd just met.

Mary Andrews frowned. "They're not animals in a menagerie, you know. If Papa doesn't come back today, I've no doubt they'll leave."

"The tall one—Adam, you said? If he has a letter of introduction, he'll be back."

"He said he did, but I never actually saw it—he might just be pretending."

"Why would he do that? If they were going to rob you, they would already have done so. Besides, they don't look like the criminal sort."

Mary smiled briefly. "Thieves seldom advertise their intentions, Hetty. But I agree—they didn't come to rob us. If I knew where Papa was staying, I'd send after him."

Hetty idly twisted a golden curl around her finger. "So your father still takes mysterious trips—have you ever found out why?"

Mary looked away from Hetty's piercing blue eyes and shook her head. "As a matter of fact, I haven't asked," she said, telling a partial truth. Mary hadn't asked because she'd been told not to—but she knew more about her father's errands than she dared to tell Hetty. "Anyway, what would you do with the frontiersmen if they decided to stay in Philadelphia?"

Hetty smiled, displaying her dimple. "Why, I'd introduce them to society, of course. Wouldn't their buckskins look wonderful in the midst of all the ruffled and stuffed shirts at the next cotillion?"

Mary winced at the thought. "I doubt very much if either of that pair would willingly attend such an event—and even if they did, they'd certainly know better than to wear buckskins."

Hetty's lips curved in a slight smile. "But that would spoil the fun," she said.

"They wouldn't find it at all entertaining," Mary replied.

"Perhaps not, but I certainly would," Hetty said. "And the way you're rushing to defend them tells me that Mistress Merry has more than a passing interest in the matter herself."

"You are quite mistaken, my dear," Mary said, attempting to sound like a haughty English grande dame and succeeding only in making Hetty laugh.

"Ah, now you sound like the Merry Andrews I remember. How I missed your quick wit all those months!"

With the subject safely away from the frontiersmen, Mary smiled back at Hetty and rose. "Come now and see my new gowns. They're not as grand as yours, but you can tell me which I ought to wear to your father's gala."

❧

"I don't think Mistress Mary has any idea when her father will be back," Adam told David that evening when once more John Andrews had failed to appear. They had just returned to the carriage house after taking supper in the kitchen, where Polly had informed them that her mistress was dining with friends, then had hovered over them throughout the meal as if she feared they might otherwise steal the plates.

"I thought so from the first," David said. "Yet she seems t' want t' keep us about. Odd girl, she is."

"Oh, I don't know about that," Adam said. "Perhaps she really is trying to do what she thinks her father would want. But I agree that it's time we moved on. First thing tomorrow, we'll take your pelts to market. Then I'll find the Reverend Ian MacPherson."

David nodded. "Pa's countin' on me t' get a fair price for the pelts. If you're with me, I'm not as likely to get cheated."

Adam looked amused. "Why? I've never traded pelts in my life."

"No, but you look like you have, an' sometimes that's all that matters."

"Appearances aren't everything," Adam said, thinking not just about David's business transaction, but about the strange girl who had offered them a distant hospitality.

What does Mary Andrews really think about us? Adam wondered. But he was careful not to ask himself if he cared.

❧

"Tell Miss Andrews that we'll be back later," Adam told Polly the next morning as he and David prepared to leave. They made their way through Philadelphia's wide streets, already thronged with market-goers, to a row house where a single sign bearing a crude representation of a beaver pelt signaled the place of business that David sought.

A bell attached to the door tinkled as they opened it, and the unmistakable odor of animal skins assailed them as they stepped inside. Robbie McCall, the white-haired broker David's father had dealt with for years, greeted David with hearty affection and insisted that he report all the family news before he'd even look at David's bundles.

" 'Tis good t' see ye again and a pleasure t' meet your cousin. Sit down;

make yourself to home. Alex! Come and make a place for these lads to sit."

McCall's apprentice, a sullen, dark-skinned boy wrapped in a stained leather apron, appeared from the back room and gathered up several pelt bundles from the only other chairs in the office.

"So, young man, will ye be followin' after yer father in the trade now?"

"No, Sir," David replied. "I intend to do something different."

"Different, is it?" McCall leaned back in his chair and looked appraisingly at David. "Well, ye're not a big 'un, but ye seem strong enough. Are ye come to seek work in the city, then?"

David shook his head. "No, Sir. From what I've seen, I don't think I'd take kindly to city life."

McCall nodded, unsurprised. "Might ye be givin' some thought to the army, then?"

"Nay, I've no interest in makin' a soldier."

"And you?" McCall asked, turning to Adam. "Dozens of frontiersmen are comin' to Philadelphia every day, signin' up on one side or another. I'm sure they'd welcome such a strappin' young man as yerself. I hear the British are offerin' fine bounties these days."

From the questioning tone in his voice, Adam understood that McCall wanted to know where his loyalties lay without giving away his own. "Neither of us came here to fight anyone," he said.

McCall's eyes held Adam's for a long moment, then he nodded as if he understood something Adam had left unsaid. "Still, ye may find ye have no choice. The time is comin' when every colonial will have t' choose sides."

"It seems that time may already have come—as soon as David and I reached the city yesterday, we got caught up in a brawl that seemed to be between Patriots and Loyalists."

"Aye, such clashes are commonplace these days. My advice to ye both is t' consider which side ye'll take when th' fightin' starts in earnest—an' mark my words, that time's a-comin', sooner than any of us might want."

Seeing the serious expressions his words had brought to Adam's and David's faces, McCall stood and put his hand on David's shoulder. "But that's enough of an old man's rantin'. Come now and let's have a look at those pelts ye brought."

❧

Mary was disappointed when Polly told her that Adam and David had gone off practically at dawn and left no word when they would be returning. As soon as she dressed, Mary went to the carriage house to satisfy herself that their things were still there. While there, she noticed the linen shirt that Adam had tried to mend.

"Polly, find my sewing basket, please," she called when she came back into the house bearing the shirt.

"Surely you ain't gonna work on that rag!" Polly exclaimed, warily eyeing Adam's garment.

"Somebody needs to," Mary replied. "Adam Craighead may be quite at home in the wilderness, but he knows nothing about sewing."

Polly sniffed. "An' why should he, when a lady of quality lowers herself to take on the task?"

Mary shot an exasperated look at Polly, whose notions about proper society were far different from her own. "Since when does performing a service lower anyone? Do you not recall that even our Lord washed His disciples' feet?"

"I also remember Mr. John sayin' that even Satan can quote Scripture," Polly muttered.

"Oh, I'm Satan now, am I?" Mary teased, and reluctantly Polly's mouth twitched in a near-smile.

"Don't twist my words, Miss Merry. You may trust that pair o' buckskins, but I'll rest me easier when they've gone on their way."

"I'm sure that won't be much longer—but in the meantime, I see nothing wrong in seeing that Adam Craighead has at least one decent shirt."

❧

At McCall's insistence, Adam and David took lunch with him at a popular establishment only a few doors from the peltry business. When questioned about why part of its sign had been painted out, leaving only the word "Stag" under a picture of a large buck deer, McCall explained that the owner had thought it prudent to remove the "Royal" that had preceded it.

"When he put it up, the British had just chased away the French, and nothin' was too good for His Majesty's troops. Every store owner in town wanted to get some sort o' British symbol on his sign."

"Now that y' mention it, I don't think we've seen many such symbols since we've come, have we, Adam?" David said.

"Not that I recall, but then we weren't looking for any," Adam said.

"Oh, there's still some about, lots of places where the Loyals gather," McCall said. "But I say a man needs a place t' get a good joint o' meat and a hunk o' bread wi'out havin' t' talk politics—and the Stag is just th' place. Eat hearty, lads."

Between McCall's penchant for storytelling and the dozens of men who stopped by the plank table to talk to the peltry merchant, it was far into the afternoon before Adam and David parted with McCall. At the merchant's advice, they bought a thin leather strip for David to wrap the peltry money in and hide beneath his hunting shirt.

"Philadelphia's as full as thieves as fleas on a dog," McCall warned them. "Put a reg'lar wampum belt on the outside o' your shirt and next thing y' know, it's cut off an' yer money's gone. And don't get the trade goods until yer ready to go back, neither, less'n yer willin' t' sleep wi' one eye open all the time."

"The more I hear about Philadelphia, the less I like it," David said as they made their way back to the street where John and Mary Andrews lived. "I can't imagine that anybody'd want t' live here."

"McCall knows that visitors are often taken advantage of. The people who live here don't seem to be afraid for their lives."

"Well, they don't seem all that friendly, either, 'cept for McCall, and in his case it's prob'ly just good business t' be nice to us. I'm ready to move on from here myself."

Adam nodded. "All right. If John Andrews still isn't at home, we'll go on to Neshaminy tonight."

"I'll go round and pack up our gear," David said when they reached the house.

"I'll see if he's here, then I'll join you," Adam said.

When Mary opened the front door to admit him, the look on her face told Adam that her father still hadn't returned.

"You and your friend are welcome to stay in the carriage house as long as you like," she added after confirming her father's absence.

"I hope nothing has happened to him," Adam said, reading the concern expressed in her eyes. "The peltry merchant warned us to watch out for thieves."

Mary's reddened cheeks baffled Adam. "I'm not worried about his safety," she said. "I just thought that he'd be here by now. I know you must have other matters to attend to."

"Yes, we do. As a matter of fact, we must go on to Neshaminy this evening."

Mary looked surprised. "But soon it'll be suppertime, and it's a long way to Neshaminy. At least stay the night."

"No, we can't. You've done enough for us already."

"It was no more than my father would have wanted," Mary said quickly, avoiding looking at Adam directly. "Before you go, I have something to give you. Wait here—I'll be right back."

Adam stood in the hallway and admired Mary's grace as she mounted the stairs. She returned only moments later, holding something white.

"Your shirt," she said, handing it to him.

He looked in surprise at the garment, which had been neatly mended with almost invisible stitches. "How came you by this?" he asked, bringing faint color to her cheeks.

"I went to the carriage house this morning to see if you'd taken your things with you. I couldn't help but see that the shirt needed a woman's hand."

I ought to tell her she has no business meddling in my possessions, Adam thought, but he couldn't reject Mary's gesture of goodwill. "I'm afraid you're right," he said instead. "Thank you—or should I thank Polly?"

Mary raised her chin slightly and looked him in the eyes. "Polly can't sew as well as you. No, Mr. Craighead, these did every stitch."

She extended her hands, spreading her fingers as if to prove that she was, indeed, a capable seamstress. Without stopping to think about how it might be taken, Adam took her hands in his and held them. Mary looked startled, but she made no move to pull away from his grasp.

"David and I do appreciate your welcome, Miss Andrews," he said. "And perhaps we'll yet be able to convey our respects to your father."

"How long will you stay at Neshaminy?" Mary asked.

"A day or two, perhaps. A friend of my father's lives there," he added, then chastised himself for appearing to presume that she cared.

"You must come back here before you leave Philadelphia. My father will be home soon—perhaps this very evening."

Adam watched Mary's expression closely and wondered if she could read his expression as well as he read hers. *She's not just being polite,* he realized, and the thought so unsettled him that he dropped her hands as if they had suddenly become burning coals.

"Tell him I'm sorry I missed seeing him," he murmured, then turned to go, too embarrassed to see the effect of his strange behavior on Mary.

"Wait!" Mary called out, and Adam stopped and turned to face her again.

"What is it?" he asked.

"Shall I tell my father that you'll be back, then?"

Once more their eyes met, and Adam nodded, his throat suddenly tight. "Yes, I'll be back. But if he isn't here, I must go on."

"I understand," Mary said. Then her expression brightened. "Why don't you leave your letter of introduction here? I'll give it to my father as soon as he comes back."

Why didn't I think of that? Adam thought. "I suppose I could," he said aloud. His letter of introduction to John Andrews would mean nothing to anyone else. "I'll give it to you before we go."

I'll see him once more, at any rate, Mary thought as Adam left her. And if the letter didn't bear a seal, she might even find out just what it was that Adam Craighead wanted from her father.

Chapter 6

Are you ready to go now?" David asked Adam when he entered the room over the carriage house. He had folded the quilts neatly and their packed saddlebags lay by the stairs. Without the bundles of pelts, their possessions now seemed meager.

Adam nodded. "Yes, after I find that letter to John Andrews. Miss Andrews offered to give it to him for me."

David grinned. "What else did she offer? She wanted us to stay around longer, too, didn't she?"

"She extended her original offer of hospitality, if that's what you mean," Adam said, determined to ignore his cousin's teasing. "She also said Polly would be heartbroken when you left."

David threw his head back and laughed. "Aye, Adam, y' know 'tis a sin t' lie like that—y' ought t' be ashamed!"

Adam assumed an expression of mock solemnity. "And ashamed I would be, but the fact is, that girl has her eye on you, Cousin. The least you can do is give her a proper farewell and thank her for waiting on us these two days."

David's smile faded. "Aye, she's fussed and grumbled, but she's fed us well, and we're bound t' have made more work. But such thanks are best come from you. I've not got your gift o' fair talkin'."

"I have no such gift that I know of," Adam said. "But I will tell Polly and our hostess that you are properly grateful. Now, if I can just find that letter—"

A few minutes later, letter in hand, Adam went to the rear door, where Polly greeted him as if unsurprised that their guests were going. Mary sat in the drawing room, making tiny stitches in what appeared to be some sort of coverlet.

"Don't disturb yourself, Ma'am," Adam said when Mary started to rise when she saw him. "I'll just leave this letter on the table. David asked me to thank you and Miss Polly for taking us in. We'll be on our way now, before the day gets older."

Mary looked as if she wanted to say something more, but with Polly hovering behind Adam, apparently eager to see him and David on their way, she merely nodded and repeated her invitation for them to return after their trip to Neshaminy.

Wishing he had been able to speak to Mary alone, Adam promised to stop by on their return trip. He turned and left through the rear door, which Polly all too agreeably shut behind him.

Mary abandoned her sewing to watch from the window as Adam and David rode away, then she turned toward the table where Adam's letter lay.

"It's sealed with wax, Mistress," Polly said, as if she knew that Mary had planned to read it.

"Most letters are, Polly," Mary said casually. "Put it on Papa's desk with his mail."

Polly picked up the letter and walked toward the window, holding it up to the light. "Looks like parchment. The way it's folded, y' can almost make out a few of the words, though."

"Polly! The very idea, trying to read a letter addressed to someone else— I'm surprised at you."

"Yes, Mistress," Polly said, but her half-smile belied her attempt to sound penitent.

Mary watched Polly take Adam's letter across the hall where John Andrews had his office and wished it hadn't been sealed. But her father would soon be home, and he'd tell her what it said. Until then, she'd just have to be patient.

🙚🙙

"You didn't tell me how far Neshaminy was," David said a few hours later. Night had fallen, and although the sky was filled with bright stars and there was a bit of a moon to guide them, they couldn't ride very fast. The air had chilled considerably once the sun had gone down, and the buckskin shirt that had seemed so comfortable in the daytime was now inadequate.

"I didn't know it was this far myself," Adam said, although he vaguely recalled that Mary had tried to tell him it wouldn't be an easy hour's journey. *We should have stayed in Philadelphia tonight,* he thought but knew better than to say so to David.

"And when we get there, will y' know where it is y' are?"

"It's not a large place—everyone will know Ian MacPherson," Adam said with more confidence than he felt.

They rode in silence through several sleeping villages, where packs of dogs came out to give them a noisy greeting, but no humans stirred to see who passed in the night.

"I'm nigh unto fallin' asleep right here in the saddle," David complained after a long while.

"I'm tired, too," Adam admitted. "There's a fair-sized barn yonder—it's bound to have a hayrick."

"Then let's try it."

The barn, a sturdy stone building far larger than the modest farmhouse that stood a few hundred feet from it, did indeed have an abundant supply of fragrant hay. Adam and David tethered their horses and soon had spread their blankets over a convenient mound of hay near the door.

"This is better than sleepin' on the floor in Philadelphia," David said, his voice drowsy.

"I suppose so," Adam said. *But at least Mary Andrews had been nearby then.* Adam's last thought before he fell asleep was that he already wanted to see her again.

❧

When Mary awoke the next morning to a cloudy day, her first thought was of Adam and David. She wondered if they had reached Neshaminy the night before. Mary began each day with prayer, and this day she found herself asking God to care for the two young men and bring them safely back.

"Mornin', Mistress." Polly seemed unusually cheerful as she brought in Mary's breakfast tray, and she didn't waste much time in revealing the reason. "The master's back home."

"When did he get here?" Mary asked.

"Late, Thomas said. Master woke him up to care for his horse and said he was tired and didn't want to be bothered this morning, so y'd best wait t' make him read his mail."

"Oh, Polly! If I wasn't so hungry, I'd throw this bun at you," Mary said.

"Throw all y' like; it won't change a thing. Too bad the young men went off like that, so near t' the time they coulda seen Master John—that is, if that's really why they came here."

Mary raised her eyebrows at Polly's words. "What on earth are you suggesting? What other reason would they have for coming here? Just as Ad— Mr. Craighead said, he has a letter of introduction to my father. Like as not, Papa can help him in some way."

"An' if he can't, y' will," Polly supplied. "I give 'em two days at the most before they're back on the doorstone again."

"I hope you're right," Mary said. "And when they do come back, Papa will be here—even if I have to tie him down to keep him from leaving again."

The image brought a brief smile to Polly's usually dour face. "I'd like t' see that—and it might be all that'll keep him here, at that."

"What makes you say so?" Mary asked, sensing that Polly knew more than her fleeting smile indicated.

"Thomas said he wanted the carriage to be made ready for this afternoon."

"Oh, he did, did he? Well, I may have something to say about that. Let me know as soon as Papa's up, will you?"

"Yes, Mistress. Enjoy yer breakfast," Polly added, grinning from the doorway.

Adam and David awoke with the dawn, somewhat stiff from their cold ride the night before, but eager to complete their journey.

"We should tell the farmer that we spent the night here," Adam said. "He might be willing to feed us and our horses for a few coins."

"You'd best go alone," David said. "One look at me and the man might think he's about to be scalped and raise the alarm."

"You don't look at all like a vicious Indian," Adam said.

"Not to y', because you know me. But I saw how that Mary Andrews and her maid looked at me at first. I'm sure they both thought I keep a sharp tomahawk handy t' use on the likes o' them."

There was a bitterness in David's tone that Adam had never heard before. "Even if they thought that at first, they soon knew better. Sometimes we have to give people a chance before we make any judgments about them."

David's sudden laugh startled Adam. "Maybe I was wrong—I'm beginnin' t' think y' might make a pretty fair preacher after all."

"I'm sorry if it sounded like I was preaching," Adam said, embarrassed at the realization that he might have been doing just that. "I'd best go try my skills out on the farmer—watch for my signal—they might just invite us in."

Another hour found Adam and David on the road again, well-fed by the German farmer in whose barn they had slept. In his strange blend of German and English, the farmer had assured them that they were near Neshaminy, and, refusing their coins, had invited them to come back anytime.

"That was a nice fellow," David commented as they rode away.

"Yes, he was. Did you notice how he kept pointing to that huge Bible when I tried to give him the money? I think he was trying to tell us that he took us in because of his religion."

"Maybe, but where I come from, it's the thing t' do t' take care o' the stranger amongst us—because we never know when we might need help."

"It was the same way with the Lenni-Lenape in the old days," Adam said. "But times are changing fast—they learned the hard way that not everyone comes in peace."

"The day is too fair for such gloomy talk," David said after a moment. "Want t' see who can get to Neshaminy first?"

"I already know that, Cousin—" Adam began, but David spurred his horse, and the race was on.

So they came laughing to Neshaminy, reining in their horses and arguing good-naturedly about who had arrived first. Adam turned to a middle-aged man who had stopped to watch them and asked his opinion.

"Tell me, Sir, which of us reached yonder fence first?"

The man looked from Adam to David and back again before speaking. "Ye shouldna be racing on a public road, lads," he said in a well-modulated voice. " 'Tis a danger to all who might chance your way."

Adam felt his face warm at the gentle admonition. "I'm sorry, Sir—we didn't think about that."

"We're not very used to real roads," David added.

The man smiled faintly. "That I could tell," he said. "What brings ye to Neshaminy?"

"I'm looking for a minister named MacPherson, Ian MacPherson," Adam said. "Might you be able to direct me to him?"

"I might, considering I am the man ye seek," he said. "That's my house yonder. I was just on my way there after a sick call. And who might ye be?"

Adam dismounted and was surprised to see that Ian MacPherson was such a tall man. "I'm Adam Craighead, and I'm sorry we had to meet like this, Sir," he said. "My father would be very disappointed in me, I'm sure."

MacPherson's hazel eyes searched Adam's, and as a flicker of recognition kindled there, he smiled broadly and reached out to grasp Adam's hand.

"Ye must be Caleb's son—now I can see the resemblance."

"Yes, Sir. He asked me to give you his regards—and this." Adam drew the letter from his saddlebag.

"And who might this lad be?" the minister prompted when Adam did not immediately introduce him to David.

"I'm sorry, Sir," Adam said again, feeling more awkward and uncouth by the moment. "This is David McKay, my cousin. His father is my mother's brother," he added when MacPherson seemed to be having some trouble making the connection.

"Welcome to ye both," MacPherson said, extending his hand to David. "Come along to the house now—my wife will be glad to give ye breakfast."

"Thank you, but we've already eaten," Adam said.

"Then ye must eat again," MacPherson said. The corners of his eyes crinkled in concert with the smile lines around his mouth, almost the only lines in his fair-skinned face.

This is no dour Scots minister, Adam thought with relief, having pictured Ian MacPherson in a completely different way. "We might just do that, Sir," Adam replied.

❧

Mary busied herself about the house as well as she could, trying to pass the time until her father was ready to see her. He had risen not long after she had, but some men arrived soon after, and he remained closeted in his office with them for more than an hour. Then, just as Mary thought she'd have a chance to tell him about Adam Craighead, another group of men arrived, and with a shrug that said "I'm sorry, but I can't help this," John Andrews went back into his office.

"I don't think those men will ever leave," Mary told Polly at lunchtime. "Why don't you knock on the door and ask if they care to take lunch?"

Polly looked at her mistress as if she had taken leave of her senses. "Y' know Master John'd have my head if I did such a thing—he's not t' be disturbed when th' door's shut, unless it's really important."

"If you're hungry enough, lunch can certainly be important," Mary said. "Or if the house should burn—"

"Mistress!" Polly said sharply. "I've not heard y' talk so strangely before. Mayhap y' need a dose of spring tonic."

Recalling the evil-smelling and worse-tasting concoction of sulphur and molasses that had been forced down her throat each March in her childhood, Mary made a face. "No, thank you! All I need is some time with my father, and I will have it, one way or another. After this batch of men leaves, I'm going in there, and you must tell anyone who comes to see him that they'll have to wait."

Polly rolled her eyes and was about to speak when they heard the office door open, then the murmur of voices and the sound of the front door closing.

Mary sprang from the table and ran into the hall, where she embraced her father. "So you finally came back!" she exclaimed.

John Andrews looked down at Mary with a puzzled expression. "I must have been gone longer than I thought to get such a welcome. But I know exactly what you want, and this time, you're going to get it."

It was Mary's turn to look puzzled as she drew back and looked at her father.

"What do you mean?"

"I've been preoccupied lately, and we haven't spent much time together. But today I intend to make it up to you."

"I know you can't help it, Papa," Mary began, but he held up a silencing hand.

"There are many things that can't be helped, true enough—but today we won't talk of that. I have a surprise for you."

Mary laced her fingers and brought them to her chin. "What is it?" she asked, then looking at the amusement in her father's eyes, she thought she knew.

"You brought me a riding horse!" she exclaimed, then threw her arms around him. "Thank you, Papa!"

John Andrews pulled away and shook his head. "No, Mary—that wasn't our bargain."

"Then what—" Mary began, realizing just as her father spoke what it must be.

"Lancaster," he said, smiling with pleasure at the thought that he was making his daughter happy. "I'm taking you to Lancaster this afternoon."

Chapter 7

The MacPhersons' house was small but comfortable. Adam and David were ushered into the main room, a combination kitchen, dining room, and sitting room, dominated by shelves filled with more books than Adam had ever seen in one place. Ian MacPherson's wife, Nancy, insisted on serving them a hearty breakfast. Although Adam feared that he'd made a poor first impression with Ian MacPherson, he soon found the minister to be a warm man who treated Adam and David as kindly as if they had been his own sons.

"Alas, Adam, in His infinite mercy and wisdom, God dinna see fit to gift Mrs. MacPherson and me wi' bairns of our own," Ian replied when Adam inquired about their family.

"Perhaps 'twas because He knew my husband and I would be needed to take in babes that had none to look after them," Nancy MacPherson said.

"That's right," Ian said proudly. "Thanks to my wife, no young one around Neshaminy has ever been put away in an orphan asylum."

"My parents did the same thing," Adam replied, remembering the succession of frightened children, their parents killed or captured by Indians, that Ann and Caleb Craighead had tended until they could be restored to relatives or homes could be found for them where they would be kindly used.

"Have ye brothers or sisters?" Ian MacPherson asked Adam.

"Only one still living, a sister some fourteen years older. Sarah wed and left home when I was still quite young."

Ian turned his attention to David. "And what of your family, Lad?"

"My father traps and hunts half the year. My mother's dead. I have one sister and four brothers, all younger."

"Tell him your brothers' names," Adam urged.

"Matthew, Mark, Luke, and John," David recited.

Ian MacPherson smiled. "Good names, those."

"Everyone calls them the Gospels," Adam said.

"I can see why." Ian turned back to David. "And I ken why ye've left home. There comes a time when every young man has to make his own way. For me, it was in '35. The Lord showed me the way to the American Plantation as clear as if He had me by the hand."

"It must have been hard for you to leave Scotland and go so far away," said Adam, who had begun to miss his wilderness home far more than he had ever thought possible.

"Aye, but I was in the Lord's will, and that made the difference."

There was an awkward silence, then Nancy MacPherson rose and took her bonnet from a peg by the door. "I must look to some chores now—Mr. McKay, will you come along?"

David looked grateful for the opportunity to go outside. "Yes, Ma'am. I need to check our horses' hoofs. Those Philadelphia cobblestones nigh ruint them."

"Not to mention the damage done from tearin' down the road," Ian said with a faint smile. "We've a fine blacksmith here. Mrs. MacPherson will show ye where to find him."

As soon as the door closed behind them, the minister picked up Adam's letter and broke its wax seal.

"I don't know what my father wrote," Adam said as the minister began to scan the closely written pages.

Ian MacPherson smiled as he started to read, then his expression grew more sober, until by the time he finished, he seemed moved almost to tears. Adam sat quietly, trying hard not to look at the minister until he refolded the letter and spoke to Adam.

"Forgive me—perhaps I shouldna ha'e read it before ye, but I was eager to know your father's mind. Caleb Craighead is as fine a man of God as I ever met. As I thought might be the case, he's burdened about your future."

"I know that," Adam said, still wondering what his father could have written that would bring tears to his oldest friend's eyes.

The minister stood and walked over to a stand on which a large Bible rested. He opened it and turned to Adam. "Do ye know chapter forty of the book of Isaiah?"

"Yes—my father reads it often. 'Comfort ye, comfort ye my people, saith your God.' Isn't that how it begins?"

Ian MacPherson nodded and continued quoting with his eyes half-shut, not looking at the verses. " 'The voice of him that crieth in the wilderness, Prepare ye the way of the Lord, make straight in the desert a highway for our God. Every valley shall be exalted, and every mountain and hill shall be made low: and the crooked shall be made straight, and the rough places plain: and the glory of the Lord shall be revealed, and all flesh shall see it together: for the mouth of the Lord hath spoken it.' "

He turned and looked searchingly at Adam. "Do ye believe those words, Lad?"

Adam's mouth felt suddenly dry and his head unaccountably light. *What does this man want from me?* he asked himself, although he knew the answer. "Yes, Sir. My father called that chapter his divine orders."

"Orders, indeed," Ian MacPherson said. "When Caleb Craighead came here lookin' for his fare to be redeemed, he testified that God had directed him to leave off schoolteaching and to cross the ocean as a minister of the gospel. His faith convinced me he was sincere, and I was happy to raise his passage money. Now Caleb asks me to help ye find your vocation."

"Is that what he wrote you?" Adam asked, certain that there must have been something else in the letter to so affect the man.

"That, and some things just between us. I never had a son of my own, Adam, but I ken something of how it maun be. If ye were mine, I'm sure I'd want ye to follow in my footsteps, too. But unless it is a path ye freely choose yourself, the journey will be for naught."

Ian MacPherson's eyes seemed to be looking into Adam's soul, probing to see what kind of person Caleb Craighead's son had turned out to be, and perhaps feeling disappointed at what he found.

"My father thinks I have a vocation for the ministry," Adam said when he could speak again.

"What do ye think?"

Adam looked away from the minister's steady gaze and shook his head. "I cannot say I have had any such call. Anyhow, I know I'm not good enough myself to guide anyone else."

Ian MacPherson shook his head sadly. "Surely ye know the Scriptures better than that. The Lord canna wait for a man to be perfect before He uses him."

Adam remained silent, unable to think of a rebuttal. "My father's a great man and he's helped many people. I know he wishes I'd take up his work with the Indians, but I don't see myself doing that."

"There are many ways to minister, Adam. All must find our own place in the kingdom. For several of us here in Neshaminy, keeping a school of sorts to train ministers has been our life's work."

"My father mentioned the Log Cabin School," Adam said, relieved for the opportunity to shift the conversation to a less personal level. "Is it still operating?"

Ian MacPherson joined Adam on the settee. "Aye, but the times ha'e changed. Now young men of a scholarly bent can go over to college in the New Jersey Colony and learn more elevated Greek and Hebrew than we can teach them. At the same time, men of God are in such scarce supply in the wilderness that some near-illiterates undertake to preach with no schooling at all."

"I heard of one such man," Adam said, smiling at the memory of his father's relish in telling the tale. "It seems that he owned a Bible but had trouble keeping it right side up when he preached from it."

Ian MacPherson nodded. "Aye, until someone told him that the page numbers came at the bottom."

"But then he lost that Bible, and the next one he got had the numbers at the top of the page, and once more people had to tell him he was holding it upside down," Adam said, continuing the story.

"So finally the poor man said right side up and upside down were of Satan, and he'd hear those words no more," Ian MacPherson finished with a flourish.

Adam chuckled. "Do you suppose that really happened?"

"I fear that it certainly could ha'e. At any rate, it makes a good tale."

"Not all tales are equally worthy to tell," Adam said, unconsciously quoting one of his father's favorite expressions.

"Spoken like Caleb Craighead's son, for certain. Well, Lad, if ye should ha'e a vocation, ye'll also ha'e our help. Your father tells me ye ha'e studied Latin and a smattering of Greek and Hebrew. Ye could be licensed with very little more schooling."

Adam's gesture took in the book-lined walls. "I'd very much like to read from your library, Sir. I thank you for your offer, and I'll consider it."

Ian MacPherson looked disappointed. " 'Considering' is a human reaction done with the mind. Ye must seek guidance from the heart."

Adam realized he'd once more revealed his lack of spiritual depth and felt his face warm. "Of course. I know that 'Thy will be done' has to be more than an empty phrase."

"Pray, Son; pray as the Bible tells us, without ceasing. Then ye'll ken His will for sure. God always sends signs to those who prayerfully seek them."

Adam nodded. "Yes, Sir."

Ian MacPherson stood and smiled down at Adam. "In the meantime, Mrs. MacPherson and I would be pleased for ye and your cousin to stay here with us as long as ye have need to."

"It's kind of you to offer, but David and I must return to Philadelphia right away."

As Adam spoke, the door opened and David and Mrs. MacPherson entered.

"The smith says he can shoe our horses first thing tomorrow," David said.

"Then we'll be on our way, with many thanks for your hospitality," Adam said.

Nancy MacPherson looked disappointed. "Oh dear, I was so hoping that the pair of you would be pupils."

"Not me!" David said with such force that the others laughed.

"We'll have to leave that matter to the Lord, Wife. In the meantime, Adam, I'll show ye what ye'd study, should ye decide to come back."

That's unlikely, Adam thought. *Father would love to have the chance to read some of these books, but I'm no scholar.* "Does a man really need to know so much to preach?" Adam said aloud.

"The Word tells us that we must study to show ourselves approved of God." Ian MacPherson looked closely at Adam. "Ha'e ye your own Bible?" he asked.

Adam shook his head. "No. I thought I might find one in Philadelphia," he added, although he had almost forgotten that his father had urged him to use some of his precious coins to do so.

Ian MacPherson selected a well-worn book from the shelf and handed it to Adam. "This belonged to a friend of mine and your father's who departed this life last month. Before he died, he asked me to give it to someone who needed it. I know he'd be pleased for Caleb Craighead's son to ha'e it."

"I can't accept this—" Adam began, but Ian MacPherson thrust the book into his hands.

"Ye can and ye will, and there's an end to it," he said, and for a moment Adam got a glimpse of another side of Ian MacPherson. He could well imagine the gentle teacher delivering an impassioned sermon that could affect his hearers, perhaps for all eternity. Ministering was a heavy responsibility, all right. That anyone in his right mind would think that Adam could do it was still a mystery to him.

"I thank you, then." Adam took the book and leafed through the pages. "This reminds me of Father's Bible; it's so full of margin notes."

Ian MacPherson nodded. "Read it every day, Adam. Make notes of your own. 'Tis where all our study begins and ends—ye don't need to be a scholar to come to the Scriptures."

As he held the minister's gift, Adam felt strangely warmed. About one thing, at least, he agreed with Ian MacPherson. Whatever his future might hold, the advice and wisdom found in those pages could help him through it.

Chapter 8

Did you hear me, Mary? I said I would take you to Lancaster this afternoon," John Andrews said.

Stunned, Mary looked aghast at her father. "Lancaster? We can't go anywhere today."

It was her father's turn to look as if he doubted Mary's sanity. "What do you mean, we can't go there today? Did you not ask—nay, *beg*—to be taken to Lancaster as soon as I came back home?"

Her father seldom showed anger, but his ruddy cheeks and the set of his mouth marked his displeasure. Mary laid a placating hand on his arm. "Yes, I recall that I did, but that was before—that is, things have changed now."

"And just what has changed so quickly, pray tell? Hetty must have persuaded you to go with her to some frippery—is that it?"

"No, Papa. The general's gala is next week. But while you were gone, you had a caller, and he'll be back in a day or so. You'll miss meeting him if we go to Lancaster."

John Andrews looked puzzled. "I wasn't aware that you'd become my business agent. Just who is this that I mustn't miss seeing?"

Mary's cheeks colored. "He left his letter of introduction. It's there on your desk."

Her father frowned slightly. "I've asked you not to disturb the papers on my desk—" he began, but Mary interrupted him.

"I didn't disturb them, Papa. I just put his letter on top." Mary moved over by her father, who hastily gathered up some papers that had evidently been left by his earlier visitors. She caught a glimpse of a broadside bearing the words "the Sons of Liberty," then found Adam's letter, which had been pushed to one side. "There it is."

John Andrews sank back into his chair as he picked up the letter. "At least you didn't read it for me," he said, and Mary knew she had been forgiven.

She pulled a chair up to the desk and leaned forward in anticipation as he broke the wax seal and began to read. But try as she might to make out the words, she was too far away to tell more than that the letter had been closely written in a fine hand. Foiled at her effort to read the letter Adam had brought, Mary watched her father's face as his eyes moved over the page, rapidly at first, and then more slowly as he reread it.

Finally he put it down and looked up, gazing into the distance as if he were seeing some vision. "Ann McKay," he said softly. "After all these years—"

"Ann McKay?" Mary questioned. "The letter is from a woman?"

Once more aware of his daughter, John Andrews looked at her and nodded. "It's from your namesake, as a matter of fact. Just the other day you asked me if she still lived—this letter is proof that she does."

"I don't understand," Mary said, wondering at the effect such a few lines of writing had on her father. "McKay was Adam's cousin's name."

"Cousin? What cousin? What on earth happened here while I was away?"

Taking a deep breath, Mary recounted the events of the past few days. "They went on to Neshaminy, but I told Mr. Craighead to come back when you were here, and he is planning to do so," she concluded.

"You entertained two frontiersmen here alone for two days? What were you thinking? You could have been murdered in your bed!"

"They stayed in the carriage house, and anyway, I knew immediately they weren't the murdering kind," Mary said. "I presume if you knew Mr. Craighead's mother, you must know the family can be trusted. They're some kind of missionaries or something, I think Mr. Craighead said."

"Yes, those men probably are trustworthy, but in the future, you mustn't allow anyone that you don't already know to enter the house whilst I am away. I have good reason for so saying," he added when Mary seemed about to protest.

"All right, Papa. I promise. Now tell me what the letter says."

John Andrews allowed himself a small smile. " 'Tis my letter, not yours; but since you've met the young man in question, and I haven't, perhaps you can tell me if he is worth helping."

"Is that what the letter is about?" Mary asked, somehow disappointed.

"That's what letters of introduction are always about," her father said. " 'This will introduce you to so-and-so, who is of sterling character and reputation, and so on. Please extend him every courtesy and help him find work, and so on and so on.' This letter isn't much different."

"Adam Craighead didn't say he had come to Philadelphia looking for work," Mary said.

"Then what reason did he give for his sudden appearance on our doorstep? And tell me about this cousin—Ann's letter doesn't mention anyone else."

"You called her Ann McKay—is she Adam's mother?"

"Yes, and she had a brother named Jonathan. I take it that this David must be his son. What business had they in Philadelphia?"

"Apparently they have pelts to sell—I believe David McKay came from North Carolina."

"This letter says that Adam Craighead lives by the Monongahela."

"Tell me about Adam's mother. How came you to know her, and when?"

Mary's impatience to hear about her namesake seemed to amuse her father. "It was a long time ago. Ann and her brother lived with my parents while their father was looking for a place to settle. Ann cared for my mother, who as you know was something of an invalid."

"And?" Mary prompted when her father stopped talking long before she considered the whole story to have been told.

"And that's all—they lived there for only a few months, then Ann married Caleb Craighead, and I never saw either of them again."

"You know Adam's father, too?" Mary asked.

"Yes. In fact, he—"

"Mr. Andrews!" Thomas ran into the room without knocking, something Mary had never seen him do before. From the look on his face, she knew that something extraordinary had happened.

"What is it, Thomas?" John Andrews stood immediately, braced to take whatever action might be needed.

"I just heard it, Sir," Thomas said. "There's been a fight outside of Boston. Th' redcoats went after th' ammunition depot at Concord. Talk is a lot of militia were hurt."

Mary looked at her father's grim expression and felt with him the gravity of the situation.

"What about the British?"

"They were chased back to Boston, Sir."

"What does that mean, Papa?" Mary asked, afraid that she already knew.

John Andrews sighed heavily. "I'm not sure, but it could mean we can no longer avoid a fight."

"But Boston—the Massachusetts Colony is far away," she murmured.

"So is England—but apparently not far enough to keep His Majesty from attacking his own." John Andrews turned to the servant. "Let me know if you hear anything else. And Thomas—"

Thomas had turned to go, but he stopped. "Yes, Sir?"

"I'll still need the carriage this afternoon but not to go to Lancaster. That trip will have to be postponed."

"You can't leave again so soon—you just got here!" Mary cried.

Her father's expression softened. "I won't be leaving town just yet, never fear. But there are people I must see. And don't worry—as you say, Boston is a long way off; and for the time being, nothing like that is about to happen in Philadelphia."

Mary watched her father leave, her heart heavy. *Nothing will happen here,* he had said, but she knew it was unlikely that any conflict in Massachusetts could long be confined to that colony.

Then another thought made her feel even more forlorn. Adam and David might not need to plan their futures after all. If war came, circumstances would do that for them.

Let Adam come back soon, Mary prayed.

❧

The blacksmith who tended to Adam's and David's horses turned out to be talkative. He had once hunted around the Monongahela and punctuated his work with a dozen stories of narrow escapes from the Indians. By the time he'd finished his work, the morning was half-gone.

"It'll be too late t' get any goods by the time we get back t' the city," David said when they were once more on their way.

"Remember what McCall told us—you oughtn't buy anything until you're ready to leave, anyway."

"I haven't even got there yet, an' I'm ready to leave right now," David replied. He was silent for a moment, then turned to look at Adam. "Have y' given any more thought to comin' back to Carolina wi' me?"

The question had first been raised at Stones' Crossing, but Adam had avoided giving his cousin a definite answer, unsure as he was of what he might find in Philadelphia. "I want to hear what Mr. Andrews has to say first, but I know you can use some help, and I'd like to see my sister again."

"I wish we could be on our way this very day," David said. "Seems I've been amongst strangers forever."

I know, Adam thought, but he had no desire to leave Philadelphia immediately. "We'll definitely have to spend another night in the city." *I have to see Mary Andrews again,* he could have added.

"If that man Andrews isn't to home yet, I don't intend to stay an' have that Polly girl breathin' down my neck."

Adam laughed. "We'll go there first, but even if Mr. Andrews is back home, we'll find a likely inn."

"Even if Mistress Mary should turn her big brown eyes on y' again?"

"I don't know what makes you say that," Adam said.

"Oh, I think y' do," David said. "Just wait—you'll see I'm right."

❧

John Andrews came home before dark, but before Mary could speak to him alone, several of the men who often called on him came by, and they remained closeted throughout the evening.

I'll talk to him tomorrow, she promised herself as she prepared for bed. Adam and David might come back from Neshaminy the next day, and she intended to make sure that this time they would meet her father.

☙

"Will you tell me what these all-night meetings mean?" Mary asked her father the next morning.

John Andrews looked tired, but not as concerned as he had appeared to be the day before. "You know everyone who was here last night—we've been doing business since before you were born. The mere threat of fighting will produce a great demand for certain goods, and we want to make sure that they'll be available when our customers have need of them."

"And talking half the night no doubt really helps," Mary said lightly.

"It seems to help you and Hetty when you get together," he returned. "Which reminds me—what is this about her father's party?"

"It's a gala," Mary said. "It'll be General Hawkins's first chance to entertain since they came back from England."

"No doubt it'll be quite an elegant event. I suppose you intend to go?"

"Hetty would never forgive me if I didn't. You're to come, too—she said the calligraphers were nearly finished with the invitations."

He shook his head. "No, thank you. You know I've no stomach for that sort of carrying on."

"But you haven't been to a party in months," Mary reminded him. "I know you always enjoy the music."

"The music is fine—it's the company I'd find offensive. Don't look like that, Mary. You may go if you like."

"Maybe you'll change your mind before then," Mary said, knowing that was unlikely.

"We'll see," he said, dismissing the subject. "You can go to the warehouse with me today if you like—there's a great deal of work to be done."

Ordinarily, Mary welcomed the opportunity to go to work with her father. She liked the bustle of the commerce around the docks and enjoyed copying the invoices and bills of lading that would be attached to goods that would make their way throughout the colonies. But today was different.

"I didn't sleep very well last night," Mary said. "Maybe I should stay here and rest."

John Andrews looked closely at his daughter. "This is about that Craighead man, isn't it? Polly said you seemed to be interested in him."

The color that flooded Mary's face betrayed her and made any denial useless. "They both seem to be worthy young men," she said. "Perhaps you'll have the opportunity to find that out for yourself soon."

"Perhaps. But should they come back, I don't want you to invite them to stay here."

"But, Papa—" Mary began.

"It's my place to do that, should I think it fitting. Send them on to the warehouse if they happen by before I get home."

"Yes, Papa," Mary agreed.

Now all Mary could do was wait—and hope that Adam kept his promise to return.

Chapter 9

Y e're goin' t' wear that curtain out, pullin' it aside so much," Polly said to Mary late that afternoon. "Y' don't want company t' know you're anxious about seein' them."

Mary turned from the window, chagrined that Polly had read her so well. "I'm not anxious about anything, Polly. I'm free to look out of my own window as often as I like."

"Yes, Mistress, I reckon that's one thing that's not yet been taxed. Should I put an extra joint o' meat in the pot, just in case th' men you're not anxious about should happen t' come back?"

Mary forced herself to sit down and pick up some mending that she'd been halfheartedly working on all day. "I suppose you might as well. Papa might bring home someone for supper—we ought to be prepared, just in case."

"I'd say you was more th'n prepared," Polly mumbled as she left the room.

Mary smiled, not fooled by Polly's grumbling. Despite her words, Mary guessed that Polly also hoped that Adam and David—especially David—would come back soon.

Mary had just gone upstairs to put her mending away when the door knocker sounded. She made herself wait while Polly took her time answering the door, and it was only when Polly called up that someone was there to see her that Mary smoothed her skirts, adjusted her cap, and slowly descended the stairs.

Adam stood in the hallway, even taller and more imposing than Mary remembered. His eyes followed her all the way down the stairs.

"Evening, Mistress Mary," he said. When she held out her hand to him, Adam hesitated a moment. He knew that propriety said his lips could merely hover over the surface of her hand and not touch it, but Adam took the opportunity to firmly kiss Mary's hand, press it afterward, and hold it a second longer than propriety allowed.

"I trust you had a pleasant trip?" Mary asked, her question including David.

"Yes, thank you, Ma'am," David said.

"Is Mr. Andrews here?" Adam asked.

"He went to the warehouse—if you like, you may go there to see him, or you're welcome to wait here," Mary said.

"I believe we've heard that story before," Adam said.

Mary hadn't blushed when Adam kissed her hand, but now she did. "He really does want to meet you both. I gave him your letter," she added, answering Adam's unspoken question.

"And? What did he say about it?"

"Only that he knew your mother when she stayed with my grandparents. He seemed to be pleased to hear from her."

"I see," said Adam, who had somehow hoped to hear more.

"We ought to go now," David said.

Mary's eyes pleaded for Adam to stay. "The warehouse isn't far. You could go there in our carriage."

"No, I think not," Adam said, responding to David's violent headshaking. "We must be on our way. Tell your father I'll come back tomorrow morning."

"But he'll be home soon; I know it." Mary took a step closer to Adam as if her nearness might change his mind.

"Perhaps—but we mustn't stay longer," Adam said.

"Won't you at least have supper with us? Polly put on an extra joint—it's no trouble at all."

At the mention of Polly's name, David's face darkened and he gestured toward the door. "Y' promised, Adam," he reminded his cousin.

"Thank you, Mistress, but we really must leave."

"We'll see you tomorrow, though?"

Adam looked at Mary, helpless to resist the appeal in her eyes if he'd wanted to. "Yes."

"Until tomorrow, then." Mary opened the front door for them. Even after Adam and David had untied their horses and walked down the street, she stood looking after them.

❧

"I'm beginning to think that this Adam Craighead and his cousin are really phantoms," John Andrews said that evening as he and Mary took their supper together. "Why didn't they come to the warehouse as I suggested?"

"It was late, and since I wasn't allowed to invite them to stay here, I suppose they were concerned about finding somewhere to stay. They said they'd come back tomorrow."

"I hope so," John Andrews said. "I confess I'm curious to see how Ann's son has turned out."

"What was she like?" Mary asked.

Her father's eyes softened. "As a girl, Ann McKay was graceful and gentle, kinder to my mother than my own sister was. Yet she could also be quite forceful if need be."

"Why, Papa! I believe you must have been half in love with her!" Mary exclaimed.

He smiled ruefully. "Half? No, far more than that. I wanted to marry her."

The notion that her father could ever have loved anyone other than her mother was new and faintly disturbing, and it was a moment before Mary spoke again. "Why didn't you marry her, then?"

John Andrews shrugged. "She chose Caleb Craighead—she met him first. But that was all a long time ago."

"Before you met my mother?"

"Oh, yes—and I've never looked back, then or since."

"But you named me after her, didn't you?"

"Yes. I suppose I hoped that you would grow up to be the kind of young lady that Ann McKay was when I first knew her."

"That's quite a tribute," Mary said. "I'd like to meet her."

"Unless you're willing to trek into the wilderness, it's not likely. But apparently you think rather well of her son."

"So will you when you meet him."

"I'll reserve my judgment until then. In the meantime, pass the chutney."

❧

Adam came alone and on foot early the next morning. Intentionally demure in a plain, beige morning gown topped by a half-apron, Mary passed the slow-moving Polly to answer his knock herself. In the shirt she'd mended for him and with his hair pulled back and tied neatly, Adam looked different— but not a whit less like a frontiersman.

"Good morning," Mary returned his greeting. "My father is expecting you," she added formally. She had started toward the office door when it opened and John Andrews emerged.

"You must be Adam Craighead," he said. Extending his hand, he studied his guest.

As Adam had surmised, Mary's father was shorter and less broad-shouldered than he was, but the older man's strength was evident in the firmness of his handshake. Adam nodded. "Aye, Sir. 'Tis a pleasure to meet you at last. I was beginning to fear I'd missed the chance."

"So was I. What about your cousin—David McKay, I think Mary called him?"

"He's doing some trading before starting back to North Carolina."

John Andrews turned to Mary. "Ask Polly to brew us a cup of the herbals she found yesterday."

"Yes, Sir." Mary hadn't expected to be a party to the conversation between Adam and her father, but taking the tea to them would give her some idea of how they were getting along. *Papa just has to like Adam,* she thought as she went to the kitchen.

"Sit down here," John Andrews invited Adam, indicating a chair. He closed his office door and pulled up a chair opposite Adam instead of taking his usual place behind his desk.

"Thank you, Sir." Adam looked around the small, sparsely furnished room. His glance lingered on the jumble of papers covering the desk.

"I read your mother's letter," John Andrews said. "Are you aware of its contents?"

"Yes and no. I didn't read it myself, but Mother told me she asked you to help me if I decided to stay in the city."

John Andrews leaned back in his chair and folded his arms across his chest. "What did she tell you about me?"

His unexpected question caught Adam off guard. "Very little, Sir. My mother said you were a good friend to her and my father. She said she hadn't seen you in many years, but she knew you still did business in Philadelphia."

John Andrews nodded. "Did she say anything else about me?"

What else could she have said? Adam wondered. "She told me that you're one of the finest people she's ever known."

A strange look passed over John Andrews's face. "Your mother didn't always have a high opinion of me," he said. He uncrossed his arms and leaned forward, his eyes searching Adam's face. "Your features resemble them both."

Adam felt uncomfortable under the close scrutiny, but he did not shrink from it. *I suppose he needs to satisfy himself about my character,* Adam told himself.

John Andrews finished his inspection and leaned back in his chair. "What would you like for me to do for you, Adam Craighead?"

This time the question was not unexpected but unanswerable. "I don't know, Sir. Mother thought I might like living in the city, but from what I've seen of it so far, I'm not sure."

John Andrews smiled faintly. "I don't wonder that a lad fresh from the wilderness would think ill of the jumble of people in Philadelphia."

"It's not just all the people here—everything seems to be so unsettled. David and I got in the middle of a brawl the first thing, and now we hear there's been some kind of battle in the Massachusetts Colony."

John Andrews nodded. "Aye, that's true. But Pennsylvania's not like some of the other colonies. Here, the large numbers of Quakers tend to hold down the hotheads on both sides."

"Do you think these disputes with Britain will come to war?"

Before Mr. Andrews could answer, there was a light rap at the door and Mary entered, bearing a tray with tea service and a plate of shortbread.

"Where's Polly?" her father asked.

"She went to market," Mary replied. *And I sent her there,* she could have added but did not.

Adam watched Mary set the tray down on a small tea table, which she then moved between him and her father. She filled Adam's cup first and handed it to him, along with a dainty square of linen, then repeated the process for her father. "The shortbread is fresh baked. Is there anything else I can get for you, Papa?"

The picture of daughterly sweetness, Mary didn't look at Adam until her father had replied in the negative. Then as she turned away from John Andrews, Mary smiled at Adam in the manner of a fellow conspirator.

"If anyone else asks for me, tell them to wait," her father called out as she closed the door behind her.

"I know your business must occupy a great deal of time," Adam said. "I mustn't keep you from it."

"Nonsense! I always have time for old friends. If you don't stay in Philadelphia, have you some idea of what you might like to do?"

Adam took a sip of the hot tea, which tasted so like the brew his mother had given him for his childhood stomachaches that he almost choked. "Something involving trade, perhaps—moving goods from place to place within the colonies, rather than having to depend on England for it all."

John Andrews looked startled. "Has Mary been talking to you about my business?" he asked, and it was Adam's turn to look surprised.

"No, Sir. Why do you ask?"

"Never mind. If you have time, perhaps you'd like to see my warehouse," John Andrews said.

"Yes, I would."

Adam's host rose and made a face as he replaced his cup on the tray. "Dreadful stuff, that—it makes one long for real English tea."

Mary materialized in the hallway as the office door opened. "Are you leaving so soon?" she asked Adam.

"Mr. Craighead is going to the warehouse with me," her father said before Adam had to make a reply.

"I'll get my bonnet," Mary said.

"You aren't invited, Mistress Mary Ann," her father said quickly.

Mary tried to hide her disappointment. "I'll tell Thomas to fetch the carriage."

"No—we'll walk. It's a lovely day and I'm sure Mr. Craighead is quite able to get there on his own power."

"Yes, Sir. I'll be glad to stretch my legs."

"Good. And on the way, I want to hear all about your family."

Mary watched helplessly as the pair walked down the street, Adam shortening his stride to match her father's. *I could keep up with them,* she thought. But that wasn't the reason her father hadn't wanted her along.

Maybe he's going to offer Adam a job, she hoped and smiled at the thought.

Chapter 10

M r. Andrews and Adam had been gone for more than two hours when Hetty came to call, wearing a pale blue gingham dress that accented her eyes to perfection.

"Well, where are they?" she asked, looking around as if she expected Adam and David to emerge from behind the furniture.

"Where are who?" Mary asked, feigning ignorance.

"Why, our frontiersmen, of course. They came back from wherever they went, didn't they?"

"Yes, but I doubt that either would consider themselves 'ours.' Adam Craighead went with Papa to the warehouse. He said David McKay was buying trade goods."

Hetty looked disappointed. "I wish they were here. I want to see their faces when they get this."

Mary saw that the stiff white invitation to the general's gala bore both Adam's and David's names. "What does your father say about inviting frontiersmen to such a formal occasion?"

Hetty took off her bonnet and turned to the smoky gold-framed mirror. She patted her blond curls, then turned back to smile at Mary. "He doesn't know about it, but when he sees what life they bring to the party, I'm sure he'll be delighted."

"You assume a great deal," Mary warned. "Even if they're still in Philadelphia next week, what makes you think they'd consider going to the gala?"

"You and I will have to convince them, of course."

Her friend's words made Mary uneasy, and she shook her head. "I'm not sure it's such a good idea, Hetty. Frontiersmen are the rage in London because they're so rare there. That's not the case in Philadelphia."

"Maybe not, but frontiersmen that look like those two are rare anywhere."

"I'll give the invitation to Adam Craighead, but I don't expect him and his cousin to accept it."

Exasperated, Hetty all but snatched the card from Mary's hand. "I'll give it to him myself, then. He should be back soon—there can't be much to see at a dirty old warehouse." Without waiting to be asked, she swept into the drawing room and settled herself in her favorite chair.

"Are you sure you want to wait? It could be a long time." Mary followed Hetty and sat down beside her, feeling unaccountably annoyed. *I don't want her to be here when Adam comes back,* she acknowledged, then felt ashamed of herself for being so petty.

Hetty's distinctive laugh had always reminded Mary of a scale played on a harpsichord, but today it had a disturbing edge. "I'll wait," she said. "There's nothing I'd rather do at the moment."

"Then tell me about the arrangements for the gala," Mary said, resigned that Hetty had no intention of leaving.

It was well after Hetty and Mary had taken a light lunch that Adam Craighead returned, alone. Hetty stayed in the drawing room while Mary admitted him.

"Where's Papa?" she asked.

"Mr. Andrews had to see to an incoming shipment. He asked me to tell you he'd probably be late again."

"Come in," Mary invited, when Adam seemed determined not to move from the doorway.

"I should be going—" he began, then stopped as Hetty came into the hallway, beaming at him.

"Don't leave yet, Mr. Craighead!" she exclaimed. "I have something for you."

A look of bewildered embarrassment briefly swept over Adam's face, and Mary cringed inwardly. *He and David would be fish out of water at Hetty's party,* she thought.

"Miss Hawkins, is it?" he said, recovering enough to remember his manners.

"Indeed, Mr. Craighead. I presume you can read?" she added, handing him the invitation.

"Hetty!" Mary exclaimed, but her friend merely laughed again.

"I can read the words, but I don't understand their intention, Miss Hawkins. Why would a British general invite us to his party?"

In response to Adam's expression of genuine puzzlement, Hetty came close enough to put a hand on his arm. "Because I want you to come, and he is my father," she said smoothly. "Please say that you will."

Adam glanced back to the invitation and shook his head. "I'm sorry, Miss Hawkins, but I'm afraid we can't accept your kind invitation."

Good for you! Mary cheered silently.

Hetty dropped her hand and stepped back as if Adam had slapped her. "And why not, pray? I'm certain you would both find the evening most enjoyable."

"Perhaps we would, Miss Hawkins, but the fact is, we'll be gone from here by then."

Mary looked at Adam in alarm. *Why must you leave so soon?* she wanted to ask but not in Hetty's presence.

"Surely you can stay a few more days," Hetty said in the honeyed tones she used to get her way with her father. "What must you do that is so urgent that it cannot wait?"

"Several things. For one, my cousin and I must start to Carolina, where he is expected."

Hetty drew her fair brows together in a frown. "A few more days won't make that much difference—you can come to the gala first."

"I'm sorry. We can't," Adam said, perhaps more shortly than he had intended.

Hetty's lips pouted, then curved in a winsome smile. "All right. But should you be delayed or happen to change your mind, the invitation remains open."

"I don't think we will." Adam turned back to Mary, who had been a silent party to the exchange. "I must go now, Mistress. David will fear I've fallen among thieves if I don't get back soon."

Stay longer, Mary's eyes pleaded. "Will you come by before you leave?" she asked aloud.

I want to, Adam's eyes told her. "I doubt it. Thank you again for your kindness to us." Adam turned back to Hetty with a half-bow. "And thank your father for his invitation, Mistress Hawkins. Good day."

"Did you see that bow!" Hetty exclaimed when the door had closed behind Adam. "Oh, what I would give to have that man at the gala!"

Adam walked rapidly back to the inn where he and David were lodging, in part hoping to vent his frustration. He'd wanted to have a more private good-bye with Mary, to tell her—

Adam stopped so suddenly that a boy carrying two loaves of bread almost ran into him. "Sorry," Adam muttered, then walked on, considering what he would have said to Mary if she'd been alone. Her father had seemed to like him and hinted that he might have a job for him, should Adam decide to settle in Philadelphia. Yet there was something strange about the nature of Mr. Andrews's business. On the surface, he imported goods for distribution to other merchants. But Adam sensed that something else was going on, something that possibly involved aid to the Patriots, something that almost surely could be considered treasonable.

Adam had told the peltry merchant that he'd chosen neither side, yet he knew the time was coming—and that right soon—when he could be forced to make that decision. Growing up on a frontier where red-coated soldiers had fought the enemies that had once stolen him away from his family, Adam had always proudly considered himself to be a British subject. Yet in the past few years, the Crown's agents had oppressed colonists with what many regarded as cruel measures.

Who is in the right? Adam asked, knowing there were always two sides to any dispute but finding no ready answer. Then he recalled Ian MacPherson's admonition: "God always sends signs to those who prayerfully seek Him."

Heedless of the people hurrying past him, Adam stopped and bowed his head. "Please send me a sign, Lord," he said aloud.

By the time Adam reached the inn, he'd made at least one decision—he would see Mary Andrews once more before leaving Philadelphia.

"I was beginning t' worry that you'd tangled wi' some mob or another," David greeted Adam. "Word is that there's fights breakin' out all over the city."

"I didn't see any today, but down at the docks I met a man who'd just come from Boston. He said what we heard yesterday about that battle in the Massachusetts Colony was correct."

"What were y' doin' at the docks? Did y' not get to see th' Andrews man?"

"I saw him—in fact, I was with him at the time—his warehouse is by the docks."

"Did he offer t' give y' work?" David asked.

"All but. He said he'd been thinking of starting up some kind of trade with the other colonies. He asked if I wanted to come in with him on it."

"What did y' tell him?"

"That I'd have to think on it. I told him I was going to Carolina first."

David had been listening soberly, but now he allowed himself a quiet smile. "I was hopin' y' wouldn't change your mind. Fact is, I don't know how I'd get all the goods back wi'out your help."

"You must have made all the trades you were aiming to, then."

"Mostly. I've yet t' see one fellow, then all that's left will be the loadin' up and movin' on."

"There's one more thing that I have to do," Adam said.

"Oh? What's that?"

"I'm going back to the Andrews's house."

David lifted a questioning eyebrow. "Why? Did y' leave something there?"

I suppose that's one way to look at it, Adam thought. "Maybe," he replied.

❧

The streets were dark and vaguely mysterious as Adam made his way to Mary's street a few hours later. He reckoned that the large shipment that had arrived that afternoon would take Mr. Andrews some time to inventory. Therefore, Mary should be home alone.

Unless she went to her friend's house, he thought. Well, he'd do without seeing Mary if it meant also seeing Hetty Hawkins. Something about Mary's friend made him uneasy, something he couldn't quite put a name to.

Let Mary be here, Adam pleaded silently as he reached her doorstep. A faint light gleamed from the drawing room window, but at first there was no response to his knock. After waiting what seemed forever, Adam knocked again.

"I'm comin'; give me time," a voice grumbled as the door swung open.

Adam let his breath out in a sigh of relief and smiled. "Good evening, Polly. Is your mistress at home?"

Ignoring his question, Polly peered around Adam. "Are y' alone?"

"Yes. David stayed with the trade goods. Is Mistress Mary here?" he repeated.

"Who is it, Polly?" a now-familiar voice called, and Adam answered for himself.

"Adam Craighead, Ma'am. May I come in?"

"Of course—Polly, fetch another candlestick."

Adam followed Mary into the drawing room and stood somewhat awkwardly until she motioned for him to join her on the sofa.

"That will be all, Polly," Mary said when the girl had set the candlestick on the window table.

"I'll be in th' kitchen if y' need me," she muttered as she left.

Adam started to speak and then stopped, unable to form any sensible words.

"Once more I must tell you that Papa isn't back yet," Mary said, her faint smile indicating that she wasn't serious.

Adam nodded. "This time I'm glad. I came to see you."

Mary's eyes shone in the candlelight, which also cast wavering shadows that highlighted her even features. "For what reason?"

She's not going to make this easy, Adam thought. He cleared his throat and made a show of looking down at his hands. "To say good-bye. And to ask you to tell your father that I appreciate his offer. Maybe one day I can accept it."

Mary looked surprised. "Papa offered you work and you're leaving?"

Adam shrugged. "I'd like to stay longer, but I can't. It's a long way to Carolina, and David needs my help."

"I see," said Mary, not sure that she did. "Do you plan to stay on in Carolina, then?"

"I don't know," Adam said. Summoning all his courage, he looked into her eyes.

Come back soon, they told him. "You'll always find a welcome in this house," Mary said aloud. "Papa said that your parents once meant a great deal to his family."

"Yes. Apparently they knew each other quite well," Adam said. *As I want to know you, Mary.*

"Did you know that I was named for your mother?" Mary asked.

"Not until Mr. Andrews told me."

"I didn't know who Ann was until today, myself."

The other truth they each had learned that day lay between them, unspoken. John Andrews had loved Ann McKay, but she had chosen Caleb Craighead.

"It's getting late—I must go," Adam said after a long moment in which neither spoke.

"Yes—Papa will be home soon."

Adam laughed. "How many times have you said that to me, Mistress Mary?"

"Call me Mary Ann," she said. "I like the 'Ann'—I wish I'd always been known by both names."

"Then good night, Mary Ann."

Adam stood and looked down at Mary, who remained seated and regarded him with pleading eyes. "Do you really have to go? I'd like to hear more about your mother."

Adam hesitated, then sat back down. "My mother isn't big in stature, but she's always been a very strong person. She's always helped my father do his work, and she has the gift of brewing herbs and healing."

"I'd like to meet her someday," Mary said wistfully.

"Come to the Monongahela, then," Adam said. "I'd like you to see our village."

"It's a long way from Philadelphia, isn't it?"

"Many days' journey, although not as far as Carolina."

"What will you do when you get to your cousin's?" Mary asked.

"I don't know yet," Adam said. "It may sound strange, but—"

He stopped, realizing that perhaps he shouldn't tell her what Ian MacPherson had said.

Mary leaned forward and took one of Adam's hands in hers as if doing so might encourage him to speak. "You can tell me anything," she said earnestly, and Adam believed her.

"I don't yet know what I'm going to do, but I trust God to send me a sign. When He does, if I am to come back here, you'll see me again."

Mary looked puzzled. "How will you find this sign?"

"I don't know. By being ready to recognize it, perhaps."

Tears shone in Mary's eyes. "I pray that God will keep you safe wherever He sends you."

"Oh, Mary—Mary Ann—" Adam picked up the hand she had placed in his and pressed it against his cheek, feeling close to tears himself.

Mary pressed her other hand to his lips. "Hush," she said softly.

Adam dropped her hand and reached for her as she moved forward to come into his arms. Then Mary lifted her head from Adam's shoulder and kissed him, so startling him that it took him a moment to realize what was happening. Once he did, Adam returned her kiss and added a few more of his own, finally cradling her head on his shoulder.

They sat together in sweet silence, bound in a loose embrace, until Polly came stomping noisily into the hall and they moved apart.

Adam sighed. "I really must go this time," he said.

Mary stood, feeling suddenly shy. "Yes, I suppose you must."

"Mistress Merry, do y' need anything?" Polly asked from the hallway.

"No, thank you, Polly," Mary said, surprised that her voice could sound so normal. "Mr. Craighead is just leaving."

"I should hope so," Polly muttered, just out of his earshot.

"My cousin said to tell you good-bye, Polly," Adam said as he walked to the door.

"The same t' him, I'm sure," Polly said.

With Polly determined to stand watch until Adam had left, good-byes were brief and formal. But as the door closed behind Adam, his last, long look echoed Mary's own unspoken words.

He'll be back, she thought. With or without a sign, Adam Craighead would be back—she was sure of it.

Chapter 11

April gave way to May, and each day Mary Andrews found herself thinking of Adam Craighead, wondering how far he and David might have traveled that day, and longing to hear from him.

"There's no regular mail service to Carolina," her father told her in response to the carefully casual question Mary posed one day. "However, I deal with a number of bargemen and peddlers who often carry letters along with their goods. Adam Craighead could send something to you by them."

Mary half-smiled, seeing that her father knew exactly what was on her mind. "Would you know where to send a letter to him?" she asked.

John Andrews frowned. "I fear I didn't pay much heed to what he said about where they were going. The McKays live somewhere on the Yadkin River, probably not too far from Salisbury."

"Can you show it to me on a map?" Mary asked.

But when her father had at length uncovered the crudely lettered parchment that his Southern agent had prepared some months earlier, Mary almost wished she hadn't asked. Her finger traced the wavering lines of a stage route from Philadelphia to Baltimore, where a lighter line indicated that the road became cruder. From Fredericksburg, one road led west over the Virginia mountains to Culpeper, then southwest to Orange and Lynch's Ferry, and on to Salem in the North Carolina Colony. Between Salem and Salisbury lay the Yadkin River, near which Adam had said the McKays lived.

"It looks like a long journey," Mary said, overwhelmed at the knowledge that Adam would be so far away.

Her father looked over her shoulder and pointed out a shorter route. "That's the way packets carry goods from the Delaware River to Norfolk. The water route does away with many tedious overland miles."

"I don't see any roads east from Norfolk," Mary commented.

"No, but by swinging northwest past Williamsburg and on to Richmond, they could pick up the Western Road on to Salem."

"In any case, it looks to be a hard journey," Mary said.

"Five hundred land miles, I judge—but why do you ask? Are you planning to visit the Southern Colonies, by any chance?"

Aware that her father was teasing her, Mary nodded solemnly. "Why not? It'd be a change of air, anyway."

John Andrews rolled up the parchment and put it aside. "If you want that, I'll take you to Lancaster."

"I don't want to go to Lancaster just yet," Mary said quickly. *If I leave Philadelphia, hearing from Adam Craighead will be more difficult,* she thought.

Her father raised an eyebrow in the way he had of showing that he doubted her. "No, but perhaps you should. The way you and Hetty go from one party to another these days must be exhausting."

"Do I look so exhausted?" Mary asked, her smile showing that she was quite aware that she did not.

"No," her father admitted, "but I'll be glad when the hot weather puts an end to most of these frolics."

So will I, in a way, Mary might have said. She had enjoyed the music and the dancing and had been flattered by the attentions of the swarms of British soldiers who all seemed alike. "The weather, or their duties. Hetty tells me that her father is leaving Philadelphia soon."

Mr. Andrews looked interested. "Really? Did she say where he might go?"

"I'm not sure that she knows—something about raising a regiment of colonials somewhere or another. She didn't seem to be concerned about it," Mary added when her father frowned.

"That young woman isn't concerned about much," he said. "I hope my Mary Ann can keep the good head she has on her shoulders."

"She can certainly try," Mary answered demurely. Her father's use of her middle name reminded Mary afresh of Adam and the miles that separated them.

Her father's expression grew serious. "I haven't said this to you before because I didn't think there was need of it—but you mustn't take too much notice of the young redcoats you meet at these parties."

"I haven't, nor do I intend to," Mary reassured him. *There is someone else on my mind.*

He nodded, seemingly satisfied. "Good. I shan't be here to see you off to the next party, but I trust you will continue to conduct yourself as the Christian your mother and I raised you to be."

"You are going away again?" Mary asked, and he nodded.

"I must."

"Then I trust you will conduct yourself as a Christian, too," Mary said solemnly.

"I shall certainly try." He took his daughter's hand. "There's something about Ann McKay—Adam Craighead's mother—that I didn't tell you."

"Oh?" Mary asked. The mere mention of Adam's name made her heart beat faster.

"When I came to Philadelphia in my youth, I was wild and undisciplined. I began to gamble and I soon got into some rather serious trouble. When I thought I had to run away from the law, Ann and her brother went with me. When I asked her to marry me, she told me she'd realized that she wanted the same faith her parents had. She had just accepted Christ into her life, and she urged me to do the same."

Mary could scarcely believe what she was hearing. Her father had always behaved with such absolute decorum and integrity that it was impossible to imagine that he could ever have done otherwise. "So you became a Christian because of Adam's mother?" she prompted when he fell silent.

"Yes, in a way, but it was only when I met Caleb Craighead that I made the commitment to Christ that I've tried to keep since. Caleb thought that Ann and I would marry. After I told him otherwise, he sought her out."

"Is Adam aware of this?" Mary asked.

"I don't know. After he left, it occurred to me that perhaps I should have mentioned it."

"You can tell him when he comes back," Mary said.

John Andrews smiled. "You seem very certain that we'll see him again," he said.

"Yes, Papa, I think Adam Craighead will come back. I just don't know when."

❧

" 'Tis no wonder there's no mail service to the North Carolina Colony," Adam said after a particularly rough day's travel had brought them out of Virginia and into North Carolina. "Any news that has to come by this route will be a great deal older by the time it gets there, if it ever does."

David McKay dismounted and unrolled his blanket. "This trail's better than the Great Valley Road," he pointed out. "Besides, a man could use th' coastal packets t' send mail."

"Mayhap we should have used them ourselves—I think Uncle Jonathan had the right idea when he told you to ship the bulky goods by water."

David grinned. "Why, Adam, I'm surprised at you! Looks to me like y' just want t' get this trip done with, 'stead of enjoyin' th' scenery along th' way."

"The country's a right fair sight, and I welcome your company, Cousin. But I keep wondering what's happening back in Philadelphia. Why, we might already be in a war and not even know it."

"I think you're worryin' about somethin' in Philadelphia, all right—an' her name is Mary," David said.

"I do think of her some," Adam admitted. *Whenever I'm awake*, he silently added. Mary was in the last thoughts he had before he slept each night.

"Prob'ly more'n she thinks o' us," David said. "Better get some sleep now—we can make Salem in two more days if th' weather holds."

☙

"This seems to be the best attended party of the season," Hetty said to Mary one evening in early June. "Just look at all these people!"

The girls stood at the doorway of the upper floor ballroom of the Massie house, where the last major party of the season was about to get under way. Hetty had saved her best lightweight dress for the occasion, a dark blue satin with ivory lace at the neck and sleeves. Mary's peach-colored gown had seen several parties already, but her addition of a dozen small lace butterflies had given the bodice an entirely new look.

The musicians, garbed in blue silk knee breeches and wearing powdered wigs, had just mounted a raised platform at one end of the hall and were noisily tuning their instruments. A number of women of all ages had already taken seats along one long side wall. Opposite them, the men stood and waited for the lead-out to begin.

"There aren't as many soldiers here tonight as usual," Mary commented.

Hetty opened her fan and used it as a screen for her remarks about the men who had looked up to nod and bow as they entered. "No men in buckskins, either. How they would liven this sad assembly!"

Mary smiled in spite of herself. "Is it so sad? I see the ensign that was so attentive to you at the Galloways' party—and isn't that the captain you were telling me about?"

As Mary spoke, a tall, blond soldier started toward them. He was about Adam Craighead's height and size, but Mary thought Edward Simmons was a rather pale imitation.

"Good evening, ladies. Now that you're here, the party has begun," he said.

"Captain Simmons, how nice to see you again," Hetty purred as he bent to kiss her hand.

"Thank you, Miss Hawkins." He turned to Mary. "Miss Mary Andrews, I believe?" He held her hand a moment longer than necessary after kissing it, so reminding Mary of Adam that her cheeks colored.

Misreading the cause of her agitation, Edward Simmons smiled smugly. "Will you do me the honor of accompanying me on the lead-out, Mistress Andrews?"

Mary glanced at Hetty, whose mouth betrayed her displeasure. *I can't help it*, Mary signaled with her eyes, but Hetty looked away and fanned rapidly as the ensign finally noticed her and came forward, smiling.

"Of course, Captain Simmons," Mary replied.

From that lead-out, through a dozen quadrilles and minuets and supper afterward, Edward Simmons was never far from Mary's side. Only once during the evening did she and Hetty find themselves seated near enough for conversation, and that with Ensign Nelson Cutter between them.

"Isn't this a marvelous party!" Hetty's eyes glittered, but Mary knew her friend well enough to detect the forced gaiety.

As Mary and the captain took the floor for the next figure, Mary attempted to direct his thoughts toward Hetty. "You must dance with Miss Hawkins. She was so looking forward to seeing you again."

Edward Simmons stared intently at Mary as if he hadn't heard her. He took her hand and silently led her through the intricate figure as if it required all his concentration.

Later, when the party was over and Captain Simmons had accompanied Mary to the street to wait for her carriage, he surprised her by seizing her hand and pressing it to his lips. "May I call on you, Miss Andrews?" he asked.

Taken aback, Mary could think of nothing to say. A flat refusal would be grossly impolite, yet she was reluctant to say anything that he might take as encouragement.

"Forgive me for being so presumptuous, but you must know that I very much want to see you again. May I, Mistress Mary?"

Hetty and the ensign appeared beside them, and Mary knew that Hetty must have heard the captain's question. "Not right away, Captain Simmons." Mary gently disengaged her hand.

"Then when?" he persisted.

"I don't know. I may be leaving the city soon," she added.

"And so may I, Mistress Mary. All the more reason for us not to delay meeting again, don't you agree?"

"Come, Mary, you're holding up the carriages," Hetty said sharply.

Welcoming the interruption, Mary murmured, "Good evening," and accepted Thomas's aid in entering her cabriolet.

Hetty climbed in beside her, and with final salutes from Ensign Cutter and Captain Simmons, the girls were borne away.

"Did you have a good time?" Mary asked when it became obvious that Hetty wouldn't speak first.

"Not as good a time as you, I imagine. What did you do to Captain Simmons to have him eating out of your hand like that?"

"Nothing—and he certainly didn't eat out of my hand," Mary said with some asperity. "He used a plate, same as everyone else."

"Humph! Well, if you decide you don't want him, send him my way." Although Hetty sounded half serious, Mary chose to treat her remark as a jest.

"What, and let him join that long line of languishing lovers you've accumulated since you came back from England? Give the poor man a chance."

"That's exactly what I intend to do—give him a chance to break his heart," Hetty said, and Mary welcomed her laughter with relief.

Chapter 12

David and Adam reached the banks of the Yadkin River late on a Thursday afternoon. They saw no one in the vicinity, and David had to call a loud "Hallo!" several times before the ferryman heard them.

"That can't be Joshua Stone," Adam commented as a grizzled old man slowly brought the flat-keeled boat that served as a ferry across the river.

"It's not—that's Moses Murray. Joshua lets him live in th' ferry house in return for runnin' the ferry."

"Well, if it ain't Master Davey McKay!" the old man exclaimed when he was close enough to recognize the young man's face. "The folks hereabout have been wonderin' when you'd git here. Is this your cousin?"

"Aye, Adam Craighead, from the Monongahela."

As they made the return trip across the river, Murray repeated the latest news, asked if David and Adam knew anything more, and seemed to be disappointed when they said they did not.

"The folks was hopin' y'd bring some good news," he said as the raft bumped against the landing. "But news or no, I 'spect they'll be glad t' see y' both."

Although Adam had never before been to North Carolina, and it had been a few years since he had seen his sister, he was made warmly welcome. Within a few minutes of arriving at the sprawl of houses by the river, Adam felt completely at home.

"You haven't changed a bit, Sarah," Adam said to his sister when she finally let him out of her embrace.

"Ah, Adam, you know 'tis wicked to lie," she said, but her hazel eyes smiled. "I hope you've a mind to stay with us awhile, now that you're here," she added.

"It'll take me some time just to figure out who all these young ones belong to. I had no idea you had such a large family."

Sarah laughed. "They're not all our kin—the entire neighborhood came as soon as they heard you were here. Look at them," Sarah said, waving her hand at the children that had gathered around David. "I'm sure you could tell that those dark-haired and dark-eyed boys are the Gospels, and the girl is their sister, Susannah. The rest of the children in the yard are neighbors—

Boones and Bryans and Moores, mostly."

"Who is that?" Adam asked, pointing toward another group that had just come out of the house.

"You don't recognize your own nephews? The taller boy's Prentiss and behind him, that's Isaac. The barefoot girl with the red hair—"

"That's your daughter, Hannah," Adam finished for her. "She looks so much like Joshua's mother I'd know her anywhere."

"Yes, her red hair always gives her away," Sarah said.

"You and Joshua have a fine family. I only wish Mother and Father could be here to see them."

At the mention of their parents, Sarah's eyes saddened and she clasped Adam's hand. "Uncle Jonathan tells me that all is not well with them," she said.

"Father had a rough winter, but if Mother's herbals hold out, he should be much better by now."

"I pray that it is so," Sarah said earnestly. " 'Tis hard to accept that we might never again meet in this life."

"I know," Adam said. He wished he could think of some comfort to offer his sister.

She straightened and attempted to smile. "Joshua and Uncle Jonathan will be sorry to miss your homecoming."

"Where are they? The ferryman said they'd both gone somewhere."

"They're out in the county after rifles."

"Rifles?" Adam repeated.

"Yes—you must have heard about the fighting in Massachusetts. Think-ing that it's coming this way sooner or later, the local militia aims to sign up every able-bodied man who isn't an out-and-out Tory. But there are no weapons to give them."

"I'd think every man around these parts would already be armed," Adam said. "I never yet saw a frontier settlement that lacked for weapons."

"Well, ours does. Most of the men hereabouts do have rifles, but they want to leave them with their women so they can defend themselves if need be. If you and David had just known in time, you could have brought us some from Pennsylvania."

"There are a few weapons in the goods we brought back, but hardly enough to outfit a militia," Adam said.

"And who is this, Missus Stone?" A burly, red-faced man came up to Adam and Sarah. With his hands on his hips, he looked Adam over. "He looks t' be fit for our militia, less'n he's one o' them Loyalist polecats."

"This is my brother, Adam Craighead, Mr. McWhorter. He just traveled all the way from Philadelphia with Davey McKay."

The man looked impressed. "Philadelphia City, is it? Well, y' must tell us all that's happenin' there, Lad. *Then* we'll see about signin' y' up."

"Not until he's had his supper, at least," Sarah said firmly.

"First thing t'morrow, then," McWhorter said.

The man walked away laughing, but Adam knew he was serious about enlisting him in the militia. If he stayed in Carolina, he would be called on to help defend it.

𝕰𝕼

As the summer heat began to make Philadelphia almost unbearable and the tension between the British and colonists grew daily, Mary's father continued to disappear for days at a time. When Mary confronted him and demanded to know what he was doing, he seemed relieved to tell her.

"We're gathering stores for the Patriots and moving as much as we can from the warehouse to points outside Philadelphia. It's slow work and most of it must be done by night."

"If you're caught—" Mary began, but he wouldn't allow her to finish.

"I don't intend to be."

"Could my friendship with Hetty be putting you in danger?" Mary asked, voicing what she had reluctantly come to suspect.

"Perhaps you know the answer to that better than I do. Has Hetty seemed to be curious about what I do?"

"Sometimes, but she hasn't mentioned it lately. In fact, since the Massies' party, I've seen very little of Hetty."

"That's just as well. I don't wish to interfere with your choice of friends, but lately I've noticed things about the way that young lady behaves that I don't care to see you imitate. Perhaps it's good for you both that you'll be apart for a time."

Mary raised questioning eyes to her father. "What do you mean?"

"As usual, you'll go to Lancaster for July and August. 'Tis cooler there, and I think perhaps you're ready for the change."

"What about you? Where will you be?"

"I must remain here."

"You'll want Polly and Thomas to stay here, then."

"Yes, but since I've kept on the Lancaster servants, you won't need them."

"I'll miss Polly," Mary said.

"Well, perhaps you can teach Doris to do your hair—I'm sure she'll be willing enough to learn."

Maybe it's a good thing that Polly will stay in Philadelphia, Mary thought. The girl could be the link between her and Adam Craighead. If Adam should happen to write—or better yet, if he came back to Philadelphia—Polly would

312

see to it that Mary knew about it as soon as possible.

"What do you say?" her father asked when Mary did not immediately reply.

"Yes, I think Doris will make a fine lady's maid. When shall I be ready to go?"

John Andrews seemed relieved that Mary was willing to go to Lancaster. "In about a week, I think. I'll send word by Jenkins so all will be in readiness. And of course you must have time to tell all your admirers that you're leaving."

"Oh, yes, I have so many it will take the better part of a week to write them all," Mary said lightly, but she knew what her father meant. Although General Hawkins had taken away a number of British soldiers, Captain Edward Simmons had stayed behind, and his dogged attentions to Mary had become wearying.

"Perhaps you should call on Miss Hawkins," Mary had told him the first time he had showed up on her doorstep, plumed hat under his arm, his heels clicked together in almost-Prussian precision.

With a look of horror he had shaken his head. "But she's a *general*'s daughter," he said, as if that made such a thing impossible.

"The general isn't even in Philadelphia anymore—and I know that Hetty would be happy to see you," Mary said, but to no avail.

"I wish you would be happy to see me, too, Miss Andrews," he said so earnestly that Mary finally gave up and allowed him a short visit.

Even though she felt uncomfortable with a small social lie, Mary instructed Polly to tell Captain Simmons she was unavailable when he called on her, and she returned all his notes unopened. Still the young officer had persisted, as if each rebuff made him more determined to win her.

"Men are a strange lot, aren't they, Polly?" Mary said one night after a neatly dressed manservant had delivered a nosegay of fringed pinks and white roses "from my captain, M'lady."

Polly twisted her mouth and shrugged. "I s'pose so, Miss Merry. I sure never heard tell o' a man as determined as that poor Captain Simmons."

"For all the good it does him," Mary said. "Take the flowers away—I don't want them."

"I don't mind havin' their sweet smell in my room, Mistress. And that captain—don't he put you to mind o' that Craighead man, not even a little bit?"

Only from the moment I first saw him, and every time since. It is the only reason I tolerate him at all. Mary could acknowledge the thought to herself, but not even to Polly could she give the words voice.

"There's no comparison between them," Mary said aloud.

"That's the way I thought matters was," Polly said, nodding her head.

"I won't even ask you what you mean by that," Mary said briskly. "There is one thing I want you to do for me after I go to Lancaster."

"Yes, Miss Merry?"

"I don't want Captain Simmons to know where I am. You can tell him I went out of town—that's all he needs to know. But if I should get a letter from Adam Craighead—or anyone else other than the captain—" she added, seeing the look on Polly's face, "send it on to me as soon as possible. Do you understand?"

Polly grinned. "Yes, Mistress. *Very* well."

"Take the flowers and go, then—I'll see you in the morning."

Chapter 13

"Well, boys, ye made much better time than I thought ye would," Jonathan McKay said when he and Joshua Stone returned a few days later.

"I couldn't get away from Philadelphia soon enough," David said.

"What about you, Adam?" Joshua asked.

"I'm not sure I'd want to live in the city forever, but it was interesting," Adam said.

"Aye, that it is," Jonathan agreed. "I'm glad Davey got t' see it, but I'm not a whit surprised that he won't abide there."

"Did y' find any rifles, Pa?" David asked, pointing to the cloth-wrapped bundle strapped to his horse's side.

"Only one or two rusty pieces of no use a-tall. Except for seein' some old friends and meetin' some newcomers, 'twas a wasted trip."

"Time to wash up—supper's laid by," Sarah Stone said, temporarily ending the men's conversation.

Later, as he and Jonathan sat alone, Adam turned the conversation from family news to present circumstances. "What is this rifle business about, Uncle Jonathan? Is there really need for so many arms?"

"Aye, Lad, even though th' British aren't yet a-hammerin' at our doorstep an' may never do so, there's many Loyalists hereabouts lookin' for an excuse t' start a fight. Our county committee of safety voted to be loyal to Britain but against taxes imposed anywhere but here. Soon as they heard of the fight in Massachusetts, they passed a resolution that the cause of the town of Boston is the common cause of all colonies. Then they seized all the gunpowder in the county and called for militia volunteers. There's no doubt that they expect a fight."

"So you and Joshua have taken the Patriots' side," Adam said, making it a half-question.

"Aye, that we have, and for a reason, Lad. The British never did aught for the McKays when we were in Ireland, and whatever help they claim to ha'e give us against the French we've long since repaid many times over in our taxes."

"Still, isn't it hard to think of yourself as anything but British?"

"I ken what ye say, but they've let us know that colonials don't deserve th'

315

same rights as British citizens. Then there's th' business about holdin' back th' land beyond the mountains—now that the French are gone, there's no reason to keep settlers away from th' Northwest."

"I've heard that some people hereabouts plan to go to the Kentucky land."

Jonathan McKay nodded. "Squire and Daniel Boone are surveyin' it now, after makin' a road o' sorts over the mountains. A few folks will go there. Most won't. We maun be ready to arm the ones that're left."

"You may have to make the rifles yourselves," Adam said. " 'Tis not a hard thing to do."

"Aye, I've done some gunsmithing. What's called for is a firelock with a three-quarter-inch bore, a barrel eight inches over a yard long, topped by an eighteen-inch bayonet. The ramrod has t' be steel, with the upper end of the upper loop trumpet-mouthed."

"Easy enough, provided you have a stash of the needed materials on hand."

Jonathan shook his head. "Not as such, but most households ha'e odds and ends that can be melted down."

"You can have anything but the cooking pots," said Sarah Stone, who had joined them in time to hear the last part of their conversation. "I refuse to risk the children's vittles preparing for a war that might never come."

"It's already come, Sarah—we just don't know what might be happening in the other colonies," her uncle said. "We must arm a militia—we have no choice."

"Perhaps you could get some rifles over at the coast," Adam suggested.

Jonathan grunted. "The only things you'll find there are Loyalists as thick as fleas on a huntin' dog and the king's ships takin' Carolina tar and pitch away after unloading rum and molasses—neither of which makes very good gun barrels."

"Then you'll have to make rifles from almost nothing, just like we do in the wilderness."

Jonathan turned to Adam, searching his face. "Bide here a time and gunsmith for us, Adam. Ye need to get to know your kin."

"I'll have to think about it," Adam said.

"That's not what Father would say," Sarah reminded him, and Adam smiled. Despite the difference in their ages, they had been brought up by the same parents, and Adam well knew what Sarah meant.

"I'll pray about the matter," he corrected.

"Don't be in a hurry to leave us, Lad," Jonathan said. "Y'r whole life's yet before ye."

❧

Mary Andrews returned from Lancaster after two months, during which she rested far more than she liked. War fever had gripped that town as well as the city of Philadelphia, and all the talk made Mary fear for her father's activities on behalf of the Patriots. She also worried about Adam and David. Neither man had seemed eager to become a soldier, but Mary suspected that both would take the Patriots' side and might, for all she knew, already have signed on with the Carolina militia.

"Miss Merry, it's sure good t' have y' home." Polly's warm greeting reminded Mary of how much she had missed the girl's chatter.

"I'm glad to be back. Has anything interesting happened?"

Polly rolled her eyes and put a fist on her hip. "Now what d' y' mean by that, Miss Merry? I'm sure the master gave y' all the news."

"Papa told me what interested him, but I thought perhaps something else might have happened that he didn't know about."

"Well, Miss Hetty came by a few times to ask when y'd be back—had two different British officers wi' her, like she wanted t' be sure I saw 'em."

"What did they look like?" Mary asked.

"One was sorta red-faced and stout, t'other was some ensign—think y' already met him."

"What about Captain Simmons?" Mary asked, and Polly grinned.

"He did come by some for awhile. Then he finally figgered out you really was gone and not jes' out a-callin'. He wanted t' know where you were, but I tole him it wa'n't none o' his business. I've not seen him since."

"Poor fellow," Mary said, smiling back at Polly. "I imagine he's gotten over his infatuation by now. Is there anything else I should know?"

Polly shook her head. "No, Mistress, but Miss Hetty did ask me to tell you she wants t' see you as soon as y' get back."

"Hetty will have to wait—I must wash off this road dust first."

While she bathed, Mary pondered what she ought to do about Hetty. They had been friends for too long for Mary not to see her at all, yet she realized that continuing their close relationship might be dangerous for her father.

Then there was the matter of being friendly with the British soldiers. Most that Mary had met seemed to be decent young men who had generally been posted to the colonies unwillingly. But when—or if—fighting broke out between the British and the Patriots, they would be her enemies. It would be better for Mary to avoid the British soldiers altogether—but to do so might also invite suspicion and thus endanger her father.

I wish Hetty had just stayed in England. Mary sighed. Her life would certainly have been simpler.

❧❧

Summer came in lush beauty to the land around the Yadkin River. Adam fished with Davey and the Gospels and also got to know his nephews, Prentiss and Isaac, who plied him with questions about his life among the Lenni-Lenape. David's sister, Susannah, was fascinated with the bracelet Adam wore and asked him to try to get someone to make her one like it.

"I can do better than that," Adam said and handed it to her. He'd been wearing it from habit since the day he'd first seen Mary Andrews. Anyway, Karendouah was miles away, and Adam had long ago dismissed her from his thoughts.

The bracelet was too large for Susannah's slender wrist, so Adam showed her how to separate the strands and retie them. Soon even the Gospels were cutting strips of leather and plaiting them Indian fashion. Adam stayed busy making and mending rifles whenever he could get the materials, and with Jonathan and Davey he ranged far into the countryside. Sometimes they watched the militia drill to the somewhat ragged accompaniment of a drum and fiddle, but as neither planned to stay in Carolina permanently, Adam and David didn't join it.

At his sister's urging, Adam began to go with her to visit the sick and read to them from his Bible.

"The people hereabouts have no one to minister to them, and they're hungry for the Word."

"I'm not a minister," Adam reminded her.

"No, but you can read the Scriptures to them and pray for them. The healing of the body always goes better when the spirit is calm."

Although awkward and self-conscious at first, Adam soon realized that what he read or prayed was not as important as the fact that he represented a link between God and those his sister sought to help. Adam had no trouble praying sincerely for their healing, but his private devotions were quite a different matter.

Recalling the advice that Ian MacPherson had given him, Adam tried to pray earnestly. Yet he felt no sense that God heard him, much less that He would give him a sign to direct his life. With each passing day, Adam felt more restless and less certain of what he was meant to do.

On the other hand, his cousin Davey knew exactly what course he wanted his life to take. One day as he and Adam fished by themselves in Dutchman's Creek, Davey told his cousin his decision.

"Next trip that Dan'l and Squire Boone make to the Kaintuck, I'm goin' with 'em."

"What does Uncle Jonathan have to say about that?" Adam asked.

"I haven't told him yet, but he shouldn't be surprised. Pa knows I've been a-wantin' to go over there."

"He'll miss trapping with you come October."

Davey shrugged. "The Gospels'll be old enough soon, and anyways, Pa's got other things on his mind these days. Why don't y' go with me, Adam? They say that th' land o' milk an' honey's got nothin' on Kaintuck."

"Yes, but from what I've heard, it's also a vicious land. The Indians—"

David made a derisive sound and shook his head. "Y' need say n' more— I see that you lack the stomach for pioneerin'."

"It's all I've ever known, Davey," Adam said, seeking to mollify his cousin. "If I'd wanted to keep pioneering, I'd have stayed where I was."

" 'Tis not th' same," Davey insisted. "There's no land left in Pennsylvania anymore. If y' heard the Boones talk about the Kaintuck, y'd want to come, too."

Adam shook his head. "It's not for me, but if pioneerin' is your heart's desire, then I wish you godspeed. I just wish that I could be as certain about what I want to do as you are."

David's declaration made Adam more restless. Although he'd written his parents that he'd probably stay in Carolina through the winter and make some decision about his future in the spring, Adam didn't want to wait that long. *Send me a sign,* he had prayed, but none had come.

Well, Adam thought as he walked alone on a high, remote ridge early one morning, *if God chooses not to send a sign, I suppose I'll just have to do the best I can on my own.*

At that moment, Adam heard a strange, almost human cry. At first he thought one of the valley sheep had strayed into the hills and become snared in the underbrush, then he realized that the sound seemed to be coming from the sky. Adam climbed onto a rock outcropping near the top of the hill to gain a better view. What he saw all but took his breath away.

A bald eagle soared in the sky above the treetops, gliding from side to side as its keen eye scanned the ground beneath its powerful wings. Without warning, it suddenly plummeted to the earth, and Adam's first thought was that an unseen Indian must have brought it down with a well-placed arrow.

But then the bird reappeared, having captured its prey, and a few flaps of its wings brought it to a tree atop an adjoining hill. Fascinated, Adam crouched on the rock and watched. Although he was too far away to make out the details of the scene, the eagle seemed to be feeding its young. It soon left the nest behind, however, and once more split the sky with its wedge-shaped wings.

Adam had seen eagles before, of course, but never had he been so close to one. Never had he been able to see how beautiful its strength was, how powerful yet graceful it was as it sailed in the air. *God did well when He made you,* Adam thought, making it a prayer of praise. He was aware of a strange warmth, much as he had felt when as a child he had surrendered his life to Jesus.

Reminded of the words that Ian MacPherson had quoted, Adam spoke them aloud. " 'They that wait upon the Lord shall renew their strength; they shall mount up with wings as eagles; they shall run and not be weary; they shall walk, and not faint.' "

Adam dropped to his knees on the flinty surface of the rock and clasped his hands together in desperate supplication. *Lord, I've tried to wait on You; I really have,* he prayed. *I want to do Your will, but I don't know where to go or what to do. If You want me to leave this place, send me a sign, Lord, and I'll do my best to understand it.*

Adam opened his eyes and let out his breath in a ragged sigh. His prayer might lack the eloquence of his father's, but it had been as sincere. Adam stood and shaded his eyes with his hand as he scanned the skies in search of the eagle. Nothing appeared.

It must have seen me, Adam thought. Fearless as eagles were, they avoided people, and one feeding eaglets would be doubly wary. Disappointed, Adam bent to pick up his rifle.

Suddenly, the air resounded with the eagle's distinctive cry, and Adam looked up in time to see not one, but two eagles soaring high overhead. They flapped their wings, then glided, climbing higher and higher as they flew to the northeast.

Adam watched them fade into specks, then disappear altogether. He stayed where he was a long time in hopes that they might return, but he knew he had seen the last of them.

Chapter 14

That evening when Adam told Sarah and Joshua what he had seen, they looked clearly puzzled.

"There's not ever been an eagle in these parts that I know about," Sarah said. "Uncle Jonathan claims our ridges aren't high or lonely enough to suit them."

"And you say there were eaglets in the nest?" Joshua asked. "This isn't their usual nesting time."

"Maybe you saw a goshawk," Sarah said. "Some of them are almost as large as eagles."

I know what I saw, Adam thought, but he knew it was useless to argue the point. "Maybe," he said. "Anyway, whatever it was reminded me that it's time I was moving on, myself."

"Not so soon!" Sarah cried. "I thought you'd stay with us through the winter, at least."

Joshua looked concerned. "Early fall storms can be hard on travelers in these parts. If you plan to go home, you'd best not wait."

Adam nodded. "I agree, and I intend to leave immediately. But I'm not going home just yet."

Sarah looked at her younger brother knowingly. "I think I can guess where you're going—and for what reason."

Joshua looked at his wife in surprise. "What's this?"

"Davey must have been talking out of turn," Adam said.

"Not only Davey, Adam. Do you have any idea how often you've spoken about Mary Andrews and her father?"

Adam's face reddened, bringing smiles to the others. "John Andrews did offer me work in his business," he said, but Adam knew that as far as his family was concerned, his return to Philadelphia was the decision of a love-sick youth.

Later, when they were alone, Sarah brought up the subject of Mary Andrews. "I hope she'll be a worthy helpmeet to you," she said. "Should you decide on the ministry, you'll need such a woman."

"She might have something to say about that," Adam said. "Anyway, I have heard no such call."

His sister laid the palm of her hand against Adam's cheek and smiled faintly. "I wonder if you've really been listening. Perhaps it was no accident that you saw two eagles."

"Do you think it could have been a sign?"

"I don't know, Adam—but I believe the Lord is dealing with you. Whatever else you do, you must take time to listen to Him."

"I'll try," Adam promised.

The next day, Adam waved a last good-bye from the ferry, then turned northeast, the direction the eagles had taken. However he might interpret their flight, Adam thought his sister was right about one thing. It was no accident that there had been two of them.

❧

"Miss Merry! Wake up!"

Polly's frantic voice brought Mary instantly awake. "What is it? What's the matter?"

Polly stood by her bed, a candlestick illuminating the fear in her face. "Get dressed and go out the back door," Polly said. "Hurry!"

Mary pulled a petticoat over her head, then struggled into a cotton day gown. "Where are we going, and why?" she asked as Polly thrust Mary's shoes and stockings into her arms.

"Never mind. Just *go*." To punctuate her words, Polly pushed Mary toward the door.

When she reached the staircase, Mary began to understand Polly's urgency. From the doorstep came angry voices calling for John Andrews to come to the door.

"Open it or we'll break it down!" someone called, as another apparently began kicking at the door.

Mary needed no further urging to quit the premises in haste. At the kitchen door, Polly stopped and motioned for Mary to wait while she opened the door a cautious crack.

"They don't seem t' ha' thought o' guardin' th' back door," Polly whispered. "Run for the carriage house."

Still barefoot, Mary did as she was told. Inside, Thomas waited with the cabriolet. As soon as Polly and Mary were seated, he walked the horse down the alley until he was a safe distance away from the house, then maneuvered onto the street and whipped the horse to a trot.

"That was close," Polly said when it was apparent that they were going to make good their escape.

"Who were those men?" Mary asked, although she had a pretty good idea. Several threatening letters had lately been delivered to the house, warning John

Andrews to "mend his ways" and "mind who you trade with."

"They were a mob, Mistress," Polly said darkly. "One man alone at first, an' when I said th' master wasn't to home, he didn't believe me. 'We'll see about that,' he says, an' the nex' thing I know, there's a ha' dozen about, bangin' on th' door and demandin' t' be let in. I don't see how y' could sleep through all that din."

"I was dreaming of a storm," Mary said, not adding that in the dream, she and Adam had been running through an open field beneath menacing clouds, accompanied by loud peals of thunder. "What will they do to the house?"

"Nothin', I hope," Polly said, but both she and Mary knew their dwelling was likely not to escape the mob's wrath.

"Anyway, I'm glad Papa wasn't home," Mary said.

Reaching the docks, Thomas stopped the carriage and slid down from the driver's seat. "I'm just goin' to check the warehouse an' see if Master John's there," he said. He tried to speak reassuringly, but Mary could hear the undercurrent of fright in his voice.

"Hurry—I don't care to be left alone on the docks in the dead of night."

"The docks 're prob'ly safer in the night than the day," Polly muttered.

She and Mary watched Thomas walk rapidly toward the dark bulk of Andrews Import Company.

"As soon as those men find that Papa isn't at home, they'll probably make straight for the warehouse," Mary predicted.

"Thomas'll be back t' us by then," Polly said with more hope than conviction.

Mary buckled her shoes and climbed down from the carriage.

"What are y' doin', Miss Merry?" Polly sounded half-alarmed, half-annoyed, and Mary laughed.

"What else would I be doing on such a fine night as this? We're going to take a little carriage ride."

"Miss Merry, have y' lost y'r mind altogether?"

Without bothering to answer, Mary climbed up to the driver's seat and gathered the reins, prepared to come to Thomas's rescue if necessary. After what seemed to be an eternity, she saw him coming back to the carriage. But before she could express her relief that he was all right, Mary saw that he was being followed by several shouting men.

Quickly, she slapped the reins and maneuvered the carriage so that Thomas could vault onto the seat. Mary wielded the carriage whip to keep the other men from attempting to do the same.

"Drive!" Mary cried, but Thomas, rapidly leaving the shouting men behind, needed no encouragement.

"What was that all about?" Mary asked when Thomas finally slowed the cabriolet and they had a chance to catch their breath.

"I dunno, Mistress. Those men weren't the reg'lar night guards. I couldn't make out any faces, but they was wearing some kind o' ribbon in their vests, best as I could tell."

"That doesn't make sense," Mary said. "The Sons of Liberty sometimes wear a ribbon rosette as a sign of their allegiance, but there would be no reason for them to chase away Thomas, whom they all know on sight."

"The men what came to th' door earlier had such ribbons," said Polly, who had leaned halfway out of the carriage so she could hear the conversation.

Thomas brought the vehicle to a stop near a streetlamp on a quiet side street. In its faint light Mary could see the concern that etched his face.

"Are y' sure, Polly?" he asked sharply, and she nodded.

"I'd stake m' life on it," she said.

"There'd be no reason for the Sons of Liberty to harm Papa, would there?" Mary asked.

"Of course not. But I'm wonderin'—"

Although Thomas didn't finish his sentence, Mary knew what he could have said. *Maybe those men weren't Sons of Liberty at all. Maybe they were Loyalists merely pretending to be Patriots.*

Mary shivered and hugged her forearms as if she were chilled. "Thomas, Polly and I will wait here while you walk back to the house and see what's happening. If the men are gone, we'll return home."

"Yes, Mistress. The two o' y' watch out, now," he said before he disappeared into the night.

Polly and Mary waited in silence. A long time passed before Thomas returned.

"Well?" Polly asked, but one look at Thomas's face in the faint glow of the streetlamp told Mary more than she wanted to know.

"Y' can't go back there, Mistress Mary. The house is all afire."

Chapter 15

Traveling alone and in a welcome spell of dry weather, Adam made the return trip to Philadelphia in less time than he and David had covered the same distance. On his best day he made about sixty miles, but out of consideration for his horse, he usually traveled fifty or so. He slept on the ground a safe distance from the road, with his rifle cradled in his arm and his horse hobbled nearby.

In every town, the possibility of war and its effects were openly and often loudly discussed. Adam rode from Lynch's Ferry to Culpeper with a peddler who complained that no one was buying imported goods anymore. "I'd be tarred an' feathered if I offered t' sell so much as a paper o' pins from over the ocean," he said.

"You must be having a hard time making a living," Adam said.

"Aye, but I'd rather starve than fatten the British merchants. I've found a few sources o' local goods, and these are all my store now."

Immediately Adam was reminded of Mary's father. "I know a Philadelphia merchant who started looking for such goods some months back."

"Aye? He should soon be a wealthy man, then. I hear tell many of the ladies of quality in th' East have taken t' wearin' homespun along wi' their servants, and their menfolk won't cross them."

"Maybe it's just a passing fancy," Adam said, while acknowledging to himself that it might be one more indication that the colonies were heading for a dramatic showdown with their parent country.

"And mebbe you'll swap your buckskins for osanburg," the peddler said, eyeing Adam's clothing with interest. "Osanburg's what y' need t' be a-wearin' in the city."

"No, thanks," Adam said.

"I'll give y' a buck for th' pants, then, and throw in the osanburgs for free. City ladies are right fond o' osanburg."

"Maybe, but my lady in Philadelphia likes my buckskins," Adam said.

The peddler grinned and touched his hand to his forehead in a rough salute. "Then gi' my greetin' to your lady, and luck t' yourself, Sir."

As the man rode away, Adam's smile faded. The closer he got to Philadelphia and to the possibility of seeing Mary again, the more unsure of himself he felt. He truly believed that his future was somehow bound with hers and that whatever he did, he wanted her by his side. However, Adam wasn't sure that Mary felt the same way. Her father, who had welcomed Adam as the son of old friends, might feel quite differently about having a poor frontiersman as a son-in-law.

Worst of all, perhaps he hadn't received any sign at all but had merely allowed his desire to see Mary Andrews overrule his judgment. When Adam got to Philadelphia, what would he find?

"Take therefore no thought for the morrow: for the morrow shall take thought for the things of itself. Sufficient unto the day is the evil thereof."

The passage came into Adam's mind unbidden and reminded him of the many times he'd heard his parents quote it.

Whatever awaited in Philadelphia, Adam prayed for the strength to face it.

⁂

"Miss Merry? Wake up."

Mary's eyes flew open, and for a horrible moment she felt a formless fear as she realized she wasn't in her familiar bed. She rubbed her eyes and looked around. "What is it?" she asked groggily.

"I'm sorry if I gave y' a start—y' was dozin' so peaceful I hated to disturb y', after y' not sleepin' any last night. But we're here, Mistress—back in Lancaster, where y'll be safe."

"Is Papa here?" Mary asked the servant who came out to meet them.

Doris shook her head. "No, Mistress Mary, an' we wasn't expectin' you, either. But come in, Child, y' look all done in."

"She is," Polly said and told Doris what had happened to the Andrews' town house.

"How terrible!" she exclaimed. "But don't worry none about your Master Andrews—I'm sure he'll come lookin' for you here straightaway."

Mary felt a stab of fear as she realized that Lancaster was the first place that anyone would look for her father, and therefore the last place he should be.

"Thomas, as soon as you've rested, you must go back to Philadelphia and find Papa. Warn him he mustn't come here."

"But Miss Merry—" Polly began, but Mary interrupted her.

"Whoever burned our house and took over the warehouse can mean only harm to Papa."

"I think he already knows that, Mistress," Thomas said gently. "Master Andrews is able to take care of himself, all right."

"Then at least let him know that I'm safely here," Mary said.

Thomas nodded. "I will, Mistress."

"Come on to bed wi' y' now," Polly said, leading Mary by the hand to the room where she always stayed when she was in Lancaster. "Ye're too tired t' think straight. Things'll seem much better after a good sleep."

❧

The last few miles between Wilmington and Philadelphia seemed to last forever, yet as Adam neared the city, he made himself stop at an inn. He stuck his head under the courtyard pump, then stripped off his shirt and washed his upper body. His chest scar throbbed and felt tight, as it sometimes did before a change in the weather. Yet the setting sun was surrounded by red clouds, an omen that usually indicated fair weather.

A big storm's coming soon, Adam told himself. But rain or shine, he'd soon see Mary. Thinking of their meeting, Adam hoped that she'd answer the door herself; but even if she didn't, he'd know by the look on her face how things stood between them. Perhaps it would be another sign to guide him on his way, another indication of whether God had led him to Mary Andrews for a purpose.

The next morning dawned fair, but a few clouds had begun to gather in the west as Adam led his horse through the crowded streets of Philadelphia. He forced himself to slow down as he turned the corner into Mary's street. Eagerly, Adam's eyes turned toward the familiar green door and white-curtained windows that marked the Andrews house. What he saw brought him to an abrupt halt.

Adam gaped in disbelief at the blackened hull that had been Mary's home. The adjacent houses had been less damaged but appeared to be vacant.

"What happened here?" Adam asked a stocky leather-aproned workman who was planing lumber in front of the house on the right.

The man glanced with disdain at Adam's buckskins. "Are y' from so far in the woods that y' can't tell when a house has burnt?"

"Aye, I see that well enough," Adam said mildly. "Might you know if the people escaped harm?"

The workman shrugged. "I suppose so, since 'tis said that no one was t' home at the time. Mr. Franklin's fire brigade kept the fire from takin' these dwellin's, but as y' can see, they're still a fair mess."

"Do you know where the people who lived here are now?"

The workman turned the plank and ran his hand across its surface before he replied. "I don't get paid t' answer questions."

"If I give you a coin—" Adam began, but the man's gesture stopped him.

"Give me what y' like; I can't tell y' what I don't know. If the folk who lived here are still in the city, I've not seen 'em."

Adam looked at the ashes that had been Mary's elegant home and felt almost physically ill. "How long ago was the fire?"

"A couple of weeks, more or less. I been workin' here less'n a week, myself."

Adam thanked the workman and walked to the end of the block, then up the alley behind the houses. The back wall still stood, looking almost untouched except for the heavy black soot that streaked the empty windows and the rear door. The carriage house hadn't burned, but the upstairs window had been broken out, and it was evident that the now-empty building had been looted.

Adam's horse lowered his head and nickered, seeing the pile of hay that still stood in the carriage horse's stall. "No time for that now," Adam murmured.

Quickly, Adam made his way toward John Andrews's warehouse, his mind churning with fears and unanswered questions. Even if John Andrews himself wasn't there, someone was bound to know if he and Mary were safe and where he could find them. Just knowing that much would help relieve his mind, though Adam knew he wouldn't rest until he could see Mary and assure himself that she was all right.

The strong scent of the sea told Adam that he was near his goal, and he quickened his pace. The streets had become more congested, and he dismounted to thread his way through the carriages, peddlers, and draymen thronging the docks. Adam was almost in front of the warehouse before he saw it—or rather, saw where it should have been. A pile of ashes and jumbled, blackened debris was all that remained.

Mary's house didn't burn by accident, and neither did the warehouse, Adam thought. It was one thing for a home to burn, perhaps through careless neglect of a candle or lamp, but it was too much of a coincidence that the same family's business would also be destroyed accidentally.

Dazed, Adam stared at the ruins for several moments. Then he turned and made his way across the street to a tavern.

It was not yet lunchtime, and only a few customers sat around the tables as Adam approached a serving woman and asked what had happened to the warehouse.

"It burned in th' night a couple weeks ago," she said matter-of-factly. "Can I fetch y' a tankard?"

Adam shook his head. "No, thank you. Do you know Mr. Andrews—the man who owned that building?"

The woman shook her head and turned to leave.

"Wait—is there someone else here that might know what happened?" Adam asked quickly.

Fear touched the woman's face, and again she shook her head. "You'd best leave," she said in a low voice. "We know nothin'."

Adam went back outside, pondering what to do next. He was almost certain that the serving woman knew John Andrews and could have told why the warehouse had been burned, but fear kept her from any discussion about it.

Fear of what? he wondered. John Andrews hadn't openly discussed politics with Adam, but there was no doubt in Adam's mind that Mary's father supported the Patriots.

If the British authorities had found out about it, they would have arrested the man and perhaps confiscated his property, but it would make no sense for them to burn it. On the other hand, a group of Loyalists might act unofficially, with the British looking the other way, to take care of quickly by mob rule what would take the courts months to consider.

"Pardon me, Sir, but I heard what y' asked in yonder."

Adam turned to look at the old man who had come up to address him. "Do you know anything about the warehouse fire? I particularly want to know if the Andrews family is all right."

"We canna talk here on the street. Follow behind me, a few steps back."

Can I trust this stranger? Adam wondered. But if he wanted any information about Mary, he had no choice but to comply.

Chapter 16

Adam untied his horse and did as the man had directed. He walked a block away from the docks, then turned north and entered a narrow lane where the dwellings were considerably smaller than those on Mary's street. The old man stopped in front of a ramshackle livery stable.

"Leave yer horse here," he directed.

"But—"

"It's all right," he said gruffly. "Tie it yonder—no one will steal it."

"I hope not," Adam said.

"Not from the city, are y'?" the old man said when he had ushered Adam into stuffy quarters uncomfortably close to the stable.

"No, I'm not. Now will you please tell me what happened to the Andrews?"

"First y' must tell me your connection wi' them."

"John Andrews and my parents were friends years ago. I met him and his daughter a few months ago. He told me I could help him in his warehouse if I decided to stay in Philadelphia."

"Well, that's unlikely now, I'd say. Far as I know, nobody was hurt in the fires. You knew the house was a-burnt, too?"

Adam nodded. "I went there first."

The man's eyes narrowed shrewdly. "Mistress Mary is a pretty little thing, at that. Well, the house and warehouse both went up on th' same night, an' no one's seen either father or daughter since, that I know of."

"Who did it?" Adam asked. "Those buildings didn't burn by accident."

"That's a question y' don't want t' ask around here," the old man said. "No one knows fer sure, but they say that the men that torched them wore Sons of Liberty ribbons."

"You mean they were Patriots?" Adam asked, incredulous.

The old man shrugged. "All I'm tellin' y' is that someone's out t' get John Andrews fer some reason y' don't have any business knowin'. If y' take my advice, y'll go back t' where y' came from and forgit that y' ever knew anybody by that name."

"You really don't know where they are?" Adam said. "I mean them no harm."

The old man smiled mirthlessly, showing gaps where he had lost several teeth. "I'm sure y' don't, specially where Mistress Mary is concerned. But even askin' questions about 'em could bring y' to harm."

"Surely you overstate the case," Adam said.

The old man rose and motioned for Adam to leave. "No. I've had my say, an' if you've half th' wits t' match yer looks, y'll do as I say."

Adam retrieved his horse and started back toward the docks, wondering what he should do next. One thing was certain—he couldn't take the man's advice. He didn't know how he was going to be able to do it, but he had to find Mary.

Dark clouds had covered the sun and a stiff breeze began to blow. The storm Adam had anticipated was about to break. *Show me what I should do, Lord*, he prayed as once again he stood before the ruined warehouse.

You must go to Neshaminy.

The thought came into Adam's mind almost in the form of an order, and suddenly Adam felt a sense of relief. Of course that was what he should do. With his connections with so many people in Philadelphia, Ian MacPherson could help him. Mounting his horse, Adam turned and headed out of the city.

🙢

"Are you alone, Son?" was Ian MacPherson's only question when Adam arrived, wet and bedraggled, at his doorstep.

"Yes, Sir. David McKay stayed on in Carolina."

"Come inside and get out of those wet clothes," his wife ordered. "You look like a drowned rat."

After he'd changed his clothes and had supper, Adam briefly told Ian MacPherson what had happened since they had parted. "So now I need your help," he finished.

"I'd hoped ye'd come to say ye were ready t' pursue the ministry, but of course I'll do what I can t' help ye find your friends. I know John Andrews t' be an upright man."

"I feel that I was led to come back to Philadelphia, although I still don't know why. Perhaps I was meant to help them."

"We'll pray about it, then ye maun get some rest. In the morning we'll speak of what ye can do," Ian MacPherson replied.

🙢

Barely a week after she had left Philadelphia for Lancaster, Mary was on her way back to it. The jolting discomfort of the cabriolet, which hadn't been designed for long-distance travel, mirrored her life since the fateful night her house had been burned.

"We'd make better time riding double on the carriage horse," Mary said as the cabriolet stopped again, this time when a Conestoga wagon in front of them lost its wheel and blocked the way.

"I b'lieve y're in some hurry t' get back t' the city," Polly said.

"I'm tired of being idle. I ought to be helping Papa any way I can," she said.

"I'm still not so sure th' city's safe for either of y'."

"Whoever burned us out didn't want to harm us—they'd not have made so much racket before setting the fire. They meant to warn Papa. I don't believe we're in any danger."

"I hope you're right, Miss Merry," Polly said without much conviction. "I'd like nothin' more than t' think that things'll get back t' th' way they was."

"So they will, Polly, but it'll take time."

Mary spoke confidently, but in her heart she knew that their lives could never be the same. She recalled how her relief at knowing that her father was safe had been tempered by the realization that his livelihood had been lost along with their home. "What will we do now? How will we live?" Mary had asked him.

John Andrews had pillowed Mary's head on his shoulder and spoken quietly of his trust that God would provide for them. "I've already found a place for us to stay, and I still have work to do. We'll be all right."

"But don't you still fear the men that did this to us?"

John had drawn back and looked into his daughter's eyes. "Not as much as I fear letting those cowards break my resolve."

"What about our friends?" Mary asked.

"For the time being, you must tell no one that you're back or where you're staying."

"Even Hetty?" Mary asked.

"Especially Hetty, I'm afraid. No one really knows who set out to ruin us, but I'm sure they were Loyalists disguised as Patriots. If you do happen to meet and she asks, you know nothing."

"That's true enough, at least," Mary said. "I pray that in this case, not knowing will be protection enough."

As the cabriolet neared Philadelphia and her new quarters, Mary yawned, closed her eyes, and pretended to sleep. She wanted to think about Adam and how she might be able to let him know where she was if he came back to Philadelphia.

No, she corrected herself, *when he comes back*. At the moment, how Adam might find her was of greater concern than her material losses.

❧

Adam returned to Philadelphia with two letters of recommendation, one to a friend of Ian MacPherson's who ran a dray business in the city, and another to the Widow McAnally, who sometimes rented her spare room to recommended Christian gentlemen. Arriving late in the afternoon, Adam decided to seek lodging first.

"I reckon ye'll do if the minister says so," the widow said, eyeing Adam's buckskins with doubt. "I don't put up wi' drinkin' an' carousin'," she warned.

"I am glad to hear it. Neither do I, Ma'am." Adam's sincerity so convinced his new landlady that she hurried away to prepare his supper.

The next morning Adam called on the drayman, a wiry man of middle years who was so glad to see someone actually asking to work that Adam was sure he would have been hired without the minister's letter.

"So many o' the young men are goin' for th' army now," he said. "Can y' start right away?"

"Later today, perhaps, but I'm concerned about finding some friends whose home burned whilst I was away. Might you know John Andrews, by any chance?"

A guarded look came over the man's face. "Everyone knows that he was burned out not long back."

"Yes. I heard he hadn't been hurt. Might you know where I could find him?"

"No, but in his place, I'd ha'e left town altogether. I'll count on havin' ye back here after noon."

"I'll be here." Adam shook Mr. Scott's hand, then turned back to the main street. Throngs of people were about, all total strangers. Adam might wish to meet Mary Andrews on the street, but he knew that was unlikely. However, there was one person in Philadelphia who should be able to help him find Mary, and soon he found someone to direct him to General Hawkins's house.

The reaction of the maid who answered the door reminded Adam of his first visit to Mary's home. After giving his name, Adam was invited into the Hawkins' house. In the elegant drawing room, Hetty's mother greeted him with interest.

"So you are the frontiersman that Hetty wanted to invite to my husband's gala," she said. "Hetty will be so sorry to miss you—she went shopping this morning."

"That's all right, Ma'am. I just got back to Philadelphia and saw that the Andrews' house had burned. I thought perhaps you might know where the family lives now."

Helen Hawkins frowned slightly. "A terrible business, that was. I understand that Patriots destroyed their warehouse, too. But I cannot tell you where the Andrews are now."

Adam felt keenly disappointed. "I thought perhaps you'd know, since your daughter and Mistress Mary are such good friends."

Mrs. Hawkins looked faintly annoyed as she stood, signaling that she wished Adam to leave. "I'm sorry I can't help you, Mr.—?"

"Craighead," Adam said, although he was fairly certain she couldn't have forgotten his name so quickly. "Would you please tell Hetty that I asked? I've taken lodgings near the market. I'll be working for Samuel Scott."

Mrs. Hawkins wrinkled her nose as if she smelled something unpleasant. "The drayman?"

"Yes, Ma'am. Mistress Hawkins can ask for me there."

"Good day, Mr. Craighead."

"You will tell her, won't you?" he persisted, but Mrs. Hawkins turned to the maid who had just reappeared.

"Mr. Craighead is leaving. Please see him out."

Once outside, Adam realized he had gleaned no new information except for Mrs. Hawkins's strange statement that the Patriots had caused the fires. *She knows more than she's willing to tell me,* he thought and wondered why. Perhaps she feared that he intended to pay suit to her daughter. Such an idea might once have struck Adam as funny, but under the circumstances it merely added to his anger and frustration.

Adam retreated down the street to a point where he would be out of sight but could still see anyone who approached the Hawkins house. Mrs. Hawkins had told him that Hetty was shopping. If so, she should soon be home—the sun was almost directly overhead, signaling that the noon hour was at hand. He folded his arms across his chest and prepared to wait.

"Is that you, Mr. Craighead?"

A voice behind Adam startled him, and he turned to see Hetty Hawkins walking toward him, a small parcel tucked under one arm.

"Yes, Ma'am—I went to your house, but your mother said you were out."

Hetty turned her blue eyes to his and smiled. "How sweet of you to wait for me," she said. "Where's your friend? Can you come in and take luncheon with us?"

"David's still in Carolina, and I must get back to work. I saw that the Andrews' house had burned—a workman told me they were all right, but I'd like to pay my respects. Can you tell me where they're staying?"

Hetty's smile faded for an instant, then reappeared. "They? Perhaps you've come back to see John Andrews, then? His warehouse burned, too, you know. I doubt that he'll be able to hire you now."

The daughter is more maddening than her mother, Adam thought. He forced himself to be civil. "Do you know where they are?" he repeated.

Hetty lowered her eyes and was silent for a moment. Then she lifted her chin and her eyes challenged his. "I cannot give you their address," she said.

"But you do know where they are?"

"If you want to see Mary—"

"Yes, I want to see her. Just tell me where she is—I won't tell anyone else."

Hetty put her hand on Adam's sleeve and applied slight pressure. "I can't tell you where she is, but I can ask her to meet you somewhere this evening."

"That is very kind of you," Adam managed to say. "How about the east side of the market?"

"What time?"

"Seven?"

Hetty shook her head. "That's too early—make it eight."

Adam inclined his head. "Eight it is. Thank you, Mistress Hawkins."

Hetty moved her hand from his sleeve. Her lips curved in the familiar half-smile that reminded him of a cat who had just enjoyed a saucer of cream.

"You will tell her?"

Hetty laughed, a soft, musical sound low in her throat. "Of course. Welcome back to Philadelphia, Mr. Craighead."

Chapter 17

I thought ye'd be back sooner," was all Samuel Scott said when Adam returned to the drayman's livery stable.

"I'll work hard enough to make up for it," Adam said.

"Did ye find what ye sought?" Scott asked, somewhat mollified by Adam's offer.

"No, but I expect to soon."

"Good. Now come and gi'e me a hand wi' this, Lad. Th' load must be at the docks this afternoon."

As the day warmed, the work grew harder, but Adam didn't mind. At least it occupied the time before the scheduled meeting with Mary Andrews.

Suppose she doesn't come? Adam tried to suppress his fear that Mary might not want to see him. In the midst of such thoughts, Adam smiled, imagining Ian MacPherson shaking his head disapprovingly at the way Adam was fretting.

"Ye do all ye can on your own, Lad, then ye ask the Lord to take the matter as far as is needed, an' make an end to it there. Worryin' is a sign that ye lack faith."

That's easy enough for Ian MacPherson to say, Adam thought that evening as he washed off the day's grime and exchanged his buckskins for osanburg knee breeches. He put on the shirt Mary had mended, topped by a waistcoat, and worked his feet into the city-stiff buckled shoes that Ian MacPherson had insisted on giving him. With his hair smoothed back and tied with a black ribbon, Adam looked very much like any other young colonial ready to court his sweetheart.

"Goin' out, are ye?" his landlady asked when he came to supper.

"I thought I might. Is there aught you need from the market, Ma'am?"

"Not at this hour, Sir," she said gruffly. "Ye'd best watch yer step around there. At night the market's likely t' have cutpurses an' thieves—an' other kinds o' folks ye ought to be careful of."

"I'll be careful," Adam promised. "Thank you for your concern," he added with a smile.

Mrs. McAnally adjusted her mobcap and looked flustered. "Neverth'less, I expect ye in at a decent hour."

"I'll probably not be gone long," Adam said, hoping otherwise.

It was less than a mile from Adam's lodgings to the market, and he arrived before full dark, far earlier than the time Hetty had told him to be there. Adam paced back and forth near the edge of the market where he could see—and be seen by—anyone who came near. As twilight deepened into night, most of the market stalls closed and the earlier crowds faded away.

She's not coming, Adam thought when the night watchman came by for the second time and eyed him as if he might be up to no good. Adam had almost decided to leave when a hooded figure detached itself from the deepest shadows and glided toward him. His heart pounding in anticipation, Adam moved to meet her.

Neither spoke as they met in a mutual embrace. Adam was startled when he felt soft hands on his cheeks, pulling his face toward hers. As the girl tilted back her head in an invitation for him to kiss her, the cloak's hood fell away, revealing blond hair, pale in the moonlight. Adam dropped his arms and stepped back as if he had been slapped.

"You're not Mary Andrews!"

The girl's musical laugh left Adam no doubt as to her identity. "How soon would you have known if I hadn't lost my hood?" Hetty asked.

As soon as our lips touched, Adam thought. "Soon—you and Mistress Andrews are quite unalike. Where is she?"

Hetty replaced her hood and took Adam's hand. "Come along. We can sit over there."

Adam allowed her to lead him to a crude bench near a food-seller's stall, where the faint aroma of meat pies and cheeses still lingered. As soon as they reached the bench, Adam took his hand from Hetty's. Once more her distinctive laugh rang through the night air.

"Where is Mistress Andrews?" he repeated.

"Mary wouldn't come, but I'm here," Hetty said.

"Why wouldn't she come? What did she say?" Adam persisted.

"Oh, Mr. Craighead, don't sound so angry," Hetty said sweetly. "Mary had no idea that you were interested in her, you know."

"That was not my understanding, Mistress Hawkins."

She leaned closer to Adam and spoke softly. "My name is Hetty. I would like you to call me that. And what should I call you?"

"Anything you like," Adam replied shortly. His surprise at seeing Hetty had been replaced by a growing hurt that Mary could dismiss him so lightly. *I didn't think she was like that,* he thought. Could he have been so mistaken about her feelings for him?

"Oh, Adam, I know you're disappointed." Hetty placed her hand on his forearm. "But it's for the best that you not see her again, since—" She broke off and glanced away as if she couldn't bear to go on.

"Since what?"

When Hetty didn't immediately reply, Adam put both his hands on her upper arms and applied slight pressure.

"I didn't want to tell you," Hetty said then, speaking in a rush, "but Mary is engaged to be married to a British soldier. Under the circumstances—"

Adam felt as if he had been kicked in the stomach. He dropped his hands from Hetty's arms and leaned away from her.

"Are you sure?" he managed to ask.

Hetty nodded. "Yes, I'm afraid it's true. From the time they met, the captain and Mary have been inseparable."

"When are they to be married?" asked Adam.

"The date hasn't been set yet—you know, with the fires, it's been difficult to make plans. But they don't want to wait."

"I see," said Adam, who neither saw nor wanted to see. "You could have told me this morning. Why didn't you?"

Hetty reached for Adam's hands and folded hers around them. "Because I thought it was her place to tell you. For your sake, I'm sorry that she chose not to, but I did want to see you again."

"Why?" Adam asked, and again Hetty's soft laughter floated across the market.

"Because from the first moment I saw you, I wanted to know you better. Perhaps now we can—"

"No!" Adam pulled his hands away from hers and stood. "Tell Mary I must see her. I can have nothing else to say to you until I have seen her."

Hetty stood and faced him, her chin tilted. "All right, I'll give her your message. But don't hope for too much."

"Tell Mary I'll be here tomorrow night—same time and place."

Hetty nodded and sounded almost businesslike. "Very well. You can depend on me, Mr. Craighead."

Can I? Adam wondered as Hetty Hawkins walked away. He supposed he should have offered to see her safely home, but she hadn't seemed to expect it. For that Adam was glad, absorbed as he was with his disappointment and hurt.

Surely Mary will come tomorrow night, Adam told himself, without a great deal of hope that she would.

❧❧

"Are you sure you can spare this many of your things?" Mary asked. She hadn't been back in Philadelphia more than two days before she and Hetty had met at the dressmaker's, and after a tearful reunion, Hetty had insisted that Mary come home with her and choose some clothing from her own clothespress.

"Of course—I just had a final fitting on three new dresses. I don't really need these."

"They should see me through until Madame DuBois can finish my order," Mary said. "That is, as long as I don't go anywhere more formal than the market."

Hetty made a face and busied herself replacing the other dresses in the press. "There's certainly no danger of that. Anyone would have to be out of their mind to try to entertain formally in Philadelphia in the summer."

"I'm a bit surprised to see you and your mother still here," Mary said. "I thought you'd go to the shore as usual."

Hetty shook her head so vigorously that her curls bounced. "Not with the way things are now. Papa says there are too many Patriots around there now—and after what they did to you, I'm sure you understand why we must stay here."

The Patriots didn't do anything to us, Mary inwardly protested. *It was Loyalists pretending to be Patriots.* But it would be foolish to discuss such matters with Hetty.

"You haven't mentioned your suitors," Mary said to change the subject. "Polly tells me that you had an officer on either arm the last time she saw you."

Hetty's smile showed her dimple. "Yes, and several more awaiting their turns. But most have gone off for some kind of training with the Prussians. Philadelphia is practically deserted these days."

"I've seen those German troops around the city," Mary said. "I hear there are thousands of them."

"Perhaps. Not one can speak decent English, their teeth are very bad, and they keep to themselves."

Mary smiled at Hetty's recital, well able to imagine what might have occurred to cause her to be so emphatic. "I take it that you don't consider them to be suitor material, then?"

Hetty rolled her eyes heavenward. "Certainly not! But turnabout is fair play. You must tell me if you've heard from the handsome frontiersman—what was his name? Adam something?"

"Adam Craighead," Mary said, feeling foolishly reluctant to speak of him in Hetty's presence. "No, and since the fire he'd not know how to find me if he did come back to Philadelphia."

"That's a pity," Hetty murmured. "But cheer up, Merry. When Papa's regiment comes back to town, things will be more lively."

❦

Adam waited until it was nearly dark to make his way to the market. He had dressed with the same care he had taken the evening before, but this time he felt far less confident.

He hadn't been there long when someone wearing a cloak like Hetty's appeared and walked toward him. Adam had a brief hope that Mary might have a similar cloak, but as the figure came closer, his heart sank.

"I tried, Adam, but I was too late," Hetty said before he could speak.

"What do you mean?"

Hetty looked at the ground as if what she had to say was too painful for her to watch him receive it. "She's gone, eloped with the captain. They went to New Jersey to be married."

"How do you know?" Adam asked.

Hetty raised her face and looked at him earnestly. "Polly told me," she said. "I'm sorry, Adam," she added and took a step toward him. Her expression was filled with such pity and concern that Adam was convinced she was telling the truth.

"I'd like to talk to Polly," he managed to say. "Surely it can do no harm to tell me where I can find her."

"I'm afraid that won't be possible," Hetty said smoothly. "Polly was about to leave to join Mary. They will live near the captain's post for the time being, and since Mr. Andrews is no longer in the city, Polly thought her place was with Mary."

"Mr. Andrews has left Philadelphia? Where did he go?"

"Polly said he left just before Mary did, but she didn't know where he was going. There is talk that the Patriots are still seeking to do him harm."

"Do you have an address for Mary in New Jersey?" Adam asked.

Hetty sounded faintly exasperated. "You frontiersmen are a stubborn lot, aren't you? Even if I knew the address—which I don't—it would be quite useless for you to attempt to contact Mary. She and the captain are obviously very much in love, and—"

"Never mind," Adam muttered. He'd already heard more than he wanted about that subject.

Hetty took a step forward and laid a sympathetic hand on Adam's arm. "I'm sorry, Adam. But perhaps you will allow me to be your friend."

Adam looked at Hetty's pleading eyes, aware only that she wasn't Mary. It was too soon to think past that. "Thank you," he said huskily.

Chapter 18

"Miss Merry, I'm leavin' for the market now. Is there anything special you'd like me t' get for y'?" Polly spoke from the door of the small room that Mary occupied in the rented house where they'd been living since their return from Lancaster.

Mary looked up from her needlework and shrugged. "Not really. Is it wise to go to the market in such threatening weather?"

"Th' rain may hold off a time. Anyhow, we must ha'e food."

"Then hurry," Mary said. "See if you can find a decent fowl for our supper."

"I'll try. Good-bye, Mistress."

With her shopping basket over her arm, Polly hurried to the market, a sprawling rectangle where all manner of goods and foodstuffs were bought and sold year-round. She made her selections as quickly as she could and had started back when a peal of thunder announced a downpour. Polly stepped back from the street and sought shelter in the overhang of a nearby shop. Through the ropes of falling rain, she watched in amusement as a drayman urged on his horse, which had halted in the middle of the road and refused to budge.

"Give 'im a taste o' th' whip, Lad!" a bystander called, and when the drayman turned to see who had spoken, Polly found herself staring into the face of Adam Craighead—or a man who could be his twin.

At the same moment, Adam saw and recognized her. Immediately he joined her.

"Y' shouldn't leave th' wagon, Sir," Polly cautioned.

"That horse isn't going anywhere—every time it rains, he stops until he's sure I'm drenched to the skin before he'll move again."

"I'm right surprised t' see y'," Polly said. "Mistress Mary was a-wonderin' where y' an' Master McKay were."

"Davey is still in Carolina. I heard about—I heard what happened," Adam said, finding it too painful to be more specific.

" 'Twas a terrible time, but praise God no one was hurt," Polly said, and Adam realized she was referring to the fire.

"Yes, I know about that, too—but I'm talking about Mistress Mary."

Polly looked puzzled. "Nothin' has happened t' her that I know of."

"She's gone to New Jersey, hasn't she?"

Polly's eyes opened wide in astonishment. "New Jersey?" she repeated. "Whyever would y' think Miss Merry went there?"

Adam felt the blood rushing to his face and he had to fight for self-control. "She isn't married, then?"

Polly shook her head vigorously. "No, Sir. Where'd y' get that idea?"

"Someone told me," Adam said, feeling it was better to leave Hetty out of it. "I've been trying to find out where you were staying, but no one seemed to know."

"That's because the master fears th' men may come back," Polly said. "He tells Miss Merry that everything will be all right, but I know better."

"Where is she, Polly? I must see her."

Her eyes narrowed and she shook her head. "I'm not t' tell, Sir. Master Andrews wouldn't like it."

"But surely you must know that I'd do nothing to harm her."

"I'll tell her y' said so," Polly said. "Th' rain's slacked and y' must get th' wagon out of th' way." Before Adam could move to stop her, Polly turned and fled. Regretfully he returned to his work, his mind churning.

Somehow Adam managed to get through the rest of the day. His relief in knowing that Mary wasn't married was no less intense than his disgust with himself that he had so readily believed it. As soon as he had finished his work, Adam went directly to Hetty's house, not taking time to change out of his work-stained buckskins.

"Tell Mistress Hawkins that Adam Craighead wants to see her," he said.

Hearing his voice, Mrs. Hawkins came to the door. "My daughter does not wish to see you, Mr. Craighead," she said firmly.

"That isn't what she told me, Ma'am," Adam said, but the door closed in his face before he had finished speaking.

Now what do I do?

Adam walked back to his lodgings, his thoughts dark. That Hetty had deceived him was bad enough, but Polly Smith's refusal to divulge where Mary lived was even worse. There was one glimmer of hope. If Polly told Mary that she'd seen him, there weren't so many draymen in the city that she wouldn't be able to locate him.

If Mary is meant to be with me, please let her find me soon, Adam prayed as he drifted off to sleep.

❧

It was raining hard when Mary opened the door to admit Hetty shortly after Polly had left for the market. "What brings you out on such a terrible day?" she asked.

Hetty took off her cloak and shook it before hanging it on the hall tree. "I have something to tell you," she said, and from her tone Mary knew it must be important.

"Come into the parlor. I'd offer you refreshment, but Polly's gone to the market."

Hetty sat beside Mary on the sofa. "I'm glad she's not here. What I have to tell you must be between us for the time being."

"Has something happened?" Mary asked, trying to imagine what could cause Hetty such concern.

"Yes, but I've been afraid to tell you."

"Tell me what?" Mary prompted.

"That Adam Craighead and I are in love."

Mary felt stunned, then incredulous. "That is a poor jest—" she began.

"No, it's true," Hetty said in a rush. "He came back just after you went to Lancaster, and naturally when he saw the house had burned, he came to me to find out what had happened. I told him that you were safe, then he—that is, we—"

Hetty broke off, too overcome to continue, and began sobbing into a lace handkerchief she kept on hand for such an emergency.

"Why did you wait until now to tell me?" Mary asked, her voice cold. "Why didn't you say something when I came back from Lancaster?"

Hetty continued sobbing into her handkerchief, muffling her reply. "Well, at f–first I didn't know where to find you, and then when we met, I–I just couldn't! I–I knew how h–h–hurt you'd be."

"Hurt!" Mary exclaimed. She stood and paced the floor, looking away from Hetty's teary face. "It's much deeper than that, Hetty. I thought you were my friend."

"Oh, Mary, I am!" Hetty rose and put out a hand in supplication. "But Adam and I, w–we couldn't help ourselves, and now Mama refuses to let him in the house—"

"I don't want to hear about it," Mary said. She took Hetty's cloak from the hall tree and thrust it toward her. "Just go and leave me alone."

"We may have to elope," Hetty said as she shrugged into the cloak. "Adam says he can't stand to be without me—"

Fighting the impulse to cover her ears, Mary took Hetty's arm and all but dragged her to the door. "Out!"

"I'd hoped you'd understand," Hetty cried as Mary closed the door in her face.

Trembling with rage and hurt, Mary went to her room and threw herself on the bed, racked by the most intense suffering she'd felt since her mother's death. Losing her home and knowing her father was still in peril had been hard to bear, but then Mary had still clung to the hope that Adam Craighead would come back and that they could face the future as one. Now, Mary had lost not only that hope but her best friend, as well.

"How could God let such a thing happen to me?" Mary cried into the silence. Only her own sobs could be heard in reply.

❧

Adam still hoped that Mary would seek him out, but in case she didn't, he determined to find her through Polly Smith. He spent as much time around the market as he could that day, hoping that she might happen by. When she didn't, he inquired of several merchants until he found a stall-keeper who knew her.

"A scrawny little dark-haired thing, ain't she?" the poultry seller said in response to Adam's query. "Works for the man what got burnt out last month."

"Yes, that's the one—do you know where she lives?"

"No, but I'll tell her y' asked—she oughter be right glad t' know that."

Adam shook his head. "No, I want to surprise her. I'll make it worth your while to get her address," he added, seeing the uncertainty on the old woman's face.

"Well, why didn't y' say so in the first place? I'll ask around—stop by this evenin' an' mayhap I'll have news for y'."

❧

By the time Mary heard Polly return, she'd cried until she had no more tears left. Not wanting Polly to see her red-rimmed eyes and pale cheeks, Mary told her she was resting.

"I have a headache and I'd like to be left alone," she said through the closed door.

"Y'd best hear what I have t' say," Polly replied. "I ha'e important news."

Mary walked to her bedroom door, but she didn't open it. "I'm in no mood to be riddled," she warned.

"I'm not riddlin' y'. Let me in, Miss Merry. This is important."

The urgency in the girl's voice made Mary fear that something had befallen her father. "It had better be," she muttered as she opened the door. Although Mary immediately turned away, Polly's gasp told her she had seen the grief written in her face.

"What's wrong, Miss Merry?" Polly entered the room and followed Mary to the lone window, where she stood with her back to Polly.

"I told you I have a headache. Just give me your news and leave me to die in peace."

Polly's lips twitched, and she nodded approvingly. "Well, Miss Merry, if y' can make a jest, I s'pose things can't be all that bad."

Mary turned to face Polly, her expression grim. "I'm not jesting. If you really have nothing to tell me—"

"But I do, Miss Merry—an' it's welcome news."

Mary sighed and folded her arms. "I'm listening."

Polly leaned forward, her eyes shining. "Well, if y' noticed, it did rain buckets soon 's I'd left fer th' market. I was shelterin' in front o' a shop when I looked up an' saw a drayman tryin' to get his horse t' move."

"Get to the point, Polly," Mary prompted when the girl paused.

"I'm tryin', Miss Merry—this drayman an' I looked at one another, an' straight off I saw who 'twas." Polly paused for dramatic effect, then grinned. "Adam Craighead—th' frontiersman himself."

"That is your welcome news?" Mary said bitterly. Through eyes that were beginning to fill with more tears, Mary saw the puzzled look on Polly's face.

"He's been tryin' t' find y' ever since he got back from Carolina. I thought y'd be pleased t' know it."

Mary took a deep breath and brushed away the tears with the back of her hand. "I hope you didn't tell him where we live."

Polly shook her head. "No, Mistress. I wanted t'; he seemed so anxious t' see y', but I recalled what the master said about not tellin' anyone, so I didn't. But I think I know how y' can find him."

Mary walked past Polly and sat down on the bed. "I doubt that Mr. Craighead wants to see me, and I certainly have no wish to see him. Now please go away and leave me alone."

"But, Miss Merry—"

"Go!" Mary ordered.

"I'll bring y' a poultice for y'r head," Polly said.

The damp cloth, saturated with fragrant herbs, eased Mary's throbbing temples but otherwise brought her no comfort. She tried to put Adam and Hetty from her mind but succeeded only in summoning vivid mental images of them together.

Hetty's perfect skin and blue eyes had captured many men's hearts, but Mary had thought Adam would be immune to her friend's charms. Apparently she had been badly mistaken. Hetty's way of dealing with men was so foreign to Mary that it had never occurred to her to imitate the other girl.

Maybe I should have, she thought forlornly. But Adam had seemed to be genuinely fond of her. *A man who can change his allegiance so quickly isn't worth a single tear.*

Yet Polly said that Adam wanted to see her. Why? To tell her he had fallen in love with her best friend? *No, thank you, Mr. Craighead. I am far better off without him,* Mary told herself, but her heart had not yet agreed.

❧❧

Slowed by the downpour, Adam was late getting his work done that day. When he had finally delivered his last load, he hurried to the market without taking time to change his clothes. One look at the poultry seller's face told Adam that her mission had been successful.

"I know where y' can find th' servant girl y' seek," she said. She bit the offered coin and satisfied herself that it was genuine before she spoke again. "Y'll need t' act fast—word is the fam'ly's about t' leave town."

"Where are they going?" he asked, but the woman shook her head. "All I can tell y' is they're now stayin' on Thimble Lane, near the tannery. Y' can't miss it if y' follow yer nose."

Adam returned to his lodgings, where he ate supper in haste before changing into his best clothes.

"Y' must be plannin' somethin' special tonight, Mr. Craighead," Mrs. McAnally said when Adam emerged from his room.

"Yes, Ma'am. I'm going to see a very special young lady."

The woman smiled. "Well, ye look very keen. Th' lady ought t' be proud t' take yer arm."

"I hope so," Adam said.

Mary had never seen him geared out in osanburg. What she would think of it was the least of Adam's concerns as he made his way toward Thimble Lane.

Chapter 19

Adam pinched his nostrils shut as he passed the tannery and turned into Thimble Lane. It was a narrower street than the one on which the Andrews had formerly lived, and obviously occupied by far less prosperous residents. *Perhaps the fires reduced John Andrews to poverty,* Adam thought, *as well as forced him to hide from those who might still seek to do him harm.*

Adam stopped and looked around, but no one was about on the streets, and the poultry seller hadn't told him in which house the Andrews lived. He stood uncertainly in the middle of the street for a moment, then a man emerged from a house halfway down the block and came toward him. When he came close enough to hear him, Adam spoke.

"Good evening. I'm looking for a family that just moved to Thimble Lane, a man and his daughter. Might you know where I could find them?"

The man regarded Adam with obvious suspicion. "Why d' y' want t' know?"

"They're my friends. I just came back from Carolina and heard that they're in these parts."

"Carolina, is it?" The man's eyes narrowed. "How feels that colony about war wi' Britain?"

Aware that the question was some sort of test, Adam shrugged. "About as in Pennsylvania. People expect there could be a fight."

"And who will win it?"

"Only God knows that," Adam replied with sincere conviction.

"Mebbe," the man replied. "Try the last house on the left—they may be th' ones y' seek."

"Thank you kindly, Sir." Adam touched his forehead in a brief salute, then hurried to the end of the block.

The house on Thimble Lane lacked a knocker, but Adam rapped on it with a force that brought an immediate response.

"Who's there?" a cautious voice on the other side called out.

"Adam Craighead. Is that you, Miss Polly?"

The door opened, and once more Polly Smith seemed surprised to see Adam.

"How did y' find us?" she asked.

"Never mind that. I'm here to see Mistress Mary."

Polly frowned and looked up and down the street. "I hope nobody a-followed y'."

"I'm sure they didn't. Please tell your mistress I'm here."

Polly shook her head. "I don't think she'll see y', but wait there an' I'll ask."

The servant girl left Adam standing on the doorstep as the summer twilight darkened to night. When she returned, Mary's answer was written in her face. "It's as I said—she won't see y'."

"Why not? Did she say?"

"T' tell th' truth, Miss Mary's not herself just now. She was fine when I went t' th' market, but by th' time I got back t' tell her I'd seen y', she'd been cryin' an' wouldn't tell me why."

"What did she say when you told her you'd seen me?"

"That she wanted nothin' t' do wi' y'. Then she said she had a headache an' wanted t' be left alone. Until just now, I hadn't spoken t' her since."

"I think I know what might be wrong," Adam said. "If you'll just let me see her, I'm sure we can straighten out this. . .misunderstanding."

Polly shook her head. "It wouldn' be any use for y' t' see Miss Merry t'night. Let her get some rest and y' come back t'morrow—by then mayhap she'll be seein' things some different."

Every impulse urged Adam to brush past Polly and find Mary, take her into his arms, and tell her he loved her. But no matter how much he longed to see Mary, Adam realized that forcing his way might only make matters worse. He had a pretty good idea that Hetty Hawkins was somehow behind Mary's sudden change of heart, and he intended to get her to admit it.

"Perhaps you're right," Adam said. "I'll be back tomorrow, and I *will* see her then."

Polly nodded and looked relieved. "I'm glad t' hear it. Good evening, Master Craighead."

Adam strode away, wishing he had thought to ride his horse. It was some distance to the Hawkins' house, and the only way he knew to get there was to return to the market and start from there. By the time Adam had done so, it was already past the hour when many households retired for the evening.

At the Hawkins' house, lights gleamed from almost every window. As Adam approached the front door and glanced in at the front window, he saw figures moving about in the drawing room. *Something unusual is happening,* he thought. Perhaps the general's duties had brought him back to Philadelphia, and the household had stayed up late to welcome him. Adam preferred not to see General Hawkins, who hadn't seemed to care for him very much, but he would if he had to do so to reach Hetty.

Resolutely Adam knocked. To his surprise, General Hawkins himself opened the door. His brow furrowed as if he found Adam's face familiar but had no name to match it.

"Adam Craighead, Sir. We met at the Andrews' house several months past."

"Who is it?" Adam heard Mrs. Hawkins call.

General Hawkins turned from Adam to answer her. "It's no one to be concerned about, Dear. I'll be back in a moment." Then he addressed Adam. "If you've come to enlist, I can direct you to the proper place."

"No, Sir. This is a personal matter."

General Hawkins looked faintly annoyed. "Oh? What personal business have you with this household?"

"I must see your daughter, Sir. I know it's late—" Adam began, but the general interrupted him.

"Hetty has retired for the evening. If you wished to see her, you should have called at a decent hour."

While her father was still speaking, Hetty appeared and took his arm. "I'm still up, Papa. Do let Mr. Craighead come inside, since he's already here."

General Hawkins shrugged. "Very well, but only for a short while. We must all rise early."

"Come in here." Hetty pulled Adam into a small parlor off the drawing room and closed the door behind her. Immediately, she reached out to put her arms around his neck, but Adam caught her wrists and held them as he glared at her. "What—" she began.

"I want to know what you told Mary about me," Adam said.

"Let go—you're hurting me," Hetty protested.

"Not until you answer me," Adam said grimly. "I want the truth."

"I'll scream and Papa will have you arrested," Hetty threatened.

"I'm sure you would, at that." Adam released Hetty's wrists and folded his arms across his chest. "You seem to be rather good at lying."

Hetty's face reddened. "Oh, Adam, don't be angry. Everything I did was for you—"

"Stop it!" he exclaimed. He clenched his fists in an attempt to stifle the urge to shake Hetty until her teeth rattled. "I want to know what you told Mary."

Hetty's lower lip trembled, and tears spilled from her blue eyes. "I told her I'd seen you," she said.

"That isn't all, is it? What else did you say?"

Hetty looked down at the floor and wrung her hands. "I meant no harm,

Adam. I just thought if she knew how we felt about each other—"

"What!" Adam stepped forward and put his hands atop her shoulders. "You told her I cared for you?"

Hetty looked miserable. "I know you would have, Adam, if you had the chance. Just because Mary saw you first—"

Adam dropped his arms to his sides and shook his head. "I don't want to hear anything more about that. You must go with me to Mary's house and tell her the truth—if any truth's in you at all."

Again the color rose in Hetty's cheeks. "I meant every word that I said to Mary. If you won't return my affection, then it's your loss."

"You won't apologize to Mary, then?"

Hetty shook her head. "No. What happened was a misunderstanding, that's all. I'm thankful I saw your true nature in time—if Mary's fool enough to want you, she's welcome to you."

"Hetty! Are you in there with Mr. Craighead? Come out this minute!"

At the sound of her mother's voice, Hetty turned and opened the door. "Yes, Mama. Mr. Craighead's just leaving. He won't be coming back."

Mrs. Hawkins looked at Adam almost triumphantly. "I told you that he wasn't suitable for you," she said. "Now you see that I was right."

Hetty's smile was barely more than a smirk. "Yes, Mama. Good-bye, Mr. Craighead."

Adam decided to try one last appeal. "If you should change your mind about seeing Mistress Ma—" he began, but Hetty interrupted him.

"I won't. Mama and I are leaving Philadelphia tomorrow to go to Papa's headquarters in New York." Hetty seemed to relish Adam's surprise.

"Then I wish you a safe journey, Ma'am," Adam said, half-bowing to Mrs. Hawkins.

Somehow Adam managed to get out of the Hawkins' house without saying anything he might later regret, although his mind was still seething with dark thoughts about Hetty when he approached his lodgings and saw that a cabriolet had stopped in front of the house.

That looks like the Andrews' carriage—maybe Mary changed her mind and has come to see me. Adam quickened his steps and arrived at the carriage just as its occupant stepped down from it.

"Good evening, Adam," John Andrews said.

Adam tried to hide his disappointment. "Mr. Andrews—I thought you were out of town."

"So I was, and soon will be again. Get into the carriage, Lad. We must talk."

Surprised, Adam did as he was told, and the cabriolet headed back toward the market. "How did you know where to find me?"

"The drayman Scott directed me here. Had I known you were in the city, you could have been working for me instead."

"When I came back and found you'd been burned out, I went to Neshaminy. The Reverend MacPherson saw to it that I had work and a place to stay while I looked for you. It was only today that I discovered your lodgings."

"I don't aim to be easily found," John Andrews said. "But I'm glad to see you, Lad. I need your help."

"In what way?"

"For the next few days, at least, someone must look after Mary."

Adam was glad the darkness masked his expression. "Is something wrong?"

"Aye, the same thing that was wrong before I was burned out. Those Loyalist rascals won't rest until they stop me from trading goods for the Patriots' use. It's too dangerous for my daughter to stay in Philadelphia, but they also know where to find us in Lancaster."

"What will you do then, Sir?"

"That remains to be seen. In the meantime, I want Mary to leave the city tonight."

"So soon?" Adam asked.

"Yes. The Loyalists know where we are now, and this time I fear they might do harm to my daughter. I know she likes you, Adam. I want her to be in a safe place until I can arrange to move my operations elsewhere."

Adam was having difficulty comprehending what John Andrews had apparently already planned. "You're asking me to take Mary somewhere?"

"Yes. I can't spare Thomas just now, and I'm sure you can use a rifle if you have to. Furthermore, I can trust my daughter with you. Will you help us?"

"I already have a job. The drayman—" Adam began, but John Andrews interrupted him.

"I've already spoken to Scott and to your landlady, as well. We all agree that you should take Mary to Neshaminy. Ian MacPherson has been my friend for many years—he'll be glad to take her in."

Adam swallowed hard. "I'll help you any way I can, Sir, but Mar—your daughter might not want to go with me."

"I doubt that. You know, Adam, God sent you here just when we needed you. I prayed that you'd decide to come back."

It was a moment before Adam could speak. "I prayed to be shown the right path. I'm still not sure about everything, but for now I'll do whatever I can to help you."

"Good. Here we are. Wait in the parlor. I'll tell Polly to waken Mary."

Mary had fallen asleep before supper, and Polly didn't have the heart to wake her up. Several times Mary had roused briefly, only to remember afresh the pain that Hetty's visit had brought. She closed her eyes tightly and willed herself back into a troubled sleep. Once she imagined that she heard Adam's voice, and another time she thought that her father had come home. She could hear him conversing in low tones with Polly, but she was too weary to get up. Moments later, all was quiet and Mary had slept once more.

Now, however, the voices were loud and insistent, and Mary sat upright and listened in the darkness for some hint of what was happening. There was a light rap on her door, and Polly entered, bearing a single candle.

"What's all the racket about?" Mary asked. Her mouth felt dry and her chest ached from weeping.

"Master Andrews is back, Miss Merry. He wants us t' get ready to leave town."

Mary swung her feet over the side of the bed and frowned. "Tonight?"

"Yes, Mistress. Y' might want t' change that gown, since y've been sleepin' in it. I'm t' pack your things."

Fully awake, Mary stuffed her feet into her kid slippers. "I can't believe Papa'd expect us to travel to Lancaster in the middle of the night!" she exclaimed. "Has something happened?"

"I don't know, Mistress," Polly answered. "But you'd best take a bite o' supper before we go, and y' can see what he has t' say."

Mary looked down at her day dress and decided it would make no sense to change it, only to have whatever she put in its place even more wrinkled by the jostling carriage. "If I have to travel, it'll be in this," she said.

"Wait, Miss Merry. Let me get th' tangles from your hair, at least."

"No one will see it," Mary said, but she sat at her dressing table and allowed Polly to ply the brush. A glimpse in the mirror showed Mary that her tears had done no lasting damage. The circles under her eyes might be deeper than usual, or merely shadows cast by the candle's light.

"Now you'll do," Polly said with satisfaction.

"Do for what?" Mary asked tartly, but Polly, gathering Mary's few remaining possessions, merely smiled.

Something is going on, Mary thought as she went down the stairs. Polly seemed entirely too pleased with herself.

"Papa?" she called when she reached the hallway. A light glowed in the sitting room, and Mary walked toward it, fully expecting to see her father. Instead, a man outfitted in osanburg knee breeches stood in the middle of the room, someone as tall as Adam Craighead. Then he stepped forward and Mary let out a cry of surprise.

"Adam Craighead! What are you doing here? I told Polly I didn't want to see you."

"Your father brought me here tonight, but I'd have come back tomorrow and stayed until I made you listen to me."

Mary half-turned as if to leave. "What could you possibly have to say that you think I would want to hear?"

Adam forced himself to stay where he was, his eyes riveted on hers. "Only one thing. I love you, Mary. I always have, and God willing, I always will."

Mary brought her hands together and steepled her fingers. " 'Tis a strange way you have of showing it, asking my best friend to marry you," Mary said.

Adam went to Mary and put his hands loosely on her upper arms. "I never asked Hetty to marry me. I went to her to try to find out where you were, and she told me you'd gone to New Jersey to marry a British officer. She lied to us both."

Mary had been standing still and tensed, keeping her distance. As he spoke, Mary looked deeply into Adam's eyes and knew that he spoke the truth. Tears came to her eyes, and Mary stepped forward and rested her head on his shoulder. "Hetty was always my best friend. How could she do such a wicked thing to us?"

Adam tightened his arms around Mary and moved his lips against her forehead, soothing her as a father might a fretful child. "Hush. Don't waste your tears on Mistress Hetty. The selfish always come to grief, and usually by their own scheming."

"I don't want to think about her ever again," Mary murmured.

"Then don't," Adam said. "Think of us instead."

"Don't talk—just shelter me here in your arms forever."

Adam smiled and looked down at Mary. With his thumb, he brushed away her most recent tears. "You haven't said you love me," he said.

Mary pulled away from his embrace and tilted her head to one side. "I wouldn't have cried over you if I didn't love you."

"I know," Adam replied. He bent his lips to hers in a tender kiss that ended only when John Andrews entered the room and cleared his throat loudly.

"We must go now."

Mary turned without embarrassment to face her father. "Papa, Adam has something to ask you."

Adam looked surprised, then he realized what Mary must mean. "Sir, I would like permission to seek your daughter's hand."

Conflicting emotions vied in John Andrews's face before he held out a hand to each of them. "It appears that your request is somewhat after the fact, but I shall take it under consideration."

"Oh, Papa! Go ahead and tell Adam you'll be glad to have me settled—I've heard you say it often enough!"

Polly stuck her head into the room, and from her pink cheeks and bright eyes, it was clear that she'd probably been in the hallway for some time. "Master, Thomas says we'd best go now."

"Very well." Mr. Andrews released his daughter and Adam's hands. "Thomas will drive you all to Mr. Craighead's lodgings, then take you and Polly on to Neshaminy and bring the carriage back. I'll go on to Lancaster then."

Mary turned puzzled eyes to her father. "What about Adam?"

"He can ride his own horse to Neshaminy at first light," John Andrews said. "Adam will keep me informed of your whereabouts until I've found a safe place for us to live."

"I suppose I'm in your employ, then?" Adam questioned.

"Of course. I can't very well let my daughter be courted by a drayman."

Mary hugged her father, then silently they went out into the starless night.

Chapter 20

After the carriage had gone on to Neshaminy, John Andrews sat in the parlor of Adam's lodgings and told him that he was almost certain that someone had told a Loyalist spy where to find him. Immediately Adam thought of a likely suspect.

"Might Mary's friend Hetty Hawkins have given you away?"

John Andrews looked thoughtful. "I would like to think not, but it's possible that Hetty could have made some innocent remark about us that was passed on to General Hawkins."

"I don't trust the girl," Adam said. "She told both Mary and me rather serious falsehoods."

Mary's father sighed. "That doesn't surprise me. I always knew that Hetty was more worldly than Mary, but I never thought she was dishonest. If I had, I wouldn't have permitted their friendship."

"Hetty and her mother are leaving town tomorrow."

"Would that they had sooner," John Andrews muttered. "Get you on to bed now. We've much traveling ahead of us."

❧

Adam rose before dawn, gathered his few possessions, and left without awakening John Andrews, who was sleeping on the parlor sofa. Mrs. McAnally seemed genuinely sorry to see him go, and after asking him to tell Ian MacPherson to send her another such lodger, she pressed Adam's hand and told him she'd pray for him. "I think the Lord has great things in store for y'," she said firmly. "I hope y' can let Him have His way."

"So do I," Adam told her, but as he rode toward Neshaminy, he wondered how much of what had happened was due to his feelings for Mary, and how much to being under God's direction. *Mary is the right wife for me; I'm sure of it,* Adam thought, but he still felt no special purpose for his life.

In the early morning quiet, Adam prayed intensely, *I still seek Your sign, Lord, and I will be obedient to it and to You.*

Soon afterward, Adam met Thomas returning with the Andrews' cabriolet. Thomas lifted his whip in greeting and called out that Mistress Mary and Miss Polly had safely reached the minister's. "Master Andrews waits for you at Mrs. McAnally's," Adam called back, then each rode on.

When he reached Neshaminy, Adam was greeted warmly by Ian MacPherson's wife.

"Mistress Andrews and the servant girl were very weary, so I sent them upstairs to rest," she said. "Come and eat now—the reverend will be back soon."

"Where is he?" Adam asked.

"Lecturing," she replied. "Hebrew or Greek or some such—I can't keep up with all that he teaches."

"Are there many ministerial students?"

Mrs. MacPherson glanced appraisingly at Adam. "As many as the Lord sends. I daresay there's always room for one more."

Mary and Polly were still upstairs when Ian MacPherson came home. He greeted Adam with affection, but also with a restraint that Adam had never before seen. "Come outside for a bit, Adam. I ha'e some news ye maun hear."

Something in his tone alarmed Adam, and even before he heard the minister's words, Adam felt a sense of foreboding.

Ian MacPherson took Adam to the crest of a small hill overlooking his house and the scattered buildings that made up the Neshaminy settlement. An ancient tree had been cut down the winter before, and the minister motioned for Adam to sit with him on its wide stump.

"You've had some word from my parents," Adam said, guessing the cause of the minister's concern.

"Yes, I'm afraid so. Your mother writes that your father has taken a turn for the worse."

Adam felt his heart tighten. "He always worked too hard."

"It seems that his time may be near. 'Twould mean much to him to see ye once more and to know that ye've settled at least part of your future."

Adam glanced sharply at Ian MacPherson, who smiled faintly. "Mistress Andrews told me that ye two have an understanding. I'm sure 'twill please your parents to know ye'll have such a worthy helpmeet."

"Her father and my mother were special friends," Adam said, not knowing how else to phrase it.

Ian MacPherson nodded. "I know the whole story," he said. "That their children should find one another is quite amazing."

"I think it's more than that," Adam said and told the minister about his experience in North Carolina. "I don't know if it was really a sign, or whether I just wanted to believe it was," he concluded. "But it led me back to her."

"Aye, Lad. I believe that ye ken it meant that, and even more. Now the question is, what will ye do about it?"

When Adam and the minister returned to the house, Mary and Polly were helping Mrs. MacPherson prepare supper. Seeing Adam, Mary ran to him and impulsively hugged him, then drew back as she realized that the minister and his wife might not approve of her behavior.

"I'm glad you got here safely," Mary said, and the compassion in her face told Adam that she knew about his father's illness.

"We need to talk," Adam said. "I know I promised to help your father, but I feel I must go to the Monongahela immediately."

Mary nodded and her eyes welled with sympathetic tears. "I understand. We'll have to pass through Lancaster on our way there, anyway—you can tell Papa what is happening then."

Adam looked at Mary in surprise. "We? Surely you're not thinking of going with me."

"Why not?"

"It—it wouldn't be proper," Adam blurted out.

"We're going to be married anyway—under the circumstances, Reverend MacPherson could suspend the banns and marry us here and now."

Adam shook his head. "No, Mary. We can't do that to your father. He deserves to see us wed."

"Well, married or not, I'm going with you, and that's that!" Mary announced.

Adam looked helplessly from Ian MacPherson to his wife and back to Polly, who was crying noisily into her apron. "Won't someone tell her she can't do this?"

Ian MacPherson took Adam's hand and squeezed it. "Oh, but she can, Lad, and I believe she will. Ye can get a license in Lancaster, then John Andrews can go to the Monongahela with ye an' be present when Caleb Craighead hears your vows."

Adam and Mary looked at each other, and both nodded. "Yes," Adam said. "That would be the best. I just pray that we can get back to Father in time."

"Ye should be on your way as soon as ye can manage it," Ian Mac-Pherson said.

Mary turned to the minister. "Will you pray for us first?"

"Of course. There's always time for that."

Ian MacPherson offered to lend them his carriage, but Adam wouldn't hear of it. "My horse is sturdy enough to carry Mary and me to Philadelphia, and Samuel Scott can find us a mount for Mary. We'll make much better time on horseback."

"I wish I could go wi' y', Miss Merry," Polly said mournfully.

"So do I, Polly, but we'll be back for you as soon as we can. In the meantime, you must make yourself useful to the reverend and his wife."

Mrs. MacPherson put her arm around Polly's slight shoulders. "Don't you worry a mite about that—we'll welcome her company."

A half hour later, with Mary riding pillion behind Adam, her arms holding him loosely around his waist, they returned to Philadelphia. There Adam left Mary with Mrs. McAnally while he found her a horse.

"I like y'r choice o' a wife," the woman whispered to Adam when he returned with a bay gelding for Mary.

"So do I," he replied.

As they left Philadelphia, Adam took comfort that Mary was at his side. Her presence couldn't take away the sadness of his father's illness, but her love and quiet understanding made it more tolerable.

"This is a fine horse Mr. Scott gave you," Mary told Adam. "I always wanted my own horse, but Papa kept putting me off about it."

"You ride quite well, though. Someone must have taught you."

Mary's lips pressed together in a grim line. "That someone was Hetty. We were closer than sisters for years. Now I can't bear to think of her."

"She could have done us both great harm, I'll admit, but she didn't succeed. We should forgive her and pray that she'll learn the error of her ways before it's too late."

Mary looked at Adam appraisingly. "Spoken like a true minister of the gospel, but you don't know Hetty as well as I do. Many times over the years I tried to convince her that she needed spiritual guidance, but she never listened."

"What about her parents? Aren't they Christians?"

"I suppose they think they are, but their churchgoing always seemed to be a matter of who would see them and what they would wear, as if the services were just another social event."

"That's unfortunate."

"Yes, but there's nothing we can do about it. We're almost to Lancaster—it's time we considered how to persuade Papa to go on with us."

When the young couple found John Andrews and Adam explained the situation about Caleb Craighead, John welcomed their suggestion that they all travel to the Monongahela together.

"I haven't been this far west in many years," Mary's father said after they'd crossed the Susquehanna and Adam pointed out the way to Stones' Crossing. "I'd almost forgotten how much land there is out here."

"All of it hereabouts is occupied or claimed," Adam said. "Even as far west as the Monongahela, no big tracts are left."

"I ought to visit some of the merchants who've settled here. Perhaps we could work out some arrangement that would help us all."

"Oh, Papa! Does everything you do have to be connected with business?"

Mary asked, and after that her father said no more, although Adam noticed that he seemed quite interested in every trading post they passed, particularly those on bodies of water.

Eventually the road became an ever-narrower trail, until at last they came into territory where Adam knew every path by heart. They rode single file, with Adam in the lead, and the closer they came to Adam's village, the more silent and withdrawn he became.

"There should be someone about," he said when he stopped near the edge of a deep forest. "We haven't seen anyone for the last five miles—I don't like it."

"What could be the matter?" John Andrews asked.

"I don't know, but I'm going to ride ahead and see what's happening. You and Mary wait here."

The village was eerily quiet as Adam entered it. A few fires burning under cooking pots testified that someone was still there, but no one tended them. Then as he approached the lodge of the chief, the low keening of the Death Song reached his ears, and Adam's blood ran cold. He dismounted and stood with his head bowed in sorrow, fearful that he had arrived too late.

"Adam! Is it really you?"

He turned as his mother came to his side, smaller and paler than he remembered, but her face remarkably calm and unlined. Wordlessly they embraced. "Thank God you're here," she said against his chest.

"What is this?" Adam asked. He released her and gestured toward the silent village.

Ann Craighead's eyes filled with tears. " 'Tis the Lenni-Lenape's way of saying good-bye to their minister," she said thickly.

"I got word that Father was ill," Adam said. "I prayed we'd get here in time."

Ann looked questioningly at her son. "We? You're not alone?"

"No. John and Mary Andrews are with me."

Adam's mother put a hand to her throat and turned even paler. "John Andrews is here? Your father will be happy to see him."

Adam raised his head sharply. "He still lives?"

"Aye, but he's very weak. Perhaps ye should see him alone first."

"Take me to him, then."

Caleb Craighead rested in the cabin he had built many years before, and Adam's first impression was how small and wasted his father's large frame seemed. His father's hair had turned white, and his skin was almost as ashen. His eyes were closed, but when his wife spoke his name, Caleb opened them and looked directly into his son's face.

"Can it be ye, Adam?" he said with more vigor than Adam would have thought possible.

"Aye, Father. I've come to seek your blessing." Adam knelt beside his father and grasped his frail hands.

"That ye've always had, Lad."

Adam's eyes filled with tears as his father raised a hand to Adam's forehead and murmured a prayer. Adam was unable to speak for a moment. "Someone came with me that you must meet," he finally managed to say. "Mother, can you fetch them? They're just at the edge of the forest."

"I'll send someone after them," Ann Craighead replied.

"I'm glad ye came back, Son. I don't fear death, but I am concerned about ye."

"Don't be—God has taken care of me, and I have faith He always will. When I was in Carolina, I think He sent me a sign."

Caleb briefly inclined his head. "Go on," he whispered.

"I'd asked God to show me what I should do, and then I saw a pair of eagles. Joshua and Sarah told me there were no eagles in that part of Carolina, but I know what I saw."

"What d'ye take the sign to mean?"

"I'm not sure, but there were two eagles, and I'm certain I've found the one God wants me to marry."

Caleb almost smiled. "That's an important decision, Lad. Are ye so sure?"

Adam heard footsteps behind him and looked back to see Mary and her father enter the cabin. "Here she is, Father—you can see for yourself."

Caleb nodded at Mary, then looked past her to her father. Caleb extended both hands to him. "John Andrews—after all these years—"

" 'Tis quite some time since the day an earnest young minister turned my life toward the Lord, but I'll never forget it—or you."

Caleb looked at Mary, who was struggling not to cry. "Is this your young lady, Adam?"

Adam took Mary's hand and drew her closer to his father's side. "Aye, Sir. Her name is Mary Ann Andrews. We hope you'll perform our marriage."

Ann Craighead uttered a sharp cry and put a hand to her mouth. "Oh, Adam! I don't know if he has the strength."

"Of course I do!" Caleb said so fiercely that they all laughed. "Mary Ann, is it? Come here, Child, and let me look at you."

Mary knelt beside Caleb and took one of his hands between hers. "I am honored to meet you, Sir," she said.

"Are ye both sure ye know what ye're doing?" he asked her. "Marriage is a sacred bond, not to be lightly entered upon."

Mary inclined her head. "Adam and I know that," she said. "Will you marry us?"

Ann's eyes met her son's and she nodded. "Can ye hold the book, Husband?" she asked.

Caleb closed his eyes and shook his head. "No need. I know the words here." He touched his chest, then opened his eyes. "Take the bride's hand, Adam—I trust that she won't bite ye."

Adam smiled. "I've heard those words often enough," he said, remembering the many times Caleb Craighead had said such words to couples who stood before him to be married. He turned to Mary and took her hand in his. "We've no ring," he said.

"Use mine." Ann Craighead slipped off her wedding band and handed it to Adam. When he hesitated, she thrust it into his palm and closed his fingers around it. "Just for the ceremony, of course. Ye maun get your own later."

"I suppose we're ready, then," Adam said.

"Let us pray," Caleb said, and the brief ceremony began.

❧

They stayed in the village by the Monongahela for a week, time enough for Mary to meet Adam's Lenni-Lenape friends who were still in the village.

"So many have left," Adam remarked. Many of the young men had decided to cast their lot with a related clan by the headwaters of the Ohio, including the warrior who had wed Karendouah.

"Why do they go?" Adam asked his old friend Tel-a-ka, knowing what the answer would be.

"Hunting no good now. White man takes deer, takes buffalo, builds his villages where our ancestors always found meat."

"What will you do?" Adam asked.

Tel-a-ka shrugged. "The people talk of the land beyond the Endless Mountains. They say it is a fair country."

From his tone Adam knew Tel-a-ka didn't agree, but Adam knew the time might soon come when the Clan of the Bow would no longer be able to sustain itself where they were. "May God guide you, my brother," Adam said, and Tel-a-ka nodded.

"My people will do as we are led," he said.

As the week wore on, John Andrews had time to renew his friendship with Caleb and Ann before Caleb slipped into a peaceful sleep from which he did not awaken.

Tel-a-ka, as chief of the Clan of the Bow, took charge of the burial preparations, but when the time came for the body to be laid to rest in a quiet glen, it was Adam who delivered the funeral sermon and said the final prayers.

"Ye should go now," Ann Craighead said a few days later. "It was God's blessing that ye came when ye did, but I'll not ask ye to stay longer."

"I don't want to leave you here alone. Won't you come back with us?" Adam asked, suspecting what his mother's answer would be.

"Nay, Son, I'm not alone. These are my people. They'll look after me."

"But more and more of the Lenni-Lenape are going away every year, Mother. It was Father's wish that we should take care of you."

"And I'll let you, when the time comes that I need it. But not now. There's too much of my life with your father in this place."

Adam kissed his mother's cheek. "I understand. But later you might change your mind. Will you promise to let me know when you're ready to leave?"

Ann nodded. "I promise."

John Andrews had been standing apart from the others, but now he joined them. "Adam, I know you can see Mary safely back to Lancaster without me. I believe I'll stay on awhile and make some trade contacts in the area. That is, if I won't be imposing on you," he added to Ann.

Her cheeks showed brief color. "Of course not. The lodge where ye've been staying is yours for as long as ye like."

"What about your business, Papa?" Mary asked.

"I've enough laid by for such a time as this. There's not much I can do as long as the Loyalists watch my every move, anyway."

Ann Craighead put a hand on her son's shoulder. "From what I hear, it seems that war against the British is bound to come. Will ye and the family in Carolina join it?"

"If we have to defend what is rightfully ours, we will, but we're not seeking it."

Ann looked worried. "I would that the British were not, either. I'll pray for ye all daily, that God'll protect ye."

"We'll await you in Lancaster," Mary said as she and her father said good-bye the next morning.

"Take your time, Sir," Adam added, knowing how badly his mother would need a friend in the days ahead.

"God bless ye both," Ann called after them.

"Your mother is a fine woman," Mary said when they had ridden some time in silence. "I can see why our fathers both loved her."

"Did you know you remind me of her?"

Mary looked surprised. "I don't look anything like your mother."

"Not in appearance, perhaps, but you're alike in spirit."

Mary reached out and touched Adam's hand. "That's the nicest compliment you could ever give me," she said.

The next day brought Adam and Mary to the tallest peak on the journey, and they stopped at its summit to rest their horses. The young couple sat with their backs to a rock, idly looking up at the cloudless blue sky. Suddenly, two huge birds flew over their heads.

"Eagles!" Mary whispered. She stood with Adam, and they held hands as they watched a magnificent pair of bald eagles soar overhead, alternately gliding and moving their powerful wings. "Where do you suppose they came from?" Mary craned her neck in a vain attempt to find their nest.

"Eagles always build in the tallest tree on the highest land," Adam said.

"Look! Now they're circling. They must see some prey."

Three times the magnificent birds formed arcs overhead, then in unison they slowly flew away in a slanting path that led south and east, and finally out of Mary and Adam's sight.

Neither spoke for a long moment, then Adam drew Mary to him and held her for a moment against his heart. "Now I know what God wants me to do."

"The eagles were your sign?" she asked.

"I believe so. Did you note the path they took?"

"I'm not very good at directions. Weren't they going south?"

"Southeast—toward Carolina."

Mary looked puzzled. "Carolina? What's there?"

"People who need me. When I was there I didn't want to see it, but now it seems so clear—I'll have to prepare myself first, but—"

"You'll be a minister," Mary finished for him.

"Yes. Father was right—he always said I should be a minister, but I doubted I had a calling."

"I thought from the first that you had the gift for it—but I prayed that you'd decide to work for my father so you'd stay near me."

Adam searched Mary's face. "And now?"

"I want whatever God wants for you."

"For us both, Mary," he corrected, drawing her close to his heart again. "Like the eagles, we'll always be together."

Sign of the Dove

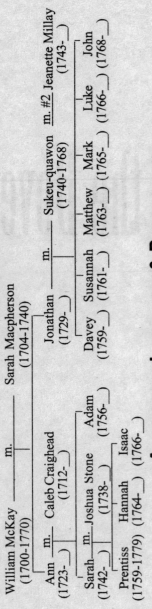

McKays of Pennsylvania

William McKay (1700-1770) — m. — Sarah Macpherson (1704-1740)

Ann (1723-) — m. — Caleb Craighead (1712-)

Jonathan (1729-) — m. — Sukeu-quawon (1740-1768)   m. #2 Jeanette Millay (1743-)

Adam (1756-)

Sarah (1742-) — m. Joshua Stone (1738-)

Prentiss (1759-1779)   Hannah (1764-)   Isaac (1766-)

Davey (1759-)   Susannah (1761-)

Matthew (1763-)   Mark (1765-)   Luke (1766-)   John (1768-)

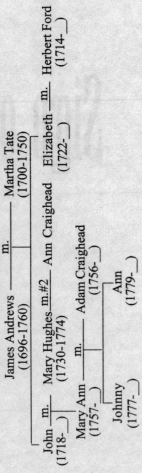

Andrews of Lancaster & Philadelphia

James Andrews (1696-1760) — m. — Martha Tate (1700-1750)

Mary Hughes m.#2 (1730-1774)   Ann Craighead   Elizabeth (1722-) — m. — Herbert Ford (1714-)

John (1718-) — m. Mary Ann (1757-)

Adam Craighead (1756-)   Ann (1779-)

Johnny (1777-)

Chapter 1

North Carolina, October 1781

The Stones' springhouse stood in the deep shade of sycamore, elm, and chestnut trees, a cool haven surrounded by thick beds of several kinds of mint. Water from an everlasting spring emerged from the bottom of an encircling hill and flowed over the stone floor, keeping anything set in it cool in the summer and preventing it from freezing during the winter.

A few years earlier, Joshua Stone had built a miniature log cabin shelter beside the springhouse so his daughter could work in comfort in all but the coldest weather.

For at least eight of her seventeen years, Hannah Stone had kept the dairy vessels clean and had carefully separated the cream from the milk. When the cream was just right to be made into butter, Hannah poured it into the red cedar churn her father had made years ago when he and her mother came to North Carolina from Pennsylvania. Dairying was hard work, but Hannah didn't mind it. She welcomed an excuse to leave her noisy household behind for the peace and quiet of the springhouse glen.

On this still-warm, early October day, Hannah's wiry red hair blended with the bright fall leaves as she bent, bareheaded as usual, over the milk emptins. Hannah had been especially glad to escape from the preparations her mother was making to welcome Nate McIntyre, her father's oldest and best friend and her uncle Jonathan's longtime winter hunting companion.

"I'll need fresh butter for the pound cake," Sarah Stone had told Hannah that morning. "You'd best churn soon's the cream's ready."

"What's so special about Uncle Nate? You've never made a fuss for him before."

"It's not just for Nate—since the boys came back, they never had a proper welcome. They all like Nate, so I thought it'd be a good time to celebrate."

We never had a party for the boys because they didn't all come back from the fighting, Hannah thought. She would never forget the look on her mother's face when they'd learned that Prentiss, the Stones' firstborn, had lost his life in a skirmish with the British in a nameless South Carolina meadow.

"It's been a long time since we were all together," Hannah said. "Will it just be Uncle Nate and our family?"

Her daughter's question brought a wry smile to Sarah's usual sober expression. "I suspect half of Rowan County may drop by when they find out Nate's here. If you want to invite some of your friends, go ahead. A few more won't matter."

"I wasn't thinking of inviting anyone—but I'd best make extra butter," Hannah said.

Now as she fitted the dasher into the lid of the churn, Hannah wished she could invite Clay Scott. He had recently come home, wounded, from his Continental army service and so far hadn't appeared in public. Inviting him to a party that included only her family would be too obvious—he might feel uncomfortable. But if everyone else came, it'd be all right.

Hannah moved the dasher up and down in the steady rhythm that would bring the cream to butter. Sometimes she sang as she churned, having found that the ballads she'd learned from her mother fit her churning stroke well. Today, however, Hannah moved the dasher to the names of all the members of her family who were near enough to come to the gathering.

"Mother and Father and me and Isaac—that's the Stones. Uncle Jonathan, Aunt Jeanette, Thomas and Marie and little Jacques; Davey and Polly and baby Mary; Susannah and her James; Matthew, Mark, Luke, and John—that's all the McKays."

Hannah frowned, trying to keep count. "Then Uncle Adam and Aunt Mary and their Johnny and Ann, and that makes twenty-two," she said aloud.

"What about me? Do I count?" A male voice Hannah recognized at once spoke behind her, so startling her that she almost upset the churn.

As she had done all her life, Hannah smiled and turned to give Nate McIntyre a welcoming hug. "Uncle Nate! We weren't expecting you so soon."

But as Hannah reached out to him, Nate put his hands on top of her forearms and gently pushed her away.

Confused, Hannah took another step back and gazed at him. Year after year as he and Jonathan McKay had met by the Yadkin each fall to go trapping and long-hunting, then returned together in the spring, this tall man with the full black beard and dark, bright eyes had always looked the same to Hannah. But on this day, something about Nate McIntyre had subtly changed.

"I came early to talk to ye," he said. Even the tone of his voice seemed different. Nate had come to the colonies from the Scottish Highlands, and he still spoke with a pronounced burr and a lilt in his voice. But the man Hannah looked at seemed almost somber, as if he brought sad news.

"Is something the matter?" she asked.

"No, Lass." He nodded toward the churn. "Go on—ye can churn whilst I talk. Your mother wouldna take it kindly if I spoiled the butter for her."

Hannah returned to her task and waited for Nate to continue. When he did not immediately do so, she asked, "Has the cat got your tongue, Uncle Nate? I never knew you to be short of words."

Nate looked uncomfortable and shifted his weight from one foot to the other and sighed. "This is harder than I thought 'twould be," he said. "To begin with, ye know that I'm not really your uncle."

Hannah nodded. "Yes, but you've always been like another member of our family. We all—"

Nate raised his hand in protest and spoke quickly. "I don't belong to your family or anyone else's—and of late that's caused me some grief. Ye aren't to call me 'uncle' anymore or think of me in that way. Do ye understand?"

"Yes, Mr. McIntyre," Hannah replied, then focused her gaze on the churn.

" 'Mister' is almost as bad. Tell me, Lass, do ye think of me as old?"

Hannah glanced sharply at Nate, thinking he must be teasing her, but one look at his face convinced her he was quite serious. "You look exactly the same to me as always—I never thought of you as any age at all."

Nate smoothed his beard in the way he had of doing when he was pre-occupied with a problem. "Well, I reckon that's a start, anyway. Ye see, Hannah, I've decided it's time I made a change in my life."

Hannah looked back at the dasher. "And what might that be, Sir?" she asked when it seemed that Nate would say no more without prompting.

"I've bought land in Kentucky—a beautiful spread, flat to hilly, watered by an everlasting spring and two creeks. I grew a corn crop on it last summer, so I can claim the acreage next to it. One more hunting season, then I aim to put down roots on my own place. What do ye think of that, Lass?"

Why is he telling me this? Hannah wondered. She said the first thing that came into her head. "I hear that Kentucky is a fair but dangerous land."

"Oh, I know ye're thinking of all that befell the Boones, but that was some time ago. The Indians pretty much leave folks alone now, and more and more people are moving there every day. I was lucky to get my land when I did."

"Mr. McIntyre—" Hannah began, but he put his hand on her shoulder and pressed it briefly.

"Can ye not call me 'Nate'? 'Tis not such an old man's name."

"I don't think I should. Mother doesn't like me to be disrespectful to my elders."

If Hannah had slapped him, Nate couldn't have looked more pained. His distress made her reach one hand out to his, while still maintaining a steady hold on the dasher with the other. "I'll call you Nate when they're not around if it will please you," she said.

He took her outstretched hand and replaced it on the dasher. "Never mind. It may take some time for ye to think of me in any way other than as your father and uncle's old friend, but I hope ye'll try."

"All right—Nate," Hannah said.

He smiled and picked up his pack. "Ye see, it's easy once ye try. I can see I'm botherin' ye—I'll leave ye to your churning and make my presence known at the house. Likely Sarah can put me to better use than aggravating her daughter."

"Don't go yet," Hannah said. She feared she'd hurt his feelings and wanted to make amends. "Did you bring us some new music?"

Nate hesitated for a moment, then opened his pack and withdrew a mouth organ. "This is a tune ye may have heard before." He wiped the mouth organ on his hunting shirt, then put it to his lips and began to play a haunting, half-familiar melody.

"What is it?" she asked when he finished.

"Ye'll know plain enough when ye hear the words."

Hannah had always loved to hear Nate sing, and for the past few years she had often sung with him, her reedy true soprano blending with his near-tenor. Nate lifted his chin and half-closed his eyes. When he began singing, the words immediately made Hannah's skin prickle and almost brought tears to her eyes.

> "Oh, don't ye see that lonesome dove
>   That flies from tree to vine
> She's mourning for her own true love
>   Just like I mourn for mine
> Just like I mourn for mine
>   Just like I mourn for mine, my love
> Believe me what I say
>   Ye are the darling of my heart
> Until my dying day—"

Nate broke off and put the mouth organ back in his pack. "There's more, but that's the idea of it."

"It's lovely," Hannah said. "You must sing the rest of it tonight."

"Perhaps. Is my fiddle still safe?"

Hannah nodded. "I suppose so. Father keeps it in the attic, locked up in that wooden box you made for it. I've not seen it since you were last here."

Nate nodded. "Likely it needs re-stringing—I brought some catgut with me. I'll be on my way now."

"Thank you for the song," Hannah said, then seeing the look on Nate's face, wished she hadn't spoken of it.

"I had ye in mind when I learnt it," he said.

"Thanks, but I doubt it'd be very good to churn by. The butter needs no more watering." Hannah smiled and was relieved when Nate smiled back.

"I have a few other ballads that might serve for that—perhaps ye'll hear them tonight."

"I hope so—Nate."

Her use of his name brought a fleeting smile, then with a half-wave he picked up his pack and started toward the house. Hannah watched him until he was out of sight, then sighed. Dismissing the puzzling encounter, she gave her full attention to bringing the thickening cream to butter.

❧

"I thought you said this was going to be a family party," Hannah said late that afternoon when more than two dozen friends and neighbors began streaming into the yard.

"When did the Stones ever turn away anyone from our house?" Sarah asked. "Besides, all are bringing food and their own trenchers, and it's still warm enough to eat outside. 'Twill be no bother at all."

Her mother's eyes shone, and Hannah knew Sarah Stone was in her element with a house full of company and an abundance of victuals to offer them.

"I don't see the Scotts here," Hannah said after a time.

"Vera's laid up with the rheumatism again. She sent word asking me to stop by tomorrow."

"I thought Clay might come without his grandmother," Hannah said.

"From what Vera says, Clay's leg must be in pretty bad shape. Oh, look—there's Adam! Good—I feared that silly Hughes boy wouldn't get the word to him in time."

Hannah turned to see her uncle, Adam Craighead, help his wife, Mary, down from the sturdy horse he rode on his ministerial rounds. Their son, Johnny, reached his chubby arms out to Sarah, who eagerly took him.

"Where's Ann?" Sarah asked. "You should have brought her, too."

"We left her with Polly—her baby Mary has the colic, and Ann's fussy with teething. Davey should be along in awhile, though."

"I'm disappointed," Sarah said. "I don't see those babies near often enough."

While Hannah and her mother played with Johnny and talked to Adam and Mary, Nate emerged from the house, carrying his fiddle. Immediately everyone gathered around, greeting him and calling out the names of tunes for him to play.

"Hold, friends! At least let the man have his supper before you put him to work!" Joshua Stone's words brought friendly jeers of disapproval from his neighbors and a smile from Nate.

"When no one wants to hear my music, then's the time to quit playing it," he said. Laying the wide end of the fiddle against his breastbone, Nate drew the bow across the strings, adjusted them until they were in tune, then launched into a lively reel tune.

"He's hopeless!" Sarah exclaimed. "Come, Hannah—while everyone's occupied with Nate, we can begin to lay out the food."

"Is Aunt Jeanette coming down?" Hannah asked as they entered the Stones' summer kitchen, located in a building behind the house.

Sarah shook her head. "No, she says she feels weaker today, but I think it's just that she doesn't like to have so many people about."

Marie Millay, Jonathan McKay's olive-skinned, dark-eyed stepdaughter, was using a wooden paddle to withdraw golden loaves of bread from the brick oven. Hearing Sarah's last remark, she looked up and nodded. "Mama will be all right as soon as everyone leaves."

Marie pronounced "mama" like "ma-*ma*," with the accent on the last syllable, one of the few things that betrayed her family's French roots. Forced to flee their native country because of religious persecution, Jeanette Millay's parents had both come to Pennsylvania as children. Widowed early and with two small children to support, Jeanette had set up a trading post on the Great Wagon Road, and it was there that the widower Jonathan McKay had met and married her in 1775, then brought her to the Yadkin to live with his motherless children.

"Who's looking after Jacques, then?" Sarah Stone asked when she realized the boy wasn't with his half sister.

"Susannah took him somewhere," Marie said.

"When did they get here? I didn't even see her," Sarah exclaimed.

"Susannah and Davey came together—he went to Salisbury to get her. Her husband stayed at home."

Hannah and her mother exchanged a knowing glance, but neither said anything. It was well-known that Susannah's husband had served briefly with the British in an ill-fated unit formed from former Highlanders. As a Tory, he no doubt thought it prudent to avoid gatherings where he'd meet veterans of the Continental Line and Carolina Militia—which included, at one time or another, every adult male in the Stone, Craighead, and McKay families, as well as Nate McIntyre.

"Well, I'll see her later," Sarah said. "Hannah, where's the butter? Lay it here beside the bread. It's a good thing you made an extra churning."

When all the food had been laid out, Sarah sent Hannah's brother Isaac, a gawky lad of fifteen who had been pulling meat from the roasted pig, to find Adam Craighead.

Isaac wasted no time exchanging pleasantries. " 'Tis time to pray so we can eat," he told his uncle.

"Then ask Nate to stop playing his fiddle. I think most of the folks would as soon listen to him as eat, anyway."

Hannah stood on the porch and watched her brother approach first Adam, then Nate, who immediately put down the fiddle.

"Go on; we want to hear more!" someone cried.

Nate turned to Adam. "Reverend, here's one ye should all know. Mayhap ye can all sing this with Hannah—I know she kens it well."

Even before he had played the first note, Hannah had guessed that it would be the Old Hundred, which was often sung, unaccompanied, when they gathered to worship. After a few bars of introduction, Nate began again, and the crisp evening air rang with the sound of many voices lifted in praise.

> "Praise God from whom all blessings flow;
>   Praise Him, all creatures here below;
> Praise Him above, ye heavenly host;
>   Praise Father, Son, and Holy Ghost."

I will never forget this moment, Hannah thought. Never had she heard any hymn sung to the accompaniment of the fiddle. Her eyes filled with tears as the last note vibrated in the stillness, then died away.

In the reverent silence that followed, Adam Craighead raised his voice in a prayer of thanks for their safe delivery from the ravages of war and added a petition that it soon be ended. After invoking blessings for their food, he concluded with an "amen" that was echoed through the crowd. Then the noise began again as the guests moved, at Joshua's urging, toward the supper tables.

Hannah stood on the porch as if rooted, speaking or nodding to everyone who passed by. Nate, who had taken his time wrapping his fiddle in velvet and replacing it in its wooden case, was the last one to reach the porch.

"That was beautiful," she said.

Nate's eyes shone as he looked down at Hannah. Gently he took one of her hands in his. "Yes, it was. Come, let's have some supper. I'm fair starved after all that playin'."

Nate was to have no rest that evening, however. As soon as the supper trenchers had been cleared away, everyone gathered around Nate and urged him to sing for them.

"Ah, ye don't want to hear me," he protested, but soon was called down.

"Have you a war ballad for us this time, my lad?" asked an old man who had fought the French and despaired that his age had kept him from going after the British.

"There's a broadside about called 'The Cornwallis Country Dance,'" Nate said. "Mayhap ye've heard it?"

After a chorus of "No!" and further urging from his audience, Nate dug in his pocket for his mouth harp and struck a few notes. "Ye ken this tune well—it's the 'Yankee Doodle.'" Nate stood in the center of the gathering, his eyes half-closed and his head thrown back, and began to sing.

"Cornwallis led a country dance,
    The like was never seen, sir.
Much retrograde and much advance
    And all with Gen'ral Greene, sir.
They rambled up and rambled down,
    Joined hands and then they run, sir.
Our Gen'ral Greene to Charlestown,
    And the Earl to Wilmington, sir—"

Nate went on for several more stanzas, at times hard to hear over the general laughter that accompanied the song. Then Nate reached the last stanza:

"His music soon forgets to play.
    His feet can no more move, sir.
And all his bands now curse the day
    They jigged to our shore, sir.
Now Tories all, what can ye say?
    Come, is not this a griper
That while your hopes are danced away
    'Tis ye must pay the piper?"

As Nate finished singing, everyone broke into loud applause. Hannah looked over to where Susannah had been sitting and saw her cousin had slipped away. Sarah had apparently noticed her absence as well, for she rose from her place and left without a word.

"That was a lively tune, and a good 'un! What else have you for us?" the old man asked.

Nate looked at Hannah, and for a moment she feared that he was going to sing the song about the lonesome dove. Instead, he motioned for her to

374

join him. "I do have something I've not done here before, but Hannah will have to help me."

"Help the man, Hannah!" "Go on!" "Hurry up, Girl!"

Hannah made her way to Nate's side with some trepidation, fearful that he somehow would embarrass her. "I'm not sure I want to do this," she said, too low for the others to hear.

"Of course ye do," he replied. "I'll play the chorus through for ye. After I sing a verse, ye sing the chorus. 'Tis a short song," he added, correctly reading the doubt reflected on her face.

"I don't know—" Hannah began.

"No—that's all there is to it," Nate said cheerfully. "Ye sing 'No, sir, no sir, no; No sir, no sir, no sir, no.' Do ye think ye can recall such a lot of words?"

"No, Sir," Hannah said bringing laughter from those close enough to have heard the exchange.

"Here we go then," Nate said and played through a lively melody before he began to sing the first verse.

> "Tell me one thing, tell me truly;
>   Tell me why ye scorn me so?
> Tell me why when asked a question
>   Ye will always answer no?"

Nate nodded and Hannah sang the chorus, putting in one extra "No, sir," but otherwise successfully completing it. Everyone laughed, then Nate sang another verse.

> "If when walking in the garden
>   Plucking flowers all wet as can be
> Will ye be offended
>   If I have a walk and talk with ye?"

Hannah successfully sang the chorus, then Nate sang again.

> "If when walking in the garden
>   I should ask ye to be mine
> And should tell ye that I love ye
>   Would ye then my heart decline?"

I knew he had something up his sleeve, Hannah thought. "Sing it with me, ladies," she invited, and amid much laughter, several of the women joined in.

"Ye cheated, Hannah Stone," Nate said under his breath, so only she heard it.

"And you deserved it, *Sir*," Hannah replied.

"Sing 'Froggie,' Uncle Nate!" begged Johnny Craighead when it was quiet again.

"Nay, I'll play it and ye all sing along—everyone knows the words."

Nate once more put his fiddle to his chest and struck up "Froggie Went a-Courtin'," which old and young alike joyfully sang.

Grateful that she was no longer the center of attention, Hannah moved away from Nate to take up little Jacques, who had been asleep but roused at the opening strains of what he called "the foggie song."

"I'll put him to bed now," Hannah said when the song ended. She took him to the loft where the children slept and laid him on a quilt, where he almost immediately fell asleep. As she came down the stairs, Hannah heard Nate singing a plaintive song that made her long to see dark-haired Clay Scott.

"Black, black, black is the color of my true love's hair," Nate sang.

"Oooh, don't you love to hear him sing?" Marie whispered. "I could listen to him all night."

Hannah nodded and tried to blink away the tears that threatened to fill her eyes. The song ended, and Nate seemed to awake from a spell as he acknowledged the applause of his audience.

"That's as much as I ha'e breath for tonight, folks," Nate said against their urging for an encore. "But if my fiddle stays in tune and ye've a mind to it, I might play some reels for ye before Jonathan McKay and I leave."

Everyone cheered and clapped again, then scattered to gather their children and belongings.

"I wish Nate McIntyre'd come a-courtin' down my way," Hannah heard Sallie Porter say wistfully.

"Not likely—old hunters like him don't settle down easy," Meg Todd told her.

"He's still a young enough man for me—" Sallie said before the girls moved out of Hannah's hearing.

Hannah gathered up dishes and helped take down the makeshift board tables, all the while humming the last tune Nate had sung. She sometimes sang it as she churned, changing the words to fit Clay Scott, a handsome lad with laughing blue eyes and curly hair the color of a crow's wing.

Hannah was unaware that Nate watched her from the doorway, nor could she know that he sometimes sang his own version of the song, in which his true love's hair wasn't black at all, but as bright a red as a scarlet maple in autumn.

Chapter 2

Those who had come from a distance stayed overnight, most in the house that Jonathan McKay had built next door to the Stones. After Jonathan's first wife, Sukey, died, the younger children had moved in with the Stones while their father hunted from October to mid-March.

When he married Jeanette Millay and brought her and her two children to his house, only Luke and John, the youngest of his four sons who were called "the Gospels," had chosen to move in with their stepmother. Jonathan's oldest son, David, had already left home by the time his father remarried, and Susannah, his only daughter, had married soon after her father. With the Tory-Patriot lines drawn as the Revolution began, she seldom came home from Salisbury.

Nate always stayed with Jonathan McKay, but since the birth of little Jacques, Jeanette was often unwell, so most of the time they took their meals next door with the Stones. Hannah was serving corn mush to the early risers when Jonathan and Nate came into the Stones' house for breakfast the next morning. As she put bowls out for them, Hannah covertly compared the two men she had always called "uncle." Jonathan McKay was really her great-uncle on her mother's side of the family, while Nate McIntyre was no kin to them at all.

Like Nate, Jonathan wore his curly hair long, only occasionally pulling it back in a queue. Both men had full beards. But Jonathan, almost ten years older than Nate, had streaks of gray in his brown hair, while Nate's was still a sooty black. Jonathan was shorter and more stoutly built than Nate, who bordered on thinness. Both men had the tanned, leathery skin of those who stay out-of-doors in all weathers.

Uncle Nate isn't bad-looking, Hannah acknowledged. He wanted to settle down, he had told her. Well, in that case there had been several young women at the party who would be glad enough to marry him. No doubt he'd see them all again when he played for the reels he had promised. Then—

"You're mighty quiet this morning," Nate said. "Cat got your tongue?"

Hannah set steaming cups of coffee beside each man's place before she put her hand to her mouth. "No, Sir—it's still there," she said, and Jonathan laughed.

"Don't ye know by now ye can't best our Hannah? She's a sharp one."

Sarah Stone sat near the fireplace, rocking Adam and Mary's little boy. She frowned at her uncle's sally. "Too sharp for the young men hereabouts, I fear. She's scared more than one away with her plain talk."

"A man that's afraid of a woman's tongue isn't much of a man," Hannah said. She could have reminded them that the two proposals she had turned down had come from completely unsuitable men whom her parents hadn't liked in the first place, but Jonathan already knew about them and it was certainly none of Nate's business.

Nate seemed amused. "Ah, Hannah, ye seem so calm most of the time, it's easy to forget that ye've a temper to match your red hair."

"Only when she's provoked, Nate, and that you know quite well. It's just that she states things plainly, which some folk hereabouts don't like," Sarah said.

" 'Tis a rare trait in a woman," Jonathan said. "That's one thing I always admired about the Lenni-Lenape—they tell the truth."

There was a moment of silence as each thought of Sukey, Jonathan's first wife. Her Indian name was Sukeu-quawon, and she'd been loved by everyone who knew her. Then Sarah eased young Johnny Craighead from her lap and stood. "Come along, Hannah. I promised Vera Scott we'd come over first thing this morning. Uncle Jon, will you look after your great-nephew until Adam and Mary come in for breakfast?"

"Great-nephew is it, now?" He frowned as if he hadn't ever thought to give a name to their relationship. " 'Tis bad enough to be a grandfather several times over without being a great-anything as well."

"I envy ye, Jonathan. I wish I had some family to call me 'great,' " Nate said.

"I suppose we could adopt you—then you could be our 'Great Nate,' " Sarah said, smiling at the notion.

"I thought ye said ye had to go somewhere," Nate growled in mock displeasure.

Sarah Stone nodded. "Yes, that we do. Hannah, fetch my medicinals and meet me in the yard."

Hannah had rather enjoyed the men's bantering, but since she was eager to see Clay Scott, she quickly carried out her mother's instructions. Clay had lived with his grandmother since the rest of his family had been killed in an Indian attack in Pennsylvania when he was barely eight. He'd escaped by hiding in the woods, then he'd walked several miles to the nearest neighbor.

Hannah had tried to imagine what she would have done in his place and decided that Clay must be the bravest boy she had ever known. He'd been among the first to sign up to fight, not with the local militia, but with the Continental Line. While the local militia had served brief enlistments, then come home and tended to their business before signing up again, Clay had been gone almost continuously for the last four years. Each time he had come back, he had seemed more handsome; and the last time, the past winter, he had noticed Hannah, too, probably for the first time since she had grown up.

"I'll be looking for you when I come back," Clay had told her when he had left, promising with his blue eyes more than he said.

"Where's your bonnet, young lady?" her mother asked when she joined Hannah.

Hannah sighed heavily. "I don't need it—it's not far to the Scotts' house."

"Go back and get it," Sarah ordered. "If you'd worn it as you should have these past years, you wouldn't have such a face full of freckles."

No one else seems to mind my freckles but you, Hannah thought, but she would never say such a thing aloud. Her family took the biblical admonition to "honor thy father and mother" quite literally.

Hannah ran back to the house to take her bonnet from its peg by the rear door. When she reached for it, she heard her uncle and Nate talking in the kitchen. She hadn't meant to eavesdrop, but hearing her name, she stopped and listened for a moment.

"Hannah's more mature than ye think," Jonathan's voice said.

"She may not think so," Nate said.

"The lass does a woman's work around here."

"Yet she's still childlike in many ways. I canna press her too soon."

Hannah snatched at her bonnet and fled, incensed. How dare Uncle Jonathan and Nate talk about her like she had no mind of her own! *Childlike,* Nate had called her. *Childlike, indeed!* she stormed. She'd show them both that Hannah Stone was a woman, ready to take on a woman's life. When she and Clay Scott wed, they'd know how wrong they were about her—

"You didn't have to run," Sarah said mildly when Hannah returned, breathing heavily. "The bonnet does no good in your hand—put it on and come along."

By the time they reached the Scotts' cabin, Hannah had calmed down, and long before they stepped over the threshold, the thought that she'd soon see Clay Scott had pushed all other thoughts from her mind.

Vera Scott came to meet them, moving with obvious difficulty. "Ah, Sarah, I knew you'd be good as your word. I hope there's something in that basket for my rheumatics. I've never known it to be so bad."

"Yes, I brought several infusions. Try this powdered spikenard root first—if it doesn't do you good, wait a day and then use this infusion of hyssop leaves. And you might also rub mustard on the sorest places—seems that the heat often relieves the sorest joints."

"Bless you, Child. I'd like you to take a look at Clay while you're here. The army surgeons said they'd done all they could, but since he came home, his leg's gotten a deal worse."

"What happened to it?" Sarah asked as she and Hannah followed Mrs. Scott into a rear room where Clay lay on a narrow cot with his heavily bandaged right leg propped on a feather bolster.

"I'd best let him tell you that. Clay, Miz Stone's here to see your leg. Explain to her exactly what happened."

Clay looked up, nodded at Sarah Stone, then looked past her to Hannah and smiled. Although he seemed shockingly thin, Clay's blue eyes had lost none of their luster. He was clean-shaven, and his face was still deeply tanned, framed by hair that was longer—and darker—than Hannah had seen it.

Black is the color of my true love's hair. The refrain played through Hannah's mind until she forced herself to stop it.

"I took a musket ball through the fleshy part of my calf—it went in one side and came out the other. We were wading a swamp and I sort of lay in the water and played dead when the British came through checking. By the time my captain could fish me out, I had leeches all over me. The surgeon bandaged my leg and told me to go home, that I wouldn't be fit for duty 'til it healed. That was about two weeks ago—it took me a long time to get back."

"Do you mind if I have a look?" Sarah asked.

Clay shrugged. "Go ahead, if you like. Grandmother thinks you might have something to help it heal."

Hannah watched her mother gently peel away the linen dressing that covered Clay's leg from knee to ankle. The wound was in the fullest part of his calf, an irregularly shaped black circle surrounded by swollen red flesh.

"It's not yet putrified," Sarah said, "but it can get that way easily enough. The leg must be soaked in hot water several times a day and dressed with plantain."

Vera Scott shook her head and held out gnarled and trembling hands. "Clay can tell you I can barely keep us fed. I can't tote water and go out and look for plantain. I'm too—"

"Of course you can't," Sarah interrupted. She spoke soothingly. "Hannah and I will see to Clay's leg."

"I can't let you do that, Miz Stone," Vera Scott protested. "You've your hands full with a houseful of young ones to take care of."

"They mostly tend themselves," Sarah said, then turned to Hannah. "We'll need fresh plantain. Find several bunches that haven't gone to seed. I'll see to heating the water."

"I thank you, Ma'am," Hannah heard Clay Scott tell her mother.

Hannah picked up her mother's herbal basket and made her way into the Scotts' fallow meadowland, where she soon found enough plantain to begin Clay's treatment. *Hannah and I can take care of him,* her mother had said.

For the past two years, Sarah Stone had taken Hannah with her on many of her calls to the sick, and just as her mother, Ann McKay Craighead, had taught Sarah to find healing plants and care for simple wounds, so Sarah was passing on her lore to Hannah. Living miles from trained medical doctors, they'd had to rely on their own wits to treat a variety of ills and accidents. Of late, a trained surgeon had come to Salisbury, and Isaac had expressed an interest in being apprenticed to him. If the doctor agreed to take him, someday Sarah's son might replace her as the local healer. But in the meantime, their neighbors respected Sarah's skill and often asked for her help.

"I do this for you in the name of Jesus," she often told people who tried to give her something in return. "I need nothing for myself."

"You ought to let them give you what they can," Hannah had once told her mother. "It makes them feel better."

"I don't heal for any reward," Sarah had said.

"I know, but the Bible says 'It is more blessed to give than to receive.' Uncle Adam would probably say you shouldn't deny people the blessing of giving to you if they want to."

"I never thought of it that way," Sarah had said, and since then, she had accepted the eggs and butter, corn and tanned leather that grateful patients brought.

Mother probably wouldn't have brought me with her today if she knew how I feel about Clay, Hannah thought. She would have to be careful not to let her affection show.

When Hannah returned to Clay's room, he greeted her with a weak smile.

"I see you found what you were looking for," he said, and she nodded and turned away, afraid that her expression might betray her.

Dear Lord, help me take care of Clay, she prayed, and she wasn't thinking simply of tending his wound.

By the time Hannah and Sarah had dressed Clay's leg and returned home, Susannah and David were preparing to leave.

"I wish you'd stay longer," Sarah said, but Susannah was adamant that she must go.

Sarah turned to David, who had only lately come back to North Carolina from Pennsylvania. "Davey, why don't you bring Polly and the children for a nice, long visit sometime? Being used to a big city, she must miss being around people."

David McKay grinned. "Y' don't know how much she hated Philadelphia,

Aunt Sarah. She was some sorry to miss hearin' Nate make his music, but I promised her we'd be sure to come back when he and Pa return from their huntin'."

"There should be a great party then, indeed," Susannah said. "Pa claims this is his last hunting season."

"He's said that before, and naught has come of it," Sarah reminded her.

"Aye, but with Nate leaving him, I think this time he means it."

Sarah looked surprised. "What do you mean? Nate's hunting with him, isn't he?"

"This one last time. Nate's bought land in Kentucky—he was telling us about it this morning while you and Hannah were gone."

"I hope you're right. It's high time your pa stayed put and took care of his wife and family."

Susannah smiled faintly. "You and Uncle Joshua have done that for him all these years. We may never have said we appreciate it, but we all do."

Sarah hugged her niece. "I know it. And Susannah—I pray that by the time your father's home for good, your husband will feel he can come here with you."

Tears came to Susannah's lovely brown eyes, and she turned away in an attempt to hide them. "Davey, we'd better go," she said. "Good-bye, Aunt Sarah, Hannah."

"Why couldn't she have wed a local boy?" Sarah said, musing aloud. Then she turned to Hannah and squared her shoulders. "We must get inside and see to lunch."

Nate and Jonathan had gone to the blacksmith's, Mary Craighead told Sarah when she inquired about them. "They're also looking for a place where Adam can preach and Nate can play some reels."

"I'm glad he decided to stay long enough to hold a service," Sarah said. "If we can't persuade Adam to live here, the least he can do is preach for us from time to time."

"You know I'd like nothing better than to live among my husband's people, but the Lord hasn't directed him here yet."

Detecting a slight note of resignation in Mary's voice, Hannah impulsively hugged her uncle's pretty wife. "Well, at least you're here for awhile. Where's Johnny? I haven't had a chance to spoil him yet."

Mary laughed. "You're the only one who hasn't, I'm afraid. He's napping in the loft, and you'd best leave him be. You'll learn when you have your own never to wake a sleeping baby."

Sarah glanced at her daughter. "Hannah ought to know that. She's certainly tended enough young ones around here. Help me stir up some corn cakes. The men'll be wanting to eat when they get back."

Between attending to her chores and playing with Johnny when he awoke, Hannah stayed busy the rest of the day. She saw Nate only briefly, when he came in to get his fiddle before he and her uncles left together to prepare the Hendersons' barn for the evening's activities. Adam would hold a preaching service first, then they would all have supper before returning to the barn.

Hannah watched people enter the barn and place their quilts and blankets over the hay that had been strewn on the barn's dirt floor. She knew Clay Scott wouldn't be there, but she couldn't help comparing him with the other young men who, like him, had just returned from their militia service. However, there was really no comparison. To Hannah, not one had half the appeal that Clay did. She settled herself beside Mary and Johnny, prepared to help keep the boy amused if he became restless.

The crowd quieted when Adam Craighead mounted the makeshift pulpit he and Jonathan McKay had rigged. Hannah wasn't yet fully accustomed to hearing her uncle preach, but as he told them who he was and why he was there, then invited them to bow their heads in prayer, she was able to lose herself in his message and forget who was bringing it. Adam gave thanks that so many husbands and sons and brothers had come home from the war, which, praise God, finally seemed to be near an end. He asked comfort for those who mourned their dead and ease to those hurt in the fighting. He gave praise to God that He worked in all situations and was always ready to help those who called upon Him.

After the prayer, Nate helped Adam line out several psalms. Then everyone joined in on their favorite hymn:

"O God, our help in ages past,
     Our hope for years to come.
Our shelter from the stormy blast,
     And our eternal home!"

Then Adam once more stood before them, an impressive man over six feet tall, with hazel eyes and long blond hair.

He still looks more like a frontiersman than a preacher, Hannah thought as her uncle opened his Bible.

" 'Tis always comforting for the saints to know that heaven will be their final home, but we all live in this world. His Word tells us that God has given each of us a commission to carry out."

Adam read several passages from the Bible, concluding with one from Matthew: "Behold, I send you forth as sheep in the midst of wolves: be ye therefore wise as serpents, and harmless as doves."

As harmless as doves.

The words echoed in Hannah's mind. Why hadn't she noticed that passage before? How could a disciple be wise as a serpent, when the Evil One himself had taken the form of a serpent to try to bring all men to his own level? And doves—there were doves in the woods behind the springhouse, and their mournful cry always made Hannah feel sad. Suddenly she was reminded of Nate's song about a lonesome dove.

Hannah glanced over to where Nate sat with her parents, evidently intent on Adam's words. She knew Nate was a believer who sometimes prayed in public, but Hannah had never heard him speak of his religion. In fact, Nate never said much about himself at all. What he'd told her in the springhouse the day before was the most he'd ever said about his personal life.

"Who are the wolves of this life?" Adam asked forcefully.

With a guilty start, Hannah realized that she hadn't been paying attention to his sermon. She straightened and fixed her full attention on Adam as he talked about wolves, a subject that his listeners could understand only too well. Even now, when the Yadkin area had been settled for over half a century, wolves were still a problem, as anyone who had tried to raise a few sheep for their wool could testify.

But there were other wolves that Jesus wanted His followers to beware of, Adam went on. Men would be false, and families would betray each other, but true disciples should never fear. "Fear not them which kill the body, but are not able to kill the soul: but rather fear him which is able to destroy both soul and body in hell."

"He preaches a powerful sermon," Hannah heard someone say when Adam had finished his exhortations to the faithful and pleas to the unrepentant.

"We need preaching like that more often," another said.

Hannah turned to Mary and smiled. "Even Johnny seemed to be paying attention," she said. "It must be wonderful to have such a powerful preacher in your own house."

Mary threw her head back and laughed, a melodious sound that caused many to cast puzzled looks her way. "If you ever wed a minister, you might think some different."

"Do you mean to tell me that Uncle Adam isn't a saint at home?" Hannah asked, adopting Mary's lighthearted tone.

"My husband is a wonderful man, but he does like to practice what he preaches—I hear his sermons many times before he feels they're ready."

"I have heard that practice makes perfect," Hannah said. "In this case, it seems to have so done."

"There is no such thing as perfection in this life," Adam said, coming up in time to hear Hannah's last statement. "Unless, of course, it's that roast pig we had last night. I do hope there's some left for supper."

Hannah's family went back to their house to eat, but many who had come from longer distances had brought their food with them and were still at the barn when it was time for the reels to begin. They all turned expectantly when Nate entered, and some called out favorite tunes they wanted him to play.

"Clear the floor," he directed, and soon there was an area large enough for several dozen to take part at once. With the oldest folk minding the littlest ones, adults of all ages formed a double line. Nate put his fiddle to his chest, tested the strings, and then launched into a minuet, followed by a quadrille and a set of squares that left everyone breathless.

Hannah danced with her brother Isaac and her cousin Mark, then with her father and uncle before Zeke Tait, one of the returned militiamen, claimed her for a set.

After it was over, Nate put down his fiddle, wiped his sweating brow, and looked straight at Hannah just as Zeke suggested that they go outside for some fresh air.

"I need some water, Lass," Nate said.

"I'll fetch it," she said, welcoming an excuse to get away from Zeke. Her uncle Jonathan had drawn a fresh bucket from the Hendersons' well before they entered the barn, and Hannah filled a gourd from it and brought it to Nate.

"Thank ye kindly, Miss Hannah," he said. He gulped it in a single draught, then wiped his mouth on his shirt sleeve and returned the gourd. "Now ye can go back to that young man that's making calf's eyes at ye."

Hannah glanced back at Zeke, who was, indeed, watching her and Nate rather closely. "He's not my young man," she said and deliberately sat down beside Nate.

"I know," he said, looking at her in a strange way that made Hannah shiver without knowing why.

Then the Henegar girls, giggling and simpering, came over to ask Nate to sing, and Hannah left.

She walked past Zeke, replaced the gourd dipper in the oaken water bucket, then kept going to where her parents stood talking to some neighbors. She didn't look back at Zeke, but from the corner of her eye she saw Betsy Hines heading toward him, and in a moment they left the barn together.

If Clay Scott had been here and asked me to walk out with him, I would have, she thought. However, Hannah had no wish to be linked with Zeke in local gossip. More than one engagement had been announced after such an encounter, and Hannah certainly didn't want word that she was taken to get back to Clay.

"You look winded," her mother told Hannah. "You'd best sit out the next set."

"I think we'll hear a songfest instead," she said. "The Henegar girls asked Nate to sing."

Sarah Stone glanced toward Nate, surrounded by a half-dozen women of all ages. "Like flies to honey," she murmured with a faint edge of disgust. Her husband grinned.

"The ladies have always been fond of Nate. Too bad he's never found one that struck his fancy."

"It's getting late," Sarah said, glancing around. Most of the youngest children had gone to sleep as soon as Nate had stopped playing, and now even the couples who had gone outside began to drift back inside.

As if he had heard Sarah, Nate stood and motioned for everyone to sit down. "We'll have a song or two now, then call it an evening. What's your pleasure?"

Several people called out tunes, and in turn Nate went through "Froggie Went a-Courtin'," which they all sang together, then lined out "Cornwallis Country Dance," which they hadn't heard. Then Nate looked toward Hannah, and for a moment she feared he'd ask her to sing the "No, Sir" song with him. *I won't do it,* she told herself and put on a sour face to indicate her unwillingness to perform.

"It's late and we all have work to do on the morrow," he said. "Name what ye wish to go home on."

There was a momentary silence, then somewhere a male voice called out, "Canaan's Shore!" Immediately there was a murmur of agreement. Nate put his fiddle to his chest and played a chord, then as he began the melody, everyone sang in unison.

"Oh, Fathers, will you meet me?
    Oh, Fathers, will you meet me?
Oh, Fathers, will you meet me
    On Canaan's happy shore?"

The next verse moved to mothers, then through a whole catalog of relatives, down to cousins, before the final triumphant stanza.

"By the grace of God we'll meet you,
    By the grace of God we'll meet you,
By the grace of God we'll meet you
    On Canaan's happy shore."

In the silence that followed the last chord, Adam stood and raised his hand in an unplanned benediction. "The Lord bless you and keep you; the Lord be gracious unto you; the Lord lift His countenance upon you and give you peace."

Then with a universal sigh of mingled regret and content, the crowd began to disperse. Almost everyone stopped by to thank Nate for his music.

"Come, Hannah," her mother said. "We have much to do tomorrow, getting Nate and your uncle on their way."

"I wish they could stay longer," Hannah said, meaning it sincerely. The new Nate both puzzled and disturbed her, but she loved his music and wished he had had the time to teach her more songs.

"I know—but they want to be off before the first frost, and from the feel of the air tonight, that won't be much longer."

Hannah shivered in the crisp night air and wrapped her shawl more closely around her shoulders. *I'm glad Nate didn't sing that "Lonesome Dove" song,* she thought. She would surely have disgraced herself by crying, and no one—least of all Hannah—would have known why.

Chapter 3

Hannah always arose early to attend to her dairying chores. The next morning, with so many visitors in the house, she went directly to the springhouse without stopping for breakfast. Steam rose from the spring, and the rays of the new sun jeweled the dew-drenched mint beds and silvered each spiderweb. The Indian summer morning was beautiful enough to make Hannah draw her breath in appreciation, but she knew there was no time to spend in idle admiration.

Hannah set to work. With her hands busy, her mind was free to think about what would happen later in the day. After Nate and Uncle Jonathan had gone on their way, Hannah and her mother would treat Clay Scott's wound. His grandmother would want to know all about the gathering at the Hendersons' barn. Her mother would probably give her a summary of Uncle Adam's sermon—she was good at that sort of thing. Mrs. Scott was fond of Nate McIntyre's music, and no doubt she'd ask what tunes he had sung. Clay Scott had been one of General Greene's men who'd chased Cornwallis through Carolina; he'd enjoy hearing the "Cornwallis Country Dance."

I must get Nate to recite the words and let me write them down, Hannah thought, but there wouldn't be much time to do that before he left. *I won't dawdle over the dairying today,* Hannah resolved.

"Ye're out early, Lass."

Startled, Hannah looked up as Nate suddenly appeared beside the spring. He had the woodsman's knack of walking silently, and garbed in his hunting buckskins, he looked every bit the part. A light breeze ruffled the fringe on his shirt and lifted the dark hair around his coonskin cap.

"There's work to be done here," Hannah said. "Surely you aren't leaving already?"

"Nay. But I wanted to see ye alone, and I reckoned this to be the best time and place for it."

"Oh?" Deliberately Hannah directed her attention to her work, straining clabbered milk through cheesecloth. It was the first step in making the cheese for which the Stones were famous throughout the Yadkin. Something told her she shouldn't look at Nate.

He stepped across the narrowest part of the spring and entered the springhouse to stand directly in front of her. "Do ye recall the time when ye followed after us and cried to be taken along?"

Hannah shook her head and continued to knead the cheesecloth. "Not really. I remember once you lifted me up on your horse a-ways from home. Is that the time you mean?"

"Prob'ly. Ye were around four years old then, runnin' after us as fast as your little legs would carry ye and bawling like an orphaned calf." Nate's voice was warm as he continued his reminiscence. " 'Take me wi' ye, Unca Nate!' ye cried, and I lifted you up beside me on the saddle and rode ye home from the ferry. Ye don't recall it at all, Lass?"

For an instant Hannah could almost taste her salty tears on that long-ago morning. She almost remembered something else—but then the shadowy memory fled. She shook her head. "I said something that made you laugh, but I don't recall why."

"I've never forgotten what ye said that day. Ye asked me to wait until ye grew up so ye could marry me."

I did not! Hannah's first, almost automatic, thought was chased down by another, and she quickly looked away from Nate's amused glance. "That was a long time ago," she said. "What makes you think of it now?"

Rather than answering her question, Nate asked one of his own. "Do ye ken how I answered ye then?"

Without looking, Hannah knew Nate was gazing intently into her face, perhaps expecting to see some evidence that she did, indeed, know the words he'd spoken then. Hannah shook her head. "You probably told me not to be such a silly goose."

"I think ye know better."

Hannah looked back to Nate, but the denial on her lips died as she saw him as he had seemed to her that day more than a decade before, a tall and handsome hero she wanted to claim as her own. That day he had gently brushed away her tears with the back of his huge hand and solemnly kissed her forehead.

I promise ye, Hannah Stone. I'll not wed another.

Hannah felt awkward and embarrassed as sudden tears stung her eyes. *There's certainly nothing to cry about,* she told herself.

"I'd forgotten all about it," she forced herself to say.

"Aye, but I never did."

Hannah finished shaping the mound of cheese on her board and laid it aside. She wiped her hands on her apron and ventured to look at Nate. "Why do you speak of it now? That must have been at least thirteen years ago."

Nate leaned forward and extended his hands as if he intended to grasp hers in them, then he straightened up and folded his arms across his chest.

"Because I did wait for ye, Lass," he said softly. "And because now I hope ye'll wait a little while longer for me."

Hannah's heart hammered in her chest and her pulse roared in her temples. She knew Nate expected her to make some response, but she had no idea how to continue with this, the strangest conversation of her life.

When it became obvious that Hannah would say nothing, Nate took a step forward and put his arms around her. She lowered her head to avoid meeting his eyes, but Nate lifted her chin with his right hand, forcing her to look at him.

"Hear me out, Hannah. Ye must know that I'm asking ye to marry me."

Marry Nate?

What he had been hinting at for the past two days had now been openly spoken, yet Hannah couldn't believe that the man she'd always thought of as a friendly older uncle could possibly want to marry her. And Nate certainly didn't hold the kind of attraction for Hannah that Clay Scott did.

"Well?" Nate said when Hannah still made no response.

"I didn't know," she said faintly.

Abruptly Nate dropped his arms to his sides and stepped backward. A dull red color washed over his neck and forehead, the only skin not hidden by his beard. "Well, now ye do," he said, almost gruffly.

"Oh." Although she knew it was woefully inadequate, Hannah could think of nothing else to say.

Nate took a deep breath, drew himself to his full height, and spoke rapidly and earnestly. "I've put away quite a bit of money over the years. Even after buying the Kentucky land, there's plenty left for us to live on. Ye'll not want for anything it's in my power to give ye."

"But—" Hannah began.

"Don't say anything now. Joshua tells me ye're not spoken for. All I ask is that ye keep me in your mind these next few months. Wait for me, Hannah, as I've waited these years for ye."

Although he hadn't moved any closer, Nate's imploring voice had the impact of a caress. His tone didn't beseech—she would have had little patience with that—but rather enveloped her in his unmistakable sincerity.

What can I say to him? Hannah wondered. She had known how to deal with the others who had paid her court, all young men she'd dismissed without a second thought. Nate McIntyre was different. He was a good man, and he'd probably make a steady, reliable husband. But he wasn't Clay Scott, and even in Nate's arms, Hannah hadn't been affected as much as she was by the mere thought of Clay.

Nate waited quietly, his eyes holding hers, until Hannah could speak. "My father has agreed to this?" she asked in a voice that wavered despite her best efforts to steady it.

Nate shook his head. "He knows nothing of my plans. Of course, when the time comes, I'll beg your hand in the proper way."

At least Father hasn't already agreed to wed me to Nate. Hannah felt a surge of relief that helped her say what she had to. "I'm sorry, Unc—Nate. I can't promise anything now. When you come back—"

He flinched when she almost called him "uncle," then recovered and smiled ruefully. "When I come back, I'll ask ye properly. That's a second promise I'll keep if ye'll let me."

Hannah nodded curtly. "All right. But much can happen in six months. If you should decide to court someone else, I'd not mind."

Nate chuckled, then broke into a full smile. "Thank ye, Ma'am. Generosity is a fine trait in a woman."

Believing that Nate was making fun of her, Hannah turned away and busily gathered the dairy things. "I must wash these now, else anymore milk put into them will likely spoil," she said, as if he had sought her out for a lecture on dairying.

"And I maun be back before they send the dogs for me." Nate took the largest pail from Hannah's hand and leaned over to lightly brush her cheek with his lips.

Then, as if nothing at all had passed between them, they walked back toward the house. At the back stoop where Hannah would scrub the milk buckets, Nate set down the bucket and raised his hand to his brow in a half-salute.

"I'll see ye later," he said and sauntered off in search of the other men.

"Are you feeling well, Hannah?" her mother asked when Hannah came into the kitchen after giving the emptins the most thorough washing they'd ever had. "I've not seen you so pale since that spell you had last winter."

Hannah put her hand to her cheek as if she might feel the paleness of which her mother had spoken. "I'm not sick," she said. Seeing her mother's anxious look, Hannah added, "It's just that I haven't eaten yet," although she'd never felt less hungry.

"That's a blessing. With all that's going on now, we've no time to be ill. The men have gone to collect the dogs. Sit down and eat before they come back."

Her mother put a bowl of hot cornmeal mush before her, then to Hannah's relief, she left to check on her nephew. Hannah scraped most of the mush into the pigs' slop bucket, then went up to the sleeping loft. A glance in the looking glass assured her that some of her usual color had returned. No one would ever suspect that anything out of the ordinary had occurred to her. She took off her dairying apron, then went back downstairs and joined her mother and young Johnny on the Stones' wide-planked front porch.

"Uncle Jonathan and Nate are getting a late start," Sarah remarked. "They're usually already across the ferry and well on their way by this hour."

"Did something happen?" Hannah asked.

"Nothing special. They've thought up a dozen things to do before they ride out. You'd think this was the first time they'd trekked into the wilderness, instead of the last."

"How many years have Uncle Jonathan and Nate McIntyre been hunting together, anyway?" Hannah asked.

Sarah moved her fingers in the air and counted silently. "Ever since the year after we came to the Yadkin, I reckon. Nate came to visit Joshua and wound up partnering with Uncle Jonathan."

"That must have been before I was born," Hannah said. *Nate really has known me all my life and then some,* she thought.

Sarah looked at her daughter with amusement. "Yes. In fact, I recall Nate seeing you in the cradle and saying you'd be an uncommonly pretty baby if you hadn't gotten your father's red hair."

"What a terrible thing to say!" Hannah exclaimed.

"Of course he wasn't serious. You know how Nate is—always making some sort of sally. Deep down, he cares for us all. He has no family, you know. I don't know what he can be thinking of, planning to traipse off alone to Kentucky next spring."

"I suppose he can take care of himself," Hannah said. Deciding she'd heard all she wanted about Nate McIntyre, she pointed to Johnny Craighead, happily playing with the wooden blocks Joshua had made for his own sons years before. "I wish Uncle Adam would stay with us awhile. I know we'd all like to see more of Johnny."

Sarah's expression softened as she looked at her nephew. "Aye. He's the spittin' image of his father when he was a lad. But Adam has already told me they can't stay past the noon hour. We'll give them a decent meal and see them on their way."

"Then we'll go back to Vera Scott's?" Hannah asked, trying not to sound too interested.

Sarah sighed. "Yes, I'm afraid so. I didn't like the look of Clay's leg at all. We need to find something else to treat it with, too—the plantain will be killed by the first heavy frost, and the wound will need care for some time."

Hannah looked away, not wanting her mother to see how pleased she was to be included in the treatment plans. *"We* need to find something else," her mother had said.

"I think I hear the dogs," Hannah said, and soon after, the men rode into sight.

Jonathan and Nate were accompanied by Adam, Joshua, and Isaac. Around their heels raced the hunting dogs that had been penned nearby. Their excited yelps filled the air, proof that they were eager to accompany their masters for another season.

Johnny ran out to meet them, then began to cry when one of the frolicking hounds knocked him off his feet. Although Adam immediately dismounted to go to his son's aid, it was Nate who reached him first. He scooped the boy up on his shoulder and brought him to the porch, where his mother, hearing the commotion, had come outside to see what was happening.

"No harm done, Lad. They only meant to be friendly," Nate said.

Now safe in his mother's arms, Johnny grinned and pointed toward the hounds. "Nice doggies," he said.

"Hunting dogs aren't pets to play with," Mary warned. "Do you understand that you must leave them alone?"

Johnny nodded and wriggled in Mary's arms until she reluctantly set him down. Immediately he ran to his father, who picked him up and placed the delighted child on his shoulder.

From the corner of her eye, Hannah saw Nate watch them intently with something like envy on his face. *Nate would make a good father,* she realized.

Looking at him, Hannah wondered idly why Nate had never married. He and her father had scouted together during the French and Indian fighting, then gone their separate ways for a time. *Maybe he had a wife and she was killed by the Indians,* Hannah speculated. Her mother had told her enough about those days so that Hannah knew many settlers had died at the hands of renegade Indians, while others, like her mother and her uncle Adam, had been held captive. Some had been well-treated, but most of those taken were either killed outright or ill-used.

I should have asked Nate why he's waited so long to decide he needs a wife, Hannah thought, but it was too late for any private conversations now. There wasn't even time for Nate to let her copy the words to his new ballads.

As if he could read her thoughts, Nate turned toward Hannah. "I left the 'Cornwallis Country Dance' broadside and a few others by the fiddle case. I thought ye might want to learn them."

"Yes, I would. Thank you." Hannah was surprised that her voice sounded so steady. She knew if she held out her hand, her fingers would be all atremble, although she wasn't certain why that should be the case.

"We'll be looking forward to hearing you play for us again in March, Nate," Sarah said. "You will come back here before you go off to Kentucky for good, won't you?"

Hannah lowered her head, fearing what Nate might say to her mother.

"Aye, ye can count on it. Thank ye for putting me up and for all the kindness ye've all shown." Nate accepted Sarah's brief embrace, shook hands with Joshua and Adam and, to the boy's delight, even with little Johnny. Then he turned toward Mary and Hannah and nodded. "Good-bye, Miss Mary. 'Tis a fine lad ye have there."

Hannah almost held her breath as Nate looked at her with the same friendly expression he had for the other members of her family. "Watch over my fiddle case, Lass," he said. "I'll be back for it in the spring."

Hannah nodded. "I wish you a safe journey," she said and meant it.

Jonathan, who had been bidding his own family farewell next door, came out of the house with his wife and daughter. "We'd best go now, Nate."

"Aye, 'tis growing late," Nate agreed.

With a final wave, the men mounted their sturdy horses and rode away in a cloud of dust amid a chorus of barking dogs.

"I'd think that racket would be enough to scare off any game within a hundred miles," Mary commented.

"You'd be surprised how quiet the dogs are when they hunt," Adam told her. "They know their job—and few hunters would ever dare go into the wilderness without at least one dog."

"I hope they'll be safe this time," said Jeanette McKay. She had made an effort to get up and see her husband off, but she looked pale and drawn. "I almost wish I didn't know it was their last season. I'll worry constantly until they come back."

Adam laid a comforting hand on Jeanette's arm. "The Lord's always protected them before. I see no reason for Him to stop now."

Jeanette smiled weakly. "I wish you were around to tell me that every day. When you say things like that, I can almost believe you're right."

"Of course I am—and the best part is, even when I'm gone, God will give you His peace. All you have to do is ask Him."

"Yes, but it's not the same as having a man of God tell it to me."

"Mama, I think you'd better go back to bed," Marie said to Jeanette.

"Are you all right, Jeanette?" Sarah peered at her uncle's wife with professional concern. "You and Hannah must have the same ailment; both of you are so pale."

Jeanette waved her hand in a gesture of dismissal. "I'm just a little tired from all the excitement. I believe I might lay down for a bit."

"I'll send you some dinner," Sarah promised.

"I'll help you ready it," Hannah volunteered. *After dinner, I'll see Clay Scott.* The thought made Hannah's chores much more tolerable.

However, after Adam and his family had left, Sarah took time to straighten the sleeping loft and gather the linens to be aired the next day. By the time she had finished, the afternoon sun was casting long shadows.

"How short the days are becoming!" Sarah exclaimed as she and Hannah started walking toward the Scotts' place. "I fear that Uncle Jonathan and Nate won't make their usual distance this day."

Almost guiltily, Hannah realized she hadn't thought of the hunters since they had ridden out of sight. "At least the weather is still fair," she said.

"Aye, and I pray it holds for them."

At that time of the day, there were few people about on the road, usually one of the most traveled in the Yadkin area. As they walked, Hannah tried to imagine the faraway places that Nate and her uncle reached each year.

The boundaries of her known world stretched only a few miles in any direction. Due east lay the Yadkin River, her father's ferry, and the town of Salem, which had been settled by German Moravians. To the southeast was Salisbury, where her father conducted his legal and business affairs and where Susannah and her husband lived. To the north and west, imposing mountains rose in grandeur.

Only a few years back, their Yadkin neighbor Daniel Boone had followed a buffalo trace and found a gap through the mountains into the land the Indians called "Kain-tuck." Hannah had been to the north only a few times, and never to Pennsylvania, which her parents and their parents before them had called home.

"There's another empty house," Sarah remarked, nodding toward what had been, until a few months ago, the Bowmans' cabin. But they had sold out to their neighbor John Foster, who needed more land to provide for his large family, and gone to live in Kentucky.

"I hope the Bowmans fare well in Kentucky," Hannah said. She wondered if their land was close to Nate's and wished she had asked him just where his claim was located. *Not that it would matter,* she thought. As little as Hannah knew about her own colony of North Carolina, she knew even less about Kentucky.

"Ill or well, they'll not be back here. Some folks just have itchy feet, and that's the way the Bowmans have always been. Never satisfied, always thinking that something better might be over the next ridge. Such folk are never content. I feel truly sorry for them."

Hannah cast a sideways glance at her mother, whose mouth was set in a rather firm line to match the strength of her convictions. "Yet didn't your parents leave Ireland and Father's folk leave England to come to Pennsylvania? Then all of you left it to come here."

"Aye, but that was a different matter," Sarah said. "The old folk had no choice but to come here or starve; there was nothing else. Then as Pennsylvania began to fill up, we saw we had no future there. We came here and worked hard and prospered. I've no wish to seek a fairer land this side of glory, myself."

"You don't ever wonder what lies yonder?" Hannah asked, nodding to the distant smudge of mountains on the western horizon.

"Sometimes, but after hearing the tales of the Boones and the Bryans about the land over the mountains, they're welcome to it. We'd best quicken our pace a bit, or nightfall will overtake us before we can get back home," she added and immediately matched action to her words.

As a result of their brisk walk, Hannah and her mother were almost out of breath when they reached the Scotts' house. Vera Scott greeted them warmly, and although she still moved cautiously and leaned heavily on her walking stick, she declared her rheumatism was much better.

"I wish you could do half as well for Clay," she said. "The boy insisted on getting up this morning and nothing I could say would stop him from trying to chop me some kindling. I'd turn him over my knee if I could; he's that stubborn."

Hannah and Sarah followed Mrs. Scott into the room where her grandson sat propped up in bed. Instead of his previous pallor, Clay's cheeks glowed unnaturally.

Sarah laid the back of her hand on his forehead. "I believe you've started a fever," she said. "I hear you've not been resting your leg. May I look at it?"

At his nod, Sarah lifted the dressing and inspected the wound. From her mother's expression, Hannah guessed that she didn't like what she saw.

Sarah probed at the edges of the wound with a corner of the dressing. "Does this hurt?"

Clay winced and drew in his breath sharply. "Yes, Ma'am, it sure does."

Sarah turned to Hannah, who stood in the doorway, watching in silence. "Heat some water as you did yesterday, but this time bring the bucket in first. We'll pour the water over his leg and let him soak it well before we put on a fresh dressing."

Hannah turned to do as she was told. So far, the visit hadn't gone as she had hoped. Clay had barely glanced at her and didn't seem to care that she was there. *He must be in pain,* she thought, not wanting to admit that there could be any other reason for Clay to ignore her.

When Hannah returned with the bucket, her mother was telling Vera Scott that some arrangements would have to be made for the household chores. "If Clay's leg is to heal properly, he mustn't strain it. Every time he does, the wound will open afresh."

"I can't lie here and let Grandma do all the work," Clay protested. "What kind of man would let an old woman tend to chores that are rightly his?"

"A man that wants to stay alive and keep both his legs, for one thing," Sarah said tartly. "If infection should set up in earnest, you know what might happen."

Clay shuddered. "I saw it often enough, but usually those men had broken bones as well. The army surgeon said I was one of the lucky ones."

"I'll warrant you could be worse off, but that's no excuse to try to see how bad it'll get."

Vera Scott turned to Sarah, distraught. "But what can we do about it, Sarah? Since the war began, there's no help to be had in these parts, even if we had the means to pay for it. But as you know, Clay's not seen a shilling of pay for months, and—"

Sarah laid her hand on the old woman's shoulder and shook it gently. "Hush! Getting yourself all worked up can only worsen your rheumatism and not do a bit of good otherwise. There is something that can be done."

Mrs. Scott's chin trembled and she clasped both Sarah's hands in hers. "What is it, then?"

"My son Isaac can see to the heavy chores—he's used to helping his father and he knows what must be done. And for the rest of it—"

Sarah's voice trailed off and she turned to Hannah, who reached out a reassuring hand to Clay's grandmother.

"I'll be happy to help you any way I can, Mrs. Scott," Hannah said with a sincerity that needed no feigning.

She didn't dare look directly at Clay Scott, but from the corner of her eye Hannah saw his pleased smile and rejoiced in it.

He really does want to see me again, she told herself and turned away before he could see how much the knowledge had affected her.

Chapter 4

The Yadkin area had always been a friendly place where neighbor helped neighbor with no thought of repayment or reward, so Sarah Stone's offer of the services of two of her children for an indefinite time was not really unusual. Still, as they walked home that evening in the deepening twilight, Sarah thanked Hannah for putting Vera Scott at ease about accepting their help.

"Had you pulled a long face, she'd never have let you nor Isaac on the place again, and Clay would probably feel obligated to do more than he should. This way, he'll have a good chance to keep his leg."

Hannah felt a chill not wholly related to the cooling evening. "You really think he could lose it? I wasn't sure you meant it."

Sarah sounded irritated. "Of course I did, and the sooner Clay Scott realizes it, too, the better."

Hannah tried to imagine Clay with a missing leg. She had seen a few men who had lost an arm or leg from accidents or war. She hadn't turned from the sight, but it was hard to act natural around them. Some had given up in resigned hopelessness, while others grimly tried to do all the work they had once done, making both themselves and their families miserable in the attempt.

God doesn't look on the outward appearance but knows the heart of a man. Hannah paraphrased the Old Testament verse that had been impressed on her mind from her childhood. In marriage, a man and woman vowed to stay together no matter what might happen to their circumstances—or to their appearances.

"We won't let him lose his leg," Hannah said.

"We?" Sarah sounded puzzled at the force with which Hannah had spoken.

"You and Isaac and I," Hannah said hastily. "If we all work together and give Clay's leg a chance to heal, he'll be good as new, won't he?"

"Only the Lord knows that for certain. But with His help, we can certainly try to do our best."

Amen, Hannah added silently.

Marie met them at the front gate, her brow dark with worry. "I thought you'd never get back," she said. "Mama's taken a bad chill."

Sarah sighed. "I feared she might be coming down with the fever again. All the signs were there."

"So did I, but she didn't want to worry Uncle Jonathan," Marie said, using the term that she and her brother had always used to refer to their stepfather.

"I'll look in on her right away—thank goodness Nate thought to bring me a fresh supply of cinchona powder. Hannah, you can help Jane with supper tonight."

Without waiting for Hannah to answer, Sarah and Marie hurried off to Uncle Jonathan's house.

The happiness Hannah had felt earlier in the day fled, leaving weariness in its place. It had already been a long day, and Hannah knew that by the time she'd helped to prepare and serve the evening meal, she'd be physically exhausted. The resentment Hannah tended to feel for her uncle's step family resurfaced, nagging at her.

As Hannah helped Jane assemble the makings of their supper, she thought of the day when she and Marie had first met. Hannah had been eleven then, and Marie ten. Thomas, Marie's older brother, had immediately taken up with Hannah's brother Prentiss, but Marie had viewed them all with a suspicion that had been promptly returned.

"What do you put on your hair to make it like that?" Marie had asked Hannah almost as soon as they had been introduced.

"The same thing you put on yours, I reckon," Hannah had replied. In truth, both girls had unusual hair, Hannah's because of its bright red hue, and Marie's because it was extremely dark and curly.

"The Millays do look like those gypsies that passed through Salisbury not long back," Hannah overheard her mother tell her father after supper that first evening. "Mayhap they have Romany blood."

Her father had explained that the Millay family was of French Huguenot ancestry, forced to leave their home many years before. "Those people went through a great deal for their religion. I admire them for their courage."

There are gypsies in France, too. The Millays could have left France because of their blood rather than their religion, Hannah had thought at the time. Now, six years later, her mind knew better, but her heart had still never quite accepted her uncle's stepfamily on equal terms with her own. Hannah still recalled the hurt she'd felt when her own parents sometimes seemed to be fonder of Thomas and Marie than of their own children.

"You favor Marie and Thomas over us," Hannah had once accused her mother.

"Nay, Hannah. Put yourself in their place, Lass, and think how you'd feel if you had to come to a new place where you knew no one. With Uncle Jonathan gone so much of the time, they've no one else to rely on. If nothing else, Christian charity ought to make you be friends with your stepcousins."

Thomas and Marie are no kin of mine, Hannah had thought, but she'd made an effort to follow the biblical admonition, "Be ye kind one to another," and she'd long since accepted her uncle's new family. Hannah was genuinely fond of little Jacques, and she got along well with Aunt Jeanette and Thomas. But with Marie, things had always been different. Hannah and Marie were outwardly cordial, but they weren't really close. Though neither openly spoke of it, Hannah knew that her mother understood the way things were between them. She was relieved that Sarah Stone no longer tried to encourage the girls to pretend a friendship which neither wanted.

"Isaac, your father has said he can spare you for a time," Sarah told her son at supper. "You're badly needed at the Scotts' place to chore for them."

Isaac looked from his mother to his father, as if waiting for Joshua Stone to confirm Sarah's words. "Doing what?" he asked when his father nodded.

Briefly Sarah told him the situation at the Scott household. "If you and Hannah can take over the work for a time, Clay Scott has a chance to keep his leg. Otherwise, I fear the worst."

Isaac brightened. "Will you let me doctor it, too?"

"I suppose so—if Dr. Willson takes you on as his apprentice, you'll be seeing a lot worse."

"Tell me about Clay's leg—what is the wound like?" Isaac asked.

Sarah frowned her disapproval. "You know we don't speak of such things when we're at table. Come tomorrow. You'll see for yourself."

Marie, who had been feeding her brother Jacques on a low settle by the fireplace, entered the conversation. "The Scotts won't know what to think when the three of you take over all their chores."

Joshua shook his head. "Only Isaac and Hannah will be doing the Scotts' work. Mrs. Stone has more than enough to handle without taking on another household."

Sarah looked annoyed. "You know that's not the way of it. The children all help out, and while the Scotts have no help at all, we have a servant."

"And could use another," Joshua said. "But I'd never be the one to stop you from doing good works."

Sarah smiled at her husband. "As if you could, anyway."

Marie wiped her brother's chin. "Jacques, you're a fair mess, and it's nigh unto your bedtime."

"Yes, you'd best take him on now. I suspect we could all stand to go to bed early this night. There'll be plenty for us all to do tomorrow."

There'll be more to my visit to the Scotts' than work, Hannah thought.

"I'm afraid Indian summer is about to end," Vera Scott said the next day after she greeted her helpers and thanked them for coming. "Every joint in my body's a-achin', and that can only mean we're in for a real howler of a storm. I'd be much obliged if your boy could get in a deal of firewood today."

"Isaac brought our sharpest axe for just that reason. But first off, I want him to see Clay's leg. Both he and Hannah will learn to apply the poultices and change the dressings so they can take turns helping me."

"There's talk as how Isaac might go to 'prentice with Doctor Willson in Salisbury," Vera Scott said. "I tell you right now, Miz Stone, you know more physic than that man Willson." She shook her finger at Isaac. "You'd best learn from your ma and leave that man alone."

"You well know I'm no surgeon," Sarah said briskly. "You had a bad time with that tooth Willson pulled, but also mind that you waited until it'd abscessed before you sought his help. You can't blame him for that."

"Maybe so, but what has Willson ever done for my rheumatism, Sarah? Nothing, that's what. Without your potions, I wouldn't be a-walkin' at all, and you know that's a fair fact. Why, as I was just telling Clay—"

"Grandma!"

Clay Scott's call interrupted her, and somewhat sheepishly Vera Scott waved her cane toward his door. "Go on and see to him, then. I'll just stay here and rest my aching bones."

"Here's the makings for wintergreen tea." Sarah handed the old lady a small pottery jar. "It should give you a bit more ease on rainy days. Come, Hannah and Isaac—let's see how our other patient fares today."

As before, Clay sat up in bed, a bolster supporting his bad leg.

"You remember my son, Isaac, I'm sure."

Clay nodded. "Quite well, but he wasn't quite so tall the last I saw him."

"I'm fifteen and already as tall as my father," Isaac said with pride. His voice had deepened, but to his chagrin it still sometimes cracked toward the end of his sentences.

"No doubt you'll top Mr. Stone when you've done growing," Clay said.

"He's grown enough to be of some help around here, and that's a fact."

Sarah bent to remove Clay's dressing and motioned for Hannah and Isaac to come closer. "I want Hannah and Isaac to learn how to attend to this."

Clay's face darkened. "Can't Grandma do it and spare you the trouble?"

" 'Tis no trouble at all, and with her rheumatism, you mustn't expect your grandmother to help you as she once did."

"Spoil me, you mean." Clay repeated what many had said over the years.

Sarah ignored the comment and gestured for her son to come even closer.

She pulled the dressing away. "Here, Isaac—you've not seen a wound like this before."

Isaac's tanned face blanched at the sight of the jagged hole in Clay's calf, now swollen and red with infection. He drew in a deep breath but seemed to be rendered speechless. Clay looked from Isaac to Hannah, who stood with her arms folded at her waist, obviously unaffected by the sight.

"I've seen worse," Hannah said in reply to Clay's unspoken question. "You're lucky the ball didn't break your shinbone."

"So they told me." Clay kept his eyes on Hannah's as her mother changed the dressing and drenched the wound with fresh infusion, keeping up a running commentary on what she was doing and why.

"Hold the dressings, Isaac, and hand me the strips as I need them," Sarah directed.

Now over his initial shock, Isaac watched his mother's ministrations with great interest. "How do you know how tight to wrap the bandage?"

"If it's too tight, I'll holler. If it falls off my leg, it's too loose," Clay said.

Clay's remark made Hannah smile, but her mother ignored it. " 'Tis a fair question and a good one, Son. Too tight, and you do more damage than good. Too loose, and you do no good at all. Unwrap what I just put on and see if you can do it the same way."

Isaac bent awkwardly to the task until the bandage slipped and one of his long fingers brushed the tender skin near the wound, causing Clay to wince.

"Ouch!" he exclaimed.

Immediately, Isaac's face reddened and he thrust the bandages into his mother's hands and backed away. "You'd best finish afore I kill him."

Sarah smiled faintly. "There's no danger of that—you were doing fine until you lost your nerve. Go make a start chopping the wood, and I'll let Hannah try her hand."

Hannah took the linen strips and began winding them as her mother had done. When she finished, Sarah pronounced it adequate. " 'Tis a bit loose directly over the wound, though—next time keep the same tension throughout."

"I was afraid I'd hurt him," Hannah said.

Clay grinned with something of his old charm. "Why shouldn't you hurt me? Everyone else does," he said.

"I'm sure you're quite mistreated, Sir." Sarah handed her basket to Hannah. "Tidy this up and bundle the used dressings. They'll need boiling— I'll start heating the water."

Hannah had been hoping to be left alone with Clay, but now that she was, she felt shy and awkward. She didn't look at him until she had wrapped the used dressings in a deerskin pouch Sarah brought along for that purpose.

"Where can I put these fresh dressings so they'll be handy?" she asked.

Clay looked around the room, then pointed to a shelf on the wall to the right of his bed. "That's probably safe as any," he said.

"Don't forget to tell Mother or Isaac where they are," Hannah said.

Clay raised his eyebrows in the way he had of challenging statements. "Won't you be coming back?"

Hannah nodded. "Probably, but mostly to do chores. Until you're better, I expect Mother will want to tend you herself."

"She's good, but that clumsy brother of yours I could do without. If he makes a doctor, heaven help the Yadkin folk!"

Clay hadn't spoken seriously, and Hannah allowed herself a fleeting smile before she made a feeble effort to take up for Isaac. "He's young now. He'll gradually learn to do better."

"That's why it's called the 'practice' of medicine, I suppose. But I'd just as soon have him practice woodchopping and let you and Miz Stone do the physicking."

"I'll tell her you said that," Hannah said.

"Hannah! Come give me a hand!"

"I must go now," Hannah said. "Stay off your leg. I'll see you tomorrow."

"I'll count the hours until your return, each more painful than the last," he said in the manner of an actor repeating a well-rehearsed line.

Was Clay serious? Hannah hoped so, but he had the reputation of saying much that he didn't mean, particularly to young ladies. Hannah risked a brief smile.

"You'd be better off counting your blessings instead. Good-bye, Clay."

I mustn't let him know how I feel about him too soon, Hannah told herself. A man liked to feel he was the pursuer, and a prize won too easily wasn't likely to be highly regarded.

In order to make herself available for Clay to court her, Hannah would have to do the Scotts' chores, hard work that she wouldn't normally welcome. However, under the present circumstances, it was exactly what she wanted.

The storm that Vera Scott had predicted arrived that evening, putting a permanent end to the pleasant fall weather, stripping the trees' brilliant foliage, and plunging the Yadkin into a killing frost the next day. Soon Hannah would have to do her churning indoors, but she wrapped herself in a long woolen shawl, determined to stay outside as long as she could.

The daily trips to the Scotts' house continued, but often Sarah went alone, saying that Hannah had done so well with the chores that she wasn't needed that day. Isaac continued to work there daily, but he had shied away from having anything to do with Clay's dressing.

"To tell the truth, I'm about to decide not to go for a doctor," Isaac told Hannah one evening after another of his attempts to change Clay's dressing as well as his mother had failed. "I don't seem to have the knack of it."

"If you still want to doctor, you should at least give it a try," Hannah told him. "Dr. Willson will let you know soon enough if he thinks you have the makings of a doctor."

"That's what I'm afraid of," Isaac said glumly. "If I don't, what will I do?"

"I'm sure Father would be glad to have you run the ferry for him when the time comes," Hannah said, but Isaac shook his head violently.

"And keep me a child the rest of his life? No, thank you. Matthew seems to like the work. Father should apprentice him when he comes back from the war, and not look to me to help him."

"Don't worry. Things will work out," Hannah said, but her heart ached for both her brother and their father. It was Prentiss, the son who had been killed fighting the British, who was to have inherited the ferry and the publick house and the adjoining land. Isaac wasn't Prentiss and could never be, and Hannah hoped that when Isaac went to Salisbury at New Year's, he'd find contentment with doctoring.

A man has to do what God means him to, or he won't find peace. Uncle Adam said those very words when he came to the Yadkin, made a minister like his father before him in spite of previously not thinking he was suited for it.

May God help Isaac find his calling, too, Hannah prayed silently. At least she didn't have to worry about finding a vocation, she thought as she went about her chores. When a girl asked God to send her a good husband, a man who would be a good provider and take care of her and their family, she had done all she could. The rest was up to God—and, of course, to the man that He would send.

Clay Scott, Hannah thought. Maybe God had allowed Clay to be wounded so they would be brought together as she cared for him. Of course, right now Clay couldn't be a good provider, but the Scott land was among the best in the county, and when Clay got back on his feet and started to work it, he'd be able to support a wife without any trouble at all. The cabin was a bit small and would need to be added to if Clay's grandmother still lived when he brought home a bride. But that was no problem; her father and Isaac and the Gospels had helped many settlers increase the size of their homes, and in turn had been helped by them when the time had come to make the McKays' and Stones' houses larger.

"Hannah, are you daydreaming again? Twice I've asked if you've finished with Clay's new infusion."

Startled, Hannah nodded and rose to strain the solution, made from dried stone root rhizomes, that would be put on Clay's wound in the coming days. *I'm glad Mother can't read my mind,* she thought.

With the cooler weather, the women of the household took turns spinning the dyed wool and flax into yarn, then fashioning it into needed garments and household goods. Under the tutelage of their stepmother, whose ancestors had been weavers in France, the Gospels had also become proficient with the loom, even to the youngest. Often they set up their looms around the large fireplace at the Stone house.

To lighten the monotony of the work, the older family members told stories of the old days, and sometimes everyone sang to the accompaniment of Joshua's mouth harp. With Sarah's care and the bitter draughts made from powdered cinchona bark, Jeanette recovered enough from her latest attack of chills and fever to join them.

"I wisht Uncle Nate was here to play us a tune on his fiddle," Mark said one evening, and everyone murmured agreement.

"I wisht I knew where he and Pa are," Luke said. "Do y' reckon they heard that the British gave up?"

"Not likely," Joshua replied. "It took nigh unto a week for us to get the news ourselves, and if the men take their usual route, they'll be far from any news of the East."

Jeanette pulled her shawl closer around her thin shoulders and shivered. "I just pray they're all right," she said wanly.

"So do I," echoed her daughter. "I've had a bad feeling from the start."

Sarah shot a sharp glance in Marie's direction. " 'Bad feelings,' as you call them, are nothing more than the devil's way of troubling us. Pray for their safety instead, and you'll be a deal better off."

Marie's cheeks reddened and she bent to her mending without replying.

"As we all do each day," said Hannah quickly.

But as a matter of fact, except for the daily family prayers in which God's protection was routinely invoked for just about everyone they knew, Hannah hadn't given much thought to Nate and Uncle Jonathan.

Out of sight, out of mind. The old saying came to Hannah, and she supposed it was true in some cases. But she knew it wasn't always true. Even on the days she didn't see Clay Scott, he was never far from her thoughts.

Does he feel the same way about me? Soon, Hannah hoped, she'd know the answer to that from Clay himself. Until then, she could only hope that he did.

For awhile it seemed that Clay's leg would heal without complications, but almost overnight it once more became so seriously inflamed that Sarah feared gangrene.

"The wound must be cleansed twice a day without fail," she declared. "I'll come first thing every morning, and Hannah can tend to it in the afternoon."

Despite patiently carrying out that unpleasant task, Hannah was alarmed that Clay grew steadily worse. Some days he hardly seemed to know that she was there, and his grandmother reported that he slept most of the time. As she changed his foul dressings, Hannah found herself saying the same prayer over and over. *Make Clay better, God. Heal his leg and restore his strength.*

Sometimes she thought to add "If it be Thy will," but most of the time she didn't. Why wouldn't it be God's will to heal the sick? After all, Jesus had devoted a large amount of His time on earth to doing just that, and certainly Clay had done nothing to deserve to lose either life or limb.

After several weeks of intensive treatment, during which Sarah was challenged to use all her healing skills, Clay's leg began to show slow improvement. However, the wound continued to drain, and the dressings had to be tended even more carefully. As his fever went down, Clay began to take more notice of Hannah again, and one day when she was wrapping his leg, he reached for her hand and pulled her toward him.

"Sit down here and rest for awhile," he said. "You always seem to be so busy these days."

Embarrassment made Hannah speak abruptly. "There's still work to do around here, you know."

Clay frowned, and immediately Hannah realized she'd said the wrong thing.

"I don't need to be reminded how much trouble I'm causing."

"You know I didn't mean that," Hannah said quickly. "I'm here to help your grandmother, as well as to tend to your leg. What I don't do she tries to, and that just makes her rheumatism worse."

Clay nodded. "I suppose having one of us in my shape is bad enough— if you had to tend to Grandma, too, you'd never get home at all. But surely you can take time to tell me what's happening out there, at least."

Clay's voice was plaintive, and his gesture took in the world outside his windowless room, from which he had long been away.

Hannah sat stiffly on the edge of Clay's narrow bed, taking care not to jar his bad leg. "Not much is happening that I know of. My uncle Adam has agreed to preach here once a month if a meetinghouse can be built, and Father and some of the other men are looking for a suitable place to put it. They hope a regular pastor will be willing to come here, once there's a meetinghouse."

Clay looked bored. "What about play-parties? I sure would love to hear a fiddle tune again."

"The last one was at corn-shucking time, and you were so sick I doubt you could've heard me even if I'd told you about it. No one's played the fiddle around here in public since Nate McIntyre left."

"I'm sorry I missed hearing him. Didn't you tell me he had some new ballads?"

Hannah nodded. "I wasn't sure you'd recall it—that was just before you got so sick."

"I remember more than you think I do." Clay looked steadily at Hannah, who quickly directed her glance to her folded hands.

Did he hear me praying for him? Well, if so, that was nothing to feel shamed about. Hannah looked back at him. "I'll bring the words to the 'Cornwallis Country Dance' tomorrow," she said. "You'll probably like it. I must go now."

Clay took her right hand in his and squeezed it hard. "Thank you," he said.

Embarrassed, Hannah stood and gently disengaged her hand. "For what? Mother and I have been glad to help. We need no thanks."

"I think you do, and as soon as I'm able, I intend to make it up to you."

There was no mistaking the meaning of Clay's steady look. It was the nearest Clay had come to declaring his feelings for her, and oblivious to the snow that had begun to blanket the countryside, Hannah felt a warm glow as she walked home that afternoon.

Chapter 5

Throughout the Yadkin those days, the weather was the main topic of conversation. Everyone hoped there wouldn't be another winter like 1779–1780, when the ground had frozen in November and not thawed until March. The almanack had predicted a "usual" winter, however, and when the first snow melted and wasn't immediately followed by another, the folk around the Yadkin breathed a collective sigh of relief.

The colder weather had also brought a respite from the fever. Jeanette McKay seemed to be almost fully recovered, but little Jacques came down with a croupy cough despite the pine tar syrup that Sarah made for him by the pint. Then Hannah, who was seldom ill, took a case of sniffles that soon grew so bad that her mother ordered her to stay inside until she was over it.

"What about the dairying?" Hannah protested. "I promised to make extra cheese for the Martins, and—"

"We'll manage the day-to-day chores ourselves, and the Martins can wait."

"Mrs. Martin's lazy daughters ought to be making their own cheese," Jeanette McKay said. She and Marie had, as usual, taken their evening meal with the Stones, and now they both sat on the other side of the fireplace, as far away from Hannah's coughing and sneezing as they could get and still be warmed by the fire.

"Mrs. Martin says they've ruined too much good milk already," Hannah said. "And then there's the Scotts—"

Sarah frowned. "With Clay's infection just now beginning to get better, the last thing he needs is another illness."

"I don't even have to see him—you can change the dressings every other day, just as you've been doing, and I'll tend to the other chores," Hannah said in a raspy voice.

"No, Hannah," Sarah said firmly. "You must take care of yourself—I don't want you to get lung fever again."

Marie looked up from the stocking she was darning. "I'll go in her place, Aunt Sarah."

Jeanette McKay laughed shortly. "I can't believe my ears, Sarah—my daughter offering to do someone else's chores, when it's all I can do to make her tend to her own."

Marie flashed a brief look of anger at her mother. "I do more than my share of work as it is. If you'd just make the Gospels turn their hand every now and again—"

"That's enough, young lady!" Jeanette exclaimed. "You'll not speak to me in that tone."

"Yes, Mama," Marie said with more resignation than conviction. It was obvious to their listeners that the disagreement between mother and daughter had not begun that day, nor would it likely end soon.

"Others' burdens always seem lighter," Sarah said in the strained silence that followed.

"Specially when they never have to carry them," Joshua said, joining the conversation. "I'm sure Vera Scott will be happy to see you, Marie. 'Tis kind of you to offer to help them."

Vera Scott isn't the only one who may be glad to see Marie, Hannah thought grimly, then chided herself for her petty jealousy. Clay would no doubt enjoy seeing a new face (*a* pretty *new face,* Hannah added). Anyway, Clay probably still viewed Marie as no more than his friend Thomas's pesky little sister. She had caused them both much grief by dogging their steps when she'd first come to live in her stepfather's house.

Marie's full lips curved in a brief smile, and she lowered her head as if Joshua's praise had embarrassed her. "It's the least I can do for the helpless," she murmured.

Hannah had trouble falling asleep that night, then awoke several times in the night with a steady, undeniable ache in her chest. *Lord, I can't be sick now. Make me better soon,* she prayed.

"It's just as I feared," Sarah told Hannah the next morning. "You've all the signs of lung fever. A hot mustard plaster will make you feel some better, but you absolutely must stay in bed."

Hannah wanted to protest, but she was too tired. She drank the hot herb tea that her mother brought her, then fell into a deep sleep from which she didn't awaken until long after Marie had returned from her first day at the Scotts' house.

I'll be able to go back tomorrow, Hannah tried to tell herself, knowing it was unlikely. When the next day came and she felt worse, Hannah didn't have the strength to care.

From what seemed to be a long way off, Hannah heard her mother and Marie talking about her. She strained to hear their words.

"Worst case she's ever had," Sarah said.

"Clay Scott will be sorry to hear it," Marie replied.

Sarah said something that Hannah couldn't catch and apparently left the room. Then there was a strange sound, as of someone being amused.

Was Marie laughing, or did I imagine it? Hannah tried to call out to her and ask, but her throat felt too tight for speech. Wearily she closed her eyes and fell back into darkness.

🙠

"Just how long have I been lying here like this?" Hannah asked her mother on the morning that she awoke, clearheaded and fairly pain-free for the first time in what seemed like ages.

"Awhile," Sarah replied.

From the look of relief on her mother's face, Hannah knew she must have been ill, indeed. *No wonder I feel so weak.*

Sarah continued to sponge Hannah's face. "You should try to get up now and sit by the fire. I'll brew something to give you strength."

"I'm sorry I've made so much trouble," Hannah said.

"Nonsense—mostly you've slept, which is the best possible remedy for lung fever."

Hannah started to ask about Clay Scott, but just then Sarah helped her to her feet, and her head swam so much that Hannah had to use all her strength just to stand upright. "Ohhh," she moaned.

"Put your arm around my waist and hold up your head," Sarah said. "You'll feel better in a moment."

A short time later, seated in a chair by the fire with a quilt draped around her shoulders, Hannah felt strong enough to speak again. "I don't see how Clay Scott can ever walk again, as long as he's been in bed, when it only took a little lung fever to make me weak as a kitten."

Sarah looked at Hannah with amusement. "Surely you don't think that Clay has been in bed all this time? He's been hopping about on the one leg for some time to keep up his strength—Vera watched to make sure he put no weight on his bad leg. Marie tells me that lately he's started walking a few steps on his own, with her help."

"You haven't seen him yourself?" Hannah asked.

"No—I hadn't been going over there regular since the bad infection cleared up. With you and Isaac doing such a good job, there was no need. And now that Clay is mending so well, I daresay he'll soon be able to take over all but the heaviest of the chores."

"Then they won't need us anymore," Hannah said.

Sarah looked sharply at her daughter. "You almost sound sorry for it— I'd think you would've had enough of doing for Vera Scott to last a lifetime by now."

"She's not so bad." Hannah attempted a weak smile. "The fact is, I think your medicine has helped her rheumatism more than she lets on, too—she'd begun doing more of the work herself even before I got sick."

"Then I suppose we've just about worked ourselves out of a job, which is just as well. We'll be having some things to tend to here," Sarah said.

"What do you mean?"

Sarah took a letter from her apron pocket. "This came yesterday, from my mother and John Andrews. It seems that they've finally decided to leave Pennsylvania long enough to visit us as soon as the weather permits."

"They're coming *here?*" Hannah's tone suggested that North Carolina was the last place her grandmother and her second husband could ever want to come.

"Yes, *here*. I'll read it to you." Sarah smoothed out the paper and held it up to the light:

My dear Sarah and Joshua and all the family,

We thank God that you are all well, as Jonathan and Nate told us a few days past. They stayed just long enough to pass on the family news, and had no more than gone on their way west again when we heard that Cornwallis had given up 7,000 men near your area, so the war for independence is finally over. Praise God!

Now that things are more settled, we can come to see our families in the Yadkin. John and I long to see all our children and their children once more on this earth. Nate said he especially wants us to be there in March when he and Jonathan come home.

A merchant friend of John's is leaving immediately for the South and I must close and trust this letter to his care. Until we meet again, may God bless and keep us all.

Mother

"Grandmother is really coming here, after all these years? I can't believe it," Hannah said.

"I know—'tis almost too good to be true. Your father thinks that if we build a small house for them in the fallow field behind Uncle Jonathan's, they might be persuaded to stay a longer while. He's already calculating what would be needed to do it."

"I'd like to read the letter, please," Hannah said.

"Here, but mind you don't tear it."

Quickly Hannah scanned the brief message. Her grandmother wrote a stiff, old-fashioned hand, with sloping letters and fancy capitals generously strewn throughout. What really interested Hannah, however, was the mention that Nate had wanted her grandmother to be at the Yadkin when he and Jonathan came back home. Hannah wondered what her parents had made of it, but she handed it back with no mention of its contents.

Sarah replaced the letter in her pocket, where Hannah guessed it wouldn't stay very long. "It seems that we have Nate to thank for pinning them down to a date. I expect they'll start from Lancaster soon after the thaw."

"How long will it take them to get here?"

Sarah shrugged. "I don't know. The roads are better now than when we came to these parts, but it's still a good distance. Ten days, perhaps—two weeks if the weather turns ill or floods slow them. But the important thing is they've decided to come. When my mother says she'll do something, it'll be done."

Hannah half-smiled. "That reminds me of my mother."

Sarah returned her daughter's smile. "And of yourself, too, of course. All of us—Jonathan and Adam, too—have her stubborn McKay ways, I suppose."

Later that day, Hannah tried to imagine how her grandmother might look. Her mother had told her how she remembered her, but it had been years since Sarah had last seen her mother, and time would have changed them both.

Did Nate tell them to come in March so they could see their granddaughter married? Well, that's quite possible; and it just might happen, but perhaps not the way Nate has intended. If Clay Scott fully recovers by then, which seems to be more than likely, there very well could be a wedding, all right.

Hannah was slow to regain her strength, and when she was at last well enough to go back to the Scotts', the weather turned nasty and forced her to remain indoors. By the time Hannah finally stood again on the Scott threshold, more than a month had passed since her last visit; and Hannah hesitated before she raised her hand and knocked, something she had never done when she had come to do their chores.

Expecting Vera Scott to come to the door, Hannah had the jar of soup Sarah had sent for the noon meal at the ready. Instead, it was Clay who opened the door. For an instant, Hannah almost didn't recognize him. For one thing, it was the first time she'd seen Clay standing unaided since he'd left to go off to war. Somehow, he seemed much shorter than she'd recalled. For another thing, she'd not expected him to be wearing the kind of loose homespun trousers and linsey-woolsey shirt that her father wore. Somehow, she had thought of him as he'd looked in his military uniform.

But that's foolish—Clay Scott was invalided out of the Continental Line, Hannah told herself. *He's done with uniforms for good.*

To make Hannah feel even stranger, Clay's welcoming smile died on his lips. Obviously, not only hadn't he expected to see Hannah, he appeared to be quite disappointed that she wasn't someone else.

"I thought you'd be Marie," he said in confirmation. "I hope she isn't ill?"

Thank you for inquiring after my health, Mr. Scott. The words badly wanted saying, and Hannah had to grit her teeth to keep them from emerging. "Not to my knowledge," she said instead. "But I'm sure you know that little Jacques hasn't been well this winter. She's probably tending him."

Clay nodded, then seemed to recollect his manners. "Come in, do. Is that soup? Grandma was just saying she wished she had a good joint of meat to start a pot of soup."

Hannah tried not to stare at Clay's limp as he walked away. "This soup is done. It only wants warming," she told Vera Scott.

Clay's grandmother turned from sliding bread into the fireplace wall oven and nodded in greeting. "I wasn't looking to see you for some time, sick as I hear you've been."

"I've been fine for a week or more, but Mother said it was too cold for me to get out." Hannah handed her the soup jar. "Mother thought you might like some white bean soup. There's quite a bit of ham hock in it, too."

"So I see," Vera Scott said, and from the tone of her voice Hannah guessed that bean soup wasn't her favorite. "If you're here thinking to do more of our chores, I suspect you'll be glad to know you're not needed."

"I came to bring the soup and to see for myself that our patient is as much improved as I had heard." Hannah glanced at Clay, who grinned and extended his arms from his sides and slowly pivoted as if to show that he was whole again.

"Thanks to excellent nursing, I'm almost good as new. I'm not ready for a quadrille just yet, of course, but by the time Nate McIntyre gets back here with his fiddle, Marie and I can show Yadkin folk how it's done."

Marie and I. Not *you and I. Marie and I.*

Mechanically Hannah returned Clay's smile, then nodded to Mrs. Scott and walked back to the front door. "I must go now—the Gospels have been taking their meals with us since Jacques has been so ill, and I haven't yet caught up on my work at home. So many have asked for our cheese, and of course I'm behind on the butter-making, too."

Hannah knew that she was chattering in the senseless way that she had so often faulted in others, but she couldn't help it. She had to keep talking or scream, and as numb as she felt, she knew she mustn't scream.

Clay followed Hannah outside and closed the door behind them. His bright blue eyes fastened on hers and he took both her hands in his. "Thank you for all you did for me," he said. "I owe you and your mother my leg, at least, and probably my life, too."

Hannah's chest felt constricted and her throat convulsed as if she might choke at any moment, but she managed to make a barely audible reply. "I was glad to do it."

"I know it wasn't—pleasant. Did you know that Marie fainted the first time she saw my leg?"

"No one told me that," Hannah said, surprised.

Clay smiled as if in fond remembrance. "She's not the nurse you are—you've your mother's gift for healing; no doubt about it."

Hannah took her hands from Clay's and tried not to sound spiteful. "I presume Marie was useful with the chores, though?"

Clay tucked his hands under his armpits as if to warm them. "You know Marie isn't as strong as you are, Hannah, but Grandma's felt enough better to do quite a bit lately. Marie needs help with the heavy work, but—"

Hannah felt a momentary flash of anger at Clay's words. *I will not stand here and listen to him praise Marie's weakness,* she vowed.

"I really have to go now. I'm glad to see that you are both doing so well."

Hannah turned away from him, but Clay reached out a restraining hand. "Wait—there's something I want you to know."

Reluctantly Hannah turned to face him, hoping Clay wouldn't notice the tears that threatened to blur her vision. "What is it?"

"Marie and I—well, we'd like to get married right away, but her mother wants us to wait until her stepfather comes back home. Until then, I think we ought to keep our engagement a secret, even from your folks. You won't tell anyone?"

Despite her best efforts against it, the edge of irritation that Hannah felt showed in her tone. "Why should I? It's nothing to me. Good-bye, Clay."

Hannah turned from him with her head held high, thankful that Clay Scott couldn't see the foolish tears that now streamed from her eyes and fell on her warmest cloak, an almost-black wool that she had thought matched Clay's hair when she had dyed it with the darkest stains she could gather.

Black is the color of my true love's hair. The refrain echoed in Hannah's mind until finally, out of sight of the Scotts' house, she gave way to her grief, wailing and sobbing as she'd not done for years.

Maybe not since the time I cried after Nate McIntyre, Hannah thought.

Black is the color of my true love's hair, Nate had sung. He'd looked at her the way she'd wanted Clay to look at her, the way he never would. Clay Scott's tender glances were all for Marie now, while she—

Hannah made fists of her hands and flailed the air, taking small comfort in the feeble act of defiance.

"Why must life be so unfair?" Hannah asked bitterly. Only the cold wind answered her.

If only I hadn't become ill, then Marie wouldn't have gone to the Scotts' house. By now, Hannah and Clay would no doubt have been as close as he and Marie seemed to be. Or at least they would have been heading in that direction.

Marie wasted no time, Hannah thought bitterly. But then, Marie must have known she couldn't, because she knew—she had to know—that Hannah cared for Clay. The wind blew harder, stinging her wet cheeks, and Hannah shivered and wrapped her cloak more closely about her. Never had she felt more alone and abandoned or more sorry for herself.

This won't do, Hannah told herself. *You're behaving like a spoiled child, and all the tears and temper tantrums in the world won't change anything.* It would be hard, but Hannah knew she must try to accept her rejection and make the best of it.

No one must know that I ever cared about Clay, Hannah resolved. She would have to learn to feign indifference around him. And as for Marie, Hannah intended never to show the anger and disappointment she felt toward the one who, no better than a common thief, had deliberately set out to steal Clay Scott from her.

The wind shrieked, and for some reason its power brought to mind a New Testament passage her father was fond of quoting: "Vengeance is mine; I will repay, saith the Lord." Then Hannah recalled another New Testament verse dealing with the treatment of one's enemies. She smiled at the picture of heaping coals of real fire on Marie's black curls, which would blaze and burn away. *Marie's so vain about her hair, it'd serve her right.*

Hannah's smile died quickly as she realized how disappointed her uncle Adam would be in her if he knew she had such evil thoughts. *Maybe I ought to talk to him about it,* Hannah thought uneasily.

Adam Craighead had a way of explaining God's ways to Hannah that praying and reading the Bible on her own never had. "You're young yet, Lass. When you've lived a few years longer, then you can understand a bit more. But never expect to understand everything that happens this side of heaven— 'tis not meant for us to know as much as Lord God Jehovah," he had once told her.

Well, Hannah thought, *it might still be some weeks before I see Uncle Adam again,* and in the meantime, she had to live through this day and the next and all the days that would follow. Days without Clay Scott.

Help me, God, Hannah prayed, not knowing what more to ask. For the present, it would be enough for Hannah to get back home and wash the tears from her face without being seen. After that, she'd take each moment as it came and do the best she could with it. Hannah held her skirts a few inches above the road, bent her head, and ran the rest of the way home.

In the weeks that followed, Hannah discovered that it was one thing to resolve to forget Clay and ignore Marie but another to carry out such a resolve. Her run home in the cold wind brought on a relapse, and Hannah almost welcomed the opportunity to take to her bed again. When she finally emerged after a few days, pale and wan, everyone assumed that Hannah's unaccustomed quietness was due to the effects of her illness and made no particular note of it.

"I'm glad you're feeling better," Marie said that evening. "The Scotts have been quite concerned about you."

No doubt they have, Hannah thought. "Tell them I thank them, but I'm not up to going visiting just yet."

"I'm sure they'll understand," Marie said, and Hannah thought she detected a note of relief in her voice.

Even when Hannah felt strong enough to resume her dairying and treating the sick with her mother, she decided it was best to avoid the Scotts. Several times when Sarah asked her to take them food or infusions, Hannah passed them on to Marie, who was more than willing to go in Hannah's place.

As winter deepened, Jeanette and Marie spent more time in their own home, for which Hannah was grateful. However, they still took many evening meals with the Stones. More than once, Hannah caught Marie regarding her with a peculiar look, as if she half-wanted to say something to Hannah but didn't know if she should. Putting herself in Marie's place, Hannah thought it must be hard on Marie not to be able to talk to anyone about her secret engagement.

If I knew I'd be marrying Clay Scott in a few months, I'd want to tell the whole world, she thought. And when Jeanette McKay asked Sarah and Hannah to help her and Marie spin her finest flax into yarn which the Gospels would then loom into linens, Hannah had to turn away to hide the tears that sprang to her eyes. "Marie has reminded me that our beds are nearly bare," Jeanette said. However, Hannah was certain that Marie intended the linens for her dowry.

One day after Hannah and her mother had worked alone for some time in silence, Sarah put down her spindle and turned to face Hannah.

"I have something to discuss with you," she began, then stopped.

Hannah felt a faint prickle of alarm. "What is it? I'm listening."

Sarah sighed and folded her hands in her lap. "I stopped by Vera Scott's yesterday, and she asked why you hadn't been to see them lately. It seems that you've been sending Marie on the errands I sent you on. I want to know why."

Hannah looked at her mother in genuine surprise. So that was it—she was disappointed to think that Hannah had failed to carry out her orders. "I didn't think it mattered who went to the Scotts', as long as someone did."

Sarah set her mouth together in a straight line of displeasure. "That is not what I asked. Why didn't you go yourself?"

Her smooth spinning rhythm disrupted, Hannah bent to retwist the broken yarn before replying. "I didn't feel up to it," she said truthfully.

"Then you should have told me. I'd have made other arrangements myself."

Hannah inclined her head. "All right. It won't happen again."

"I should hope not! I told Vera that you'd recovered from your illness, and she said a very strange thing. Perhaps you can help me understand it."

Hannah hand-turned the wheel and concentrated on regaining her spinning rhythm without looking at her mother, but when Sarah didn't continue, Hannah prompted her. "What did Mrs. Scott say?"

"She said you mustn't let Clay keep you from coming to see her. When I asked her what she meant, she flustered and turned me away, saying you'd know. Just what is there between you and Clay Scott, anyway?"

Hannah shook her head. "Nothing, Mother. I can't imagine why Mrs. Scott would say such a thing."

"Well, something's amiss about it all. I can't lay my finger to it just now, but as your grandfather Craighead used to say, 'The truth will always come out; tell it or not.' If you've something that ought to be said, now is the time to speak of it."

For a moment Hannah considered burrowing her head in Sarah's lap and tearfully confessing how all her hopes of marrying Clay Scott had been brought to nothing, and all because of Marie. But she knew that such an action would ultimately do more harm than good. Instead, Hannah stopped the spinning wheel and met her mother's concerned gaze, her eyes steady.

"There's nothing to say, Mother, except that I am truly sorry to have caused you concern."

Sarah looked relieved, and Hannah knew that her mother had accepted her denial. "You've always been strong-minded and willful, but I've never known you to lie. I'll not speak of this to your father—there's no need to worry him, now that he's so occupied with plans for the meetinghouse."

Hannah seized the opportunity to direct her mother's thoughts elsewhere. "When will the meetinghouse be finished?"

"They say by New Year's, when Adam is to deliver the consecration message, but splitting the roof shingles is taking longer than they expected. At this rate, Adam may find himself preaching under the open sky to a half-frozen congregation."

"I wouldn't care," Hannah said. "I can't wait to see him and Mary and the children again."

"Yes, that'll be grand—and your father can certainly use Adam's help if the house he wants to build for Mother is to be finished by the end of February."

"February? I thought you said they'd be here in March," Hannah said.

"Yes, but I want to have everything ready in case they should arrive early. Isaac is making a bedstead, and Adam's to bring a wagonload of other furniture. And that reminds me, Hannah—we ought to be making some more linens for ourselves as soon as we finish these. With so much company around the place, we'll be hard-pressed to make our store go around."

"They can use that coverlet I made last fall," Hannah said. She'd seen the pattern in a house on Dutchman's Creek where she and her mother had gone doctoring and immediately had gathered the dyes for the bright blue pattern. The hue matched Clay's eyes, she had thought then. She'd daydreamed about him as she had made the coverlet, then put it away in the chest she'd been gradually filling for the last two years. Now she'd have no use for the coverlet, and since it would only serve to remind her of Clay Scott, Hannah was quite willing to give it away.

Sarah smiled at her daughter's generosity. "Thank you. If we can't get another finished in time, I'll borrow it. But then back it goes into your dower chest. You never know when you might need it," she added.

Hannah said nothing, but unaccountably she thought of Nate McIntyre. As was the custom, Jonathan McKay had sent a packet of gifts to his family for Christmas, and with it had been a letter from Nate. It was addressed to them all, thanking them again for their hospitality in the fall and reminding them that he would see them in March.

I have some new songs for Hannah, and something else that for now will have to be a surprise, he wrote.

"Maybe Uncle Nate's found himself a wife," Isaac ventured as they took turns making lighthearted guesses as to what he could mean.

"Not likely," Joshua said, and Hannah was glad that no one was looking at her just then. Things were bad enough already—she certainly didn't need to be teased about Nate McIntyre.

But after everyone had gone to bed that night, Hannah crept downstairs and retrieved the letter from the mantel. She lighted a candle from the embers of the banked fire and reread every word as if it might contain some secret message just for her.

Hannah wondered what Nate might be bringing, and if it really was just for her, which was not clear in his wording. Even more, she was concerned with what would happen when he came back. *Will Nate McIntyre still want to marry me?* Hannah had replaced the letter on the mantel and shivered, not entirely from the chill of the room.

Black is the color of my true love's hair. Nate had sung those words to Hannah, words Hannah had longed to sing to Clay Scott. Now it seemed clear that she'd never have the chance.

"Lord, why does life have to be so unfair?" Hannah had murmured. Then with a heavy sigh, she had blown out the candle and went back to bed.

Chapter 6

Despite Sarah's doubts, the meetinghouse roof was finally installed; rough, backless benches were hewn—only temporary, the men said, until they had time to make better—and the building stood ready for consecration on the first Sunday of 1782.

Although a raw rain had been falling steadily all day, a large crowd turned out for the occasion. By midmorning, every bench was filled, and many people stood around the sides of the meetinghouse and crowded around the door.

"Don't this just show how much we need a regular preacher?" Hannah heard someone say.

"Folk hereabouts turn out for anything," another said.

Then another voice spoke, one Hannah hadn't heard for some time. "All these people pressed so close should warm you, Grandma. Hannah will move over a bit and make room for you, I'm sure."

Hannah turned to meet Clay Scott's blue eyes and felt a physical shock. She'd seen Clay once or twice, now that he was getting out more, but only from a distance. She hadn't thought of meeting him here, so she wasn't as prepared as she would have liked.

"Hello, Clay, Mrs. Scott. Do sit down, Ma'am."

"I don't know, Child. With the misery in my back like it is, I shouldn't be here a-tall, but I do love good preaching; and since I missed hearing your uncle the last time, I determined not to let another chance pass me by."

"What will you do?" Hannah asked Clay. She surmised that standing would be painful to his hurt leg, which he still obviously favored and probably always would.

Clay smiled and his blue eyes twinkled with excitement. "Don't worry about me. Can you see to Grandma after the preaching's over?"

Hannah nodded. "Father brought the carriage. He'll be glad to take her home."

"Good. She probably oughtn't even be out on a day like this, but nothing would do her—she wanted to hear Adam Craighead preach. Be careful, Grandma."

Clay kissed the old lady's cheek, nodded again to Hannah, made his way through the crowd to the door, and then outside.

No doubt he's going to the McKays' house now, Hannah realized. Only minutes before the Stones and McKays were ready to come to the meetinghouse, Marie had complained of feeling unwell and stayed behind.

She and Clay must have planned this time to be together. The thought brought Hannah a stab of pain. Even though she didn't think about Clay as often as she once had, she still keenly felt his loss.

"Clay's probably going to see Marie," Vera Scott said matter-of-factly. Startled that his grandmother had voiced what she was thinking, Hannah merely nodded in agreement.

Mrs. Scott must know about their engagement, Hannah thought. And judging by her tone of voice, she approved. No doubt the old lady looked forward to having someone to take over all the housework and do the cooking for her. Hannah sighed. From her own experience she knew that Vera Scott wasn't always pleasant to be around, especially on the days when her rheumatism pained her the most. No doubt Marie had already discovered that, and it didn't matter to her anymore than it would to Hannah, had she been in Marie's place.

"What're they waiting for? I'm ready for the service to begin," Vera Scott announced.

Just then a man in a black frock coat entered, and Hannah recognized the Reverend Elias Smalley, whose congregation met in Salisbury and who had agreed to join Adam Craighead in consecrating the meetinghouse.

"I hope this part don't last too long," a man behind Hannah said in a loud whisper. "I hear the reverend favors long prayers."

"Wish I'd thought to bring some corn pone to chaw on," Vera Scott whispered to Hannah. "I fear my innards'll start to a-rumbling long afore this service is done."

Adam greeted Pastor Smalley, then turned and raised his hand for quiet. Elias Smalley mounted to the pulpit and in sonorous tones invoked the blessings of the Lord on everyone in Carolina, the people in the whole Yadkin, those there assembled, and on the dwelling in which they were gathered.

Smalley's prayer at last over, Adam joined him at the pulpit and lined out some Psalms, which were sung with ragged enthusiasm.

Nate would have these walls ringing if he could be here, Hannah thought. For a moment she imagined Nate standing beside Uncle Adam as they'd done in the Hendersons' barn back in October. She was surprised at how easily the image came to her mind.

I hope Nate and Uncle Jonathan are still safe. Hannah made the thought into a prayer, then settled back to listen as her uncle began to preach about what the church was, and what their responsibility would be to the man they hoped would come to lead them.

As Adam Craighead continued to speak, Hannah wished once more that he could be persuaded to stay in the Yadkin instead of merely preaching for them once a month. Hannah thought she might be able to talk to him about the burden of jealousy and pain she'd felt ever since she'd learned that Clay and Marie were engaged. Yet even as she rehearsed what she could say, Hannah realized how petty it would sound. She could almost see the reproof in her uncle's grave hazel eyes as he would gently tell her she must give her anger, pain, and jealousy to Christ and let Him deal with it.

Hannah defended herself in imagination. *But you don't understand how I feel.*

Maybe not, but God does. When you give Him all your life, including the pain, then He can heal your spirit, Uncle Adam would probably say.

Although it was no longer quite so chilly in the meetinghouse, Hannah shivered and hugged her arms as if to hold on to the pain she wasn't yet ready to surrender.

No, Hannah decided, *I won't speak to Uncle Adam this time.* Perhaps when he came again in February, if she felt no better, she might mention it to him. But for now, pain and hurt had become Hannah's most constant companions, and she wasn't sure she was ready to send them away just yet.

The consecration, preaching, and singing continued for several hours, and even Hannah's limbs felt stiff as she stood to leave. Mrs. Scott needed help to stand, and even then could move only with great difficulty.

"Sarah, I have need of that pain elixir you made when Clay was so bad off. This weather and that bench have hobbled me for fair," she said when she reached the Stones' carriage.

"I keep some made up. Come home with us now and I'll fetch it—and then stay to eat with us while you're about it."

"That's kind of you, Sarah. I don't believe I could lift a skillet in the shape I'm in, much less cook a whole meal."

Hannah climbed into the carriage beside Vera Scott and wondered that the older woman didn't seem concerned about where her grandson was or where he would dine.

"What about Clay?" Sarah Stone asked. "He didn't stay for the service. Should we go by your place and fetch him?"

Vera Scott shook her head. "No, no—Clay can take care of himself now, thanks to your good doctoring. No need to go out of your way on his account."

That's just as well, Hannah thought on the short ride home. *"No need to go out of your way on his account."* Hannah considered the truth of Vera Scott's words in her own situation. That was the way she attempted to deal with

Marie and Clay. If she kept busy with her own concerns and never went out of her way to think about or see them, in time her hurt would heal. Someday maybe she could see Clay's black hair without thinking of the love ballad Nate had sung about his true love's hair.

Joshua stopped the carriage close by the front porch and helped Vera Scott hobble into the house while Sarah went after the elixir. In a moment, the McKays' carriage arrived. The younger Gospels, making up for the time they had to be quiet in the meetinghouse, burst into the Stones' house in a whirl of noise and motion. Jeanette hushed them and left Jacques with Mark while she went next door to check on Marie.

A few moments later Jeanette returned, alone. She stopped in the doorway and leaned on the frame for support. Although her mouth opened and closed, no sound came out. Seeing her distress, everyone grew silent.

Something is terribly wrong, Hannah thought. *Could harm have come to Marie?*

Sarah thrust the pain elixir into Vera Scott's hands and rushed to Jeanette's side. "What is it? What is wrong?"

Jeanette put a trembling hand to her throat, and tears began to spill from her eyes. "She's gone," she whispered in a voice too low to be heard more than a few feet away. But Hannah heard, and a cold shock went through her body.

He's gone—Prentiss is gone, Sarah Stone had cried out when the news came that her son had been killed. It was a term commonly used in those parts to mean that someone had died. To say that someone was dead was considered to be too harsh, too final, so they said "gone" instead. But Marie—as far as anyone knew, anyway—was in perfect health. What could have happened?

Sarah grabbed the sobbing Jeanette's shoulders and shook her hard. "Gone? What do you mean?" she demanded.

Jacques, alarmed at his mother's tears, began to wail loudly himself, but everyone else, including the Gospels, seemed frozen in place as they waited for Jeanette to pull herself together enough to speak.

"Marie's gone!" Jeanette repeated.

"Come on, Isaac." Joshua motioned to his son, and they pushed past Jeanette and hurried toward the McKays' house.

"No," Jeanette finally managed to say. "Marie's not there. She's *gone.*"

Hannah let out her breath in a sigh of relief, and suddenly everyone was talking at once.

"Sit down and I'll get you some water," Sarah said, leading Jeanette to the settle. "Sit with her, Hannah."

Not knowing what else to do, Hannah put her arms around Jeanette and murmured the kinds of comforting words she had so often heard her mother say in similar situations. Jeanette had just finished a dipper of fresh well water from Sarah when Joshua and Isaac returned.

Joshua held out a sheet of paper, evidently some sort of letter. "I found this on the floor by Marie's bed. Did you see it, Jeanette?"

Jeanette wiped her eyes with the handkerchief Sarah had pressed into her hand. "Yes," she said thickly. "I read it."

"What does it say?" Sarah asked. Joshua handed it to her, and she quickly scanned the few lines and turned back to Jeanette. "Do you mind if I tell them?"

Jeanette shook her head. "No. Everyone in the Yadkin will know soon enough."

Sarah looked again at the note, then gave it to Jeanette. "Marie says that she and Clay Scott decided not to wait until March to ask for her stepfather's blessing. They have gone to be married elsewhere."

From the moment her father had come back from the McKays' house with the letter in his hand, Hannah had guessed its content, so she did not join in the others' gasp of surprise.

"Married! I didn't even know they were courting!" Sarah exclaimed.

Vera Scott looked dazed. "I don't understand. They said they'd wait until Jonathan McKay came home and Clay would be in better shape to support them," she said, as if trying to explain it to herself as well.

Sarah looked back to Jeanette, who had stopped crying and gained some measure of composure. "Did you know Clay and Marie were engaged?"

Jeanette nodded. "Marie told me they wanted to marry, but I thought it was probably just a notion that she'd get over. I told her she'd have to have Jonathan's blessing, and I figured by the time he got home she'd have thought better of it, what with Clay so crippled, and her so young—"

Vera Scott turned to Jeanette and spoke with an edge of anger in her voice. "My grandson's not too crippled to support a wife, and your daughter's old enough to know her mind, too."

"Marie's just a baby!" Jeanette countered. "Clay Scott took advantage of her youth and innocence, or she'd never have thought of running away from her home."

"What makes you think it was Clay's idea to elope?" Vera Scott asked. "He told me he was well content to leave things as they were until spring."

"Please hush, both of you," Sarah said firmly. "There's no good to be done by placing blame. What's done is done, and all the arguing in the world can't undo it. Aunt Jeanette, go home and wash your face. Mrs. Scott, try to sit quietly and let the elixir have a chance to work. Adam and Mary will be here in a moment. They mustn't catch this household in such turmoil, and on the Lord's Day, too."

Mother didn't say they ought to be ashamed of themselves, but her tone certainly did, Hannah thought. She had always admired her mother's ability to get to the heart of a situation and sort it out while everyone else stood by and wrung their hands.

And of course, what Sarah had said was true. Clay and Marie were determined to marry, and the sooner their families accepted it, the better. It would cause a great deal of tongue-wagging and headshaking for awhile, but then another topic of gossip would come along, and soon everyone would forget that the Scotts, that nice young couple, had once scandalized the Yadkin.

In the confusion, Adam Craighead had entered the house and was standing in the middle of the room before anyone noticed him. "Why the long faces? Was my sermon that bad?"

Sarah looked relieved to see her brother and immediately went to him and embraced him. "It has nothing to do with you. We've just had a bit of a shock," she began, but Isaac blurted out the news before his mother could break it gently.

"Marie and Clay Scott ran off to get married!"

Adam looked surprised. "I didn't know they were engaged," he said. "From the way you all look, I feared something really bad had happened."

Something really bad did happen, Uncle Adam, Hannah wanted to say. *The man I love has eloped and taken with him what was left of my broken heart. I will never, ever, be the same again.*

Sarah nodded toward Vera Scott, who sat with her hands over her eyes. "I'm sure Aunt Jeanette and Mrs. Scott find it bad enough. However, what's done is done. May God forgive them, misguided as they are."

Adam nodded. "Perhaps Aunt Jeanette and Clay's grandmother will be as ready to forgive them as God is."

Vera Scott looked up at Adam and sighed. "Clay don't need to ask forgiveness from me. He had my blessing to marry Marie Millay, and he well knew it."

"Perhaps you ought to go see Aunt Jeanette now," Sarah suggested to Adam. "Hannah, help Mary with the children while I see if Jane has our dinner nearly done. We'll all feel better after we've had something to eat."

I won't, Hannah thought darkly. *I'll never feel better again.*

Hannah stood and motioned for Isaac to take Johnny, while she approached Adam's wife and held out her hands to her uncle and aunt's chubby little girl.

"Come to Cousin Hannah," she invited.

Mary Craighead looked surprised as the child let Hannah take her. "Ann won't usually go to strangers. You must have a way with children, Hannah."

"They seem to like me well enough," Hannah replied. "Come, little one. Cousin Hannah has a rag dolly you can play with. Would you like to see it?"

The child's long blond curls bobbed as she nodded her head, her big brown eyes large. "Yeth, Anna."

Hannah bent her head to Annie's and kissed her smooth forehead. For a moment she felt almost overwhelmed by a feeling of love for her little cousin.

I will have children of my own someday. The words came to Hannah suddenly, part hope, part vow.

In her mind's eye, Hannah saw herself standing with her shadow children. She cradled one in her arms, while several others held on to her skirts. They wouldn't, as she had once daydreamed, have Clay Scott's dark hair and laughing blue eyes, but as Hannah climbed to the sleeping loft with Annie in her arms, she could almost believe that by then, it wouldn't matter.

❧

Nearly ten days passed before Marie and Clay Scott returned to the Yadkin, and it was another day after that before Hannah saw them. She was on her way back from the springhouse with the day's churning when she saw Clay emerge from the McKays' house with a bundle of linens.

Hannah had dreaded the moment that she would encounter Clay and Marie as husband and wife, but seeing Clay before he saw her, she at least had some time to prepare herself for the encounter.

Sarah Stone stood on the McKays' porch with Jeanette, and she was the first to notice Hannah. "Here she comes. Clay, look who's here."

Clay turned from the wagon and seemed embarrassed to see her. He nodded curtly. "Good morning, Hannah."

Hannah returned his nod. "Morning, Clay. Where's Marie?"

"In the house with Jacques. He's really missed her."

"I'm sure she missed him, as well," Hannah said.

"Hannah, go divide today's churning and give Clay and Marie a chunk of butter," Sarah directed. "I doubt that Vera Scott has any in the house."

"No, Ma'am, Grandma's larder is pretty low right now, and we've not yet had the chance to fill it. We'll be much obliged for it."

"Bring them some of the joint Jane's cooking for our dinner, too," Sarah added as Hannah turned to leave. "There's much more there than we can eat."

In no hurry to rejoin the newlyweds, Hannah took her time taking the joint of beef from the fire and slicing off a large chunk. She wrapped it and the butter in a clean square of linen but decided against putting them in a basket. When food was received in any sort of container, the recipient was expected to return it filled with something else. Hannah didn't think her mother would want Marie or Vera Scott to feel obligated to carry out the custom when they might be having a hard time managing their own meals.

When Hannah returned to the McKays' house, Marie stood on the front porch beside Clay. *She doesn't look a bit different,* Hannah thought with a shock of surprise. She didn't know what she had expected, but somehow it seemed to Hannah that, as Clay Scott's wife, Marie ought to look radiantly happy. In fact, Marie and her mother were both crying, while Clay stood watching them with obvious discomfort.

"You don't know how much everyone has missed you," Jeanette sobbed. "Little Jacques has cried himself to sleep every night since you left, and I—"

Jeanette stopped, unable to continue speaking, and Marie put her arms around her mother and sobbed along with her until Sarah stepped forward and put an arm around each of them. "Here, here, this won't do at all!" she exclaimed. "This is no time for such caterwauling. Marie, tell your mama good-bye and go on home with your husband. Aunt Jeanette, Marie's not going to China, you know. You and Jacques will see her nigh every day."

Jeanette and Marie drew apart, but neither seemed cheered by Sarah's words, and neither spoke.

"Do you need any more help loading things?" Hannah asked Clay.

"No, this is all." Clay took Marie's hand. "Let's go home now."

With painful slowness, Clay maneuvered his lame leg down the steps and hoisted himself onto the wagon seat. He reached out to help Marie up beside him, then the wagon jolted out of the yard and away from the house that had been Marie's home for so many years.

"I hope he'll be good to her," Jeanette said, then went inside her house and closed the door behind her.

"Aunt Jeanette seems awfully upset," Hannah said. "Shouldn't you go see about her?"

Sarah Stone shook her head. "She's not done with her grieving yet. 'Tis not a thing one wants company to do."

"Would you grieve like that for me if I should marry?" Hannah asked.

Sarah's lips parted in a smile. "Nay! I might grieve some if no one ever asks you at all, which is mighty unlikely. But you've a long time yet to worry about that."

"Do you think that Marie is too young to marry?" Hannah asked.

Sarah shrugged. "Time will tell, I suppose. Many have wed younger and been happy, but—well, it depends." She put her arm around her daughter's waist and hugged her lightly. "For my part, I'm in no hurry for my only daughter to leave me."

❦

February came in with a hard freeze. Toward the end of the month, the weather moderated and a thaw set in. With the expected return of the hunters and the anticipated arrival of Ann and John Andrews, work at the Stone and McKay households proceeded at a hectic pace.

Glad for the opportunity to stay busy, Hannah wholeheartedly threw herself into the preparations for their guests. Marie visited her mother often, but Hannah seldom saw her for more than a few minutes at a time. When Clay and Marie took supper with the Stones, as they did at least once a week, Hannah found she could talk with them almost normally.

The sharp pain Hannah had once felt at the mere thought of Clay had subsided to a dull, manageable ache. Often she went for hours, if not days, without thinking of Clay at all. However, she avoided being alone with him. For that reason, when Clay Scott stopped by on a day when everyone else had gone to work on the dwelling where the Andrewses would stay, Hannah almost didn't let him in the house.

"I know you're in there, Hannah," Clay called out after knocking several times failed to bring her to the door. "The cold hurts my leg—can't I come in?"

Hannah sighed and opened the door. "You can warm yourself. Then you must be on your way." Hannah turned away, careful not to look into his eyes.

"You weren't this cruel before." Clay made his way to the fireplace and stood beside Hannah, stretching his hands to the fire. "I'll never forget how good you were to me when I was laid up."

"I'm not being cruel now," Hannah said.

"Then why did I have to beg for you to let me in?"

Hannah was aware that Clay was looking at her intently, but she gazed steadfastly into the ever-changing patterns made by the flames. "I think you know why, Clay. You're a married man now, and it's not seemly for you to visit here when I am alone."

"Who's to know that?"

Hannah glanced at Clay from the corner of her eye, then returned her attention to the flames. "You and I know it, and that's all that matters. What brings you here? If you need some physic, Mother—"

Clay put his hands on Hannah's arms and turned her to face him. His blue eyes had never been more intent or disturbing, and Hannah could not make herself look long at them.

"Don't talk to me like that, Hannah. You know we've always felt something special for each other, and that doesn't need to change."

Clay's voice was soft and persuasive, and for a moment Hannah felt the old, familiar yearning his presence always seemed to bring. When she did not immediately speak or move away from his grasp, Clay groaned and pulled her toward him. For a moment Hannah let herself rest in his embrace as she had once dreamed of doing. His arms around her were solid and reassuring. She allowed her head to lie on his shoulder for a moment, but when Clay lowered his face to hers and kissed her lips, Hannah immediately broke away from his embrace and stepped back.

Clay's anguish showed in his face and in his voice as well. "Don't try to deny your feelings, Hannah. The way you came into my arms told me all I need to know—" He stepped forward to embrace her again, but this time she resisted.

"No!" Hannah pushed away from Clay so violently that her skirt whirled dangerously close to the flames in the fireplace. Clay grabbed her and pulled her back, continuing to grip her forearms. "Let me go!" she exclaimed.

"Not until you listen to what I came to say." Clay spoke with quiet intensity. "I'll never know how Marie managed to talk me into marrying her. Maybe it was because I'd nearly died and wasn't thinking straight. Anyhow, it was a big mistake, and it didn't take me long to know so."

Oh, Clay, how could you have let her spoil our chance to be together? Hannah longed to be folded into the shelter of his arms and to accept the love his eyes offered her, but something held her back. *He must never know how I truly feel,* Hannah told herself.

For a moment Hannah stood silent, then she returned his steady gaze. "You must never say such a thing, or even think it!" she finally managed to say.

"I can't help it, Hannah. I love you and I always will. I didn't know what to do about it until yesterday." Clay pulled a folded paper from his pocket. "This came from my captain, the one who pulled me out of the swamp. He wants me to come over to Cape Fear and work in his pitch and tar business. All I've been able to think of since is that this is our chance, Hannah."

"Our chance for what? You don't make sense, Clay."

Clay's face glowed with excitement. "Don't you see? We can go together to Cape Fear. No one knows us there. We'll start anew together—"

For a moment Hannah pictured a life with Clay, but almost instantly she realized it couldn't be the life she had once dreamed of sharing with him. Hannah's voice shook, but her resolve was rock-solid. "You already have a wife, Clay Scott. Have you forgotten God's commandment against adultery?"

Clay took a half step backward as if Hannah had struck him. "It wouldn't be adultery," he said in a low voice. "Marie and I—no minister would marry us."

"You mean you're not even—" Hannah began but stopped, unable to finish the thought.

Clay shrugged and half-smiled as if remembering the occasion. "I bribed a half-drunken justice of the peace to fill out a paper and mumble a few words before us, so Marie thinks we're wed. But I don't think it was legal and binding, so there's nothing to stop you and me from getting married for real."

"I wouldn't say that." Hannah's initial shock quickly yielded to anger. She strode across the room, flung open the door, and motioned for Clay to leave. "I want you to go now and forget that you were ever here. I won't listen to another word about it."

Clay slowly made his way to the door, making a show of limping even more than usual. There he stopped and gazed sorrowfully into Hannah's eyes.

"At least think about it. Marie already spends more time with her mother than at home. She may be upset for a little while, but in the long run it'll be best for all concerned if we just admit we made a mistake and go on."

Hannah shook her head and tried to push Clay through the doorway. "Perhaps you made a mistake, but I don't intend to add to it. Go!"

"But, Hannah—" Clay was still trying to plead his case when she finally got him out of the doorway enough to close it. Quickly she pulled the door latch to the inside and leaned her head against the wall, trembling all over.

The one man that Hannah had thought she loved had come to her and begged her to elope with him. At a tremendous cost to her one-time dreams, she'd been strong enough to turn him down. But from this point on, Hannah knew that nothing would ever be the same for her.

Dear God, help me, Hannah prayed. Then she thought of Marie, and tears of sorrow and self-pity welled up in her eyes. *If only Marie hadn't interfered and taken Clay from me, none of this would have happened.*

Hannah wiped her eyes and squared her shoulders. It would be senseless to waste any more time crying. There was nothing that could be done to restore Clay to her, but Hannah knew that she must do something to ensure that the marriage that Marie had schemed to bring about was valid. She couldn't say anything to her parents or Aunt Jeanette, but Adam Craighead would be coming again the first Sunday in March.

I must tell him that there's a possibility that Clay and Marie aren't legally married. Her uncle knew about the laws—he'd know what must be done to see to it that their bonds would be as binding as Marie already thought they were. But that was all Hannah would say to him about the matter.

No one must ever know what else had passed between her and Clay.

Chapter 7

The day before Adam Craighead was due to preach again, Hannah and her mother were taking advantage of a fair and windy day to air linens. Mark, the Gospel then taking his turn helping Joshua at the ferry, came running toward them, breathless with the news that John and Ann Andrews had just arrived on the other side of the Yadkin and would soon be in their midst.

"I told you they might come early!" Sarah told Hannah. "The men finished the work on their cabin in good time. Take off that apron, Hannah—there's a tear in the pocket—and try to smooth your hair. Where did I put my other bonnet? Oh, if only I'd had some notice that they were coming today!"

Her mother's uncharacteristic agitation amused Hannah. "I've never seen you so upset about company."

"This is family, not company—and I can scarcely believe that Mother is really here, after all these years."

The travelers arrived with an escort. Isaac and Mark had returned to the ferry and joined Joshua in riding with them. Sarah and Hannah stood by the gate as the party rode up.

Hannah searched out the lone woman in the group. *So that's my grandmother,* she thought. Ann Andrews accepted Isaac's help in dismounting, then was immediately engulfed in her daughter's embrace.

Hannah had expected her grandmother to look like most of the older ladies around the Yadkin: plump, perhaps, with a deeply lined face, few or no teeth, and gray or white hair. In reality, Sarah's mother was slender to the point of thinness. Her face was etched with a few deep lines, but her jawline was firm, indicating that she still had most of her teeth. The hair revealed when she threw back the hood of her traveling cloak was soft ash blond, threaded with many strands of silver.

She's beautiful, Hannah thought with awe, but her grandmother's physical appearance was only a small part of it. The rare radiance of Ann Andrews's face also revealed the true beauty from within of one who lives close to God.

While Hannah waited for her mother to let her grandmother go long enough to take notice of her, she watched John Andrews dismount and shake hands with Luke and John, the McKay boys he hadn't met at the ferry. He had grown white-haired and somewhat stout over the years, but he was still a distinguished-looking man. In his features Hannah could detect similarities to those of his daughter, Mary Craighead, and his grandchildren.

"Hannah, come greet your grandmother," Sarah said at last.

Hannah and Ann Andrews were exactly the same height, but as Hannah put her arms around her grandmother's shoulders, she was aware of how much more frail the older woman was than her appearance suggested.

Her grandmother put out a tender hand and traced the contours of Hannah's face. "Ah, Lass, let me look at ye. That hair—it seems only yesterday that I first met Isabel Prentiss on the voyage over. We were no older than ye now are. Ye put me greatly to mind of her, except for your eyes—they're like your mother's and your grandfather's."

"So I've been told," Hannah said. "I wish that I could have known Grandfather Craighead."

Ann looked sad for a moment. "So do I, Child, but knowing that a bit of him lives on in all of ye gives me great comfort."

"We'd better go inside, Mother," Sarah said. "I know you must be weary after such a long journey. Jane has hot tea waiting."

Ann Andrews took Hannah's hand in hers and motioned to her husband. "This is Sarah's Hannah," she said.

Hannah half-curtsied as she had been taught to show respect to visitors. "Welcome to our home, Sir."

John Andrews took Hannah's arm and smiled down at her. "You look just as I expected from what Nate McIntyre said."

Hannah was glad that her mother and grandmother had walked on toward the house and that the boys were too busy with the Andrews' baggage to heed their conversation. "He spoke to you about me?" Hannah asked.

"Quite a bit. But of course it was in the strictest confidence—" John Andrews began, then was interrupted by the arrival of Joshua, who had returned to make sure that the boys had all the luggage.

What had Nate said about her? The question nagged Hannah all that afternoon, but she never had the opportunity to ask either Mr. Andrews or her grandmother about it privately.

Even if Nate told them he had asked me to marry him, that was months ago. He's probably changed his mind by now, Hannah thought. At one time she would have been relieved to think that he was no longer interested in her, but now Hannah found herself recalling the way Nate had looked when he'd asked her to share his new life in Kentucky.

A girl could do worse than marry an older man, especially if he has money and is willing to spend it on her. Hannah had heard those words only last year, when Eleanor Hopkins, the Lynches' bond servant, had wed the widower Amos Hargrove, who was more than twice her age. He had bought up Eleanor's remaining time and moved her into his big fieldstone house on Dutchman's Creek, where she had her own servants and reportedly was treated like a queen. But Hannah had privately wondered how a young girl like Eleanor could stand to wed a man like stout, red-faced Amos Hargrove, whose features seemed frozen in a perennial scowl.

Later, after Eleanor and Amos Hargrove had been married for some time, Hannah learned that she had been the man's first choice. "Your father never seriously considered Mr. Hargrove's suit, of course," Sarah had assured Hannah when she saw her horror at the thought. "Amos isn't the first widower to look for a young wife, and he surely won't be the last. A man alone seldom stays that way if he can find a willing helpmeet."

Nate had always been a man alone, and apparently he wanted to change that before he moved to Kentucky. Yet Hannah was almost certain that there had been more than the practical necessity of having a helpmeet behind Nate's proposal. She thought he was also fond of her, or at least he had seemed to be in October. But in six months, many things could change. Certainly much was different around the Yadkin since Nate had seen Hannah.

I'll know as soon as I see him if Nate still wants to marry me, Hannah thought. If he didn't, she couldn't blame him—looking back, she knew she'd given him little cause to hope that she would agree to be his wife. On the other hand, if he still felt the same way about her, marrying Nate McIntyre would effectively remove Clay Scott as a constant source of concern.

In the meantime, the arrival the next morning of Adam and his family kept Hannah's mind off herself. The emotional reunion of Adam Craighead with his mother and Mary Andrews Craighead with her father brought tears to all eyes. Little Annie Craighead immediately won her grandmother's heart when she toddled to her without prompting and called her "Mama Ann," a name which she apparently made up on the spot. Johnny Craighead was more reserved, but John Andrews was pleased that his grandson shook hands with him and looked him in the eye "like a little gentleman," as he expressed it.

"It's blessed we are all, indeed," Ann said, summing up what each had been thinking. "How proud Caleb Craighead would be of our children and their bairns!"

"I think he knows how we've turned out," Sarah said softly. "I just wish that we could have been nearer one another over the years. And that Uncle Jonathan could have been here for this day."

Ann sighed. " 'Tis na wise to be worried about the things that canna be changed. Jonathan will be back soon and we'll all be together again. Then my earthly joy will be quite complete."

It was quite late in the evening before John and Ann Andrews finally retired to the dwelling that Joshua had built for them, and Adam and his family settled down to sleep in Hannah's room. Hannah lay on a quilt pallet in the attic, too excited to fall asleep. Her grandmother's words raced through her mind: *Jonathan will be back soon and we'll all be together again. Then my earthly joy will be complete.*

With Jonathan McKay would also come Nate McIntyre. Staring into the darkness, Hannah wished she could be certain that Nate still wanted to marry her. She imagined the look on Clay Scott's face when he heard that Hannah was to marry someone else and leave the Yadkin forever. Clay might profess—and even feel—sorrow, but Hannah knew that they had no future together. Even though she'd once hoped otherwise, Clay's recent behavior had made that clear. He would always be her first love, but Hannah knew that Clay lacked a strong moral compass.

On the other hand, there was no question that Nate McIntyre was a firm Christian and trustworthy in every way. Hannah didn't feel about him as she had Clay, and she was somewhat hazy about the details of what their life in Kentucky might be like. *But I will go with him if he asks me.*

In fact, Hannah had to admit, she would just about go anywhere with anyone as long as Clay and Marie Scott weren't there. *I must ask Adam what should be done in their case,* Hannah thought uneasily. Having knowledge that there might be a legal problem to their wedding, Hannah felt an obligation to remedy it, even though it didn't seem of much concern to Clay. Marie and her mother and Uncle Jonathan would certainly want the marriage to be legal and binding.

I'd better stop worrying and pray. Hannah knelt on the splintery attic floor and thanked God for the reunion her family had just enjoyed. She asked that something be done to ensure that Clay and Marie's marriage would be legal, and that Uncle Jonathan and Nate McIntyre would soon safely return. *And let Nate McIntyre still want to marry me,* she added.

Hannah slipped back onto her pallet and pulled the covers up under her chin. Then, aware that she had omitted something important, she resumed her kneeling posture. *Dear Lord, I ask these things only if they be in Thy will. Amen.*

Hannah lay back down, closed her eyes, and added a final plea: *But please let them be in Your will. Amen!*

❧

The preaching service the next day was once more well-attended. Everyone lingered afterward, eager to meet Ann and John Andrews, so the family was late returning to the Stones' house.

"I hope you're not going to rush off like you usually do," Sarah said to her brother. "It would break Mother's heart for you not to bide here awhile."

"We'll stay as long as we can, but Mother understands I have duties that can't be too long neglected."

Overhearing the conversation, Hannah bided her time and waited for the opportunity to speak to her uncle in private. Later that day, having been sent a message that Ann and John Andrews had arrived, Davey McKay; his wife, Polly; and their daughter, Mary, arrived, swelling the number of visitors by three.

Polly had been indentured to John Andrews when Davey and Adam had first met her and Mary Andrews in Philadelphia, and both she and her former employer were delighted to be reunited.

"What happened to that scrawny black-haired little girl that used to stomp up and down my stairs and burn the meat? I hardly know this lovely young woman," John Andrews said.

Mary, who regarded Polly more as a dear friend than a former servant, answered for her. "She grew up and married well," she said. "Davey's taken good care of her."

"Aye, and he'd better! 'Tis good to see you again, Davey. How do you fare these days? Is business good, now that the British have given up on their upstart colonies?"

Ann threw up her hands in mock horror. "Business, always business!" she exclaimed. "Never how pretty a place is, or what nice folks may live there, but how is the business. What can be done wi' such a man?"

"I'd say ye did the right thing to bring him here, Aunt Ann. There's more ways to make money around here than in Pennsylvania, and that's a fact." Davey McKay spoke earnestly, but his wife laughed.

" 'Tis a fact that his head is full of ideas he's no money to carry out," Polly said. "But these folk didn't come all this way to hear y' rattle on—I expect Mr. John might want to see our little Mary."

Hannah had been holding the child since Davey and Polly's arrival, and now she brought the dark-haired little girl closer for inspection.

"And so I do," he declared. "What a pretty little thing she is! In fact, I've never seen such healthy children anywhere. Do you not have the fever in these parts?"

"Aye, the Lord has blessed us with healthy babes, and Aunt Sarah's a good healer," Davey replied. "Uncle Jonathan always said that betwixt my mother and Aunt Sarah, babies never had a chance to stay sick very long."

"Sukey taught me many new ways of healing," Sarah said, and for a moment those who had known her fell silent, remembering the gentle Delaware

Indian woman who had borne Jonathan McKay six healthy children before the birth of the last took Sukey's own life.

"When do y' think the hunters will be back?" Davey finally asked. "I've a notion to stay here 'til then, if Aunt Jeanette can find the room for us all, that is."

"I'm sure she'll be more than happy to have you, especially now that Marie's gone," Sarah assured him.

"As for when your father and Nate will be back, it should be soon," Joshua said. "A fellow crossing the ferry yesterday said he was sure he'd seen Jonathan McKay on the Trading Trail near Fincastle not a week ago. If that's so, he could be here any day."

What about Nate? Hannah thought, but fortunately Sarah asked the question so she didn't have to.

"You mean he was alone? I hope nothing has happened to Nate. He planned to come back with Uncle Jonathan."

"I wouldn't worry about him," Davey said. "Like as not, they went their separate ways to do their tradin'. Seems to me like Nate said somethin' about takin' his pelts to Philadelphia to get the best price. Well do Adam and I know how far it is from here to there."

"Well, just as soon as Nate comes, we'll have a play-party the likes of which the Yadkin has never seen," Sarah declared. "We'll get James and Susannah here from Salisbury, and with everyone together, what a time we'll have!"

John Andrews, who sat next to Hannah, winked at her. "I guess there'll be another reason to celebrate, eh?"

Hannah was glad that no one else had heard his remark. "I don't know, Sir. It wouldn't be seemly to say anything until Mr. McIntyre gets here."

"Ah, so you've not told your parents, then—Nate doubted that you would, but I thought you might have. McIntyre's a fine fellow, you know, and with the war finally over and the British out of the way of our trade, he's smart to be going to Kentucky. It's a fine place to do business just now."

Hannah felt uncomfortable with the thought that Nate had seemingly shared all his plans with the Andrews. "I don't know about that, but I hope you won't repeat anything that Mr. McIntyre might have said concerning me."

John Andrews smiled and winked again. "My lips are sealed, young lady. He spoke to me in confidence, and so it will remain. But let me be the first to offer you my best wishes, just in case."

He must think Nate will marry me, Hannah realized. But John Andrews hadn't seen Nate for months, and many things could have changed since then. In anguished impatience to know the outcome of the rest of her life, Hannah silently prayed that Nate would come back soon.

It was late the following afternoon before Hannah finally found the opportunity to speak privately to her uncle. Asked to gather prickly ash and dogwood bark for her mother to make infusions, Hannah invited Adam to go with her. He carried the gathering basket and sharp knife as Hannah hitched her skirts and plunged into the woods behind the springhouse.

"One of my earliest and fondest memories is of herb-gathering with Sarah and Mother," Adam said. "Most of the time they made me stay at home with Father, but I always begged to go along."

"Mother seldom speaks of those days," Hannah said. "They must not have been very happy."

"Then it wasn't a matter of being happy but simply surviving. After Sarah and I were taken by the Seneca, nothing was ever the same."

"You were so young then; you mustn't recall much about it."

"A bit here and there, but I'll always carry the reminder." Adam gestured toward his chest, which Hannah knew bore a twisted scar.

"Mother must remember every detail, but she's said little about it."

"When bringing them to mind causes pain, some experiences are best forgotten."

Such as my encounter with Clay Scott, Hannah thought. She stopped and pointed out a young dogwood. "Mother wants to make a soak for sore muscles from dogwood bark. Strip off a narrow piece lengthwise, with the grain," she directed. "Otherwise, the tree might die of the shock."

Adam smiled faintly. "I see that you have developed your mother's talent for ordering people around."

"Did I sound bossy? I didn't mean to—I suppose that's just my way. Let's get another strip from that larger dogwood, then we'll need some chunks of bark from yonder prickly ash. Chewing it ought to ease Aunt Jeanette's toothache."

"It's good that you've learned to gather and make medicals—'tis a badly needed skill. Vera Scott said yesterday that she credits Sarah and you for saving Clay's life."

Hannah swallowed hard and tried to think of what she should say. The mention of Clay's name offered an opening for her to speak of him and Marie, yet now that she had the opportunity, Hannah didn't know how to begin. "If so, it was Mother's doing, not mine. All I did was change Clay's dressings and chore for the Scotts."

"That was important, though. After all, Jesus tells us that what is done to the least of His children is counted as service to Him, as well."

"Yes, I know." *I must speak now or never,* Hannah told herself. She took a deep breath and turned to face her uncle. "Sir, there's a matter I must speak to you about."

Immediately Adam gave Hannah his full attention. His grave hazel eyes regarded her with interest. "Surely you're not concerned about your salvation, Hannah?"

"No, Sir. I reckon that's as secure as it'll ever be. But something has come up that I don't know what to do about."

"Perhaps if you tell me, I can help."

Hannah stared at the ground and uneasily shifted her weight. There was a moment of silence while she sought the right words. "I have reason to believe that Clay and Marie aren't legally wed," she finally managed to say.

Adam sounded astonished. "What makes you think so?"

Hannah raised her eyes to his and spoke earnestly. "It was something Clay said. No one else knows, not even Marie—and no one else must know. It's bad enough that they didn't wait for Uncle Jonathan's blessing. I don't know what he might do if he found out they aren't even really man and wife."

Adam placed a comforting hand on her shoulder. "Don't worry, Hannah. If it is true, the matter can be remedied easily enough. No doubt they'll be happy to repeat their vows in the presence of their families when Uncle Jonathan returns."

Relieved, Hannah impetuously threw her arms around her uncle, upsetting the gathering basket and sending half the bark to the ground. "Oh, thank you, Uncle Adam! You always know exactly what to do."

"The Lord knows that's not true," he said, but he smiled as he bent to retrieve the strips of bark.

Another thought struck Hannah, and once more she turned to her uncle. "There's one more thing—" she began, but he did not let her finish.

"Don't worry—what you told me will stay between us."

From the way Adam looked at her, Hannah was almost positive that he must know that she cared for Clay Scott. She wanted to assure him that she no longer did, but perhaps it was best just to leave things as they were. "I'm glad you understand," Hannah said. "We'd better go now, or it'll be too dark for you to take the children to the ferry."

The next morning Hannah awoke with a strange feeling that this might be the day that Jonathan McKay returned home. After what her father had said, she no longer expected Nate to be with him, but when the word came that afternoon that Uncle Jonathan had reached the ferry, she joined the others who had already started out to meet him on the road.

They hadn't gotten very far when in the distance they spotted Joshua and Davey, and riding alongside them, Jonathan McKay.

"Oh, look how thin he is!" Jeanette exclaimed.

"No more than usual," said Sarah. "Hunters always lose weight in the wilderness, but he'll soon fatten up."

"His beard and hair are much whiter, too," Jeanette said. "There's no telling what he's been through this time."

"At least, praise God, he's come back to us safely," Sarah said, but Jeanette, already running toward her husband, didn't hear her.

Jonathan dismounted and embraced his wife. "Where's little Jacques?" he asked her.

" 'Tis his nap time. Jane is watching him. He'd have been too cross had I wakened him now."

Jonathan nodded and turned to greet the others. "Nate didn't come back with you?" Sarah asked when he embraced her.

Glad that her mother had asked the question that might have seemed strange for her to pose, Hannah tried not to appear too interested in her uncle's reply.

"Nay. He's probably somewhere betwixt here and Philadelphia—he has much to attend to before going to Kentucky," he said.

"I was hoping he'd be on hand to play for us now that we're all here," Jeanette said. "Joshua has probably told you that your sister and John Andrews arrived last week?"

"Aye. I'm glad they were able to get away so soon." Jonathan turned back to Jeanette.

"Joshua tells me ye have some other important news," he said.

Jeanette flushed and looked away. "Not yet, Jonny," she said in a low voice. "I'll tell you when we get home."

"Hannah and I'll let the folks know you're safely arrived," Sarah said quickly. "We'll expect you all to supper this evening."

Davey and Joshua rode back to the ferry, and Sarah and Hannah turned toward the house, leaving Jonathan and Jeanette alone.

"Your father shouldn't have said anything at all to Uncle Jonathan," Sarah said.

"I suppose he thought it'd be easier on him to be a bit forewarned," Hannah said.

"I doubt if it will help. My uncle has always cared for Jeanette's children like they were his own flesh and blood, and the news that Marie wouldn't wait even a few weeks for his blessing will be hard for him to bear."

"Uncle Jonathan will be upset at first, but I think he'll soon get over it," Hannah said. "Having the family together again will be a great distraction."

Sarah ventured a small smile. "For them, perhaps, but not for us. We must make provisions to feed all of these people. We'd best get home and make sure there's food enough in the larder."

By the time the Scotts arrived for supper that night, Jeanette had broken the news of Clay and Marie's elopement. Jonathan went immediately to the Scotts' to see them before they all joined the rest of the family at the Stones' home.

Whatever had passed between Marie and her stepfather, Hannah noted that her uncle seemed a great deal more restrained than he usually was on his return from long-hunting. However, he seemed more sad and hurt than angry or outraged. Clay and Marie sat flanked by his grandmother and her mother, as if they had to protect them from the others. Marie's eyes were red-rimmed, while Clay sat rigid and unsmiling. Both looked like children who had just been punished and sent to a corner to consider their transgressions.

Adam blessed the food and thanked God that the family had been reunited after so many years apart. The children had been fed earlier but weren't inclined to believe that they should go to bed just yet. They raced around the board tables that had been set to accommodate the diners and made conversation almost impossible until their respective mothers tired of the din and took them away.

In the sudden silence that followed the children's departure, Adam spoke to Clay and Marie. "I've not yet performed a wedding at the new meeting-house," he said. "Would you two like to repeat your vows there? I'm sure it would please your families."

Clay's face darkened for a moment as if in anger, but he said nothing. Marie looked startled and turned to see how her mother regarded the suggestion.

"Oh, could you, Adam? It would mean a great deal to Jonny and me to know that Marie was wed in God's house and with the blessing of her family."

Jonathan turned to Marie, a look of consternation on his face. "Ye weren't married in a church, Lass?"

Marie's cheeks pinkened. "No, Uncle Jonathan. Something about repeating the banns," she murmured, but Clay interrupted her.

"I have a marriage certificate signed by Justice Thurman," he said defensively.

"And you'll have another signed by me," Adam said.

"Oh, that's a wonderful idea!" Jeanette exclaimed. She turned to her husband. "Don't you think so?"

Jonathan looked uncomfortable, but he nodded stiffly. "I suppose it can't hurt anything," he said.

Uncle Adam knew exactly what to say, Hannah thought. She smiled at her uncle in relieved gratitude. Looking around her family circle, Hannah felt a sudden tide of love for them. They'd all been through many hard times, but they never stopped loving each other—or the Lord. No matter what might lie ahead in the days to come, Hannah was thankful for the heritage of faith her family had made possible for her to claim for herself.

"We lack only one thing to celebrate this marriage—" Sarah began.

"Nate McIntyre's music," Joshua finished for her.

"Oh, yes!" Vera Scott exclaimed. "If he was just here now, what a play-party we could have!"

"I hope Nate won't tarry too much longer a-gettin' here," Davey said. "Polly and I can't bide here much longer."

"Then ye can come back when Nate plays for the party," Jonathan said, and Hannah knew then that it was all right. All was settled except for one thing: whether another wedding would also be celebrated then.

Chapter 8

Susannah arrived the next day, alone, saying that her husband, James, would be along in a day or two to pay his respects to the family.

"Even though the war is over, people still call James and Susannah Tories, and it goes hard with them," Sarah told Hannah privately. "They're considering leaving Carolina altogether; it's gotten so bad."

"Where would they go?"

Hannah wasn't surprised when her mother shrugged and said, "To Kentucky, perhaps. That seems to be the place to remove to these days."

That means that Susannah and James might even be my neighbors one day. Although she couldn't yet say anything about it to Susannah, the possibility brought Hannah faint comfort.

The next day the families gathered at the meetinghouse, where Adam read the standard Westminster marriage service for Clay and Marie. Jeanette wept as her daughter entered on Clay's arm, wearing her best dress and carrying a bouquet of greenery and daffodils that Hannah had gathered early that morning. After the ceremony, everyone went to the Scotts', where Clay's grandmother provided a wedding breakfast.

"That service was a wonderful idea, Reverend," Vera Scott told Adam. "I'm so happy that you suggested it. We all felt bad that we weren't there when Clay and Marie said their vows."

"It was my pleasure, Ma'am," Adam replied gravely.

Clay managed to speak to Hannah when no one was looking their way. "I hope you're satisfied," he asked. "Don't think I don't know whose idea this was."

"It certainly wasn't my idea for you to marry Marie in the first place," Hannah said, then immediately wished she could take back the words.

"It wasn't mine, either," Clay said. "If only—"

"I hope you and Marie will be very happy," Hannah said loudly as she saw her mother approaching.

Later, only Hannah noticed how Adam drew Clay to one side and appeared to speak quite earnestly to him.

"I told Clay I would record the marriage at the county seat," Adam told her when she questioned him about it after they got home.

"Then it's legal?" she asked, and Adam nodded.

"That knot is tied on earth as well as in heaven. I reckon you'll have to find something else to worry about now," he teased.

"That shouldn't be hard to do around here," Hannah said tartly.

The next day Adam reluctantly departed, leaving his wife and children with the Stones and promising to return when Nate arrived. Davey and Polly left the following day, expressing disappointment that they'd missed seeing him.

"Maybe Nate's decided not to come here at all," Hannah suggested to her uncle that evening.

"He said he'll be here, Lass, and I've ever known him to be a man of his word."

Surely Uncle Jonathan must know that Nate asked me to marry him, Hannah thought, but since he hadn't said or done anything to indicate it, she certainly wouldn't bring it up.

Patience, Hannah told herself, but it was hard to be patient when the rest of her life awaited the arrival of the man who might hold her fate in his hands. Many nights Hannah slept poorly, and during the days she often dreamed at her chores, imagining what might happen when Nate McIntyre finally reached the Yadkin again. The days turned to weeks, and when March was more than half-over, still Nate hadn't come.

Early one morning as Hannah walked to the springhouse, she considered how she should conduct herself when she saw Nate. *Like as not,* she reasoned, *I'll at least have warning that he's on his way from the ferry.* Hannah would have time to put on a fresh apron and tuck her wiry red curls under her mobcap. She'd stand back and let everyone else greet Nate first, she decided. She'd look calm and demure and wait for Nate to make the first move. If he indicated that he still wanted to marry her, then she'd bestow on him a seemly show of affection—but not until then. Hannah had been hurt once. She was in no hurry to invite more heartache in case Nate had changed his mind about wanting to marry her.

Reaching the springhouse, Hannah hummed as she fit the dasher to the churn. It seemed a very long time ago that Nate had stood in this very place and sung about a lonesome dove. In the distance, a mourning dove's call floated on the still air, and Hannah cupped her hands to her mouth and repeated the notes the way Aunt Sukey had taught her to do.

"We Delaware can make the birds talk to us. Sometimes the Lenni-Lenape warriors use the birds' calls to signal each other so their enemies will not know they are near," Sukey had told Hannah.

"The Seneca warriors who took me and Adam used the owl's call as one of their signals," Sarah had said then. Although Hannah wished that her mother would talk more about being an Indian captive, only rarely did she mention it, and she never said much. "That was long ago and far away, and only the here and now matters," her mother would say when anyone pressed for more details.

Hannah waited a long moment without hearing the dove again, then repeated the notes, holding the final one until she ran out of breath.

This time, an answer came almost immediately from the woods east of the springhouse, and instinctively Hannah turned, half expecting to see a mourning dove perched on a branch in one of the surrounding elm trees.

Instead, a tall figure walked out of the woods. Tendrils of the morning mist parted and swirled around his leggings. He looked very much like an apparition, but when he spoke, Hannah knew that what she saw was real.

"You're pretty good at that," Nate McIntyre said.

Hannah gasped and held on to the dasher pole to steady herself. She had left the house bareheaded, in her oldest, most tattered dress, and with her hair still in its single nighttime braid. She gulped air and tried to speak, but she barely managed a whisper.

"So are you."

Hannah knew she shouldn't stare at Nate, but she couldn't help it. He was taller and thinner than she remembered, but the greatest change was in his face. He had shaved his beard, apparently fairly recently, revealing the lines etched deeply around his mouth. The ruddy glow of his complexion, combined with his dark hair and eyes, made Nate look somehow foreign, exotic, and gypsylike. However, his garb was still that of the hunter and woodsman. He wore obviously new, unstained buckskins, and his hair was pulled back from his face and tied with a rawhide strap.

Nate stopped a few feet short of Hannah and held out his hands, palms up, in a gesture of appeal. "Do I look so bad to ye, Lass?" he said quietly.

You look older and wilder, and not at all the way I thought that you would, Hannah could have said, but she merely shook her head.

"Will ye come to me, then?"

Is this Nate's way of repeating his proposal? Hannah realized that her carefully made plans for their reunion had come to naught. By seeing her alone first, Nate must mean to make sure of Hannah's mind before he spoke to her father.

Hannah looked down at her knuckles, white from gripping the dasher pole, and felt a moment of panic. Her whole life might depend on what she did in the next few seconds, and now that the time of decision was upon her, Hannah felt suddenly unsure of herself.

Help me, Lord, she prayed.

It seemed that an eternity passed, but in reality it could only have been a few seconds before Hannah felt the blood returning to her face. She took a deep breath and raised her eyes to meet his. "Yes," she whispered, too low to be heard.

Hannah half-turned and put a foot out, but before she could take even one step, Nate quickly sprang forward. With a loud whoop, he picked Hannah up and twirled her about until she cried out in alarm. When he set her down, Hannah looked into his eyes and knew that he hadn't changed his mind about marrying her, after all. If she wanted him, Nate McIntyre was hers.

Nate smiled down at her. "Did ye get my letter a few months back?" he asked.

"You wrote me a letter? No, I didn't."

"Not to ye alone, but to the family. I tried to let ye know I was bringing a surprise."

Hannah nodded. "Aye, we got that letter. Besides shaving off your beard, what's the other surprise?"

Nate ran the back of his hand across his cheeks as if he hadn't remembered his beard was gone. "Did ye like it? I can always grow it back."

"It's not that I don't like it—I'm just not used to it," Hannah said. *Or to the idea that you'll become my husband.*

"There'll be plenty of time for that, I reckon. Come and see what I brought ye."

Nate took Hannah's hand and led her through the woods to a small clearing where several horses were tethered to a low-bending sapling. She recognized Nate's saddle horse, the same one he'd ridden for years, and his packhorse, a wide-backed animal he'd rescued some time back from a trader who'd beaten it half to death. But the other one she didn't recognize. It was a pale shade of buckskin, with an even lighter mane and tail.

Nate patted the animal's withers and turned to Hannah. "Well, what do ye think of her?"

"She's mine?" Hannah blinked and put a timid hand out to touch the horse's velvety nose. She felt that she might be in the midst of a waking dream, and that soon she'd open her eyes and be back at the springhouse, with the butter spoilt in the churn.

"All yours," Nate said, while his eyes sent the message, *As I am, Hannah.*

"Does she have a name?"

"She answers to Shadow, but ye can always change it."

"No, Shadow suits her. Can I ride her now?"

Nate laughed. "Lacking a saddle or blanket? I think not. But ye can lead her to the house if ye like."

"Oh, I can't be seen garbed like this!" Hannah exclaimed, suddenly remembering how disheveled she must look.

"I brought ye a dress, too," Nate said almost shyly, "It's in my saddlebag, but I reckon mebbe this wouldna be the proper time for ye to be tryin' it on."

"No, it wouldn't—and anyhow, I've got to get back to the butter before it ruins, and you must be wanting breakfast. You're bound to find someone at the table. With so many in the house, it seems we're feeding people constantly."

You're chattering like an idiot, Hannah chided herself. Nate didn't seem to notice.

"Ah, Hannah, I'm happy that ye came to the springhouse this morning. I came the long way around to keep from being seen at the ferry. I spent last night in the woods, hoping that I'd see ye first, before the others knew I was here."

I'm glad you did, Hannah thought, but she was somehow reluctant to let him know it. "Everyone's been looking for you for days and wondering when you'd come."

"It's been a long, hard trip, but thank the Lord, I'm safely here at last."

Nate put his arms around Hannah and held her close. His buckskin shirt was soft under her cheek, but Hannah felt tense and self-consciously awkward in his embrace. *Nate's taller and thinner than Clay,* she thought, and tried to put from her mind how much better she had fit into Clay Scott's arms.

Nate released Hannah and traced the outline of her lips with his fingertip, then bent and lightly kissed her forehead. "I suppose it's time I talked with Joshua about us," he said.

Us, Hannah thought, and shivered slightly. It was still hard for her to think of Nate and herself as a pair. Hannah inclined her head in a brief nod.

"After that, I have some new songs for all to hear. Tend to your work and hurry back to the house."

"I will," Hannah promised, but Nate had already turned away to unhitch the horses.

In a daze Hannah returned to the springhouse. She was almost surprised to find everything was just as she had left it. The dasher handle tilted at an angle where she had dropped it to go to Nate. Hannah's fingers trembled as she clasped the handle and began to churn again. The liquid sloshing of the cream told her that her earlier work had gone for naught; it would be some time yet before the butter came.

That's just as well, Hannah told herself. The others would greet Nate and talk to him while he ate breakfast. She would have time to sneak up the back stairs, change her clothes, and brush her hair, then reappear as if she had no idea at all that Nate McIntyre had arrived. Or would Nate have told them that he had seen her?

Hannah sighed. To be engaged to a man—and if Hannah understood what had passed between them that morning, she and Nate would marry if her father approved—and yet to know no more about him than she knew about what Nate might do was somewhat unsettling.

Maybe we can get to know one another better before we go to Kentucky, Hannah thought, but there'd probably be little time for that. Soon the dogwood would bloom, the universal sign that it was time to plant corn. Nate would certainly want to be in Kentucky by then. Hannah put both hands around the dasher and said a prayer of thanks for Nate's safe return. *And, Lord, help us both through the uncertain days ahead,* she added.

As Hannah knew would be the case, as soon as the Stone and McKay households knew that Nate McIntyre had returned, he immediately became the center of attention. After a long talk with Jonathan McKay, Nate visited with Hannah's grandmother and John Andrews for some time. He related the news that he had heard in Philadelphia and gave John Andrews some of the most recent newspapers, which the older man took gratefully and retired to read. It was midmorning before Sarah realized that Nate hadn't yet seen Joshua and sent Luke to tell him that his friend had returned.

"Why didn't you use the ferry?" Joshua asked Nate almost immediately.

"I'll explain it to ye on the way to the stable," Nate said. "There's something there I want ye to see."

Hannah watched the men walk away and wished she could hear what Nate was saying to her father. She thought it likely that Nate would show Father the horse he brought her and then ask for her hand. Hannah found chores that kept her near the back porch so she would see them as soon as they returned.

When I see their faces, I'll know how Father took Nate's request, Hannah told herself, but an hour later when the men finally scraped their shoes on the stone beside the back porch and entered the house, nothing in either of their expressions hinted at the outcome of their meeting.

"Where's my wife?" Joshua asked Jane. He didn't even glance at Hannah, who stood kneading bread at the trestle table near the cooking fire.

"She's over to Miz Jeanette's, plannin' that party," Jane replied. Immediately Joshua strode off, alone, toward the McKay house.

Her hands still sticky with dough, Hannah followed Nate into the main house. "What did Father say?" she asked him.

"He wants to speak with your mother before giving me an answer."

"Why? You're Father's dearest friend, and Mother has known you almost as long as he has."

Nate smiled wryly. "Too long, perhaps. Joshua had assumed me past marrying anyone, much less a lass young enough to be my daughter."

"That's not fair!" Hannah exclaimed.

"What are you complainin' about now?" asked Isaac, who entered the house just in time to overhear Hannah's last remark. Then he saw her companion and grinned broadly. "Uncle Nate! I didn't know you were back. How are you?"

Nate put his right hand out to Isaac and clapped him on the shoulder with the other. "Hello, Isaac. I'm better than I have any right to be, I'm sure. Your father tells me the doctor has taken ye on—I'm surprised to see ye here in the middle of the day."

"I came for some physics. Dr. Willson has a fever patient in need of Mother's decoctions."

"She's at Aunt Jeanette's," Hannah told him.

"I'll go on over, then." Isaac turned to Nate. "When's the party going to be?"

"What party is this that everyone seems to know about but me?" Nate asked.

"Why, the wedding party, of course," Isaac replied.

Nate looked questioningly at Hannah. "Wedding?"

"Didn't anyone tell you that Marie just got married? Everyone's been waiting to have the celebration until you could be here to play your fiddle for it."

"Oh, that." Nate seemed amused. "Yes, I heard that Marie and the Scott fellow had eloped. Joshua said there'd be a party tomorrow evening. I hadn't thought of it as being just for them."

"It won't be," Hannah said quickly. "As usual, everyone who wants to come will be invited."

"Then I must test my fiddle," Nate said. "Do ye know where it is, Hannah?"

"I'll get it for you."

Hannah had visited its storage place in the attic several times since her father had put the fiddle there in October. Now, as always, when Hannah opened the box and removed the instrument, she took pleasure in its simple beauty and the sheen of its highly polished wood.

"I can teach ye to play if ye've a mind to learn," Nate said from the doorway.

Hannah shook her head. "I fear I'd ruin it."

"Nonsense. Ye hold it so—" Nate turned the fiddle in her hands. Awkwardly Hannah fitted it to a spot just below her collarbone. "Now draw the bow over the strings."

Hannah's attempt produced an almost-human screech of distress. Nate chuckled and stood behind her. He put his right hand over hers to guide the bow and placed the fingers of his left hand over the fiddle's neck.

"Now try again," he directed. This time, the sound was more pleasing, and Nate guided her hand as he fingered a few more notes. "Not bad—you could learn," he said.

Hannah was keenly aware of Nate's nearness and the light pressure of his hand on hers. Abruptly she lowered the fiddle and turned and offered it to him. Nate took it but kept hold of her right hand while he replaced the fiddle in its box. He looked at Hannah intently.

"There is so much I want to share with ye, Hannah." Nate lowered his head and moved toward her. *He's about to kiss me,* Hannah realized.

However, just before Nate's lips touched hers, Hannah's mother called out her name. Nate took a step back from Hannah just as Sarah and Joshua entered the attic.

To her dismay, Hannah saw that her mother had been crying, while her father's expression was uncharacteristically stern.

Sarah fiercely embraced Hannah as if to hold her back from some great danger. "Oh, Hannah, how can you even think of going to Kentucky after all the horrible things that have happened there?" she cried.

The obvious distress of her usually calm parents disturbed Hannah. She looked at Nate, her eyes imploring him to speak for her.

"As I told Joshua, the dangers that the early settlers faced are now largely past," he said. "I wouldna take Hannah into harm's way."

Sarah took her daughter's hand and looked levelly at Joshua and Nate. "So you say. Leave us now, please. I will speak with Hannah in private."

"But, Wife—" Joshua began, then was immediately silenced by Sarah's expression.

"We'll be downstairs," Nate said. *Take courage, Lass,* his eyes told Hannah.

When the men had gone, Sarah sank down on a stack of cherry wood planks that Joshua was drying to fashion into a larger dining table. She motioned for Hannah to sit beside her but remained silent for a long moment.

"I scarce know where to begin," Sarah said, then again fell silent.

"I thought you and Father liked Nate," Hannah finally said, her tone almost making it a question.

"We do, but neither of us ever thought—had you ever once even hinted that Nate McIntyre was courting you, it'd be different. I'm hurt that you didn't confide in your own mother."

Sarah looked as if she might cry again, and hastily Hannah took her mother's hand in hers and squeezed it. "I wasn't sure that Nate was serious. He said very little to me, and that just before he and Uncle Jonathan left. Also, I figured he'd probably change his mind."

Sarah shook her head sadly. "Well, he didn't. He wants to wed you, but to his credit, only with our blessing."

"And will you and Father give it?" Hannah drew in her breath and waited for her mother's reply.

Sarah sighed. "It's not that simple. We know Nate to be a good man, and if he intended to settle hereabouts, we could overlook the matter of his age. But traipsing off to Kentucky and you a mere girl—Hannah, you have no idea what life in the wilderness is like."

"I realize it's not easy. But Nate knows the land like the back of his own hand. I'm sure he'll take good care of me."

Sarah made a derisive sound. "Like our neighbor Dan'l Boone took care of his wife? I well recall how Rebecca came back here after Indians killed her eldest boy and kidnapped their daughter Jemima and the Calloway girls."

"But Rebecca Boone went back to Kentucky," Hannah pointed out.

"Yes, but it took Dan'l months to persuade her to return. And since then, you know how many others from the Yadkin that we've heard about being burned out or captured—or killed. It's not the kind of life your father and I want for our only daughter."

"The frontier will be much safer now that the war is over—I heard Father say so himself not long ago. Anyway, I'm sure Nate wouldn't take me into known danger."

"Aye, but the fact remains that even without the British urging them on, many Indians will keep trying to force settlers away from their old hunting ground. They'll fight to the last man before they'll give up."

Her mother's bitter tone surprised Hannah. "I never heard you speak so ill of Indians. I know you loved the tribe that you grew up among and felt burdened for all those that hadn't heard the gospel."

Sarah dabbed at her eyes with a handkerchief. "The Lenni-Lenape were like my own brothers and sisters, that's true, but even so I never understood all of their ways. Other tribes well deserved to be called 'savages.' I can never, never forget some of the horrors they committed, both on whites and their own. I don't think many Indians have changed their ways since then."

"I always thought you and Adam were well used by the Seneca," Hannah said, making it a question.

Sarah's expression told her daughter otherwise. "No human held by another against their will is well used. God spared Adam and me by His grace. But just as Adam bears that scar on his chest, mine is here, on my heart."

No wonder Mother never wanted to talk about those days, Hannah thought. "I understand," she said softly. "But you and Father and Uncle Adam—and Aunt Sukey and Uncle Jonathan, too—all managed to survive. So will we."

Sarah smiled sadly. "So you already think of you and Nate as 'we,' do you? I recall when it was the same with your father and me."

It isn't that way with us yet, Hannah thought but knew she must not say. Although she felt near to tears herself, Hannah attempted a reassuring smile.

"Will you give us your blessing, then?"

Sarah stood and brushed dust from her skirts. "That is up to your father. But I will speak to him."

"Thank you." Hannah knew the value of her mother's influence, and she gave Sarah a quick hug.

Downstairs, her grandmother sat with Joshua, and their expressions told Hannah that they must have been discussing Nate's proposal.

"Come outside with me, Hannah," Ann Andrews invited. "I want to see your mother's herb garden."

It was a short walk to the plot of ground where Sarah Stone grew herbs and vegetables. Hannah helped her grandmother negotiate the low fence designed to keep out the sheep.

"This plot makes me think of the one I had at Stones' Crossing," Ann Andrews said. "I see Sarah put signs up so ye'll know where to find the plants even when they're not blooming—that's important."

"Yes. Unfortunately, many of the things Mother uses come from bogs and barrens and won't grow in our garden. But with what's here, she can treat almost anything."

Ann nodded. "Aye, I see wintergreen and allheal and comfrey and Indian root. I gave your mother cuttings or seeds and rhizomes for all of them, and many more."

"She still uses the book of physic you made for her," Hannah said.

Ann nodded. "Aye. To us then, Carolina was a completely unknown land. I had no way to know whether Sarah could find the herbals she'd need, so I made sure that she'd have at least some physic ready."

"It must have been hard on you to see Mother move so far away from you and Grandfather," Hannah said.

Ann shook her head. "Times were different then. We were saddened, of course, but we had already been through much, and we'd learned to trust the Lord to keep us all safely folded."

Hannah glanced at her grandmother. "I suppose you know that Nate wants me to go to Kentucky?"

"Aye, so he told us in Lancaster these many months past. He asked us not to mention it to anyone else."

"My parents seem to be set against my marriage to Nate."

Her grandmother frowned slightly and shook her head. "Nay, Lass, I think they're just agin having ye go to the frontier. 'Tis hard for them to bear, knowing what they do about the life."

"But Kentucky isn't like Pennsylvania was in their day," Hannah protested.

Ann put her hand on Hannah's cheek and searched her eyes for a long moment before she nodded. "Aye, Hannah. I can see ye're a brave girl, but ye ought to know what lies ahead."

"You and Grandfather went into the wilderness, and so did Mother and Father," Hannah pointed out. "No one stopped you."

"And perhaps so shall ye and Nate. If the Lord intends it, then all will be well."

"I hope you'll remind my parents of that," Hannah said.

"I already have, my dear. Now help me find the black root for Mr. Andrews. He won't admit it, but his digestion's been out of sorts lately and I intend to give him a good dosing."

Hannah hoped to see Nate when she returned to the house, but he had gone to the ferry with her father. Her mother immediately put her to work on the preparations for the dinner which would be served at the house following the party in the Hendersons' barn.

As she worked, Hannah watched her mother for any sign that she and her father had finally made up their minds about her marriage to Nate but saw none. Neither woman mentioned the issue. Night fell, and Joshua came in, alone, to take the evening meal.

"Nate and the Gospels are at the McKays'," he said in response to Hannah's questioning glance. "We figured it was best under the circumstances," he added.

Although she did not usually challenge her parents about anything, Hannah now confronted her father. "I know that Nate has asked you for my hand. When will you give him your answer?"

Joshua Stone put his hand on Hannah's shoulder and half-smiled. "In a year or so, perhaps, when you're a woman grown," he replied. From his tone, she thought he might merely be teasing her.

However, Hannah's mother had overheard the exchange, and she spoke more seriously as she joined them. "Your father and I intend to seek Adam's counsel in the matter. He'll be here tomorrow."

Chapter 9

For Hannah, the night passed slowly. In the sleepless hours, she considered her situation. Her mother seemed particularly reluctant for Hannah to go to Kentucky, raising fears for her safety that Hannah had never considered. Yet the dangers that might await in the Kentucky wilderness seemed nothing in comparison to the constant heartache Hannah would feel being in almost daily sight of Marie and Clay Scott.

I can't stay here, Hannah told herself. If Nate went on to Kentucky without her, then God would have to show her another way to get out of the Yadkin. In the meantime, she could only pray that Adam would take her part when he spoke to her parents.

Adam rode in alone the next morning and said that the rest of his family were coming with James and Susannah in the large carriage they had inherited from James's grandfather. Since he had been a British official, the carriage had borne the king's crest, which James had hastily removed. However, even after Davey McKay had replaced the royal crest with a circle of thirteen stars to represent the independent colonies, the carriage and its occupants still met with occasional jeers.

"I'm glad that you came alone," Sarah told Adam the moment he dismounted.

"Oh?" Adam looked from his sister to Hannah, who had joined them. Adam regarded her sober expression and the dark circles under her eyes with alarm. "What is it? Has something happened to Mother?"

"Nay, she's fine. However, Joshua and I must speak with you on a most important matter."

"Can it wait 'til I wash off the road dust?"

"Of course. Hannah, have Jane bring water immediately, and then fetch your father. I think he's with Mother and John Andrews."

Hannah did her mother's bidding. When she reached her grandmother's cabin, she saw that both Joshua and Nate were indeed there, and that Nate was talking, the center of attention.

"So I got my original four hundred acres and a preemption of a thousand more. When I go back with surveying equipment, I should be able to make a good patent for several thousand more—" Nate saw Hannah and stopped in midsentence as he stood. "Come in," he invited. "I was just telling your folks about Kentucky."

"I'm sorry to interrupt you, but Uncle Adam is here. Mother wants Father to join them."

Immediately Joshua stood and nodded his farewell to the others. "Stay here," he said to Hannah. "We'll send for you if you're needed."

As soon as her father left, Nate turned to Hannah and smiled. "No doubt my talk was tiring everyone, so your arrival was quite timely."

"Sit down, both of ye," Ann Andrews invited. "And Nate, do go on. From what ye say, Kentucky must be a fair land, indeed."

He nodded. "Aye, that it is, Ma'am. There's more game there than ye ever saw in your life, and streams so full of fish ye can 'most pluck them out with your hands, like the bears do."

"Are there many bears?" John Andrews asked. "I try to stock bear grease in my stores, but it's getting hard to find in Pennsylvania."

"Oh, yes, Sir, there're lots of bears. Kentucky has natural salt licks, and there ye can always find all manner of creatures—bear and deer and elk and moose, too."

"There must be panthers and wildcats as well," Ann Andrews said matter-of-factly.

"Panthers!" Hannah exclaimed. She'd never seen one herself, but she'd heard stories of how in the old days they'd sometimes creep into a cabin at night and take a sleeping child.

"Them and wildcats and wolves, too, but all the settlers have dogs. Their barking either keeps the beasts away or gives fair warning they're nigh."

"Caleb used to burn a fire at night for that purpose, but I never got used to the cries of wolves and panthers. To this day, my blood runs cold just to think of it," Ann said.

"Is all your land in forest?" John Andrews asked Nate, and Hannah suspected that his intent was to change a subject that distressed his wife.

"About half is wooded, but there's also open land, and some rolling hills quite suitable for livestock."

"I take it that you don't intend to farm on a big scale," John Andrews said.

Nate grinned. "Nay, I'm no farmer. I'll always have a vegetable garden and a plot of corn to feed the animals and grind for meal, of course. But most of the land will be an inheritance for my children."

My children, Hannah thought. *Not our children.* Nate hadn't even glanced at her when he said the words, but of course it would be presumptuous on his part to include Hannah until they were wed.

"What about hunting?" asked Ann in the silence that followed Nate's declaration. "Will ye still be doing that?"

"Aye, some, but on my own land or thereabouts—and mostly for food, not pelts. No more trekking into the wilderness for months on end for me. I've had my fill of that life. I want to settle in one place long enough to take root."

Nate looked back at Hannah, and his expression left no doubt that he wanted her to be with him.

"We wish ye well, I'm sure," Hannah's grandmother said. "But I'll readily confess that I'm glad it's ye that'll be going there and not me. As long as it was my husband's calling to preach on the frontier, I went with him and that willingly. But no more!"

"Not even for a visit? I'll be happy to show ye around, and no one could be more welcome."

John Andrews chuckled. "We'll keep it in mind," he said. "But look, here comes a lad—one of the Gospels, I'm sure, but I get them mixed up."

Ann squinted her eyes to make out the slight figure running toward the cabin. "That's John, the youngest," she said. " 'Tis said Luke's too lazy to run."

At the door the boy stopped, too winded to speak for a moment. "Ha. . . Hannah," he finally managed to gasp, "Un. . .Uncle Adam wants t' see y'. He said he'd be a-waitin' at the springhouse."

Hannah and Nate exchanged a quick glance, then Hannah rose and excused herself.

"Tell the reverend I'll see him later," Nate said, and she nodded.

As she hurried to the springhouse, Hannah turned over in her mind the brief encounters she and Nate McIntyre had had there. This time, her uncle would be waiting to question her about Nate. Aware that the outcome of their interview might well affect the course of her life, Hannah felt her heart pounding and her pulse roaring in her ears.

When he saw Hannah, Adam rose from the rock where he sat and put down a book he had been reading. "There's no need for you to hurry so," he said mildly. "I wasn't planning to leave before you got here."

I'm acting more like a child than a woman ready to wed, Hannah thought. She tried to compose herself before she spoke. "What do you have to tell me?"

Adam laughed. "What makes you think I have anything to tell you?"

His unexpected smile made Hannah feel even more insecure. "I thought Mother and Father—" she began, but he quickly interrupted her.

"Our talk is between us alone. However, they did tell me that Nate McIntyre has asked your hand in marriage. What are your feelings about the matter, Hannah?"

Whatever she had thought her uncle might say, Hannah hadn't anticipated that question. She opened her mouth, then closed it again without speaking.

"I admit that I was surprised," he went on when she said nothing. "Especially when Sarah told me that Nate had spoken to you as early as last October."

Hannah looked at the ground and probed a fallen twig with the toe of her slipper. "I didn't think he was serious then."

"Or might it be that you thought a girl your age couldn't consider marrying a man as old as Nate McIntyre?"

Hannah looked at her uncle in surprise. "Is that what they told you?"

"It doesn't matter. I want to hear from your own lips whether you really do want to marry Nate McIntyre."

Despite her best efforts to make it firm, Hannah's voice wavered slightly. "Yes, I want to marry him."

Adam's eyes seemed to be probing her very soul. "Might you also see this marriage as a way to leave the Yadkin?"

Hannah returned his gaze and inclined her head slightly. "Yes."

"If that's all it is, you certainly don't have to marry for that reason. I'm sure that Mother and John Andrews would be more than pleased to take you back to Pennsylvania with them."

Hannah shook her head violently. "No! I wouldn't want to do that."

"Then I must ask one question, Hannah, and take care how you answer. Do you really love Nate McIntyre?"

Why did he ask me that? It was a question that she hadn't thought anyone would raise. Everyone knew many happy, enduring marriages that had begun as a matter of convenience or circumstance rather than of often-fleeting romantic notions.

Hannah swallowed hard and forced herself to return her uncle's steady gaze. "I care for Nate a great deal. And God knows I'll try my best to make him a good wife."

Wordlessly Adam put his arms around Hannah and drew her to him. When she began to cry, he patted her back and murmured words of comfort. "There's no call for tears, Lass. Whatever happens, it'll be for the right," he said.

In the security of her uncle's comforting embrace, Hannah could almost believe it. But in her deepest heart, a nagging question remained.

Will everything really be for the right? Or could agreeing to a loveless match be the biggest mistake of her life?

Sarah said nothing to Hannah when she returned from the springhouse, but Hannah suspected that her mother's preoccupied air wasn't entirely due to her business with the preparations for the supper that would follow the party.

She's worrying whether they should give Nate their blessing, Hannah guessed. She wished she knew what advice her uncle would give them. Hannah wanted to see Nate, but her mother told her he'd taken his horses to be shod and wouldn't be back for awhile.

As the day wore on, Hannah convinced herself that her parents would probably decide to send Nate on to Kentucky without her. Perhaps they had already reached that decision. By the time Hannah went upstairs to get ready for the party, she felt a great deal more dread than anticipation.

Hannah forced a hairbrush through her wiry red curls and considered her uncertain future. If her parents approved the match, she and Nate could be married right away in a service that would be identical to the one just held for Clay and Marie. If they didn't approve, there was little Hannah could do about it. Nate had promised he would not marry her without their permission, and even if Nate would be willing to elope with her, Hannah respected her parents too much to go against their wishes or to do anything that would sever the ties between them.

Hannah sighed. She supposed Nate might wait a few more months in the hope that her parents might change their minds and give their blessing, but such a request wouldn't be fair to Nate. He'd already waited for her a long time, and Hannah instinctively knew that if they were to marry at all, it would have to be now.

By the time Hannah joined her family and their guests—who now included Adam and Mary, Davey and Polly, and James and Susannah—her mood was far from festive.

Susannah linked her arm in Hannah's as they walked, apart from the others, to the Hendersons' barn. "You look too sad for a play-party. Do you have the miseries?"

Hannah smiled faintly. "I suppose so, in a way, but I'm glad to see you looking happier. Are things finally better for you and James in Salisbury?"

The dark, brooding look that Susannah had worn for so many months momentarily returned. "I wish I could say so, but I fear nothing about our situation will improve as long as we stay in Carolina. James wants us to move to Kentucky. He and Uncle Nate have been talking about it ever since we got here."

"How do you feel about going to live in the wilderness?"

Susannah shrugged. "According to Uncle Nate, Kentucky's not a wilderness anymore. Towns and villages are springing up everywhere, he says, and James can find all the work he wants."

"Then you don't mind?"

"Of course I mind," Susannah said somewhat shortly. "I mind that we are still called Tories and no one will give James their custom because of it. I mind that we have to leave what has always been our home, but what can I do if James is set on it? He's my husband."

" 'Whither thou goest, I will go,' " Hannah murmured.

"What did you say?" asked Susannah, looking strangely at Hannah.

"I was thinking of the story of Ruth and Boaz," Hannah said. "But of course when Ruth said 'Whither thou goest, I will go,' she was a widow speaking to her mother-in-law. That doesn't apply in your situation."

Susannah smiled. "Nay, James's mother isn't likely to ask me to go anywhere with her, nor would I be quite so willing as Ruth to glean in alien corn on her account. But with James, I will go anywhere."

And so should it be, Hannah thought. "James is a fortunate man," she said aloud.

When they reached the Hendersons' barn, several dozen people had already assembled, but neither Nate nor the guests of honor were in evidence. Hannah and Susannah claimed a place conveniently located near the water bucket and exchanged greetings with their friends and neighbors. A buzz of anticipation ran through the gathering crowd when Nate made his entrance. Clean-shaven and resplendent in his new buckskins, Nate McIntyre drew many an admiring female glance. *He won't have any trouble finding someone else to go to Kentucky with him if I can't,* Hannah realized with a pang that surprised her in its intensity.

Nate looked around, acknowledging the shouted greetings and scattered applause, until he saw Hannah. Only a few noticed the almost imperceptible nod he made in her direction or saw Hannah nod back. From his expression, Hannah decided her father had not yet delivered any answer.

"Now the party can begin!" someone called.

"Let the man tune up first!" Lem Tucker shouted. Lately he had acquired his own fiddle. He hadn't yet played it in public, but its mere ownership gave him some claim to importance.

"No need for that." Nate held his fiddle aloft and drew the bow across it to show that it was ready. Then, amid applause and laughter, he put it to his chest and began a lively air.

As he finished it with a flourish, the guests of honor entered, almost as if they had waited to make sure they'd be the center of attention. Marie smiled broadly, but Clay's expression was rather somber. He walked slowly, as if trying not to give in to his bad leg.

"Will Clay Scott's limp get any better?" Susannah whispered to Hannah.

"I doubt it. Mother says it's a miracle he can use that leg at all."

Jonathan McKay led Clay and Marie to the center of the gathering. Despite her best intentions not to, Hannah found herself watching Clay and Marie. Marie seemed quite pleased with herself and the man beside her, but Clay—

All the fuss is embarrassing him, Hannah tried to tell herself, but the fact was that Clay looked as if he'd rather be anywhere else, with anyone else, than here in the Hendersons' barn with his new wife and all the Yadkin watching. *He's still the handsomest man here,* Hannah thought. *If only Marie hadn't interfered, this evening would be different.*

"Play a lively tune, Lad!" Lem Tucker said, and those of all ages who had come to form the lines and squares of the schottisches and quadrilles cheered in approval as Nate started a Scottish reel.

Susannah rose to partner her husband, but Hannah declined Isaac's invitation to join him in the square. Nate played several tunes in succession, then set down his fiddle and announced it was time for all to take a brief rest.

As Hannah had expected, Nate started toward her. The crowd around the water bucket stood aside, and Isaac handed the dipper to Nate. "Wet your whistle so's you can sing for us, Uncle Nate," Isaac said. "I want to hear that 'Cornwallis Country Dance' tune again."

"Even with the war over these months?" Nate asked, but the enthusiastic reaction of the others was proof enough that the Carolina patriots hadn't yet tired of poking fun at the British.

'Tis no wonder poor James and Susannah can't bide here longer, Hannah thought. It could be a long time before anti-British sentiment completely died out.

Nate handed the dipper off to someone else and sat down beside Hannah. "How are ye, Lass? I've not seen ye much of late."

"I think 'twas planned that way," she said. "Has my father said aught to you today?"

"He has spoken much about nothing that matters. It is his way, you know."

" 'Tis not a way I care for."

"Wait—you'll see." Nate smiled enigmatically and rose, stretching lazily in the unhurried manner he'd always had of doing everything. With a farewell nod, he went back to the makeshift platform and again took up his fiddle.

Seeing that Nate had returned, a crowd gathered around him and began to call for more requests than a dozen Nates could have managed in a whole week of singing.

"That's enough!" Nate finally called out good-naturedly. "I reckon I'll just play what strikes my own fancy, since I can't suit all of yours. First, here's something ye all seem to favor."

The first chords of the "Cornwallis Country Dance" brought expressions of approval. When a few began to sing it along with him, Nate stopped singing to fancy-up the fiddle accompaniment. When it ended, he played "Froggie Went a-Courtin' " for the children and then started another set of reels.

At the end of the last, Nate put down his fiddle. "Folks, I understand there's some newlyweds amongst us. Stand up and let everyone see ye."

Amid laughter and applause Clay and Marie stood. Marie blushed becomingly, while Clay, his face white against his black hair, managed a weak smile and quickly sat back down.

"This is for ye and any other courtin' couples that might be hereabouts," Nate said. He tilted back his head and with half-closed eyes began the ballad that always made Hannah think of Clay.

" 'Black, black, black is the color of my true love's hair—Her lips are something wond'rous fair—' "

From the moment Nate began to sing, even the children grew quiet. On the other side of Hannah, James reached for his black-haired Susannah's hand. Hannah shivered and fought back tears of self-pity.

Oh, Marie, why did you come between us? By rights, Nate ought to be singing that song for Clay and me. However, since that was impossible, Hannah knew she shouldn't dwell on what might have been.

The spell that Nate's voice wove was so complete that the last note died away in complete silence, the greatest compliment any musician can receive. Then everyone began to applaud wildly. Nate turned toward Hannah and held out his hand.

"Come here," he mouthed, and with a sinking heart Hannah realized Nate must intend for her to sing the "No, Sir" song with him.

A murmur swept through the crowd as she rose and joined him, followed by a scattering of applause amid good-natured comments.

"Don't ask me to sing in front of all these people," Hannah told Nate.

"I'm not. I'll do the singin'—ye just stand right there and listen."

Like Hannah, most of the others expected the "No" song and smiled in anticipation. However, the first sad, sweet notes from Nate's fiddle told them he had something quite different in mind. He played through the melody once, then turned and sang directly to Hannah as if they were alone at the springhouse.

" 'O, don't ye see that lonesome dove that flies from tree to vine?' "

Why is Nate doing this? was Hannah's first thought. Then as Nate sang, " 'He weeps, he moans for his own true love, just as I weep for mine,' " a tremor passed through her body. Surely Nate knew her father well enough to realize that Joshua wouldn't like for Hannah to be made part of such a public display. Hannah dared not look toward her father, fearing what she might see in his face. Nate sang on, adding several new verses to the saga of the lonesome dove who pined away for his love and the man who did the same.

" 'Believe me what I say—Ye are the darling of my heart—Until my dying day, love—Until my dying day.' "

The last words were almost whispered, then after a momentary silence, everyone applauded.

"Well, how did ye like it?" Nate asked Hannah.

" 'Tis lovely, but too sad." From the corner of her eye, Hannah saw her father striding toward them, and she tensed, fearing the worst. But when he reached them, Hannah saw that the intense look on her father's face was not anger, after all, but an opposite, deep emotion. He embraced Hannah, then shook Nate's hand with both of his.

Standing between them, Joshua Stone turned to the gathering and held up both hands for quiet. "I thought you might all like to know that Nate McIntyre here has asked for my daughter Hannah's hand in marriage."

There was a collective gasp, followed by whispered murmuring. Hannah instinctively looked at Clay Scott. Seeing his shocked surprise, she quickly lowered her eyes and hoped he hadn't noticed her watching him.

Her father paused to let his announcement sink in, then continued. "I reckon there's only one other thing left to say—and that is, you're all invited to the wedding!"

Hannah turned to her father. She had to speak loudly to be heard over the noisy approval of the gathering. "Why didn't you tell us before now?"

"Because I didn't make up my mind for certain until I heard Nate sing that song. I'd prayed for some sign, and somehow right then I knew that it was right for you two to be together."

"When's the weddin' gonna be, Stone?" Lem Tucker called out. Everyone laughed when Joshua shrugged his shoulders and looked quizzically at Nate and Hannah.

"That's a matter to be decided between them and Ad—uh, the Reverend Craighead," Joshua said.

A huge grin split Nate's face and once again he pumped Joshua's hand. "The sooner the better," he said. "I figure we need to be on my land by the first of April."

"That's not much time," Joshua said.

Nate looked to Hannah. "Can ye be ready so soon, Lass?"

"I. . .I suppose so." Hannah was too overwhelmed by the realization that she really had permission to marry Nate McIntyre to think about all of the preparations that would be involved.

Joshua raised his hands to halt the buzz of conversation. "Before we go, maybe the Reverend Craighead would like to say a few words."

Adam had been standing only a few steps away. He came forward and embraced Hannah and shook hands with both Nate and Joshua before he turned and spoke.

"I think most of you know that Nate McIntyre needs to be in Kentucky by corn-planting time, so I expect I'll be hearing their vows right soon."

Adam looked at Hannah and took her hand. "We'll all miss our Hannah, but we commit her and Nate to the care of the Lord and trust that all will be well as they journey to their new home."

In the silence that followed Adam's words, Mary Craighead's clear alto began "Blest Be the Tie That Binds," and soon everyone joined in, with Nate taking up the tune on his fiddle.

Hannah saw her mother crying as she sang, triggering her own tears and an almost-overwhelming sadness. *How can I leave my family and our home and all our neighbors and friends?*

Then Hannah glanced over at Clay and Marie and had her answer. She had no choice—a way had opened for her to leave a painful situation, and no matter what she had to leave behind or what might await on the other side, she had to go.

Chapter 10

Hannah and Nate's unexpected engagement soon became the chief topic of discussion at the supper that had been intended only to celebrate Clay and Marie's marriage. However, Clay, at least, seemed relieved not to be the center of attention. Nate sat by Hannah and couldn't stop smiling. He repeated what he had already told the family about his Kentucky land and his plans to go into business there.

Having accepted her husband's decision in the matter, Sarah Stone was already deep into planning the wedding. "I wish I'd had more notice of this marriage," she complained. "A proper dowry can't be gotten up overnight, you know."

"Hannah needs to bring me no dower," Nate said.

Sarah sighed and shook her head. "That shows how ignorant you are of what it takes to make a home, Nate McIntyre. Have you a store of linens and a cook pot? Do you have a milk cow and sheep? Have you wool and flax laid by for spinning and a wheel to spin it on, Sir?"

Nate raised his hands in surrender even before Sarah finished her questioning. "Ye know I don't, but all those things can be gotten as needed."

"So you say, but I'll not have my daughter going into the wilderness without even the most common necessities of life, and that's that, Mr. McIntyre."

"How long will it take you to gather them?" Nate asked, chastened.

Sarah frowned and waved her fingers in the air as if counting before she finally said, "A week, at the least."

Nate nodded. "That should leave us enough traveling time." He looked at Hannah, who had remained silent during the discussion of her future. "How about it, Lass? Will a week do?"

Still unused to the idea that she was truly going anywhere, Hannah nodded. "Whatever Mother says is agreeable with me."

"Then you'll stay right here and not marry," Sarah said quickly. Everyone laughed, but from the corner of her eye Hannah saw Clay Scott looking at her strangely, and she wondered what he thought about her impending wedding.

It doesn't matter, Hannah told herself. She wanted nothing more to do with Clay and Marie; that part of her life would be a closed book once she married Nate and went to Kentucky.

Later that night, Hannah's grandmother, then her mother, gave her some advice about how she should conduct herself as a married woman.

Your husband must always come first, they said. The lives of both women had always demonstrated they shared that belief, so the idea wasn't foreign to Hannah. When at last they stopped talking and Hannah went to bed, she couldn't sleep.

Am I really ready for the responsibilities of marriage? she wondered. *Especially marriage to an older man, used to doing everything his way.*

Hannah stared into the darkness for a long time before she knelt and prayed she would be a good wife to Nate. By keeping her husband happy, a wife would find her own happiness, her mother had said. *I'll try my best,* Hannah thought drowsily. But she knew it wouldn't be easy.

Nate came over the next morning while the Stones were still at breakfast and told Hannah to get her riding clothes. " 'Tis time ye and Shadow got used to one another," he said.

"I usually just tie up my skirts to ride," Hannah said. "Will that do?"

"Around here, but not on the trail. I'll give ye some leggings if ye have none."

"She can have mine," Sarah said quickly. "It's been ages since I needed them."

Joshua looked at Sarah fondly. "At least Hannah won't have to paint her face and play Indian like you once did," he said.

Nate laughed. "Oh, I'd 'most forgotten that story," he said. "Let's see, that must have been about when? About 1758, was it?"

"Did you see her then, Nate?" Hannah asked, trying to imagine that her mother and her future husband had been young together.

"Nay, I'd gone back to scouting by then, but I've heard the story often enough to know it by heart myself."

"And laugh about it, too, I suppose," Sarah said tartly.

Joshua smiled fondly at her. "Well, you have to admit that it was funny when it rained and Sukey's stain started coming off."

Hannah smiled, happy that her parents could still remember with fondness the journey that had brought them together so many years before. *I wonder if Nate and I will share memories like that someday,* she thought.

"To you, perhaps. I don't recall being at all amused," Sarah said. She turned to Hannah. "You'd best go along now—there is much work for us to do to get you ready for your own journey."

"We won't be gone long," Nate promised.

He took Hannah's hand as they walked to the stable, then helped her mount the waiting horse. "I borrowed one of Joshua's saddles—I'll get one for ye in Salisbury later today."

"I don't need anything fancy," Hannah said.

Nate looked at her fondly. "Aye, Hannah, let me spoil ye in the ways I can," he said. "There's so much I won't be able to help ye with—later."

Hannah wasn't sure what he meant, but she nodded. "I'm not used to being fussed over," she said.

"Then it's time you began."

They walked their horses to the road, where Hannah made her new mount trot, then canter.

"This is far enough—time to turn back," Nate said when they had covered several miles.

"I'll race you home," she challenged.

Nate laughed. "Your father warned me you might lead me a merry chase, but I didn't expect it to start quite so soon. All right, Hannah. On your mark, get set—"

At the "Go!" Hannah dug her heels into Shadow's side and slapped the horse's withers with the reins. Shadow reared sideways, pranced a few steps, then settled down into a flat run that slowed only when Hannah reined her in at the Stones' meadow.

Without waiting for Nate to help her, Hannah slid from the saddle and patted Shadow's lathered flanks. "You're a beauty," she said to the horse. "I can already see that we're going to get along."

Nate dismounted and went to Hannah. "I hope ye can say the same about us," he said.

Hannah nodded. "So do I," she said.

Without taking her into his arms, Nate took a step forward, then bent and kissed Hannah on the lips. "I'm honored to have ye to wife," he said quietly.

"I'm honored that you asked me," Hannah replied.

He kissed her again, and this time when Nate's arms tightened around her, Hannah felt a moment of panic as she realized that he probably expected her to return his kiss with as much feeling as it had been given.

I can't, she thought.

He's going to be your husband. You must, something told her. With her eyes shut tight, Hannah pressed her lips to Nate's until he pulled away. Hannah opened her eyes to find Nate regarding her with a strange look on his face.

"Ye may not love me yet, but I love ye enough for the both of us. It'll be all right," he said.

"Oh, Nate—" Hannah began, but Nate covered her lips with a light, brief kiss.

"Not another word," he said. "Go on back to the house and do whatever it is that your mother wants. I'll tend to Shadow, then I'm going on to Salisbury for some things. I don't know when I'll be back. We'll talk later."

However, no such opportunity presented itself immediately. Nate stayed in Salisbury for several days. In the meantime, her mother kept Hannah busy from morning until night as they sorted, discarded, and packed items for her journey. When Nate returned and pronounced the stack far too large, even with the new packhorse he had brought back from Salisbury, the sorting process had to begin anew. Hannah had time to do no more than exchange a few words with Nate, always in the presence of the others.

The wedding arrangements had been quickly made. Adam would deliver a sermon at the meetinghouse on Sunday, after which the family would gather for Nate and Hannah's simple marriage ceremony. Immediately after, the couple would start on their way to Kentucky.

With her future thus settled, Hannah should have felt both joy and relief. Yet Friday night when the whirl of activity had subsided, Hannah realized she felt neither. Sarah noticed her daughter's sadness, but she attributed it to their impending parting and said nothing.

Early Saturday morning, Adam volunteered to help Hannah harvest some medicinal herbs to take with her to Kentucky.

"What's wrong, Hannah?" he asked her as soon as they were out of the house.

"Nothing, so far as I know. What makes you think aught is amiss?"

"The look in your eyes. If you're just having second thoughts about marrying, that's natural and nothing to be concerned about."

Hannah shook her head and avoided looking directly at Adam. "I'm already homesick, even thinking about leaving."

"Yes, I'm sure that's part of it. But it seems to me that you may also be concerned about some burden you're taking with you."

Hannah glanced at her uncle, surprised as always at the way he seemed to have of sensing others' problems. "And what is that?" she asked.

"A kind of burden that will eventually wear you down. If there's anyone here that you haven't forgiven or asked forgiveness from, you'll never have peace, no matter how many miles you put behind you."

Hannah frowned. "I'm not sure I know what you mean."

"If you think ill of someone, you might believe that you can forget it by staying away from them. But you can't, Hannah."

How does Uncle Adam manage to know things about me that I hardly admit to myself? Hannah ventured a sideways glance at Adam. "If that's so, what can be done about it?"

"You've studied the Scriptures—you know what Jesus told us in the

Sermon on the Mount."

"The Beatitudes?" Hannah mentally reviewed them and found none that seemed to fit.

"No, after that. Jesus speaks of what we must do to feel at peace with ourselves."

"There should be a physic for that," Hannah said.

"In a way there is—always remember that God's Word serves that very purpose. And speaking of physic, we'd best start our gathering before the sun gets higher."

All that morning as Hannah helped her mother bundle and label the herbs, she pondered her uncle's words. After lunch Hannah slipped away and took the family Bible to the attic, the one place in the house where she could be alone. Hannah thumbed through its well-worn pages until she found and read the entire Sermon on the Mount. She turned back to Matthew 5:23–24, the verses Adam had alluded to:

> *"Therefore if thou bring thy gift to the altar, and there rememberest that thy brother hath ought against thee; Leave there thy gift before the altar, and go thy way; first be reconciled to thy brother, and then come and offer thy gift."*

Hannah read the passage several times without seeing what it had to do with her. She knew of no one who had anything against her. *Unlike Marie,* Hannah told herself, *I've never knowingly hurt anyone. Marie ought to be asking me for forgiveness. Because of Marie, Clay was forced into a bad marriage. He should be married to me instead. If Uncle Adam only knew how Marie schemed to steal Clay Scott away, he wouldn't be so quick to speak of burdens to me—*

"Read it again."

Something stopped Hannah's self-righteous tirade. Slowly Hannah read the passage aloud. As she did so, the words that hadn't made any impression on her mind began to speak directly to her heart.

First be reconciled to thy brother, Jesus ordered. Making peace wasn't necessarily up to the person who had done wrong. It was also the responsibility of the one who had been wronged.

Hannah sat back and closed her eyes as she considered what the passage should mean to her. *Marie and I don't like each other very much, and we never have.* A few months ago, Uncle Adam had said that Christians didn't have to like people to love them in the Lord. Hannah hadn't understood, and with her usual directness, she had asked him how such love was possible.

"Think of how your parents feel when you misbehave," he had told her then. "You did wrong and they didn't like what you did, but they still love you. It is the same with God. Since we know He loves us and will forgive us even when we sin, then we are obligated to show the same spirit to others."

Hannah tried to pray for God to help her, but she kept seeing the triumphant expression on Marie's face and feeling anew the sorrow that Marie had caused her. Surely, when Hannah was far away in Kentucky with Nate, the memory of Marie's betrayal and Hannah's bitterness would both fade.

No, it won't. Hannah's eyes flew open as Adam's words echoed and re-echoed through her mind: *You'll never have peace, no matter how many miles you put behind you.*

Jesus had made the remedy quite plain. *First be reconciled to thy brother.*

Hannah quickly returned the Bible to its shelf and went into the kitchen to get her bonnet. Her mother and grandmother sat at the table, writing out directions for use of the physics Hannah would take to Kentucky. They looked up when she entered.

"You might help us do this," Sarah said.

"I will later. There's something I must do now."

"Ye look strange, Child," Ann said. "Is everything all right?"

Hannah bent to kiss her grandmother's cheek, then straightened and shook her head. "No, but it will be soon, I hope."

"Wedding jitters," Hannah heard her mother declare as she went out.

"I don't think so," Ann said quietly. "Hannah may have more need of our prayers now than she ever will in the wilderness."

All the way to the Scotts' house, Hannah prayed for the right words to say to Marie. Yet she felt a moment of panic when she reached their door. *Maybe no one is at home,* she hoped.

The door opened almost immediately. Facing Hannah was Clay Scott. Somehow, she hadn't thought that she'd have to see him. For a moment Hannah froze, equally unable to speak or to leave.

"Hannah! What's wrong? Has something happened?" Clay asked.

Hannah swallowed hard and looked past him. "No, I just came to see Marie. Is she here?"

Clay looked relieved and smiled, not quite the boyish smile that had once so captivated Hannah, but one which suggested that they shared a secret no one else knew. "She's with her mother," he said. *As usual,* his tone suggested.

"Oh," Hannah said flatly. "I've been too busy this morning to get over there, so I didn't know—"

Clay stepped out on the porch and closed the door behind him. "I'm glad you're here. There's something I want you to know."

Still uncomfortable being alone with Clay, Hannah folded her arms and waited for him to continue. His face reddened, and he seemed to be having a difficult time framing his words.

"That day I came to your house—" he began, then stopped.

"I thought we agreed to forget it," Hannah said, but she was quite aware that neither had.

Clay sighed. "Well, it was wrong and I shouldn't have done it. I don't know what got into me that day. Marie kept running home to her mother, and she and Grandma weren't getting along—then I got that letter from my captain. All I could think of was how well you and I always got along and how good it would be to leave here and start all over with you."

Hannah regarded him evenly. "I know. I accept your apology. You needn't say anything more."

Again Clay looked relieved. "Thank you, but that's not all. I've done a lot of thinking lately. When your father said you were going to Kentucky with Nate McIntyre, I realized that's what Marie and I should do, too."

"You're going to Kentucky?" Hannah's composure was seriously shaken. *Lord, I don't think I can stand that much.*

Clay chuckled humorlessly. "Nay, that place is too wild for anyone in my shape. But I do plan to take my captain's offer."

Hannah let out her breath in a sigh of relief. "What does Marie think about living in Cape Fear?"

Clay shrugged. "You know Marie—she doesn't want to leave her mother and that little brother of hers. But she won't be outdone. She said if Hannah Stone could go all the way to Kentucky, she can certainly manage Cape Fear."

She still has to keep up with me, Hannah thought and immediately tried to dismiss such ideas.

"I'm happy for you both, then," Hannah said with sincerity that she didn't have to feign.

"And I wish the same for you and Nate."

Clay's blue eyes seemed to be looking into her very heart, where, Hannah knew, there would always be a place for him as her friend. She nodded her acknowledgment, then turned to go.

"Wait—you never said why you're looking for Marie."

"I just want to talk to her. We've not seen much of each other lately."

"I know. But don't say anything about Cape Fear yet—I thought it best to wait until after your wedding to tell everyone."

"I won't. Will you and Marie be coming to the wedding?"

Clay considered her question a moment, then nodded shortly. "If you and Nate want us there."

"Yes, of course we do."

"All right." As if she were one of his male friends, Clay extended his hand to Hannah, and she shook it. "And Hannah—thank you."

Hannah didn't ask why Clay thanked her. No doubt he had figured out that she'd been behind the suggestion that he and Marie should repeat their vows. While Clay had probably resented it at the time, Hannah realized that the ceremony must have begun a profound change for Clay and Marie.

Thank You, Lord, Hannah prayed on the way to the McKay house. *Now please help me talk to Marie.*

Jeanette McKay answered Hannah's knock and looked surprised to see her.

"Since when must you knock at this door, Hannah Stone? Come in. Nate isn't here, though—he and your father are at the ferry."

Jacques toddled over to her and held up his arms to be picked up. Instead, Hannah bent over and hugged him. "Hello, little one. We haven't had much time to play lately, have we?" Then Hannah turned back to Jeanette. "I really came to see Marie. Is she here?"

"Yes, in the kitchen, working on dinner. With all the extra folks here these days, she's been quite a help."

"I hope putting everyone up hasn't been too much strain for you," Hannah said.

"Nay, I feel much stronger now that Jonny's back, and it's not that much extra work. I'm glad you're here. You and Marie haven't seen much of one another since—" Jeanette stopped, then somewhat awkwardly added, "lately."

Hannah found Marie standing at the kitchen table, shaping corn bread into hand-shaped portions. She glanced at Hannah, then looked back at the cornmeal mixture as if it required all her powers of concentration. "I'm right surprised you have time to go a-visiting these days," she said.

"I needed to get away for awhile," Hannah said truthfully. "Also, I wanted to speak to you alone."

Marie looked at Hannah with a puzzled expression. "Me? What about?"

This isn't going to be easy, Hannah realized. She wet her lips and took a deep breath. "I don't want to leave the Yadkin with any ill feelings between us. If I've done aught to offend you, I ask your forgiveness. I really want you and Clay to be happy."

Marie's face darkened and her mouth twisted. "How can you—of all people—say such a thing!"

"Because it's true," Hannah replied. "I admit that I resented it when you married Clay—"

"I knew you did, but Clay kept saying I was imagining it," Marie interrupted. "Then one day I overheard Grandma Scott tell Clay that he should have married you, as he'd always planned, that I wasn't worthy of him—"

Overcome by emotion, Marie bent her head and began to weep. Quickly Hannah put her arms around Marie's slight shoulders and fought back her own tears. "There was never anything binding between us," Hannah said. "Clay chose and married you, and you both deserve the chance to be happy."

"If Clay had it to do over, he probably wouldn't pick me again, though," Marie said. "I've seen it in his eyes whenever he's around you—"

"Hush!" Hannah cried, lightly shaking Marie's shoulders. "Clay Scott is your husband and you must look ahead to your future together. Believe me; Clay loves you."

Marie wiped her wet cheeks with the back of her hand and looked dubious. "Are you sure?"

Hannah nodded. "Yes, and you should be, too."

Marie put her arms around Hannah's neck and hugged her. "Thank you for telling me," she said. "I've always been so afraid of losing him—"

Hannah pulled away from Marie and lightly placed her hand on her lips as a sign for quiet. "You must never speak that way again."

"All right," Marie said meekly.

"One more thing—I want you and Clay to come to my wedding."

Marie nodded. "I'll see that we do."

Walking across the yard to her house, Hannah felt as if a great load had been lifted from her shoulders.

That wasn't so bad, she thought with relief. Now she could leave the Yadkin with a clear conscience. Occupied with her own thoughts, Hannah didn't notice Adam until he spoke to her from the front porch. He sat on a backless bench set against the house wall, his Bible lying open across his knees.

"Hello, Hannah. You certainly look a sight happier than you did this morning."

Hannah sat down beside him and nodded. "I am." For some reason, the tears she had managed to hold back in the presence of Clay and Marie now began to spill out and run down her cheeks. "I d–don't know why I'm crying," she said in a moment. "You were r–right—I made amends where it was needed, and I do f–feel so much better."

Adam smiled. "I knew so the moment I saw your face. But you'd better sit here a spell before you go inside. Your mother already doubts you really want to marry. Seeing you now would probably confirm that opinion."

Hannah sniffed and wiped her eyes with the edge of her apron. "Maybe she's right," she said. "I've been around Nate all my life, but I don't really know much about him."

"You know that he's a good man and that he cares for you deeply," Adam said. "What else matters?"

I shouldn't have mentioned Nate, Hannah realized. She managed a shaky smile. "Nothing. I heard Mother say I had wedding jitters, and I reckon she's right."

In an attempt to change the subject, Hannah picked up the paper Adam had been writing on. She squinted in an effort to make out the closely written words. "Is this your sermon for tomorrow?"

"It's notes on a passage that came to me when Nate sang that song about the lonesome dove. Even though I preached from it not long ago, I thought it'd be fitting for you and Nate as you go into the wilderness." Adam glanced down at his Bible and pointed a finger to the verses. " 'Behold, I send you forth as sheep in the midst of wolves: be ye therefore wise as serpents, and harmless as doves.' "

Hannah read the next few verses over his shoulder and shook her head slightly. "Jesus was talking about the persecution of the disciples. I don't see how that applies to us."

"Ah, Hannah, look at verses 19 and 20: 'When they deliver you up, take no thought how or what ye shall speak: for it shall be given you in that same hour what ye shall speak. For it is not ye that speak, but the Spirit of your Father which speaketh in you.' "

That's exactly what happened when I saw Clay and Marie, Hannah realized. "I hadn't thought of it that way before," she said aloud.

"That's why you should always cherish God's Word, Hannah. No matter what other weapons you and Nate carry into the wilderness, there is none more powerful than the Sword of the Spirit."

Hannah nodded. "I'll remember," she said.

Adam closed the Bible and stood. "I suppose you can go inside now," he said. "Sarah said something about a dress you need to try on."

"A dress?" Hannah repeated, then she remembered that Nate had told her he had brought her a dress. With all that had happened since, she hadn't given another thought about it.

"Your wedding dress, no doubt."

"Do I look all right?" Hannah invited her uncle's scrutiny.

Adam cocked his head to one side and surveyed her appearance. "Take off your apron—they'll wonder why it's so wet. Yes, now you'll do."

Hannah found her mother with Mary Craighead and Polly McKay. All three were making fine stitches in garments that they immediately put aside when they saw her.

"Uncle Adam said there's a dress for me to try on," Hannah said.

Sarah sounded relieved. "Well, I must say 'tis good to see you in a better mood. Yes, Luke brought this over awhile ago, said it was a gift from Nate.

No doubt it's for your wedding."

The package was wrapped in rough burlap, but the top had been left open, allowing a glimpse of something white.

"Oh!" was all Hannah could say when she opened it and withdrew a dress made of the finest material she had ever seen. Its neck and sleeves were adorned with panels of lace, rarely seen in their part of Carolina.

"Nate must have brought it from Philadelphia," said Mary, a native of that city.

Polly McKay nodded in agreement. "Yes, and I'd say he paid a pretty penny for it, too."

Sarah took the dress from Hannah and held it up to her, judging its length. "Go put it on, Hannah."

Hannah took the dress back from her mother and doubtfully noted how narrow the set-in waist was. "What if I can't wear it?"

"If it doesn't fit, we can probably alter it," Mary said.

"I'll help you with it," Sarah volunteered.

Hannah went to her parents' room, the only one with a full-length pier glass, and quickly removed her everyday linsey-woolsey dress. Gingerly she lifted the cloud of white material over her head and placed her arms in the sleeves, one at a time and with great care, lest she snag the material. Sarah laced the bodice, then stepped back to let Hannah look at herself.

Surrounded by the contrasting whiteness of the material, Hannah's skin glowed, and even her wiry hair took on a darker, richer hue. The tapering waist, snug without being tight, and fully gathered skirt set off a new slenderness and femininity.

"Is that really me?" she said aloud.

Sarah wiped away a furtive tear and nodded. "Aye. Nate chose well—only the hem wants taking up a bit. Otherwise, the dress might have been made to your own measurements."

Hannah looked back at her reflection and that of her mother beside her. Without warning, Hannah was engulfed in a wave of sadness. "Oh, Mother, I'm going to miss you!"

With tears in her eyes, Sarah put her arms around her daughter and held her tight for a moment, then she pulled away and attempted a weak smile. "I know how you feel, Lass. And someday, when your own daughter says the same thing to you, you'll know how I feel, too. But we must always look ahead, not back. And speaking of looking ahead, I'll start on hemming your dress now, else you might find yourself tripping on the hem and falling at your wedding."

The image coaxed a smile to Hannah's lips. "That wouldn't be a very good start, would it?"

Mention of the wedding reminded Hannah that she hadn't seen Nate all day. *I'm really glad Father consented to our marriage,* she thought and suddenly wanted to tell Nate so.

"I'll be back in a little while," Hannah told her mother, and without stopping for her bonnet, she ran to the stable.

Luke looked up in surprise as she came in. "Why, Hannah, what are you doing here? I was just brushing the horse Nate brought y'. She's a beauty—have you rid her yet?"

Hannah nodded her head. "Yes, and I intend to do so again. Help me saddle her, Luke."

"I'm not sure y' ought to go off by yourself," he said doubtfully. "Pa'd have my hide if harm came to y' on my account."

"I'm just going to the ferry. Shadow won't even work up a lather."

"If y' say so," said Luke, but he still looked dubious as he tightened the saddle cinch and helped Hannah mount.

Hannah left the stable yard at a sedate walk, then urged Shadow to a canter when she reached the road. At her father's public house, Hannah dismounted and tied Shadow's reins to the hitching rail alongside Nate's horse. Inside the dim interior, Mark scattered fresh sawdust on the floor, apparently alone.

He looked up, as surprised to see Hannah as his brother had been at the stable. "Hullo, Hannah. What brings y' this way?"

"I need to see Na—Mr. McIntyre," she said.

Luke grinned and gestured toward the ferry. "Last I saw of Uncle Nate, he was helpin' Uncle Joshua splice in some new cable. Like as not, he's still there."

I wish he'd been alone, Hannah thought as she left the public house and walked the worn path to the ferry.

At first she saw no one except the old ferryman, dozing under a budding sycamore. Then she heard her name and turned to see Nate coming from the ferryman's shed.

"What brings ye here?" he asked when he reached her.

Hannah sighed. "You're the third person who's asked me that in the last few minutes," she said. "Everyone must think I stay home all the time."

"Well, ye have to admit it's all ye've done of late. Is something amiss?"

Hannah shook her head and felt somewhat foolish. "I rode Shadow over," she said, as if that explained everything.

"Oh?" Nate looked at her quizzically. A half-smile played around his mouth, and Hannah had the uneasy feeling that he knew why she was there better than she did herself. "Does the new saddle suit ye?"

Hannah nodded. "It's very nice. Will you ride back to the house with me?"

Nate glanced toward the shed. "I'll tell Joshua I'm leaving—we just finished with the ferry cable."

Watching Nate stride away from her, Hannah felt her heart begin to beat faster. *This time tomorrow, we'll be man and wife,* she thought in wonder.

Nate returned in a moment and silently they walked together to their horses. Nate helped Hannah mount, then swung into his own saddle. Side by side they rode back toward the Stones'.

When they reached the woods, Hannah halted her horse and turned to Nate.

"I want to go to the springhouse," she said.

Without asking her why, Nate nodded and dismounted. Hannah waited while he looped their reins around a sapling, then raised his arms to help her down. He kept one arm around her waist as they walked the few steps to the springhouse.

"This will always be a special place for me," Nate said when they once more stood on the flat rock by the spring.

"And for me, too," she said, then paused as she cast about for a way to tell him what was on her heart. "Thank you for the dress. It's the most beautiful one I ever saw."

Nate's eyes glowed and he took both her hands in his. "Does it fit?"

Hannah nodded. "Aye, except for being a little long. Mother is hemming it."

"Good. I tried to describe ye to the dressmaker, who I judged to be about your height. I told her ye came to here on me," he said, pointing to his chest. "But she wouldn't come close enough to me to measure it properly."

"You had the dress made just for me?"

Nate nodded. "Aye. That's one reason I was so long in Philadelphia—that, and haggling for good prices for my trade goods. I want the best for ye, Lass."

Hannah looked into Nate's eyes, unaware of how much her expression told him. "I want the same for you, Nate."

"Something has happened—ye look different."

Hannah nodded. "I asked forgiveness of one I wronged," she said. "Only then did I realize how—how much I care for you."

"Oh, Hannah! As soon as I saw ye at the ferry I dared to hope—"

As Nate had once done to her, Hannah laid her hand over his mouth. "Hush," she said quietly. In perfect agreement of that point, Nate swept Hannah into his arms and held her there.

We do fit together, after all, Hannah marveled as Nate bent to kiss her.

With a sense of homecoming, Hannah raised her face to his and returned his kiss with an enthusiasm that surprised them both.

"I think I love you, Nate McIntyre," Hannah whispered when she could again speak.

"And ye know already how much I care for ye, Hannah Stone." Nate pulled away from her to look into her face again, and Hannah saw that there were tears in his eyes.

"I'll never betray the trust ye do me by wedding me."

"And I'll do my best to make you a good wife," Hannah said solemnly.

They kissed again, then Hannah laid her head on his shoulder and chuckled.

"What do ye find so funny about kissing me?" Nate asked fondly.

"Nothing, but I just realized that soon I'll be Hannah McIntyre." It was the first time she had said her future name out loud, and Nate smiled.

"Ye can't claim that name until the morrow," he reminded her. "And for now, Hannah Stone probably has better things to do than spend more time with a worthless old hunter. Up to the house with ye, now."

"So you're ordering me about already, and us not properly wed? Perhaps I ought to call the whole thing off, after all."

Nate grinned at Hannah. "I don't think ye can, Lass. Stones never go back on their word, ye know."

"And what about McIntyres?" she asked lightly.

Nate's smile faded and he took her in his arms again. "This McIntyre never gives up, no matter how long it takes."

In the security and warmth of Nate's embrace, Hannah matched his tone. "Then neither will I."

Nate kissed her again. "Aye, so be it, then."

On the morrow, they would exchange the formal vows that would legally bind them for life, but as Hannah stood with Nate by the springhouse, she felt that what had just passed between them had been equally momentous.

No matter what happens to us from now on, Hannah thought, *Nate and I will always have each other. With God's help, we'll find the strength to meet every challenge—together.*

A Letter to Our Readers

Dear Readers:

In order that we might better contribute to your reading enjoyment, we would appreciate you taking a few minutes to respond to the following questions. When completed, please return to the following: Fiction Editor, Barbour Publishing, Inc., P.O. Box 719, Uhrichsville, OH 44683.

1. Did you enjoy reading *Pennsylvania?*
   □ Very much. I would like to see more books like this.
   □ Moderately. I would have enjoyed it more if   _____

   _____

   _____

2. What influenced your decision to purchase this book?
   (Check those that apply.)
   □ Cover   □ Back cover copy   □ Title   □ Price
   □ Friends   □ Publicity   □ Other

3. Which story was your favorite?
   □ *Love's Gentle Journey*   □ *Sign of the Eagle*
   □ *Sign of the Bow*   □ *Sign of the Dove*

4. Please check your age range:
   □ Under 18   □ 18–24   □ 25–34
   □ 35–45   □ 46–55   □ Over 55

5. How many hours per week do you read? _____

Name _____

Occupation _____

Address _____

City _____ State _____ Zip _____

If you enjoyed
Pennsylvania
then read:

The ENGLISH GARDEN

*Centuries of Botanical Delight Brought
to Life in Four Romantic Novellas*

Woman of Valor by Jill Stengl
Apple of His Eye by Gail Gaymer Martin
A Flower Amidst the Ashes by DiAnn Mills
Robyn's Garden by Kathleen Y'Barbo

If you enjoyed

Pennsylvania

then read:

German Enchantment

*A Legacy of Customs and Devotion
in Four Romantic Novellas*

Where Angels Camp by Dianne Christner
The Nuremberg Angel by Irene B. Brand
Dearest Enemy by Pamela Griffin
Once a Stranger by Gail Gaymer Martin

JEARTSONG ❤ PRESENTS

Love Stories
Are Rated G!

That's for godly, gratifying, and of course, great! If you love a thrilling love story but don't appreciate the sordidness of some popular paperback romances, **Heartsong Presents** is for you. In fact, **Heartsong Presents** is the only inspirational romance book club featuring love stories where Christian faith is the primary ingredient in a marriage relationship.

Sign up today to receive your first set of four, never-before-published Christian romances. Send no money now; you will receive a bill with the first shipment. You may cancel at any time without obligation, and if you aren't completely satisfied with any selection, you may return the books for an immediate refund!

Imagine. . .four new romances every four weeks—two historical, two contemporary—with men and women like you who long to meet the one God has chosen as the love of their lives. . .all for the low price of $9.97 postpaid.

To join, simply complete the coupon below and mail to the address provided. **Heartsong Presents** romances are rated G for another reason: They'll arrive Godspeed!

YES! Sign me up for Hearts❤ng!

NEW MEMBERSHIPS WILL BE SHIPPED IMMEDIATELY!
Send no money now. We'll bill you only $9.97 postpaid with your first shipment of four books. Or for faster action, call toll free 1-800-847-8270.

NAME _____

ADDRESS _____

CITY _____ STATE _____ ZIP _____

MAIL TO: HEARTSONG PRESENTS, P.O. Box 721, Uhrichsville, Ohio 44683
www.heartsongpresents.com